FROM THE PAGES OF
PYGMALION AND
THREE OTHER PLAYS

I am, and have always been, and shall now always be, a revolutionary writer, because our laws make law impossible; our liberties destroy all freedom; our property is organized robbery; our morality is an impudent hypocrisy; our wisdom is administered by inexperienced or malexperienced dupes, our power wielded by cowards and weaklings, and our honor false in all its points. I am an enemy of the existing order for good reasons.

> (from Shaw's preface to *Major Barbara*, pages 43–44)

"He knows nothing; and he thinks he knows everything. That points clearly to a political career." (from *Major Barbara*, page 127)

"You have learnt something. That always feels at first as if you had lost something." (from *Major Barbara*, page 132)

If you cannot have what you believe in you must believe in what you have.

> (from Shaw's preface to *The Doctor's Dilemma*, page 166)

"I find that the moment I let a woman make friends with me, she becomes jealous, exacting, suspicious, and a damned nuisance. I find that the moment I let myself make friends with a woman, I become selfish and tyrannical. Women upset everything." (from *Pygmalion*, page 394)

"The great secret, Eliza, is not having bad manners or good manners or any other particular sort of manners, but having the same manner for all human souls: in short, behaving as if you were in Heaven, where there are no third-class carriages, and one soul is as good as another."

> (from *Pygmalion*, pages 451–452)

"The surest way to ruin a man who doesn't know how to handle money is to give him some." (from *Heartbreak House*, page 568)

"His heart is breaking: that is all. It is a curious sensation: the sort of pain that goes mercifully beyond our powers of feeling. When your heart is broken, your boats are burned: nothing matters any more. It is the end of happiness and the beginning of peace." (from *Heartbreak House*, page 596)

Pygmalion
and Three Other Plays

GEORGE

BERNARD SHAW

With an Introduction and Notes
by JOHN A. BERTOLINI

GEORGE STADE
Consulting Editorial Director

BARNES & NOBLE CLASSICS
NEW YORK

ⅉℬ

Barnes & Noble Classics

New York

Published by Barnes & Noble Books
122 Fifth Avenue
New York, NY 10011

www.barnesandnoble.com/classics

Major Barbara was first published in 1907, *Doctor's Dilemma* in 1909,
Pygmalion in 1916, and *Heartbreak House* in 1919.

Published in 2004 by Barnes & Noble Classics with new Introduction,
Notes, Biography, Chronology, Inspired By, Comments & Questions,
and For Further Reading.

Introduction, Notes, and For Further Reading
Copyright © 2004 by John A. Bertolini.

Note on George Bernard Shaw, The World of George Bernard Shaw and His Plays,
Inspired by *Pygmalion and Three Other Plays*, and Comments & Questions
Copyright © 2004 by Barnes & Noble, Inc.

Pygmalion and Three Other Plays
ISBN-13: 978-1-59308-078-5
ISBN-10: 1-59308-078-6
LC Control Number 2003112512

Produced and published in conjunction with:
Fine Creative Media, Inc.
322 Eighth Avenue
New York, NY 10001

Michael J. Fine, President and Publisher

Printed in the United States of America

QM

7 9 11 13 15 17 19 20 18 16 14 12 10 8

GEORGE BERNARD SHAW

Dramatist, critic, and social reformer George Bernard Shaw was born on July 26, 1856, into a poor yet genteel Dublin household. His diffident and impractical father was an alcoholic disdained by his mother, a professional singer who ingrained in her only son a love of music, art, and literature. Just shy of his seventeenth birthday, Shaw joined his mother and two sisters in London, where they had settled three years earlier.

There he struggled—and failed—to support himself by writing. He first wrote a string of novels, beginning with the semi-autobiographical *Immaturity*, completed in 1879. Though some of his novels were serialized, none met with great success, and Shaw decided to abandon the form in favor of drama. While he struggled artistically, he flourished politically; for some years his greater fame was as a political activist and pamphleteer. A stammering, shy young man, Shaw nevertheless joined in the radical politics of his day. In the late 1880s he became a leading member of the fledgling Fabian Society, a group dedicated to progressive politics, and authored numerous pamphlets on a range of social and political issues. He often mounted a soapbox in Hyde Park and there developed the enthralling oratory style that pervades his dramatic writing.

In the 1890s, deeply influenced by the dramatic writings of Henrik Ibsen, Shaw spurned the conventions of the stage in "unpleasant" plays, such as *Mrs. Warren's Profession*, and in "pleasant" ones like *Arms and the Man* and *Candida*. His drama shifted attention from romantic travails to the great web of society, with its hypocrisies and other ills. The burden of writing seriously strained

Shaw's health; he suffered from chronic migraine headaches. Shaw married fellow Fabian and Irish heiress Charlotte Payne-Townshend.

By the turn of the century, Shaw had matured as a dramatist with the historical drama *Caesar and Cleopatra*, and his masterpieces *Man and Superman* and *Major Barbara*. In all, he wrote more than fifty plays, including his antiwar *Heartbreak House* and the polemical *Saint Joan*, for which he was awarded the Nobel Prize. Equally prolific in his writings about music and theater, Shaw was so popular that he signed his critical pieces with simply the initials GBS. (He disliked his first name, George, and never used it except for the initial.) He remained in the public eye throughout his final years, writing controversial plays until his death. George Bernard Shaw died at his country home on November 2, 1950.

TABLE OF CONTENTS

THE WORLD OF
GEORGE BERNARD SHAW
AND HIS PLAYS

1856   George Bernard Shaw is born on July 26, at 33 Upper Synge Street in Dublin, to George Carr Shaw and Lucinda Elizabeth Gurly Shaw.

1865   George John Vandeleur Lee, Mrs. Shaw's singing instructor, moves into the Shaw household. Known as Vandeleur Lee, he has a reputation as an unscrupulous character.

1869   Embarrassed by controversy and gossip related to his mother's relationship with Vandeleur Lee, young "Sonny," as Shaw was called by his family, leaves school.

1871   He begins work in a Dublin land agent's office.

1873   Shaw's mother, now a professional singer, follows Vandeleur Lee to London, where they establish a household that includes Shaw's sisters, Elinor Agnes and Lucille Frances (Lucy). Shaw's mother tries to earn a living performing and teaching Vandeleur Lee's singing method.

1876   Elinor Agnes dies on March 27. Shaw joins his mother, his sister Lucy, and Vandeleur Lee in London. Although he tries to support himself as a writer, for the next five years Shaw remains financially dependent on his mother.

1877   Shaw ghostwrites music reviews that appear under Vandeleur Lee's byline in his column for the *Hornet*, a London newspaper. This first professional writing "job" lasts until the editor discovers the subterfuge.

1879   Shaw completes and serializes his first novel, *Immaturity*. He works for the Edison Telephone Company and later

will record his experience in his second novel, *The Irrational Knot*. Henrik Ibsen's play *A Doll's House* premieres.

1880   Shaw completes *The Irrational Knot*.

1881   He becomes a vegetarian in the hope that the change in his
diet will relieve his migraine headaches. He completes *Love
Among Artists*. *The Irrational Knot* is serialized in *Our Corner*,
a monthly periodical.

1882   Shaw hears Henry George's lecture on land nationaliza-
tion, which inspires some of his socialist ideas. He attends
meetings of the Social Democratic Federation and is introduced to the works of Karl Marx.

1883   The Fabian Society—a middle-class socialist debating
group advocating progressive, nonviolent reform rather
than the revolution supported by the Social Democratic
Federation—is founded in London. Shaw completes the
novel *Cashel Byron's Profession*, drawing on his experience as
an amateur boxer. He writes his final novel, *An Unsocial Socialist*.

1884   Shaw joins the fledgling Fabian Society; he contributes to
many of its pamphlets, including *The Fabian Manifesto*
(1884), *The Impossibilities of Anarchism* (1893), and *Socialism
for Millionaires* (1901), and begins speaking publicly around
London on social and political issues. *An Unsocial Socialist*
is serialized in the periodical *Today*.

1885   The author's father, a longtime alcoholic, dies; neither his
estranged wife nor his children attend his funeral. Shaw
himself never drinks or smokes. He begins writing criticism of music, art, and literature for the *Pall Mall Gazette*,
the *Dramatic Review*, and *Our Corner*. *Cashel Byron's Profession*
is serialized in the periodical *Today*.

1886   Shaw begins writing art and music criticism for the *World*.
Cashel Byron's Profession is published.

1887   Swedish dramatist and writer August Strindberg's play *The
Father* is performed. The Social Democratic Federation's

planned march on Trafalgar Square ends in bloodshed as police suppress the protesters; Shaw is a speaker at the event. His novel *An Unsocial Socialist* is published in book form.

1888   Shaw begins writing music criticism in the *Star* under the pen name Corno di Bassetto ("basset horn," perhaps a reference to the pitch of his voice).

1889   He edits the volume *Fabian Essays in Socialism*, to which he contributes "The Economic Basis of Socialism" and "The Transition to Social Democracy."

1890   Ibsen completes *Hedda Gabler*.

1891   Ibsen's *Ghosts* is performed in London. Shaw publishes *The Quintessence of Ibsenism*, a polemical pamphlet that celebrates Ibsen as a rebel for leftist causes.

1892   Sidney Webb, a founder and close associate of Shaw, is elected to the London City Council along with five other Fabian Society members. *Widowers' Houses*, Shaw's first "unpleasant" play, is performed on the London stage.

1893   Shaw writes *The Philanderer* and *Mrs. Warren's Profession*, his two other "unpleasant" plays. The latter is refused a license by the royal censor because its subject is prostitution; as a result, the play is not performed until 1902. *Widowers' Houses* is published.

1894   Seeking a wider audience, Shaw begins a series of "pleasant" plays with *Arms and the Man*, produced this year, and *Candida*, a successful play about marriage greatly influenced by Ibsen's *A Doll's House*.

1895   Shaw writes another "pleasant" play, *The Man of Destiny*, a one-act about Napoleon, and drama criticism for the *Saturday Review*.

1896   Shaw completes the fourth "pleasant" play, *You Never Can Tell*. He meets Charlotte Payne-Townshend, a wealthy Irish heiress and fellow Fabian. The Nobel Prizes are established for physics, medicine, chemistry, peace, and literature.

1897   *Candida* is produced. *The Devil's Disciple*, a drama set dur-
       ing the American Revolution, is successfully staged in New
       York. Shaw is elected as councilor for the borough of St.
       Pancras, London; he will serve in this position until 1903.

1898   Shaw writes *Caesar and Cleopatra* and publishes *Mrs. Warren's
       Profession* and *The Perfect Wagnerite*. His first anthology of
       plays, *Plays Pleasant and Unpleasant*, is published. He falls ill
       and, believing his illness fatal, marries his friend and nurse
       Charlotte Payne-Townshend; his wife's fortune makes
       Shaw wealthy.

1899   *You Never Can Tell* premieres. Shaw writes *Captain Brass-
       bound's Conversion*.

1900   The Fabian Society, the Independent Labour Party, and the
       Social Democratic Federation join forces to form the
       Labour Representation Party, which is politically allied to
       the trade union movement. The party wins two seats in the
       House of Commons. *Captain Brasshound's Conversion* is pro-
       duced. *Three Plays for Puritans* collects *The Devil's Disciple*,
       Caesar and Cleopatra, and *Captain Brassbound's Conversion*.

1901   Strindberg's *Dance of Death* is completed. The Social Revo-
       lutionary Party, instrumental in the Bolshevik Revolution,
       is formed in Russia. Shaw writes about the eternal obsta-
       cles in male-female relations in his epic *Man and Superman*,
       which he subtitles "A Comedy and a Philosophy." He also
       publishes *The Devil's Disciple* and sees *Caesar and Cleopatra*
       produced for the first time.

1902   A private production of *Mrs. Warren's Profession* is staged at
       the New Lyric Theatre in London.

1903   Shaw publishes *Man and Superman*. *The Admirable Bashville* is
       produced.

1904   *John Bull's Other Island* premieres in London.

1905   Shaw writes the play *Major Barbara*, through which he at-
       tempts to communicate many of his moral and economic
       theories, including the need for a more fair distribution of

wealth. It is produced this year, as is *Man and Superman*. In New York City, *Mrs. Warren's Profession* is publicly staged for the first time. Oscar Wilde's *De Profundis* is published posthumously. The Sinn Fein party, dedicated to Irish independence, is founded in Dublin.

1906   The Labour Representation Party wins twenty-nine seats and shortens its name to the Labour Party. Henrik Ibsen dies. Shaw's *The Doctor's Dilemma*, a satire on the medical profession, is produced.

1909   Shaw writes *The Shewing-Up of Blanco Posnet* and the one-act farce *Press Cuttings*, both banned by the royal censor.

1910   Shaw writes *Misalliance*, which he compares to Shakespeare's *The Taming of the Shrew*.

1912   He publishes *Misalliance*, and his satire *Androcles and the Lion* is staged for the first time.

1913   A German language version of *Pygmalion*, another satire Shaw wrote in 1912, premieres in Vienna.

1914   With World War I imminent, Shaw publishes a polemical antiwar tract, *Common Sense About the War*, which provokes a popular backlash and public denouncement. *Pygmalion* is produced for the first time in English.

1917   Dejected over the war, Shaw writes *Heartbreak House*.

1919   *Heartbreak House* is published in New York.

1920   The canonization of Joan of Arc gives Shaw the idea for a new play. *Heartbreak House* is produced in New York.

1921   Shaw publishes five linked plays begun during the war under the title *Back to Methuselah*, a dramatic work that begins in the Garden of Eden and ends in the year A.D. 31,920.

1923   Shaw writes *Saint Joan*, which is produced and hailed as a masterpiece.

1924   *Saint Joan* is published.

1925   Shaw is awarded the Nobel Prize for Literature for *Saint Joan*. He donates the prize money to fund an English translation of the works of August Strindberg.

1928   Shaw publishes his nonfiction *The Intelligent Women's Guide to Socialism and Capitalism* and writes *The Apple Cart*, a dramatic comedy set in the future.

1929   *The Apple Cart* is produced.

1931   Shaw visits Russia, where he meets Josef Stalin and Maxim Gorky. He completes the play *Too True to Be Good*, which explores how war can undermine established morals.

1932   *Too True to Be Good* is staged for the first time.

1933   An international celebrity, Shaw makes his first trip to America. *On the Rocks* and *Village Wooing* are produced.

1934   Shaw writes the plays *The Simpleton of the Unexpected Isles*, *The Six of Calais*, and the first draft of *The Millionairess* during a cruise to New Zealand. *Simpleton* is produced this year.

1938   *Geneva*, a play that imagines a successful League of Nations, premieres.

1939   Shaw writes *Good King Charles's Golden Days*, which is produced this year. He wins an Academy Award for the screenplay for *Pygmalion*, over which he exercised tight control.

1943   His wife, Charlotte, dies after a long illness.

1947   Shaw completes the play *The Buoyant Billions*.

1948   *The Buoyant Billions* is produced in Zurich.

1949   Shaw's puppet play, *Shakes Versus Shav*, is produced.

1950   George Bernard Shaw dies on November 2 from complications related to a fall from a ladder. He bequeaths funds for a competition to create a new English alphabet based on phonetics rather than Roman letters. The competition, won in 1958 by Kingsley Read, results in the Shavian alphabet.

INTRODUCTION

In one of Katharine Hepburn's early films, *Morning Glory* (from a 1933 play by Zoe Akins), Hepburn plays a self-confident, self-reliant, fearless, and outspoken young woman, ambitious to become a great actress in New York—in short, Hepburn plays herself. In the film, in an exchange with a producer (played by the ever-dapper Adolphe Menjou), Hepburn explains that she has done several major roles back home in her local Vermont theater company, including a role "in Shaw's *You Never Can Tell*." Menjou then asks, "*Bernard* Shaw?" and she replies, "The one and only." They continue:

"You think Shaw's clever?"

"He's the greatest living dramatist."

"You really think so?"

"I know it."

She goes on to explain that she once wrote to Shaw and received a reply (which she carries with her), and that she will always have a Shaw play in her repertoire "as long as I remain in the theater." The version of herself Hepburn plays here amounts to a version of the headstrong Shavian heroine. In the real theater world, Hepburn played the title role in one of Shaw's late but not-quite-great plays, *The Millionairess*, in a New York and London production (1952). Some twelve years earlier, when she was starring in the film *The Philadelphia Story*, Shaw himself had suggested that she was just the sort of actress to play his millionairess. But even apart from her actual stage experience with Shaw, Hepburn, like her parents before her, was a Shavian—that is, influenced by Shaw's ideas; full of unorthodox views, especially about religion;

independent-minded; strong-willed. That was the appeal of Shaw in the 1930s, when the number of his plays that were part of the active repertory of the world's theater—say twenty plays—was greater than that of almost any other playwright, Shakespeare, as always, excepted.

The modernists—Eliot, Joyce, Beckett—and modernism had not yet completely triumphed, so that Virginia Woolf and Leonard Woolf could argue about Shaw's place in modernism, Virginia maintaining that Shaw was out of date, and Leonard asserting that if it had not been for Shaw's work of educating the first generation of the twentieth century about everything, the modernists would have found no audience. So Shaw still could seem ahead of his time—enough ahead of his time for a most modern woman like Katharine Hepburn (and the character she played in *Morning Glory*) to admire him as a culture hero, an advanced thinker, and a modern playwright.

The four plays in the present volume are test cases both for Shaw's achievement in drama and for the destinies of his head-strong heroines. The plays also give more trouble than those in Barnes & Noble Classics's other edition of Shaw—*Mrs. Warren's Profession*, *Candida*, *The Devil's Disciple*, and *Man and Superman*— more trouble in that they have more unresolved chords than his earlier plays, and so are more difficult to understand; they re-flect a Shaw troubled by the role of the artist in the world and by the world's role in the universe. *Heartbreak House*, the last play in this edition, was written during World War I; it ex-presses Shaw's struggle not to be defeated by all the evidence that the Devil in *Man and Superman*, who argued that Man is pri-marily a destroyer with his heart in his weapons, was right after all. Just the number of the war dead—the prodigiousness of which can be gauged by considering that United States fatalities for the whole of the Vietnam war, some 54,000, about equaled the number killed on one side on a single day of battle on the Western Front.

Major Barbara and its two predecessor plays—*Man and Superman* (1903) and *John Bull's Other Island* (1904; Shaw's only major play about and set in his native Ireland)—form a trilogy on the theme of human destiny within a social order and a cosmic perspective, as Bernard Dukore has suggested in *Shaw's Theatre* (see "For Further Reading"). All three plays use forceful images of heaven and hell, and debate propositions and ideas that would transform the world from a hellish place to a more heavenly one. But where *Man and Superman* projects an optimistic vision of human potential, both *John Bull's Other Island* and *Major Barbara* end more ambiguously—that is, with the sense that any hope that humankind will put an end to war and waste remains in the realm of madness or fantasy—though Shaw still commits his characters to the fervent attempt to turn hope into reality. By the time Shaw wrote *Heartbreak House*, during World War I, he found himself a powerless witness to death and destruction on a massive scale such as the world had not seen. *Heartbreak House* records most precisely the reaction of the playwright to be like that of a man looking down from the top ledge of a skyscraper who becomes afraid, not that he will fall, but that he will jump. The tension in the play derives from Shaw's instinct to resist yet give full expression to the allure of the jump that would let him be finally done with the world.

John Bull's Other Island made Shaw famous and popular in 1904. Previously he had been something of a coterie dramatist with a few mildly successful plays to his credit. But the topicality of *John Bull's Other Island*—together with the fortuitous attendance at a performance by King Edward, during which he laughed frequently and noticeably, and apparently with such gusto that he broke his chair—raised Shaw's recognition and reputation to a hitherto unattained level. Certainly Shaw's Irish play has its hilarious moments and episodes; but it is also suffused with sadness over the spiritual paralysis Shaw diagnoses as deriving from his countrymen's tormenting imagination, which drives them to flee

from reality to the bottle and futile dreams. The play's embodi-
ment of this tragic condition is a defrocked priest, Father Keegan,
who expresses in the last scene an ideal social and metaphysical
order:

> In my dreams [Heaven] is a country where the State is the
> Church and the Church the people: three in one and one
> in three. It is a commonwealth in which work is play and
> play is life: three in one and one in three. It is a temple in
> which the priest is the worshipper and the worshipper the
> worshipped: three in one and one in three. It is a godhead
> in which all life is human and all humanity divine: three in
> one and one in three. It is, in short, the dream of a mad-
> man.

Yeats in his old age cited this speech of Keegan along with a
very few other passages in literature as moving him greatly; the
line "How can we know the dancer from the dance?" from Yeats's
poem "Among School Children" seems to echo Keegan. At its core
Keegan's dream proposes that all life is holy because it is whole,
that the material and the metaphysical are indivisible, that the social and the spiritual are equally in need of attention. And though
that proposition is presented as and perhaps acknowledged to be
a madman's dream, it lies at the heart of the ideas that Shaw's next
big play, *Major Barbara*, confronts.

MAJOR BARBARA

Major Barbara was successfully revived by the Roundabout Theatre
in New York in 2001. The revival elicited the following encomium
from Margo Jefferson, writing in *The New York Times Book Review*
(August 5), after she has noted that "Shaw was a true artist, a master of multiple forms":

The language and the complexity of the world Shaw made still excite. It isn't just the war of wills between Barbara Undershaft, the society girl who turns to the Salvation Army in her need to do good and save souls, and her father, whose munitions empire commits him to war and destruction. It is out-of-work cockneys, young men about town and rich dowagers, all living on habit, instinct and the calculation needed to bridge the gap between what they have and what they want. And, in all Shaw's work, it is the rigorous musicality of his language.

Jefferson is surely right that Shaw's achievement in *Major Barbara* has two aspects: the variety and plenitude of the world he unfolds before us; and the designing and composing of sentences into harmony, counterpoint, and rhythmical ideas. But let me add a third aspect: the shaping and arranging of action. And it is not for naught that Shaw knew Shakespeare's plays as he knew Beethoven's nine symphonies note for note. But Shaw's view of Shakespeare has often been misunderstood—Shaw loved Shakespeare's art but did not love what he took to be Shakespeare's stoic-pessimistic view of life. He said once that no one would ever write a better play than *Othello*, because humanly speaking, Shakespeare had done the thing as well as it could be done; in the same way no one could improve on Mozart's music. Shaw learned much from Shakespeare—how much is especially evident in *Major Barbara*. One of Shakespeare's triumphant strategies for getting a maximum of meaning out of dramatic form is to parallel actions and stage images in one dramatic scene with another, thereby causing the audience to compare the behavior of one character to that of another. Characters and actions become metaphors—that is, we come to understand a character or an action better, or to rethink our attitude toward it, by its being set parallel to another character in an analogous situation, or by the placement of a similar action in a different context.

For example, *Major Barbara* enacts a drama of loss of self and rebirth in terms of finding one's home and one's work. The protagonist of the play, Barbara Undershaft, is the daughter of an aristocratic mother, Lady Britomart, and a fabulously wealthy and powerful munitions maker, Andrew Undershaft, who is also a foundling (the play has a strong fairy tale/parable quality). In the first act, Andrew Undershaft returns home, to a great house in fashionable Wilton Crescent, after a long absence from family life; he proves so fascinating to his grown children, especially Barbara, that by the end of the act, his wife has been reduced to tears because all her children have deserted her to follow their father into another room, where Andrew has agreed to participate in a nondenominational religious concert. Finally, though, even Lady Britomart is lured by the music and joins her husband and children.

The second act is in every way patterned after the action of the first, though in appearance they could not be more different. Barbara has invited her father the next day to watch her work at her Salvation Army shelter in a neighborhood that is the exact opposite of Wilton Crescent. There, her millionaire father finds cold, brutality, hunger, hypocrisy, and the work of conversion, where Wilton Crescent seemed to provide warmth, comfort, formality, and conversation. But Shaw's aim is to show that both places are alike in being devoid of authentic religious feeling and genuine spiritual nourishment. Shaw does so by having Undershaft do wittingly to Barbara in the second act what he does unwittingly to her mother in the first act: undermine her sense of self and position. In Lady Britomart, the undermining is limited and temporary, but in Barbara's case it induces in her a dark night of the soul that makes her resign her job with the Salvation Army. For her father shows his spiritually vital daughter, whose greatest hunger is to affect and transform the souls of people, that her organization can be bought.

When the Salvation Army general, Mrs. Baines, arrives and

announces that a number of shelters will close unless the Army secures substantial donations from wealthy benefactors, Undershaft offers to make a £5,000 contribution, which in turn will compel equal contributions from, among others, a whisky distiller. The general cheerfully accepts, but Barbara is horrified to see the Army "sell itself" by taking donations from a whisky distiller and a munitions maker. Her principled posture makes her resign in a state of tearful despair. (For those who believe with Oscar Wilde that life imitates art and not the other way around, I note that, according to the Associated Press on January 3, 2003, the Salvation Army refused a donation of $100,000 from a lotto winner in Naples, Florida, on the grounds that the Salvation Army counsels families who have lost their homes due to gambling, and would therefore be hypocritical in accepting such a donation!) When the shelters are saved the Army members gather together behind a band that includes both Barbara's father and her fiancé, and march off for a great celebration at the Assembly Hall, leaving the deserted Barbara, stripped of her identity as a saver of souls and stripped of her real home, which was the shelter.

Both the first and second acts, therefore, end with a woman in tears and feeling that everything she valued has been taken from her, put in that state by Andrew Undershaft, her misery accompanied by the sound of music from another place. And just as Shakespeare in *Henry IV, Part One* describes Hotspur calling for his horse after he has plotted to rebel against the king, and then Falstaff in the next scene calling for his horse during the Gadshill robbery, in order to make us think about what Hotspur's rebellion has in common with Falstaff's robbery, in *Major Barbara* Shaw parallels Lady Britomart and Barbara in order to make us see more complexly the nature of Barbara's loss. Since Barbara has now lost the two things that above all give us our sense of ourselves—work and home—she will spend the third act trying to find new versions of both, which together mean a new self.

But you need not take my word that setting up parallel actions is Shaw's method, for he says so himself in the preface, when he explains how he has shown us two attempts on the part of transgressors to pay off the Salvation Army: Bill Walker for having struck Jenny Hill, and Horace Bodger for selling whisky to the poor:

> But I, the dramatist, whose business it is to shew the connexion between things that seem apart and unrelated in the haphazard order of events in real life, have contrived to make it [that the Army will take Bodger's atonement money but not Bill's] known to Bill, with the result that the Salvation Army loses its hold of him at once (p. 35).

Here we see Shaw doing just what Aristotle in his *Poetics* says is the mark of genius in the poet (because it cannot be learned): intuiting the hidden similarity between two apparent dissimilars, or making metaphors. Shaw makes Bill Walker see the comparison so that we will see it, just as Shakespeare makes Prince Hal see the connection between the apparent opposites Falstaff the coward and Hotspur the daredevil, which is that both live outside of all order.

The friends to whom Shaw read *Major Barbara* were strongly moved by the power of the second act, in which Andrew Undershaft demonstrates the power of the pound over religion, and in doing so makes his daughter feel as if she has lost all purpose in life. In one of the play's most profound aphorisms, Undershaft reproves Barbara for feeling self-pity by observing to her: "You have learnt something. That always feels at first as if you had lost something" (p. 132). Perceiving something new often means abandoning a cherished view or opinion, and it often hurts to do so, but Shaw puts the emphasis on "at first." In other words, one can find compensations for losses; one can mend a broken heart.

And so Barbara does when she gets to her father's cannon-works town with its powerful foundry, its well-tended workers' dwellings, its families, and its children. She sees that here is a real challenge for her: Can she induce well-fed and well-paid workers to pay attention to their spiritual selves, to their salvation? She decides to renew hope and marry the man who will take over the cannon works from her father. That man turns out to be Cusins. From the premiere of the play in 1906 people have found its ending ambiguous: Do Barbara and Cusins succumb to the allure of materialism in agreeing to take over the cannon works from Undershaft? Or do they intend to use their new power to "make war on war"? Shaw leaves the question unresolved, though he clearly leans toward the latter possibility. In any case, as he said in the postscript to the preface to *Back to Methuselah* (1921), which he wrote in 1944 for the Oxford World's Classics edition: It is the job of classic works to "try to solve, or at least to formulate, the riddles of creation."

Cusins formulates one of the riddles of creation in an exchange with Barbara over how the cannon works are to be used. Cusins says he will use them to give power to the people. But Barbara laments the power to destroy and kill. Cusins replies: "You cannot have power for good without having power for evil too" (p. 155). Another way of formulating that idea is: Undershaft's weapons and explosives are as good or as bad as the man making them (to adapt a line from the film *Shane*). Barbara sees the cannon works as her opportunity to raise "hell to heaven." Her most immediate impulse, however, is to escape to heaven, away from the "naughty, mischievous children of men." But her courage returns, and she unites herself to both Cusins and her father (while she also reaffirms her bond with her mother, an affirmation that is the seal of her reborn self). Jonathan Wisenthal (in *The Marriage of Contraries*) has argued persuasively that the end of the play anticipates a tripartite union of three kinds of power: material (Undershaft), intellectual (Cusins), and spiritual (Barbara). But Shaw is well aware that such a union, like Father Keegan's vision of three in one, is not realized in the play, and may be only a madman's dream.

THE DOCTOR'S DILEMMA

The comical satire of the medical profession in Shaw's play hardly differs from Molière's portrayal of doctors and patients in his comedies devoted to the subject (*The Imaginary Invalid*, *The Doctor in Spite of Himself*, *Doctor Love*). Shaw makes the same points that Molière makes (points that bear repeating for every generation): that there are fashions in diseases as there are in dresses; that people will use real, pretended, and imagined illnesses to manipulate and dominate their nearest and dearest; that doctors have obsessions in treatments and cure-alls, and resist innovation; that they will pretend to knowledge they do not have and are jealous of professional rivals; and that they behave as all other professionals do in using jargon to prevent outsiders from keeping close tabs on them. And though Shaw has much fun with all of this—especially the surgeon determined to remove everyone's "nuciform sac" as a universal cure for what ails you—the satirical comedy is not the real point of the play.

Nor is the real point the ethical dilemma denoted by the title. Doctor Ridgeon has developed a new, effective cure for tuberculosis but can treat only so many patients. He must choose, therefore, who to save: the artist, Louis Dubedat, who creates authentic art but is immoral in his treatment of others—indiscriminately exploitative, deceitful in all things, honest in none, monumentally selfish, and automatically unscrupulous—or the dull but decent Doctor Blenkinsop, a gentle and considerate soul, generous to a fault, congenial to all, genuinely honest, but an ineffectual doctor, innocuous company, and generally useless to society. One further complication is that Doctor Ridgeon has fallen in love with the artist's wife, Jennifer, who not only worships her husband but utterly blinds herself to his crimes.

The very symmetry of this dilemma has misled even some of the best critical minds into faulting the play for contrivance (for example, Lionel Trilling in *The Experience of Literature*). But the Shavian symmetry aims not for contrivance but for the theme of the Double, the use of paired characters to dramatize the relationship between inner and outer life in individuals, a theme Shaw had addressed already in *The Devil's Disciple*, but to which here he gives a deeper development and darker variation. The scalawag Dick Dudgeon of the earlier play, who was not truly villainous but only unorthodox and unconventional in his manners and morals, here becomes the truly opprobrious artist-scoundrel Dubedat, while the minister and man of peace, Anthony Anderson, who turns into a man of war and rebellion, becomes Dr. Ridgeon, medical miracle worker and murderer.

Judith Anderson becomes Jennifer Dubedat. We may note that in the transformation Shaw shifts the woman's position in the triangle: In the later play, she is the wife not of the socially respectable older man, but of the transgressive young artist; and she has become the erotic object of the older Ridgeon, who sees in her some fantasy of female artistic beauty, a fantasy for which he is willing to kill by withholding his medical skill. The perfect irony of Ridgeon's infatuation is matched by Jennifer's tragi-comic fantasy of her husband as the noble artist. The poisonous ending of the play keeps her a primarily comic figure because she remains perfectly happy in her deluded picture of her dead husband, while Ridgeon is turned into a mainly tragic figure by the mere addition of self-knowledge. He comes to see himself through the woman's eyes: a jealous old man who "committed a purely disinterested murder" (p. 357).

That Shaw self-consciously reworked the psychological pattern of the woman's role in the rivalry of the Doubles from *The Devil's Disciple* to *The Doctor's Dilemma* can be seen from his having given Jennifer a line virtually identical to a line he gave Judith— a line, moreover, that describes the relationship of the two men to be that of psychological twins. In the earlier play, Judith reproaches Dick Dudgeon for being jealous of her husband: "Can you not forgive him for being so much better than you are?" In the later play, Jennifer reproaches Ridgeon: "Can you not forgive him for being superior to you? for being cleverer? for being braver? for being a great artist?" (p. 326). Where the earlier pair's rivalry centered on a question of relative moral worth, each wanting to be the better man, each discovering the truth about himself, the later play's pair of Doubles compete as twin artists. (For Shaw the defining characteristic of the artist was that he or she should create new thought; hence, he regarded scientists like Ridgeon, inventor of a new treatment for tuberculosis, or Henry Higgins, the phoneticist in *Pygmalion*, as artists in that broad sense.)

There is yet another link between the two plays. Shaw asserted that the idea for *The Doctor's Dilemma* resulted from hearing his friend, the great physician Sir Almoth Wright (upon whom and whose development of opsonin Shaw based Ridgeon's story), when asked if he could take on an extra patient, say that he would have to consider whose life was more worth saving. In *The Devil's Disciple* the saving of lives (and souls) based on moral worth is at issue, for Dick saves the minister's life, and the minister in turn wants to save Dick's soul but changes to saving his life. Implicit in each play is the question: Whose lives are worth saving? In the more optimistic and comic vision of *The Devil's Disciple*, there is obviously so much goodness in each of the two men that the answer to the question would seem: Everyone's life is worth saving. In the darker *Doctor's Dilemma*, the answer would seem: hardly anyone's.

The most prevalent paradigm for stories of Doubles—*The Strange Case of Dr. Jekyll and Mr. Hyde* and *The Picture of Dorian Gray*, to take examples contemporary with *The Doctor's Dilemma*—is that the destruction of one's Double means the destruction of oneself. When Doctor Ridgeon kills Louis Dubedat he is trying to kill his

unrealized self. In an unguarded moment, after discovering Dubedat's true nature to be that of an unscrupulous liar, cheat, and
monstrous egotist, Ridgeon remarks to his old patron and friend,
Sir Patrick: "I'm not at all convinced that the world wouldnt be a
better world if everybody behaved as Dubedat does than it is now
that everybody behaves as Blenkinsop does" (pp. 300–301). That
is, he feels the world would be better if everyone behaved with regard to self-interest and without regard to the interest of others.
Sir Patrick challenges Ridgeon to explain why he then does not
behave so. Ridgeon replies that he cannot. He would like to act
that way but cannot get up the courage. He calls it a dilemma, and
thus explains the title: To think one way and to live another is the
doctor's dilemma. Finally, though, he tries to resolve his dilemma
by killing Louis. But as the play's final scene—one of Shaw's greatest—shows, in doing so he destroys himself, for Jennifer categor-
ically rejects his attempt to take Louis's place in her bed and in her
heart. She has married someone else, according to her husband's
dying wish.

Historian and critic Jacques Barzun says that if you open a Shaw
play to any scene and begin reading, you quickly become convinced that the characters are talking about life and death matters.
So intensely do they listen to one another and turn every assertion, query, and rejoinder into blows, thrusts, and shots, that one
feels both of them cannot possibly emerge from the "discussion"
alive. This is particularly true of Ridgeon's final confrontation with
Jennifer. The scene anticipates the ferocious struggle between
Higgins and Eliza in *Pygmalion*—another play in which an older
man has a potential sexual relationship with a younger woman that
ends in a checkmate.

PYGMALION

The parallels between Eliza Doolittle and Jennifer Dubedat result chiefly from their involvement—their struggles—with
older men whose apparent coldness stems from their scientists'

approach to life and human relations. And just as Shaw revealed that Jennifer occupied a niche in his imagination similar to Judith's (in *The Devil's Disciple*) by giving the former an expanded version of a line belonging to the latter, so too does Shaw give Eliza one of Jennifer's lines. In that no-quarter-given final dialogue between Jennifer and Ridgeon, Jennifer expresses her frustration at trying to converse with him: "I don't understand that. And I cant argue with you" (p. 357). In Eliza's last verbal smack-down with Higgins, she expresses a similar sense of futility: "I cant talk to you: you turn everything against me" (p. 456). Both women are complaining about more than traditional male-female miscommunication (though there is plenty of that in their dialogue); each is rebelling against Ridgeon's and Higgins's automatic treatment of them as creatures, as means to an end rather than ends in themselves. In Ridgeon's case, he wants to possess Beauty itself in the person of Jennifer, whose beauty first attracts him through one of her husband's drawings of her, for then he would take the place of the artist, Louis, who is capable of creating beauty.

Higgins's case is more deranged. The man admits he has never married because he has never found a woman enough like his mother—a woman, Shaw takes pains to point out, who surrounds herself with art. Now, a son who looks for a replicate of his mother in a wife is a son who wants to take his father's place, to be his own father (note that Higgins's father is never so much as referred to in the play). Higgins has mastered the art of speech, of phonetics, so that he can identify people's hidden origins, as he does with the crowd that gathers around Eliza when she suspects he is a detective ready to arrest her for prostitution and is protesting her innocence. As soon as he hears their accents, he tells them where they were born, all the while concealing his own identity. (There is something of Shakespeare's "Duke of dark corners" in *Measure for Measure*, walking amongst his people incognito, as well as of Shakespeare's Prospero about Higgins.) Pickering even asks him if he does this in a music hall for a living, as if Higgins were a magician. (Shaw had a similar experience when, while lecturing dock workers on elocution, they called him a "quick-change artist.")

Higgins belongs with Ibsen's Master Builder (in *The Master Builder*, 1892) and Rubek the sculptor (in *When We Dead Awaken*, 1899) among modern drama's most profound studies of the artist's psychology, for the Professor of Speech forgets the difference between life and art. When he undertakes the experiment of turning the "draggle-tailed guttersnipe" Eliza Doolittle into a "duchess at an ambassador's garden party," Higgins imagines that he is a god creating out of nothing, out of the "squashed cabbage leaves of Covent Garden." He fails to see that he has only transported her from one kind of limiting garden to another. As part of the fantasy of creator he lives out, he must become Eliza's father: "I'll be worse than two fathers to you." He considers the "gift of articulate speech" he is to give Eliza a "divine" one, but it is really the parent's gift to the child; more particularly, the mother gives language to the child (which is why we speak the "mother tongue"). Much later in the play, Shaw will make this point comically by having Henry's mother, Mrs. Higgins, trick her son into not whistling by provoking a remark from him, and explain herself by saying, "I only wanted to make you speak" (p. 445).

In making Eliza speak, Higgins becomes her parent; he becomes a creator, instead of someone who is himself created. He can fantasize that he is an original, in the way all artists want to believe that their art is original. That is why Shaw has Higgins tell everyone where they originated; and why Shaw makes Higgins identify himself professionally to Pickering as one who does "a little as a poet on Miltonic lines" (p. 378). (When Shaw prepared the play to be filmed, he excised this reference to Milton, perhaps because it was too revealing of his anxieties about his own originality), for Milton's Satan (in *Paradise Lost*) claims not to have been created by God: He considers himself to be coeval with God. In other words, Satan considers himself self-begotten, the author of himself; he has no origin outside himself. Nor does Higgins. Shaw plays a great deal with images of Higgins as a satanic tempter, as when Eliza feels "tempted" by his offer of chocolates, or when Mrs. Pearce reproaches him for "tempting" Eliza; he even munches an apple, the biblical symbol of temptation, as he suggests to her that she might marry someone or other.

But when his Frankenstein's "creature," Eliza, comes to life, he treats her as his creation, not as a fellow creature. Higgins has been slow to see that Eliza has fully as much soul as he, that she is full of humanity and self-respect, that she has ambition and goodness in her. The sailor-hat Shaw gives her to wear befits her willingness to voyage into life, though her voyage begins with a tempest of rain over Covent Garden. Higgins fails to recognize the gumption she shows in seeking him out to improve her speech so she can earn enough to live a decent life. To him she is only the subject of an experiment whereby he may demonstrate his art; to him she has no feelings that he need bother about. But he is wrong: Eliza feels intensely. Indeed, the powerful drive of her feelings brings her to life in the fourth act and drives her to independence from Higgins in the fifth act. (Like *The Doctor's Dilemma*, *Pygmalion* has five acts, showing the affinity between the two plays, but also showing that Shaw is particularly conscious here of the Shakespearean model.)

Higgins says to Pickering that all the attractive young, rich American women he teaches "might as well be blocks of wood," as far as their sexually tempting him is concerned. And at first he regards Eliza this way—as a block of wood out of which he will carve a duchess. When Leontes looks upon his wife Hermione's statue in Shakespeare's *The Winter's Tale*, he becomes ashamed, remembering the grave injustice he did her, and asks rhetorically: "Does not the stone rebuke me for being more stone than it?" (act

5, scene 3). Eliza's flexible humanity rebukes Higgins for being stone cold. It is an accusation that stings and provokes Higgins to one of his great outbursts about the life of science, of art being utterly unlike the life of the gutter, not immediate, not warm. (The speech actually reflects an intensely dramatic letter Shaw sent to Mrs. Patrick Campbell, while she was rehearsing the part of Eliza Doolittle, in which he reproaches her for rejecting him.) Eliza retorts that she was not seeking from him what the gutter gave; she wanted from him respect for her as a fellow human being, some regard for her feelings. She rightly says that she will not care for someone who does not care for her. But she does not quite succeed in penetrating his defense system until she shows the shrewdest understanding of where his pride lies. She threatens to set herself up as a rival artist by becoming a teacher of phonetics. That finally makes Higgins actually think of her as an original herself, and not just a copy of him. When at the end of the play Eliza rebuffs Higgins's final attempt to bully her, she tells Higgins to buy his own gloves, and then "sweeps out"; she becomes mobile, while he remains, statue-like, standing in place.

HEARTBREAK HOUSE

The Doctor's Dilemma and *Pygmalion*, for all their embedding in social problems—doctors having a pecuniary interest in their patients' illnesses, language as class barrier—grew out of Shaw's preoccupations with the figure of the artist, the dangers of self-absorption combined poisonously with lack of self-knowledge. *Heartbreak House* grew out of and during the four-year cataclysm World War I, the family feud among the ruling houses of Europe, which nearly ended them all, along with everyone else. To Shaw, who forged—and I mean forged—through an intense exercise of will and faith an optimism about the future course of the human race in the face of his own subcutaneous suspicions that human beings harbor within a fugitive desire for self-destruction, the war was a nightmare come true.

He first reacted, as writers tend to do, by writing something—a pamphlet he called "Common Sense About the War." In it he argued that first of all, now that we (Great Britain and its allies) are in the war we must prosecute it vigorously to the finish, but we must seize the opportunity when it is over to insure that it is the last war. While conceding the necessity of victory, though, Shaw argued that we must not deal with the defeated Germans from a morally superior position. He also opined that if the Germans behaved badly to the civilian population in Belgium, we have behaved badly to subjects of our empires, that the Germans' militarism differs little from ours. He challenged the rhetoric of the war by suggesting that if those who insist we must crush Germany totally mean it, then why do we not try to kill all the German women instead of the men?

Such equations and flippancy infuriated the reading populace and the literati, who mostly supported the war and Britain's role in it. Shaw turned almost overnight from a tolerated, popular provocateur into a national persona non grata. He was denounced left and right, called the vilest names (fellow playwright and former friend Henry Arthur Jones, in an open letter, called Shaw "a freakish homunculus, germinated outside of lawful procreation"); Theodore Roosevelt vilified him. Shaw's books were removed from bookstore shelves; people asserted they would get up and leave the room if Shaw entered; for a while it seemed he might suffer Oscar Wilde's fate upon being imprisoned for sodomy, that of being deliberately ignored. To Shaw such attacks mattered little, for his courage and indifference to personal criticism was—well, extraordinary.

I know of no better example from Shaw's life that illustrates this quality of extraordinariness in him than the episode of his expulsion from the Dramatists' Club. At an October 27, 1915, meeting, there was a discussion among the members of their desire not to encounter Shaw at the Club, given his attitude toward the war. The Secretary, H. M. Paul, then wrote to Shaw that his company was undesired by some of the members. Did Shaw sue them? Did he whine to the newspapers that his freedom of speech was being suppressed? No, he wrote back to Paul that as the constitution of the Club made no provision for expelling members, here is how they must go about it: "The proper procedure is as follows. They must draw up a resolution that I be expelled from the Club, and state their reasons. Of this full notice must be given so that every member of the Club shall be warned that it is going to be moved." Etc. Now, it takes a miraculous amount of good temper (or a miraculous absence of rancor) to write such a letter. Who among our public literary figures would be capable of such a gesture in such a political context?

For Shaw, a comic sense of things was not only indispensable, but a stay against despair. Yet he felt the wounds of the war through the grief of friends who lost loved ones in battle. When Mrs. Patrick Campbell's son, Alan, was killed in 1917, Shaw wrote to her expressing his anger over the war: "These things simply make me furious. I want to swear. I *do* swear. Killed just because people are blasted fools." At other times, Shaw was able to channel his anger into a kind of humor that can only be described as dangerous—and courageous.

When St. John Ervine, a fellow playwright and future biographer of Shaw, was wounded by a shell and had to have a leg amputated, Shaw wrote to cheer him up. First he recounted to Ervine how he, Shaw, had once broken a leg and had to get around on crutches but found that he could do without his "leg just as easily as without eyes in the back of my head." Shaw then asserted that Ervine was actually better off than he himself was: "You will be in a stronger position. I had to feed and nurse the useless leg. You will have all the energy you hitherto spent on it to invest in the rest of your frame. For a man of your profession two legs are an extravagance." Shaw went on to enumerate other benefits to losing the leg, such as an increased pension, and no more going to the Front. Finally Shaw reached the logical conclusion: "The more the case is gone into the more it appears that you are an exceptionally happy and fortunate man, relieved of a limb to which you owed none of your fame, and which indeed was the cause of your conscription" (*Collected Letters*, vol. 3, pp. 550–551). Wit does not usually seem a humane weapon, but such a letter shows the same kind of comic courage Aristophanes exhibited when he condemned war by imagining women on a sex strike.

Heartbreak House was written in a context where one could consider writing such a letter, and the play's mixed tones show it. Shaw claimed that the play wrote itself. By turns whimsical, farcical, melancholy, tragi-comic, and visionary, *Heartbreak House* sometimes drifts and sometimes sails full speed ahead—whithersoever. Shaw said that it represented the European elite before the war—by which he meant the people whose concerns should have been history, political economy, and government, but were instead sex, aesthetics, leisure activities, and money, and so people who let their countries blunder into war. Shaw arranges for various representative members of this society to gather for a weekend in the country in ancient Captain Shotover's house, which is designed to resemble a ship and therefore carries the metaphoric suggestion that it is the Ship of State. (People have been misled by Shaw's subtitle, "A Fantasia in the Russian Manner on English Themes," to see a strong resemblance to Chekhov's plays, but *Heartbreak House* is at least equally indebted to Tolstoy's *The Fruits of Enlightenment* or Gorky's *The Lower Depths*.)

Shaw claimed repeatedly that he did not know what his play meant, and indeed it is full of mystery. The play is launched with a young woman falling asleep while reading *Othello*, so that the rest of the play seems to be her dream, a bed-voyage. It begins and ends respectively with the averting of a small and a large destruction. In between, identities become confused and fluid as in dreams. The Captain insists on mistaking Mazzini Dunn for his old boatswain, Billy Dunn, though they do not look alike, and when the real Billy shows up unexpectedly, Shotover asks him, "Are there two of you?"—and gets one of the play's biggest laughs (in a play that has fewer laughs than almost any other of Shaw's plays). Billy explains to his Captain the confusion by noting that there were two branches of the Dunn family, the drinking Dunns and the thinking Dunns.

Captain Shotover as an inventor, adventurer, and architect succeeds Ridgeon and Higgins as a figure for the artist, but an artist who has gone slightly mad from disappointment with reality, whose heart was broken when his daughter rejected his ways and left home, and who himself has taken refuge in rum. To fill the void made by his daughter's desertion, he enters into a spiritual marriage with young Ellie Dunn, who had been in actuality planning herself to marry an older man, the crude capitalist Alfred Mangan. In that way, Shotover continues in the Shavian/Shakespearean line of spiritual affinities between fathers and daughters. In *Major Barbara*, Cusins says to Undershaft: "A father's love for a grown-up daughter is the most dangerous of all infatuations. I apologize for mentioning my own pale, coy, mistrustful fancy in the same breath with it" (p. 98). Like Undershaft, too, Shotover invents and keeps explosives.

To the play's contemporaries who lived through World War I, *Heartbreak House*, however indirectly, expressed the feelings of sadness, futility, and madness the war provoked (T. E. Lawrence, known as Lawrence of Arabia, who became a great friend of Shaw, called it "the most blazing bit of genius in English literature"). The play never alludes explicitly to the context of the war, though. The closest it comes to doing so is at the end, when a zeppelin flies over the house during an air raid and bombs are dropped. The ghostly inhabitants of Heartbreak House are variously terrified and thrilled by the energy, sound, and destructive power of the air machines. At the end, Captain Shotover calls the raid Judgment Day, while the heroines, Ellie Dunn and Hesione Hushabye, hope that the zeppelin will return the next night. Does Shaw mean that these people, the failed leaders of the best society, are played out and long only for the world to be destroyed? Or is their thrilling to the wonder and raw energy of the sky machine a sign of their renewal? Their purgation? (Shaw had always bet on young women, like Ellie, to become "active verbs" and change the world.)

I think Shaw himself meant both possibilities to be weighed, for the direction Europe would take in 1919 was as unknown to Shaw as it was to Europe. But since both Shaw and Europe would see another World War twenty years later, it would seem that Ellie and Hesione had their hope fulfilled; the air machines indeed did come back. Shaw survived that war, too, and did not die until 1950, writing plays—practicing the craft of Shakespeare, as he put it— and prefaces, fables, screenplays, and political treatises, and enough letters for ten lives.

Shaw once inscribed one of his books as a gift to a friend. The friend subsequently fell on hard times and had to sell the valuable volume to a secondhand bookstore. Shaw found himself browsing the very bookstore at a later date and stumbled upon the volume inscribed by him. He immediately purchased it and re-sent it to his friend with the additional inscription: "With the renewed compliments of the author, G. Bernard Shaw." The current neglect of Shaw may have nothing to do with hard economic times, but the present two editions of his plays by Barnes & Noble Classics should be understood to be placed before the public—with the renewed compliments of their author.

JOHN A. BERTOLINI was educated at Manhattan College and Columbia University. He teaches English and dramatic literature, Shakespeare, and film at Middlebury College, in Vermont, where he is Ellis Professor of the Liberal Arts. He is the author of *The Playwrighting Self of Bernard Shaw* and editor of *Shaw and Other Playwrights*; he has also published articles on Alfred Hitchcock, Renaissance drama, and British and American dramatists. He is writing a book on Terence Rattigan's plays.

PYGMALION
AND
THREE OTHER PLAYS

MAJOR BARBARA

PREFACE TO MAJOR BARBARA

FIRST AID TO CRITICS

BEFORE DEALING WITH the deeper aspects of Major Barbara, let me, for the credit of English literature, make a protest against an unpatriotic habit into which many of my critics have fallen. Whenever my view strikes them as being at all outside the range of, say, an ordinary suburban churchwarden, they conclude that I am echoing Schopenhauer, Nietzsche, Ibsen, Strindberg, Tolstoy,[1] or some other heresiarch* in northern or eastern Europe.

I confess there is something flattering in this simple faith in my accomplishment as a linguist and my erudition as a philosopher. But I cannot tolerate the assumption that life and literature is so poor in these islands that we must go abroad for all dramatic material that is not common and all ideas that are not superficial. I therefore venture to put my critics in possession of certain facts concerning my contact with modern ideas.

About half a century ago, an Irish novelist, Charles Lever, wrote a story entitled A Day's Ride: A Life's Romance. It was published by Charles Dickens in Household Words, and proved so strange to the public taste that Dickens pressed Lever to make short work of it. I read scraps of this novel when I was a child; and it made an enduring impression on me. The hero was a very romantic hero, trying to live bravely, chivalrously, and powerfully by

---

*Leader of a heresy (belief contrary to orthodox tenets of a religion).

dint of mere romance-fed imagination, without courage, without means, without knowledge, without skill, without anything real except his bodily appetites. Even in my childhood I found in this poor devil's unsuccessful encounters with the facts of life, a poignant quality that romantic fiction lacked. The book, in spite of its first failure, is not dead: I saw its title the other day in the catalogue of Tauchnitz.*

Now why is it that when I also deal in the tragi-comic irony of the conflict between real life and the romantic imagination, no critic ever affiliates me to my countryman and immediate forerunner, Charles Lever, whilst they confidently derive me from a Norwegian author of whose language I do not know three words, and of whom I knew nothing until years after the Shavian *Anschauung*† was already unequivocally declared in books full of what came, ten years later, to be perfunctorily labelled Ibsenism. I was not Ibsenist even at second hand; for Lever, though he may have read Henri Beyle, *alias* Stendhal, certainly never read Ibsen. Of the books that made Lever popular, such as Charles O'Malley and Harry Lorrequer, I know nothing but the names and some of the illustrations. But the story of the day's ride and life's romance of Potts (claiming alliance with Pozzo di Borgo) caught me and fascinated me as something strange and significant, though I already knew all about Alnaschar and Don Quixote and Simon Tappertit and many another romantic hero mocked by reality.[2] From the plays of Aristophanes to the tales of Stevenson that mockery has been made familiar to all who are properly saturated with letters.

Where, then, was the novelty in Lever's tale? Partly, I think, in a new seriousness in dealing with Potts's disease.‡ Formerly, the contrast between madness and sanity was deemed comic: Hogarth shews us how fashionable people went in parties to Bedlam to

---

laugh at the lunatics. I myself have had a village idiot exhibited to me as something irresistibly funny. On the stage the madman was once a regular comic figure: that was how Hamlet got his opportunity before Shakespear touched him. The originality of Shakespear's version lay in his taking the lunatic sympathetically and seriously, and thereby making an advance towards the eastern consciousness of the fact that lunacy may be inspiration in disguise, since a man who has more brains than his fellows necessarily appears as mad to them as one who has less. But Shakespear did not do for Pistol and Parolles what he did for Hamlet. The particular sort of madman they represented, the romantic make-believer, lay outside the pale of sympathy in literature: he was pitilessly despised and ridiculed here as he was in the east under the name of Alnaschar, and was doomed to be, centuries later, under the name of Simon Tappertit. When Cervantes relented over Don Quixote, and Dickens relented over Pickwick, they did not become impartial: they simply changed sides, and became friends and apologists where they had formerly been mockers.

In Lever's story there is a real change of attitude. There is no relenting towards Potts: he never gains our affections like Don Quixote and Pickwick: he has not even the infatuate courage of Tappertit. But we dare not laugh at him, because, somehow, we recognize ourselves in Potts. We may, some of us, have enough nerve, enough muscle, enough luck, enough tact or skill or address or knowledge to carry things off better than he did; to impose on the people who saw through him; to fascinate Katinka (who cut Potts so ruthlessly at the end of the story); but for all that, we know that Potts plays an enormous part in ourselves and in the world, and that the social problem is not a problem of story-book heroes of the older pattern, but a problem of Pottses, and of how to make men of them. To fall back on my old phrase, we have the feeling—one that Alnaschar, Pistol, Parolles, and Tappertit never gave us—that Potts is a piece of really scientific natural history as distinguished from comic story telling. His author is not throwing a stone at a creature of another and inferior order, but making a confession, with the effect that the stone hits everybody full in the conscience and causes their self-esteem to smart very sorely. Hence the failure of Lever's book to please the readers of Household Words. That pain in the self-esteem nowadays causes critics to raise a cry of Ibsenism. I therefore assure them that the sensation first came to me from Lever and may have come to him from Beyle, or at least out of the Stendhalian atmosphere. I exclude the hypothesis of complete originality on Lever's part, because a man can no more be completely original in that sense than a tree can grow out of air.

Another mistake as to my literary ancestry is made whenever I violate the romantic convention that all women are angels when they are not devils; that they are better looking than men; that their part in courtship is entirely passive; and that the human female form is the most beautiful object in nature. Schopenhauer wrote a splenetic essay which, as it is neither polite nor profound, was probably intended to knock this nonsense violently on the head. A sentence denouncing the idolized form as ugly has been largely quoted. The English critics have read that sentence; and I must here affirm, with as much gentleness as the implication will bear, that it has yet to be proved that they have dipped any deeper. At all events, whenever an English playwright represents a young and marriageable woman as being anything but a romantic heroine, he is disposed of without further thought as an echo of Schopenhauer. My own case is a specially hard one, because, when I implore the critics who are obsessed with the Schopenhaurian formula to remember that playwrights, like sculptors, study their figures from life, and not from philosophic essays, they reply passionately that I am not a playwright and that my stage figures do not live. But even so, I may and do ask them why, if they must give the credit of my plays to a philosopher, they do not give it to an English philosopher? Long before I ever read a word by Schopenhauer, or even knew whether he was a philosopher or a chemist, the Socialist revival of the eighteen-eighties brought me into contact, both literary and personal, with Mr. Ernest Belfort Bax, an English Socialist and philosophic essayist, whose handling of modern feminism would provoke romantic protests from Schopenhauer himself, or even Strindberg. At a matter of fact I hardly noticed Schopenhauer's disparagements of women when they came under my notice later on, so thoroughly had Mr. Bax familiarized me with the homoist* attitude, and forced me to recognize the extent to which public opinion, and consequently legislation and jurisprudence, is corrupted by feminist sentiment.

But Mr. Bax's essays were not confined to the Feminist question.† He was a ruthless critic of current morality. Other writers have gained sympathy for dramatic criminals by eliciting the alleged "soul of goodness in things evil";‡ but Mr. Bax would propound some quite undramatic and apparently shabby violation of our commercial law and morality, and not merely defend it with the most disconcerting ingenuity, but actually prove it to be a positive duty that nothing but the certainty of police persecution should prevent every right-minded man from at once doing on principle. The Socialists were naturally shocked, being for the most part morbidly moral people; but at all events they were saved later on from the delusion that nobody but Nietzsche had ever challenged our mercanto-Christian morality. I first heard the name of Nietzsche from a German mathematician, Miss Borchardt, who had read my Quintessence of Ibsenism, and told me that she saw what I had been reading: namely, Nietzsche's Jenseits von Gut und Böse.§ Which I protest I had never seen, and could not have read with any comfort, for want of the necessary German, if I had seen it.

Nietzsche, like Schopenhauer, is the victim in England of a sin-

---

*One who vaunts the worth of the male gender.

†That is, the question of whether women are morally superior to men.

‡Quotation from Shakespeare's *Henry V* (act 4, scene 1).

§English translation: *Beyond Good and Evil* (1886).

gle much quoted sentence containing the phrase "big blonde beast."[3] On the strength of this alliteration it is assumed that Nietzsche gained his European reputation by a senseless glorification of selfish bullying as the rule of life, just as it is assumed, on the strength of the single word Superman (Übermensch) borrowed by me from Nietzsche, that I look for the salvation of society to the despotism of a single Napoleonic Superman, in spite of my careful demonstration of the folly of that outworn infatuation. But even the less recklessly superficial critics seem to believe that the modern objection to Christianity as a pernicious slave-morality was first put forward by Nietzsche. It was familiar to me before I ever heard of Nietzsche. The late Captain Wilson, author of several queer pamphlets, propagandist of a metaphysical system called Comprehensionism, and inventor of the term "Crosstian-ity"* to distinguish the retrograde element in Christendom, was wont thirty years ago, in the discussions of the Dialectical Society, to protest earnestly against the beatitudes of the Sermon on the Mount as excuses for cowardice and servility, as destructive of our will, and consequently of our honor and manhood. Now it is true that Captain Wilson's moral criticism of Christianity was not a historical theory of it, like Nietzsche's; but this objection cannot be made to Mr. Stuart-Glennie, the successor of Buckle as a philosophic historian,[†] who has devoted his life to the elaboration and propagation of his theory that Christianity is part of an epoch (or rather an aberration, since it began as recently as 6000 B.C. and is already collapsing) produced by the necessity in which the numerically inferior white races found themselves to impose their domination on the colored races by priestcraft, making a virtue

---

*Shaw borrows F. J. Wilson's term for the morbid dwelling on Christ's suffering.

†John S. Stuart-Glennie (1832–1909?) was a Scots writer and historian; English historian Henry Thomas Buckle (1821–1862) is the author of *History of Civilization in England*.

and a popular religion of drudgery and submissiveness in this world not only as a means of achieving saintliness of character but of securing a reward in heaven. Here you have the slave-morality view formulated by a Scotch philosopher* long before English writers began chattering about Nietzsche.

As Mr. Stuart-Glennie traced the evolution of society to the conflict of races, his theory made some sensation among Socialists—that is, among the only people who were seriously thinking about historical evolution at all—by its collision with the class-conflict theory of Karl Marx. Nietzsche, as I gather, regarded the slave-morality as having been invented and imposed on the world by slaves making a virtue of necessity and a religion of their servitude. Mr. Stuart-Glennie regards the slave-morality as an invention of the superior white race to subjugate the minds of the inferior races whom they wished to exploit, and who would have destroyed them by force of numbers if their minds had not been subjugated. As this process is in operation still, and can be studied at first hand not only in our Church schools and in the struggle between our modern proprietary classes and the proletariat, but in the part played by Christian missionaries in reconciling the black races of Africa to their subjugation by European Capitalism, we can judge for ourselves whether the initiative came from above or below. My object here is not to argue the historical point, but simply to make our theatre critics ashamed of their habit of treating Britain as an intellectual void, and assuming that every philosophical idea, every historic theory, every criticism of our moral, religious and juridical institutions, must necessarily be either imported from abroad, or else a fantastic sally (in rather questionable taste) totally unrelated to the existing body of thought. I urge them to remember that this body of thought is the slowest of growths and the rarest of blossomings, and that if there is such a

---

*In later editions Shaw added here "of my acquaintance," after he had become friends with Stuart-Glennie.

thing on the philosophic plane as a matter of course, it is that no individual can make more than a minute contribution to it. In fact, their conception of clever persons parthenogenetically bringing forth complete original cosmogonies by dint of sheer "brilliancy" is part of that ignorant credulity which is the despair of the honest philosopher, and the opportunity of the religious impostor.

THE GOSPEL OF ST. ANDREW UNDERSHAFT

It is this credulity that drives me to help my critics out with Major Barbara by telling them what to say about it. In the millionaire Undershaft I have represented a man who has become intellectually and spiritually as well as practically conscious of the irresistible natural truth which we all abhor and repudiate: to wit, that the greatest of evils and the worst of crimes is poverty, and that our first duty—a duty to which every other consideration should be sacrificed—is not to be poor. "Poor but honest," "the respectable poor," and such phrases are as intolerable and as immoral as "drunken but amiable," "fraudulent but a good after-dinner speaker," "splendidly criminal," or the like. Security, the chief pretence of civilization, cannot exist where the worst of dangers, the danger of poverty, hangs over everyone's head, and where the alleged protection of our persons from violence is only an accidental result of the existence of a police force whose real business is to force the poor man to see his children starve whilst idle people overfeed pet dogs with the money that might feed and clothe them.

It is exceedingly difficult to make people realize that an evil is an evil. For instance, we seize a man and deliberately do him a malicious injury: say, imprison him for years. One would not suppose that it needed any exceptional clearness of wit to recognize in this an act of diabolical cruelty. But in England such a recognition provokes a stare of surprise, followed by an explanation that the outrage is punishment or justice or something else that is all right, or perhaps by a heated attempt to argue that we should all be robbed and murdered in our beds if such senseless villainies as sentences of imprisonment were not committed daily. It is useless to argue that even if this were true, which it is not, the alternative to adding crimes of our own to the crimes from which we suffer is not helpless submission. Chickenpox is an evil; but if I were to declare that we must either submit to it or else repress it sternly by seizing everyone who suffers from it and punishing them by inoculation with smallpox, I should be laughed at; for though nobody could deny that the result would be to prevent chickenpox to some extent by making people avoid it much more carefully, and to effect a further apparent prevention by making them conceal it very anxiously, yet people would have sense enough to see that the deliberate propagation of smallpox was a creation of evil, and must therefore be ruled out in favor of purely humane and hygienic measures. Yet in the precisely parallel case of a man breaking into my house and stealing my wife's diamonds I am expected as a matter of course to steal ten years of his life, torturing him all the time. If he tries to defeat that monstrous retaliation by shooting me, my survivors hang him. The net result suggested by the police statistics is that we inflict atrocious injuries on the burglars we catch in order to make the rest take effectual precautions against detection; so that instead of saving our wives' diamonds from burglary we only greatly decrease our chances of ever getting them back, and increase our chances of being shot by the robber if we are unlucky enough to disturb him at his work.

But the thoughtless wickedness with which we scatter sentences of imprisonment, torture in the solitary cell and on the plank bed, and flogging, on moral invalids and energetic rebels, is as nothing compared to the stupid levity with which we tolerate poverty as if it were either a wholesome tonic for lazy people or else a virtue to be embraced as St. Francis embraced it. If a man is indolent, let him be poor. If he is drunken, let him be poor. If he is not a gentleman, let him be poor. If he is addicted to the fine arts or to pure science instead of to trade and finance, let him be poor. If he chooses to spend his urban eighteen shillings a week or his agricultural thirteen shillings a week on his beer and his family instead of saving it up for his old age, let him be poor. Let nothing be done for "the undeserving": let him be poor. Serve him right! Also—somewhat inconsistently—blessed are the poor!

Now what does this Let Him Be Poor mean? It means let him be weak. Let him be ignorant. Let him become a nucleus of disease. Let him be a standing exhibition and example of ugliness and dirt. Let him have rickety children. Let him be cheap and let him drag his fellows down to his price by selling himself to do their work. Let his habitations turn our cities into poisonous congeries of slums. Let his daughters infect our young men with the diseases of the streets and his sons revenge him by turning the nation's manhood into scrofula, cowardice, cruelty, hypocrisy, political imbecility, and all the other fruits of oppression and malnutrition. Let the undeserving become still less deserving; and let the deserving lay up for himself, not treasures in heaven, but horrors in hell upon earth. This being so, is it really wise to let him be poor? Would he not do ten times less harm as a prosperous burglar, incendiary, ravisher or murderer, to the utmost limits of humanity's comparatively negligible impulses in these directions? Suppose we were to abolish all penalties for such activities, and decide that poverty is the one thing we will not tolerate—that every adult with less than, say, £365 a year, shall be painlessly but inexorably killed, and every hungry half naked child forcibly fattened and clothed, would not that be an enormous improvement on our existing system, which has already destroyed so many civilizations, and is visibly destroying ours in the same way?

Is there any radicle of such legislation in our parliamentary system? Well, there are two measures just sprouting in the political soil, which may conceivably grow to something valuable. One is the institution of a Legal Minimum Wage. The other, Old Age Pensions. But there is a better plan than either of these. Some time ago I mentioned the subject of Universal Old Age Pensions to my fellow Socialist Mr. Cobden-Sanderson, famous as an artist-craftsman in bookbinding and printing. "Why not Universal Pensions for Life?" said Cobden-Sanderson. In saying this, he solved the industrial problem at a stroke. At present we say callously to each citizen: "If you want money, earn it," as if his having or not having it were a matter that concerned himself alone. We do not even secure for him the opportunity of earning it: on the contrary, we allow our industry to be organized in open dependence on the maintenance of "a reserve army of unemployed" for the sake of "elasticity." The sensible course would be Cobden-Sanderson's: that is, to give every man enough to live well on, so as to guarantee the community against the possibility of a case of the malignant disease of poverty, and then (necessarily) to see that he earned it.

Undershaft, the hero of Major Barbara, is simply a man who, having grasped the fact that poverty is a crime, knows that when society offered him the alternative of poverty or a lucrative trade in death and destruction, it offered him, not a choice between opulent villainy and humble virtue, but between energetic enterprise and cowardly infamy. His conduct stands the Kantian test,[4] which Peter Shirley's does not. Peter Shirley is what we call the honest poor man. Undershaft is what we call the wicked rich one: Shirley is Lazarus, Undershaft Dives.* Well, the misery of the world is due to the fact that the great mass of men act and believe as Peter Shirley acts and believes. If they acted and believed as Undershaft acts and believes, the immediate result would be a revolution of incalculable beneficence. To be wealthy, says Undershaft, is with me a point of honor for which I am prepared to kill at the risk of my own life. This preparedness is, as he says, the final test of sincerity. Like Froissart's medieval hero,† who saw that "to rob

---

Dives is Latin for "rich"; Shaw is referring to the biblical story of Lazarus and the Rich Man (see Luke 16:19–31).

†Reference to Aymerigot Marcel, governor of Aloise, described in *Chronicles*, an account of the Hundred Years' War by Jean Froissart (1333?–c.1405).

and pill was a good life," he is not the dupe of that public sentiment against killing which is propagated and endowed by people who would otherwise be killed themselves, or of the mouth-honor paid to poverty and obedience by rich and insubordinate do-nothings who want to rob the poor without courage and command them without superiority. Froissart's knight, in placing the achievement of a good life before all the other duties—which indeed are not duties at all when they conflict with it, but plain wickednesses—behaved bravely, admirably, and, in the final analysis, public-spiritedly. Medieval society, on the other hand, behaved very badly indeed in organizing itself so stupidly that a good life could be achieved by robbing and pilling. If the knight's contemporaries had been all as resolute as he, robbing and pilling would have been the shortest way to the gallows, just as, if we were all as resolute and clearsighted as Undershaft, an attempt to live by means of what is called "an independent income" would be the shortest way to the lethal chamber. But as, thanks to our political imbecility and personal cowardice (fruits of poverty, both), the best imitation of a good life now procurable is life on an independent income, all sensible people aim at securing such an income, and are, of course, careful to legalize and moralize both it and all the actions and sentiments which lead to it and support it as an institution. What else can they do? They know, of course, that they are rich because others are poor. But they cannot help that: it is for the poor to repudiate poverty when they have had enough of it. The thing can be done easily enough: the demonstrations to the contrary made by the economists, jurists, moralists and sentimentalists hired by the rich to defend them, or even doing the work gratuitously out of sheer folly and abjectness, impose only on the hirers.

The reason why the independent income-tax payers are not solid in defence of their position is that since we are not medieval rovers through a sparsely populated country, the poverty of those we rob prevents our having the good life for which we sacrifice

them. Rich men or aristocrats with a developed sense of life—
men like Ruskin and William Morris and Kropotkin*—have enormous social appetites and very fastidious personal ones. They are
not content with handsome houses: they want handsome cities.
They are not content with be-diamonded wives and blooming
daughters: they complain because the charwoman is badly
dressed, because the laundress smells of gin, because the semp-
stress is anemic, because every man they meet is not a friend and
every woman not a romance. They turn up their noses at their
neighbors' drains, and are made ill by the architecture of their
neighbors' houses. Trade patterns made to suit vulgar people do
not please them (and they can get nothing else): they cannot sleep
nor sit at ease upon "slaughtered" cabinet makers' furniture. The
very air is not good enough for them: there is too much factory
smoke in it. They even demand abstract conditions: justice, honor,
a noble moral atmosphere, a mystic nexus to replace the cash
nexus. Finally they declare that though to rob and pill with your
own hand on horseback and in steel coat may have been a good
life, to rob and pill by the hands of the policeman, the bailiff, and
the soldier, and to underpay them meanly for doing it, is not a
good life, but rather fatal to all possibility of even a tolerable one.
They call on the poor to revolt, and, finding the poor shocked at
their ungentlemanliness, despairingly revile the proletariat for its
"damned wantlessness" (*verdammte Bedürfnislosigkeit*).

So far, however, their attack on society has lacked simplicity.
The poor do not share their tastes nor understand their art-
criticisms. They do not want the simple life, nor the esthetic life;
on the contrary, they want very much to wallow in all the costly
vulgarities from which the elect souls among the rich turn away
with loathing. It is by surfeit and not by abstinence that they will
be cured of their hankering after unwholesome sweets. What they
do dislike and despise and are ashamed of is poverty. To ask them

---

*Prince Pyotr Kropotkin (1842–1921), Russian geographer and anarchist.

to fight for the difference between the Christmas number of the Illustrated London News and the Kelmscott Chaucer* is silly: they prefer the News. The difference between a stockbroker's cheap and dirty starched white shirt and collar and the comparatively costly and carefully dyed blue shirt of William Morris is a difference so disgraceful to Morris in their eyes that if they fought on the subject at all, they would fight in defence of the starch. "Cease to be slaves, in order that you may become cranks" is not a very inspiring call to arms; nor is it really improved by substituting saints for cranks. Both terms denote men of genius; and the common man does not want to live the life of a man of genius: he would much rather live the life of a pet collie if that were the only alternative. But he does want more money. Whatever else he may be vague about, he is clear about that. He may or may not prefer Major Barbara to the Drury Lane pantomime; but he always prefers five hundred pounds to five hundred shillings.

Now to deplore this preference as sordid, and teach children that it is sinful to desire money, is to strain towards the extreme possible limit of impudence in lying, and corruption in hypocrisy. The universal regard for money is the one hopeful fact in our civilization, the one sound spot in our social conscience. Money is the most important thing in the world. It represents health, strength, honor, generosity and beauty as conspicuously and undeniably as the want of it represents illness, weakness, disgrace, meanness and ugliness. Not the least of its virtues is that it destroys base people as certainly as it fortifies and dignifies noble people. It is only when it is cheapened to worthlessness for some, and made impossibly dear to others, that it becomes a curse. In short it is a curse only in such foolish social conditions that life itself is a curse.

---

*Reference to *The Works of Geoffrey Chaucer* (1896), beautifully illustrated by English painter Edward Burne-Jones and printed by William Morris (English artist and founder of Kelmscott Press); this edition of Chaucer's works represents aestheticism.

For the two things are inseparable: money is the counter that enables life to be distributed socially: it *is* life as truly as sovereigns
and bank notes are money. The first duty of every citizen is to insist on having money on reasonable terms; and this demand is not
complied with by giving four men three shillings each for ten or
twelve hours' drudgery and one man a thousand pounds for nothing. The crying need of the nation is not for better morals, cheaper
bread, temperance, liberty, culture, redemption of fallen sisters
and erring brothers, nor the grace, love and fellowship of the Trinity, but simply for enough money. And the evil to be attacked is
not sin, suffering, greed, priestcraft, kingcraft, demagogy, mo-
nopoly, ignorance, drink, war, pestilence, nor any other of the
scapegoats which reformers sacrifice, but simply poverty.

Once take your eyes from the ends of the earth and fix them on
this truth just under your nose; and Andrew Undershaft's views
will not perplex you in the least. Unless indeed his constant sense
that he is only the instrument of a Will or Life Force which uses
him for purposes wider than his own, may puzzle you. If so, that
is because you are walking either in artificial Darwinian darkness,
or in mere stupidity. All genuinely religious people have that consciousness. To them Undershaft the Mystic will be quite intelligible, and his perfect comprehension of his daughter the Salvationist
and her lover the Euripidean republican natural and inevitable.
That, however, is not new, even on the stage. What is new, as far
as I know, is that article in Undershaft's religion which recognizes
in Money the first need and in poverty the vilest sin of man and
society.

This dramatic conception has not, of course, been attained *per
saltum*.* Nor has it been borrowed from Nietzsche or from any
man born beyond the Channel. The late Samuel Butler,† in his own

---

*By leaping (Latin).

†English poet (1612–1680); author of the long satirical poem *Hudibras*, mentioned below.

department the greatest English writer of the latter half of the XIX century, steadily inculcated the necessity and morality of a conscientious Laodiceanism* in religion and of an earnest and constant sense of the importance of money. It drives one almost to despair of English literature when one sees so extraordinary a study of English life as Butler's posthumous Way of All Flesh making so little impression that when, some years later, I produce plays in which Butler's extraordinarily fresh, free and future-piercing suggestions have an obvious share, I am met with nothing but vague cacklings about Ibsen and Nietzsche, and am only too thankful that they are not about Alfred de Musset and Georges Sand.[5] Really, the English do not deserve to have great men. They allowed Butler to die practically unknown, whilst I, a comparatively insignificant Irish journalist, was leading them by the nose into an advertisement of me which has made my own life a burden. In Sicily there is a Via Samuele Butler. When an English tourist sees it, he either asks "Who the devil was Samuele Butler?" or wonders why the Sicilians should perpetuate the memory of the author of Hudibras.

Well, it cannot be denied that the English are only too anxious to recognize a man of genius if somebody will kindly point him out to them. Having pointed myself out in this manner with some success, I now point out Samuel Butler, and trust that in consequence I shall hear a little less in future of the novelty and foreign origin of the ideas which are now making their way into the English theatre through plays written by Socialists. There are living men whose originality and power are as obvious as Butler's; and when they die that fact will be discovered. Meanwhile I recommend them to insist on their own merits as an important part of their own business.

---

*Indifference to religion; as charged against the Laodiceans in the Bible, Revelation 3:14–22.

THE SALVATION ARMY

When Major Barbara was produced in London, the second act was reported in an important northern newspaper as a withering attack on the Salvation Army, and the despairing ejaculation of Barbara deplored by a London daily as a tasteless blasphemy. And they were set right, not by the professed critics of the theatre, but by religious and philosophical publicists like Sir Oliver Lodge and Dr. Stanton Coit, and strenuous Nonconformist journalists like Mr. William Stead, who not only understand the act as well as the Salvationists themselves, but also saw it in its relation to the religious life of the nation, a life which seems to lie not only outside the sympathy of many of our theatre critics, but actually outside their knowledge of society. Indeed nothing could be more ironically curious than the confrontation Major Barbara effected of the theatre enthusiasts with the religious enthusiasts. On the one hand was the playgoer, always seeking pleasure, paying exorbitantly for it, suffering unbearable discomforts for it, and hardly ever getting it. On the other hand was the Salvationist, repudiating gaiety and courting effort and sacrifice, yet always in the wildest spirits, laughing, joking, singing, rejoicing, drumming, and tambourining: his life flying by in a flash of excitement, and his death arriving as a climax of triumph. And, if you please, the playgoer despising the Salvationist as a joyless person, shut out from the heaven of the theatre, self-condemned to a life of hideous gloom; and the Salvationist mourning over the playgoer as over a prodigal with vine leaves in his hair, careering outrageously to hell amid the popping of champagne corks and the ribald laughter of sirens! Could misunderstanding be more complete, or sympathy worse misplaced?

Fortunately, the Salvationists are more accessible to the religious character of the drama than the playgoers to the gay energy and artistic fertility of religion. They can see, when it is pointed out to them, that a theatre, as a place where two or three are gathered together, takes from that divine presence an inalienable sanctity of which the grossest and profanest farce can no more deprive it than a hypocritical sermon by a snobbish bishop can desecrate Westminster Abbey. But in our professional playgoers this indispensable preliminary conception of sanctity seems wanting. They talk of actors as mimes and mummers, and, I fear, think of dramatic authors as liars and pandars, whose main business is the voluptuous soothing of the tired city speculator when what he calls the serious business of the day is over. Passion, the life of drama, means nothing to them but primitive sexual excitement: such phrases as "impassioned poetry" or "passionate love of truth" have fallen quite out of their vocabulary and been replaced by "passional crime" and the like. They assume, as far as I can gather, that people in whom passion has a larger scope are passionless and therefore uninteresting. Consequently they come to think of religious people as people who are not interesting and not amusing. And so, when Barbara cuts the regular Salvation Army jokes, and snatches a kiss from her lover across his drum, the devotees of the theatre think they ought to appear shocked, and conclude that the whole play is an elaborate mockery of the Army. And then either hypocritically rebuke me for mocking, or foolishly take part in the supposed mockery!

Even the handful of mentally competent critics got into difficulties over my demonstration of the economic deadlock in which the Salvation Army finds itself. Some of them thought that the Army would not have taken money from a distiller and a cannon founder: others thought it should not have taken it: all assumed more or less definitely that it reduced itself to absurdity or hypocrisy by taking it. On the first point the reply of the Army itself was prompt and conclusive. As one of its officers said, they would take money from the devil himself and be only too glad to get it out of his hands and into God's. They gratefully acknowledged that publicans not only give them money but allow them to collect it in the bar—sometimes even when there is a Salvation meeting outside preaching teetotalism. In fact, they questioned the verisimilitude of the play, not because Mrs. Baines took the money, but because Barbara refused it.

On the point that the Army ought not to take such money, its justification is obvious. It must take the money because it cannot exist without money, and there is no other money to be had. Practically all the spare money in the country consists of a mass of rent, interest, and profit, every penny of which is bound up with crime, drink, prostitution, disease, and all the evil fruits of poverty, as inextricably as with enterprise, wealth, commercial probity, and national prosperity. The notion that you can earmark certain coins as tainted is an unpractical individualist superstition. None the less the fact that all our money is tainted gives a very severe shock to earnest young souls when some dramatic instance of the taint first makes them conscious of it. When an enthusiastic young clergyman of the Established Church first realizes that the Ecclesiastical Commissioners receive the rents of sporting public houses, brothels, and sweating dens; or that the most generous contributor at his last charity sermon was an employer trading in female labor cheapened by prostitution as unscrupulously as a hotel keeper trades in waiters' labor cheapened by tips, or commissionaire's labor cheapened by pensions; or that the only patron who can afford to rebuild his church or his schools or give his boys' brigade a gymnasium or a library is the son-in-law of a Chicago meat King, that young clergyman has, like Barbara, a very bad quarter hour. But he cannot help himself by refusing to accept money from anybody except sweet old ladies with independent incomes and gentle and lovely ways of life. He has only to follow up the income of the sweet ladies to its industrial source, and there he will find Mrs. Warren's profession and the poisonous canned meat and all the rest of it. His own stipend has the same root. He must either share the world's guilt or go to another planet. He must save the world's honor if he is to save his own. This is what all the Churches find just as the Salvation Army and Barbara find it in the play. Her discovery that she is her father's accomplice; that the Salvation Army is the accomplice of the distiller and the dynamite maker; that they can no more escape one another than they can escape the air they breathe; that there is no salvation for them through personal righteousness, but only through the redemption of the whole nation from its vicious, lazy, competitive anarchy: this discovery has been made by everyone except the Pharisees and (apparently) the professional playgoers, who still wear their Tom Hood shirts* and underpay their washerwomen without the slightest misgiving as to the elevation of their private characters, the purity of their private atmospheres, and their right to repudiate as foreign to themselves the coarse depravity of the garret and the slum. Not that they mean any harm: they only desire to be, in their little private way, what they call gentlemen. They do not understand Barbara's lesson because they have not, like her, learnt it by taking their part in the larger life of the nation.

BARBARA'S RETURN TO THE COLORS

Barbara's return to the colors may yet provide a subject for the dramatic historian of the future. To go back to the Salvation Army with the knowledge that even the Salvationists themselves are not saved yet; that poverty is not blessed, but a most damnable sin; and that when General Booth chose Blood and Fire for the emblem of Salvation instead of the Cross, he was perhaps better inspired than he knew: such knowledge, for the daughter of Andrew Undershaft, will clearly lead to something hopefuller than distributing bread and treacle at the expense of Bodger.

It is a very significant thing, this instinctive choice of the military form of organization, this substitution of the drum for the organ, by the Salvation Army. Does it not suggest that the Salvationists divine that they must actually fight the devil instead of

---

*Reference to English poet Thomas Hood's "The Song of the Shirt" (1843), which laments the hard laboring lives of seamstresses.

merely praying at him? At present, it is true, they have not quite ascertained his correct address. When they do, they may give a very rude shock to that sense of security which he has gained from his experience of the fact that hard words, even when uttered by eloquent essayists and lecturers, or carried unanimously at enthusiastic public meetings on the motion of eminent reformers, break no bones. It has been said that the French Revolution was the work of Voltaire, Rousseau and the Encyclopedists. It seems to me to have been the work of men who had observed that virtuous indignation, caustic criticism, conclusive argument and instructive pamphleteering, even when done by the most earnest and witty literary geniuses, were as useless as praying, things going steadily from bad to worse whilst the Social Contract and the pamphlets of Voltaire were at the height of their vogue. Eventually, as we know, perfectly respectable citizens and earnest philanthropists connived at the September massacres because hard experience had convinced them that if they contented themselves with appeals to humanity and patriotism, the aristocracy, though it would read their appeals with the greatest enjoyment and appreciation, flattering and admiring the writers, would none the less continue to conspire with foreign monarchists to undo the revolution and restore the old system with every circumstance of savage vengeance and ruthless repression of popular liberties.

The nineteenth century saw the same lesson repeated in England. It had its Utilitarians, its Christian Socialists, its Fabians (still extant): it had Bentham, Mill, Dickens, Ruskin, Carlyle, Butler, Henry George,* and Morris. And the end of all their efforts is the Chicago described by Mr. Upton Sinclair, and the London in which the people who pay to be amused by my dramatic representation of Peter Shirley turned out to starve at forty because there are younger slaves to be had for his wages, do not take, and

---

*American thinker and economist (1839–1897), whose 1884 London lecture on society and economics led Shaw into socialism.

have not the slightest intention of taking, any effective step to organize society in such a way as to make that everyday infamy impossible. I, who have preached and pamphleteered like any
Encyclopedist, have to confess that my methods are no use, and
would be no use if I were Voltaire, Rousseau, Bentham, Mill, Dickens, Carlyle, Ruskin, George, Butler, and Morris all rolled into
one, with Euripides, More, Molière, Shakespear, Beaumarchais,
Swift, Goethe, Ibsen, Tolstoy, Moses and the prophets all thrown
in (as indeed in some sort I actually am, standing as I do on all
their shoulders). The problem being to make heroes out of cowards, we paper apostles and artist-magicians have succeeded only
in giving cowards all the sensations of heroes whilst they tolerate
every abomination, accept every plunder, and submit to every oppression. Christianity, in making a merit of such submission, has
marked only that depth in the abyss at which the very sense of
shame is lost. The Christian has been like Dickens' doctor* in the
debtor's prison, who tells the newcomer of its ineffable peace and
security: no duns;† no tyrannical collectors of rates, taxes, and
rent; no importunate hopes nor exacting duties; nothing but the
rest and safety of having no further to fall.

Yet in the poorest corner of this sod-destroying Christendom
vitality suddenly begins to germinate again. Joyousness, a sacred
gift long dethroned by the hellish laughter of derision and obscenity, rises like a flood miraculously out of the fetid dust and
mud of the slums; rousing marches and impetuous dithyrambs rise
to the heavens from people among whom the depressing noise
called "sacred music" is a standing joke; a flag with Blood and Fire
on it is unfurled, not in murderous rancor, but because fire is
beautiful and blood a vital and splendid red;[6] Fear, which we flatter by calling Self, vanishes; and transfigured men and women

---

*That is, Doctor Haggage in Charles Dickens's *Little Dorrit* (1855–1857), a
novel that Shaw considered an indictment of capitalism.
†Persistent debt collectors.

carry their gospel through a transfigured world, calling their leader General, themselves captains and brigadiers, and their whole body an Army: praying, but praying only for refreshment, for strength to fight, and for needful MONEY (a notable sign, that); preaching, but not preaching submission; daring ill-usage and abuse, but not putting up with more of it than is inevitable; and practising what the world will let them practise, including soap and water, color and music. There is danger in such activity; and where there is danger there is hope. Our present security is nothing, and can be nothing, but evil made irresistible.

WEAKNESSES OF THE SALVATION ARMY

For the present, however, it is not my business to flatter the Salvation Army. Rather must I point out to it that it has almost as many weaknesses as the Church of England itself. It is building up a business organization which will compel it eventually to see that its present staff of enthusiast-commanders shall be succeeded by a bureaucracy of men of business who will be no better than bishops, and perhaps a good deal more unscrupulous. That has always happened sooner or later to great orders founded by saints; and the order founded by St. William Booth is not exempt from the same danger. It is even more dependent than the Church on rich people who would cut off supplies at once if it began to preach that indispensable revolt against poverty which must also be a revolt against riches. It is hampered by a heavy contingent of pious elders who are not really Salvationists at all, but Evangelicals of the old school. It still, as Commissioner Howard* affirms, "sticks to Moses," which is flat nonsense at this time of day if the Commissioner means, as I am afraid he does, that the Book of Genesis contains a trustworthy scientific account of the origin of species, and that the god to whom Jephthah sacrificed his daughter is any less obviously a tribal idol than Dagon or Chemosh.

---

*T. Henry Howard, Salvation Army chief of staff (1912–1919).

Further, there is still too much other-worldliness about the Army. Like Frederick's grenadier, the Salvationist wants to live for ever[7] (the most monstrous way of crying for the moon); and though it is evident to anyone who has ever heard General Booth and his best officers that they would work as hard for human salvation as they do at present if they believed that death would be the end of them individually, they and their followers have a bad habit of talking as if the Salvationists were heroically enduring a very bad time on earth as an investment which will bring them in dividends later on in the form, not of a better life to come for the whole world, but of an eternity spent by themselves personally in a sort of bliss which would bore any active person to a second death. Surely the truth is that the Salvationists are unusually happy people. And is it not the very diagnostic of true salvation that it shall overcome the fear of death? Now the man who has come to believe that there is no such thing as death, the change so called being merely the transition to an exquisitely happy and utterly careless life, has not overcome the fear of death at all: on the contrary, it has overcome him so completely that he refuses to die on any terms whatever. I do not call a Salvationist really saved until he is ready to lie down cheerfully on the scrap heap, having paid scot and lot and something over, and let his eternal life pass on to renew its youth in the battalions of the future.

Then there is the nasty lying habit called confession, which the Army encourages because it lends itself to dramatic oratory, with plenty of thrilling incident. For my part, when I hear a convert relating the violences and oaths and blasphemies he was guilty of before he was saved, making out that he was a very terrible fellow then and is the most contrite and chastened of Christians now, I believe him no more than I believe the millionaire who says he came up to London or Chicago as a boy with only three halfpence in his pocket. Salvationists have said to me that Barbara in my play would never have been taken in by so transparent a humbug as Snobby Price; and certainly I do not think Snobby could have taken in any experienced Salvationist on a point on which the Salvationist did not wish to be taken in. But on the point of conversion all Salvationists wish to be taken in; for the more obvious the sinner the more obvious the miracle of his conversion. When you advertize a converted burglar or reclaimed drunkard as one of the attractions at an experience meeting, your burglar can hardly have been too burglarious or your drunkard too drunken. As long as such attractions are relied on, you will have your Snobbies claiming to have beaten their mothers when they were as a matter of prosaic fact habitually beaten by them, and your Rummies of the tamest respectability pretending to a past of reckless and dazzling vice. Even when confessions are sincerely autobiographic there is no reason to assume at once that the impulse to make them is pious or the interest of the hearers wholesome. It might as well be assumed that the poor people who insist on shewing appalling ulcers to district visitors are convinced hygienists, or that the curiosity which sometimes welcomes such exhibitions is a pleasant and creditable one. One is often tempted to suggest that those who pester our police superintendents with confessions of murder might very wisely be taken at their word and executed, except in the few cases in which a real murderer is seeking to be relieved of his guilt by confession and expiation. For though I am not, I hope, an unmerciful person, I do not think that the inexorability of the deed once done should be disguised by any ritual, whether in the confessional or on the scaffold.

And here my disagreement with the Salvation Army, and with all propagandists of the Cross (to which I object as I object to all gibbets) becomes deep indeed. Forgiveness, absolution, atonement, are figments: punishment is only a pretence of cancelling one crime by another; and you can no more have forgiveness without vindictiveness than you can have a cure without a disease. You will never get a high morality from people who conceive that their misdeeds are revocable and pardonable, or in a society where absolution and expiation are officially provided for us all. The de-

mand may be very real; but the supply is spurious. Thus Bill
Walker, in my play, having assaulted the Salvation Lass, presently
finds himself overwhelmed with an intolerable conviction of sin
under the skilled treatment of Barbara. Straightway he begins to
try to unassault the lass and deruffianize his deed, first by getting
punished for it in kind, and, when that relief is denied him, by fin-
ing himself a pound to compensate the girl. He is foiled both ways.
He finds the Salvation Army as inexorable as fact itself. It will not
punish him; it will not take his money. It will not tolerate a redeemed ruffian; it leaves him no means of salvation except ceasing
to be a ruffian. In doing this, the Salvation Army instinctively
grasps the central truth of Christianity and discards its central superstition: that central truth being the vanity of revenge and punishment, and that central superstition the salvation of the world by
the gibbet.

For, be it noted, Bill has assaulted an old and starving woman
also; and for this worse offence he feels no remorse whatever, because she makes it clear that her malice is as great as his own. "Let
her have the law of me, as she said she would," says Bill: "what I
done to her is no more on what you might call my conscience than
sticking a pig." This shews a perfectly natural and wholesome state
of mind on his part. The old woman, like the law she threatens him
with, is perfectly ready to play the game of retaliation with him:
to rob him if he steals, to flog him if he strikes, to murder him if
he kills. By example and precept the law and public opinion teach
him to impose his will on others by anger, violence, and cruelty,
and to wipe off the moral score by punishment. That is sound
Crosstianity. But this Crosstianity has got entangled with something which Barbara calls Christianity, and which unexpectedly
causes her to refuse to play the hangman's game of Satan casting
out Satan. She refuses to prosecute a drunken ruffian; she con-
verses on equal terms with a blackguard whom no lady could be
seen speaking to in the public street: in short, she behaves as ille-
gally and unbecomingly as possible under the circumstances. Bill's

conscience reacts to this just as naturally as it does to the old woman's threats. He is placed in a position of unbearable moral inferiority, and strives by every means in his power to escape from it, whilst he is still quite ready to meet the abuse of the old woman by attempting to smash a mug on her face. And that is the triumphant justification of Barbara's Christianity as against our system of judicial punishment and the vindictive villain-thrashings and "poetic justice" of the romantic stage.

For the credit of literature it must be pointed out that the situation is only partly novel. Victor Hugo long ago gave us the epic of the convict and the bishop's candlesticks, of the Crosstian policeman annihilated by his encounter with the Christian Valjean. But Bill Walker is not, like Valjean, romantically changed from a demon into an angel. There are millions of Bill Walkers in all classes of society to-day; and the point which I, as a professor of natural psychology, desire to demonstrate, is that Bill, without any change in his character whatsoever, will react one way to one sort of treatment and another way to another.

In proof I might point to the sensational object lesson provided by our commercial millionaires to-day. They begin as brigands: merciless, unscrupulous, dealing out ruin and death and slavery to their competitors and employees, and facing desperately the worst that their competitors can do to them. The history of the English factories,* the American trusts, the exploitation of African gold, diamonds, ivory and rubber, outdoes in villainy the worst that has ever been imagined of the buccaneers of the Spanish Main. Captain Kidd would have marooned a modern Trust magnate for conduct unworthy of a gentleman of fortune. The law every day seizes on unsuccessful scoundrels of this type and punishes them with a cruelty worse than their own, with the result that they come out of the torture house more dangerous than they went in, and renew

---

*British colonial trading posts were run by factors, or agents, and thus were called factories.

their evil doing (nobody will employ them at anything else) until they are again seized, again tormented, and again let loose, with the same result.

But the successful scoundrel is dealt with very differently, and very Christianly. He is not only forgiven: he is idolized, respected, made much of, all but worshipped. Society returns him good for evil in the most extravagant overmeasure. And with what result? He begins to idolize himself, to respect himself, to live up to the treatment he receives. He preaches sermons; he writes books of the most edifying advice to young men, and actually persuades himself that he got on by taking his own advice; he endows educational institutions; he supports charities; he dies finally in the odor of sanctity, leaving a will which is a monument of public spirit and bounty. And all this without any change in his character. The spots of the leopard and the stripes of the tiger are as brilliant as ever; but the conduct of the world towards him has changed; and his conduct has changed accordingly. You have only to reverse your attitude towards him——to lay hands on his property, revile him, assault him, and he will be a brigand again in a moment, as ready to crush you as you are to crush him, and quite as full of pretentious moral reasons for doing it.

In short, when Major Barbara says that there are no scoundrels, she is right: there are no absolute scoundrels, though there are impracticable people of whom I shall treat presently. Every practicable man (and woman) is a potential scoundrel and a potential good citizen. What a man is depends on his character; but what he does, and what we think of what he does, depends on his circumstances. The characteristics that ruin a man in one class make him eminent in another. The characters that behave differently in different circumstances behave alike in similar circumstances. Take a common English character like that of Bill Walker. We meet Bill everywhere: on the judicial bench, on the episcopal bench,* in the

---

*Bishops of the Church of England, when sitting as a ruling body.

Privy Council, at the War Office and Admiralty, as well as in the Old Bailey dock or in the ranks of casual unskilled labor. And the morality of Bill's characteristics varies with these various circumstances. The faults of the burglar are the qualities of the financier: the manners and habits of a duke would cost a city clerk his situation. In short, though character is independent of circumstances, conduct is not; and our moral judgments of character are not: both are circumstantial. Take any condition of life in which the circumstances are for a mass of men practically alike: felony, the House of Lords, the factory, the stables, the gipsy encampment or where you please! In spite of diversity of character and temperament, the conduct and morals of the individuals in each group are as predicable and as alike in the main as if they were a flock of sheep, morals being mostly only social habits and circumstantial necessities. Strong people know this and count upon it. In nothing have the master-minds of the world been distinguished from the ordinary suburban season-ticket holder more than in their straightforward perception of the fact that mankind is practically a single species, and not a menagerie of gentlemen and bounders, villains and heroes, cowards and daredevils, peers and peasants, grocers and aristocrats, artisans and laborers, washerwomen and duchesses, in which all the grades of income and caste represent distinct animals who must not be introduced to one another or intermarry. Napoleon constructing a galaxy of generals and courtiers, and even of monarchs, out of his collection of social nobodies; Julius Cæsar appointing as governor of Egypt the son of a freedman—one who but a short time before would have been legally disqualified for the post even of a private soldier in the Roman army; Louis XI making his barber his privy councillor: all these had in their different ways a firm hold of the scientific fact of human equality, expressed by Barbara in the Christian formula that all men are children of one father. A man who believes that men are naturally divided into upper and lower and middle classes morally is making exactly the same mistake as the man who believes that they are naturally divided in the same way socially. And just as our persistent attempts to found political institutions on a basis of social inequality have always produced long periods of destructive friction relieved from time to time by violent explosions of revolution; so the attempt—will Americans please note—to found moral institutions on a basis of moral inequality can lead to nothing but unnatural Reigns of the Saints relieved by licentious Restorations; to Americans who have made divorce a public institution turning the face of Europe into one huge sardonic smile by refusing to stay in the same hotel with a Russian man of genius* who has changed wives without the sanction of South Dakota; to grotesque hypocrisy, cruel persecution, and final utter confusion of conventions and compliances with benevolence and respectability. It is quite useless to declare that all men are born free if you deny that they are born good. Guarantee a man's goodness and his liberty will take care of itself. To guarantee his freedom on condition that you approve of his moral character is formally to abolish all freedom whatsoever, as every man's liberty is at the mercy of a moral indictment, which any fool can trump up against everyone who violates custom, whether as a prophet or as a rascal. This is the lesson Democracy has to learn before it can become anything but the most oppressive of all the priesthoods.

Let us now return to Bill Walker and his case of conscience against the Salvation Army. Major Barbara, not being a modern Tetzel, or the treasurer of a hospital, refuses to sell Bill absolution for a sovereign. Unfortunately, what the Army can afford to refuse in the case of Bill Walker, it cannot refuse in the case of Bodger. Bodger is master of the situation because he holds the purse strings. "Strive as you will," says Bodger, in effect: "me you cannot do without. You cannot save Bill Walker without my money." And the Army answers, quite rightly under the circumstances, "We will

---

*Reference to Russian writer Maxim Gorky (pen name of Aleksey Peshkov, 1868–1936).

take money from the devil himself sooner than abandon the work of Salvation." So Bodger pays his conscience-money and gets the absolution that is refused to Bill. In real life Bill would perhaps never know this. But I, the dramatist, whose business it is to shew the connexion between things that seem apart and unrelated in the haphazard order of events in real life, have contrived to make it known to Bill, with the result that the Salvation Army loses its hold of him at once.

But Bill may not be lost, for all that. He is still in the grip of the facts and of his own conscience, and may find his taste for black-guardism permanently spoiled. Still, I cannot guarantee that happy ending. Let anyone walk through the poorer quarters of our cities when the men are not working, but resting and chewing the cud of their reflections; and he will find that there is one expression on every mature face: the expression of cynicism. The discovery made by Bill Walker about the Salvation Army has been made by everyone of them. They have found that every man has his price; and they have been foolishly or corruptly taught to mistrust and despise him for that necessary and salutary condition of social existence. When they learn that General Booth, too, has his price, they do not admire him because it is a high one, and admit the need of organizing society so that he shall get it in an honorable way: they conclude that his character is unsound and that all religious men are hypocrites and allies of their sweaters and oppressors. They know that the large subscriptions which help to support the Army are endowments, not of religion, but of the wicked doctrine of docility in poverty and humility under oppression; and they are rent by the most agonizing of all the doubts of the soul, the doubt whether their true salvation must not come from their most abhorrent passions, from murder, envy, greed, stubbornness, rage, and terrorism, rather than from public spirit, reasonableness, humanity, generosity, tenderness, delicacy, pity and kindness. The confirmation of that doubt, at which our newspapers have been working so hard for years past, is the morality of militarism; and the justification of militarism is that circumstances may at any time make it the true morality of the moment. It is by producing such moments that we produce violent and sanguinary revolutions, such as the one now in progress in Russia* and the one which Capitalism in England and America is daily and diligently provoking.

At such moments it becomes the duty of the Churches to evoke all the powers of destruction against the existing order. But if they do this, the existing order must forcibly suppress them. Churches are suffered to exist only on condition that they preach submission to the State as at present capitalistically organized. The Church of England itself is compelled to add to the thirty-six articles in which it formulates its religious tenets, three more in which it apologetically protests that the moment any of these articles comes in conflict with the State it is to be entirely renounced, abjured, violated, abrogated and abhorred, the policeman being a much more important person than any of the Persons of the Trinity. And this is why no tolerated Church nor Salvation Army can ever win the entire confidence of the poor. It must be on the side of the police and the military, no matter what it believes or disbelieves; and as the police and the military are the instruments by which the rich rob and oppress the poor (on legal and moral principles made for the purpose), it is not possible to be on the side of the poor and of the police at the same time. Indeed the religious bodies, as the almoners† of the rich, become a sort of auxiliary police, taking off the insurrectionary edge of poverty with coals and blankets, bread and treacle, and soothing and cheering the victims with hopes of immense and inexpensive happiness in another world when the process of working them to premature death in the service of the rich is complete in this.

---

*Shaw refers to the unsuccessful Russian Revolution of 1905.
†Distributors of charity.

CHRISTIANITY AND ANARCHISM

Such is the false position from which neither the Salvation Army nor the Church of England nor any other religious organization whatever can escape except through a reconstitution of society. Nor can they merely endure the State passively, washing their hands of its sins. The State is constantly forcing the consciences of men by violence and cruelty. Not content with exacting money from us for the maintenance of its soldiers and policemen, its gaolers and executioners, it forces us to take an active personal part in its proceedings on pain of becoming ourselves the victims of its violence. As I write these lines, a sensational example is given to the world. A royal marriage* has been celebrated, first by sacrament in a cathedral, and then by a bullfight having for its main amusement the spectacle of horses gored and disembowelled by the bull, after which, when the bull is so exhausted as to be no longer dangerous, he is killed by a cautious matador. But the ironic contrast between the bullfight and the sacrament of marriage does not move anyone. Another contrast—that between the splendor, the happiness, the atmosphere of kindly admiration surrounding the young couple, and the price paid for it under our abominable social arrangements in the misery, squalor and degradation of millions of other young couples—is drawn at the same moment by a novelist, Mr. Upton Sinclair, who chips a corner of the veneering from the huge meat packing industries of Chicago, and shews it to us as a sample of what is going on all over the world underneath the top layer of prosperous plutocracy. One man[†] is sufficiently moved by that contrast to pay his own life as the price of one terrible blow at the responsible parties. Unhappily his poverty leaves him also ignorant enough to be duped by

---

*Between Alfonso XIII of Spain and Victoria Eugénie, granddaughter of Queen Victoria, on May 31, 1906.

†Reference to Spanish anarchist Mateo Morral, who threw a bomb at King Alfonso XIII's wedding party and later committed suicide.

the pretence that the innocent young bride and bridegroom, put
forth and crowned by plutocracy as the heads of a State in which
they have less personal power than any policeman, and less influence than any chairman of a trust, are responsible. At them accordingly he launches his sixpennorth of fulminate,* missing his
mark, but scattering the bowels of as many horses as any bull in
the arena, and slaying twenty-three persons, besides wounding
ninety-nine. And of all these, the horses alone are innocent of the
guilt he is avenging: had he blown all Madrid to atoms with every
adult person in it, not one could have escaped the charge of being
an accessory, before, at, and after the fact, to poverty and prostitution, to such wholesale massacre of infants as Herod never
dreamt of, to plague, pestilence and famine, battle, murder and
lingering death—perhaps not one who had not helped, through
example, precept, connivance, and even clamor, to teach the dynamiter his well-learnt gospel of hatred and vengeance, by ap-
proving every day of sentences of years of imprisonment so
infernal in its unnatural stupidity and panic-stricken cruelty, that
their advocates can disavow neither the dagger nor the bomb
without stripping the mask of justice and humanity from themselves also.[8]

Be it noted that at this very moment there appears the biography of one of our dukes, who, being Scotch, could argue about
politics, and therefore stood out as a great brain among our aristocrats. And what, if you please, was his grace's favorite historical
episode, which he declared he never read without intense satisfaction? Why, the young General Bonapart's pounding of the Paris
mob to pieces in 1795, called in playful approval by our respectable classes "the whiff of grapeshot,"[9] though Napoleon, to
do him justice, took a deeper view of it, and would fain have had
it forgotten. And since the Duke of Argyll was not a demon, but a
man of like passions with ourselves, by no means rancorous or

---

*An explosive.

cruel as men go, who can doubt that all over the world proletarians of the ducal kidney are now revelling in the "whiff of dynamite"[10] (the flavor of the joke seems to evaporate a little, does it
not?) because it was aimed at the class they hate even as our argute
duke hated what he called the mob.

In such an atmosphere there can be only one sequel to the
Madrid explosion. All Europe burns to emulate it. Vengeance!
More blood! Tear "the Anarchist beast" to shreds. Drag him to the
scaffold. Imprison him for life. Let all civilized States band together to drive his like off the face of the earth; and if any State refuses to join, make war on it. This time the leading London
newspaper, anti-Liberal and therefore anti-Russian in politics,
does not say "Serve you right" to the victims, as it did, in effect,
when Bobrikoff, and De Plehve, and Grand Duke Sergius,* were
in the same manner unofficially fulminated into fragments. No:
fulminate our rivals in Asia by all means, ye brave Russian revolu-
tionaries; but to aim at an English princess—monstrous! hideous!
hound down the wretch to his doom; and observe, please, that we
are a civilized and merciful people, and, however much we may
regret it, must not treat him as Ravaillac and Damiens[11] were
treated. And meanwhile, since we have not yet caught him, let us
soothe our quivering nerves with the bullfight, and comment in a
courtly way on the unfailing tact and good taste of the ladies of our
royal houses, who, though presumably of full normal natural tenderness, have been so effectually broken in to fashionable routine
that they can be taken to see the horses slaughtered as helplessly
as they could no doubt be taken to a gladiator show, if that happened to be the mode just now.

Strangely enough, in the midst of this raging fire of malice, the
one man who still has faith in the kindness and intelligence of

---

*Nikolai Bobrikov (1839–1904), Vyacheslav Plehve (1846–1904), and Sergei
Alexandrovich Romanov (1857–1905) were Russian officials assassinated by revo-
lutionaries.

human nature is the fulminator, now a hunted wretch, with nothing, apparently, to secure his triumph over all the prisons and scaffolds of infuriate Europe except the revolver in his pocket and his readiness to discharge it at a moment's notice into his own or any other head. Think of him setting out to find a gentleman and a Christian in the multitude of human wolves howling for his blood.[12] Think also of this: that at the very first essay he finds what he seeks, a veritable grandee of Spain, a noble, high-thinking, unterrified, malice-void soul, in the guise——of all masquerades in the world!——of a modern editor.* The Anarchist wolf, flying from the wolves of plutocracy, throws himself on the honor of the man. The man, not being a wolf (nor a London editor), and therefore not having enough sympathy with his exploit to be made bloodthirsty by it, does not throw him back to the pursuing wolves—gives him, instead, what help he can to escape, and sends him off acquainted at last with a force that goes deeper than dynamite, though you cannot make so much of it for sixpence. That righteous and honorable high human deed is not wasted on Europe, let us hope, though it benefits the fugitive wolf only for a moment. The plutocratic wolves presently smell him out. The fugitive shoots the unlucky wolf whose nose is nearest; shoots himself; and then convinces the world, by his photograph, that he was no monstrous freak of reversion to the tiger, but a good looking young man with nothing abnormal about him except his appalling courage and resolution (that is why the terrified shriek Coward at him): one to whom murdering a happy young couple on their wedding morning would have been an unthinkably unnatural abomination under rational and kindly human circumstances.

Then comes the climax of irony and blind stupidity. The wolves, balked of their meal of fellow-wolf, turn on the man, and proceed to torture him, after their manner, by imprisonment, for

---

*Reference to Jose Nakens, editor of the revolutionary newspaper *El Motin*, who provided temporary refuge for Morral (see note on page 37).

refusing to fasten his teeth in the throat of the dynamiter and hold him down until they came to finish him.

Thus, you see, a man may not be a gentleman nowadays even if he wishes to. As to being a Christian, he is allowed some latitude in that matter, because, I repeat, Christianity has two faces. Popular Christianity has for its emblem a gibbet, for its chief sensation a sanguinary execution after torture, for its central mystery an insane vengeance bought off by a trumpery expiation. But there is a nobler and profounder Christianity which affirms the sacred mystery of Equality, and forbids the glaring futility and folly of vengeance, often politely called punishment or justice. The gibbet part of Christianity is tolerated. The other is criminal felony. Connoisseurs in irony are well aware of the fact that the only editor* in England who denounces punishment as radically wrong, also repudiates Christianity; calls his paper The Freethinker; and has been imprisoned for two years for blasphemy.

SANE CONCLUSIONS

And now I must ask the excited reader not to lose his head on one side or the other, but to draw a sane moral from these grim absurdities. It is not good sense to propose that laws against crime should apply to principals only and not to accessories whose consent, counsel, or silence may secure impunity to the principal. If you institute punishment as part of the law, you must punish people for refusing to punish. If you have a police, part of its duty must be to compel everybody to assist the police. No doubt if your laws are unjust, and your policemen agents of oppression, the result will be an unbearable violation of the private consciences of citizens. But that cannot be helped: the remedy is, not to license everybody to thwart the law if they please, but to make laws that will command the public assent, and not to deal cruelly and stu-

---

*Reference to George William Foote (1850–1915), a passionate opponent of orthodox Christianity.

pidly with lawbreakers. Everybody disapproves of burglars; but the modern burglar, when caught and overpowered by a householder, usually appeals, and often, let us hope, with success, to his captor not to deliver him over to the useless horrors of penal servitude. In other cases the lawbreaker escapes because those who could give him up do not consider his breach of the law a guilty action. Sometimes, even, private tribunals are formed in opposition to the official tribunals; and these private tribunals employ assassins as executioners, as was done, for example, by Mahomet before he had established his power officially, and by the Ribbon lodges of Ireland in their long struggle with the landlords. Under such circumstances, the assassin goes free although everybody in the district knows who he is and what he has done. They do not betray him, partly because they justify him exactly as the regular Government justifies its official executioner, and partly because they would themselves be assassinated if they betrayed him: another method learnt from the official government. Given a tribunal, employing a slayer who has no personal quarrel with the slain; and there is clearly no moral difference between official and unofficial killing.

In short, all men are anarchists with regard to laws which are against their consciences, either in the preamble or in the penalty. In London our worst anarchists are the magistrates, because many of them are so old and ignorant that when they are called upon to administer any law that is based on ideas or knowledge less than half a century old, they disagree with it, and being mere ordinary homebred private Englishmen without any respect for law in the abstract, naïvely set the example of violating it. In this instance the man lags behind the law; but when the law lags behind the man, he becomes equally an anarchist. When some huge change in social conditions, such as the industrial revolution of the eighteenth and nineteenth centuries, throws our legal and industrial institutions out of date, Anarchism becomes almost a religion. The whole force of the most energetic geniuses of the time in philosophy,

economics, and art, concentrates itself on demonstrations and re-
minders that morality and law are only conventions, fallible and
continually obsolescing. Tragedies in which the heroes are bandits,
and comedies in which law-abiding and conventionally moral folk
are compelled to satirize themselves by outraging the conscience
of the spectators every time they do their duty, appear simultane-
ously with economic treatises entitled "What is Property? Theft!"
and with histories of "The Conflict between Religion and Science."

Now this is not a healthy state of things. The advantages of living in society are proportionate, not to the freedom of the individual from a code, but to the complexity and subtlety of the code
he is prepared not only to accept but to uphold as a matter of such
vital importance that a lawbreaker at large is hardly to be tolerated
on any plea. Such an attitude becomes impossible when the only
men who can make themselves heard and remembered throughout the world spend all their energy in raising our gorge against
current law, current morality, current respectability, and legal
property. The ordinary man, uneducated in social theory even
when he is schooled in Latin verse, cannot be set against all the
laws of his country and yet persuaded to regard law in the abstract
as vitally necessary to society. Once he is brought to repudiate the
laws and institutions he knows, he will repudiate the very conception of law and the very groundwork of institutions, ridiculing
human rights, extolling brainless methods as "historical," and tol-
erating nothing except pure empiricism in conduct, with dynamite as the basis of politics and vivisection as the basis of science.
That is hideous; but what is to be done? Here am I, for instance,
by class a respectable man, by common sense a hater of waste and
disorder, by intellectual constitution legally minded to the verge
of pedantry, and by temperament apprehensive and economically
disposed to the limit of old-maidishness; yet I am, and have always
been, and shall now always be, a revolutionary writer, because our
laws make law impossible; our liberties destroy all freedom; our
property is organized robbery; our morality is an impudent

hypocrisy; our wisdom is administered by inexperienced or mal-experienced dupes, our power wielded by cowards and weaklings, and our honor false in all its points. I am an enemy of the existing order for good reasons; but that does not make my attacks any less encouraging or helpful to people who are its enemies for bad reasons. The existing order may shriek that if I tell the truth about it, some foolish person may drive it to become still worse by trying to assassinate it. I cannot help that, even if I could see what worse it could do than it is already doing. And the disadvantage of that worst even from its own point of view is that society, with all its prisons and bayonets and whips and ostracisms and starvations, is powerless in the face of the Anarchist who is prepared to sacrifice his own life in the battle with it. Our natural safety from the cheap and devastating explosives which every Russian student can make, and every Russian grenadier has learnt to handle in Manchuria, lies in the fact that brave and resolute men, when they are rascals, will not risk their skins for the good of humanity, and, when they are sympathetic enough to care for humanity, abhor murder, and never commit it until their consciences are outraged beyond endurance. The remedy is, then, simply not to outrage their consciences.

Do not be afraid that they will not make allowances. All men make very large allowances indeed before they stake their own lives in a war to the death with society. Nobody demands or expects the millennium. But there are two things that must be set right, or we shall perish, like Rome, of soul atrophy disguised as empire.

The first is, that the daily ceremony of dividing the wealth of the country among its inhabitants shall be so conducted that no crumb shall go to any able-bodied adults who are not producing by their personal exertions not only a full equivalent for what they take, but a surplus sufficient to provide for their superannuation and pay back the debt due for their nurture.

The second is that the deliberate infliction of malicious injuries

which now goes on under the name of punishment be abandoned;
so that the thief, the ruffian, the gambler, and the beggar, may
without inhumanity be handed over to the law, and made to understand that a State which is too humane to punish will also be
too thrifty to waste the life of honest men in watching or re-
straining dishonest ones. That is why we do not imprison dogs. We
even take our chance of their first bite. But if a dog delights to
bark and bite, it goes to the lethal chamber. That seems to me sensible. To allow the dog to expiate his bite by a period of torment,
and then let him loose in a much more savage condition (for the
chain makes a dog savage) to bite again and expiate again, having
meanwhile spent a great deal of human life and happiness in the
task of chaining and feeding and tormenting him, seems to me idiotic and superstitious. Yet that is what we do to men who bark and
bite and steal. It would be far more sensible to put up with their
vices, as we put up with their illnesses, until they give more trouble than they are worth, at which point we should, with many
apologies and expressions of sympathy, and some generosity in
complying with their last wishes, place them in the lethal chamber[13] and get rid of them. Under no circumstances should they be
allowed to expiate their misdeeds by a manufactured penalty, to
subscribe to a charity, or to compensate the victims. If there is to
be no punishment there can be no forgiveness. We shall never have
real moral responsibility until everyone knows that his deeds are
irrevocable, and that his life depends on his usefulness. Hitherto,
alas! humanity has never dared face these hard facts. We frantically
scatter conscience money and invent systems of conscience bank-
ing, with expiatory penalties, atonements, redemptions, salva-
tions, hospital subscription lists and what not, to enable us to
contract-out of the moral code. Not content with the old scape-
goat and sacrificial lamb, we deify human saviors, and pray to
miraculous virgin intercessors. We attribute mercy to the inexorable; soothe our consciences after committing murder by
throwing ourselves on the bosom of divine love; and shrink even

from our own gallows because we are forced to admit that it, at least, is irrevocable—as if one hour of imprisonment were not as irrevocable as any execution!

If a man cannot look evil in the face without illusion, he will never know what it really is, or combat it effectually. The few men who have been able (relatively) to do this have been called cynics, and have sometimes had an abnormal share of evil in themselves, corresponding to the abnormal strength of their minds; but they have never done mischief unless they intended to do it. That is why great scoundrels have been beneficent rulers whilst amiable and privately harmless monarchs have ruined their countries by trusting to the hocus-pocus of innocence and guilt, reward and punishment, virtuous indignation and pardon, instead of standing up to the facts without either malice or mercy. Major Barbara stands up to Bill Walker in that way, with the result that the ruffian who cannot get hated, has to hate himself. To relieve this agony he tries to get punished; but the Salvationist whom he tries to provoke is as merciless as Barbara, and only prays for him. Then he tries to pay, but can get nobody to take his money. His doom is the doom of Cain, who, failing to find either a savior, a policeman, or an almoner to help him to pretend that his brother's blood no longer cried from the ground, had to live and die a murderer. Cain took care not to commit another murder, unlike our railway shareholders (I am one) who kill and maim shunters* by hundreds to save the cost of automatic couplings, and make atonement by annual subscriptions to deserving charities. Had Cain been allowed to pay off his score, he might possibly have killed Adam and Eve for the mere sake of a second luxurious reconciliation with God afterwards. Bodger, you may depend on it, will go on to the end of his life poisoning people with bad whisky, because he can always depend on the Salvation Army or the Church of England to nego-

---

*Laborers who perform the dangerous work of coupling and uncoupling railway cars.

tiate a redemption for him in consideration of a trifling percentage of his profits.

There is a third condition too, which must be fulfilled before
the great teachers of the world will cease to scoff at its religions.
Creeds must become intellectually honest. At present there is not
a single credible established religion in the world. That is perhaps
the most stupendous fact in the whole world-situation. This play
of mine, Major Barbara, is, I hope, both true and inspired; but
whoever says that it all happened, and that faith in it and understanding of it consist in believing that it is a record of an actual occurrence, is, to speak according to Scripture, a fool and a liar, and
is hereby solemnly denounced and cursed as such by me, the author, to all posterity.

London, June 1906.

MAJOR BARBARA

ACT I

It is after dinner on a January night, in the library in Lady Britomart[14] *Undershaft's house in Wilton Crescent. A large and comfortable settee is in the middle of the room, upholstered in dark leather. A person sitting on it (it is vacant at present) would have, on his right, Lady Britomart's writing-table, with the lady herself busy at it; a smaller writing-table behind him on his left; the door behind him on Lady Britomart's side; and a window with a window-seat directly on his left. Near the window is an armchair.*

Lady Britomart is a woman of fifty or thereabouts, well dressed and yet careless of her dress, well bred and quite reckless of her breeding, well mannered and yet appallingly outspoken and indifferent to the opinion of her interlocutors, amiable and yet peremptory, arbitrary, and high-tempered to the last bearable degree, and withal a very typical managing matron of the upper class, treated as a naughty child until she grew into a scolding mother, and finally settling down with plenty of practical ability and worldly experience, limited in the oddest way with domestic and class limitations, conceiving the universe exactly as if it were a large house in Wilton Crescent, though handling her corner of it very effectively on that assumption, and being quite enlightened and liberal as to the books in the library, the pictures on the walls, the music in the portfolios, and the articles in the papers.

Her son, Stephen, comes in. He is a gravely correct

young man under 25, taking himself very seriously, but still in some awe of his mother, from childish habit and bachelor shyness rather than from any weakness of character.

STEPHEN   What's the matter?

LADY BRITOMART   Presently, Stephen.

[*STEPHEN submissively walks to the settee and sits down. He takes up The Speaker.*]

LADY BRITOMART   Dont begin to read, Stephen. I shall require all your attention.

STEPHEN   It was only while I was waiting—

LADY BRITOMART   Dont make excuses, Stephen. [*He puts down The Speaker.*] Now! [*She finishes her writing; rises; and comes to the settee.*] I have not kept you waiting v e r y long, I think.

STEPHEN   Not at all, mother.

LADY BRITOMART   Bring me my cushion. [*He takes the cushion from the chair at the desk and arranges it for her as she sits down on the settee.*] Sit down. [*He sits down and fingers his tie nervously.*] Dont fiddle with your tie, Stephen: there is nothing the matter with it.

STEPHEN   I beg your pardon. [*He fiddles with his watch chain instead.*]

LADY BRITOMART   Now are you attending to me, Stephen?

STEPHEN   Of course, mother.

LADY BRITOMART   No: it's n o t of course. I want something much more than your everyday matter-of-course attention. I am going to speak to you very seriously, Stephen. I wish you would let that chain alone.

STEPHEN [*hastily relinquishing the chain*]   Have I done anything to annoy you, mother? If so, it was quite unintentional.

LADY BRITOMART [*astonished*]   Nonsense! [*With some remorse.*]   My poor boy, did you think I was angry with you?

STEPHEN   What is it, then, mother? You are making me very uneasy.

LADY BRITOMART [*squaring herself at him rather aggressively*] Stephen: may I ask how soon you intend to realize that you are a grown-up man, and that I am only a woman?

STEPHEN [*amazed*]   Only a—

LADY BRITOMART   Dont repeat my words, please: it is a most aggravating habit. You must learn to face life seriously, Stephen. I really cannot bear the whole burden of our family affairs any longer. You must advise me: you must assume the responsibility.

STEPHEN   I!

LADY BRITOMART   Yes, you, of course. You were 24 last June. Youve been at Harrow and Cambridge. Youve been to India and Japan. You must know a lot of things, now; unless you have wasted your time most scandalously. Well, a d - v i s e me.

STEPHEN [*much perplexed*]   You know I have never interfered in the household—

LADY BRITOMART   No: I should think not. I dont want you to order the dinner.

STEPHEN   I mean in our family affairs.

LADY BRITOMART   Well, you must interfere now; for they are getting quite beyond me.

STEPHEN [*troubled*]   I have thought sometimes that perhaps I ought; but really, mother, I know so little about them; and what I do know is so painful—it is so impossible to mention some things to you— [*he stops, ashamed*]

LADY BRITOMART   I suppose you mean your father.

STEPHEN [*almost inaudibly*]   Yes.

LADY BRITOMART   My dear: we cant go on all our lives not mentioning him. Of course you were quite right not to open the subject until I asked you to; but you are old enough now to be taken into my confidence, and to help me to deal with him about the girls.

STEPHEN   But the girls are all right. They are engaged.

LADY BRITOMART [*complacently*]   Yes: I have made a very good match for Sarah. Charles Lomax will be a millionaire at 35. But that is ten years ahead; and in the meantime his trustees cannot under the terms of his father's will allow him more than £800 a year.

STEPHEN   But the will says also that if he increases his income by his own exertions, they may double the increase.

LADY BRITOMART   Charles Lomax's exertions are much more likely to decrease his income than to increase it. Sarah will have to find at least another £800 a year for the next ten years; and even then they will be as poor as church mice. And what about Barbara? I thought Barbara was going to make the most brilliant career of all of you. And what does she do? Joins the Salvation Army; discharges her maid; lives on a pound a week; and walks in one evening with a professor of Greek whom she has picked up in the street, and who pretends to be a Salvationist, and actually plays the big drum for her in public because he has fallen head over ears in love with her.

STEPHEN   I was certainly rather taken aback when I heard they were engaged. Cusins is a very nice fellow, certainly: nobody would ever guess that he was born in Australia; but—

LADY BRITOMART   Oh, Adolphus Cusins will make a very good husband. After all, nobody can say a word against Greek: it stamps a man at once as an educated gentleman. And my family, thank Heaven, is not a pig-headed Tory one. We are Whigs,* and believe in liberty. Let snobbish people say what they please: Barbara shall marry, not the man they like, but the man *I* like.

---

*Tory and Whig are the names of political parties that are, respectively, conservative and liberal.

STEPHEN   Of course I was thinking only of his income. However, he is not likely to be extravagant.

LADY BRITOMART   Dont be too sure of that, Stephen. I know your quiet, simple, refined, poetic people like Adolphus—quite content with the best of everything! They cost more than your extravagant people, who are always as mean as they are second rate. No: Barbara will need at least £2000 a year. You see it means two additional households. Besides, my dear, y o u must marry soon. I dont approve of the present fashion of philandering bachelors and late marriages; and I am trying to arrange something for you.

STEPHEN   It's very good of you, mother; but perhaps I had better arrange that for myself.

LADY BRITOMART   Nonsense! you are much too young to begin matchmaking: you would be taken in by some pretty little nobody. Of course I dont mean that you are not to be consulted: you know that as well as I do. [STEPHEN closes his lips and is silent.] Now dont sulk, Stephen.

STEPHEN   I am not sulking, mother. What has all this got to do with—with—with my father?

LADY BRITOMART   My dear Stephen: where is the money to come from? It is easy enough for you and the other children to live on my income as long as we are in the same house; but I cant keep four families in four separate houses. You know how poor my father is: he has barely seven thousand a year now; and really, if he were not the Earl of Stevenage, he would have to give up society. He can do nothing for us. He says, naturally enough, that it is absurd that he should be asked to provide for the children of a man who is rolling in money. You see, Stephen, your father must be fabulously wealthy, because there is always a war going on somewhere.

STEPHEN   You need not remind me of that, mother. I have hardly ever opened a newspaper in my life without seeing our name in it. The Undershaft torpedo! The Undershaft quick firers! The Undershaft ten inch! the Undershaft disappearing rampart gun! the Undershaft submarine! and now the Undershaft aerial battleship! At Harrow they called me the Woolwich Infant.* At Cambridge it was the same. A little brute at King's† who was always trying to get up revivals, spoilt my Bible—your first birthday present to me—by writing under my name, "Son and heir to Undershaft and Lazarus, Death and Destruction Dealers: address, Christendom and Judea." But that was not so bad as the way I was kowtowed to everywhere because my father was making millions by selling cannons.

LADY BRITOMART   It is not only the cannons, but the war loans that Lazarus arranges under cover of giving credit for the cannons. You know, Stephen, it's perfectly scandalous. Those two men, Andrew Undershaft and Lazarus, positively have Europe under their thumbs. That is why your father is able to behave as he does. He is above the law. Do you think Bismarck or Gladstone or Disraeli could have openly defied every social and moral obligation all their lives as your father has?[15] They simply wouldnt have dared. I asked Gladstone to take it up. I asked The Times to take it up. I asked the Lord Chamberlain to take it up. But it was just like asking them to declare war on the Sultan.‡ They w o u l d n t. They said they couldnt touch him. I believe they were afraid.

STEPHEN   What could they do? He does not actually break the law.

LADY BRITOMART   Not break the law! He is always breaking the law. He broke the law when he was born: his parents were not married.

STEPHEN   Mother! Is that true?

---

*Joking name, in typical British humor, for a large cannon of the Royal Arsenal Woolwich in London.
†That is, King's College of Cambridge University.
‡Ruler of Turkey.

LADY BRITOMART   Of course it's true: that was why we separated.

STEPHEN   He married without letting you know this!

LADY BRITOMART [*rather taken aback by this inference*]   Oh no. To do Andrew justice, that was not the sort of thing he did. Besides, you know the Undershaft motto: Unashamed. Everybody knew.

STEPHEN   But you said that was why you separated.

LADY BRITOMART   Yes, because he was not content with being a foundling himself: he wanted to disinherit you for another foundling. That was what I couldnt stand.

STEPHEN [*ashamed*]   Do you mean for—for—for—

LADY BRITOMART   Dont stammer, Stephen. Speak distinctly.

STEPHEN   But this is so frightful to me, mother. To have to speak to you about such things!

LADY BRITOMART   It's not pleasant for me, either, especially if you are still so childish that you must make it worse by a display of embarrassment. It is only in the middle classes, Stephen, that people get into a state of dumb helpless horror when they find that there are wicked people in the world. In our class, we have to decide what is to be done with wicked people; and nothing should disturb our self-possession. Now ask your question properly.

STEPHEN   Mother: you have no consideration for me. For Heaven's sake either treat me as a child, as you always do, and tell me nothing at all; or tell me everything and let me take it as best I can.

LADY BRITOMART   Treat you as a child! What do you mean? It is most unkind and ungrateful of you to say such a thing. You know I have never treated any of you as children. I have always made you my companions and friends, and allowed you perfect freedom to do and say whatever you liked, so long as you liked what I could approve of.

STEPHEN [*desperately*]   I daresay we have been the very imperfect children of a very perfect mother; but I do beg you to let me alone for once, and tell me about this horrible business of my father wanting to set me aside for another son.

LADY BRITOMART [*amazed*]   Another son! I never said anything of the kind. I never dreamt of such a thing. This is what comes of interrupting me.

STEPHEN   But you said——

LADY BRITOMART [*cutting him short*]   Now be a good boy, Stephen, and listen to me patiently. The Undershafts are descended from a foundling in the parish of St. Andrew Undershaft* in the city. That was long ago, in the reign of James the First. Well, this foundling was adopted by an armorer and gun-maker. In the course of time the foundling succeeded to the business; and from some notion of gratitude, or some vow or something, he adopted another foundling, and left the business to him. And that foundling did the same. Ever since that, the cannon business has always been left to an adopted foundling named Andrew Undershaft.

STEPHEN   But did they never marry? Were there no legitimate sons?

LADY BRITOMART   Oh yes: they married just as your father did; and they were rich enough to buy land for their own children and leave them well provided for. But they always adopted and trained some foundling to succeed them in the business; and of course they always quarrelled with their wives furiously over it. Your father was adopted in that way; and he pretends to consider himself bound to keep up the tradition and adopt somebody to leave the business to. Of course I was not going to stand that. There may have been some reason for it when the Undershafts could only marry

*Saint Andrew Undershaft is a church in London.

women in their own class, whose sons were not fit to govern great estates. But there could be no excuse for passing over m y son.

STEPHEN [*dubiously*]   I am afraid I should make a poor hand of managing a cannon foundry.

LADY BRITOMART   Nonsense! you could easily get a manager and pay him a salary.

STEPHEN   My father evidently had no great opinion of my capacity.

LADY BRITOMART   Stuff, child! you were only a baby: it had nothing to do with your capacity. Andrew did it on principle, just as he did every perverse and wicked thing on principle. When my father remonstrated, Andrew actually told him to his face that history tells us of only two successful institutions: one the Undershaft firm, and the other the Roman Empire under the Antonines.[16] That was because the Antonine emperors all adopted their successors. Such rubbish! The Stevenages are as good as the Antonines, I hope; and you are a Stevenage. But that was Andrew all over. There you have the man! Always clever and unanswerable when he was defending nonsense and wickedness: always awkward and sullen when he had to behave sensibly and decently!

STEPHEN   Then it was on my account that your home life was broken up, mother. I am sorry.

LADY BRITOMART   Well, dear, there were other differences. I really cannot bear an immoral man. I am not a Pharisee, I hope; and I should not have minded his merely d o i n g wrong things: we are none of us perfect. But your father didnt exactly d o wrong things: he said them and thought them: that was what was so dreadful. He really had a sort of religion of wrongness. Just as one doesnt mind men practising immorality so long as they own that they are in the wrong by preaching morality; so I couldnt forgive Andrew for preaching immorality while he practised morality. You would all have grown up without principles, without any knowledge of right and wrong, if he had been in the house. You know, my dear, your father was a very attractive man in some ways. Children did not dislike him; and he took advantage of it to put the wickedest ideas into their heads, and make them quite unmanageable. I did not dislike him myself: very far from it; but nothing can bridge over moral disagreement.

STEPHEN   All this simply bewilders me, mother. People may differ about matters of opinion, or even about religion; but how can they differ about right and wrong? Right is right; and wrong is wrong; and if a man cannot distinguish them properly, he is either a fool or a rascal: thats all.

LADY BRITOMART [touched]   Thats my own boy [she pats his cheek]! Your father never could answer that: he used to laugh and get out of it under cover of some affectionate nonsense. And now that you understand the situation, what do you advise me to do?

STEPHEN   Well, what c a n you do?

LADY BRITOMART   I must get the money somehow.

STEPHEN   We cannot take money from him. I had rather go and live in some cheap place like Bedford Square or even Hampstead than take a farthing of his money.

LADY BRITOMART   But after all, Stephen, our present income comes from Andrew.

STEPHEN [shocked]   I never knew that.

LADY BRITOMART   Well, you surely didnt suppose your grandfather had anything to give me. The Stevenages could not do everything for you. We gave you social position. Andrew had to contribute s o m e t h i n g. He had a very good bargain, I think.

STEPHEN [bitterly]   We are utterly dependent on him and his cannons, then?

LADY BRITOMART   Certainly not: the money is settled. But

he provided it. So you see it is not a question of taking money from him or not: it is simply a question of how much. I dont want any more for myself.

STEPHEN   Nor do I.

LADY BRITOMART   But Sarah does; and Barbara does. That is, Charles Lomax and Adolphus Cusins will cost them more. So I must put my pride in my pocket and ask for it, I suppose. That is your advice, Stephen, is it not?

STEPHEN   No.

LADY BRITOMART [*sharply*]   Stephen!

STEPHEN   Of course if you are determined——

LADY BRITOMART   I am not determined: I ask your advice; and I am waiting for it. I will not have all the responsibility thrown on my shoulders.

STEPHEN [*obstinately*]   I would die sooner than ask him for another penny.

LADY BRITOMART [*resignedly*]   You mean that *I* must ask him. Very well, Stephen: it shall be as you wish. You will be glad to know that your grandfather concurs. But he thinks I ought to ask Andrew to come here and see the girls. After all, he must have some natural affection for them.

STEPHEN   Ask him here!!!

LADY BRITOMART   Do n o t repeat my words, Stephen. Where else can I ask him?

STEPHEN   I never expected you to ask him at all.

LADY BRITOMART   Now dont tease, Stephen. Come! you see that it is necessary that he should pay us a visit, dont you?

STEPHEN [*reluctantly*]   I suppose so, if the girls cannot do without his money.

LADY BRITOMART   Thank you, Stephen: I knew you would give me the right advice when it was properly explained to you. I have asked your father to come this evening. [*Stephen bounds from his seat.*] Dont jump, Stephen: it fidgets me.

STEPHEN [*in utter consternation*]   Do you mean to say that my father is coming here to-night——that he may be here at any moment?

LADY BRITOMART [*looking at her watch*]   I said nine. [*He gasps. She rises.*] Ring the bell, please. [*STEPHEN goes to the smaller writing table; presses a button on it; and sits at it with his elbows on the table and his head in his hands, outwitted and overwhelmed.*] It is ten minutes to nine yet; and I have to prepare the girls. I asked Charles Lomax and Adolphus to dinner on purpose that they might be here. Andrew had better see them in case he should cherish any delusions as to their being capable of supporting their wives. [*The butler enters: LADY BRITOMART goes behind the settee to speak to him.*] Morrison: go up to the drawingroom and tell everybody to come down here at once. [*MORRISON withdraws. LADY BRITOMART turns to STEPHEN.*] Now remember, Stephen: I shall need all your countenance and authority. [*He rises and tries to recover some vestige of these attributes.*] Give me a chair, dear. [*He pushes a chair forward from the wall to where she stands, near the smaller writing table. She sits down; and he goes to the arm-chair, into which he throws himself.*] I dont know how Barbara will take it. Ever since they made her a major in the Salvation Army she has developed a propensity to have her own way and order people about which quite cows me sometimes. It's not ladylike: I'm sure I dont know where she picked it up. Anyhow, Barbara shant bully m e; but still it's just as well that your father should be here before she has time to refuse to meet him or make a fuss. Dont look nervous, Stephen; it will only encourage Barbara to make difficulties. *I* am nervous enough, goodness knows; but I dont shew it.

SARAH and BARBARA come in with their respective young men, CHARLES LOMAX and ADOLPHUS CUSINS.[17] *SARAH is slender, bored, and mundane. BARBARA is robuster, jollier, much more energetic. SARAH is fashionably dressed: BARBARA is in Salvation Army uniform. LOMAX, a young man about town, is like many other young men about town. He is afflicted with a frivolous sense of humor which plunges him at the most inopportune moments into paroxysms of imperfectly suppressed laughter. CUSINS is a spectacled student, slight, thin haired, and sweet voiced, with a more complex form of LOMAX's complaint. His sense of humor is intellectual and subtle, and is complicated by an appalling temper. The life-long struggle of a benevolent temperament and a high conscience against impulses of inhuman ridicule and fierce impatience has set up a chronic strain which has visibly wrecked his constitution. He is a most implacable, determined, tenacious, intolerant person who by mere force of character presents himself as——and indeed actually is——considerate, gentle, explanatory, even mild and apologetic, capable possibly of murder, but not of cruelty or coarseness. By the operation of some instinct which is not merciful enough to blind him with the illusions of love, he is obstinately bent on marrying BARBARA. LOMAX likes SARAH and thinks it will be rather a lark to marry her. Consequently he has not attempted to resist LADY BRITOMART's arrangements to that end.*

All four look as if they had been having a good deal of fun in the drawingroom. The girls enter first, leaving the swains outside. SARAH comes to the settee. BARBARA comes in after her and stops at the door.

BARBARA   Are Cholly and Dolly to come in?

LADY BRITOMART [*forcibly*]   Barbara: I will not have Charles called Cholly: the vulgarity of it positively makes me ill.

BARBARA   It's all right, mother. Cholly is quite correct nowadays. Are they to come in?

LADY BRITOMART   Yes, if they will behave themselves.

BARBARA [*through the door*]   Come in, Dolly, and behave yourself.

BARBARA comes to her mother's writing table. CUSINS enters smiling, and wanders towards LADY BRITOMART.

SARAH [*calling*]   Come in, Cholly. [*LOMAX enters, controlling his features very imperfectly, and places himself vaguely between SARAH and BARBARA.*]

LADY BRITOMART [*peremptorily*]   Sit down, all of you. [*They sit. CUSINS crosses to the window and seats himself there. LOMAX takes a chair. BARBARA sits at the writing table and SARAH on the settee.*] I dont in the least know what you are laughing at, Adolphus. I am surprised at you, though I expected nothing better from Charles Lomax.

CUSINS [*in a remarkably gentle voice*]   Barbara has been trying to teach me the West Ham Salvation March.

LADY BRITOMART   I see nothing to laugh at in that; nor should you if you are really converted.

CUSINS [*sweetly*]   You were not present. It was really funny, I believe.

LOMAX   Ripping.

LADY BRITOMART   Be quiet, Charles. Now listen to me, children. Your father is coming here this evening. [*General stupefaction.*]

LOMAX   [*remonstrating*]   Oh I say!

LADY BRITOMART   You are not called on to say anything, Charles.

SARAH   Are you serious, mother?

LADY BRITOMART   Of course I am serious. It is on your account, Sarah, and also on Charles's. [*Silence. CHARLES looks painfully unworthy.*] I hope you are not going to object, Barbara.

BARBARA   I! why should I? My father has a soul to be saved like anybody else. Hes quite welcome as far as I am concerned.

LOMAX [*still remonstrant*]   But really, dont you know! Oh I say!

LADY BRITOMART [*frigidly*]   What do you wish to convey, Charles?

LOMAX   Well, you must admit that this is a bit thick.

LADY BRITOMART [*turning with ominous suavity to CUSINS*]   Adolphus: you are a professor of Greek. Can you translate Charles Lomax's remarks into reputable English for us?

CUSINS [*cautiously*]   If I may say so, Lady Brit, I think Charles has rather happily expressed what we all feel. Homer, speaking of Autolycus, uses the same phrase. πυκινὸν δόμον ἐλθεῖν[18] means a bit thick.

LOMAX [*handsomely*]   Not that I mind, you know, if Sarah dont.

LADY BRITOMART [*crushingly*]   Thank you. Have I y o u r permission, Adolphus, to invite my own husband to my own house?

CUSINS [*gallantly*]   You have my unhesitating support in everything you do.

LADY BRITOMART   Sarah: have you nothing to say?

SARAH   Do you mean that he is coming regularly to live here?

LADY BRITOMART   Certainly not. The spare room is ready for him if he likes to stay for a day or two and see a little more of you; but there are limits.

SARAH   Well, he cant eat us, I suppose. *I* dont mind.

LOMAX [*chuckling*]   I wonder how the old man will take it.

LADY BRITOMART   Much as the old woman will, no doubt, Charles.

LOMAX [*abashed*]   I didnt mean—at least—

LADY BRITOMART   You didnt t h i n k, Charles. You never do; and the result is, you never mean anything. And now please attend to me, children. Your father will be quite a stranger to us.

LOMAX   I suppose he hasnt seen Sarah since she was a little kid.

LADY BRITOMART   Not since she was a little kid, Charles, as you express it with that elegance of diction and refinement of thought that seem never to desert you. Accordingly—er—[*impatiently*] Now I have forgotten what I was going to say. That comes of your provoking me to be sarcastic, Charles. Adolphus: will you kindly tell me where I was.

CUSINS [*sweetly*]   You were saying that as Mr. Undershaft has not seen his children since they were babies, he will form his opinion of the way you have brought them up from their behavior to-night, and that therefore you wish us all to be particularly careful to conduct ourselves well, especially Charles.

LOMAX   Look here: Lady Brit didnt say that.

LADY BRITOMART [*vehemently*]   I did, Charles. Adolphus's recollection is perfectly correct. It is most important that you should be good; and I do beg you for once not to pair off into opposite corners and giggle and whisper while I am speaking to your father.

BARBARA   All right, mother. We'll do you credit.

LADY BRITOMART   Remember, Charles, that Sarah will want to feel proud of you instead of ashamed of you.

LOMAX   Oh I say! theres nothing to be exactly proud of, dont you know.

LADY BRITOMART   Well, try and look as if there was.

MORRISON, pale and dismayed, breaks into the room in unconcealed disorder.

MORRISON   Might I speak a word to you, my lady?

LADY BRITOMART   Nonsense! Shew him up.

MORRISON   Yes, my lady. [*He goes.*]

LOMAX   Does Morrison know who it is?

LADY BRITOMART   Of course. Morrison has always been with us.

LOMAX   It must be a regular corker for him, dont you know.

LADY BRITOMART   Is this a moment to get on my nerves, Charles, with your outrageous expressions?

LOMAX   But this is something out of the ordinary, really—

MORRISON [*at the door*]   The—er—Mr. Undershaft. [*He retreats in confusion.*]

ANDREW UNDERSHAFT comes in. All rise. LADY BRITOMART meets him in the middle of the room behind the settee.

ANDREW is, on the surface, a stoutish, easygoing elderly man, with kindly patient manners, and an engaging simplicity of character. But he has a watchful, deliberate, waiting, listening face, and formidable reserves of power, both bodily and mental, in his capacious chest and long head. His gentleness is partly that of a strong man who has learnt by experience that his natural grip hurts ordinary people unless he handles them very carefully, and partly the mellowness of age and success. He is also a little shy in his present very delicate situation.

LADY BRITOMART   Good evening, Andrew.

UNDERSHAFT   How d'ye do, my dear.

LADY BRITOMART   You look a good deal older.

UNDERSHAFT [*apologetically*]   I a m somewhat older. [*With a touch of courtship.*] Time has stood still with you.

LADY BRITOMART [*promptly*]   Rubbish! This is your family.

UNDERSHAFT [*surprised*]   Is it so large? I am sorry to say my memory is failing very badly in some things. [*He offers his hand with paternal kindness to LOMAX.*]

LOMAX [*jerkily shaking his hand*]   Ahdedoo.

UNDERSHAFT   I can see you are my eldest. I am very glad to meet you again, my boy.

LOMAX [*remonstrating*]   No but look here dont you know— [*Overcome.*] Oh I say!

LADY BRITOMART [*recovering from momentary speechlessness*] Andrew: do you mean to say that you dont remember how many children you have?

UNDERSHAFT   Well, I am afraid I—. They have grown so much—er. Am I making any ridiculous mistake? I may as well confess: I recollect only one son. But so many things have happened since, of course—er—

LADY BRITOMART [*decisively*]   Andrew: you are talking nonsense. Of course you have only one son.

UNDERSHAFT   Perhaps you will be good enough to introduce me, my dear.

LADY BRITOMART   That is Charles Lomax, who is engaged to Sarah.

UNDERSHAFT   My dear sir, I beg your pardon.

LOMAX   Notatall. Delighted, I assure you.

LADY BRITOMART   This is Stephen.

UNDERSHAFT [*bowing*]   Happy to make your acquaintance, Mr. Stephen. Then [*going to CUSINS*] you must be my son. [*Taking CUSINS' hands in his.*] How are you, my young friend? [*To LADY BRITOMART.*] He is very like you, my love.

CUSINS   You flatter me, Mr. Undershaft. My name is Cusins: engaged to Barbara. [*Very explicitly.*] That is Major Barbara Undershaft, of the Salvation Army. That is Sarah, your second daughter. This is Stephen Undershaft, your son.

UNDERSHAFT   My dear Stephen, I b e g your pardon.

STEPHEN   Not at all.

UNDERSHAFT   Mr. Cusins: I am much indebted to you for explaining so precisely. [*Turning to SARAH.*] Barbara, my dear—

SARAH [*prompting him*]   Sarah.

UNDERSHAFT   Sarah, of course. [*They shake hands. He goes over to BARBARA.*] Barbara—I am right this time, I hope.

BARBARA   Quite right. [*They shake hands.*]

LADY BRITOMART [*resuming command*]   Sit down, all of you. Sit down, Andrew. [*She comes forward and sits on the settee. CUSINS also brings his chair forward on her left. BARBARA and STEPHEN resume their seats. LOMAX gives his chair to SARAH and goes for another.*]

UNDERSHAFT   Thank you, my love.

LOMAX [*conversationally, as he brings a chair forward between the writing table and the settee, and offers it to UNDERSHAFT*] Takes you some time to find out exactly where you are, dont it?

UNDERSHAFT [*accepting the chair*]   That is not what embarrasses me, Mr. Lomax. My difficulty is that if I play the part of a father, I shall produce the effect of an intrusive stranger; and if I play the part of a discreet stranger, I may appear a callous father.

LADY BRITOMART   There is no need for you to play any part at all, Andrew. You had much better be sincere and natural.

UNDERSHAFT [*submissively*]   Yes, my dear: I daresay that will be best. [*Making himself comfortable.*] Well, here I am. Now what can I do for you all?

LADY BRITOMART   You need not do anything, Andrew. You are one of the family. You can sit with us and enjoy yourself.

LOMAX's too long suppressed mirth explodes in agonized neighings.

LADY BRITOMART [*outraged*]   Charles Lomax: if you can behave yourself, behave yourself. If not, leave the room.

LOMAX   I'm awfully sorry, Lady Brit; but really, you know, upon my soul! [*He sits on the settee between LADY BRITOMART and UNDERSHAFT, quite overcome.*]

BARBARA   Why dont you laugh if you want to, Cholly? It's good for your inside.

LADY BRITOMART   Barbara: you have had the education of a lady. Please let your father see that; and dont talk like a street girl.

UNDERSHAFT   Never mind me, my dear. As you know, I am not a gentleman; and I was never educated.

LOMAX [*encouragingly*]   Nobody'd know it, I assure you. You look all right, you know.

CUSINS   Let me advise you to study Greek, Mr. Undershaft. Greek scholars are privileged men. Few of them know Greek; and none of them know anything else; but their position is unchallengeable. Other languages are the qualifications of waiters and commercial travellers: Greek is to a man of position what the hallmark is to silver.

BARBARA   Dolly: dont be insincere. Cholly: fetch your concertina and play something for us.

LOMAX [*doubtfully to UNDERSHAFT*]   Perhaps that sort of thing isnt in your line, eh?

UNDERSHAFT   I am particularly fond of music.

LOMAX [*delighted*]   Are you? Then I'll get it. [*He goes upstairs for the instrument.*]

UNDERSHAFT   Do you play, Barbara?

BARBARA   Only the tambourine. But Cholly's teaching me the concertina.

UNDERSHAFT   Is Cholly also a member of the Salvation Army?

BARBARA   No: he says it's bad form to be a dissenter.* But I dont despair of Cholly. I made him come yesterday to a meeting at the dock gates, and took the collection in his hat.

LADY BRITOMART   It is not my doing, Andrew. Barbara is old enough to take her own way. She has no father to advise her.

BARBARA   Oh yes she has. There are no orphans in the Salvation Army.

UNDERSHAFT   Your father there has a great many children and plenty of experience, eh?

BARBARA [*looking at him with quick interest and nodding*]   Just so. How did y o u come to understand that? [*LOMAX is heard at the door trying the concertina.*]

LADY BRITOMART   Come in, Charles. Play us something at once.

LOMAX   Righto! [*He sits down in his former place, and preludes.*]

UNDERSHAFT   One moment, Mr. Lomax. I am rather interested in the Salvation Army. Its motto might be my own: Blood and Fire.

LOMAX [*shocked*]   But not your sort of blood and fire, you know.

UNDERSHAFT   My sort of blood cleanses: my sort of fire purifies.

BARBARA   So do ours. Come down to-morrow to my shelter—the West Ham shelter—and see what we're doing. We're

---

*That is, a member of a Christian sect other than the Church of England.

going to march to a great meeting in the Assembly Hall at Mile End. Come and see the shelter and then march with us: it will do you a lot of good. Can you play anything?

UNDERSHAFT   In my youth I earned pennies, and even shillings occasionally, in the streets and in public house parlors by my natural talent for stepdancing. Later on, I became a member of the Undershaft orchestral society, and performed passably on the tenor trombone.

LOMAX [*scandalized*]   Oh I say!

BARBARA   Many a sinner has played himself into heaven on the trombone, thanks to the Army.

LOMAX [*to BARBARA, still rather shocked*]   Yes; but what about the cannon business, dont you know? [*To UNDERSHAFT.*] Getting into heaven is not exactly in your line, is it?

LADY BRITOMART   Charles!!!

LOMAX   Well; but it stands to reason, dont it? The cannon business may be necessary and all that: we cant get on without cannons; but it isnt right, you know. On the other hand, there may be a certain amount of tosh about the Salvation Army—I belong to the Established Church* myself—but still you cant deny that it's religion; and you cant go against religion, can you? At least unless youre downright immoral, dont you know.

UNDERSHAFT   You hardly appreciate my position, Mr. Lomax—

LOMAX [*hastily*]   I'm not saying anything against you personally, you know.

UNDERSHAFT   Quite so, quite so. But consider for a moment. Here I am, a manufacturer of mutilation and murder. I find myself in a specially amiable humor just now because, this morning, down at the foundry, we blew twenty-seven dummy soldiers into fragments with a gun which formerly destroyed only thirteen.

---

*Particular religion supported financially by the state.

LOMAX [*leniently*]   Well, the more destructive war becomes, the sooner it will be abolished, eh?

UNDERSHAFT   Not at all. The more destructive war becomes the more fascinating we find it. No, Mr. Lomax: I am obliged to you for making the usual excuse for my trade; but I am not ashamed of it. I am not one of those men who keep their morals and their business in watertight compartments. All the spare money my trade rivals spend on hospitals, cathedrals and other receptacles for conscience money, I devote to experiments and researches in improved methods of destroying life and property. I have always done so; and I always shall. Therefore your Christmas card moralities of peace on earth and goodwill among men are of no use to me. Your Christianity, which enjoins you to resist not evil, and to turn the other cheek, would make me a bankrupt. M y morality—m y religion—must have a place for cannons and torpedoes in it.

STEPHEN [*coldly—almost sullenly*]   You speak as if there were half a dozen moralities and religions to choose from, instead of one true morality and one true religion.

UNDERSHAFT   For me there is only one true morality; but it might not fit you, as you do not manufacture aerial battleships. There is only one true morality for every man; but every man has not the same true morality.

LOMAX [*overtaxed*]   Would you mind saying that again? I didnt quite follow it.

CUSINS   It's quite simple. As Euripides says, one man's meat is another man's poison morally as well as physically.

UNDERSHAFT   Precisely.

LOMAX   Oh, t h a t. Yes, yes, yes. True. True.

STEPHEN   In other words, some men are honest and some are scoundrels.

BARBARA   Bosh. There are no scoundrels.

UNDERSHAFT   Indeed? Are there any good men?

BARBARA   No. Not one. There are neither good men nor

scoundrels: there are just children of one Father; and the sooner they stop calling one another names the better. You neednt talk to me: I know them. Ive had scores of them through my hands: scoundrels, criminals, infidels, philanthropists, missionaries, county councillors, all sorts. Theyre all just the same sort of sinner; and theres the same salvation ready for them all.

UNDERSHAFT   May I ask have you ever saved a maker of cannons?

BARBARA   No. Will you let me try?

UNDERSHAFT   Well, I will make a bargain with you. If I go to see you to-morrow in your Salvation Shelter, will you come the day after to see me in my cannon works?

BARBARA   Take care. It may end in your giving up the cannons for the sake of the Salvation Army.

UNDERSHAFT   Are you sure it will not end in your giving up the Salvation Army for the sake of the cannons?

BARBARA   I will take my chance of that.

UNDERSHAFT   And I will take my chance of the other. [*They shake hands on it.*] Where is your shelter?

BARBARA   In West Ham. At the sign of the cross. Ask anybody in Canning Town. Where are your works?

UNDERSHAFT   In Perivale St. Andrews. At the sign of the sword. Ask anybody in Europe.

LOMAX   Hadnt I better play something?

BARBARA   Yes. Give us Onward, Christian Soldiers.

LOMAX   Well, thats rather a strong order to begin with, dont you know. Suppose I sing Thourt passing hence, my brother. It's much the same tune.

BARBARA   It's too melancholy. You get saved, Cholly; and youll pass hence, my brother, without making such a fuss about it.

LADY BRITOMART   Really, Barbara, you go on as if religion were a pleasant subject. Do have some sense of propriety.

UNDERSHAFT   I do not find it an unpleasant subject, my dear. It is the only one that capable people really care for.

LADY BRITOMART [*looking at her watch*]   Well, if you are determined to have it, I insist on having it in a proper and respectable way. Charles: ring for prayers. [*General amazement. STEPHEN rises in dismay.*]

LOMAX [*rising*]   Oh I say!

UNDERSHAFT [*rising*]   I am afraid I must be going.

LADY BRITOMART   You cannot go now, Andrew: it would be most improper. Sit down. What will the servants think?

UNDERSHAFT   My dear: I have conscientious scruples. May I suggest a compromise? If Barbara will conduct a little service in the drawingroom, with Mr. Lomax as organist, I will attend it willingly. I will even take part, if a trombone can be procured.

LADY BRITOMART   Dont mock, Andrew.

UNDERSHAFT [*shocked—to BARBARA*]   You dont think I am mocking, my love, I hope.

BARBARA   No, of course not; and it wouldnt matter if you were: half the Army came to their first meeting for a lark. [*Rising.*] Come along. Come, Dolly. Come, Cholly. [*She goes out with UNDERSHAFT, who opens the door for her. CUSINS rises.*]

LADY BRITOMART   I will not be disobeyed by everybody. Adolphus: sit down. Charles: you may go. You are not fit for prayers: you cannot keep your countenance.

LOMAX   Oh I say! [*He goes out.*]

LADY BRITOMART [*continuing*]   But you, Adolphus, can behave yourself if you choose to. I insist on your staying.

CUSINS   My dear Lady Brit: there are things in the family prayer book that I couldnt bear to hear you say.

LADY BRITOMART   What things, pray?

CUSINS   Well, you would have to say before all the servants that we have done things we ought not to have done, and left undone things we ought to have done, and that there is no health in us. I cannot bear to hear you doing yourself such an injustice, and Barbara such an injustice. As for myself, I flatly deny it: I have done my best. I shouldnt dare to marry Barbara—I couldnt look you in the face—if it were true. So I must go to the drawingroom.

LADY BRITOMART [*offended*]   Well, go. [*He starts for the door.*] And remember this, Adolphus [*he turns to listen*]: I have a very strong suspicion that you went to the Salvation Army to worship Barbara and nothing else. And I quite appreciate the very clever way in which you systematically humbug me. I have found you out. Take care Barbara doesnt. Thats all.

CUSINS [*with unruffled sweetness*]   Dont tell on me. [*He goes out.*]

LADY BRITOMART   Sarah: if you want to go, go. Anything's better than to sit there as if you wished you were a thousand miles away.

SARAH [*languidly*]   Very well, mamma. [*She goes.*]
   LADY BRITOMART, with a sudden flounce, gives way to a little gust of tears.

STEPHEN [*going to her*]   Mother: whats the matter?

LADY BRITOMART [*swishing away her tears with her handkerchief*] Nothing. Foolishness. You can go with him, too, if you like, and leave me with the servants.

STEPHEN   Oh, you mustnt think that, mother. I—I dont like him.

LADY BRITOMART   The others do. That is the injustice of a woman's lot. A woman has to bring up her children; and that means to restrain them, to deny them things they want, to set them tasks, to punish them when they do wrong, to do all the unpleasant things. And then the father, who has nothing to do but pet them and spoil them, comes in when all her work is done and steals their affection from her.

STEPHEN   He has not stolen our affection from you. It is only curiosity.

LADY BRITOMART [*violently*]   I wont be consoled, Stephen.

There is nothing the matter with me. [*She rises and goes towards the door.*]

STEPHEN   Where are you going, mother?

LADY BRITOMART   To the drawingroom, of course. [*She goes out. Onward, Christian Soldiers, on the concertina, with tambourine accompaniment, is heard when the door opens.*] Are you coming, Stephen?

STEPHEN   No. Certainly not. [*She goes. He sits down on the settee, with compressed lips and an expression of strong dislike.*]

END OF ACT I.

ACT II

*The yard of the West Ham shelter of the Salvation Army is
a cold place on a January morning. The building itself, an
old warehouse, is newly whitewashed. Its gabled end
projects into the yard in the middle, with a door on the
ground floor, and another in the loft above it without any
balcony or ladder, but with a pulley rigged over it for
hoisting sacks. Those who come from this central gable end
into the yard have the gateway leading to the street on
their left, with a stone horse-trough just beyond it, and, on
the right, a penthouse shielding a table from the weather.
There are forms* at the table; and on them are seated a
man and a woman, both much down on their luck,
finishing a meal of bread (one thick slice each, with
margarine and golden syrup) and diluted milk.*

*The man, a workman out of employment, is young,
agile, a talker, a poser, sharp enough to be capable of
anything in reason except honesty or altruistic
considerations of any kind. The woman is a commonplace
old bundle of poverty and hard-worn humanity. She looks
sixty and probably is forty-five. If they were rich people,
gloved and muffed and well wrapped up in furs and
overcoats, they would be numbed and miserable; for it is a
grindingly cold, raw, January day; and a glance at the
background of grimy warehouses and leaden sky visible
over the whitewashed walls of the yard would drive any*

---

*Benches.

idle rich person, straight to the Mediterranean. But these two, being no more troubled with visions of the Mediterranean than of the moon, and being compelled to keep more of their clothes in the pawnshop, and less on their persons, in winter than in summer, are not depressed by the cold: rather are they stung into vivacity, to which their meal has just now given an almost jolly turn. The man takes a pull at his mug, and then gets up and moves about the yard with his hands deep in his pockets, occasionally breaking into a stepdance.

THE WOMAN   Feel better arter your meal, sir?

THE MAN   No. Call that a meal! Good enough for you, praps; but wot is it to me, an intelligent workin man.

THE WOMAN   Workin man! Wot are you?

THE MAN   Painter.

THE WOMAN [*sceptically*]   Yus, I dessay.

THE MAN   Yus, you dessay! I know. Every loafer that cant do nothink calls isself a painter. Well, I'm a real painter: grainer, finisher, thirty-eight bob a week when I can get it.

THE WOMAN   Then why dont you go and get it?

THE MAN   I'll tell you why. Fust: I'm intelligent—fffff! it's rotten cold here [*he dances a step or two*]—yes: intelligent beyond the station o life into which it has pleased the capitalists to call me; and they dont like a man that sees through em. Second, an intelligent bein needs a doo share of appiness; so I drink somethink cruel when I get the chawnce. Third, I stand by my class and do as little as I can so's to leave arf the job for me fellow workers. Fourth, I'm fly enough to know wots inside the law and wots outside it; and inside it I do as the capitalists do: pinch wot I can lay me ands on. In a proper state of society I am sober, industrious and honest: in Rome, so to speak, I do as the Romans do. Wots the consequence? When

trade is bad—and it's rotten bad just now—and the employers az to sack arf their men, they generally start on me.

THE WOMAN   Whats your name?

THE MAN   Price. Bronterre O'Brien* Price. Usually called
Snobby Price, for short.

THE WOMAN   Snobby's a carpenter, aint it? You said you was
a painter.

PRICE   Not that kind of snob, but the genteel sort. I'm too uppish, owing to my intelligence, and my father being a Chartist
and a reading, thinking man: a stationer, too. I'm none of your
common hewers of wood and drawers of water;† and dont
you forget it. [*He returns to his seat at the table, and takes up his
mug.*] Wots y o u r name?

THE WOMAN   Rummy Mitchens, sir.

PRICE [*quaffing the remains of his milk to her*]   Your elth, Miss
Mitchens.

RUMMY [*correcting him*]   Missis Mitchens.

PRICE   Wot! Oh Rummy, Rummy! Respectable married
woman, Rummy, gittin rescued by the Salvation Army by pre-
tendin to be a bad un. Same old game!

RUMMY   What am I to do? I cant starve. Them Salvation lasses
is dear good girls; but the better you are, the worse they likes
to think you were before they rescued you. Why shouldnt they
av a bit o credit, poor loves? theyre worn to rags by their
work. And where would they get the money to rescue us if we
was to let on we're no worse than other people? You know
what ladies and gentlemen are.

---

*Snobby is named after a well-known Chartist, James Bronterre O'Brien
(1805–1864); Chartists were nineteenth-century English political reformers who
advocated for the working classes.

†Snobby quotes the Bible (see Joshua 9:21, King James Version) to disdain mere
manual laborers.

PRICE   Thievin swine! Wish I ad their job, Rummy, all the same. Wot does Rummy stand for? Pet name praps?

RUMMY   Short for Romola.[19]

PRICE   For wot!?

RUMMY   Romola. It was out of a new book. Somebody me mother wanted me to grow up like.

PRICE   We're companions in misfortune, Rummy. Both on us got names that nobody cawnt pronounce. Consequently I'm Snobby and youre Rummy because Bill and Sally wasnt good enough for our parents. Such is life!

RUMMY   Who saved you, Mr. Price? Was it Major Barbara?

PRICE   No: I come here on my own. I'm goin to be Bronterre O'Brien Price, the converted painter. I know wot they like. I'll tell em how I blasphemed and gambled and wopped my poor old mother——

RUMMY [*shocked*]   Used you to beat your mother?

PRICE   Not likely. She used to beat me. No matter: you come and listen to the converted painter, and youll hear how she was a pious woman that taught me me prayers at er knee, an how I used to come home drunk and drag her out o bed be er snow white airs, an lam into er with the poker.

RUMMY   Thats whats so unfair to us women. Your confessions is just as big lies as ours: you dont tell what you really done no more than us; but you men can tell your lies right out at the meetins and be made much of for it; while the sort o confessions we az to make az to be whispered to one lady at a time. It aint right, spite of all their piety.

PRICE   Right! Do you spose the Army 'd be allowed if it went and did right? Not much. It combs our air and makes us good little blokes to be robbed and put upon. But I'll play the game as good as any of em. I'll see somebody struck by lightnin, or hear a voice sayin "Snobby Price: where will you spend eternity?" I'll ave a time of it, I tell you.

RUMMY   You wont be let drink, though.

PRICE   I'll take it out in gorspellin, then. I dont want to drink
if I can get fun enough any other way.

*JENNY HILL, a pale, overwrought, pretty Salvation lass of 1 8, comes
in through the yard gate, leading PETER SHIRLEY, a half hardened,
half worn-out elderly man, weak with hunger.*

JENNY [*supporting him*]   Come! pluck up. I'll get you something
to eat. Youll be all right then.

PRICE [*rising and hurrying officiously to take the old man off Jenny's
hands*]   Poor old man! Cheer up, brother: youll find rest and
peace and appiness ere. Hurry up with the food, miss: e's fair
done. [*JENNY hurries into the shelter.*] Ere, buck up, daddy! shes
fetchin y'a thick slice o breadn treacle, an a mug o sky-blue.*
[*He seats him at the corner of the table.*]

RUMMY [*gaily*]   Keep up your old art!† Never say die!

SHIRLEY   I'm not an old man. I'm ony 46. I'm as good as ever
I was. The grey patch come in my hair before I was thirty. All
it wants is three pennorth o hair dye: am I to be turned on the
streets to starve for it? Holy God! I've worked ten to twelve
hours a day since I was thirteen, and paid my way all through;
and now am I to be thrown into the gutter and my job given
to a young man that can do it no better than me because Ive
black hair that goes white at the first change?

PRICE [*cheerfully*]   No good jawrin about it. Youre ony a
jumped-up, jerked-off, orspittle-turned-out incurable‡ of an
ole workin man: who cares about you? Eh? Make the thievin
swine give you a meal: theyve stole many a one from you. Get
a bit o your own back. [*JENNY returns with the usual meal.*]
There you are, brother. Awsk a blessin an tuck that into you.

SHIRLEY [*looking at it ravenously but not touching it, and crying like
a child*]   I never took anything before.

---

*Diluted milk.

†That is, heart.

‡Nervous, discarded, and rejected as incurable by the hospital.

JENNY [*petting him*]   Come, come! the Lord sends it to you: he wasnt above taking bread from his friends; and why should you be? Besides, when we find you a job you can pay us for it if you like.

SHIRLEY [*eagerly*]   Yes, yes: thats true. I can pay you back: its only a loan. [*Shivering.*] Oh Lord! oh Lord! [*He turns to the table and attacks the meal ravenously.*]

JENNY   Well, Rummy, are you more comfortable now?

RUMMY   God bless you, lovey! youve fed my body and saved my soul, havent you? [*JENNY, touched, kisses her.*] Sit down and rest a bit: you must be ready to drop.

JENNY   Ive been going hard since morning. But theres more work than we can do. I mustnt stop.

RUMMY   Try a prayer for just two minutes. Youll work all the better after.

JENNY [*her eyes lighting up*]   Oh isnt it wonderful how a few minutes prayer revives you! I was quite lightheaded at twelve o'clock, I was so tired; but Major Barbara just sent me to pray for five minutes; and I was able to go on as if I had only just begun. [*To PRICE.*] Did you have a piece of bread?

PRICE [*with unction*]   Yes, miss; but Ive got the piece that I value more; and thats the peace that passeth hall hannerstennin.*

RUMMY [*fervently*]   Glory Hallelujah!

BILL WALKER, a rough customer of about 25, appears at the yard gate and looks malevolently at JENNY.

JENNY   That makes me so happy. When you say that, I feel wicked for loitering here. I must get to work again.

She is hurrying to the shelter, when the new-comer moves quickly up to the door and intercepts her. His manner is so threatening that she retreats as he comes at her truculently, driving her down the yard.

BILL   I know you. Youre the one that took away my girl. Youre

---

*That is, "all understanding"; Price is quoting from the Bible, Philippians 4:7: "The peace of God, which passeth all understanding" (KJV).

the one that set er agen me. Well, I'm goin to av er out. Not
that I care a curse for her or you: see? But I'll let er know; and
I'll let y o u know. I'm goin to give er a doin thatll teach er to
cut away from me. Now in with you and tell er to come out
afore I come in and kick er out. Tell er Bill Walker wants er.
She'll know what that means; and if she keeps me waitin itll
be worse. You stop to jaw back at me; and I'll start on you:
d'ye hear? Theres your way. In you go. [*He takes her by the arm
and slings her towards the door of the shelter. She falls on her hand
and knee. RUMMY helps her up again.*]

PRICE [*rising, and venturing irresolutely towards BILL*]   Easy there,
mate. She aint doin you no arm.

BILL   Who are you callin mate? [*Standing over him threateningly.*]
Youre goin to stand up for her, are you? Put up your ands.

RUMMY [*running indignantly to him to scold him*]   Oh, you great
brute— [*He instantly swings his left hand back against her face. She
screams and reels back to the trough, where she sits down, covering her
bruised face with her hands and rocking herself and moaning with
pain.*]

JENNY [*going to her*]   Oh God forgive you! How could you
strike an old woman like that?

BILL [*seizing her by the hair so violently that she also screams, and tearing her away from the old woman*]   You Gawd forgive me again
and I'll Gawd forgive you one on the jaw thatll stop you
prayin for a week. [*Holding her and turning fiercely on PRICE.*]
Av you anything to say agen it? Eh?

PRICE [*intimidated*]   No, matey: she aint anything to do with me.

BILL   Good job for you! I'd put two meals into you and fight
you with one finger after, you starved cur. [*To JENNY.*] Now
are you goin to fetch out Mog Habbijam;* or am I to knock
your face off you and fetch her myself?

---

*"Mog" is a diminutive of Margaret; in subsequent editions, Shaw spelled
Walker's pronunciation more phonetically: "Ebbijem."

JENNY [*writing in his grasp*]   Oh please someone go in and tell
  Major Barbara— [*She screams again as he wrenches her head down;
  and PRICE and RUMMY flee into the shelter.*]

BILL   You want to go in and tell your Major of me, do you?

JENNY   Oh please dont drag my hair. Let me go.

BILL   Do you or dont you? [*She stifles a scream.*] Yes or no.

JENNY   God give me strength—

BILL [*striking her with his fist in the face*][20]   Go and shew her that,
  and tell her if she wants one like it to come and interfere with
  me. [*JENNY, crying with pain, goes into the shed. He goes to the
  form and addresses the old man.*] Here: finish your mess; and get
  out o my way.

SHIRLEY [*springing up and facing him fiercely, with the mug in his
  hand*]   You take a liberty with me, and I'll smash you over
  the face with the mug and cut your eye out. Aint you satisfied—young whelps like you—with takin the bread out o the
  mouths of your elders that have brought you up and slaved
  for you, but you must come shovin and cheekin and bullyin
  in here, where the bread o charity is sickenin in our stum-
  micks?

BILL [*contemptuously, but backing a little*]   Wot good are you, you
  old palsy mug? Wot good are you?

SHIRLEY   As good as you and better. I'll do a day's work agen
  you or any fat young soaker of your age. Go and take my job
  at Horrockses, where I worked for ten year. They want young
  men there: they cant afford to keep men over forty-five.
  Theyre very sorry—give you a character and happy to help
  you to get anything suited to your years—sure a steady man
  wont be long out of a job. Well, let em try y o u. Theyll find
  the differ. What do y o u know? Not as much as how to
  beeyave yourself—layin your dirty fist across the mouth of a
  respectable woman!

BILL   Dont provoke me to lay it acrost yours: d'ye hear?

SHIRLEY [*with blighting contempt*]   Yes: you like an old man to hit, dont you, when youve finished with the women. I aint seen you hit a young one yet.

BILL [*stung*]   You lie, you old soupkitchener, you. There was a young man here. Did I offer to hit him or did I not?

SHIRLEY   Was he starvin or was he not? Was he a man or only a crosseyed thief an a loafer? Would you hit my son-in-law's brother?

BILL   Who's he?

SHIRLEY   Todger Fairmile o Balls Pond. Him that won £20 off the Japanese wrastler at the music hall by standin out 17 minutes 4 seconds agen him.

BILL [*sullenly*]   I'm no music hall wrastler. Can he box?

SHIRLEY   Yes: an you cant.

BILL   Wot! I cant, cant I? Wots that you say [*threatening him*]?

SHIRLEY [*not budging an inch*]   Will you box Todger Fairmile if I put him on to you? Say the word.

BILL [*subsiding with a slouch*]   I'll stand up to any man alive, if he was ten Todger Fairmiles. But I dont set up to be a perfessional.

SHIRLEY [*looking down on him with unfathomable disdain*]   Y o u box! Slap an old woman with the back o your hand! You hadnt even the sense to hit her where a magistrate couldnt see the mark of it, you silly young lump of conceit and ignorance. Hit a girl in the jaw and ony make her cry! If Todger Fairmile'd done it, she wouldnt a got up inside o ten minutes, no more than you would if he got on to you. Yah! I'd set about you myself if I had a week's feedin in me instead o two months starvation. [*He returns to the table to finish his meal.*]

BILL [*following him and stooping over him to drive the taunt in*]   You lie! you have the bread and treacle in you that you come here to beg.

SHIRLEY [*bursting into tears*]   Oh God! it's true: I'm only an old pauper on the scrap heap. [*Furiously.*] But youll come to it yourself; and then youll know. Youll come to it sooner than a teetotaller like me, fillin yourself with gin at this hour o the mornin!

BILL   I'm no gin drinker, you old liar; but when I want to give my girl a bloomin good idin I like to av a bit o devil in me: see? An here I am, talkin to a rotten old blighter like you sted o givin her wot for. [*Working himself into a rage.*] I'm goin in there to fetch her out. [*He makes vengefully for the shelter door.*]

SHIRLEY   Youre goin to the station on a stretcher, more likely; and theyll take the gin and the devil out of you there when they get you inside. You mind what youre about: the major here is the Earl o Stevenage's granddaughter.

BILL [*checked*]   Garn!*

SHIRLEY   Youll see.

BILL [*his resolution oozing*]   Well, I aint done nothin to er.

SHIRLEY   Spose she said you did! who'd believe you?

BILL [*very uneasy, skulking back to the corner of the penthouse*] Gawd! theres no jastice in this country. To think wot them people can do! I'm as good as er.

SHIRLEY   Tell her so. Its just what a fool like you would do.

BARBARA, brisk and businesslike, comes from the shelter with a note book, and addresses herself to SHIRLEY. BILL, cowed, sits down in the corner on a form, and turns his back on them.

BARBARA   Good morning.

SHIRLEY [*standing up and taking off his hat*]   Good morning, miss.

BARBARA   Sit down: make yourself at home. [*He hesitates; but she puts a friendly hand on his shoulder and makes him obey.*] Now then! since youve made friends with us, we want to know all about you. Names and addresses and trades.

SHIRLEY   Peter Shirley. Fitter. Chucked out two months ago because I was too old.

---

*"Go on!"

BARBARA [*not at all surprised*]   Youd pass still. Why didnt you dye your hair?

SHIRLEY   I did. Me age come out at a coroner's inquest on me daughter.[21]

BARBARA   Steady?

SHIRLEY   Teetotaller. Never out of a job before. Good worker. And sent to the knackers* like an old horse!

BARBARA   No matter: if you did your part God will do his.

SHIRLEY [*suddenly stubborn*]   My religion's no concern of anybody but myself.

BARBARA [*guessing*]   I know. Secularist?†

SHIRLEY [*hotly*]   Did I offer to deny it?

BARBARA   Why should you? My own father's a Secularist, I think. Our Father—yours and mine—fulfils himself in many ways; and I daresay he knew what he was about when he made a Secularist of you. So buck up, Peter! we can always find a job for a steady man like you. [*SHIRLEY, disarmed, touches his hat. She turns from him to BILL.*] Whats y o u r name?

BILL [*insolently*]   Wots that to you?

BARBARA [*calmly making a note*]   Afraid to give his name. Any trade?

BILL   Who's afraid to give his name? [*Doggedly, with a sense of heroically defying the House of Lords in the person of Lord Stevenage.*] If you want to bring a charge agen me, bring it. [*She waits, unruffled.*] My name's Bill Walker.

BARBARA [*as if the name were familiar: trying to remember how*] Bill Walker? [*Recollecting.*] Oh, I know: youre the man that Jenny Hill was praying for inside just now. [*She enters his name in her note book.*]

BILL   Who's Jenny Hill? And what call has she to pray for me?

BARBARA   I dont know. Perhaps it was you that cut her lip.

---

*Slaughterers of worn-out domestic animals, such as horses.
†Atheist.

BILL [*defiantly*]   Yes, it w a s me that cut her lip. I aint afraid o
y o u.

BARBARA   How could you be, since youre not afraid of God?
Youre a brave man, Mr. Walker. It takes some pluck to do
o u r work here; but none of us dare lift our hand against a
girl like that, for fear of her father in heaven.

BILL [*sullenly*]   I want none o your cantin jaw. I suppose you
think I come here to beg from you, like this damaged lot here.
Not me. I dont want your bread and scrape and catlap.* I dont
believe in your Gawd, no more than you do yourself.

BARBARA [*sunnily apologetic and ladylike, as on a new footing with
him*]   Oh, I beg your pardon for putting your name down,
Mr. Walker. I didnt understand. I'll strike it out.

BILL [*taking this as a slight, and deeply wounded by it*]   Eah! you let
my name alone. Aint it good enough to be in your book?

BARBARA [*considering*]   Well, you see, theres no use putting
down your name unless I can do something for you, is there?
Whats your trade?

BILL [*still smarting*]   Thats no concern o yours.

BARBARA   Just so. [*Very businesslike.*] I'll put you down as [*writing*] the man who—struck—poor little Jenny Hill—in the
mouth.

BILL [*rising threateningly*]   See here. Ive ad enough o this.

BARBARA [*quite sunny and fearless*]   What did you come to us
for?

BILL   I come for my girl, see? I come to take her out o this and
to break er jawr for her.

BARBARA [*complacently*]   You see I was right about your trade.
[*BILL, on the point of retorting furiously, finds himself, to his great
shame and terror, in danger of crying instead. He sits down again
suddenly.*] Whats her name?

BILL [*dogged*]   Er name's Mog Abbijam: thats wot her name is.

_____

*Something the cat would drink.

BARBARA   Oh, she's gone to Canning Town, to our barracks there.

BILL [*fortified by his resentment of MOG's perfidy*]   Is she? [*Vindictively.*] Then I'm goin to Kennintahn arter her. [*He crosses to the gate; hesitates; finally comes back at Barbara.*] Are you lyin to me to get shut o me?

BARBARA   I dont want to get shut of you. I want to keep you here and save your soul. Youd better stay: youre going to have a bad time today, Bill.

BILL   Who's goin to give it to me? Y o u, praps.

BARBARA   Someone you dont believe in. But youll be glad afterwards.

BILL [*slinking off*]   I'll go to Kennintahn to be out o the reach o your tongue. [*Suddenly turning on her with intense malice.*] And if I dont find Mog there, I'll come back and do two years for you, selp me Gawd if I don't!

BARBARA [*a shade kindlier, if possible*]   It's no use, Bill. Shes got another bloke.

BILL   Wot!

BARBARA   One of her own converts. He fell in love with her when he saw her with her soul saved, and her face clean, and her hair washed.

BILL [*surprised*]   Wottud she wash it for, the carroty slut? It's red.

BARBARA   It's quite lovely now, because she wears a new look in her eyes with it. It's a pity youre too late. The new bloke has put your nose out of joint, Bill.

BILL   I'll put his nose out o joint for him. Not that I care a curse for her, mind that. But I'll teach her to drop me as if I was dirt. And I'll teach him to meddle with my judy. Wots iz bleedin name?

BARBARA   Sergeant Todger Fairmile.

SHIRLEY [*rising with grim joy*]   I'll go with him, miss. I want to see them two meet. I'll take him to the infirmary when it's over.

BILL [*to SHIRLEY, with undissembled misgiving*]   Is that im you was speakin on?

SHIRLEY   Thats him.

BILL   Im that wrastled in the music all?

SHIRLEY   The competitions at the National Sportin Club was worth nigh a hundred a year to him. Hes gev em up now for religion; so hes a bit fresh for want of the exercise he was accustomed to. Hell be glad to see you. Come along.

BILL   Wots is weight?

SHIRLEY   Thirteen four. [*BILL's last hope expires.*]

BARBARA   Go and talk to him, Bill. He'll convert you.

SHIRLEY   He'll convert your head into a mashed potato.

BILL [*sullenly*]   I aint afraid of him. I aint afraid of ennybody. But he can lick me. Shes done me. [*He sits down moodily on the edge of the horse trough.*]

SHIRLEY   You aint goin. I thought not. [*He resumes his seat.*]

BARBARA [*calling*]   Jenny!

JENNY [*appearing at the shelter door with a plaster on the corner of her mouth*]   Yes, Major.

BARBARA   Send Rummy Mitchens out to clear away here.

JENNY   I think shes afraid.

BARBARA [*her resemblance to her mother flashing out for a moment*]   Nonsense! she must do as shes told.

JENNY [*calling into the shelter*]   Rummy: the Major says you must come.

> *JENNY comes to BARBARA, purposely keeping on the side next BILL, lest he should suppose that she shrank from him or bore malice.*

BARBARA   Poor little Jenny! Are you tired? [*Looking at the wounded cheek.*] Does it hurt?

JENNY   No: it's all right now. It was nothing.

BARBARA [*critically*]   It was as hard as he could hit, I expect. Poor Bill! You dont feel angry with him, do you?

JENNY   Oh no, no, no: indeed I dont, Major, bless his poor heart! [*BARBARA kisses her; and she runs away merrily into the shel-*

ter. Bill writhes with an agonizing return of his new and alarming symptoms, but says nothing. RUMMY MITCHENS comes from the shelter.]

BARBARA [*going to meet RUMMY*]   Now Rummy, bustle. Take in those mugs and plates to be washed; and throw the crumbs about for the birds.

RUMMY takes the three plates and mugs; but SHIRLEY takes back his mug from her, as there is still some milk left in it.

RUMMY   There aint any crumbs. This aint a time to waste good bread on birds.

PRICE [*appearing at the shelter door*]   Gentleman come to see the shelter, Major. Says hes your father.

BARBARA   All right. Coming. [*SNOBBY goes back into the shelter, followed by BARBARA.*]

RUMMY [*stealing across to BILL and addressing him in a subdued voice, but with intense conviction*]   I'd av the lor of you, you flat eared pignosed potwalloper,* if she'd let me. Youre no gentleman, to hit a lady in the face. [*BILL, with greater things moving in him, takes no notice.*]

SHIRLEY [*following her*]   Here! in with you and dont get yourself into more trouble by talking.

RUMMY [*with hauteur*]   I aint ad the pleasure o being hintroduced to you, as I can remember. [*She goes into the shelter with the plates.*]

SHIRLEY   Thats the—

BILL [*savagely*]   Dont you talk to me, d'ye hear. You lea me alone, or I'll do you a mischief. I'm not dirt under y o u r feet, anyway.

SHIRLEY [*calmly*]   Dont you be afeerd. You aint such prime company that you need expect to be sought after. [*He is about to go into the shelter when BARBARA comes out, with UNDERSHAFT on her right.*]

---

*One with the lowly job of scrubbing pots.

BARBARA   Oh there you are, Mr. Shirley! [*Between them.*] This is my father: I told you he was a Secularist, didnt I? Perhaps youll be able to comfort one another.

UNDERSHAFT [*startled*]   A Secularist! Not the least in the world: on the contrary, a confirmed mystic.

BARBARA   Sorry, I'm sure. By the way, papa, what i s your religion—in case I have to introduce you again?

UNDERSHAFT   My religion? Well, my dear, I am a Millionaire. That is my religion.

BARBARA   Then I'm afraid you and Mr. Shirley wont be able to comfort one another after all. Youre not a Millionaire, are you, Peter?

SHIRLEY   No; and proud of it.

UNDERSHAFT [*gravely*]   Poverty, my friend, is not a thing to be proud of.

SHIRLEY [*angrily*]   Who made your millions for you? Me and my like. Whats kep us poor? Keepin you rich. I wouldnt have your conscience, not for all your income.

UNDERSHAFT   I wouldnt have your income, not for all your conscience, Mr. Shirley. [*He goes to the penthouse and sits down on a form.*]

BARBARA [*stopping SHIRLEY adroitly as he is about to retort*]   You wouldnt think he was my father, would you, Peter? Will you go into the shelter and lend the lasses a hand for a while: we're worked off our feet.

SHIRLEY [*bitterly*]   Yes: I'm in their debt for a meal, aint I?

BARBARA   Oh, not because youre in their debt; but for love of them, Peter, for love of them. [*He cannot understand, and is rather scandalized.*] There! dont stare at me. In with you; and give that conscience of yours a holiday [*bustling him into the shelter*].

SHIRLEY [*as he goes in*]   Ah! it's a pity you never was trained to use your reason, miss. Youd have been a very taking lecturer on Secularism.

BARBARA turns to her father.

UNDERSHAFT   Never mind me, my dear. Go about your work; and let me watch it for a while.

BARBARA   All right.

UNDERSHAFT   For instance, whats the matter with that out-patient over there?

BARBARA [*looking at BILL, whose attitude has never changed, and whose expression of brooding wrath has deepened*]   Oh, we shall cure him in no time. Just watch. [*She goes over to BILL and waits. He glances up at her and casts his eyes down again, uneasy, but grimmer than ever.*] It w o u l d be nice to just stamp on Mog Hab-bijam's face, wouldnt it, Bill?

BILL [*starting up from the trough in consternation*]   It's a lie: I never said so. [*She shakes her head.*] Who told you wot was in my mind?

BARBARA   Only your new friend.

BILL   Wot new friend?

BARBARA   The devil, Bill. When he gets round people they get miserable, just like you.

BILL [*with a heartbreaking attempt at devil-may-care cheerfulness*]   I aint miserable. [*He sits down again, and stretches his legs in an attempt to seem indifferent.*]

BARBARA   Well, if youre happy, why dont you look happy, as we do?

BILL [*his legs curling back in spite of him*]   I'm appy enough, I tell you. Why dont you lea me alown? Wot av I done to y o u? I aint smashed y o u r face, av I?

BARBARA [*softly: wooing his soul*]   It's not me thats getting at you, Bill.

BILL   Who else is it?

BARBARA   Somebody that doesnt intend you to smash women's faces, I suppose. Somebody or something that wants to make a man of you.

BILL [*blustering*]   Make a man o m e! Aint I a man? eh? aint I a man? Who sez I'm not a man?

BARBARA   Theres a man in you somewhere, I suppose. But why did he let you hit poor little Jenny Hill? That wasnt very manly of him, was it?

BILL [*tormented*]   Av done with it, I tell you. Chack it. I'm sick of your Jenny Ill and er silly little face.

BARBARA   Then why do you keep thinking about it? Why does it keep coming up against you in your mind? Youre not getting converted, are you?

BILL [*with conviction*]   Not ME. Not likely. Not arf.*

BARBARA   Thats right, Bill. Hold out against it. Put out your strength. Dont lets get you cheap. Todger Fairmile said he wrestled for three nights against his Salvation harder than he ever wrestled with the Jap at the music hall. He gave in to the Jap when his arm was going to break. But he didnt give in to his salvation until his heart was going to break. Perhaps youll escape that. You havnt any heart, have you?

BILL   Wot d'ye mean? Wy aint I got a art the same as ennybody else?

BARBARA   A man with a heart wouldnt have bashed poor little Jenny's face, would he?

BILL [*almost crying*]   Ow, w i l l you lea me alown? Av I ever offered to meddle with y o u, that you come naggin and provowkin me lawk this? [*He writhes convulsively from his eyes to his toes.*]

BARBARA [*with a steady soothing hand on his arm and a gentle voice that never lets him go*]   It's your soul thats hurting you, Bill, and not me. Weve been through it all ourselves. Come with us, Bill. [*He looks wildly round.*] To brave manhood on earth and eternal glory in heaven. [*He is on the point of breaking down.*] Come. [*A drum is heard in the shelter; and BILL, with a gasp, escapes from the spell as BARBARA turns quickly. ADOLPHUS enters from the shelter with a big drum.*] Oh! there you are, Dolly. Let me

_____

*That is, half.

introduce a new friend of mine, Mr. Bill Walker. This is my bloke, Bill: Mr. Cusins. [*CUSINS salutes with his drumstick.*]

BILL   Goin to marry im?

BARBARA   Yes.

BILL [*fervently*]   Gord elp im! Gawd elp im!

BARBARA   Why? Do you think he wont be happy with me?

BILL   Ive only ad to stand it for a mornin: e'll av to stand it for a lifetime.

CUSINS   That is a frightful reflection, Mr. Walker. But I cant tear myself away from her.

BILL   Well, I can. [*To BARBARA.*] Eah! do you know where I'm going to, and wot I'm goin to do?

BARBARA   Yes: youre going to heaven; and youre coming back here before the week's out to tell me so.

BILL   You lie. I'm goin to Kennintahn, to spit in Todger Fairmile's eye. I bashed Jenny Ill's face; and now I'll get me own face bashed and come back and shew it to er. E'll it me ardern I it e r. Thatll make us square. [*To ADOLPHUS.*] Is that fair or is it not? Youre a genlmn: you oughter know.

BARBARA   Two black eyes wont make one white one, Bill.

BILL   I didnt ast y o u. Cawnt you never keep your mahth shut? I ast the genlmn.

CUSINS [*reflectively*]   Yes: I think youre right, Mr. Walker. Yes: I should do it. Its curious: its exactly what an ancient Greek would have done.

BARBARA   But what good will it do?

CUSINS   Well, it will give Mr. Fairmile some exercise; and it will satisfy Mr. Walker's soul.

BILL   Rot! there aint no sach a thing as a soul. Ah* kin you tell wether Ive a soul or not? You never seen it.

BARBARA   Ive seen it hurting you when you went against it.

BILL [*with compressed aggravation*]   If you was my girl and took

---

*That is, how.

the word out o me mahth lawk thet, I'd give you suthink youd feel urtin, so I would. [*To ADOLPHUS.*] You take my tip, mate. Stop er jawr; or youll die afore your time. [*With intense expression.*] Wore aht: thets wot youll be: wore aht. [*He goes away through the gate.*]

CUSINS [*looking after him*]   I wonder!

BARBARA   Dolly! [*Indignant, in her mother's manner.*]

CUSINS   Yes, my dear, it's very wearing to be in love with you. If it lasts, I quite think I shall die young.

BARBARA   Should you mind?

CUSINS   Not at all. [*He is suddenly softened, and kisses her over the drum, evidently not for the first time, as people cannot kiss over a big drum without practice. UNDERSHAFT coughs.*]

BARBARA   It's all right, papa, weve not forgotten you. Dolly: explain the place to papa: I havnt time. [*She goes busily into the shelter.*]

UNDERSHAFT and ADOLPHUS now have the yard to themselves. UNDERSHAFT, seated on a form, and still keenly attentive, looks hard at ADOLPHUS. ADOLPHUS looks hard at him.

UNDERSHAFT   I fancy you guess something of what is in my mind, Mr. Cusins. [*CUSINS flourishes his drumsticks as if in the act of beating a lively rataplan, but makes no sound.*] Exactly so. But suppose Barbara finds you out!

CUSINS   You know, I do not admit that I am imposing on Barbara. I am quite genuinely interested in the views of the Salvation Army. The fact is, I am a sort of collector of religions; and the curious thing is that I find I can believe them all. By the way, have you any religion?

UNDERSHAFT   Yes.

CUSINS   Anything out of the common?

UNDERSHAFT   Only that there are two things necessary to Salvation.

CUSINS [*disappointed, but polite*]   Ah, the Church Catechism. Charles Lomax also belongs to the Established Church.

UNDERSHAFT   The two things are—

CUSINS   Baptism and—

UNDERSHAFT   No. Money and gunpowder.

CUSINS [*surprised, but interested*]   That is the general opinion of our governing classes. The novelty is in hearing any man confess it.

UNDERSHAFT   Just so.

CUSINS   Excuse me: is there any place in your religion for honor, justice, truth, love, mercy and so forth?

UNDERSHAFT   Yes: they are the graces and luxuries of a rich, strong, and safe life.

CUSINS   Suppose one is forced to choose between them and money or gunpowder?

UNDERSHAFT   Choose money a n d gunpowder; for without enough of both you cannot afford the others.

CUSINS   That is your religion?

UNDERSHAFT   Yes.

The cadence of this reply makes a full close in the conversation. CUSINS twists his face dubiously and contemplates UNDERSHAFT. UNDERSHAFT contemplates him.

CUSINS   Barbara wont stand that. You will have to choose between your religion and Barbara.

UNDERSHAFT   So will you, my friend. She will find out that that drum of yours is hollow.

CUSINS   Father Undershaft: you are mistaken: I am a sincere Salvationist. You do not understand the Salvation Army. It is the army of joy, of love, of courage: it has banished the fear and remorse and despair of the old hell-ridden evangelical sects: it marches to fight the devil with trumpet and drum, with music and dancing, with banner and palm, as becomes a sally from heaven by its happy garrison. It picks the waster out of the public house and makes a man of him: it finds a worm wriggling in a back kitchen, and lo! a woman! Men and women of rank too, sons and daughters of the Highest.

It takes the poor professor of Greek, the most artificial and self-suppressed of human creatures, from his meal of roots, and lets loose the rhapsodist in him; reveals the true worship of Dionysos[22] to him; sends him down the public street drumming dithyrambs [*he plays a thundering flourish on the drum*].

UNDERSHAFT   You will alarm the shelter.

CUSINS   Oh, they are accustomed to these sudden ecstasies of piety. However, if the drum worries you— [*he pockets the drumsticks; unhooks the drum; and stands it on the ground opposite the gateway*].

UNDERSHAFT   Thank you.

CUSINS   You remember what Euripides says about your money and gunpowder?

UNDERSHAFT   No.

CUSINS [*declaiming*]

> One and another
> In money and guns may outpass his brother;
> And men in their millions float and flow
> And seethe with a million hopes as leaven;
> And they win their will; or they miss their will;
> And their hopes are dead or are pined for still;
> But whoe'er can know
> As the long days go
> That to live is happy, has found h i s heaven.[23]

My translation: what do you think of it?

UNDERSHAFT   I think, my friend, that if you wish to know, as the long days go, that to live is happy, you must first acquire money enough for a decent life, and power enough to be your own master.

CUSINS   You are damnably discouraging. [*He resumes his declamation.*]

Is it so hard a thing to see
That the spirit of God—whate'er it be—
The Law that abides and changes not, ages long,
The Eternal and Nature-born; t h e s e things be strong?
What else is Wisdom? What of Man's endeavor,
Or God's high grace so lovely and so great?
To stand from fear set free? to breathe and wait?
To hold a hand uplifted over Fate?
And shall not Barbara be loved for ever?[24]

UNDERSHAFT   Euripides mentions Barbara, does he?

CUSINS   It is a fair translation. The word means Loveliness.

UNDERSHAFT   May I ask—as Barbara's father—how much a
year she is to be loved for ever on?

CUSINS   As Barbara's father, that is more your affair than mine.
I can feed her by teaching Greek: that is about all.

UNDERSHAFT   Do you consider it a good match for her?

CUSINS [*with polite obstinacy*]   Mr. Undershaft: I am in many
ways a weak, timid, ineffectual person; and my health is far
from satisfactory. But whenever I feel that I must have anything, I get it, sooner or later. I feel that way about Barbara. I
dont like marriage: I feel intensely afraid of it; and I dont
know what I shall do with Barbara or what she will do with
me. But I feel that I and nobody else must marry her. Please
regard that as settled.——Not that I wish to be arbitrary; but
why should I waste your time in discussing what is inevitable?

UNDERSHAFT   You mean that you will stick at nothing: not
even the conversion of the Salvation Army to the worship of
Dionysos.

CUSINS   The business of the Salvation Army is to save, not to
wrangle about the name of the pathfinder. Dionysos or another: what does it matter?

UNDERSHAFT [*rising and approaching him*]   Professor Cusins:
you are a young man after my own heart.

CUSINS   Mr. Undershaft: you are, as far as I am able to gather, a most infernal old rascal; but you appeal very strongly to my sense of ironic humor.

UNDERSHAFT mutely offers his hand. They shake.

UNDERSHAFT [*suddenly concentrating himself*]   And now to business.

CUSINS   Pardon me. We were discussing religion. Why go back to such an uninteresting and unimportant subject as business?

UNDERSHAFT   Religion is our business at present, because it is through religion alone that we can win Barbara.

CUSINS   Have you, too, fallen in love with Barbara?

UNDERSHAFT   Yes, with a father's love.

CUSINS   A father's love for a grown-up daughter is the most dangerous of all infatuations. I apologize for mentioning my own pale, coy, mistrustful fancy in the same breath with it.

UNDERSHAFT   Keep to the point. We have to win her; and we are neither of us Methodists.*

CUSINS   That doesnt matter. The power Barbara wields here— the power that wields Barbara herself—is not Calvinism, not Presbyterianism, not Methodism—

UNDERSHAFT   Not Greek Paganism either, eh?

CUSINS   I admit that. Barbara is quite original in her religion.

UNDERSHAFT [*triumphantly*]   Aha! Barbara Undershaft would be. Her inspiration comes from within herself.

CUSINS   How do you suppose it got there?

UNDERSHAFT [*in towering excitement*]   It is the Undershaft inheritance. I shall hand on my torch to my daughter. She shall make my converts and preach my gospel—

CUSINS   What! Money and gunpowder!

UNDERSHAFT   Yes, money and gunpowder; freedom and power; command of life and command of death.

---

*Undershaft means that Barbara might find Methodism, a religion of the common people, appealing.

CUSINS [*urbanely: trying to bring him down to earth*]   This is extremely interesting, Mr. Undershaft. Of course you know that you are mad.

UNDERSHAFT [*with redoubled force*]   And you?

CUSINS   Oh, mad as a hatter. You are welcome to my secret since I have discovered yours. But I am astonished. Can a madman make cannons?

UNDERSHAFT   Would anyone else than a madman make them? And now [*with surging energy*] question for question. Can a sane man translate Euripides?

CUSINS   No.

UNDERSHAFT [*seizing him by the shoulder*]   Can a sane woman make a man of a waster or a woman of a worm?

CUSINS [*reeling before the storm*]   Father Colossus—Mammoth Millionaire—

UNDERSHAFT [*pressing him*]   Are there two mad people or three in this Salvation shelter to-day?

CUSINS   You mean Barbara is as mad as we are!

UNDERSHAFT [*pushing him lightly off and resuming his equanimity suddenly and completely*]   Pooh, Professor! let us call things by their proper names. I am a millionaire; you are a poet; Barbara is a savior of souls. What have we three to do with the common mob of slaves and idolaters? [*He sits down again with a shrug of contempt for the mob.*]

CUSINS   Take care! Barbara is in love with the common people. So am I. Have you never felt the romance of that love?

UNDERSHAFT [*cold and sardonic*]   Have you ever been in love with Poverty, like St. Francis? Have you ever been in love with Dirt, like St. Simeon?* Have you ever been in love with disease and suffering, like our nurses and philanthropists? Such passions are not virtues, but the most unnatural of all the

---

*Saint Simeon (c. 390–459), called "Stylites" (pillar-dweller), spent the last thirty years of his life on a pillar (where, presumably, he could not wash easily).

vices. This love of the common people may please an earl's granddaughter and a university professor; but I have been a common man and a poor man; and it has no romance for me. Leave it to the poor to pretend that poverty is a blessing: leave it to the coward to make a religion of his cowardice by preaching humility: we know better than that. We three must stand together above the common people: how else can we help their children to climb up beside us? Barbara must belong to us, not to the Salvation Army.

CUSINS   Well, I can only say that if you think you will get her away from the Salvation Army by talking to her as you have been talking to me, you dont know Barbara.

UNDERSHAFT   My friend: I never ask for what I can buy.

CUSINS [*in a white fury*]   Do I understand you to imply that you can buy Barbara?

UNDERSHAFT   No; but I can buy the Salvation Army.

CUSINS   Quite impossible.

UNDERSHAFT   You shall see. All religious organizations exist by selling themselves to the rich.

CUSINS   Not the Army. That is the Church of the poor.

UNDERSHAFT   All the more reason for buying it.

CUSINS   I dont think you quite know what the Army does for the poor.

UNDERSHAFT   Oh yes I do. It draws their teeth: that is enough for me—as a man of business—

CUSINS   Nonsense. It makes them sober—

UNDERSHAFT   I prefer sober workmen. The profits are larger.

CUSINS   —honest—

UNDERSHAFT   Honest workmen are the most economical.

CUSINS   —attached to their homes—

UNDERSHAFT   So much the better: they will put up with anything sooner than change their shop.

CUSINS   —happy—

UNDERSHAFT   An invaluable safeguard against revolution.

CUSINS   —unselfish—

UNDERSHAFT   Indifferent to their own interests, which suits me exactly.

CUSINS   —with their thoughts on heavenly things—

UNDERSHAFT [*rising*]   And not on Trade Unionism nor Socialism. Excellent.

CUSINS [*revolted*]   You really are an infernal old rascal.

UNDERSHAFT [*indicating PETER SHIRLEY, who has just come from the shelter and strolled dejectedly down the yard between them*] And this is an honest man!

SHIRLEY   Yes; and what av I got by it? [*He passes on bitterly and sits on the form, in the corner of the penthouse.*]
   SNOBBY PRICE, beaming sanctimoniously, and JENNY HILL, with a tambourine full of coppers, come from the shelter and go to the drum, on which JENNY begins to count the money.

UNDERSHAFT [*replying to SHIRLEY*]   Oh, your employers must have got a good deal by it from first to last. [*He sits on the table, with one foot on the side form. CUSINS, overwhelmed, sits down on the same form nearer the shelter. BARBARA comes from the shelter to the middle of the yard. She is excited and a little overwrought.*]

BARBARA   Weve just had a splendid experience meeting at the other gate in Cripps's lane. Ive hardly ever seen them so much moved as they were by your confession, Mr. Price.

PRICE   I could almost be glad of my past wickedness if I could believe that it would elp to keep hathers stright.

BARBARA   So it will, Snobby. How much, Jenny?

JENNY   Four and tenpence, Major.

BARBARA   Oh Snobby, if you had given your poor mother just one more kick, we should have got the whole five shillings!

PRICE   If she heard you say that, miss, she'd be sorry I didnt. But I'm glad. Oh what a joy it will be to her when she hears I'm saved!

UNDERSHAFT   Shall I contribute the odd twopence, Barbara?

The millionaire's mite, eh? [*He takes a couple of pennies from his pocket.*]

BARBARA   How did you make that twopence?

UNDERSHAFT   As usual. By selling cannons, torpedoes, submarines, and my new patent Grand Duke hand grenade.

BARBARA   Put it back in your pocket. You cant buy your Salvation here for twopence: you must work it out.

UNDERSHAFT   Is twopence not enough? I can afford a little more, if you press me.

BARBARA   Two million millions would not be enough. There is bad blood on your hands; and nothing but good blood can cleanse them. Money is no use. Take it away. [*She turns to CUSINS.*] Dolly: you must write another letter for me to the papers. [*He makes a wry face.*] Yes: I know you dont like it; but it must be done. The starvation this winter is beating us: everybody is unemployed. The General says we must close this shelter if we cant get more money. I force the collections at the meetings until I am ashamed: dont I, Snobby?

PRICE   It's a fair treat to see you work it, Miss. The way you got them up from three-and-six to four-and-ten with that hymn, penny by penny and verse by verse, was a caution. Not a Cheap Jack* on Mile End Waste could touch you at it.

BARBARA   Yes; but I wish we could do without it. I am getting at last to think more of the collection than of the people's souls. And what are those hatfuls of pence and halfpence? We want thousands! tens of thousands! hundreds of thousands! I want to convert people, not to be always begging for the Army in a way I'd die sooner than beg for myself.

UNDERSHAFT [*in profound irony*]   Genuine unselfishness is capable of anything, my dear.

BARBARA [*unsuspectingly, as she turns away to take the money from*

---

*Seller of shoddy goods.

the drum and put it in a cash bag she carries]   Yes, isnt it? [*UN-DERSHAFT looks sardonically at CUSINS.*]

CUSINS [*aside to UNDERSHAFT*]   Mephistopheles! Machiavelli!

BARBARA [*tears coming into her eyes as she ties the bag and pockets it*]   How are we to feed them? I cant talk religion to a man with bodily hunger in his eyes. [*Almost breaking down.*] It's frightful.

JENNY [*running to her*]   Major, dear——

BARBARA [*rebounding*]   No, dont comfort me. It will be all right. We shall get the money.

UNDERSHAFT   How?

JENNY   By praying for it, of course. Mrs. Baines says she prayed for it last night; and she has never prayed for it in vain: never once. [*She goes to the gate and looks out into the street.*]

BARBARA [*who has dried her eyes and regained her composure*]   By the way, dad, Mrs. Baines has come to march with us to our big meeting this afternoon; and she is very anxious to meet you, for some reason or other. Perhaps she'll convert you.

UNDERSHAFT   I shall be delighted, my dear.

JENNY [*at the gate: excitedly*]   Major! Major! heres that man back again.

BARBARA   What man?

JENNY   The man that hit me. Oh, I hope hes coming back to join us.

BILL WALKER, with frost on his jacket, comes through the gate, his hands deep in his pockets and his chin sunk between his shoulders, like a cleaned-out gambler. He halts between BARBARA and the drum.

BARBARA   Hullo, Bill! Back already!

BILL [*nagging at her*]   Bin talkin ever sence, av you?

BARBARA   Pretty nearly. Well, has Todger paid you out for poor Jenny's jaw?

BILL   No he aint.

BARBARA   I thought your jacket looked a bit snowy.

BILL   So it is snowy. You want to know where the snow come from, dont you?

BARBARA   Yes.

BILL   Well, it come from off the ground in Parkinses Corner in Kennintahn. It got rubbed off be my shoulders: see?

BARBARA   Pity you didnt rub some off with your knees, Bill! That would have done you a lot of good.

BILL [*with sour mirthless humor*]   I was saving another man's knees at the time. E was kneelin on my ed, so e was.

JENNY   Who was kneeling on your head?

BILL   Todger was. E was prayin for me: prayin comfortable with me as a carpet. So was Mog. So was the ole bloomin meetin. Mog she sez "O Lord break is stubborn spirit; but dont urt is dear art." That was wot she said. "Dont urt is dear art"! An er bloke—thirteen stun four!—kneelin wiv all is weight on me. Funny, aint it?

JENNY   Oh no. We're so sorry, Mr. Walker.

BARBARA [*enjoying it frankly*]   Nonsense! of course it's funny. Served you right, Bill! You must have done something to him first.

BILL [*doggedly*]   I did wot I said I'd do. I spit in is eye. E looks up at the sky and sez, "O that I should be fahnd worthy to be spit upon for the gospel's sake!" e sez; an Mog sez "Glory Allel-loolier!"; and then e called me Brother, an dahned me as if I was a kid and e was me mother washin me a Setterda nawt. I andt just no show wiv im at all.* Arf the street prayed; an the tother arf larfed fit to split theirselves. [*To BARBARA.*] There! are you settisfawd nah?

BARBARA [*her eyes dancing*]   Wish I'd been there, Bill.

BILL   Yes: youd a got in a hextra bit o talk on me, wouldnt you?

JENNY   I'm so sorry, Mr. Walker.

---

*That is, "I hadn't just no show with him at all."

BILL [*fiercely*]   Dont you go bein sorry for me: you've no call. Listen ere. I broke your jawr.

JENNY   No, it didnt hurt me: indeed it didnt, except for a moment. It was only that I was frightened.

BILL   I dont want to be forgive be you, or be ennybody. Wot I did I'll pay for. I tried to get me own jawr broke to settisfaw you—

JENNY [*distressed*]   Oh no—

BILL [*impatiently*]   Tell y'I did: cawnt you listen to wots bein told you? All I got be it was bein made a sight of in the public street for me pains. Well, if I cawnt settisfaw you one way, I can another. Listen ere! I ad two quid saved agen the frost; an I've a pahnd of it left. A mate o mine last week ad words with the judy e's goin to marry. E give er wot-for; an e's bin fined fifteen bob. E ad a right to it er because they was goin to be marrid; but I adnt no right to it you; so put anather fawv bob on an call it a pahnd's worth. [*He produces a sovereign.*] Eres the money. Take it; and lets av no more o your forgivin an prayin and your Major jawrin me. Let wot I done be done and paid for; and let there be a end of it.

JENNY   Oh, I couldnt take it, Mr. Walker. But if you would give a shilling or two to poor Rummy Mitchens! you really did hurt her; and shes old.

BILL [*contemptuously*]   Not likely. I'd give her anather as soon as look at er. Let her av the lawr o me as she threatened! S h e aint forgiven me: not mach. Wot I done to er is not on me mawnd—wot she [*indicating BARBARA*] might call on me conscience—no more than stickin a pig. It's this Christian game o yours that I wont av played agen me: this bloomin forgivin an naggin an jawrin that makes a man that sore that iz lawf's a burdn to im. I wont av it, I tell you; so take your money and stop throwin your silly bashed face hup agen me.

JENNY   Major: may I take a little of it for the Army?

BARBARA   No: the Army is not to be bought. We want your soul, Bill; and we'll take nothing less.

BILL [*bitterly*]   I know. It aint enough. Me an me few shillins is not good enough for you. Youre a earl's grendorter, you are. Nothin less than a underd pahnd for you.

UNDERSHAFT   Come, Barbara! you could do a great deal of good with a hundred pounds. If you will set this gentleman's mind at ease by taking his pound, I will give the other ninety-nine. [*Bill, astounded by such opulence, instinctively touches his cap.*]

BARBARA   Oh, youre too extravagant, papa. Bill offers twenty pieces of silver. All you need offer is the other ten. That will make the standard price to buy anybody who's for sale. I'm not; and the Army's not.[25] [*To BILL.*] Youll never have another quiet moment, Bill, until you come round to us. You cant stand out against your salvation.

BILL [*sullenly*]   I cawnt stend aht agen music-all wrastlers and artful tongued women. I've offered to pay. I can do no more. Take it or leave it. There it is. [*He throws the sovereign on the drum, and sits down on the horse-trough. The coin fascinates SNOBBY PRICE, who takes an early opportunity of dropping his cap on it.*]

MRS. BAINES comes from the shelter. She is dressed as a Salvation Army Commissioner. She is an earnest looking woman of about 40, with a caressing, urgent voice, and an appealing manner.

BARBARA   This is my father, Mrs. Baines. [*UNDERSHAFT comes from the table, taking his hat off with marked civility.*] Try what you can do with him. He wont listen to me, because he remembers what a fool I was when I was a baby. [*She leaves them together and chats with JENNY.*]

MRS. BAINES   Have you been shewn over the shelter, Mr. Undershaft? You know the work we're doing, of course.

UNDERSHAFT [*very civilly*]   The whole nation knows it, Mrs. Baines.

MRS. BAINES   No, sir: the whole nation does not know it, or we should not be crippled as we are for want of money to carry our work through the length and breadth of the land. Let me tell you that there would have been rioting this winter in London but for us.

UNDERSHAFT   You really think so?

MRS. BAINES   I know it. I remember 1886, when you rich gentlemen hardened your hearts against the cry of the poor. They broke the windows of your clubs in Pall Mall.

UNDERSHAFT [*gleaming with approval of their method*]   And the Mansion House Fund* went up next day from thirty thousand pounds to seventy-nine thousand! I remember quite well.

MRS. BAINES   Well, wont you help me to get at the people? They wont break windows then. Come here, Price. Let me shew you to this gentleman. [*PRICE comes to be inspected.*] Do you remember the window breaking?

PRICE   My ole father thought it was the revolution, maam.

MRS. BAINES   Would you break windows now?

PRICE   Oh no maam. The windows of eaven av bin opened to me. I know now that the rich man is a sinner like myself.

RUMMY [*appearing above at the loft door*]   Snobby Price!

SNOBBY   Wot is it?

RUMMY   Your mother's askin for you at the other gate in Crippses Lane. She's heard about your confession [*PRICE turns pale*].

MRS. BAINES   Go, Mr. Price; and pray with her.

JENNY   You can go through the shelter, Snobby.

PRICE [*to MRS. BAINES*]   I couldnt face her now, maam, with all the weight of my sins fresh on me. Tell her she'll find her son at ome, waitin for her in prayer. [*He skulks off through the gate, incidentally stealing the sovereign on his way out by picking up his cap from the drum.*]²⁶

MRS. BAINES [*with swimming eyes*]   You see how we take the

---

*The Lord Mayor of London's collection of donations in times of national need.

anger and the bitterness against you out of their hearts, Mr. Undershaft.

UNDERSHAFT   It is certainly most convenient and gratifying to all large employers of labor, Mrs. Baines.

MRS. BAINES   Barbara: Jenny: I have good news: most wonderful news. [*JENNY runs to her.*] My prayers have been answered. I told you they would, Jenny, didn't I?

JENNY   Yes, yes.

BARBARA [*moving nearer to the drum*]   Have we got money enough to keep the shelter open?

MRS. BAINES   I hope we shall have enough to keep all the shelters open. Lord Saxmundham has promised us five thousand pounds—

BARBARA   Hooray!

JENNY   Glory!

MRS. BAINES   —if—

BARBARA   "If!" If what?

MRS. BAINES   —if five other gentlemen will give a thousand each to make it up to ten thousand.

BARBARA   Who is Lord Saxmundham? I never heard of him.

UNDERSHAFT [*who has pricked up his ears at the peer's name, and is now watching BARBARA curiously*]   A new creation, my dear. You have heard of Sir Horace Bodger?

BARBARA   Bodger! Do you mean the distiller? Bodger's whisky!

UNDERSHAFT   That is the man. He is one of the greatest of our public benefactors. He restored the cathedral at Hakington. They made him a baronet for that. He gave half a million to the funds of his party: they made him a baron for that.

SHIRLEY   What will they give him for the five thousand?

UNDERSHAFT   There is nothing left to give him. So the five thousand, I should think, is to save his soul.

MRS. BAINES   Heaven grant it may! Oh Mr. Undershaft, you have some very rich friends. Cant you help us towards the other five thousand? We are going to hold a great meeting this afternoon at the Assembly Hall in the Mile End Road. If I could only announce that one gentleman had come forward to support Lord Saxmundham, others would follow. Dont you know somebody? couldnt you? wouldnt you? [*her eyes fill with tears*] oh, think of those poor people, Mr. Undershaft: think of how much it means to them, and how little to a great man like you.

UNDERSHAFT [*sardonically gallant*]   Mrs. Baines: you are irresistible. I cant disappoint you; and I cant deny myself the satisfaction of making Bodger pay up. You shall have your five thousand pounds.

MRS. BAINES   Thank God!

UNDERSHAFT   You dont thank m e?

MRS. BAINES   Oh sir, dont try to be cynical: dont be ashamed of being a good man. The Lord will bless you abundantly; and our prayers will be like a strong fortification round you all the days of your life. [*With a touch of caution.*] You will let me have the cheque to shew at the meeting, wont you? Jenny: go in and fetch a pen and ink. [*JENNY runs to the shelter door.*]

UNDERSHAFT   Do not disturb Miss Hill: I have a fountain pen. [*JENNY halts. He sits at the table and writes the cheque. CUSINS rises to make more room for him. They all watch him silently.*]

BILL [*cynically, aside to BARBARA, his voice and accent horribly debased*]   Wot prawce Selvytion nah?

BARBARA   Stop. [*UNDERSHAFT stops writing: they all turn to her in surprise.*] Mrs. Baines: are you really going to take this money?

MRS. BAINES [*astonished*]   Why not, dear?

BARBARA   Why not! Do you know what my father is? Have you forgotten that Lord Saxmundham is Bodger the whisky man? Do you remember how we implored the County Council to stop him from writing Bodger's Whisky in letters of fire against the sky; so that the poor drink-ruined creatures on the embankment could not wake up from their snatches of sleep without being reminded of their deadly thirst by that wicked sky sign? Do you know that the worst thing I have had to fight here is not the devil, but Bodger, Bodger, Bodger, with his whisky, his distilleries, and his tied houses?* Are you going to make our shelter another tied house for him, and ask me to keep it?

BILL   Rotten drunken whisky it is too.

MRS. BAINES   Dear Barbara: Lord Saxmundham has a soul to be saved like any of us. If heaven has found the way to make a good use of his money, are we to set ourselves up against the answer to our prayers?

BARBARA   I know he has a soul to be saved. Let him come down here; and I'll do my best to help him to his salvation. But he wants to send his cheque down to buy us, and go on being as wicked as ever.

UNDERSHAFT [with a reasonableness which CUSINS alone perceives to be ironical]   My dear Barbara: alcohol is a very necessary article. It heals the sick——

BARBARA   It does nothing of the sort.

UNDERSHAFT   Well, it assists the doctor: that is perhaps a less questionable way of putting it. It makes life bearable to millions of people who could not endure their existence if they were quite sober. It enables Parliament to do things at eleven at night that no sane person would do at eleven in the morning. Is it Bodger's fault that this inestimable gift is deplorably abused by less than one per cent of the poor? [He turns again to the table; signs the cheque; and crosses it.]

MRS. BAINES   Barbara: will there be less drinking or more if all those poor souls we are saving come to-morrow and find the doors of our shelters shut in their faces? Lord Saxmund-

---

*Pubs owned by the breweries or distilleries that supply them.

ham gives us the money to stop drinking—to take his own business from him.

CUSINS [*impishly*]   Pure self-sacrifice on Bodger's part, clearly! Bless dear Bodger! [*BARBARA almost breaks down as ADOLPHUS, too, fails her.*]

UNDERSHAFT [*tearing out the cheque and pocketing the book as he rises and goes past CUSINS to MRS. BAINES*]   I also, Mrs. Baines, may claim a little disinterestedness. Think of my business! think of the widows and orphans! the men and lads torn to pieces with shrapnel and poisoned with lyddite* [*MRS. BAINES shrinks; but he goes on remorsely*]! the oceans of blood, not one drop of which is shed in a really just cause! the ravaged crops! the peaceful peasants forced, women and men, to till their fields under the fire of opposing armies on pain of starvation! the bad blood of the fierce little cowards at home who egg on others to fight for the gratification of their national vanity! All this makes money for me: I am never richer, never busier than when the papers are full of it. Well, it is your work to preach peace on earth and goodwill to men. [*MRS. BAINES's face lights up again.*] Every convert you make is a vote against war. [*Her lips move in prayer.*] Yet I give you this money to help you to hasten my own commercial ruin. [*He gives her the cheque.*]

CUSINS [*mounting the form in an ecstasy of mischief*]   The millennium will be inaugurated by the unselfishness of Undershaft and Bodger. Oh be joyful! [*He takes the drumsticks from his pockets and flourishes them.*]

MRS. BAINES [*taking the cheque*]   The longer I live the more proof I see that there is an Infinite Goodness that turns everything to the work of salvation sooner or later. Who would have thought that any good could have come out of war and drink? And yet their profits are brought today to the feet of salvation to do its blessed work. [*She is affected to tears.*]

*An explosive.

JENNY [*running to MRS. BAINES and throwing her arms round her*] Oh dear! how blessed, how glorious it all is!

CUSINS [*in a convulsion of irony*]   Let us seize this unspeakable moment. Let us march to the great meeting at once. Excuse me just an instant. [*He rushes into the shelter. JENNY takes her tambourine from the drum head.*]

MRS. BAINES   Mr. Undershaft: have you ever seen a thousand people fall on their knees with one impulse and pray? Come with us to the meeting. Barbara shall tell them that the Army is saved, and saved through you.

CUSINS [*returning impetuously from the shelter with a flag and a trombone, and coming between MRS. BAINES and UNDERSHAFT*] You shall carry the flag down the first street, Mrs. Baines [*he gives her the flag*]. Mr. Undershaft is a gifted trombonist: he shall intone an Olympian diapason to the West Ham Salvation March. [*Aside to UNDERSHAFT, as he forces the trombone on him.*] Blow, Machiavelli, blow.

UNDERSHAFT [*aside to him, as he takes the trombone*]   The trumpet in Zion! [*CUSINS rushes to the drum, which he takes up and puts on. UNDERSHAFT continues, aloud.*] I will do my best. I could vamp a bass* if I knew the tune.

CUSINS   It is a wedding chorus from one of Donizetti's operas;† but we have converted it. We convert everything to good here, including Bodger. You remember the chorus. "For thee immense rejoicing—immenso giubilo—immenso giubilo." [*With drum obbligato.*] Rum tum ti tum tum, tum tum ti ta—

BARBARA   Dolly: you are breaking my heart.

CUSINS   What is a broken heart more or less here? Dionysos Undershaft has descended. I am possessed.

---

*Improvise a bass-line accompaniment.
†Italian composer Gaetano Donizetti's *Lucia di Lammermoor* (1835), based on Sir Walter Scott's novel *The Bride of Lammermoor* (1819).

MRS. BAINES   Come, Barbara: I must have my dear Major to carry the flag with me.

JENNY   Yes, yes, Major darling.

CUSINS [*snatches the tambourine out of JENNY's hand and mutely offers it to BARBARA*]

BARBARA [*coming forward a little as she puts the offer behind her with a shudder, whilst CUSINS recklessly tosses the tambourine back to JENNY and goes to the gate*]   I cant come.

JENNY   Not come!

MRS. BAINES [*with tears in her eyes*]   Barbara: do you think I am wrong to take the money?

BARBARA [*impulsively going to her and kissing her*]   No, no: God help you, dear, you must: you are saving the Army. Go; and may you have a great meeting!

JENNY   But arnt you coming?

BARBARA   No. [*She begins taking off the silver S brooch from her collar.*]

MRS. BAINES   Barbara: what are you doing?

JENNY   Why are you taking your badge off? You cant be going to leave us, Major.

BARBARA [*quietly*]   Father: come here.

UNDERSHAFT [*coming to her*]   My dear! [*Seeing that she is going to pin the badge on his collar, he retreats to the penthouse in some alarm.*]

BARBARA [*following him*]   Dont be frightened. [*She pins the badge on and steps back towards the table, shewing him to the others.*] There! It's not much for £5000, is it?

MRS. BAINES   Barbara: if you wont come and pray with us, promise me you will pray f o r us.

BARBARA   I cant pray now. Perhaps I shall never pray again.

MRS. BAINES   Barbara!

JENNY   Major!

BARBARA [*almost delirious*]   I cant bear any more. Quick march!

CUSINS [*calling to the procession in the street outside*] Off we go. Play up, there! I m m e n s o g i u b i l o. [*He gives the time with his drum; and the band strikes up the march, which rapidly becomes more distant as the procession moves briskly away.*][27]

MRS. BAINES I must go, dear. Youre overworked: you will be all right tomorrow. We'll never lose you. Now Jenny: step out with the old flag. Blood and Fire! [*She marches out through the gate with her flag.*]

JENNY Glory Hallelujah! [*Flourishing her tambourine and marching.*]

UNDERSHAFT [*to CUSINS, as he marches out past him easing the slide of his trombone*] "My ducats and my daughter"![28]

CUSINS [*following him out*] Money and gunpowder!

BARBARA Drunkenness and Murder! My God: why hast thou forsaken me?*

She sinks on the form with her face buried in her hands. The march passes away into silence. BILL WALKER steals across to her.

BILL [*taunting*] Wot prawce Selvytion nah?

SHIRLEY Dont you hit her when shes down.

BILL She it me wen aw wiz dahn. Waw shouldnt I git a bit o me own back?

BARBARA [*raising her head*] I didnt take y o u r money, Bill. [*She crosses the yard to the gate and turns her back on the two men to hide her face from them.*]

BILL [*sneering after her*] Naow, it warnt enough for you. [*Turning to the drum, he misses the money.*] Ellow! If you aint took it summun else az. Weres it gorn? Blame me if Jenny Ill didnt take it arter all!

RUMMY [*screaming at him from the loft*] You lie, you dirty blackguard! Snobby Price pinched it off the drum wen e took ap iz cap. I was ap ere all the time an see im do it.

---

*Barbara repeats Christ's words of doubt just before He dies on the Cross (see the Bible, Matthew 27:46).

BILL   Wot! Stowl maw money! Waw didnt you call thief on him, you silly old mucker you?

RUMMY   To serve you aht for ittin me acrost the fice. It's cost y'pahnd, that az. [*Raising a pæan of squalid triumph.*] I done you. I'm even with you. I ve ad it aht o y—[*BILL snatches up SHIRLEY's mug and hurls it at her. She slams the loft door and vanishes. The mug smashes against the door and falls in fragments.*][29]

BILL [*beginning to chuckle*]   Tell us, ole man, wot o'clock this mornin was it wen im as they call Snobby Prawce was sived?

BARBARA [*turning to him more composedly, and with unspoiled sweetness*]   About half past twelve, Bill. And he pinched your pound at a quarter to two. *I* know. Well, you cant afford to lose it. I'll send it to you.

BILL [*his voice and accent suddenly improving*]   Not if I was to starve for it. *I* aint to be bought.

SHIRLEY   Aint you? Youd sell yourself to the devil for a pint o beer; ony there aint no devil to make the offer.

BILL [*unshamed*]   So I would, mate, and often av, cheerful. But s h e cawnt buy me. [*Approaching BARBARA.*] You wanted my soul, did you? Well, you aint got it.

BARBARA   I nearly got it, Bill. But weve sold it back to you for ten thousand pounds.

SHIRLEY   And dear at the money!

BARBARA   No, Peter: it was worth more than money.

BILL [*salvationproof*]   It's no good: you cawnt get rahnd me nah. I dont blieve in it; and Ive seen today that I was right. [*Going.*] So long, old soupkitchener! Ta, ta, Major Earl's Grendorter! [*Turning at the gate.*] Wot prawce Selvytion nah? Snobby Prawce! Ha! ha!

BARBARA [*offering her hand*]   Goodbye, Bill.

BILL [*taken aback, half plucks his cap off; then shoves it on again defiantly*]   Git aht. [*BARBARA drops her hand, discouraged. He has a twinge of remorse.*] But thets aw rawt, you knaow. Nathink pasnl. Naow mellice. So long, Judy. [*He goes.*]

BARBARA   No malice. So long, Bill.

SHIRLEY [*shaking his head*]   You make too much of him, Miss, in your innocence.

BARBARA [*going to him*]   Peter: I'm like you now. Cleaned out, and lost my job.

SHIRLEY   Youve youth an hope. Thats two better than me.

BARBARA   I'll get you a job, Peter. Thats hope for you: the youth will have to be enough for me. [*She counts her money.*] I have just enough left for two teas at Lockharts,* a Rowton doss[30] for you, and my tram and bus home. [*He frowns and rises with offended pride. She takes his arm.*] Dont be proud, Peter: it's sharing between friends. And promise me youll talk to me and not let me cry. [*She draws him towards the gate.*]

SHIRLEY   Well, I'm not accustomed to talk to the like of you—

BARBARA [*urgently*]   Yes, yes: you must talk to me. Tell me about Tom Paine's books and Bradlaugh's lectures.[31] Come along.

SHIRLEY   Ah, if you would only read Tom Paine in the proper spirit, Miss! [*They go out through the gate together.*]

END OF ACT II.

---

*The 1905 equivalent of a fast-food restaurant.

ACT III

Next day after lunch Lady Britomart is writing in the library in Wilton Crescent. Sarah is reading in the armchair near the window. Barbara, in ordinary dress, pale and brooding, is on the settee. Charles Lomax enters. Coming forward between the settee and the writing table, he starts on seeing Barbara fashionably attired and in low spirits.

LOMAX   Youve left off your uniform!

BARBARA says nothing; but an expression of pain passes over her face.

LADY BRITOMART [*warning him in low tones to be careful*] Charles!

LOMAX [*much concerned, sitting down sympathetically on the settee beside BARBARA*] I'm awfully sorry, Barbara. You know I helped you all I could with the concertina and so forth. [*Momentously.*] Still, I have never shut my eyes to the fact that there is a certain amount of tosh about the Salvation Army. Now the claims of the Church of England—

LADY BRITOMART   Thats enough, Charles. Speak of something suited to your mental capacity.

LOMAX   But surely the Church of England is suited to all our capacities.

BARBARA [*pressing his hand*] Thank you for your sympathy, Cholly. Now go and spoon with Sarah.

LOMAX [*rising and going to SARAH*] How is my ownest today?

SARAH   I wish you wouldnt tell Cholly to do things, Barbara.

He always comes straight and does them. Cholly: we're going to the works at Perivale St. Andrews this afternoon.

LOMAX   What works?

SARAH   The cannon works.

LOMAX   What! Your governor's shop!

SARAH   Yes.

LOMAX   Oh I say!

CUSINS enters in poor condition. He also starts visibly when he sees BARBARA without her uniform.

BARBARA   I expected you this morning, Dolly. Didnt you guess that?

CUSINS [*sitting down beside her*]   I'm sorry. I have only just breakfasted.

SARAH   But weve just finished lunch.

BARBARA   Have you had one of your bad nights?

CUSINS   No: I had rather a good night: in fact, one of the most remarkable nights I have ever passed.

BARBARA   The meeting?

CUSINS   No: after the meeting.

LADY BRITOMART   You should have gone to bed after the meeting. What were you doing?

CUSINS   Drinking.

LADY BRITOMART   ⎫ ⎧ Adolphus!
SARAH   ⎪ ⎪ Dolly!
BARBARA   ⎬ ⎨ Dolly!
LOMAX   ⎭ ⎩ Oh I say!

LADY BRITOMART   What were you drinking, may I ask?

CUSINS   A most devilish kind of Spanish burgundy, warranted free from added alcohol: a Temperance burgundy in fact. Its richness in natural alcohol made any addition superfluous.

BARBARA   Are you joking, Dolly?

CUSINS [*patiently*]   No. I have been making a night of it with the nominal head of this household: that is all.

LADY BRITOMART   Andrew made you drunk!

CUSINS   No: he only provided the wine. I think it was Dionysos who made me drunk. [*To BARBARA.*] I told you I was possessed.

LADY BRITOMART   Youre not sober yet. Go home to bed at once.

CUSINS   I have never before ventured to reproach you, Lady Brit; but how could you marry the Prince of Darkness?

LADY BRITOMART   It was much more excusable to marry him than to get drunk with him. That is a new accomplishment of Andrew's, by the way. He usent to drink.

CUSINS   He doesnt now. He only sat there and completed the wreck of my moral basis, the rout of my convictions, the purchase of my soul. He cares for you, Barbara. That is what makes him so dangerous to me.

BARBARA   That has nothing to do with it, Dolly. There are larger loves and diviner dreams than the fireside ones. You know that, dont you?

CUSINS   Yes: that is our understanding. I know it. I hold to it. Unless he can win me on that holier ground he may amuse me for a while; but he can get no deeper hold, strong as he is.

BARBARA   Keep to that; and the end will be right. Now tell me what happened at the meeting?

CUSINS   It was an amazing meeting. Mrs. Baines almost died of emotion. Jenny Hill went stark mad with hysteria. The Prince of Darkness played his trombone like a madman: its brazen roarings were like the laughter of the damned. 117 conversions took place then and there. They prayed with the most touching sincerity and gratitude for Bodger, and for the anonymous donor of the £5000. Your father would not let his name be given.

LOMAX   That was rather fine of the old man, you know. Most chaps would have wanted the advertisement.

CUSINS   He said all the charitable institutions would be down on him like kites on a battle field if he gave his name.

LADY BRITOMART   Thats Andrew all over. He never does a proper thing without giving an improper reason for it.

CUSINS   He convinced me that I have all my life been doing improper things for proper reasons.

LADY BRITOMART   Adolphus: now that Barbara has left the Salvation Army, you had better leave it too. I will not have you playing that drum in the streets.

CUSINS   Your orders are already obeyed, Lady Brit.

BARBARA   Dolly: were you ever really in earnest about it? Would you have joined if you had never seen me?

CUSINS [*disingenuously*]   Well—er—well, possibly, as a collector of religions—

LOMAX [*cunningly*]   Not as a drummer, though, you know. You are a very clearheaded brainy chap, Cholly; and it must have been apparent to you that there is a certain amount of tosh about—

LADY BRITOMART   Charles: if you must drivel, drivel like a grown-up man and not like a schoolboy.

LOMAX [*out of countenance*]   Well, drivel is drivel, dont you know, whatever a man's age.

LADY BRITOMART   In good society in England, Charles, men drivel at all ages by repeating silly formulas with an air of wisdom. Schoolboys make their own formulas out of slang, like you. When they reach your age, and get political private secretaryships and things of that sort, they drop slang and get their formulas out of The Spectator or The Times. Y o u had better confine yourself to The Times. You will find that there is a certain amount of tosh about The Times; but at least its language is reputable.

LOMAX [*overwhelmed*]   You are so awfully strong-minded, Lady Brit—

LADY BRITOMART   Rubbish! [*MORRISON comes in.*] What is it?

MORRISON   If you please, my lady, Mr. Undershaft has just drove up to the door.

LADY BRITOMART   Well, let him in. [*MORRISON hesitates.*] Whats the matter with you?

MORRISON   Shall I announce him, my lady; or is he at home here, so to speak, my lady?

LADY BRITOMART   Announce him.

MORRISON   Thank you, my lady. You wont mind my asking, I hope. The occasion is in a manner of speaking new to me.

LADY BRITOMART   Quite right. Go and let him in.

MORRISON   Thank you, my lady. [*He withdraws.*]

LADY BRITOMART   Children: go and get ready. [*SARAH and BARBARA go upstairs for their out-of-door wraps.*] Charles: go and tell Stephen to come down here in five minutes: you will find him in the drawing room. [*CHARLES goes.*] Adolphus: tell them to send round the carriage in about fifteen minutes. [*ADOLPHUS goes.*]

MORRISON [*at the door*]   Mr. Undershaft.

UNDERSHAFT comes in. MORRISON goes out.

UNDERSHAFT   Alone! How fortunate!

LADY BRITOMART [*rising*]   Dont be sentimental, Andrew. Sit down. [*She sits on the settee: he sits beside her, on her left. She comes to the point before he has time to breathe.*] Sarah must have £800 a year until Charles Lomax comes into his property. Barbara will need more, and need it permanently, because Adolphus hasnt any property.

UNDERSHAFT [*resignedly*]   Yes, my dear: I will see to it. Anything else? for yourself, for instance?

LADY BRITOMART   I want to talk to you about Stephen.

UNDERSHAFT [*rather wearily*]   Dont, my dear. Stephen doesnt interest me.

LADY BRITOMART   He does interest me. He is our son.

UNDERSHAFT   Do you really think so? He has induced us to bring him into the world; but he chose his parents very incongruously, I think. I see nothing of myself in him, and less of you.

LADY BRITOMART   Andrew: Stephen is an excellent son, and a most steady, capable, highminded young man. You are simply trying to find an excuse for disinheriting him.

UNDERSHAFT   My dear Biddy: the Undershaft tradition disinherits him. It would be dishonest of me to leave the cannon foundry to my son.

LADY BRITOMART   It would be most unnatural and improper of you to leave it anyone else, Andrew. Do you suppose this wicked and immoral tradition can be kept up for ever? Do you pretend that Stephen could not carry on the foundry just as well as all the other sons of the big business houses?

UNDERSHAFT   Yes: he could learn the office routine without understanding the business, like all the other sons; and the firm would go on by its own momentum until the real Undershaft—probably an Italian or a German—would invent a new method and cut him out.

LADY BRITOMART   There is nothing that any Italian or German could do that Stephen could not do. And Stephen at least has breeding.

UNDERSHAFT   The son of a foundling! nonsense!

LADY BRITOMART   My son, Andrew! And even you may have good blood in your veins for all you know.

UNDERSHAFT   True. Probably I have. That is another argument in favor of a foundling.

LADY BRITOMART   Andrew: dont be aggravating. And dont be wicked. At present you are both.

UNDERSHAFT   This conversation is part of the Undershaft tradition, Biddy. Every Undershaft's wife has treated him to it ever since the house was founded. It is mere waste of breath.

If the tradition be ever broken it will be for an abler man than Stephen.

LADY BRITOMART [*pouting*]   Then go away.

UNDERSHAFT [*deprecatory*]   Go away!

LADY BRITOMART   Yes: go away. If you will do nothing for Stephen, you are not wanted here. Go to your foundling, whoever he is; and look after h i m.

UNDERSHAFT   The fact is, Biddy—

LADY BRITOMART   Dont call me Biddy. I dont call you Andy.

UNDERSHAFT   I will not call my wife Britomart: it is not good sense. Seriously, my love, the Undershaft tradition has landed me in a difficulty. I am getting on in years; and my partner Lazarus has at last made a stand and insisted that the succession must be settled one way or the other; and of course he is quite right. You see, I havnt found a fit successor yet.

LADY BRITOMART [*obstinately*]   There is Stephen.

UNDERSHAFT   Thats just it: all the foundlings I can find are exactly like Stephen.

LADY BRITOMART   Andrew!!

UNDERSHAFT   I want a man with no relations and no schooling: that is, a man who would be out of the running altogether if he were not a strong man. And I cant find him. Every blessed foundling nowadays is snapped up in his infancy by Barnardo homes,* or School Board officers, or Boards of Guardians; and if he shews the least ability, he is fastened on by schoolmasters; trained to win scholarships like a racehorse; crammed with secondhand ideas; drilled and disciplined in docility and what they call good taste; and lamed for

---

*British physician and philanthropist Thomas Barnardo (1845–1905) founded homes for orphaned and destitute children, which were known as Doctor Barnardo's Homes.

life so that he is fit for nothing but teaching. If you want to keep the foundry in the family, you had better find an eligible foundling and marry him to Barbara.

LADY BRITOMART   Ah! Barbara! Your pet! You would sacrifice Stephen to Barbara.

UNDERSHAFT   Cheerfully. And you, my dear, would boil Barbara to make soup for Stephen.

LADY BRITOMART   Andrew: this is not a question of our likings and dislikings: it is a question of duty. It is your duty to make Stephen your successor.

UNDERSHAFT   Just as much as it is your duty to submit to your husband. Come, Biddy! these tricks of the governing class are of no use with me. I am one of the governing class myself; and it is waste of time giving tracts to a missionary. I have the power in this matter; and I am not to be humbugged into using it for your purposes.

LADY BRITOMART   Andrew: you can talk my head off; but you cant change wrong into right. And your tie is all on one side. Put it straight.

UNDERSHAFT [*disconcerted*]   It wont stay unless it's pinned— [*he fumbles at it with childish grimaces*].
    STEPHEN comes in.

STEPHEN [*at the door*]   I beg your pardon [*about to retire*].

LADY BRITOMART   No: come in, Stephen. [*STEPHEN comes forward to his mother's writing table.*]

UNDERSHAFT [*not very cordially*]   Good afternoon.

STEPHEN [*coldly*]   Good afternoon.

UNDERSHAFT [*to LADY BRITOMART*]   He knows all about the tradition, I suppose?

LADY BRITOMART   Yes. [*To STEPHEN.*] It is what I told you last night, Stephen.

UNDERSHAFT [*sulkily*]   I understand you want to come into the cannon business.

STEPHEN   *I* go into trade! Certainly not.

UNDERSHAFT [*opening his eyes, greatly eased in mind and manner*]
Oh! in that case——!

LADY BRITOMART   Cannons are not trade, Stephen. They
are enterprise.

STEPHEN   I have no intention of becoming a man of business
in any sense. I have no capacity for business and no taste for it.
I intend to devote myself to politics.

UNDERSHAFT [*rising*]   My dear boy: this is an immense relief
to me. And I trust it may prove an equally good thing for the
country. I was afraid you would consider yourself disparaged
and slighted. [*He moves towards STEPHEN as if to shake hands with
him.*]

LADY BRITOMART [*rising and interposing*]   Stephen: I cannot
allow you to throw away an enormous property like this.

STEPHEN [*stiffly*]   Mother: there must be an end of treating me
as a child, if you please. [*LADY BRITOMART recoils, deeply
wounded by his tone.*] Until last night I did not take your attitude
seriously, because I did not think you meant it seriously. But I
find now that you left me in the dark as to matters which you
should have explained to me years ago. I am extremely hurt
and offended. Any further discussion of my intentions had
better take place with my father, as between one man and another.

LADY BRITOMART   Stephen! [*She sits down again; and her eyes
fill with tears.*]

UNDERSHAFT [*with grave compassion*]   You see, my dear, it is
only the big men who can be treated as children.

STEPHEN   I am sorry, mother, that you have forced me——

UNDERSHAFT [*stopping him*]   Yes, yes, yes, yes: thats all right,
Stephen. She wont interfere with you any more: your independence is achieved: you have won your latchkey. Dont rub
it in; and above all, dont apologize. [*He resumes his seat.*] Now
what about your future, as between one man and another——I
beg your pardon, Biddy: as between two men and a woman.

LADY BRITOMART [*who has pulled herself together strongly*]   I quite understand, Stephen. By all means go your own way if you feel strong enough. [*STEPHEN sits down magisterially in the chair at the writing table with an air of affirming his majority.*]

UNDERSHAFT   It is settled that you do not ask for the succession to the cannon business.

STEPHEN   I hope it is settled that I repudiate the cannon business.

UNDERSHAFT   Come, come! dont be so devilishly sulky: it's boyish. Freedom should be generous. Besides, I owe you a fair start in life in exchange for disinheriting you. You cant become prime minister all at once. Havnt you a turn for something? What about literature, art and so forth?

STEPHEN   I have nothing of the artist about me, either in faculty or character, thank Heaven!

UNDERSHAFT   A philosopher, perhaps? Eh?

STEPHEN   I make no such ridiculous pretension.

UNDERSHAFT   Just so. Well, there is the army, the navy, the Church, the Bar. The Bar requires some ability. What about the Bar?

STEPHEN   I have not studied law. And I am afraid I have not the necessary push——I believe that is the name barristers give to their vulgarity——for success in pleading.

UNDERSHAFT   Rather a difficult case, Stephen. Hardly anything left but the stage, is there? [*STEPHEN makes an impatient movement.*] Well, come! is there a n y t h i n g you know or care for?

STEPHEN [*rising and looking at him steadily*]   I know the difference between right and wrong.

UNDERSHAFT [*hugely tickled*]   You dont say so! What! no capacity for business, no knowledge of law, no sympathy with art, no pretension to philosophy; only a simple knowledge of the secret that has puzzled all the philosophers, baffled all the lawyers, muddled all the men of business, and ruined most of the artists: the secret of right and wrong. Why, man, youre a genius, a master of masters, a god! At twenty-four, too!

STEPHEN [*keeping his temper with difficulty*]   You are pleased to be facetious. I pretend to nothing more than any honorable English gentleman claims as his birthright [*he sits down angrily*].

UNDERSHAFT   Oh, thats everybody's birthright. Look at poor little Jenny Hill, the Salvation lassie! she would think you were laughing at her if you asked her to stand up in the street and teach grammar or geography or mathematics or even drawingroom dancing; but it never occurs to her to doubt that she can teach morals and religion. You are all alike, you respectable people. You cant tell me the bursting strain of a ten-inch gun, which is a very simple matter; but you all think you can tell me the bursting strain of a man under temptation. You darent handle high explosives; but youre all ready to handle honesty and truth and justice and the whole duty of man, and kill one another at that game. What a country! what a world!

LADY BRITOMART [*uneasily*]   What do you think he had better do, Andrew?

UNDERSHAFT   Oh, just what he wants to do. He knows nothing; and he thinks he knows everything. That points clearly to a political career. Get him a private secretaryship to someone who can get him an Under Secretaryship; and then leave him alone. He will find his natural and proper place in the end on the Treasury bench.*

STEPHEN [*springing up again*]   I am sorry, sir, that you force me to forget the respect due to you as my father. I am an Englishman; and I will not hear the Government of my country insulted. [*He thrusts his hands in his pockets, and walks angrily across to the window.*]

---

*In the House of Commons (Parliament's lower house), the Treasury bench is the first row of seats on the right of the Speaker, where cabinet members sit.

UNDERSHAFT [*with a touch of brutality*]   The government of your country! *I* am the government of your country: I, and Lazarus. Do you suppose that you and half a dozen amateurs like you, sitting in a row in that foolish gabble shop, can govern Undershaft and Lazarus? No, my friend: you will do what pays u s. You will make war when it suits us, and keep peace when it doesnt. You will find out that trade requires certain measures when we have decided on those measures. When I want anything to keep my dividends up, you will discover that my want is a national need. When other people want something to keep my dividends down, you will call out the police and military. And in return you shall have the support and applause of my newspapers, and the delight of imagining that you are a great statesman. Government of your country! Be off with you my boy, and play with your caucuses and leading articles* and historic parties and great leaders and burning questions and the rest of your toys. *I* am going back to my counting house to pay the piper and call the tune.

STEPHEN [*actually smiling, and putting his hand on his father's shoulder with indulgent patronage*]   Really, my dear father, it is impossible to be angry with you. You don't know how absurd all this sounds to m e. You are very properly proud of having been industrious enough to make money; and it is greatly to your credit that you have made so much of it. But it has kept you in circles where you are valued for your money and deferred to for it, instead of in the doubtless very old-fashioned and behind-the-times public school and university where I formed my habits of mind. It is natural for you to think that money governs England; but you must allow me to think I know better.

UNDERSHAFT   And what d o e s govern England, pray?

---

*Caucuses are small councils within a political party that determine party positions; leading articles are the leading editorials in newspapers.

STEPHEN   Character, father, character.

UNDERSHAFT   Whose character? Yours or mine?

STEPHEN   Neither yours nor mine, father, but the best elements in the English national character.

UNDERSHAFT   Stephen: Ive found your profession for you. Youre a born journalist. I'll start you with a high-toned weekly review. There!

STEPHEN goes to the smaller writing table and busies himself with his letters.

SARAH, BARBARA, LOMAX, and CUSINS come in ready for walking. BARBARA crosses the room to the window and looks out. CUSINS drifts amiably to the armchair, and LOMAX remains near the door, whilst SARAH comes to her mother.

SARAH   Go and get ready, mamma: the carriage is waiting. [*LADY BRITOMART leaves the room.*]

UNDERSHAFT [*to SARAH*]   Good day, my dear. Good afternoon, Mr. Lomax.

LOMAX [*vaguely*]   Ahdedoo.

UNDERSHAFT [*to CUSINS*]   Quite well after last night, Euripides, eh?

CUSINS   As well as can be expected.

UNDERSHAFT   Thats right. [*To BARBARA.*] So you are coming to see my death and devastation factory, Barbara?

BARBARA [*at the window*]   You came yesterday to see my salvation factory. I promised you a return visit.

LOMAX [*coming forward between SARAH and UNDERSHAFT*]   Youll find it awfully interesting. Ive been through the Woolwich Arsenal; and it gives you a ripping feeling of security, you know, to think of the lot of beggars we could kill if it came to fighting. [*To UNDERSHAFT, with sudden solemnity.*] Still, it must be rather an awful reflection for you, from the religious point of view as it were. Youre getting on, you know, and all that.

SARAH   You dont mind Cholly's imbecility, papa, do you?

LOMAX [*much taken aback*]   Oh I say!

UNDERSHAFT   Mr. Lomax looks at the matter in a very proper spirit, my dear.

LOMAX   Just so. Thats all I meant, I assure you.

SARAH   Are you coming, Stephen?

STEPHEN   Well, I am rather busy—er— [*Magnanimously.*] Oh well, yes: I'll come. That is, if there is room for me.

UNDERSHAFT   I can take two with me in a little motor I am experimenting with for field use. You wont mind its being rather unfashionable. It's not painted yet; but it's bullet proof.

LOMAX [*appalled at the prospect of confronting WILTON CRESCENT in an unpainted motor*]   Oh I s a y!

SARAH   The carriage for me, thank you. Barbara doesnt mind what shes seen in.

LOMAX   I say, Dolly old chap: do you really mind the car being a guy? Because of course if you do I'll go in it. Still—

CUSINS   I prefer it.

LOMAX   Thanks awfully, old man. Come, Sarah. [*He hurries out to secure his seat in the carriage. SARAH follows him.*]

CUSINS [*moodily walking across to LADY BRITOMART's writing table*] Why are we two coming to this Works Department of Hell? that is what I ask myself.

BARBARA   I have always thought of it as a sort of pit where lost creatures with blackened faces stirred up smoky fires and were driven and tormented by my father? Is it like that, dad?

UNDERSHAFT [*scandalized*]   My dear! It is a spotlessly clean and beautiful hillside town.

CUSINS   With a Methodist chapel? Oh d o say theres a Methodist chapel.

UNDERSHAFT   There are two: a Primitive one* and a sophis-

---

*Primitive Methodists belong to a branch of the church that adheres more strictly to original Methodist doctrine.

ticated one. There is even an Ethical Society;* it is not much patronized, as my men are all strongly religious. In the High Explosives Sheds they object to the presence of Agnostics as unsafe.

CUSINS   And yet they dont object to you!

BARBARA   Do they obey all your orders?

UNDERSHAFT   I never give them any orders. When I speak to one of them it is "Well, Jones, is the baby doing well? and has Mrs. Jones made a good recovery." "Nicely, thank you, sir." And thats all.

CUSINS   But Jones has to be kept in order. How do you maintain discipline among your men?

UNDERSHAFT   I dont. They do. You see, the one thing Jones wont stand is any rebellion from the man under him, or any assertion of social equality between the wife of the man with 4 shillings a week less than himself, and Mrs. Jones! Of course they all rebel against me, theoretically. Practically, every man of them keeps the man just below him in his place. I never meddle with them. I never bully them. I dont even bully Lazarus. I say that certain things are to be done; but I dont order anybody to do them. I dont say, mind you, that there is no ordering about and snubbing and even bullying. The men snub the boys and order them about; the carmen snub the sweepers; the artisans snub the unskilled laborers; the foremen drive and bully both the laborers and artisans; the assistant engineers find fault with the foremen; the chief engineers drop on the assistants; the departmental managers worry the chiefs; and the clerks have tall hats and hymnbooks and keep up the social tone by refusing to associate on equal terms with anybody. The result is a colossal profit, which comes to me.

---

*Group that looks to reason instead of to a supernatural being as the basis for moral behavior.

CUSINS [*revolted*]   You really are a——well, what I was saying yesterday.

BARBARA   What was he saying yesterday?

UNDERSHAFT   Never mind, my dear. He thinks I have made you unhappy. Have I?

BARBARA   Do you think I can be happy in this vulgar silly dress? I! who have worn the uniform. Do you understand what you have done to me? Yesterday I had a man's soul in my hand. I set him in the way of life with his face to salvation. But when we took your money he turned back to drunkenness and derision. [*With intense conviction.*] I will never forgive you that. If I had a child, and you destroyed its body with your explosives——if you murdered Dolly with your horrible guns——I could forgive you if my forgiveness would open the gates of heaven to you. But to take a human soul from me, and turn it into the soul of a wolf! that is worse than any murder.

UNDERSHAFT   Does my daughter despair so easily? Can you strike a man to the heart and leave no mark on him?

BARBARA [*her face lighting up*]   Oh, you are right: he can never be lost now: where was my faith?

CUSINS   Oh, clever clever devil!

BARBARA   You may be a devil; but God speaks through you sometimes. [*She takes her father's hands and kisses them.*] You have given me back my happiness: I feel it deep down now, though my spirit is troubled.

UNDERSHAFT   You have learnt something. That always feels at first as if you had lost something.

BARBARA   Well, take me to the factory of death, and let me learn something more. There must be some truth or other behind all this frightful irony. Come, Dolly. [*She goes out.*]

CUSINS   My guardian angel! [*To* UNDERSHAFT.] Avaunt! [*He follows* BARBARA.]

STEPHEN [*quietly, at the writing table*]   You must not mind

Cusins, father. He is a very amiable good fellow; but he is a Greek scholar and naturally a little eccentric.

UNDERSHAFT   Ah, quite so. Thank you, Stephen. Thank you. [*He goes out.*]

STEPHEN smiles patronizingly; buttons his coat responsibly; and crosses the room to the door. LADY BRITOMART, dressed for out-of-doors, opens it before he reaches it. She looks round for the others; looks at STEPHEN; and turns to go without a word.

STEPHEN [*embarrassed*]   Mother—

LADY BRITOMART   Dont be apologetic, Stephen. And dont forget that you have outgrown your mother. [*She goes out.*]

Perivale St. Andrews lies between two Middlesex hills, half climbing the northern one. It is an almost smokeless town of white walls, roofs of narrow green slates or red tiles, tall trees, domes, campaniles, and slender chimney shafts, beautifully situated and beautiful in itself. The best view of it is obtained from the crest of a slope about half a mile to the east, where the high explosives are dealt with. The foundry lies hidden in the depths between, the tops of its chimneys sprouting like huge skittles* into the middle distance. Across the crest runs a platform of concrete, with a parapet which suggests a fortification, because there is a huge cannon of the obsolete Woolwich Infant pattern peering across it at the town. The cannon is mounted on an experimental gun carriage: possibly the original model of the Undershaft disappearing rampart gun alluded to by STEPHEN. The parapet has a high step inside which serves as a seat.

BARBARA is leaning over the parapet, looking towards the town. On her right is the cannon; on her left the end of a shed raised on piles, with a ladder of three or four steps up to the door, which opens outwards and has a little wooden landing at the threshold, with a fire bucket in the corner of the landing. The parapet stops short of the shed, leaving a gap which is the beginning of the path down the hill through the foundry to the town. Behind the cannon is a trolley carrying a huge

---

*Pins, like bowling pins, used in the game of skittles.

conical bombshell, with a red band painted on it. Further from the parapet, on the same side, is a deck chair, near the door of an office, which, like the sheds, is of the lightest possible construction.

CUSINS arrives by the path from the town.

BARBARA   Well?

CUSINS   Not a ray of hope. Everything perfect, wonderful, real. It only needs a cathedral to be a heavenly city instead of a hellish one.

BARBARA   Have you found out whether they have done anything for old Peter Shirley.

CUSINS   They have found him a job as gatekeeper and timekeeper. He's frightfully miserable. He calls the timekeeping brainwork, and says he isnt used to it; and his gate lodge is so splendid that hes ashamed to use the rooms, and skulks in the scullery.

BARBARA   Poor Peter!

STEPHEN arrives from the town. He carries a field-glass.

STEPHEN [*enthusiastically*]   Have you two seen the place? Why did you leave us?

CUSINS   I wanted to see everything I was not intended to see; and Barbara wanted to make the men talk.

STEPHEN   Have you found anything discreditable?

CUSINS   No. They call him Dandy Andy and are proud of his being a cunning old rascal; but it's all horribly, frightfully, immorally, unanswerably perfect.

SARAH arrives.

SARAH   Heavens! what a place! [*She crosses to the trolley.*] Did you see the nursing home!? [*She sits down on the shell.*]

STEPHEN   Did you see the libraries and schools!?

SARAH   Did you see the ball room and the banqueting chamber in the Town Hall!?

STEPHEN   Have you gone into the insurance fund, the pension fund, the building society, the various applications of co-operation!?

UNDERSHAFT comes from the office, with a sheaf of telegrams in his hands.

UNDERSHAFT   Well, have you seen everything? I'm sorry I was called away. [*Indicating the telegrams.*] News from Manchuria.

STEPHEN   Good news, I hope.

UNDERSHAFT   Very.

STEPHEN   Another Japanese victory?

UNDERSHAFT   Oh, I dont know. Which side wins does not concern us here. No: the good news is that the aerial battleship is a tremendous success. At the first trial it has wiped out a fort with three hundred soldiers in it.

CUSINS [*from the platform*]   Dummy soldiers?

UNDERSHAFT   No: the real thing. [*CUSINS and BARBARA exchange glances. Then CUSINS sits on the step and buries his face in his hands. BARBARA gravely lays her hand on his shoulder, and he looks up at her in a sort of whimsical desperation.*] Well, Stephen, what do you think of the place?

STEPHEN   Oh, magnificent. A perfect triumph of organization. Frankly, my dear father, I have been a fool: I had no idea of what it all meant—of the wonderful forethought, the power of organization, the administrative capacity, the financial genius, the colossal capital it represents. I have been repeating to myself as I came through your streets "Peace hath her victories no less renowned than War."* I have only one misgiving about it all.

UNDERSHAFT   Out with it.

STEPHEN   Well, I cannot help thinking that all this provision for every want of your workmen may sap their independence and weaken their sense of responsibility. And greatly as we enjoyed our tea at that splendid restaurant—how they gave us all

*Quotation from Sonnet 16, "Cromwell, our chief of men" (lines 10–11), by English poet John Milton (1608–1674).

that luxury and cake and jam and cream for threepence I really cannot imagine!—still you must remember that restaurants break up home life. Look at the continent, for instance! Are you sure so much pampering is really good for the men's characters?

UNDERSHAFT   Well you see, my dear boy, when you are organizing civilization you have to make up your mind whether trouble and anxiety are good things or not. If you decide that they are, then, I take it, you simply dont organize civilization; and there you are, with trouble and anxiety enough to make us all angels! But if you decide the other way, you may as well go through with it. However, Stephen, our characters are safe here. A sufficient dose of anxiety is always provided by the fact that we may be blown to smithereens at any moment.

SARAH   By the way, papa, where do you make the explosives?

UNDERSHAFT   In separate little sheds, like that one. When one of them blows up, it costs very little; and only the people quite close to it are killed.

STEPHEN, who is quite close to it, looks at it rather scaredly, and moves away quickly to the cannon. At the same moment the door of the shed is thrown abruptly open; and a foreman in overalls and list slippers comes out on the little landing and holds the door open for LOMAX, who appears in the doorway.

LOMAX [with studied coolness]   My good fellow: you neednt get into a state of nerves. Nothing's going to happen to you; and I suppose it wouldnt be the end of the world if anything did. A little bit of British pluck is what y o u want, old chap. [He descends and strolls across to SARAH.]

UNDERSHAFT [to the foreman]   Anything wrong, Bilton?

BILTON [with ironic calm]   Gentleman walked into the high explosives shed and lit a cigaret, sir: thats all.

UNDERSHAFT   Ah, quite so. [To LOMAX.] Do you happen to remember what you did with the match?

LOMAX   Oh come! I'm not a fool. I took jolly good care to blow it out before I chucked it away.

BILTON   The top of it was red hot inside, sir.

LOMAX   Well, suppose it was! I didnt chuck it into any of y o u r messes.

UNDERSHAFT   Think no more of it, Mr. Lomax. By the way, would you mind lending me your matches?

LOMAX [*offering his box*]   Certainly.

UNDERSHAFT   Thanks. [*He pockets the matches.*]

LOMAX [*lecturing to the company generally*]   You know, these high explosives dont go off like gunpowder, except when theyre in a gun. When theyre spread loose, you can put a match to them without the least risk: they just burn quietly like a bit of paper. [*Warming to the scientific interest of the subject.*] Did you know that, Undershaft?[32] Have you ever tried?

UNDERSHAFT   Not on a large scale, Mr. Lomax. Bilton will give you a sample of gun cotton when you are leaving if you ask him. You can experiment with it at home. [*Bilton looks puzzled.*]

SARAH   Bilton will do nothing of the sort, papa. I suppose it's your business to blow up the Russians and Japs; but you might really stop short of blowing up poor Cholly. [*BILTON gives it up and retires into the shed.*]

LOMAX   My ownest, there is no danger. [*He sits beside her on the shell.*]

LADY BRITOMART arrives from the town with a bouquet.

LADY BRITOMART [*coming impetuously between UNDERSHAFT and the deck chair*]   Andrew: you shouldnt have let me see this place.

UNDERSHAFT   Why, my dear?

LADY BRITOMART   Never mind why: you shouldnt have: thats all. To think of all that [*indicating the town*] being yours! and that you have kept it to yourself all these years!

UNDERSHAFT   It does not belong to me. I belong to it. It is the Undershaft inheritance.

LADY BRITOMART   It is not. Your ridiculous cannons and that noisy banging foundry may be the Undershaft inheritance; but all that plate and linen, all that furniture and those houses and orchards and gardens belong to us. They belong to m e: they are not a man's business. I wont give them up. You must be out of your senses to throw them all away; and if you persist in such folly, I will call in a doctor.

UNDERSHAFT [*stooping to smell the bouquet*]   Where did you get the flowers, my dear?

LADY BRITOMART   Your men presented them to me in your William Morris Labor Church.[33]

CUSINS [*springing up*]   Oh! It needed only that. A Labor Church!

LADY BRITOMART   Yes, with Morris's words in mosaic letters ten feet high round the dome. NO MAN IS GOOD ENOUGH TO BE ANOTHER MAN'S MASTER. The cynicism of it!

UNDERSHAFT   It shocked the men at first, I am afraid. But now they take no more notice of it than of the ten commandments in church.

LADY BRITOMART   Andrew: you are trying to put me off the subject of the inheritance by profane jokes. Well, you shant. I dont ask it any longer for Stephen: he has inherited far too much of your perversity to be fit for it. But Barbara has rights as well as Stephen. Why should not Adolphus succeed to the inheritance? I could manage the town for him; and he can look after the cannons, if they are really necessary.

UNDERSHAFT   I should ask nothing better if Adolphus were a foundling. He is exactly the sort of new blood that is wanted in English business. But hes not a foundling; and theres an end of it.

CUSINS [*diplomatically*]   Not quite. [*They all turn and stare at him. He comes from the platform past the shed to UNDERSHAFT.*] I think— Mind! I am not committing myself in any way as to my future course—but I t h i n k the foundling difficulty can be got over.

UNDERSHAFT   What do you mean?

CUSINS   Well, I have something to say which is in the nature of a confession.

SARAH
LADY BRITOMART
BARBARA   } Confession!
STEPHEN

LOMAX   Oh I say!

CUSINS   Yes, a confession. Listen, all. Until I met Barbara I thought myself in the main an honorable, truthful man, because I wanted the approval of my conscience more than I wanted anything else. But the moment I saw Barbara, I wanted her far more than the approval of my conscience.

LADY BRITOMART   Adolphus!

CUSINS   It is true. You accused me yourself, Lady Brit, of joining the Army to worship Barbara; and so I did. She bought my soul like a flower at a street corner; but she bought it for herself.

UNDERSHAFT   What! Not for Dionysos or another?

CUSINS   Dionysos and all the others are in herself. I adored what was divine in her, and was therefore a true worshipper. But I was romantic about her too. I thought she was a woman of the people, and that a marriage with a professor of Greek would be far beyond the wildest social ambitions of her rank.

LADY BRITOMART   Adolphus!!

LOMAX   Oh I s a y!!!

CUSINS   When I learnt the horrible truth—

LADY BRITOMART   What do you mean by the horrible truth, pray?

CUSINS   That she was enormously rich; that her grandfather was an earl; that her father was the Prince of Darkness—

UNDERSHAFT   Chut!

CUSINS   —and that I was only an adventurer trying to catch a
rich wife, then I stooped to deceive her about my birth.

BARBARA   Dolly!

LADY BRITOMART   Your birth! Now Adolphus, dont dare to
make up a wicked story for the sake of these wretched cannons. Remember: I have seen photographs of your parents;
and the Agent General for South Western Australia knows
them personally and has assured me that they are most respectable married people.

CUSINS   So they are in Australia; but here they are outcasts.
Their marriage is legal in Australia, but not in England. My
mother is my father's deceased wife's sister; and in this island
I am consequently a foundling. [*Sensation.*] Is the subterfuge
good enough, Machiavelli?

UNDERSHAFT [*thoughtfully*]   Biddy: this may be a way out of
the difficulty.

LADY BRITOMART   Stuff! A man cant make cannons any the
better for being his own cousin instead of his proper self [*she
sits down in the deck chair with a bounce that expresses her downright
contempt for their casuistry*].

UNDERSHAFT [*to CUSINS*]   You are an educated man. That is
against the tradition.

CUSINS   Once in ten thousand times it happens that the
schoolboy is a born master of what they try to teach him.
Greek has not destroyed my mind: it has nourished it. Besides, I did not learn it at an English public school.

UNDERSHAFT   Hm! Well, I cannot afford to be too particular: you have cornered the foundling market. Let it pass. You
are eligible, Euripides: you are eligible.

BARBARA [*coming from the platform and interposing between
CUSINS and UNDERSHAFT*]   Dolly: yesterday morning,
when Stephen told us all about the tradition, you became very

silent; and you have been strange and excited ever since. Were you thinking of your birth then?

CUSINS   When the finger of Destiny suddenly points at a man in the middle of his breakfast, it makes him thoughtful. [*BARBARA turns away sadly and stands near her mother, listening perturbedly.*]

UNDERSHAFT   Aha! You have had your eye on the business, my young friend, have you?

CUSINS   Take care! There is an abyss of moral horror between me and your accursed aerial battleships.

UNDERSHAFT   Never mind the abyss for the present. Let us settle the practical details and leave your final decision open. You know that you will have to change your name. Do you object to that?

CUSINS   Would any man named Adolphus—any man called Dolly!—object to be called something else?

UNDERSHAFT   Good. Now, as to money! I propose to treat you handsomely from the beginning. You shall start at a thousand a year.

CUSINS [*with sudden heat, his spectacles twinkling with mischief*]   A thousand! You dare offer a miserable thousand to the son-in-law of a millionaire! No, by Heavens, Machiavelli! you shall not cheat m e. You cannot do without me; and I can do without you. I must have two thousand five hundred a year for two years. At the end of that time, if I am a failure, I go. But if I am a success, and stay on, you must give me the other five thousand.

UNDERSHAFT   What other five thousand?

CUSINS   To make the two years up to five thousand a year. The two thousand five hundred is only half pay in case I should turn out a failure. The third year I must have ten per cent on the profits.

UNDERSHAFT [*taken aback*]   Ten per cent! Why, man, do you know what my profits are?

CUSINS   Enormous, I hope: otherwise I shall require twenty-five per cent.

UNDERSHAFT   But, Mr. Cusins, this is a serious matter of business. You are not bringing any capital into the concern.

CUSINS   What! no capital! Is my mastery of Greek no capital? Is my access to the subtlest thought, the loftiest poetry yet attained by humanity, no capital? My character! my intellect! my life! my career! what Barbara calls my soul! are these no capital? Say another word; and I double my salary.

UNDERSHAFT   Be reasonable—

CUSINS [*peremptorily*]   Mr. Undershaft: you have my terms. Take them or leave them.

UNDERSHAFT [*recovering himself*]   Very well. I note your terms; and I offer you half.

CUSINS [*disgusted*]   Half!

UNDERSHAFT [*firmly*]   Half.

CUSINS   You call yourself a gentleman; and you offer me half!!

UNDERSHAFT   I do not call myself a gentleman; but I offer you half.

CUSINS   This to your future partner! your successor! your son-in-law!

BARBARA   You are selling your own soul, Dolly, not mine. Leave me out of the bargain, please.

UNDERSHAFT   Come! I will go a step further for Barbara's sake. I will give you three fifths; but that is my last word.

CUSINS   Done!

LOMAX   Done in the eye. Why, *I* only get eight hundred, you know.

CUSINS   By the way, Mac, I am a classical scholar, not an arithmetical one. Is three fifths more than half or less?

UNDERSHAFT   More, of course.

CUSINS   I would have taken two hundred and fifty. How you can succeed in business when you are willing to pay all that money to a University don who is obviously not worth a junior clerk's wages!—well! What will Lazarus say?

UNDERSHAFT   Lazarus is a gentle romantic Jew who cares for nothing but string quartets and stalls at fashionable theatres. He will get the credit of your rapacity in money matters, as he has hitherto had the credit of mine. You are a shark of the first order, Euripides. So much the better for the firm!

BARBARA   Is the bargain closed, Dolly? Does your soul belong to him now?

CUSINS   No: the price is settled: that is all. The real tug of war is still to come. What about the moral question?

LADY BRITOMART   There is no moral question in the matter at all, Adolphus. You must simply sell cannons and weapons to people whose cause is right and just, and refuse them to foreigners and criminals.

UNDERSHAFT [*determinedly*]   No: none of that. You must keep the true faith of an Armorer, or you dont come in here.

CUSINS   What on earth is the true faith of an Armorer?

UNDERSHAFT   To give arms to all men who offer an honest price for them, without respect of persons or principles: to aristocrat and republican, to Nihilist and Tsar, to Capitalist and Socialist, to Protestant and Catholic, to burglar and policeman, to black man white man and yellow man, to all sorts and conditions, all nationalities, all faiths, all follies, all causes and all crimes. The first Undershaft wrote up in his shop IF GOD GAVE THE HAND, LET NOT MAN WITHHOLD THE SWORD. The second wrote up ALL HAVE THE RIGHT TO FIGHT: NONE HAVE THE RIGHT TO JUDGE. The third wrote up TO MAN THE WEAPON: TO HEAVEN THE VICTORY. The fourth had no literary turn; so he did not write up anything; but he sold cannons to Napoleon under the nose of George the Third. The fifth wrote up PEACE SHALL NOT PREVAIL SAVE WITH A SWORD IN HER HAND. The sixth, my master, was the best of all. He wrote up NOTHING IS EVER DONE IN THIS WORLD UNTIL MEN ARE PREPARED TO KILL ONE ANOTHER IF IT IS NOT DONE. After that, there was nothing left for the seventh to say. So he wrote up, simply, UNASHAMED.

CUSINS   My good Machiavelli, I shall certainly write some-thing up on the wall; only, as I shall write it in Greek, you wont be able to read it. But as to your Armorer's faith, if I take my neck out of the noose of my own morality I am not going to put it into the noose of yours. I shall sell cannons to whom I please and refuse them to whom I please. So there!

UNDERSHAFT   From the moment when you become Andrew Undershaft, you will never do as you please again. Dont come here lusting for power, young man.

CUSINS   If power were my aim I should not come here for it. Y o u have no power.

UNDERSHAFT   None of my own, certainly.

CUSINS   I have more power than you, more will. You do not drive this place: it drives you. And what drives the place?

UNDERSHAFT [*enigmatically*]   A will of which I am a part.

BARBARA [*startled*]   Father! Do you know what you are saying; or are you laying a snare for my soul?[34]

CUSINS   Dont listen to his metaphysics, Barbara. The place is driven by the most rascally part of society, the money hunters, the pleasure hunters, the military promotion hunters; and he is their slave.

UNDERSHAFT   Not necessarily. Remember the Armorer's Faith. I will take an order from a good man as cheerfully as from a bad one. If you good people prefer preaching and shirking to buying my weapons and fighting the rascals, dont blame me. I can make cannons: I cannot make courage and conviction. Bah! You tire me, Euripides, with your morality mongering. Ask Barbara: s h e understands. [*He suddenly takes BARBARA's hands, and looks powerfully into her eyes.*] Tell him, my love, what power really means.

BARBARA [*hypnotized*]   Before I joined the Salvation Army, I was in my own power; and the consequence was that I never knew what to do with myself. When I joined it, I had not time enough for all the things I had to do.

UNDERSHAFT [*approvingly*]   Just so. And why was that, do you suppose?

BARBARA   Yesterday I should have said, because I was in the power of God. [*She resumes her self-possession, withdrawing her hands from his with a power equal to his own.*] But you came and shewed me that I was in the power of Bodger and Undershaft. Today I feel—oh! how can I put into words? Sarah: do you remember the earthquake at Cannes, when we were little children?—how little the surprise of the first shock mattered compared to the dread and horror of waiting for the second? That is how I feel in this place today. I stood on the rock I thought eternal; and without a word of warning it reeled and crumbled under me. I was safe with an infinite wisdom watching me, an army marching to Salvation with me; and in a moment, at a stroke of your pen in a cheque book, I stood alone; and the heavens were empty. That was the first shock of the earthquake: I am waiting for the second.

UNDERSHAFT   Come, come, my daughter! dont make too much of your little tinpot tragedy. What do we do here when we spend years of work and thought and thousands of pounds of solid cash on a new gun or an aerial battleship that turns out just a hairsbreadth wrong after all? Scrap it. Scrap it without wasting another hour or another pound on it. Well, you have made for yourself something that you call a morality or a religion or what not. It doesnt fit the facts. Well, scrap it. Scrap it and get one that does fit. That is what is wrong with the world at present. It scraps its obsolete steam engines and dynamos; but it wont scrap its old prejudices and its old moralities and its old religions and its old political constitutions. Whats the result? In machinery it does very well; but in morals and religion and politics it is working at a loss that brings it nearer bankruptcy every year. Dont persist in that folly. If your old religion broke down yesterday, get a newer and a better one for tomorrow.

BARBARA   Oh how gladly I would take a better one to my soul! But you offer me a worse one. [*Turning on him with sudden vehemence.*] Justify yourself: shew me some light through the darkness of this dreadful place, with its beautifully clean workshops, and respectable workmen, and model homes.

UNDERSHAFT   Cleanliness and respectability do not need justification, Barbara: they justify themselves. I see no darkness here, no dreadfulness. In your Salvation shelter I saw poverty, misery, cold and hunger. You gave them bread and treacle and dreams of heaven. I give from thirty shillings a week to twelve thousand a year. They find their own dreams; but I look after the drainage.

BARBARA   And their souls?

UNDERSHAFT   I save their souls just as I saved yours.

BARBARA [*revolted*]   Y o u saved my soul! What do you mean?

UNDERSHAFT   I fed you and clothed you and housed you. I took care that you should have money enough to live handsomely—more than enough; so that you could be wasteful, careless, generous. That saved your soul from the seven deadly sins.

BARBARA [*bewildered*]   The seven deadly sins!

UNDERSHAFT   Yes, the deadly seven. [*Counting on his fingers.*] Food, clothing, firing, rent, taxes, respectability and children. Nothing can lift those seven millstones from Man's neck but money; and the spirit cannot soar until the millstones are lifted. I lifted them from your spirit. I enabled Barbara to become Major Barbara; and I saved her from the crime of poverty.

CUSINS   Do you call poverty a crime?

UNDERSHAFT   The worst of crimes. All the other crimes are virtues beside it: all the other dishonors are chivalry itself by comparison. Poverty blights whole cities; spreads horrible pestilences; strikes dead the very souls of all who come within sight, sound or smell of it. What y o u call crime is nothing: a murder here and a theft there, a blow now and a curse then: what do they matter? they are only the accidents and illnesses of life: there are not fifty genuine professional criminals in London. But there are millions of poor people, abject people, dirty people, ill fed, ill clothed people. They poison us morally and physically: they kill the happiness of society: they force us to do away with our own liberties and to organize unnatural cruelties for fear they should rise against us and drag us down into their abyss. Only fools fear crime: we all fear poverty. Pah! [*turning on Barbara*] you talk of your half-saved ruffian in West Ham: you accuse me of dragging his soul back to perdition. Well, bring him to me here; and I will drag his soul back again to salvation for you. Not by words and dreams; but by thirty-eight shillings a week, a sound house in a handsome street, and a permanent job. In three weeks he will have a fancy waistcoat; in three months a tall hat and a chapel sitting;* before the end of the year he will shake hands with a duchess at a Primrose League† meeting, and join the Conservative Party.

BARBARA   And will he be the better for that?

UNDERSHAFT   You know he will. Dont be a hypocrite, Barbara. He will be better fed, better housed, better clothed, better behaved; and his children will be pounds heavier and bigger. That will be better than an American cloth‡ mattress in a shelter, chopping firewood, eating bread and treacle, and being forced to kneel down from time to time to thank heaven for it: knee drill, I think you call it. It is cheap work converting starving men with a Bible in one hand and a slice of bread in the other. I will undertake to convert West Ham to Mahometanism on the same terms. Try your hand on m y men: their souls are hungry because their bodies are full.

---

*Wealthier members of a congregation could pay to have a regular seat.

†Conservative organization founded in 1883; named for the presumed favorite flower of Benjamin Disraeli (see endnote 15).

‡Material waterproofed on one side.

BARBARA   And leave the east end to starve?

UNDERSHAFT [*his energetic tone dropping into one of bitter and brooding remembrance*]   *I* was an east ender. I moralized and starved until one day I swore that I would be a full-fed free man at all costs—that nothing should stop me except a bullet, neither reason nor morals nor the lives of other men. I said "Thou shalt starve ere I starve"; and with that word I became free and great. I was a dangerous man until I had my will: now I am a useful, beneficent, kindly person. That is the history of most self-made millionaires, I fancy. When it is the history of every Englishman we shall have an England worth living in.

LADY BRITOMART   Stop making speeches, Andrew. This is not the place for them.

UNDERSHAFT [*punctured*]   My dear: I have no other means of conveying my ideas.

LADY BRITOMART   Your ideas are nonsense. You got on because you were selfish and unscrupulous.

UNDERSHAFT   Not at all. I had the strongest scruples about poverty and starvation. Your moralists are quite unscrupulous about both: they make virtues of them. I had rather be a thief than a pauper. I had rather be a murderer than a slave. I dont want to be either; but if you force the alternative on me, then, by Heaven, I'll choose the braver and more moral one. I hate poverty and slavery worse than any other crimes whatsoever. And let me tell you this. Poverty and slavery have stood up for centuries to your sermons and leading articles: they will not stand up to my machine guns. Dont preach at them: dont reason with them. Kill them.

BARBARA   Killing. Is that your remedy for everything?

UNDERSHAFT   It is the final test of conviction, the only lever strong enough to overturn a social system, the only way of saying Must. Let six hundred and seventy fools loose in the street; and three policemen can scatter them. But huddle them together in a certain house in Westminster;* and let them go through certain ceremonies and call themselves certain names until at last they get the courage to kill; and your six hundred and seventy fools become a government. Your pious mob fills up ballot papers and imagines it is governing its masters; but the ballot paper that really governs is the paper that has a bullet wrapped up in it.

CUSINS   That is perhaps why, like most intelligent people, I never vote.

UNDERSHAFT   Vote! Bah! When you vote, you only change the names of the cabinet. When you shoot, you pull down governments, inaugurate new epochs, abolish old orders and set up new. Is that historically true, Mr. Learned Man, or is it not?

CUSINS   It is historically true. I loathe having to admit it. I repudiate your sentiments. I abhor your nature. I defy you in every possible way. Still, it is true. But it ought not to be true.

UNDERSHAFT   Ought, ought, ought, ought, ought! Are you going to spend your life saying ought, like the rest of our moralists? Turn your oughts into shalls, man. Come and make explosives with me. Whatever can blow men up can blow society up. The history of the world is the history of those who had courage enough to embrace this truth. Have you the courage to embrace it, Barbara?

LADY BRITOMART   Barbara, I positively forbid you to listen to your father's abominable wickedness. And you, Adolphus, ought to know better than to go about saying that wrong things are true. What does it matter whether they are true if they are wrong?

UNDERSHAFT   What does it matter whether they are wrong if they are true?

---

*That is, the House of Commons.

LADY BRITOMART [*rising*]   Children: come home instantly. Andrew: I am exceedingly sorry I allowed you to call on us. You are wickeder than ever. Come at once.

BARBARA [*shaking her head*]   It's no use running away from wicked people, mamma.

LADY BRITOMART   It is every use. It shews your disapprobation of them.

BARBARA   It does not save them.

LADY BRITOMART   I can see that you are going to disobey me. Sarah: are you coming home or are you not?

SARAH   I daresay it's very wicked of papa to make cannons; but I dont think I shall cut him on that account.

LOMAX [*pouring oil on the troubled waters*]   The fact is, you know, there is a certain amount of tosh about this notion of wickedness. It doesnt work. You must look at facts. Not that I would say a word in favor of anything wrong; but then, you see, all sorts of chaps are always doing all sorts of things; and we have to fit them in somehow, dont you know. What I mean is that you cant go cutting everybody; and thats about what it comes to. [*Their rapt attention to his eloquence makes him nervous.*] Perhaps I dont make myself clear.

LADY BRITOMART   You are lucidity itself, Charles. Because Andrew is successful and has plenty of money to give to Sarah, you will flatter him and encourage him in his wickedness.

LOMAX [*unruffled*]   Well, where the carcase is, there will the eagles be gathered, dont you know. [*To UNDERSHAFT.*] Eh? What?

UNDERSHAFT   Precisely. By the way, m a y I call you Charles?

LOMAX   Delighted. Cholly is the usual ticket.

UNDERSHAFT [*to LADY BRITOMART*]   Biddy—

LADY BRITOMART [*violently*]   Dont dare call me Biddy. Charles Lomax: you are a fool. Adolphus Cusins: you are a Jesuit. Stephen: you are a prig. Barbara: you are a lunatic. Andrew: you are a vulgar tradesman. Now you all know my opinion; and m y conscience is clear, at all events [*she sits down again with a vehemence that almost wrecks the chair*].

UNDERSHAFT   My dear: you are the incarnation of morality. [*She snorts.*] Your conscience is clear and your duty done when you have called everybody names. Come, Euripides! it is getting late; and we all want to get home. Make up your mind.

CUSINS   Understand this, you old demon—

LADY BRITOMART   Adolphus!

UNDERSHAFT   Let him alone, Biddy. Proceed, Euripides.

CUSINS   You have me in a horrible dilemma. I want Barbara.

UNDERSHAFT   Like all young men, you greatly exaggerate the difference between one young woman and another.

BARBARA   Quite true, Dolly.

CUSINS   I also want to avoid being a rascal.

UNDERSHAFT [*with biting contempt*]   You lust for personal righteousness, for self-approval, for what you call a good conscience, for what Barbara calls salvation, for what I call patronizing people who are not so lucky as yourself.

CUSINS   I do not: all the poet in me recoils from being a good man. But there are things in me that I must reckon with: pity—

UNDERSHAFT   Pity! The scavenger of misery.

CUSINS   Well, love.

UNDERSHAFT   I know. You love the needy and the outcast: you love the oppressed races, the negro, the Indian ryot,* the Pole, the Irishman. Do you love the Japanese? Do you love the Germans? Do you love the English?

CUSINS   No. Every true Englishman detests the English. We are the wickedest nation on earth; and our success is a moral horror.

UNDERSHAFT   That is what comes of your gospel of love, is it?

---

*Farmer; peasant.

CUSINS   May I not love even my father-in-law?

UNDERSHAFT   Who wants your love, man? By what right do you take the liberty of offering it to me? I will have your due heed and respect, or I will kill you. But your love. Damn your impertinence!

CUSINS [grinning]   I may not be able to control my affections, Mac.

UNDERSHAFT   You are fencing, Euripides. You are weakening: your grip is slipping. Come! try your last weapon. Pity and love have broken in your hand: forgiveness is still left.

CUSINS   No: forgiveness is a beggar's refuge. I am with you there: we must pay our debts.

UNDERSHAFT   Well said. Come! you will suit me. Remember the words of Plato.

CUSINS [starting]   Plato! Y o u dare quote Plato to m e!

UNDERSHAFT   Plato says, my friend, that society cannot be saved until either the Professors of Greek take to making gunpowder, or else the makers of gunpowder become Professors of Greek.*

CUSINS   Oh, tempter, cunning tempter!

UNDERSHAFT   Come! choose, man, choose.

CUSINS   But perhaps Barbara will not marry me if I make the wrong choice.

BARBARA   Perhaps not.

CUSINS [desperately perplexed]   You hear!

BARBARA   Father: do you love nobody?

UNDERSHAFT   I love my best friend.

LADY BRITOMART   And who is that, pray?

UNDERSHAFT   My bravest enemy. That is the man who keeps me up to the mark.

---

*Allusion to book 5 of Plato's *Republic* (fifth century B.C.), which asserts that an ideal society cannot be realized until philosophers become kings or kings become philosophers—that is, until "political greatness and wisdom meet in one."

CUSINS   You know, the creature is really a sort of poet in his way. Suppose he is a great man, after all!

UNDERSHAFT   Suppose you stop talking and make up your mind, my young friend.

CUSINS   But you are driving me against my nature. I hate war.

UNDERSHAFT   Hatred is the coward's revenge for being intimidated. Dare you make war on war? Here are the means: my friend Mr. Lomax is sitting on them.

LOMAX [springing up]   Oh I say! You dont mean that this thing is loaded, do you? My ownest: come off it.

SARAH [sitting placidly on the shell]   If I am to be blown up, the more thoroughly it is done the better. Dont fuss, Cholly.

LOMAX [to UNDERSHAFT, strongly remonstrant]   Your own daughter, you know.

UNDERSHAFT   So I see. [To CUSINS.] Well, my friend, may we expect you here at six tomorrow morning?

CUSINS [firmly]   Not on any account. I will see the whole establishment blown up with its own dynamite before I will get up at five. My hours are healthy, rational hours: eleven to five.

UNDERSHAFT   Come when you please: before a week you will come at six and stay until I turn you out for the sake of your health. [Calling.] Bilton! [He turns to LADY BRITOMART, who rises.] My dear: let us leave these two young people to themselves for a moment. [BILTON comes from the shed.] I am going to take you through the gun cotton shed.

BILTON [barring the way]   You cant take anything explosive in here, sir.

LADY BRITOMART   What do you mean? Are you alluding to me?

BILTON [unmoved]   No, maam. Mr. Undershaft has the other gentleman's matches in his pocket.

LADY BRITOMART [abruptly]   Oh! I beg your pardon. [She goes into the shed.]

UNDERSHAFT   Quite right, Bilton, quite right: here you are.

[*He gives BILTON the box of matches.*] Come, Stephen. Come, Charles. Bring Sarah. [*He passes into the shed.*]

BILTON opens the box and deliberately drops the matches into the fire-bucket.

LOMAX   Oh I say! [*BILTON stolidly hands him the empty box.*] Infernal nonsense! Pure scientific ignorance! [*He goes in.*]

SARAH   Am I all right, Bilton?

BILTON   Youll have to put on list slippers,* miss: thats all. Weve got em inside. [*She goes in.*]

STEPHEN [*very seriously to CUSINS*]   Dolly, old fellow, think. Think before you decide. Do you feel that you are a sufficiently practical man? It is a huge undertaking, an enormous responsibility. All this mass of business will be Greek to you.

CUSINS   Oh, I think it will be much less difficult than Greek.

STEPHEN   Well, I just want to say this before I leave you to yourselves. Dont let anything I have said about right and wrong prejudice you against this great chance in life. I have satisfied myself that the business is one of the highest character and a credit to our country. [*Emotionally.*] I am very proud of my father. I— [*Unable to proceed, he presses CUSINS' hand and goes hastily into the shed, followed by BILTON.*]

BARBARA and CUSINS, left alone together, look at one another silently.

CUSINS   Barbara: I am going to accept this offer.

BARBARA   I thought you would.

CUSINS   You understand, dont you, that I had to decide without consulting you. If I had thrown the burden of the choice on you, you would sooner or later have despised me for it.

BARBARA   Yes: I did not want you to sell your soul for me any more than for this inheritance.

CUSINS   It is not the sale of my soul that troubles me: I have sold it too often to care about that. I have sold it for a pro-

---

*Made from list, a strong material that borders a weaker cloth.

fessorship. I have sold it for an income. I have sold it to escape being imprisoned for refusing to pay taxes for hangmen's ropes and unjust wars and things that I abhor. What is all human conduct but the daily and hourly sale of our souls for trifles? What I am now selling it for is neither money nor position nor comfort, but for reality and for power.

BARBARA   You know that you will have no power, and that he has none.

CUSINS   I know. It is not for myself alone. I want to make power for the world.

BARBARA   I want to make power for the world too; but it must be spiritual power.

CUSINS   I think all power is spiritual: these cannons will not go off by themselves. I have tried to make spiritual power by teaching Greek. But the world can never be really touched by a dead language and a dead civilization. The people must have power; and the people cannot have Greek. Now the power that is made here can be wielded by all men.

BARBARA   Power to burn women's houses down and kill their sons and tear their husbands to pieces.

CUSINS   You cannot have power for good without having power for evil too. Even mother's milk nourishes murderers as well as heroes. This power which only tears men's bodies to pieces has never been so horribly abused as the intellectual power, the imaginative power, the poetic, religious power than can enslave men's souls. As a teacher of Greek I gave the intellectual man weapons against the common man. I now want to give the common man weapons against the intellectual man. I love the common people. I want to arm them against the lawyer, the doctor, the priest, the literary man, the professor, the artist, and the politician, who, once in authority, are the most dangerous, disastrous, and tyrannical of all the fools, rascals, and impostors. I want a democratic power strong enough to force the intellectual oligarchy to use its genius for the general good or else perish.

BARBARA   Is there no higher power than that [*pointing to the shell*]?

CUSINS   Yes: but that power can destroy the higher powers just as a tiger can destroy a man: therefore man must master that power first. I admitted this when the Turks and Greeks were last at war. My best pupil went out to fight for Hellas. My parting gift to him was not a copy of Plato's Republic, but a revolver and a hundred Undershaft cartridges. The blood of every Turk he shot—if he shot any—is on my head as well as on Undershaft's. That act committed me to this place for ever. Your father's challenge has beaten me. Dare I make war on war? I dare. I must. I will. And now, is it all over between us?

BARBARA   [*touched by his evident dread of her answer*] Silly baby Dolly! How could it be?

CUSINS   [*overjoyed*]   Then you—you—you— Oh for my drum! [*He flourishes imaginary drumsticks.*]

BARBARA   [*angered by his levity*]   Take care, Dolly, take care. Oh, if only I could get away from you and from father and from it all! if I could have the wings of a dove and fly away to heaven!

CUSINS   And leave m e!

BARBARA   Yes, you, and all the other naughty mischievous children of men. But I cant. I was happy in the Salvation Army for a moment. I escaped from the world into a paradise of enthusiasm and prayer and soul saving; but the moment our money ran short, it all came back to Bodger: it was he who saved our people: he, and the Prince of Darkness, my papa. Undershaft and Bodger: their hands stretch everywhere: when we feed a starving fellow creature, it is with their bread, because there is no other bread; when we tend the sick, it is in the hospitals they endow; if we turn from the churches they build, we must kneel on the stones of the streets they pave. As long as that lasts, there is no getting away from them. Turning our backs on Bodger and Undershaft is turning our backs on life.

CUSINS   I thought you were determined to turn your back on the wicked side of life.

BARBARA   There is no wicked side: life is all one. And I never wanted to shirk my share in whatever evil must be endured, whether it be sin or suffering. I wish I could cure you of middle-class ideas, Dolly.

CUSINS [*gasping*]   Middle cl——! A snub! A social snub to m e! from the daughter of a foundling.

BARBARA   That is why I have no class, Dolly: I come straight out of the heart of the whole people. If I were middle-class I should turn my back on my father's business; and we should both live in an artistic drawingroom, with you reading the reviews in one corner, and I in the other at the piano, playing Schumann:* both very superior persons, and neither of us a bit of use. Sooner than that, I would sweep out the guncotton shed, or be one of Bodger's barmaids. Do you know what would have happened if you had refused papa's offer?

CUSINS   I wonder!

BARBARA   I should have given you up and married the man who accepted it. After all, my dear old mother has more sense than any of you. I felt like her when I saw this place—felt that I must have it—that never, never, never could I let it go; only she thought it was the houses and the kitchen ranges and the linen and china, when it was really all the human souls to be saved: not weak souls in starved bodies, crying with gratitude for a scrap of bread and treacle, but fullfed, quarrelsome, snobbish, uppish creatures, all standing on their little rights and dignities, and thinking that my father ought to be greatly obliged to them for making so much money for him—and so

---

*Robert Schumann (1810–1856), German Romantic composer renowned for his piano compositions.

he ought. That is where salvation is really wanted. My father shall never throw it in my teeth again that my converts were bribed with bread. [*She is transfigured.*] I have got rid of the bribe of bread. I have got rid of the bribe of heaven. Let God's work be done for its own sake: the work he had to create us to do because it cannot be done except by living men and women. When I die, let him be in my debt, not I in his; and let me forgive him as becomes a woman of my rank.

CUSINS   Then the way of life lies through the factory of death?

BARBARA   Yes, through the raising of hell to heaven and of man to God, through the unveiling of an eternal light in the Valley of The Shadow. [*Seizing him with both hands.*] Oh, did you think my courage would never come back? did you believe that I was a deserter? that I, who have stood in the streets, and taken my people to my heart, and talked of the holiest and greatest things with them, could ever turn back and chatter foolishly to fashionable people about nothing in a drawingroom? Never, never, never, never: Major Barbara will die with the colors. Oh! and I have my dear little Dolly boy still; and he has found me my place and my work. Glory Hallelujah! [*She kisses him.*]

CUSINS   My dearest: consider my delicate health. I cannot stand as much happiness as you can.

BARBARA   Yes: it is not easy work being in love with me, is it? But it's good for you. [*She runs to the shed, and calls, childlike*] Mamma! Mamma! [*BILTON comes out of the shed, followed by UNDERSHAFT.*] I want Mamma.

UNDERSHAFT   She is taking off her list slippers, dear. [*He passes on to CUSINS.*] Well? What does she say?

CUSINS   She has gone right up into the skies.

LADY BRITOMART [*coming from the shed and stopping on the steps, obstructing SARAH, who follows with LOMAX. BARBARA clutches like a baby at her mother's skirt.*] Barbara: when will you learn to be independent and to act and think for yourself? I

know as well as possible what that cry of "Mamma, Mamma,"
means. Always running to me!

SARAH [*touching LADY BRITOMART's ribs with her finger tips and
imitating a bicycle horn*] Pip! pip!

LADY BRITOMART [*highly indignant*]   How dare you say Pip!
pip! to me, Sarah? You are both very naughty children. What
do you want, Barbara?

BARBARA   I want a house in the village to live in with Dolly.
[*Dragging at the skirt.*] Come and tell me which one to take.

UNDERSHAFT [*to CUSINS*]   Six o'clock tomorrow morning,
my young friend.

THE END

THE DOCTOR'S
DILEMMA

PREFACE ON DOCTORS

IT IS NOT the fault of our doctors that the medical service of the community, as at present provided for, is a murderous absurdity. That any sane nation, having observed that you could provide for the supply of bread by giving bakers a pecuniary interest in baking for you, should go on to give a surgeon a pecuniary interest in cutting off your leg, is enough to make one despair of political humanity. But that is precisely what we have done. And the more appalling the mutilation, the more the mutilator is paid. He who corrects the ingrowing toe-nail receives a few shillings: he who cuts your inside out receives hundreds of guineas, except when he does it to a poor person for practice.

Scandalized voices murmur that these operations are necessary. They may be. It may also be necessary to hang a man or pull down a house. But we take good care not to make the hangman and the housebreaker the judges of that. If we did, no man's neck would be safe and no man's house stable. But we do make the doctor the judge, and fine him anything from sixpence to several hundred guineas if he decides in our favor. I cannot knock my shins severely without forcing on some surgeon the difficult question, "Could I not make a better use of a pocketful of guineas than this man is making of his leg? Could he not write as well—or even better— on one leg than on two? And the guineas would make all the difference in the world to me just now. My wife—my pretty ones—the leg may mortify—it is always safer to operate—he will be well in a fortnight—artificial legs are now so well made that they are really better than natural ones—evolution is towards motors and leglessness, &c., &c., &c."

Now there is no calculation that an engineer can make as to the behavior of a girder under a strain, or an astronomer as to the recurrence of a comet, more certain than the calculation that under such circumstances we shall be dismembered unnecessarily in all directions by surgeons who believe the operations to be necessary solely because they want to perform them. The process metaphorically called bleeding the rich man is performed not only metaphorically but literally every day by surgeons who are quite as honest as most of us. After all, what harm is there in it? The surgeon need not take off the rich man's (or woman's) leg or arm: he can remove the appendix or the uvula,* and leave the patient none the worse after a fortnight or so in bed, whilst the nurse, the general practitioner, the apothecary, and the surgeon will be the better.

DOUBTFUL CHARACTER BORNE BY THE MEDICAL PROFESSION

Again I hear the voices indignantly muttering old phrases about the high character of a noble profession and the honor and conscience of its members. I must reply that the medical profession has not a high character: it has an infamous character. I do not know a single thoughtful and well-informed person who does not feel that the tragedy of illness at present is that it delivers you helplessly into the hands of a profession which you deeply mistrust, because it not only advocates and practises the most revolting cruelties in the pursuit of knowledge, and justifies them on grounds which would equally justify practising the same cruelties on yourself or your children, or burning down London to test a patent fire extinguisher, but, when it has shocked the public, tries to reassure it with lies of breath-bereaving brazenness. That is the character the medical profession has got just now. It may be deserved or it may not: there it is at all events, and the doctors who

---

*Pendant fleshy lobe at the back of the mouth.

have not realized this are living in a fool's paradise. As to the honor
and conscience of doctors, they have as much as any other class of
men, no more and no less. And what other men dare pretend to
be impartial where they have a strong pecuniary interest on one
side? Nobody supposes that doctors are less virtuous than judges;
but a judge whose salary and reputation depended on whether the
verdict was for plaintiff or defendant, prosecutor or prisoner,
would be as little trusted as a general in the pay of the enemy. To
offer me a doctor as my judge, and then weight his decision with
a bribe of a large sum of money and a virtual guarantee that if he
makes a mistake it can never be proved against him, is to go wildly
beyond the ascertained strain which human nature will bear. It is
simply unscientific to allege or believe that doctors do not under
existing circumstances perform unnecessary operations and manufacture and prolong lucrative illnesses. The only ones who can
claim to be above suspicion are those who are so much sought
after that their cured patients are immediately replaced by fresh
ones. And there is this curious psychological fact to be remembered: a serious illness or a death advertizes the doctor exactly as
a hanging advertizes the barrister who defended the person
hanged. Suppose, for example, a royal personage gets something
wrong with his throat, or has a pain in his inside. If a doctor effects
some trumpery cure with a wet compress or a peppermint
lozenge nobody takes the least notice of him. But if he operates on
the throat and kills the patient, or extirpates an internal organ and
keeps the whole nation palpitating for days whilst the patient hov-
ers in pain and fever between life and death, his fortune is made:
every rich man who omits to call him in when the same symptoms
appear in his household is held not to have done his utmost duty
to the patient. The wonder is that there is a king or queen left alive
in Europe.

DOCTOR'S CONSCIENCES

There is another difficulty in trusting to the honor and conscience of a doctor. Doctors are just like other Englishmen: most of them have no honor and no conscience: what they commonly mistake for these is sentimentality and an intense dread of doing anything that everybody else does not do, or omitting to do anything that everybody else does. This of course does amount to a sort of working or rule-of-thumb conscience; but it means that you will do anything, good or bad, provided you get enough people to keep you in countenance by doing it also. It is the sort of conscience that makes it possible to keep order on a pirate ship, or in a troop of brigands. It may be said that in the last analysis there is no other sort of honor or conscience in existence—that the assent of the majority is the only sanction known to ethics. No doubt this holds good in political practice. If mankind knew the facts, and agreed with the doctors, then the doctors would be in the right; and any person who thought otherwise would be a lunatic. But mankind does not agree, and does not know the facts. All that can be said for medical popularity is that until there is a practicable alternative to blind trust in the doctor, the truth about the doctor is so terrible that we dare not face it. Molière saw through the doctors; but he had to call them in just the same. Napoleon had no illusions about them; but he had to die under their treatment just as much as the most credulous ignoramus that ever paid sixpence for a bottle of strong medicine. In this predicament most people, to save themselves from unbearable mistrust and misery, or from being driven by their conscience into actual conflict with the law, fall back on the old rule that if you cannot have what you believe in you must believe in what you have. When your child is ill or your wife dying, and you happen to be very fond of them, or even when, if you are not fond of them, you are human enough to forget every personal grudge before the spectacle of a fellow creature in pain or peril, what you want is comfort, reassurance, something to clutch at, were it but a straw. This the doctor brings you. You have a wildly urgent feeling that something must be done; and the doctor does something. Sometimes what he does kills the patient; but you do not know that; and the doctor assures you that all that human skill could do has been done. And nobody has the brutality to say to the newly bereft father, mother, husband, wife, brother, or sister, "You have killed your lost darling by your credulity."

THE PECULIAR PEOPLE*

Besides, the calling in of the doctor is now compulsory except in cases where the patient is an adult and not too ill to decide the steps to be taken. We are subject to prosecution for manslaughter or for criminal neglect if the patient dies without the consolations of the medical profession. This menace is kept before the public by the Peculiar People. The Peculiars, as they are called, have gained their name by believing that the Bible is infallible, and taking their belief quite seriously. The Bible is very clear as to the treatment of illness. The Epistle of James, chapter v., contains the following explicit directions:

> 14. Is any sick among you? let him call for the elders of the Church; and let them pray over him, anointing him with oil in the name of the Lord:
> 15. And the prayer of faith shall save the sick, and the Lord shall raise him up; and if he have committed sins, they shall be forgiven him.

The Peculiars obey these instructions and dispense with doctors. They are therefore prosecuted for manslaughter when their children die.

---

*Christian sect (founded 1838) that rejected medical treatment on biblical grounds.

When I was a young man, the Peculiars were usually acquitted. The prosecution broke down when the doctor in the witness box was asked whether, if the child had had medical attendance, it would have lived. It was, of course, impossible for any man of sense and honor to assume divine omniscience by answering this in the affirmative, or indeed pretending to be able to answer it at all. And on this the judge had to instruct the jury that they must acquit the prisoner. Thus a judge with a keen sense of law (a very rare phenomenon on the Bench, by the way) was spared the possibility of having to sentence one prisoner (under the Blasphemy Laws) for questioning the authority of Scripture, and another for ignorantly and superstitiously accepting it as a guide to conduct. To-day all this is changed. The doctor never hesitates to claim divine omniscience, nor to clamor for laws to punish any scepticism on the part of laymen. A modern doctor thinks nothing of signing the death certificate of one of his own diphtheria patients, and then going into the witness box and swearing a Peculiar into prison for six months by assuring the jury, on oath, that if the prisoner's child, dead of diphtheria, had been placed under his treatment instead of that of St. James, it would not have died. And he does so not only with impunity, but with public applause, though the logical course would be to prosecute him either for the murder of his own patient or for perjury in the case of St. James. Yet no barrister, apparently, dreams of asking for the statistics of the relative case-mortality in diphtheria among the Peculiars and among the believers in doctors, on which alone any valid opinion could be founded. The barrister is as superstitious as the doctor is infatuated; and the Peculiar goes unpitied to his cell, though nothing whatever has been proved except that his child does without the interference of a doctor as effectually as any of the hundreds of children who die every day of the same diseases in the doctor's care.

RECOIL OF THE DOGMA OF MEDICAL INFALLIBILITY ON THE DOCTOR

On the other hand, when the doctor is in the dock, or is the defendant in an action for malpractice, he has to struggle against the inevitable result of his former pretences to infinite knowledge and unerring skill. He has taught the jury and the judge, and even his own counsel, to believe that every doctor can, with a glance at the tongue, a touch on the pulse, and a reading of the clinical thermometer, diagnose with absolute certainty a patient's complaint, also that on dissecting a dead body he can infallibly put his finger on the cause of death, and, in cases where poisoning is suspected, the nature of the poison used. Now all this supposed exactness and infallibility is imaginary; and to treat a doctor as if his mistakes were necessarily malicious or corrupt malpractices (an inevitable deduction from the postulate that the doctor, being omniscient, cannot make mistakes) is as unjust as to blame the nearest apothecary for not being prepared to supply you with sixpenny-worth of the elixir of life, or the nearest motor garage for not having perpetual motion on sale in gallon tins. But if apothecaries and motor car makers habitually advertized elixir of life and perpetual motion, and succeeded in creating a strong general belief that they could supply it, they would find themselves in an awkward position if they were indicted for allowing a customer to die, or for burning a chauffeur by putting petrol into his car. That is the predicament the doctor finds himself in when he has to defend himself against a charge of malpractice by a plea of ignorance and fallibility. His plea is received with flat credulity; and he gets little sympathy, even from laymen who know, because he has brought the incredulity on himself. If he escapes, he can only do so by opening the eyes of the jury to the facts that medical science is as yet very imperfectly differentiated from common curemongering witchcraft; that diagnosis, though it means in many instances (including even the identification of pathogenic* bacilli under the microscope) only a choice among terms so loose that they would not be accepted as definitions in any really exact science, is, even at that, an uncertain and difficult matter on which doctors often differ; and that the very best medical opinion and treatment varies widely from doctor to doctor, one practitioner prescribing six or seven scheduled poisons† for so familiar a disease as enteric fever‡ where another will not tolerate drugs at all; one starving a patient whom another would stuff; one urging an operation which another would regard as unnecessary and dangerous; one giving alcohol and meat which another would sternly forbid, &c., &c., &c.: all these discrepancies arising not between the opinion of good doctors and bad ones (the medical contention is, of course, that a bad doctor is an impossibility), but between practitioners of equal eminence and authority. Usually it is impossible to persuade the jury that these facts are facts. Juries seldom notice facts; and they have been taught to regard any doubts of the omniscience and omnipotence of doctors as blasphemy. Even the fact that doctors themselves die of the very diseases they profess to cure passes unnoticed. We do not shoot out our lips and shake our heads, saying, "They save others: themselves they cannot save": their reputation stands, like an African king's palace, on a foundation of dead bodies; and the result is that the verdict goes against the defendant when the defendant is a doctor accused of malpractice.

Fortunately for the doctors, they very seldom find themselves in this position, because it is so difficult to prove anything against them. The only evidence that can decide a case of malpractice is expert evidence: that is, the evidence of other doctors; and every doctor will allow a colleague to decimate a whole countryside sooner than violate the bond of professional etiquet by giving him

---

*Disease-causing.

†Dangerous drugs, legally obtained only with a doctor's prescription.

‡Intestinal disease.

away. It is the nurse who gives the doctor away in private, because every nurse has some particular doctor whom she likes; and she usually assures her patients that all the others are disastrous noodles, and soothes the tedium of the sick-bed by gossip about their blunders. She will even give a doctor away for the sake of making the patient believe that she knows more than the doctor. But she dare not, for her livelihood, give the doctor away in public. And the doctors stand by one another at all costs. Now and then some doctor in an unassailable position, like the late Sir William Gull,* will go into the witness box and say what he really thinks about the way a patient has been treated; but such behavior is considered little short of infamous by his colleagues.

WHY DOCTORS DO NOT DIFFER

The truth is, there would never be any public agreement among doctors if they did not agree to agree on the main point of the doctor being always in the right. Yet the two guinea man never thinks that the five shilling man is right: if he did, he would be understood as confessing to an overcharge of £1:17s.; and on the same ground the five shilling man cannot encourage the notion that the owner of the sixpenny surgery† round the corner is quite up to his mark. Thus even the layman has to be taught that infallibility is not quite infallible, because there are two qualities of it to be had at two prices.

But there is no agreement even in the same rank at the same price. During the first great epidemic of influenza towards the end of the nineteenth century a London evening paper sent round a journalist-patient to all the great consultants‡ of that day, and published their advice and prescriptions; a proceeding passionately denounced by the medical papers as a breach of confidence of

---

*Physician who died in 1890.
†Low-cost doctor's office.
‡Prominent doctors.

these eminent physicians. The case was the same; but the prescriptions were different, and so was the advice. Now a doctor cannot think his own treatment right and at the same time think his colleague right in prescribing a different treatment when the patient is the same. Anyone who has ever known doctors well enough to hear medical shop talked without reserve knows that they are full of stories about each other's blunders and errors, and that the theory of their omniscience and omnipotence no more holds good among themselves than it did with Molière and Napoleon. But for this very reason no doctor dare accuse another of malpractice. He is not sure enough of his own opinion to ruin another man by it. He knows that if such conduct were tolerated in his profession no doctor's livelihood or reputation would be worth a year's purchase. I do not blame him: I should do the same myself. But the effect of this state of things is to make the medical profession a conspiracy to hide its own shortcomings. No doubt the same may be said of all professions. They are all conspiracies against the laity; and I do not suggest that the medical conspiracy is either better or worse than the military conspiracy, the legal conspiracy, the sacerdotal conspiracy, the pedagogic conspiracy, the royal and aristocratic conspiracy, the literary and artistic conspiracy, and the innumerable industrial, commercial, and financial conspiracies, from the trade unions to the great exchanges,* which make up the huge conflict which we call society. But it is less suspected. The Radicals† who used to advocate, as an indispensable preliminary to social reform, the strangling of the last king with the entrails of the last priest,‡ substituted compulsory vaccination for compulsory baptism without a murmur.

---

*Big business corporations; also, the Stock Exchange.

†Extremist members of the left wing.

‡Line variously attributed to French philosopher Denis Diderot (1713–1784) and eighteenth-century revolutionary Jean Messelier.

THE CRAZE FOR OPERATIONS

Thus everything is on the side of the doctor. When men die of disease they are said to die from natural causes. When they recover (and they mostly do) the doctor gets the credit of curing them. In surgery all operations are recorded as successful if the patient can be got out of the hospital or nursing home alive, though the subsequent history of the case may be such as would make an honest surgeon vow never to recommend or perform the operation again. The large range of operations which consist of amputating limbs and extirpating organs admits of no direct verification of their necessity. There is a fashion in operations as there is in sleeves and skirts: the triumph of some surgeon who has at last found out how to make a once desperate operation fairly safe is usually followed by a rage for that operation not only among the doctors, but actually among their patients. There are men and women whom the operating table seems to fascinate: half-alive people who through vanity, or hypochondria, or a craving to be the constant objects of anxious attention or what not, lose such feeble sense as they ever had of the value of their own organs and limbs. They seem to care as little for mutilation as lobsters or lizards, which at least have the excuse that they grow new claws and new tails if they lose the old ones. Whilst this book was being prepared for the press a case was tried in the Courts, of a man who sued a railway company for damages because a train had run over him and amputated both his legs. He lost his case because it was proved that he had deliberately contrived the occurrence himself for the sake of getting an idler's pension at the expense of the railway company, being too dull to realize how much more he had to lose than to gain by the bargain even if he had won his case and received damages above his utmost hopes.

This amazing case makes it possible to say, with some prospect of being believed, that there is in the classes who can afford to pay for fashionable operations a sprinkling of persons so incapable of

appreciating the relative importance of preserving their bodily in-
tegrity (including the capacity for parentage) and the pleasure of
talking about themselves and hearing themselves talked about as
the heroes and heroines of sensational operations, that they tempt
surgeons to operate on them not only with huge fees, but with
personal solicitation. Now it cannot be too often repeated that
when an operation is once performed, nobody can ever prove that
it was unnecessary. If I refuse to allow my leg to be amputated, its
mortification and my death may prove that I was wrong; but if I
let the leg go, nobody can ever prove that it would not have mor-
tified had I been obstinate. Operation is therefore the safe side for
the surgeon as well as the lucrative side. The result is that we hear
of "conservative surgeons" as a distinct class of practitioners who
make it a rule not to operate if they can possibly help it, and who
are sought after by the people who have vitality enough to regard
an operation as a last resort. But no surgeon is bound to take the
conservative view. If he believes that an organ is at best a useless
survival, and that if he extirpates it the patient will be well and
none the worse in a fortnight, whereas to await the natural cure
would mean a month's illness, then he is clearly justified in rec-
ommending the operation even if the cure without operation is as
certain as anything of the kind ever can be. Thus the conservative
surgeon and the radical or extirpatory surgeon may both be right
as far as the ultimate cure is concerned; so that their consciences
do not help them out of their differences.

CREDULITY AND CHLOROFORM

There is no harder scientific fact in the world than the fact that belief can be produced in practically unlimited quantity and intensity, without observation or reasoning, and even in defiance of
both, by the simple desire to believe founded on a strong interest
in believing. Everybody recognizes this in the case of the amatory
infatuations of the adolescents who see angels and heroes in obviously (to others) commonplace and even objectionable maidens

and youths. But it holds good over the entire field of human activity. The hardest-headed materialist will become a consulter of table-rappers and slate-writers* if he loses a child or a wife so beloved that the desire to revive and communicate with them becomes irresistible. The cobbler believes that there is nothing like leather. The Imperialist who regards the conquest of England by a foreign power as the worst of political misfortunes believes that the conquest of a foreign power by England would be a boon to the conquered. Doctors are no more proof against such illusions than other men. Can anyone then doubt that under existing conditions a great deal of unnecessary and mischievous operating is bound to go on, and that patients are encouraged to imagine that modern surgery and anesthesia have made operations much less serious matters than they really are? When doctors write or speak to the public about operations, they imply, and often say in so many words, that chloroform has made surgery painless. People who have been operated on know better. The patient does not feel the knife, and the operation is therefore enormously facilitated for the surgeon; but the patient pays for the anesthesia with hours of wretched sickness; and when that is over there is the pain of the wound made by the surgeon, which has to heal like any other wound. This is why operating surgeons, who are usually out of the house with their fee in their pockets before the patient has recovered consciousness, and who therefore see nothing of the suffering witnessed by the general practitioner and the nurse, occasionally talk of operations very much as the hangman in Barnaby Rudge talked of executions, as if being operated on were a luxury in sensation as well as in price.

MEDICAL POVERTY

To make matters worse, doctors are hideously poor. The Irish gentleman doctor of my boyhood, who took nothing less than a

---

*Spiritualists who conduct séances to contact the dead.

guinea, though he might pay you four visits for it, seems to have no equivalent nowadays in English society. Better be a railway porter than an ordinary English general practitioner. A railway porter has from eighteen to twenty-three shillings a week from the Company merely as a retainer; and his additional fees from the public, if we leave the third-class two-penny tip out of account (and I am by no means sure that even this reservation need be made), are equivalent to doctor's fees in the case of second-class passengers, and double doctor's fees in the case of first. Any class of educated men thus treated tends to become a brigand class, and doctors are no exception to the rule. They are offered disgraceful prices for advice and medicine. Their patients are for the most part so poor and so ignorant that good advice would be resented as impracticable and wounding. When you are so poor that you cannot afford to refuse eighteenpence from a man who is too poor to pay you any more, it is useless to tell him that what he or his sick child needs is not medicine, but more leisure, better clothes, better food, and a better drained and ventilated house. It is kinder to give him a bottle of something almost as cheap as water, and tell him to come again with another eighteenpence if it does not cure him. When you have done that over and over again every day for a week, how much scientific conscience have you left? If you are weak-minded enough to cling desperately to your eighteenpence as denoting a certain social superiority to the sixpenny doctor, you will be miserably poor all your life; whilst the sixpenny doctor, with his low prices and quick turnover of patients, visibly makes much more than you do and kills no more people.

A doctor's character can no more stand out against such conditions than the lungs of his patients can stand out against bad ventilation. The only way in which he can preserve his self-respect is by forgetting all he ever learnt of science, and clinging to such help as he can give without cost merely by being less ignorant and more accustomed to sick-beds than his patients. Finally, he acquires a certain skill at nursing cases under poverty-stricken do-

mestic conditions, just as women who have been trained as domestic servants in some huge institution with lifts, vacuum clean-
ers, electric lighting, steam heating, and machinery that turns the
kitchen into a laboratory and engine house combined, manage,
when they are sent out into the world to drudge as general servants, to pick up their business in a new way, learning the slat-
ternly habits and wretched makeshifts of homes where even
bundles of kindling wood are luxuries to be anxiously econo-
mized.

THE SUCCESSFUL DOCTOR

The doctor whose success blinds public opinion to medical
poverty is almost as completely demoralized. His promotion
means that his practice becomes more and more confined to the
idle rich. The proper advice for most of their ailments is typified
in Abernathy's* "Live on sixpence a day and earn it." But here, as
at the other end of the scale, the right advice is neither agreeable
nor practicable. And every hypochondriacal rich lady or gentleman who can be persuaded that he or she is a lifelong invalid
means anything from fifty to five hundred pounds a year for the
doctor. Operations enable a surgeon to earn similar sums in a couple of hours; and if the surgeon also keeps a nursing home, he may
make considerable profits at the same time by running what is the
most expensive kind of hotel. These gains are so great that they
undo much of the moral advantage which the absence of grinding
pecuniary anxiety gives the rich doctor over the poor one. It is
true that the temptation to prescribe a sham treatment because
the real treatment is too dear for either patient or doctor does not
exist for the rich doctor. He always has plenty of genuine cases
which can afford genuine treatment; and these provide him with
enough sincere scientific professional work to save him from the

---

*John Abernathy (1764–1831), English surgeon renowned for his popular lec-
tures.

ignorance, obsolescence, and atrophy of scientific conscience into which his poorer colleagues sink. But on the other hand his expenses are enormous. Even as a bachelor, he must, at London west end rates, make over a thousand a year before he can afford even to insure his life. His house, his servants, and his equipage (or autopage)[1] must be on the scale to which his patients are accustomed, though a couple of rooms with a camp bed in one of them might satisfy his own requirements. Above all, the income which provides for these outgoings stops the moment he himself stops working. Unlike the man of business, whose managers, clerks, warehousemen and laborers keep his business going whilst he is in bed or in his club, the doctor cannot earn a farthing by deputy. Though he is exceptionally exposed to infection, and has to face all weathers at all hours of the night and day, often not enjoying a complete night's rest for a week, the money stops coming in the moment he stops going out; and therefore illness has special terrors for him, and success no certain permanence. He dare not stop making hay while the sun shines; for it may set at any time. Men do not resist pressure of this intensity. When they come under it as doctors they pay unnecessary visits; they write prescriptions that are as absurd as the rub of chalk with which an Irish tailor once charmed away a wart from my father's finger; they conspire with surgeons to promote operations; they nurse the delusions of the *malade imaginaire** (who is always really ill because, as there is no such thing as perfect health, nobody is ever really well); they exploit human folly, vanity, and fear of death as ruthlessly as their own health, strength, and patience are exploited by selfish hypochondriacs. They must do all these things or else run pecuniary risks that no man can fairly be asked to run. And the healthier the world becomes, the more they are compelled to live by imposture and the less by that really helpful activity of which all doctors get enough to preserve them from utter corruption. For

---

*Hypochondriac (French).

even the most hardened humbug who ever prescribed ether tonics to ladies whose need for tonics is of precisely the same character as the need of poorer women for a glass of gin, has to help a
mother through child-bearing often enough to feel that he is not
living wholly in vain.

THE PSYCHOLOGY OF SELF-RESPECT IN SURGEONS

The surgeon, though often more unscrupulous than the general
practitioner, retains his self-respect more easily. The human conscience can subsist on very questionable food. No man who is occupied in doing a very difficult thing, and doing it very well, ever
loses his self-respect. The shirk, the duffer,* the malingerer, the
coward, the weakling, may be put out of countenance by his own
failures and frauds; but the man who does evil skilfully, energetically, masterfully, grows prouder and bolder at every crime. The
common man may have to found his self-respect on sobriety, honesty and industry; but a Napoleon needs no such props for his
sense of dignity. If Nelson's conscience whispered to him at all in
the silent watches of the night, you may depend on it it whispered
about the Baltic and the Nile and Cape St. Vincent, and not about
his unfaithfulness to his wife. A man who robs little children when
no one is looking can hardly have much self-respect or even self-
esteem; but an accomplished burglar must be proud of himself. In
the play to which I am at present preluding I have represented an
artist who is so entirely satisfied with his artistic conscience, even
to the point of dying like a saint with its support, that he is utterly
selfish and unscrupulous in every other relation without feeling at
the smallest disadvantage. The same thing may be observed in
women who have a genius for personal attractiveness: they expend
more thought, labor, skill, inventiveness, taste and endurance on
making themselves lovely than would suffice to keep a dozen ugly

---

*Incompetent person.

women honest; and this enables them to maintain a high opinion of themselves, and an angry contempt for unattractive and personally careless women, whilst they lie and cheat and slander and sell themselves without a blush. The truth is, hardly any of us have ethical energy enough for more than one really inflexible point of honor. Andrea del Sarto, like Louis Dubedat in my play, must have expended on the attainment of his great mastery of design and his originality in fresco painting more conscientiousness and industry than go to the making of the reputations of a dozen ordinary mayors and church-wardens; but (if Vasari is to be believed) when the King of France entrusted him with money to buy pictures for him, he stole it to spend on his wife. Such cases are not confined to eminent artists. Unsuccessful, unskilful men are often much more scrupulous than successful ones. In the ranks of ordinary skilled labor many men are to be found who earn good wages and are never out of a job because they are strong, indefatigable, and skilful, and who therefore are bold in a high opinion of themselves; but they are selfish and tyrannical, gluttonous and drunken, as their wives and children know to their cost.

Not only do these talented energetic people retain their self-respect through shameful misconduct: they do not even lose the respect of others, because their talents benefit and interest everybody, whilst their vices affect only a few. An actor, a painter, a composer, an author, may be as selfish as he likes without reproach from the public if only his art is superb; and he cannot fulfil this condition without sufficient effort and sacrifice to make him feel noble and martyred in spite of his selfishness. It may even happen that the selfishness of an artist may be a benefit to the public by enabling him to concentrate himself on their gratification with a recklessness of every other consideration that makes him highly dangerous to those about him. In sacrificing others to himself he is sacrificing them to the public he gratifies; and the public is quite content with that arrangement. The public actually has an interest in the artist's vices.

It has no such interest in the surgeon's vices. The surgeon's art is exercised at its expense, not for its gratification. We do not go to the operating table as we go to the theatre, to the picture gallery, to the concert room, to be entertained and delighted: we go to be tormented and maimed, lest a worse thing should befall us. It is of the most extreme importance to us that the experts on whose assurance we face this horror and suffer this mutilation should have no interests but our own to think of; should judge our cases scientifically; and should feel about them kindly. Let us see what guarantees we have: first for the science, and then for the kindness.

ARE DOCTORS MEN OF SCIENCE?

I presume nobody will question the existence of a widely spread popular delusion that every doctor is a man of science. It is escaped only in the very small class which understands by science something more than conjuring with retorts and spirit lamps, magnets and microscopes, and discovering magical cures for disease. To a sufficiently ignorant man every captain of a trading schooner is a Galileo, every organ-grinder a Beethoven, every piano-tuner a Helmholtz, every Old Bailey barrister a Solon, every Seven Dials pigeon dealer a Darwin, every scrivener a Shakespear, every locomotive engine a miracle, and its driver no less wonderful than George Stephenson.[2] As a matter of fact, the rank and file of doctors are no more scientific than their tailors; or, if you prefer to put it the reverse way, their tailors are no less scientific than they. Doctoring is an art, not a science: any layman who is interested in science sufficiently to take in one of the scientific journals and follow the literature of the scientific movement, knows more about it than those doctors (probably a large majority) who are not interested in it, and practise only to earn their bread. Doctoring is not even the art of keeping people in health (no doctor seems able to advise you what to eat any better than his grandmother or the nearest quack): it is the art of curing illnesses. It does happen exceptionally that a practising doctor makes a contribution to science (my play describes a very notable one); but it happens much oftener that he draws disastrous conclusions from his clinical experience because he has no conception of scientific method, and believes, like any rustic, that the handling of evidence and statistics needs no expertness. The distinction between a quack doctor and a qualified one is mainly that only the qualified one is authorized to sign death certificates, for which both sorts seem to have about equal occasion. Unqualified practitioners now make large incomes as hygienists, and are resorted to as frequently by cultivated amateur scientists who understand quite well what they are doing as by ignorant people who are simply dupes. Bone-setters make fortunes under the very noses of our greatest surgeons from educated and wealthy patients; and some of the most successful doctors on the register use quite heretical methods of treating disease, and have qualified themselves solely for convenience. Leaving out of account the village witches who prescribe spells and sell charms, the humblest professional healers in this country are the herbalists. These men wander through the fields on Sunday seeking for herbs with magic properties of curing disease, preventing childbirth, and the like. Each of them believes that he is on the verge of a great discovery, in which Virginia Snake Root will be an ingredient, heaven knows why! Virginia Snake Root fascinates the imagination of the herbalist as mercury used to fascinate the alchemists. On week days he keeps a shop in which he sells packets of pennyroyal, dandelion, &c., labelled with little lists of the diseases they are supposed to cure, and apparently do cure to the satisfaction of the people who keep on buying them. I have never been able to perceive any distinction between the science of the herbalist and that of the duly registered doctor. A relative of mine recently consulted a doctor about some of the ordinary symptoms which indicate the need for a holiday and a change. The doctor satisfied himself that the patient's heart was a little depressed. Digitalis being a drug labelled as a heart specific by the profession, he promptly administered a stiff dose. Fortunately the patient was a hardy old lady who was not easily killed. She recovered with no worse result than her conversion to Christian Science,* which owes its vogue quite as much to public despair of doctors as to superstition. I am not, observe, here concerned with the question as to whether the dose of digitalis was judicious or not; the point is, that a farm laborer consulting a herbalist would have been treated in exactly the same way.

BACTERIOLOGY AS A SUPERSTITION

The smattering of science that all—even doctors—pick up from the ordinary newspapers nowadays only makes the doctor more dangerous than he used to be. Wise men used to take care to consult doctors qualified before 1860, who were usually contemptuous of or indifferent to the germ theory and bacteriological therapeutics; but now that these veterans have mostly retired or died, we are left in the hands of the generations which, having heard of microbes much as St. Thomas Aquinas heard of angels, suddenly concluded that the whole art of healing could be summed up in the formula: Find the microbe and kill it. And even that they did not know how to do. The simplest way to kill most microbes is to throw them into an open street or river and let the sun shine on them, which explains the fact that when great cities have recklessly thrown all their sewage into the open river the water has sometimes been cleaner twenty miles below the city than thirty miles above it. But doctors instinctively avoid all facts that are reassuring, and eagerly swallow those that make it a marvel that anyone could possibly survive three days in an atmosphere consisting mainly of countless pathogenic germs. They conceive microbes as immortal until slain by a germicide administered by a

---

*Religion, founded in 1866 by Mary Baker Eddy, that eschews doctors in favor of spiritual healing.

duly qualified medical man. All through Europe people are adjured, by public notices and even under legal penalties, not to throw their microbes into the sunshine, but to collect them carefully in a handkerchief; shield the handkerchief from the sun in the darkness and warmth of the pocket; and send it to a laundry to be mixed up with everybody elses's handkerchiefs, with results only too familiar to local health authorities.

In the first frenzy of microbe killing, surgical instruments were dipped in carbolic oil, which was a great improvement on not dipping them in anything at all and simply using them dirty; but as microbes are so fond of carbolic oil that they swarm in it, it was not a success from the anti-microbe point of view. Formalin* was squirted into the circulation of consumptives until it was discovered that formalin nourishes the tubercle bacillus handsomely and kills men. The popular theory of disease is the common medical theory: namely, that every disease had its microbe duly created in the garden of Eden, and has been steadily propagating itself and producing widening circles of malignant disease ever since. It was plain from the first that if this had been even approximately true, the whole human race would have been wiped out by the plague long ago, and that every epidemic, instead of fading out as mysteriously as it rushed in, would spread over the whole world. It was also evident that the characteristic microbe of a disease might be a symptom instead of a cause. An unpunctual man is always in a hurry; but it does not follow that hurry is the cause of unpunctuality: on the contrary, what is the matter with the patient is sloth. When Florence Nightingale said bluntly that if you overcrowded your soldiers in dirty quarters there would be an outbreak of smallpox among them, she was snubbed as an ignorant female who did not know that smallpox can be produced only by the importation of its specific microbe.

---

*Solution containing formaldehyde, used as a disinfectant.

If this was the line taken about smallpox, the microbe of which has never yet been run down and exposed under the microscope by the bacteriologist, what must have been the ardor of conviction as to tuberculosis, tetanus, enteric fever, Maltese fever, diphtheria, and the rest of the diseases in which the characteristic bacillus had been identified! When there was no bacillus it was assumed that, since no disease could exist without a bacillus, it was simply eluding observation. When the bacillus was found, as it frequently was, in persons who were not suffering from the disease, the theory was saved by simply calling the bacillus an impostor, or pseudo-bacillus. The same boundless credulity which the public exhibit as to a doctor's power of diagnosis was shown by the doctors themselves as to the analytic microbe hunters. These witch finders would give you a certificate of the ultimate constitution of anything from a sample of the water from your well to a scrap of your lungs, for seven-and-sixpence. I do not suggest that the analysts were dishonest. No doubt they carried the analysis as far as they could afford to carry it for the money. No doubt also they could afford to carry it far enough to be of some use. But the fact remains that just as doctors perform for half-a-crown, without the least misgiving, operations which could not be thoroughly and safely performed with due scientific rigor and the requisite apparatus by an unaided private practitioner for less than some thousands of pounds, so did they proceed on the assumption that they could get the last word of science as to the constituents of their pathological samples for a two hours cab fare.

ECONOMIC DIFFICULTIES OF IMMUNIZATION

I have heard doctors affirm and deny almost every possible proposition as to disease and treatment. I can remember the time when doctors no more dreamt of consumption and pneumonia being infectious than they now dream of sea-sickness being in-

fectious, or than so great a clinical observer as Sydenham*
dreamt of smallpox being infectious. I have heard doctors deny
that there is such a thing as infection. I have heard them deny the
existence of hydrophobia as a specific disease differing from
tetanus. I have heard them defend prophylactic measures and
prophylactic legislation as the sole and certain salvation of
mankind from zymotic disease; and I have heard them denounce
both as malignant spreaders of cancer and lunacy. But the one objection I have never heard from a doctor is the objection that prophylaxis by the inoculatory methods most in vogue is an
economic impossibility under our private practice system. They
buy some stuff from somebody for a shilling, and inject a penny-
worth of it under their patient's skin for half-a-crown, conclud-
ing that, since this primitive rite pays the somebody and pays
them, the problem of prophylaxis has been satisfactorily solved.
The results are sometimes no worse than the ordinary results of
dirt getting into cuts; but neither the doctor nor the patient is
quite satisfied unless the inoculation "takes"; that is, unless it produces perceptible illness and disablement. Sometimes both doctor and patient get more value in this direction than they bargain
for. The results of ordinary private-practice-inoculation at their
worst are bad enough to be indistinguishable from those of the
most discreditable and dreaded disease known; and doctors, to
save the credit of the inoculation, have been driven to accuse
their patient or their patient's parents of having contracted this
disease independently of the inoculation, an excuse which naturally does not make the family any more resigned, and leads to
public recriminations in which the doctors, forgetting everything
but the immediate quarrel, naively excuse themselves by admit-
ting, and even claiming as a point in their favor, that it is often impossible to distinguish the disease produced by their inoculation

---

*Thomas Sydenham (1624–1689), English physician and pioneer in treating dis-
eases.

and the disease they have accused the patient of contracting. And both parties assume that what is at issue is the scientific soundness of the prophylaxis. It never occurs to them that the particular pathogenic germ which they intended to introduce into the patient's system may be quite innocent of the catastrophe, and that the casual dirt introduced with it may be at fault. When, as in the case of smallpox or cowpox, the germ has not yet been detected, what you inoculate is simply undefined matter that has been scraped off an anything but chemically clean calf suffering from the disease in question. You take your chance of the germ being in the scrapings, and, lest you should kill it, you take no precautions against other germs being in it as well. Anything may happen as the result of such an inoculation. Yet this is the only stuff of the kind which is prepared and supplied even in State establishments: that is, in the only establishments free from the commercial temptation to adulterate materials and scamp precautionary processes.

Even if the germ were identified, complete precautions would hardly pay. It is true that microbe farming is not expensive. The cost of breeding and housing two head of cattle would provide for the breeding and housing of enough microbes to inoculate the entire population of the globe since human life first appeared on it. But the precautions necessary to insure that the inoculation shall consist of nothing else but the required germ in the proper state of attenuation are a very different matter from the precautions necessary in the distribution and consumption of beefsteaks. Yet people expect to find vaccines and antitoxins and the like retailed at "popular prices" in private enterprise shops just as they expect to find ounces of tobacco and papers of pins.

THE PERILS OF INOCULATION

The trouble does not end with the matter to be inoculated. There is the question of the condition of the patient. The discoveries of

Sir Almroth Wright* have shewn that the appalling results which led to the hasty dropping in 1894 of Koch's tuberculin[†] were not accidents, but perfectly orderly and inevitable phenomena following the injection of dangerously strong "vaccines" at the wrong moment, and reinforcing the disease instead of stimulating the resistance to it. To ascertain the right moment a laboratory and a staff of experts are needed. The general practitioner, having no such laboratory and no such experience, has always chanced it, and insisted, when he was unlucky, that the results were not due to the inoculation, but, to some other cause: a favorite and not very tactful one being the drunkenness or licentiousness of the patient. But though a few doctors have now learnt the danger of inoculating without any reference to the patient's "opsonic index"[‡] at the moment of inoculation, and though those other doctors who are denouncing the danger as imaginary and opsonin as a craze or a fad, obviously do so because it involves an operation which they have neither the means nor the knowledge to perform, there is still no grasp of the economic change in the situation. They have never been warned that the practicability of any method of extirpating disease depends not only on its efficacy, but on its cost. For example, just at present the world has run raving mad on the subject of radium, which has excited our credulity precisely as the apparitions at Lourdes excited the credulity of Roman Catholics. Suppose it were ascertained that every child in the world could be rendered absolutely immune from all disease during its entire life by taking half an ounce of radium to every pint of its milk. The world would be none the healthier, because not even a Crown Prince—no, not even the son of a Chicago Meat King, could af-

---

*Noted immunologist and a friend of Shaw (1861–1947); partial model for Doctor Ridgeon in the play.

†German bacteriologist and Nobel laureate Robert Koch (1843–1910) developed tuberculin, a substance to diagnose tuberculosis.

‡Measurement of the amount of opsonin in the blood; opsonin is a constituent of the blood that helps phagocytes (such as white blood cells) destroy disease.

ford the treatment. Yet it is doubtful whether doctors would re-
frain from prescribing it on that ground. The recklessness with
which they now recommend wintering in Egypt or at Davos to
people who cannot afford to go to Cornwall, and the orders given
for champagne jelly and old port in households where such luxuries must obviously be acquired at the cost of stinting necessaries,
often make one wonder whether it is possible for a man to go
through a medical training and retain a spark of common sense.

This sort of inconsiderateness gets cured only in the classes
where poverty, pretentious as it is even at its worst, cannot pitch
its pretences high enough to make it possible for the doctor (himself often no better off than the patient) to assume that the average income of an English family is about £2,000 a year, and that it
is quite easy to break up a home, sell an old family seat at a sacrifice, and retire into a foreign sanatorium devoted to some "treatment" that did not exist two years ago and probably will not exist
(except as a pretext for keeping an ordinary hotel) two years
hence. In a poor practice the doctor must find cheap treatments
for cheap people or humiliate and lose his patients either by prescribing beyond their means or sending them to the public hospitals. When it comes to prophylactic inoculation, the alternative
lies between the complete scientific process, which can only be
brought down to a reasonable cost by being very highly organized
as a public service in a public institution, and such cheap, nasty,
dangerous and scientifically spurious imitations as ordinary vaccination, which seems not unlikely to be ended, like its equally
vaunted forerunner, XVIII. century inoculation, by a purely reac-
tionary law making all sorts of vaccination, scientific or not, criminal offences. Naturally, the poor doctor (that is, the average
doctor) defends ordinary vaccination frantically, as it means to
him the bread of his children. To secure the vehement and practically unanimous support of the rank and file of the medical profession for any sort of treatment or operation, all that is necessary
is that it can be easily practised by a rather shabbily dressed man

in a surgically dirty room in a surgically dirty house without any
assistance, and that the materials for it shall cost, say, a penny, and
the charge for it to a patient with £100 a year be half-a-crown.
And, on the other hand, a hygienic measure has only to be one of
such refinement, difficulty, precision and costliness as to be quite
beyond the resources of private practice, to be ignored or angrily
denounced as a fad.

TRADE UNIONISM AND SCIENCE

Here we have the explanation of the savage rancor that so amazes
people who imagine that the controversy concerning vaccination
is a scientific one. It has really nothing to do with science. The
medical profession, consisting for the most part of very poor men
struggling to keep up appearances beyond their means, find themselves threatened with the extinction of a considerable part of
their incomes: a part, too, that is easily and regularly earned, since
it is independent of disease, and brings every person born into the
nation, healthy or not, to the doctors. To boot, there is the occasional windfall of an epidemic, with its panic and rush for revaccination. Under such circumstances, vaccination would be defended
desperately were it twice as dirty, dangerous, and unscientific in
method as it actually is. The note of fury in the defence, the feeling that the anti-vaccinator is doing a cruel, ruinous, inconsiderate thing in a mood of malignant folly: all this, so puzzling to the
observer who knows nothing of the economic side of the question, and only sees that the anti-vaccinator, having nothing whatever to gain and a good deal to lose by placing himself in
opposition to the law and to the outcry that adds private persecution to legal penalties, can have no interest in the matter except
the interest of a reformer in abolishing a corrupt and mischievous
superstition, becomes intelligible the moment the tragedy of
medical poverty and the lucrativeness of cheap vaccination is
taken into account.

In the face of such economic pressure as this, it is silly to expect that medical teaching, any more than medical practice, can possibly be scientific. The test to which all methods of treatment are finally brought is whether they are lucrative to doctors or not. It would be difficult to cite any proposition less obnoxious to science than that advanced by Hahneman:* to wit, that drugs which in large doses produce certain symptoms, counteract them in very small doses, just as in more modern practice it is found that a sufficiently small inoculation with typhoid rallies our powers to resist the disease instead of prostrating us with it. But Hahnemann and his followers were frantically persecuted for a century by generations of apothecary-doctors whose incomes depended on the quantity of drugs they could induce their patients to swallow. These two cases of ordinary vaccination and homeopathy are typical of all the rest. Just as the object of a trade union under existing conditions must finally be, not to improve the technical quality of the work done by its members, but to secure a living wage for them, so the object of the medical profession today is to secure an income for the private doctor; and to this consideration all concern for science and public health must give way when the two come into conflict. Fortunately they are not always in conflict. Up to a certain point doctors, like carpenters and masons, must earn their living by doing the work that the public wants from them; and as it is not in the nature of things possible that such public want should be based on unmixed disutility, it may be admitted that doctors have their uses, real as well as imaginary. But just as the best carpenter or mason will resist the introduction of a machine that is likely to throw him out of work, or the public technical education of unskilled laborers' sons to compete with him, so the doctor will resist with all his powers of persecution every advance of science that threatens his income. And as the advance

---

*Samuel Christian Hahnemann (1755–1843), German physician who introduced homeopathy (treatment of disease by introducing small doses of a remedy that produce symptoms of the disease in a healthy person).

of scientific hygiene tends to make the private doctor's visits rarer, and the public inspector's frequenter, whilst the advance of scientific therapeutics is in the direction of treatments that involve highly organized laboratories, hospitals, and public institutions generally, it unluckily happens that the organization of private practitioners which we call the medical profession is coming more and more to represent, not science, but desperate and embittered anti-science: a statement of things which is likely to get worse until the average doctor either depends upon or hopes for an appointment in the public health service for his livelihood.

So much for our guarantees as to medical science. Let us now deal with the more painful subject of medical kindness.

DOCTORS AND VIVISECTION

The importance to our doctors of a reputation for the tenderest humanity is so obvious, and the quantity of benevolent work actually done by them for nothing (a great deal of it from sheer good nature) so large, that at first sight it seems unaccountable that they should not only throw all their credit away, but deliberately choose to band themselves publicly with outlaws and scoundrels by claiming that in the pursuit of their professional knowledge they should be free from the restraints of law, of honor, of pity, of remorse, of everything that distinguishes an orderly citizen from a South Sea buccaneer, or a philosopher from an inquisitor. For here we look in vain for either an economic or a sentimental motive. In every generation fools and blackguards have made this claim; and honest and reasonable men, led by the strongest contemporary minds, have repudiated it and exposed its crude rascality. From Shakespear and Dr. Johnson to Ruskin and Mark Twain, the natural abhorrence of sane mankind for the vivisector's cruelty, and the contempt of able thinkers for his imbecile casuistry, have been expressed by the most popular spokesmen of humanity. If the medical profession were to outdo the Anti-Vivisection Societies in a general professional protest against the practice and principles of the vivisectors, every doctor in the kingdom would gain substantially by the immense relief and reconciliation which would follow such a reassurance of the humanity of the doctor. Not one doctor in a thousand is a vivisector, or has any interest in vivisection, either pecuniary or intellectual, or would treat his dog cruelly or allow anyone else to do it. It is true that the doctor complies with the professional fashion of defending vivisection, and assuring you that people like Shakespear and Dr. Johnson and Ruskin and Mark Twain are ignorant sentimentalists, just as he complies with any other silly fashion: the mystery is, how it became the fashion in spite of its being so injurious to those who follow it. Making all possible allowance for the effect of the brazen lying of the few men who bring a rush of despairing patients to their doors by professing in letters to the newspapers to have learnt from vivisection how to cure certain diseases, and the assurances of the sayers of smooth things that the practice is quite painless under the law, it is still difficult to find any civilized motive for an attitude by which the medical profession has everything to lose and nothing to gain.

THE PRIMITIVE SAVAGE MOTIVE

I say civilized motive advisedly; for primitive tribal motives are easy enough to find. Every savage chief who is not a Mahomet learns that if he wishes to strike the imagination of his tribe—and without doing that he cannot rule them—he must terrify or revolt them from time to time by acts of hideous cruelty or disgusting unnaturalness. We are far from being as superior to such tribes as we imagine. It is very doubtful indeed whether Peter the Great could have effected the changes he made in Russia if he had not fascinated and intimidated his people by his monstrous cruelties and grotesque escapades. Had he been a nineteenth-century king of England, he would have had to wait for some huge accidental calamity: a cholera epidemic, a war, or an insurrection, before waking us up sufficiently to get anything done. Vivisection helps the doctor to rule us as Peter ruled the Russians. The notion that the man who does dreadful things is superhuman, and that therefore he can also do wonderful things either as ruler, avenger, healer, or what not, is by no means confined to barbarians. Just as the manifold wickednesses and stupidities of our criminal code are supported, not by any general comprehension of law or study of jurisprudence, not even by simple vindictiveness, but by the superstition that a calamity of any sort must be expiated by a human sacrifice; so the wickednesses and stupidities of our medicine men are rooted in superstitions that have no more to do with science than the traditional ceremony of christening an ironclad has to do with the effectiveness of its armament. We have only to turn to Macaulay's* description of the treatment of Charles II. in his last illness to see how strongly his physicians felt that their only chance of cheating death was by outraging nature in tormenting and disgusting their unfortunate patient. True, this was more than two centuries ago; but I have heard my own nineteenth-century grandfather describe the cupping and firing† and nauseous medicines of his time with perfect credulity as to their beneficial effects; and some more modern treatments appear to me quite as barbarous. It is in this way that vivisection pays the doctor. It appeals to the fear and credulity of the savage in us; and without fear and credulity half the private doctor's occupation and seven-eighths of his influence would be gone.

THE HIGHER MOTIVE. THE TREE OF KNOWLEDGE

But the greatest force of all on the side of vivisection is the mighty and indeed divine force of curiosity. Here we have no decaying tribal instinct which men strive to root out of themselves

---

*Thomas Babington Macaulay (1800–1859), a much-admired and -quoted British historian and author.

†Cupping was a medical practice of drawing blood to the surface of the body with warmed glass vessels; firing was cauterizing a wound with a heated iron.

as they strive to root out the tiger's lust for blood. On the contrary, the curiosity of the ape, or of the child who pulls out the legs and wings of a fly to see what it will do without them, or who, on being told that a cat dropped out of the window will always fall on its legs, immediately tries the experiment on the nearest cat from the highest window in the house (I protest I did it myself from the first floor only), is as nothing compared to the thirst for knowledge of the philosopher, the poet, the biologist, and the naturalist. I have always despised Adam because he had to be tempted by the woman, as she was by the serpent, before he could be induced to pluck the apple from the tree of knowledge. I should have swallowed every apple on the tree the moment the owner's back was turned. When Gray said "Where ignorance is bliss, 'tis folly to be wise,"* he forgot that it is godlike to be wise; and since nobody wants bliss particularly, or could stand more than a very brief taste of it if it were attainable, and since everybody, by the deepest law of the Life Force, desires to be godlike, it is stupid, and indeed blasphemous and despairing, to hope that the thirst for knowledge will either diminish or consent to be subordinated to any other end whatsoever. We shall see later on that the claim that has arisen in this way for the unconditioned pursuit of knowledge is as idle as all dreams of unconditioned activity; but none the less the right to knowledge must be regarded as a fundamental human right. The fact that men of science have had to fight so hard to secure its recognition, and are still so vigorously persecuted when they discover anything that is not quite palatable to vulgar people, makes them sorely jealous for that right; and when they hear a popular outcry for the suppression of a method of research which has an air of being scientific, their first instinct is to rally to the defence of that method without further consideration, with the result that they sometimes, as in the

---

*Last lines of "Ode on a Distant Prospect of Eton College," by English poet Thomas Gray (1716–1771).

case of vivisection, presently find themselves fighting on a false issue.

THE FLAW IN THE ARGUMENT

I may as well pause here to explain their error. The right to know is like the right to live. It is fundamental and unconditional in its assumption that knowledge, like life, is a desirable thing, though any fool can prove that ignorance is bliss, and that "a little knowledge is a dangerous thing"* (a little being the most that any of us can attain), as easily as that the pains of life are more numerous and constant than its pleasures, and that therefore we should all be better dead. The logic is unimpeachable; but its only effect is to make us say that if these are the conclusions logic leads to, so much the worse for logic, after which curt dismissal of Folly, we continue living and learning by instinct: that is, as of right. We legislate on the assumption that no man may be killed on the strength of a demonstration that he would be happier in his grave, not even if he is dying slowly of cancer and begs the doctor to despatch him quickly and mercifully. To get killed lawfully he must violate somebody else's right to live by committing murder. But he is by no means free to live unconditionally. In society he can exercise his right to live only under very stiff conditions. In countries where there is compulsory military service he may even have to throw away his individual life to save the life of the community.

It is just so in the case of the right to knowledge. It is a right that is as yet very imperfectly recognized in practice. But in theory it is admitted that an adult person in pursuit of knowledge must not be refused it on the ground that he would be better or happier without it. Parents and priests may forbid knowledge to those who accept their authority; and social taboo may be made effective by acts of legal persecution under cover of repressing

---

*Paraphrase of "Essay on Criticism," by English poet Alexander Pope (1688–1744); Shaw substituted "knowledge" for Pope's "learning."

blasphemy, obscenity, and sedition; but no government now openly forbids its subjects to pursue knowledge on the ground that knowledge is in itself a bad thing, or that it is possible for any of us to have too much of it.

LIMITATIONS OF THE RIGHT TO KNOWLEDGE

But neither does any government exempt the pursuit of knowledge, any more than the pursuit of life, liberty, and happiness (as the American Constitution* puts it), from all social conditions. No man is allowed to put his mother into the stove because he desires to know how long an adult woman will survive at a temperature of 500° Fahrenheit, no matter how important or interesting that particular addition to the store of human knowledge may be. A man who did so would have short work made not only of his right to knowledge, but of his right to live and all his other rights at the same time. The right to knowledge is not the only right; and its exercise must be limited by respect for other rights, and for its own exercise by others. When a man says to Society, "May I torture my mother in pursuit of knowledge?" Society replies, "No." If he pleads, "What! Not even if I have a chance of finding out how to cure cancer by doing it?" Society still says, "Not even then." If the scientist, making the best of his disappointment, goes on to ask may he torture a dog, the stupid and callous people who do not realize that a dog is a fellow-creature and sometimes a good friend, may say Yes, though Shakespear, Dr. Johnson and their like may say No. But even those who say "You may torture *a* dog" never say "You may torture *my* dog." And nobody says, "Yes, because in the pursuit of knowledge you may do as you please." Just as even the stupidest people say, in effect, "If you cannot at-

---

*It is the Declaration of Independence, not the Constitution, that states all men "are endowed . . . with certain unalienable Rights, that among these are Life, Liberty and the Pursuit of Happiness."

tain to knowledge without burning your mother you must do without knowledge," so the wisest people say, "If you cannot attain to knowledge without torturing a dog, you must do without knowledge."

A FALSE ALTERNATIVE

But in practice you cannot persuade any wise man that this alternative can ever be forced on anyone but a fool, or that a fool can be trusted to learn anything from any experiment, cruel or humane. The Chinaman who burnt down his house to roast his pig* was no doubt honestly unable to conceive any less disastrous way of cooking his dinner; and the roast must have been spoiled after all (a perfect type of the average vivisectionist experiment); but this did not prove that the Chinaman was right: it only proved that the Chinaman was an incapable cook and, fundamentally, a fool.

Take another celebrated experiment: one in sanitary reform. In the days of Nero Rome was in the same predicament as London to-day. If some one would burn down London, and it were rebuilt, as it would now have to be, subject to the sanitary by-laws and Building Act provisions enforced by the London County Council, it would be enormously improved; and the average lifetime of Londoners would be considerably prolonged. Nero argued in the same way about Rome. He employed incendiaries to set it on fire; and he played the harp in scientific raptures whilst it was burning. I am so far of Nero's way of thinking that I have often said, when consulted by despairing sanitary reformers, that what London needs to make her healthy is an earthquake. Why, then, it may be asked, do not I, as a public-spirited man, employ incendiaries to set it on fire, with a heroic disregard of the consequences to myself and others? Any vivisector would, if he had the courage of his opinions. The reasonable answer is that London can be made

---

*Reference to English essayist Charles Lamb's "A Dissertation on Roast Pig," from *Essays of Elia* (1823).

healthy without burning her down; and that as we have not enough civic virtue to make her healthy in a humane and economical way, we should not have enough to rebuild her in that way. In the old Hebrew legend, God lost patience with the world as Nero did with Rome, and drowned everybody except a single family. But the result was that the progeny of that family reproduced all the vices of their predecessors so exactly that the misery caused by the flood might just as well have been spared: things went on just as they did before. In the same way, the lists of diseases which vivisection claims to have cured is long; but the returns of the Registrar-General shew that people still persist in dying of them as if vivisection had never been heard of. Any fool can burn down a city or cut an animal open; and an exceptionally foolish fool is quite likely to promise enormous benefits to the race as the result of such activities. But when the constructive, benevolent part of the business comes to be done, the same want of imagination, the same stupidity and cruelty, the same laziness and want of perseverance that prevented Nero or the vivisector from devising or pushing through humane methods, prevents him from bringing order out of the chaos and happiness out of the misery he has made. At one time it seemed reasonable enough to declare that it was impossible to find whether or not there was a stone inside a man's body except by exploring it with a knife, or to find out what the sun is made of without visiting it in a balloon. Both these impossibilities have been achieved, but not by vivisectors. The Röntgen rays* need not hurt the patient; and spectrum analysis involves no destruction. After such triumphs of humane experiment and reasoning, it is useless to assure us that there is no other key to knowledge except cruelty. When the vivisector offers us that assurance, we reply simply and contemptuously, "You mean that you are not clever or humane or energetic enough to find one."

---

*X rays; discovered by German physicist Wilhelm Konrad Röntgen in 1895.

CRUELTY FOR ITS OWN SAKE

It will now, I hope, be clear why the attack on vivisection is not an attack on the right to knowledge: why, indeed, those who have the deepest conviction of the sacredness of that right are the leaders of the attack. No knowledge is finally impossible of human attainment; for even though it may be beyond our present capacity, the needed capacity is not unattainable. Consequently no method of investigation is the only method; and no law forbidding any particular method can cut us off from the knowledge we hope to gain by it. The only knowledge we lose by forbidding cruelty is knowledge at first hand of cruelty itself, which is precisely the knowledge humane people wish to be spared.

But the question remains: Do we all really wish to be spared that knowledge? Are humane methods really to be preferred to cruel ones? Even if the experiments come to nothing, may not their cruelty be enjoyed for its own sake, as a sensational luxury? Let us face these questions boldly, not shrinking from the fact that cruelty is one of the primitive pleasures of mankind, and that the detection of its Protean disguises as law, education, medicine, discipline, sport and so forth, is one of the most difficult of the unending tasks of the legislator.

OUR OWN CRUELTIES

At first blush it may seem not only unnecessary, but even indecent, to discuss such a proposition as the elevation of cruelty to the rank of a human right. Unnecessary, because no vivisector confesses to a love of cruelty for its own sake or claims any general fundamental right to be cruel. Indecent, because there is an accepted convention to repudiate cruelty; and vivisection is only tolerated by the law on condition that, like judicial torture, it shall be done as mercifully as the nature of the practice allows. But the moment the controversy becomes embittered, the recriminations bandied between the opposed parties bring us face-to-face with

some very ugly truths. On one occasion I was invited to speak at
a large Anti-Vivisection meeting in the Queen's Hall in London. I
found myself on the platform with fox hunters, tame stag hunters,
men and women whose calendar was divided, not by pay days and
quarter days,* but by seasons for killing animals for sport: the fox,
the hare, the otter, the partridge and the rest having each its ap-
pointed date for slaughter. The ladies among us wore hats and
cloaks and head-dresses obtained by wholesale massacres, ruthless
trappings, callous extermination of our fellow creatures. We insisted on our butchers supplying us with white veal, and were
large and constant consumers of *pâte de foie gras;* both comestibles
being obtained by revolting methods. We sent our sons to public
schools where indecent flogging is a recognized method of taming
the young human animal. Yet we were all in hysterics of indignation at the cruelties of the vivisectors. These, if any were present,
must have smiled sardonically at such inhuman humanitarians,
whose daily habits and fashionable amusements cause more suffering in England in a week than all the vivisectors of Europe do
in a year. I made a very effective speech, not exclusively against
vivisection, but against cruelty; and I have never been asked to
speak since by that Society, nor do I expect to be, as I should probably give such offence to its most affluent subscribers that its attempts to suppress vivisection would be seriously hindered. But
that does not prevent the vivisectors from freely using the "youre
another" retort, and using it with justice.

We must therefore give ourselves no airs of superiority when
denouncing the cruelties of vivisection. We all do just as horrible
things, with even less excuse. But in making that admission we are
also making short work of the virtuous airs with which we are
sometimes referred to the humanity of the medical profession as
a guarantee that vivisection is not abused—much as if our burglars

---

*Days every three months when rent and other payments are due.

should assure us that they are too honest to abuse the practice of burgling. We are, as a matter of fact, a cruel nation; and our habit of disguising our vices by giving polite names to the offences we are determined to commit does not, unfortunately for my own comfort, impose on me. Vivisectors can hardly pretend to be better than the classes from which they are drawn, or those above them; and if these classes are capable of sacrificing animals in various cruel ways under cover of sport, fashion, education, discipline, and even, when the cruel sacrifices are human sacrifices, of political economy, it is idle for the vivisector to pretend that he is incapable of practising cruelty for pleasure or profit or both under the cloak of science. We are all tarred with the same brush; and the vivisectors are not slow to remind us of it, and to protest vehemently against being branded as exceptionally cruel and as devisers of horrible instruments of torture by people whose main notion of enjoyment is cruel sport, and whose requirements in the way of villainously cruel traps occupy pages of the catalogue of the Army and Navy Stores.

THE SCIENTIFIC INVESTIGATION OF CRUELTY

There is in man a specific lust for cruelty which infects even his passion of pity and makes it savage. Simple disgust at cruelty is very rare. The people who turn sick and faint and those who gloat are often alike in the pains they take to witness executions, floggings, operations or ally other exhibitions of suffering, especially those involving bloodshed, blows, and laceration. A craze for cruelty can be developed just as a craze for drink can; and nobody who attempts to ignore cruelty as a possible factor in the attraction of vivisection and even of anti-vivisection, or in the credulity with which we accept its excuses, can be regarded as a scientific investigator of it. Those who accuse vivisectors of indulging the well-known passion of cruelty under the cloak of research are therefore putting forward a strictly scientific psychological hypothesis, which is also simple, human, obvious, and probable. It may be as wounding to the personal vanity of the vivisector as Darwin's Origin of Species was to the people who could not bear to think that they were cousins to the monkeys (remember Goldsmith's anger when he was told that he could not move his upper jaw); but science has to consider only the truth of the hypothesis, and not whether conceited people will like it or not. In vain do the sentimental champions of vivisection declare themselves the most humane of men, inflicting suffering only to relieve it, scrupulous in the use of anesthetics, and void of all passion except the passion of pity for a disease-ridden world. The really scientific investigator answers that the question cannot be settled by hysterical protestations, and that if the vivisectionist rejects deductive reasoning, he had better clear his character by his own favorite method of experiment.

SUGGESTED LABORATORY TESTS OF THE VIVISECTOR'S EMOTIONS

Take the hackneyed case of the Italian who tortured mice, ostensibly to find out about the effects of pain rather less than the nearest dentist could have told him, and who boasted of the ecstatic sensations (he actually used the word love) with which he carried out his experiments. Or the gentleman who starved sixty dogs to death to establish the fact that a dog deprived of food gets progressively lighter and weaker, becoming remarkably emaciated, and finally dying: an undoubted truth, but ascertainable without laboratory experiments by a simple enquiry addressed to the nearest policeman, or, failing him, to any sane person in Europe. The Italian is diagnosed as a cruel voluptuary: the dog-starver is passed over as such a hopeless fool that it is impossible to take any interest in him. Why not test the diagnosis scientifically? Why not perform a careful series of experiments on persons under the influence of voluptuous ecstasy, so as to ascertain its physiological symptoms? Then perform a second series on persons engaged in mathematical work or machine designing, so as to ascertain the symptoms of cold scientific activity? Then note the symptoms of a vivisector performing a cruel experiment; and compare them with the voluptuary symptoms and the mathematical symptoms? Such experiments would be quite as interesting and important as any yet undertaken by the vivisectors. They might open a line of investigation which would finally make, for instance, the ascertainment of the guilt or innocence of an accused person a much exacter process than the very fallible methods of our criminal courts. But instead of proposing such an investigation, our vivisectors offer us all the pious protestations and all the huffy recriminations that any common unscientific mortal offers when he is accused of unworthy conduct.

ROUTINE

Yet most vivisectors would probably come triumphant out of such a series of experiments, because vivisection is now a routine, like butchering or hanging or flogging; and many of the men who practise it do so only because it has been established as part of the profession they have adopted. Far from enjoying it, they have simply overcome their natural repugnance and become indifferent to it, as men inevitably become indifferent to anything they do often enough. It is this dangerous power of custom that makes it so difficult to convince the common sense of mankind that any established commercial or professional practice has its root in passion. Let a routine once spring from passion, and you will presently find thousands of routineers following it passionlessly for a livelihood. Thus it always seems strained to speak of the religious convictions of a clergyman, because nine out of ten clergymen have no religious convictions: they are ordinary officials carrying on a routine of baptizing, marrying, and churching;* praying, reciting, and preaching; and, like solicitors or doctors, getting away from their

---

*Conducting a service of thanksgiving for a new mother.

duties with relief to hunt, to garden, to keep bees, to go into society, and the like. In the same way many people do cruel and vile
things without being in the least cruel or vile, because the routine
to which they have been brought up is superstitiously cruel and
vile. To say that every man who beats his children and every
schoolmaster who flogs a pupil is a conscious debauchee is absurd:
thousands of dull, conscientious people beat their children conscientiously, because they were beaten themselves and think children
ought to be beaten. The ill-tempered vulgarity that instinctively
strikes at and hurts a thing that annoys it (and all children are annoying), and the simple stupidity that requires from a child per-
fection beyond the reach of the wisest and best adults (perfect
truthfulness coupled with perfect obedience is quite a common
condition of leaving a child unwhipped), produce a good deal of
flagellation among people who not only do not lust after it, but
who hit the harder because they are angry at having to perform an
uncomfortable duty. These people will beat merely to assert their
authority, or to carry out what they conceive to be a divine order
on the strength of the precept of Solomon recorded in the Bible,*
which carefully adds that Solomon completely spoilt his own son
and turned away from the god of his fathers to the sensuous idolatry in which he ended his days.

In the same way we find men and women practising vivisection
as senselessly as a humane butcher, who adores his fox terrier, will
cut a calf's throat and hang it up by its heels to bleed slowly to
death because it is the custom to eat veal and insist on its being
white; or as a German purveyor nails a goose to a board and stuffs
it with food because fashionable people eat *pâté de foie gras*; or as
the crew of a whaler breaks in on a colony of seals and clubs them
to death in wholesale massacre because ladies want sealskin jack-
ets; or as fanciers blind singing birds with hot needles, and muti-
late the ears and tails of dogs and horses. Let cruelty or kindness

---

*Reference to Proverbs 13:24: "He that spareth his rod hateth his son" (KJV).

or anything else once become customary and it will be practised by people to whom it is not at all natural, but whose rule of life is simply to do only what everybody else does, and who would lose their employment and starve if they indulged in any peculiarity. A respectable man will lie daily, in speech and in print, about the qualities of the article he lives by selling, because it is customary do so. He will flog his boy for telling a lie, because it is customary to do so. He will also flog him for not telling a lie if the boy tells inconvenient or disrespectful truths, because it is customary to do so. He will give the same boy a present on his birthday, and buy him a spade and bucket at the seaside, because it is customary to do so, being all the time neither particularly mendacious, nor particularly cruel, nor particularly generous, but simply incapable of ethical judgment or independent action.

Just so do we find a crowd of petty vivisectionists daily committing atrocities and stupidities, because it is the custom to do so. Vivisection is customary as part of the routine of preparing lectures in medical schools. For instance, there are two ways of making the action of the heart visible to students. One, a barbarous, ignorant, and thoughtless way, is to stick little flags into a rabbit's heart and let the students see the flags jump. The other, an elegant, ingenious, well-informed, and instructive way, is to put a sphygmograph* on the student's wrist and let him see a record of his heart's action traced by a needle on a slip of smoked paper. But it has become the custom for lecturers to teach from the rabbit; and the lecturers are not original enough to get out of their groove. Then there are the demonstrations which are made by cutting up frogs with scissors. The most humane man, however repugnant the operation may be to him at first, cannot do it at lecture after lecture for months without finally—and that very soon—feeling no more for the frog than if he were cutting up pieces of paper. Such clumsy and lazy ways of teaching are based on the cheapness of

*Device that attaches to the wrist to record the pulse graphically on paper.

frogs and rabbits. If machines were as cheap as frogs, engineers would not only be taught the anatomy of machines and the functions of their parts: they would also have machines misused and wrecked before them so that they might learn as much as possible by using their eyes, and as little as possible by using their brains and imaginations. Thus we have, as part of the routine of teaching, a routine of vivisection which soon produces complete indifference to it on the part even of those who are naturally humane. If they pass on from the routine of lecture preparation, not into general practice, but into research work, they carry this acquired indifference with them into the laboratory, where any atrocity is possible, because all atrocities satisfy curiosity. The routine man is in the majority in his profession always: consequently the moment his practice is tracked down to its source in human passion there is a great and quite sincere poohpoohing from himself, from the mass of the profession, and from the mass of the public, which sees that the average doctor is much too commonplace and decent a person to be capable of passionate wickedness of any kind.

Here then, we have in vivisection, as in all the other tolerated and instituted cruelties, this anti-climax: that only a negligible percentage of those who practise and consequently defend it get any satisfaction out of it. As in Mr. Galsworthy's play Justice the useless and detestable torture of solitary imprisonment is shewn at its worst without the introduction of a single cruel person into the drama, so it would be possible to represent all the torments of vivisection dramatically without introducing a single vivisector who had not felt sick at his first experience in the laboratory. Not that this can exonerate any vivisector from suspicion of enjoying his work (or her work: a good deal of the vivisection in medical schools is done by women). In every autobiography which records a real experience of school or prison life, we find that here and there among the routineers there is to be found the genuine amateur, the orgiastic flogging schoolmaster or the nagging warder, who has sought out a cruel profession for the sake of its cruelty.

But it is the genuine routineer who is the bulwark of the practice, because, though you can excite public fury against a Sade,* a Bluebeard,[3] or a Nero, you cannot rouse any feeling against dull Mr. Smith doing his duty: that is, doing the usual thing. He is so obviously no better and no worse than anyone else that it is difficult to conceive that the things he does are abominable. If you would see public dislike surging up in a moment against an individual, you must watch one who does something unusual, no matter how sensible it may be. The name of Jonas Hanway† lives as that of a brave man because he was the first who dared to appear in the streets of this rainy island with an umbrella.

THE OLD LINE BETWEEN MAN AND BEAST

But there is still a distinction to be clung to by those who dare not tell themselves the truth about the medical profession because they are so helplessly dependent on it when death threatens the household. That distinction is the line that separates the brute from the man in the old classification. Granted, they will plead, that we are all cruel; yet the tame-stag-hunter does not hunt men; and the sportsman who lets a leash of greyhounds loose on a hare would be horrified at the thought of letting them loose on a human child. The lady who gets her cloak by flaying a sable does not flay a negro; nor does it ever occur to her that her veal cutlet might be improved on by a slice of tender baby.

Now there was a time when some trust could be placed in this distinction. The Roman Catholic Church still maintains, with what it must permit me to call a stupid obstinacy, and in spite of St.

---

*French author Marquis de Sade (1740–1814), known for his licentious novels and pamphlets, was imprisoned for numerous sex offenses; the word *sadism* is derived from his name.

†English trader and philanthropist (1712–1786) said to have introduced the umbrella to England.

Francis and St. Anthony, that animals have no souls and no rights; so that you cannot sin against an animal, or against God by anything you may choose to do to an animal. Resisting the temptation to enter on an argument as to whether you may not sin against your own soul if you are unjust or cruel to the least of those whom St. Francis called his little brothers, I have only to point out here that nothing could be more despicably superstitious in the opinion of a vivisector than the notion that science recognizes any such step in evolution as the step from a physical organism to an immortal soul. That conceit has been taken out of all our men of science, and out of all our doctors, by the evolutionists; and when it is considered how completely obsessed biological science has become in our days, not by the full scope of evolution, but by that particular method of it which has neither sense nor purpose nor life nor anything human, much less godlike, in it: by the method, that is, of so-called Natural Selection (meaning no selection at all, but mere dead accident and luck), the folly of trusting to vivisectors to hold the human animal any more sacred than the other animals becomes so clear that it would be waste of time to insist further on it. As a matter of fact the man who once concedes to the vivisector the right to put a dog outside the laws of honor and fellowship, concedes to him also the right to put himself outside them; for he is nothing to the vivisector but a more highly developed, and consequently more interesting-to-experiment-on vertebrate than the dog.

VIVISECTING THE HUMAN SUBJECT

I have in my hand a printed and published account by a doctor of how he tested his remedy for pulmonary tuberculosis, which was, to inject a powerful germicide directly into the circulation by stabbing a vein with a syringe. He was one of those doctors who are able to command public sympathy by saying, quite truly, that when they discovered that the proposed treatment was dangerous, they experimented thenceforth on themselves. In this case the doctor was devoted enough to carry his experiments to the point of running serious risks, and actually making himself very uncomfortable. But he did not begin with himself. His first experiment was on two hospital patients. On receiving a message from the hospital to the effect that these two martyrs to therapeutic science had all but expired in convulsions, he experimented on a rabbit, which instantly dropped dead. It was then, and not until then, that he began to experiment on himself, with the germicide modified in the direction indicated by the experiments made on the two patients and the rabbit. As a good many people countenance vivisection because they fear that if the experiments are not made on rabbits they will be made on themselves, it is worth noting that in this case, where both rabbits and men were equally available, the men, being, of course, enormously more instructive, and costing nothing, were experimented on first. Once grant the ethics of the vivisectionists and you not only sanction the experiment on the human subject, but make it the first duty of the vivisector. If a guinea pig may be sacrificed for the sake of the very little that can be learnt from it, shall not a man be sacrificed for the sake of the great deal that can be learnt from him? At all events, he *is* sacrificed, as this typical case shows. I may add (not that it touches the argument) that the doctor, the patients, and the rabbit all suffered in vain, as far as the hoped-for rescue of the race from pulmonary consumption is concerned.

"THE LIE IS A EUROPEAN POWER"

Now at the very time when the lectures describing these experiments were being circulated in print and discussed eagerly by the medical profession, the customary denials that patients are experimented on were as loud, as indignant, as high-minded as ever, in spite of the few intelligent doctors who point out rightly that all treatments are experiments on the patient. And this brings us to an obvious but mostly overlooked weakness in the vivisector's position: that is, his inevitable forfeiture of all claim to have his word believed. It is hardly to be expected that a man who does not hesitate to vivisect for the sake of science will hesitate to lie about it afterwards to protect it from what he deems the ignorant sentimentality of the laity. When the public conscience stirs uneasily and threatens suppression, there is never wanting some doctor of eminent position and high character who will sacrifice himself devotedly to the cause of science by coming forward to assure the public on his honor that all experiments on animals are completely painless; although he must know that the very experiments which first provoked the anti-vivisection movement by their atrocity were experiments to ascertain the physiological effects of the sensation of extreme pain (the much more interesting physiology of pleasure remains uninvestigated) and that all experiments in which sensation is a factor are voided by its suppression. Besides, vivisection may be painless in cases where the experiments are very cruel. If a person scratches me with a poisoned dagger so gently that I do not feel the scratch, he has achieved a painless vivisection; but if I presently die in torment I am not likely to consider that his humanity is amply vindicated by his gentleness. A cobra's bite hurts so little that the creature is almost, legally speaking, a vivisector who inflicts no pain. By giving his victims chloroform before biting them he could comply with the law completely.

Here, then, is a pretty deadlock. Public support of vivisection is founded almost wholly on the assurances of the vivisectors that great public benefits may be expected from the practice. Not for a moment do I suggest that such a defence would be valid even if proved. But when the witnesses begin by alleging that in the cause of science all the customary ethical obligations (which include the obligation to tell the truth) are suspended, what weight can any reasonable person give to their testimony? I would rather swear fifty lies than take an animal which had licked my hand in good fellowship and torture it. If I did torture the dog, I should certainly not have the face to turn round and ask how any person dare suspect an honorable man like myself of telling lies. Most sensible and humane people would, I hope, reply flatly that honorable men do not behave dishonorably even to dogs. The murderer who, when asked by the chaplain whether he had any other crimes to confess, replied indignantly, "What do you take me for?" reminds us very strongly of the vivisectors who are so deeply hurt when their evidence is set aside as worthless.

AN ARGUMENT WHICH WOULD DEFEND ANY CRIME

The Achilles heel of vivisection, however, is not to be found in the pain it causes, but in the line of argument by which it is justified. The medical code regarding it is simply criminal anarchism at its very worst. Indeed no criminal has yet had the impudence to argue as every vivisector argues. No burglar contends that as it is admittedly important to have money to spend, and as the object of burglary is to provide the burglar with money to spend, and as in many instances it has achieved this object, therefore the burglar is a public benefactor and the police are ignorant sentimentalists. No highway robber has yet harrowed us with denunciations of the puling moralist who allows his child to suffer all the evils of poverty because certain faddists think it dishonest to garotte an alderman. Thieves and assassins understand quite well that there are paths of acquisition, even of the best things, that are barred to all men of honor. Again, has the silliest burglar ever pretended that to put a stop to burglary is to put a stop to industry? All the vivisections that have been performed since the world began have produced nothing so important as the innocent and honorable discovery of radiography; and one of the reasons why radiography was not discovered sooner was that the men whose business it was to discover new clinical methods were coarsening and stupefying themselves with the sensual villanies and cutthroat's casuistries of vivisection. The law of the conservation of energy holds good in physiology as in other things: every vivisector is a deserter from

the army of honorable investigators. But the vivisector does not
see this. He not only calls his methods scientific: he contends that
there are no other scientific methods. When you express your natural loathing for his cruelty and your natural contempt for his stupidity, he imagines that you are attacking science. Yet he has no
inkling of the method and temper of science. The point at issue
being plainly whether he is a rascal or not, he not only insists that
the real point is whether some hotheaded anti-vivisectionist is a
liar (which he proves by ridiculously unscientific assumptions as to
the degree of accuracy attainable in human statement), but never
dreams of offering any scientific evidence by his own methods.

There are many paths to knowledge already discovered; and no
enlightened man doubts that there are many more waiting to be
discovered. Indeed, all paths lead to knowledge; because even the
vilest and stupidest action teaches us something about vileness and
stupidity, and may accidentally teach us a good deal more: for instance, a cutthroat learns (and perhaps teaches) the anatomy of the
carotid artery and jugular vein; and there can be no question that
the burning of St. Joan of Arc must have been a most instructive
and interesting experiment to a good observer, and could have
been made more so if it had been carried out by skilled physiolo-
gists under laboratory conditions. The earthquake in San Francisco
proved invaluable as an experiment in the stability of giant steel
buildings; and the ramming of the Victoria by the Camperdown*
settled doubtful points of the greatest importance in naval war-
fare. According to vivisectionist logic our builders would be justified in producing artificial earthquakes with dynamite, and our
admirals in contriving catastrophes at naval manœuvres, in order
to follow up the line of research thus accidentally discovered.

The truth is, if the acquisition of knowledge justifies every sort
of conduct, it justifies any sort of conduct, from the illumination

---

*Reference to an accident in 1893 between two ships of the British Royal
Navy—HMS *Victoria* and HMS *Camperdown*—in which many drowned.

of Nero's feasts by burning human beings alive (another interesting experiment) to the simplest act of kindness. And in the light of that truth it is clear that the exemption of the pursuit of knowledge from the laws of honor is the most hideous conceivable enlargement of anarchy; worse, by far, than an exemption of the pursuit of money or political power, since these can hardly be attained without some regard for at least the appearances of human welfare, whereas a curious devil might destroy the whole race in torment, acquiring knowledge all the time from his highly interesting experiment. There is more danger in one respectable scientist countenancing such a monstrous claim than in fifty assassins or dynamitards. The man who makes it is ethically imbecile; and whoever imagines that it is a scientific claim has not the faintest conception of what science means. The paths to knowledge are countless. One of these paths is a path through darkness, secrecy, and cruelty. When a man deliberately turns from all other paths and goes down that one, it is scientific to infer that what attracts him is not knowledge, since there are other paths to that, but cruelty. With so strong and scientific a case against him, it is childish for him to stand on his honor and reputation and high character and the credit of a noble profession and so forth: he must clear himself either by reason or by experiment, unless he boldly contends that evolution has retained a passion of cruelty in man just because it is indispensable to the fulness of his knowledge.

THOU ART THE MAN

I shall not be at all surprised if what I have written above has induced in sympathetic readers a transport of virtuous indignation at the expense of the medical profession. I shall not damp so creditable and salutary a sentiment; but I must point out that the guilt is shared by all of us. It is not in his capacity of healer and man of science that the doctor vivisects or defends vivisection, but in his entirely vulgar lay capacity. He is made of the same clay as the ignorant, shallow, credulous, half-miseducated, pecuniarily anxious people who call him in when they have tried in vain every bottle and every pill the advertizing druggist can persuade them to buy. The real remedy for vivisection is the remedy for all the mischief that the medical profession and all the other professions are doing: namely, more knowledge. The juries which send the poor Peculiars to prison, and give vivisectionists heavy damages against humane persons who accuse them of cruelty; the editors and councillors and student-led mobs who are striving to make Vivisection one of the watchwords of our civilization, are not doctors: they are the British public, all so afraid to die that they will cling frantically to any idol which promises to cure all their diseases, and crucify anyone who tells them that they must not only die when their time comes, but die like gentlemen. In their paroxysms of cowardice and selfishness they force the doctors to humor their folly and ignorance. How complete and inconsiderate their ignorance is can only be realized by those who have some knowledge of vital statistics, and of the illusions which beset Public Health legislation.

WHAT THE PUBLIC WANTS AND WILL NOT GET

The demands of this poor public are not reasonable, but they are quite simple. It dreads disease and desires to be protected against it. But it is poor and wants to be protected cheaply. Scientific measures are too hard to understand, too costly, too clearly tending towards a rise in the rates and more public interference with the insanitary, because insufficiently financed, private house. What the public wants, therefore, is a cheap magic charm to prevent, and a cheap pill or potion to cure, all disease. It forces all such charms on the doctors.

THE VACCINATION CRAZE

Thus it was really the public and not the medical profession that took up vaccination with irresistible faith, sweeping the invention

out of Jenner's* hand and establishing it in a form which he himself repudiated. Jenner was not a man of science; but he was not a
fool; and when he found that people who had suffered from cowpox either by contagion in the milking shed or by vaccination,
were not, as he had supposed, immune from smallpox, he ascribed
the cases of immunity which had formerly misled him to a disease
of the horse, which, perhaps because we do not drink its milk and
eat its flesh, is kept at a greater distance in our imagination than
our foster mother the cow. At all events, the public, which had
been boundlessly credulous about the cow, would not have the
horse on any terms; and to this day the law which prescribes Jen-
nerian vaccination is carried out with an anti-Jennerian inoculation because the public would have it so in spite of Jenner. All the
grossest lies and superstitions which have disgraced the vaccination craze were taught to the doctors by the public. It was not the
doctors who first began to declare that all our old men remember
the time when almost every face they saw in the street was horribly pitted with smallpox, and that all this disfigurement has vanished since the introduction of vaccination. Jenner himself alluded
to this imaginary phenomenon before the introduction of vaccination, and attributed it to the older practice of smallpox inoculation, by which Voltaire, Catherine II. and Lady Mary Wortley
Montagu† so confidently expected to see the disease made harmless. It was not Jenner who set people declaring that smallpox, if
not abolished by vaccination, had at least been made much milder:
on the contrary, he recorded a pre-vaccination epidemic in which
none of the persons attacked went to bed or considered themselves as seriously ill. Neither Jenner, nor any other doctor ever,
as far as I know, inculcated the popular notion that everybody got

---

*Edward Jenner (1749–1823), English physician who discovered the smallpox
vaccine.

†English writer (1689–1762) who introduced inoculation for smallpox to England, after observing it in Turkey.

smallpox as a matter of course before vaccination was invented. That doctors get infected with these delusions, and are in their unprofessional capacity as members of the public subject to them like other men, is true; but if we had to decide whether vaccination was first forced on the public by the doctors or on the doctors by the public, we should have to decide against the public.

STATISTICAL ILLUSIONS

Public ignorance of the laws of evidence and of statistics can hardly be exaggerated. There may be a doctor here and there who in dealing with the statistics of disease has taken at least the first step towards sanity by grasping the fact that as an attack of even the commonest disease is an exceptional event, apparently overwhelming statistical evidence in favor of any prophylactic can be produced by persuading the public that everybody caught the disease formerly. Thus if a disease is one which normally attacks fifteen per cent of the population, and if the effect of a prophylactic is actually to increase the proportion to twenty per cent, the publication of this figure of twenty per cent will convince the public that the prophylactic has reduced the percentage by eighty per cent instead of increasing it by five, because the public, left to itself and to the old gentlemen who are always ready to remember, on every possible subject, that things used to be much worse than they are now (such old gentlemen greatly outnumber the laudatores tempori acti*), will assume that the former percentage was about 100. The vogue of the Pasteur treatment of hydrophobia, for instance, was due to the assumption by the public that every person bitten by a rabid dog necessarily got hydrophobia. I myself heard hydrophobia discussed in my youth by doctors in Dublin before a Pasteur Institute existed, the subject having been brought forward there by the scepticism of an eminent surgeon as to whether hydrophobia is really a specific disease or only ordinary

---

*Praisers of times past (Latin).

tetanus induced (as tetanus was then supposed to be induced) by a lacerated wound. There were no statistics available as to the proportion of dog bites that ended in hydrophobia; but nobody ever guessed that the cases could be more than two or three per cent of the bites. On me, therefore, the results published by the Pasteur Institute produced no such effect as they did on the ordinary man who thinks that the bite of a mad dog means certain hydrophobia. It seemed to me that the proportion of deaths among the cases treated at the Institute was rather higher, if anything, than might have been expected had there been no Institute in existence. But to the public every Pasteur patient who did not die was miraculously saved from an agonizing death by the beneficent white magic of that most trusty of all wizards, the man of science.

Even trained statisticians often fail to appreciate the extent to which statistics are vitiated by the unrecorded assumptions of their interpreters. Their attention is too much occupied with the cruder tricks of those who make a corrupt use of statistics for advertizing purposes. There is, for example, the percentage dodge. In some hamlet, barely large enough to have a name, two people are attacked during a smallpox epidemic. One dies: the other recovers. One has vaccination marks: the other has none. Immediately either the vaccinists or the anti-vaccinists publish the triumphant news that at such and such a place not a single vaccinated person died of smallpox whilst 100 per cent of the unvaccinated perished miserably; or, as the case may be, that 100 per cent of the unvaccinated recovered whilst the vaccinated succumbed to the last man. Or, to take another common instance, comparisons which are really comparisons between two social classes with different standards of nutrition and education are palmed off as comparisons between the results of a certain medical treatment and its neglect. Thus it is easy to prove that the wearing of tall hats and the carrying of umbrellas enlarges the chest, prolongs life, and confers comparative immunity from disease; for the statistics shew that the classes which use these articles are bigger, healthier, and live longer than the class which never dreams of possessing such things. It does not take much perspicacity to see that what really makes this difference is not the tall hat and the umbrella, but the wealth and nourishment of which they are evidence, and that a gold watch or membership of a club in Pall Mall might be proved in the same way to have the like sovereign virtues. A university degree, a daily bath, the owning of thirty pairs of trousers, a knowledge of Wagner's music, a pew in church,* anything, in short, that implies more means and better nurture than the mass of laborers enjoy, can be statistically palmed off as a magic-spell conferring all sorts of privileges.

In the case of a prophylactic enforced by law, this illusion is intensified grotesquely, because only vagrants can evade it. Now vagrants have little power of resisting any disease: their death rate and their case-mortality rate is always high relatively to that of respectable folk. Nothing is easier, therefore, than to prove that compliance with any public regulation produces the most gratifying results. It would be equally easy even if the regulation actually raised the death-rate, provided it did not raise it sufficiently to make the average householder, who cannot evade regulations, die as early as the average vagrant who can.

THE SURPRISES OF ATTENTION AND NEGLECT

There is another statistical illusion which is independent of class differences. A common complaint of houseowners is that the Public Health Authorities frequently compel them to instal costly sanitary appliances which are condemned a few years later as dangerous to health, and forbidden under penalties. Yet these discarded mistakes are always made in the first instance on the strength of a demonstration that their introduction has reduced the death-rate. The explanation is simple. Suppose a law were

---

*This could be reserved by wealthy people for an annual payment.

made that every child in the nation should be compelled to drink a pint of brandy per month, but that the brandy must be administered only when the child was in good health, with its digestion and so forth working normally, and its teeth either naturally or artificially sound. Probably the result would be an immediate and startling reduction in child mortality, leading to further legislation increasing the quantity of brandy to a gallon. Not until the brandy craze had been carried to a point at which the direct harm done by it would outweigh the incidental good, would an anti-brandy party be listened to. That incidental good would be the substitution of attention to the general health of children for the neglect which is now the rule so long as the child is not actually too sick to run about and play as usual. Even if this attention were confined to the children's teeth, there would be an improvement which it would take a good deal of brandy to cancel.

This imaginary case explains the actual case of the sanitary appliances which our local sanitary authorities prescribe today and condemn tomorrow. No sanitary contrivance which the mind of even the very worst plumber can devize could be as disastrous as that total neglect for long periods which gets avenged by pestilences that sweep through whole continents, like the black death and the cholera. If it were proposed at this time of day to discharge all the sewage of London crude and untreated into the Thames, instead of carrying it, after elaborate treatment, far out into the North Sea, there would be a shriek of horror from all our experts. Yet if Cromwell had done that instead of doing nothing, there would probably have been no Great Plague of London.* When the Local Health Authority forces every householder to have his sanitary arrangements thought about and attended to by somebody whose special business it is to attend to such things, then it matters not how erroneous or even directly mischievous may be the specific measures taken: the net result at first is sure to be an im-

---

*Epidemic of bubonic plague in 1685 that killed tens of thousands of people.

provement. Not until attention has been effectually substituted for neglect as the general rule, will the statistics begin to shew the merits of the particular methods of attention adopted. And as we are far from having arrived at this stage, being as to health legislation only at the beginning of things, we have practically no evidence yet as to the value of methods. Simple and obvious as this is, nobody seems as yet to discount the effect of substituting attention for neglect in drawing conclusions from health statistics. Everything is put to the credit of the particular method employed, although it may quite possibly be raising the death rate by five per thousand whilst the attention incidental to it is reducing the death rate fifteen per thousand. The net gain of ten per thousand is credited to the method, and made the excuse for enforcing more of it.

STEALING CREDIT FROM CIVILIZATION

There is yet another way in which specifics which have no merits at all, either direct or incidental, may be brought into high repute by statistics. For a century past civilization has been cleaning away the conditions which favor bacterial fevers. Typhus, once rife, has vanished: plague and cholera have been stopped at our frontiers by a sanitary blockade. We still have epidemics of smallpox and typhoid; and diphtheria and scarlet fever are endemic in the slums. Measles, which in my childhood was not regarded as a dangerous disease, has now become so mortal that notices are posted publicly urging parents to take it seriously. But even in these cases the contrast between the death and recovery rates in the rich districts and in the poor ones has led to the general conviction among experts that bacterial diseases are preventible; and they already are to a large extent prevented. The dangers of infection and the way to avoid it are better understood than they used to be. It is barely twenty years since people exposed themselves recklessly to the infection of consumption and pneumonia in the belief that these diseases were not "catching." Nowadays the troubles of consumptive patients are greatly increased by the growing disposition to treat them as lepers. No doubt there is a good deal of ignorant exaggeration and cowardly refusal to face a human and necessary share of the risk. That has always been the case. We now know that the medieval horror of leprosy was out of all proportion to the danger of infection, and was accompanied by apparent blindness to the infectiousness of smallpox, which has since been worked up by our disease terrorists into the position formerly held by leprosy. But the scare of infection, though it sets even doctors talking as if the only really scientific thing to do with a fever patient is to throw him into the nearest ditch and pump carbolic acid on him from a safe distance until he is ready to be cremated on the spot, has led to much greater care and cleanliness. And the net result has been a series of victories over disease.

Now let us suppose that in the early nineteenth century somebody had come forward with a theory that typhus fever always begins in the top joint of the little finger; and that if this joint be amputated immediately after birth, typhus fever will disappear. Had such a suggestion been adopted, the theory would have been triumphantly confirmed; for as a matter of fact, typhus fever *has* disappeared. On the other hand cancer and madness have increased (statistically) to an appalling extent. The opponents of the little finger theory would therefore be pretty sure to allege that the amputations were spreading cancer and lunacy. The vaccination controversy is full of such contentions. So is the controversy as to the docking of horses' tails and the cropping of dogs' ears. So is the less widely known controversy as to circumcision and the declaring certain kinds of flesh unclean by the Jews. To advertize any remedy or operation, you have only to pick out all the most reassuring advances made by civilization, and boldly present the two in the relation of cause and effect: the public will swallow the fallacy without a wry face. It has no idea of the need for what is called a control experiment. In Shakespear's time and for long after it, mummy was a favorite medicament. You took a pinch of the dust of a dead Egyptian in a pint of the hottest water you could bear to drink; and it did you a great deal of good. This, you thought, proved what a sovereign healer mummy was. But if you had tried the control experiment of taking the hot water without the mummy, you might have found the effect exactly the same, and that any hot drink would have done as well.

BIOMETRIKA

Another difficulty about statistics is the technical difficulty of calculation. Before you can even make a mistake in drawing your conclusion from the correlations established by your statistics you must ascertain the correlations. When I turn over the pages of Biometrika, a quarterly journal in which is recorded the work done in the field of biological statistics by Professor Karl Pearson and his colleagues, I am out of my depth at the first line, because mathematics are to me only a concept: I never used a logarithm in my life, and could not undertake to extract the square root of four without misgiving. I am therefore unable to deny that the statistical ascertainment of the correlations between one thing and another must be a very complicated and difficult technical business, not to be tackled successfully except by high mathematicians; and I cannot resist Professor Karl Pearson's immense contempt for, and indignant sense of grave social danger in, the unskilled guesses of the ordinary sociologist.

Now the man in the street knows nothing of Biometrika: all he knows is that "you can prove anything by figures," though he forgets this the moment figures are used to prove anything he wants to believe. If he did take in Biometrika he would probably become abjectly credulous as to all the conclusions drawn in it from the correlations so learnedly worked out; though the mathematician whose correlations would fill a Newton with admiration may, in collecting and accepting data and draw-conclusions from them, fall into quite crude errors by just such popular oversights as I have been describing.

PATIENT-MADE THERAPEUTICS

To all these blunders and ignorances doctors are no less subject than the rest of us. They are not trained in the use of evidence, nor in biometrics, nor in the psychology of human credulity, nor in the incidence of economic pressure. Further, they must believe, on the whole, what their patients believe, just as they must wear the sort of hat their patients wear. The doctor may lay down the law despotically enough to the patient at points where the patient's mind is simply blank; but when the patient has a prejudice the doctor must either keep it in countenance or lose his patient. If people are persuaded that night air is dangerous to health and that fresh air makes them catch cold, it will not be possible for a doctor to make his living in private practice if he prescribes ventilation. We have to go back no further than the days of The Pickwick Papers to find ourselves in a world where people slept in four-post beds with curtains drawn closely round to exclude as much air as possible. Had Mr. Pickwick's doctor told him that he would be much healthier if he slept on a camp bed by an open window, Mr. Pickwick would have regarded him as a crank and called in another doctor. Had he gone on to forbid Mr. Pickwick to drink brandy and water whenever he felt chilly, and assured him that if he were deprived of meat or salt for a whole year, he would not only not die, but would be none the worse, Mr. Pickwick would have fled from his presence as from that of a dangerous madman. And in these matters the doctor cannot cheat his patient. If he has no faith in drugs or vaccination, and the patient has, he can cheat him with colored water and pass his lancet through the flame of a spirit lamp before scratching his arm. But he cannot make him change his daily habits without knowing it.

THE REFORMS ALSO COME FROM THE LAITY

In the main, then, the doctor learns that if he gets ahead of the superstitions of his patients he is a ruined man; and the result is that he instinctively takes care not to get ahead of them. That is why all the changes come from the laity. It was not until an agitation had been conducted for many years by laymen, including quacks and faddists of all kinds, that the public was sufficiently impressed to make it possible for the doctors to open their minds and their mouths on the subject of fresh air, cold water, temperance, and the rest of the new fashions in hygiene. At present the tables have been turned on many old prejudices. Plenty of our most popular elderly doctors believe that cold tubs in the morning are unnatural, exhausting, and rheumatic; that fresh air is a fad and that everybody is the better for a glass or two of port wine every day; but they no longer dare say as much until they know exactly where they are; for many very desirable patients in country houses have lately been persuaded that their first duty is to get up at six in the morning and begin the day by taking a walk barefoot through the dewy grass. He who shews the least scepticism as to this practice is at once suspected of being "an old-fashioned doctor," and dismissed to make room for a younger man.

In short, private medical practice is governed not by science but by supply and demand; and however scientific a treatment may be, it cannot hold its place in the market if there is no demand for it; nor can the grossest quackery be kept off the market if there is a demand for it.

FASHIONS AND EPIDEMICS

A demand, however, can be inculcated. This is thoroughly understood by fashionable tradesmen, who find no difficulty in persuading their customers to renew articles that are not worn out and to buy things they do not want. By making doctors tradesmen, we compel them to learn the tricks of trade; consequently we find that the fashions of the year include treatments, operations, and particular drugs, as well as hats, sleeves, ballads, and games. Tonsils, vermiform appendices, uvulas, even ovaries are sacrificed because it is the fashion to get them cut out, and because the operations are highly profitable. The psychology of fashion becomes a pathology; for the cases have every air of being genuine: fashions, after all, are only induced epidemics, proving that epidemics can be induced by tradesmen, and therefore by doctors.

THE DOCTOR'S VIRTUES

It will be admitted that this is a pretty bad state of things. And the melodramatic instinct of the public, always demanding that every wrong shall have, not its remedy, but its villain to be hissed, will blame, not its own apathy, superstition, and ignorance, but the depravity of the doctors. Nothing could be more unjust or mischievous. Doctors, if no better than other men, are certainly no worse. I was reproached during the performances of The Doctor's Dilemma at the Court Theatre in 1907[4] because I made the artist a rascal, the journalist an illiterate incapable, and all the doctors "angels." But I did not go beyond the warrant of my own experience. It has been my luck to have doctors among my friends for nearly forty years past (all perfectly aware of my freedom from the usual credulity as to the miraculous powers and knowledge attributed to them); and though I know that there are medical blackguards as well as military, legal, and clerical blackguards (one soon finds that out when one is privileged to hear doctors talking shop among themselves), the fact that I was no more at a loss for private medical advice and attendance when I had not a penny in my pocket than I was later on when I could afford fees on the highest scale, has made it impossible for me to share that hostility to the doctor as a man which exists and is growing as an inevitable result of the present condition of medical practice. Not that the interest in disease and aberrations which turns some men and women to medicine and surgery is not sometimes as morbid as the interest in misery and vice which turns some others to philanthropy and "rescue work." But the true doctor is inspired by a hatred of ill-health, and a divine impatience of any waste of vital forces. Unless a man is led to medicine or surgery through a very exceptional technical aptitude, or because doctoring is a family tradition, or because he regards it unintelligently as a lucrative and gentlemanly profession, his motives in choosing the career of a healer are clearly generous. However actual practice may disillusion and corrupt him, his selection in the first instance is not a selection of a base character.

THE DOCTOR'S HARDSHIPS

A review of the counts in the indictment I have brought against private medical practice will shew that they arise out of the doctor's position as a competitive private tradesman: that is, out of his poverty and dependence. And it should be borne in mind that doctors are expected to treat other people specially well whilst themselves submitting to specially inconsiderate treatment. The butcher and baker are not expected to feed the hungry unless the hungry can pay; but a doctor who allows a fellow-creature to suffer or perish without aid is regarded as a monster. Even if we must dismiss hospital service as really venal, the fact remains that most doctors do a good deal of gratuitous work in private practice all through their careers. And in his paid work the doctor is on a different footing to the tradesman. Although the articles he sells, advice and treatment, are the same for all classes, his fees have to be graduated like the income tax. The successful fashionable doctor may weed his poorer patients out from time to time, and finally use the College of Physicians* to place it out of his own power to accept low fees; but the ordinary general practitioner never makes out his bills without considering the taxable capacity of his patients.

---

*Professional organization for physicians in Britain.

Then there is the disregard of his own health and comfort which results from the fact that he is, by the nature of his work, an emergency man. We are polite and considerate to the doctor when there is nothing the matter, and we meet him as a friend or entertain him as a guest; but when the baby is suffering from croup, or its mother has a temperature of 104°, or its grandfather has broken his leg, nobody thinks of the doctor except as a healer and saviour. He may be hungry, weary, sleepy, run down by several successive nights disturbed by that instrument of torture, the night bell; but who ever thinks of this in the face of sudden sickness or accident? We think no more of the condition of a doctor attending a case than of the condition of a fireman at a fire. In other occupations night-work is specially recognized and provided for. The worker sleeps all day; has his breakfast in the evening; his lunch or dinner at midnight; his dinner or supper before going to bed in the morning; and he changes to day-work if he cannot stand night-work. But a doctor is expected to work day and night. In practices which consist largely of workmen's clubs,* and in which the patients are therefore taken on wholesale terms and very numerous, the unfortunate assistant, or the principal if he has no assistant, often does not undress, knowing that he will be called up before he has snatched an hour's sleep. To the strain of such inhuman conditions must be added the constant risk of infection. One wonders why the impatient doctors do not become savage and unmanageable, and the patient ones imbecile. Perhaps they do, to some extent. And the pay is wretched, and so uncertain that refusal to attend without payment in advance becomes often a necessary measure of self-defence, whilst the County Court has long ago put an end to the tradition that the doctor's fee is an honorarium. Even the most eminent physicians, as such biographies as those of Paget† shew, are sometimes miserably, inhumanly poor until they are past their prime.

---

*Company doctors paid through workers' contributions.
†Sir James Paget (1814–1899), renowned English surgeon and pathologist.

In short, the doctor needs our help for the moment much more than we often need his. The ridicule of Molière, the death of a well-informed and clever writer like the late Harold Frederic* in the hands of Christian Scientists (a sort of sealing with his blood of the contemptuous disbelief in and dislike of doctors he had bitterly expressed in his books), the scathing and quite justifiable exposure of medical practice in the novel by Mr. Maarten Maartens entitled The New Religion: all these trouble the doctor very little, and are in any case well set off by the popularity of Sir Luke Fildes' famous picture,† and by the verdicts in which juries from time to time express their conviction that the doctor can do no wrong. The real woes of the doctor are the shabby coat, the wolf at the door, the tyranny of ignorant patients, the work-day of 24 hours, and the uselessness of honestly prescribing what most of the patients really need: that is, not medicine, but money.

THE PUBLIC DOCTOR

What then is to be done?

Fortunately we have not to begin absolutely from the beginning: we already have, in the Medical Officer of Health, a sort of doctor who is free from the worst hardships, and consequently from the worst vices, of the private practitioner. His position depends, not on the number of people who are ill, and whom he can keep ill, but on the number of people who are well. He is judged, as all doctors and treatments should be judged, by the vital statistics of his district. When the death rate goes up his credit goes down. As every increase in his salary depends on the issue of a public debate as to the health of the constituency under his charge, he has every inducement to strive towards the ideal of a clean bill

---

*American novelist (1856–1898).

†Reference to The Doctor, a painting by Sir Luke Fildes (1844–1927), based on the death of his son, that depicts a doctor keeping watch at the bedside of a sick child.

of health. He has a safe, dignified, responsible, independent position based wholly on the public health; whereas the private practitioner has a precarious, shabby-genteel, irresponsible, servile position, based wholly on the prevalence of illness.

It is true, there are grave scandals in the public medical service. The public doctor may be also a private practitioner eking out his earnings by giving a little time to public work for a mean payment. There are cases in which the position is one which no successful practitioner will accept, and where, therefore, incapables or drunkards get automatically selected for the post, *faute de mieux*;* but even in these cases the doctor is less disastrous in his public capacity than in his private one: besides, the conditions which produce these bad cases are doomed, as the evil is now recognized and understood. A popular but unstable remedy is to enable local authorities, when they are too small to require the undivided time of such men as the Medical Officers of our great municipalities, to combine for public health purposes so that each may share the services of a highly paid official of the best class; but the right remedy is a larger area as the sanitary unit.

MEDICAL ORGANIZATION

Another advantage of public medical work is that it admits of organization, and consequently of the distribution of the work in such a manner as to avoid wasting the time of highly qualified experts on trivial jobs. The individualism of private practice leads to an appalling waste of time on trifles. Men whose dexterity as operators or almost divinatory skill in diagnosis are constantly needed for difficult cases, are poulticing whitlows,† vaccinating, changing unimportant dressings, prescribing ether drams for ladies with timid leanings towards dipsomania, and generally wasting their time in the pursuit of private fees. In no other pro-

---

*For lack of a better (French).

†Infections of the finger or toe.

fession is the practitioner expected to do all the work involved in
it from the first day of his professional career to the last as the doctor is. The judge passes sentence of death; but he is not expected
to hang the criminal with his own hands, as he would be if the legal
profession were as unorganized as the medical. The bishop is not
expected to blow the organ or wash the baby he baptizes. The general is not asked to plan a campaign or conduct a battle at half-past
twelve and to play the drum at half-past two. Even if they were,
things would still not be as bad as in the medical profession; for in
it not only is the first-class man set to do third-class work, but,
what is much more terrifying, the third-class man is expected to
do first-class work. Every general practitioner is supposed to be
capable of the whole range of medical and surgical work at a moment's notice; and the country doctor, who has not a specialist nor
a crack consultant at the end of his telephone, often has to tackle
without hesitation cases which no sane practitioner in a town
would take in hand without assistance. No doubt this develops the
resourcefulness of the country doctor, and makes him a more capable man than his suburban colleague; but it cannot develop the
second-class man into a first-class one. If the practice of law not
only led to a judge having to hang, but the hangman to judge, or if
in the army matters were so arranged that it would be possible for
the drummer boy to be in command at Waterloo whilst the Duke
of Wellington was playing the drum in Brussels, we should not be
consoled by the reflection that our hangmen were thereby made a
little more judicial-minded, and our drummers more responsible,
than in foreign countries where the legal and military professions
recognized the advantages of division of labor.

Under such conditions no statistics as to the graduation of professional ability among doctors are available. Assuming that doctors are normal men and not magicians (and it is unfortunately
very hard to persuade people to admit so much and thereby destroy the romance of doctoring) we may guess that the medical
profession, like the other professions, consists of a small percent-

age of highly gifted persons at one end, and a small percentage of altogether disastrous duffers at the other. Between these extremes comes the main body of doctors (also, of course, with a weak and a strong end) who can be trusted to work under regulations with more or less aid from above according to the gravity of the case. Or, to put it in terms of the cases, there are cases that present no difficulties, and can be dealt with by a nurse or student at one end of the scale, and cases that require watching and handling by the very highest existing skill at the other; whilst between come the great mass of cases which need visits from the doctor of ordinary ability and from the chiefs of the profession in the proportion of, say, seven to none, seven to one, three to one, one to one, or, for a day or two, none to one. Such a service is organized at present only in hospitals; though in large towns the practice of calling in the consultant acts, to some extent, as a substitute for it. But in the latter case it is quite unregulated except by professional etiquet, which, as we have seen, has for its object, not the health of the patient or of the community at large, but the protection of the doctor's livelihood and the concealment of his errors. And as the consultant is an expensive luxury, he is a last resource rather, as he should be, than a matter of course, in all cases where the general practitioner is not equal to the occasion: a predicament in which a very capable man may find himself at any time through the cropping up of a case of which he has had no clinical experience.

THE SOCIAL SOLUTION OF THE MEDICAL PROBLEM

The social solution of the medical problem, then, depends on that large, slowly advancing, pettishly resisted integration of society called generally Socialism. Until the medical profession becomes a body of men trained and paid by the country to keep the country in health it will remain what it is at present: a conspiracy to exploit popular credulity and human suffering. Already our M.O.H.s (Medical Officers of Health) are in the new position: what is lacking is appreciation of the change, not only by the public but by the private doctors. For, as we have seen, when one of the first-rate posts becomes vacant in one of the great cities, and all the leading M.O.H.s compete for it, they must appeal to the good health of the cities of which they have been in charge, and not to the size of the incomes the local private doctors are making out of the ill-health of their patients. If a competitor can prove that he has utterly ruined every sort of medical private practice in a large city except obstetric practice and the surgery of accidents, his claims are irresistible; and this is the ideal at which every M.O.H. should aim. But the profession at large should none the less welcome him and set its house in order for the social change which will finally be its own salvation. For the M.O.H. as we know him is only the beginning of that army of Public Hygiene which will presently take the place in general interest and honor now occupied by our military and naval forces. It is silly that an Englishman should be more afraid of a German soldier than of a British disease germ, and should clamor for more barracks in the same newspapers that protest against more school clinics, and cry out that if the State fights disease for us it makes us paupers, though they never say that if the State fights the Germans for us it makes us cowards. Fortunately, when a habit of thought is silly it only needs steady treatment by ridicule from sensible and witty people to be put out of countenance and perish. Every year sees an increase in the number of persons employed in the Public Health Service, who would formerly have been mere adventurers in the Private Illness Service. To put it another way, a host of men and women who have now a strong incentive to be mischievous and even murderous rogues will have a much stronger, because a much honester, incentive to be not only good citizens but active benefactors to the community. And they will have no anxiety whatever about their incomes.

THE FUTURE OF PRIVATE PRACTICE

It must not be hastily concluded that this involves the extinction of the private practitioner. What it will really mean for him is release from his present degrading and scientifically corrupting slavery to his patients. As I have already shewn, the doctor who has to live by pleasing his patients in competition with everybody who has walked the hospitals, scraped through the examinations, and bought a brass plate, soon finds himself prescribing water to teetotallers and brandy or champagne jelly to drunkards; beefsteaks and stout in one house, and "uric acid free" vegetarian diet over the way; shut windows, big fires, and heavy overcoats to old Colonels, and open air and as much nakedness as is compatible with decency to young faddists, never once daring to say either "I dont know," or "I dont agree." For the strength of the doctor's, as of every other man's position when the evolution of social organization at last reaches his profession, will be that he will always have open to him the alternative of public employment when the private employer becomes too tyrannous. And let no one suppose that the words doctor and patient can disguise from the parties the fact that they are employer and employee. No doubt doctors who are in great demand can be as high-handed and independent as employees are in all classes when a dearth in their labor market makes them indispensable; but the average doctor is not in this position: he is struggling for life in an overcrowded profession, and knows well that "a good bedside manner" will carry him to solvency through a morass of illness, whilst the least attempt at plain dealing with people who are eating too much, or drinking too much, or frowsting* too much (to go no further in the list of intemperances that make up so much of family life) would soon land him in the Bankruptcy Court.

Private practice, thus protected, would itself protect individu-

---

*Staying in musty rooms.

als, as far as such protection is possible, against the errors and superstitions of State medicine, which are at worst no worse than the errors and superstitions of private practice, being, indeed, all derived from it. Such monstrosities as vaccination are, as we have seen, founded, not on science, but on half-crowns. If the Vaccination Acts, instead of being wholly repealed as they are already half repealed, were strengthened by compelling every parent to have his child vaccinated by a public officer whose salary was completely independent of the number of vaccinations performed by him, and for whom there was plenty of alternative public health work waiting, vaccination would be dead in two years, as the vaccinator would not only not gain by it, but would lose credit through the depressing effects on the vital statistics of his district of the illness and deaths it causes, whilst it would take from him all the credit of that freedom from smallpox which is the result of good sanitary administration and vigilant prevention of infection. Such absurd panic scandals as that of the last London epidemic, where a fee of half-a-crown per re-vaccination produced raids on houses during the absence of parents, and the forcible seizure and re-vaccination of children left to answer the door, can be prevented simply by abolishing the half-crown and all similar follies, paying, not for this or that ceremony of witchcraft, but for immunity from disease, and paying, too, in a rational way. The officer with a fixed salary saves himself trouble by doing his business with the least possible interference with the private citizen. The man paid by the job loses money by not forcing his job on the public as often as possible without reference to its results.

THE TECHNICAL PROBLEM

As to any technical medical problem specially involved, there is none. If there were, I should not be competent to deal with it, as I am not a technical expert in medicine: I deal with the subject as an economist, a politician, and a citizen exercising my common sense. Everything that I have said applies equally to all the medical techniques, and will hold good whether public hygiene be based on the poetic fancies of Christian Science, the tribal superstitions of the druggist and the vivisector, or the best we can make of our real knowledge. But I may remind those who confusedly imagine that the medical problem is also the scientific problem, that all problems are finally scientific problems. The notion that therapeutics or hygiene or surgery is any more or less scientific than making or cleaning boots is entertained only by people to whom a man of science is still a magician who can cure diseases, transmute metals, and enable us to live for ever. It may still be necessary for some time to come to practise on popular credulity, popular love and dread of the marvellous, and popular idolatry, to induce the poor to comply with the sanitary regulations they are too ignorant to understand. As I have elsewhere confessed, I have myself been responsible for ridiculous incantations with burning sulphur, experimentally proved to be quite useless, because poor people are convinced, by the mystical air of the burning and the horrible smell, that it exorcises the demons of smallpox and scarlet fever and makes it safe for them to return to their houses. To assure them that the real secret is sunshine and soap is only to convince them that you do not care whether they live or die, and wish to save money at their expense. So you perform the incantation; and back they go to their houses, satisfied. A religious ceremony—a poetic blessing of the threshold, for instance—would be much better; but unfortunately our religion is weak on the sanitary side. One of the worst misfortunes of Christendom was that reaction against the voluptuous bathing of the imperial Romans which made dirty habits a part of Christian piety, and in some unlucky places (the Sandwich Islands* for example) made the introduction of Christianity also the introduction of disease, because the formulators of the superseded native religion, like Mahomet, had been enlightened enough to introduce as religious duties such sanitary measures as ablution and the most careful and reverent treatment of

---

*Former name of Hawaii.

everything cast off by the human body, even to nail clippings and hairs; and our missionaries thoughtlessly discredited this godly doctrine without supplying its place, which was promptly taken by laziness and neglect. If the priests of Ireland could only be persuaded to teach their flocks that it is a deadly insult to the Blessed Virgin to place her image in a cottage that is not kept up to that high standard of Sunday cleanliness to which all her worshippers must believe she is accustomed, and to represent her as being especially particular about stables because her son was born in one, they might do more in one year than all the Sanitary Inspectors in Ireland could do in twenty; and they could hardly doubt that Our Lady would be delighted. Perhaps they do nowadays; for Ireland is certainly a transfigured country since my youth as far as clean faces and pinafores can transfigure it. In England, where so many of the inhabitants are too gross to believe in poetic faiths, too respectable to tolerate the notion that the stable at Bethany was a common peasant farmer's stable instead of a first-rate racing one, and too savage to believe that anything can really cast out the devil of disease unless it be some terrifying hoodoo* of tortures and stinks, the M.O.H. will no doubt for a long time to come have to preach to fools according to their folly, promising miracles, and threatening hideous personal consequences of neglect of by-laws and the like; therefore it will be important that every M.O.H. shall have, with his (or her) other qualifications, a sense of humor, lest (he or she) should come at last to believe all the nonsense that must needs be talked. But he must, in his capacity of an expert advising the authorities, keep the government itself free of superstition. If Italian peasants are so ignorant that the Church can get no hold of them except by miracles, why miracles there must be. The blood of St. Januarius† must liquefy whether the Saint is in the humor or not. To trick a heathen into

---

*Superstitious practice using magic and spells.

†Martyr (272?–305) during the reign of Roman emperor Diocletian; in Naples, a phial thought to contain his dried blood is said to liquefy each year.

being a dutiful Christian is no worse than to trick a whitewasher into trusting himself in a room where a smallpox patient has lain, by pretending to exorcise the disease with burning sulphur. But woe to the Church if in deceiving the peasant it also deceives itself; for then the Church is lost, and the peasant too, unless he revolt against it. Unless the Church works the pretended miracle painfully against the grain, and is continually urged by its dislike of the imposture to strive to make the peasant susceptible to the true reasons for behaving well, the Church will become an instrument of his corruption and an exploiter of his ignorance, and will find itself launched upon that persecution of scientific truth of which all priesthoods are accused—and none with more justice than the scientific priesthood.

And here we come to the danger that terrifies so many of us: the danger of having a hygienic orthodoxy imposed on us. But we must face that: in such crowded and poverty ridden civilizations as ours any orthodoxy is better than laisser-faire. If our population ever comes to consist exclusively of well-to-do, highly cultivated, and thoroughly instructed free persons in a position to take care of themselves, no doubt they will make short work of a good deal of official regulation that is now of life-and-death necessity to us; but under existing circumstances, I repeat, almost any sort of attention that democracy will stand is better than neglect. Attention and activity lead to mistakes as well as to successes; but a life spent in making mistakes is not only more honorable but more useful than a life spent doing nothing. The one lesson that comes out of all our theorizing and experimenting is that there is only one really scientific progressive method; and that is the method of trial and error. If you come to that, what is laisser-faire but an orthodoxy? the most tyrannous and disastrous of all the orthodoxies, since it forbids you even to learn.

THE LATEST THEORIES

Medical theories are so much a matter of fashion, and the most
fertile of them are modified so rapidly by medical practice and biological research, which are international activities, that the play
which furnishes the pretext for this preface is already slightly outmoded, though I believe it may be taken as a faithful record for the
year (1906) in which it was begun. I must not expose any professional man to ruin by connecting his name with the entire freedom of criticism which I, as a layman, enjoy; but it will be evident
to all experts that my play could not have been written but for the
work done by Sir Almroth Wright in the theory and practice of securing immunization from bacterial diseases by the inoculation of
"vaccines" made of their own bacteria: a practice incorrectly called
vaccinetherapy (there is nothing vaccine about it) apparently because it is what vaccination ought to be and is not. Until Sir Almroth Wright, following up one of Metchnikoff's* most suggestive
biological romances, discovered that the white corpuscles or
phagocytes which attack and devour disease germs for us do their
work only when we butter the disease germs appetizingly for
them with a natural sauce which Sir Almroth named opsonin, and
that our production of this condiment continually rises and falls
rhythmically from negligibility to the highest efficiency, nobody
had been able even to conjecture why the various serums that
were from time to time introduced as having effected marvellous
cures, presently made such direful havoc of some unfortunate patient that they had to be dropped hastily. The quantity of sturdy
lying that was necessary to save the credit of inoculation in those
days was prodigious; and had it not been for the devotion shewn
by the military authorities throughout Europe, who would order
the entire disappearance of some disease from their armies, and

---

*The writings of Russian biologist Ilya Metchnikoff (1845–1916) include *Immu-
nity in Infectious Diseases* (1905) and *The Nature of Man* (1903).

bring it about by the simple plan of changing the name under which the cases were reported, or for our own Metropolitan Asylums Board,* which carefully suppressed all the medical reports that revealed the sometimes quite appalling effects of epidemics of revaccination, there is no saying what popular reaction might not have taken place against the whole immunization movement in therapeutics.

The situation was saved when Sir Almroth Wright pointed out that if you inoculated a patient with pathogenic germs at a moment when his powers of cooking them for consumption by the phagocytes was receding to its lowest point, you would certainly make him a good deal worse and perhaps kill him, whereas if you made precisely the same inoculation when the cooking power was rising to one of its periodical climaxes, you would stimulate it to still further exertions and produce just the opposite result. And he invented a technique for ascertaining in which phase the patient happened to be at any given moment. The dramatic possibilities of this discovery and invention will be found in my play. But it is one thing to invent a technique: it is quite another to persuade the medical profession to acquire it. Our general practitioners, I gather, simply declined to acquire it, being mostly unable to afford either the acquisition or the practice of it when acquired. Something simple, cheap, and ready at all times for all comers, is, as I have shewn, the only thing that is economically possible in general practice, whatever may be the case in Sir Almroth's famous laboratory in St. Mary's Hospital. It would have become necessary to denounce opsonin in the trade papers as a fad and Sir Almroth as a dangerous man if his practice in the laboratory had not led him to the conclusion that the customary inoculations were very much too powerful, and that a comparatively infinitesimal dose would not precipitate a negative phase of cooking activity, and might in-

*London public-health board established in 1867 that operated, among other things, specialist hospitals for infectious diseases and tuberculosis.

duce a positive one. And thus it happens that the refusal of our general practitioners to acquire the new technique is no longer quite so dangerous in practice as it was when The Doctor's Dilemma was written: nay, that Sir Ralph Bloomfield Bonington's way of administering inoculations as if they were spoonfuls of squills* may sometimes work fairly well. For all that, I find Sir Almroth Wright, on the 23rd May, 1910, warning the Royal Society of Medicine that "the clinician has not yet been prevailed upon, to reconsider his positon," which means that the general practitioner ("the doctor," as he is called in our homes) is going on just as he did before, and could not afford to learn or practice a new technique even if he had ever heard of it. To the patient who does not know about it he will say nothing. To the patient who does, he will ridicule it, and disparage Sir Almroth. What else can he do, except confess his ignorance and starve?

But now please observe how "the whirligig of time brings its revenges."† This latest discovery of the remedial virtue of a very, very tiny hair of the dog that bit you reminds us, not only of Arndt's law of protoplasmic reaction to stimuli, according to which weak and strong stimuli provoke opposite reactions, but of Hahnemann's homeopathy, which was founded on the fact alleged by Hahnemann that drugs which produce certain symptoms when taken in ordinary perceptible quantities, will, when taken in infinitesimally small quantities, provoke just the opposite symptoms; so that the drug that gives you a headache will also cure a headache if you take little enough of it. I have already explained that the savage opposition which homeopathy encountered from the medical profession was not a scientific opposition; for nobody seems to deny that some drugs act in the alleged manner. It was opposed simply because doctors and apothecaries lived by selling

---

*Medicinal syrup derived from the squill plant, a bulbous herb.

†Thus Feste gloats over Malvolio's humiliation in Shakespeare's Twelfth Night (act 5, scene 1).

bottles and boxes of doctor's stuff to be taken in spoonfuls or in pellets as large as peas; and people would not pay as much for drops and globules no bigger than pins' heads. Nowadays, however, the more cultivated folk are beginning to be so suspicious of drugs, and the incorrigibly superstitious people so profusely supplied with patent medicines (the medical advice to take them being wrapped round the bottle and thrown in for nothing) that homeopathy has become a way of rehabilitating the trade of prescription compounding, and is consequently coming into professional credit. At which point the theory of opsonins comes very opportunely to shake hands with it.

Add to the newly triumphant homeopathist and the opsonist that other remarkable innovator, the Swedish masseur, who does not theorize about you, but probes you all over with his powerful thumbs until he finds out your sore spots and rubs them away, besides cheating you into a little wholesome exercise; and you have nearly everything in medical practice to-day that is not flat witchcraft or pure commercial exploitation of human credulity and fear of death. Add to them a good deal of vegetarian and teetotal controversy raging round a clamor for scientific eating and drinking, and resulting in little so far except calling digestion Metabolism and dividing the public between the eminent doctor who tells us that we do not eat enough fish, and his equally eminent colleague who warns us that a fish diet must end in leprosy, and you have all that opposes with any sort of countenance the rise of Christian Science with its cathedrals and congregations and zealots and miracles and cures: all very silly, no doubt, but sane and sensible, poetic and hopeful, compared to the pseudo science of the commercial general practitioner, who foolishly clamors for the prosecution and even the execution of the Christian Scientists when their patients die, forgetting the long death roll of his own patients.

By the time this preface is in print the kaleidoscope may have had another shake; and opsonin may have gone the way of phlo-

giston* at the hands of its own restless discoverer. I will not say
that Hahnemann may have gone the way of Diafoirus;† for Diafoirus we have always with us. But we shall still pick up all our
knowledge in pursuit of some Will o' the Wisp or other. What is
called science has always pursued the Elixir of Life and the
Philosopher's Stone, and is just as busy after them to-day as ever it
was in the days of Paracelsus.‡ We call them by different names:
Immunization or Radiology or what not; but the dreams which
lure us into the adventures from which we learn are always at bottom the same. Science becomes dangerous only when it imagines
that it has reached its goal. What is wrong with priests and popes
is that instead of being apostles and saints, they are nothing but
empirics who say "I know" instead of "I am learning," and pray for
credulity and inertia as wise men pray for scepticism and activity.
Such abominations as the Inquisition and the Vaccination Acts are
possible only in the famine years of the soul, when the great vital
dogmas of honor, liberty, courage, the kinship of all life, faith that
the unknown is greater than the known and is only the As Yet Unknown, and resolution to find a manly highway to it, have been
forgotten in a paroxysm of littleness and terror in which nothing
is active except concupiscence and the fear of death, playing on
which any trader can filch a fortune, any blackguard gratify his
cruelty, and any tyrant make us his slaves.

Lest this should seem too rhetorical a conclusion for our professional men of science, who are mostly trained not to believe
anything unless it is worded in the jargon of those writers who,
because they never really understand what they are trying to say,
cannot find familiar words for it, and are therefore compelled to

---

*Hypothetical substance thought to be released through burning, a theory dis-
proved by French chemist Antoine Lavoisier (1743–1794).

†In Molière's play *The Imaginary Invalid* (1673), a doctor who disdains such new-
fangled theories as circulation of the blood.

‡Sixteenth-century German alchemist and physician.

invent a new language of nonsense for every book they write, let me sum up my conclusions as dryly as is consistent with accurate thought and live conviction.

1. Nothing is more dangerous than a poor doctor: not even a poor employer or a poor landlord.

2. Of all the anti-social vested interests the worst is the vested interest in ill-health.

3. Remember that an illness is a misdemeanor; and treat the doctor as an accessory unless he notifies every case to the Public Health authority.

4. Treat every death as a possible and under our present system a probable murder, by making it the subject of a reasonably conducted inquest; and execute the doctor, if necessary, *as* a doctor, by striking him off the register.

5. Make up your mind how many doctors the community needs to keep it well. Do not register more or less than this number; and let registration constitute the doctor a civil servant with a dignified living wage paid out of public funds.

6. Municipalize Harley Street.

7. Treat the private operator exactly as you would treat a private executioner.

8. Treat persons who profess to be able to cure disease as you treat fortune tellers.

9. Keep the public carefully informed, by special statistics and announcements of individual cases, of all illnesses of doctors or in their families.

10. Make it compulsory for a doctor using a brass plate to have inscribed on it, in addition to the letters indicating his qualifications, the words "Remember that I too am mortal."

11. In legislation and social organization, proceed on the principle that invalids, meaning persons who cannot keep themselves alive by their own activities, cannot, beyond reason, expect to be kept alive by the activity of others. There is a point at which the most energetic policeman or doctor, when called upon to deal

with an apparently drowned person, gives up artificial respiration, although it is never possible to declare with certainty, at any point short of decomposition, that five minutes of the exercise would not effect resuscitation. The theory that every individual alive is of infinite value is legislatively impracticable. No doubt the higher the life we secure to the individual by wise social organization, the greater his value is to the community, and the more pains we shall take to pull him through any temporary danger or disablement. But the man who costs more than he is worth is doomed by sound hygiene as inexorably as by sound economics.

12. Do not try to live for ever. You will not succeed.

13. Use your health, even to the point of wearing it out. That is what it is for. Spend all you have before you die; and do not out-live yourself.

14. Take the utmost care to get well born and well brought up. This means that your mother must have a good doctor. Be careful to go to a school where there is what they call a school clinic, where your nutrition and teeth and eyesight and other matters of importance to you will be attended to. Be particularly careful to have all this done at the expense of the nation, as otherwise it will not be done at all, the chances being about forty to one against your being able to pay for it directly yourself, even if you know how to set about it. Otherwise you will be what most people are at present: an unsound citizen of an unsound nation, without sense enough to be ashamed or unhappy about it.

I am grateful to Hesba Stretton, the authoress of "Jessica's First Prayer," for permission to use the title of one of her stories for this play.

THE DOCTOR'S DILEMMA

ACT I

*On the 15th June 1908, in the early forenoon, a medical
student, surname Redpenny, Christian name unknown and
of no importance, sits at work in a doctor's consulting-room.
He devils for the doctor by answering his letters, acting as
his domestic laboratory assistant, and making himself
indispensable generally, in return for unspecified advantages
involved by intimate intercourse with a leader of his
profession, and amounting to an informal apprenticeship
and a temporary affiliation. Redpenny is not proud, and
will do anything he is asked without reservation of his
personal dignity if he is asked in a fellow-creaturely way. He
is a wide-open-eyed, ready, credulous, friendly, hasty youth,
with his hair and clothes in reluctant transition from the
untidy boy to the tidy doctor.*

*Redpenny is interrupted by the entrance of an old
serving-woman who has never known the cares, the
preoccupations, the responsibilities, jealousies, and
anxieties of personal beauty. She has the complexion of a
never-washed gypsy, incurable by any detergent; and she
has, not a regular beard and moustaches, which could at
least be trimmed and waxed into a masculine
presentableness, but a whole crop of small beards and
moustaches, mostly springing from moles all over her face.
She carries a duster and toddles about meddlesomely,
spying out dust so diligently that whilst she is flicking off*

one speck she is already looking elsewhere for another. In conversation she has the same trick, hardly ever looking at the person she is addressing except when she is excited. She has only one manner, and that is the manner of an old family nurse to a child just after it has learnt to walk. She has used her ugliness to secure indulgences unattainable by Cleopatra or Fair Rosamund, and has the further great advantage over them that age increases her qualification instead of impairing it. Being an industrious, agreeable, and popular old soul, she is a walking sermon on the vanity of feminine prettiness. Just as Redpenny has no discovered Christian name, she has no discovered surname, and is known throughout the doctors' quarter between Cavendish Square and the Marylebone Road simply as Emmy.

The consulting-room has two windows looking on Queen Anne Street. Between the two is a marble-topped console, with haunched gilt legs ending in sphinx claws. The huge pier-glass* which surmounts it is mostly disabled from reflection by elaborate painting on its surface of palms, ferns, lilies, tulips, and sunflowers. The adjoining wall contains the fireplace, with two arm-chairs before it. As we happen to face the corner we see nothing of the other two walls. On the right of the fireplace, or rather on the right of any person facing the fireplace, is the door. On its left is the writing-table at which Redpenny sits. It is an untidy table with a microscope, several test tubes, and a spirit lamp standing up through its litter of papers. There is a couch in the middle of the room, at right angles to the console, and parallel to the fireplace. A chair stands between the couch and the windowed wall. The windows have green Venetian blinds and rep† curtains;

*Tall mirror that covers the wall space between two windows.
†Transversely corded fabric.

and there is a gasalier; but it is a convert to electric
lighting. The wall paper and carpets are mostly green,
coeval with the gasalier and the Venetian blinds. The
house, in fact, was so well furnished in the middle of the
XIXth century that it stands unaltered to this day and is
still quite presentable.*

EMMY [*entering and immediately beginning to dust the couch*]
Theres a lady bothering me to see the doctor.

REDPENNY [*distracted by the interruption*]   Well, she cant see
the doctor. Look here: whats the use of telling you that the
doctor cant take any new patients, when the moment a knock
comes to the door, in you bounce to ask whether he can see
somebody?

EMMY   Who asked you whether he could see somebody?

REDPENNY   You did.

EMMY   I said theres a lady bothering me to see the doctor. That
isnt asking. Its telling.

REDPENNY   Well, is the lady bothering you any reason for
you to come bothering me when I'm busy?

EMMY   Have you seen the papers?

REDPENNY   No.

EMMY   Not seen the birthday honors?

REDPENNY [*beginning to swear*]   What the—

EMMY   Now, now, ducky!

REDPENNY   What do you suppose I care about the birthday
honors? Get out of this with your chattering. Dr Ridgeon will
be down before I have these letters ready. Get out.

EMMY   Dr Ridgeon wont never be down any more, young
man.

She detects dust on the console and is down on it immediately.

---

*Chandelier with gas burners.

REDPENNY [*jumping up and following her*]   What?

EMMY   He's been made a knight. Mind you dont go Dr Ridgeoning him in them letters. Sir Colenso Ridgeon is to be his name now.

REDPENNY   I'm jolly glad.

EMMY   I never was so taken aback. I always thought his great discoveries was fudge (let alone the mess of them) with his drops of blood and tubes full of Maltese fever and the like. Now he'll have a rare laugh at me.

REDPENNY   Serve you right! It was like your cheek to talk to him about science. [*He returns to his table and resumes his writing*].

EMMY   Oh, I dont think much of science; and neither will you when youve lived as long with it as I have. Whats on my mind is answering the door. Old Sir Patrick Cullen has been here already and left first congratulations—hadnt time to come up on his way to the hospital, but was determined to be first— coming back, he said. All the rest will be here too: the knocker will be going all day. What I'm afraid of is that the doctor'll want a footman like all the rest, now that he's Sir Colenso. Mind: dont you go putting him up to it, ducky; for he'll never have any comfort with anybody but me to answer the door. I know who to let in and who to keep out. And that reminds me of the poor lady. I think he ought to see her. She's just the kind that puts him in a good temper. [*She dusts REDPENNY's papers*].

REDPENNY   I tell you he cant see anybody. Do go away, Emmy. How can I work with you dusting all over me like this?

EMMY   I'm not hindering you working—if you call writing letters working. There goes the bell. [*She looks out of the window*]. A doctor's carriage. Thats more congratulations. [*She is going out when SIR COLENSO RIDGEON enters*]. Have you finished your two eggs, sonny?

RIDGEON   Yes.

EMMY   Have you put on your clean vest?

RIDGEON   Yes.

EMMY   Thats my ducky diamond! Now keep yourself tidy and dont go messing about and dirtying your hands: the people are coming to congratulate you. [*She goes out*].

SIR COLENSO RIDGEON is a man of fifty who has never shaken off his youth. He has the off-handed manner and the little audacities of address which a shy and sensitive man acquires in breaking himself in to intercourse with all sorts and conditions of men. His face is a good deal lined; his movements are slower than, for instance, REDPENNY's; and his flaxen hair has lost its lustre; but in figure and manner he is more the young man than the titled physician. Even the lines in his face are those of overwork and restless scepticism, perhaps partly of curiosity and appetite, rather than of age. Just at present the announcement of his knighthood in the morning papers makes him specially self-conscious, and consequently specially off-hand with REDPENNY.

RIDGEON   Have you seen the papers? Youll have to alter the name in the letters if you havnt.

REDPENNY   Emmy has just told me. I'm awfully glad. I—

RIDGEON   Enough, young man, enough. You will soon get accustomed to it.

REDPENNY   They ought to have done it years ago.

RIDGEON   They would have; only they couldnt stand Emmy opening the door, I daresay.

EMMY [*at the door, announcing*]   Dr Shoemaker. [*She withdraws*].

A middle-aged gentleman, well dressed, comes in with a friendly but propitiatory air, not quite sure of his reception. His combination of soft manners and responsive kindliness, with a certain unseizable reserve and a familiar yet foreign chiselling of feature, reveal the Jew:[5] in this instance the handsome gentlemanly Jew, gone a little pigeon-breasted* and stale after thirty, as handsome young Jews often do, but still decidedly good-looking.

---

*Having a projecting breastbone.

THE GENTLEMAN   Do you remember me? Schutzmacher. University College school and Belsize Avenue. Loony Schutz- macher, you know.

RIDGEON   What! Loony! [*He shakes hands cordially*]. Why, man, I thought you were dead long ago. Sit down. [*SCHUTZ- MACHER sits on the couch: RIDGEON on the chair between it and the window*]. Where have you been these thirty years?

SCHUTZMACHER   In general practice, until a few months ago. Ive retired.

RIDGEON   Well done, Loony! I wish *I* could afford to retire. Was your practice in London?

SCHUTZMACHER   No.

RIDGEON   Fashionable coast practice, I suppose.

SCHUTZMACHER   How could I afford to buy a fashionable practice? I hadnt a rap. I set up in a manufacturing town in the midlands in a little surgery at ten shillings a week.

RIDGEON   And made your fortune?

SCHUTZMACHER   Well, I'm pretty comfortable. I have a place in Hertfordshire besides our flat in town. If you ever want a quiet Saturday to Monday, I'll take you down in my motor at an hour's notice.

RIDGEON   Just rolling in money! I wish you rich g.p.'s would teach me how to make some. Whats the secret of it?

SCHUTZMACHER   Oh, in my case the secret was simple enough, though I suppose I should have got into trouble if it had attracted any notice. And I'm afraid you'll think it rather infra dig.*

RIDGEON   Oh, I have an open mind. What was the secret?

SCHUTZMACHER   Well, the secret was just two words.

RIDGEON   Not Consultation Free, was it?

SCHUTZMACHER [*shocked*]   No, no. Really!

---

*Abbreviated version of the Latin phrase *infra dignitatem*, which means "beneath one's dignity."

RIDGEON [*apologetic*]   Of course not. I was only joking.

SCHUTZMACHER   My two words were simply Cure Guaranteed.

RIDGEON [*admiring*]   Cure Guaranteed!

SCHUTZMACHER   Guaranteed. After all, thats what everybody wants from a doctor, isnt it?

RIDGEON   My dear Loony, it was an inspiration. Was it on the brass plate?

SCHUTZMACHER   There was no brass plate. It was a shop window: red, you know, with black lettering. Doctor Leo Schutzmacher, L.R.C.P.M.R.C.S.* Advice and medicine sixpence. Cure Guaranteed.

RIDGEON   And the guarantee proved sound nine times out of ten, eh?

SCHUTZMACHER [*rather hurt at so moderate an estimate*]   Oh, much oftener than that. You see, most people get well all right if they are careful and you give them a little sensible advice. And the medicine really did them good. Parrish's Chemical Food: phosphates, you know. One tablespoonful to a twelve-ounce bottle of water: nothing better, no matter what the case is.

RIDGEON   Redpenny: make a note of Parrish's Chemical Food.

SCHUTZMACHER   I take it myself, you know, when I feel run down. Good-bye. You dont mind my calling, do you? Just to congratulate you.

RIDGEON   Delighted, my dear Loony. Come to lunch on Saturday next week. Bring your motor and take me down to Hertford.

SCHUTZMACHER   I will. We shall be delighted. Thank you. Good-bye. [*He goes out with RIDGEON, who returns immediately*].

---

*Licentiate of the Royal College of Physicians, Member of the Royal College of Surgeons.

REDPENNY   Old Paddy Cullen was here before you were up, to be the first to congratulate you.

RIDGEON   Indeed. Who taught you to speak of Sir Patrick Cullen as old Paddy Cullen, you young ruffian?

REDPENNY   You never call him anything else.

RIDGEON   Not now that I am Sir Colenso. Next thing, you fellows will be calling me old Colly Ridgeon.

REDPENNY   We do, at St. Anne's.

RIDGEON   Yach! Thats what makes the medical student the most disgusting figure in modern civilization. No veneration, no manners—no—

EMMY [*at the door, announcing*]   Sir Patrick Cullen. [*She retires*].

SIR PATRICK CULLEN is more than twenty years older than RID-GEON, not yet quite at the end of his tether, but near it and resigned to it. His name, his plain, downright, sometimes rather arid common sense, his large build and stature, the absence of those odd moments of cere-monial servility by which an old English doctor sometimes shews you what the status of the profession was in England in his youth, and an occasional turn of speech, are Irish; but he has lived all his life in En-gland and is thoroughly acclimatized. His manner to RIDGEON, whom he likes, is whimsical and fatherly: to others he is a little gruff and un-inviting, apt to substitute more or less expressive grunts for articulate speech, and generally indisposed, at his age, to make much social effort. He shakes RIDGEON's hand and beams at him cordially and jocularly.

SIR PATRICK   Well, young chap. Is your hat too small for you, eh?

RIDGEON   Much too small. I owe it all to you.

SIR PATRICK   Blarney, my boy. Thank you all the same. [*He sits in one of the arm-chairs near the fireplace. RIDGEON sits on the couch*]. Ive come to talk to you a bit. [*To REDPENNY*] Young man: get out.

REDPENNY   Certainly, Sir Patrick [*He collects his papers and makes for the door*].

SIR PATRICK   Thank you. Thats a good lad. [*REDPENNY van-*

ishes]. They all put up with me, these young chaps, because I'm an old man, a real old man, not like you. Youre only beginning to give yourself the airs of age. Did you ever see a boy cultivating a moustache? Well, a middle-aged doctor cultivating a grey head is much the same sort of spectacle.

RIDGEON   Good Lord! yes: I suppose so. And I thought that the days of my vanity were past. Tell me: at what age does a man leave off being a fool?

SIR PATRICK   Remember the Frenchman who asked his grandmother at what age we get free from the temptations of love. The old woman said she didnt know. [*RIDGEON laughs*]. Well, I make you the same answer. But the world's growing very interesting to me now, Colly.

RIDGEON   You keep up your interest in science, do you?

SIR PATRICK   Lord! yes. Modern science is a wonderful thing. Look at your great discovery! Look at all the great discoveries! Where are they leading to? Why, right back to my poor dear old father's ideas and discoveries. He's been dead now over forty years. Oh, it's very interesting.

RIDGEON   Well, theres nothing like progress, is there?

SIR PATRICK   Dont misunderstand me, my boy. I'm not belittling your discovery. Most discoveries are made regularly every fifteen years; and it's fully a hundred and fifty since yours was made last. Thats something to be proud of. But your discovery's not new. It's only inoculation. My father practised inoculation until it was made criminal in eighteen-forty. That broke the poor old man's heart, Colly: he died of it. And now it turns out that my father was right after all. Youve brought us back to inoculation.

RIDGEON   I know nothing about smallpox. My line is tuberculosis and typhoid and plague. But of course the principle of all vaccines is the same.

SIR PATRICK   Tuberculosis? M-m-m-m! Youve found out how to cure consumption, eh?

RIDGEON   I believe so.

SIR PATRICK   Ah yes. It's very interesting. What is it the old cardinal says in Browning's play? "I have known four and twenty leaders of revolt."[6] Well, Ive known over thirty men that found out how to cure consumption. Why do people go on dying of it, Colly? Devilment, I suppose. There was my father's old friend George Boddington of Sutton Coldfield. He discovered the open-air cure in eighteen-forty. He was ruined and driven out of his practice for only opening the windows; and now we wont let a consumptive patient have as much as a roof over his head. Oh, it's very v e r y interesting to an old man.

RIDGEON   You old cynic, you dont believe a bit in my discovery.

SIR PATRICK   No, no: I dont go quite so far as that, Colly. But still, you remember Jane Marsh?

RIDGEON   Jane Marsh? No.

SIR PATRICK   You dont!

RIDGEON   No.

SIR PATRICK   You mean to tell me you dont remember the woman with the tuberculosus ulcer on her arm?

RIDGEON [enlightened]   Oh, your washerwoman's daughter. Was her name Jane Marsh? I forgot.

SIR PATRICK   Perhaps youve forgotten also that you undertook to cure her with Koch's tuberculin.

RIDGEON   And instead of curing her, it rotted her arm right off. Yes: I remember. Poor Jane! However, she makes a good living out of that arm now by shewing it at medical lectures.

SIR PATRICK   Still, that wasnt quite what you intended, was it?

RIDGEON   I took my chance of it.

SIR PATRICK   Jane did, you mean.

RIDGEON   Well, it's always the patient who has to take the chance when an experiment is necessary. And we can find out nothing without experiment.

SIR PATRICK   What did you find out from Jane's case?

RIDGEON   I found out that the inoculation that ought to cure sometimes kills.

SIR PATRICK   I could have told you that. Ive tried these modern inoculations a bit myself. Ive killed people with them; and Ive cured people with them; but I gave them up because I never could tell which I was going to do.

RIDGEON [*taking a pamphlet from a drawer in the writing-table and handing it to him*]   Read that the next time you have an hour to spare; and youll find out why.

SIR PATRICK [*grumbling and fumbling for his spectacles*] Oh, bother your pamphlets. Whats the practice of it? [*Looking at the pamphlet*] Opsonin? What the devil is opsonin?

RIDGEON   Opsonin is what you butter the disease germs with to make your white blood corpuscles eat them. [*He sits down again on the couch*].

SIR PATRICK   Thats not new. Ive heard this notion that the white corpuscles—what is it that whats his name?—Metchnikoff—calls them?

RIDGEON   Phagocytes.

SIR PATRICK   Aye, phagocytes: yes, yes, yes. Well, I heard this theory that the phagocytes eat up the disease germs years ago: long before you came into fashion. Besides, they dont always eat them.

RIDGEON   They do when you butter them with opsonin.

SIR PATRICK   Gammon.*

RIDGEON   No: it's not gammon. What it comes to in practice is this. The phagocytes wont eat the microbes unless the microbes are nicely buttered for them. Well, the patient manufactures the butter for himself all right; but my discovery is that the manufacture of that butter, which I call opsonin, goes

---

*Term for winning a backgammon game before the opponent removes any pieces from the board, thereby earning double points.

on in the system by ups and downs——Nature being always rhythmical, you know——and that what the inoculation does is to stimulate the ups or downs, as the case may be. If we had inoculated Jane Marsh when her butter factory was on the up-grade, we should have cured her arm. But we got in on the down-grade and lost her arm for her. I call the up-grade the positive phase and the down-grade the negative phase. Everything depends on your inoculating at the right moment. Inoculate when the patient is in the negative phase and you kill: inoculate when the patient is in the positive phase and you cure.

SIR PATRICK   And pray how are you to know whether the patient is in the positive or the negative phase?

RIDGEON   Send a drop of the patient's blood to the laboratory at St. Anne's; and in fifteen minutes I'll give you his opsonin index in figures. If the figure is one, inoculate and cure: if it's under point eight, inoculate and kill. Thats my discovery: the most important that has been made since Harvey discovered the circulation of the blood. My tuberculosis patients dont die now.

SIR PATRICK   And mine do when my inoculation catches them in the negative phase, as you call it. Eh?

RIDGEON   Precisely. To inject a vaccine into a patient without first testing his opsonin is as near murder as a respectable practitioner can get. If I wanted to kill a man I should kill him that way.

EMMY [looking in]   Will you see a lady that wants her husband's lungs cured?

RIDGEON [impatiently]   No. Havnt I told you I will see nobody? [To SIR PATRICK] I live in a state of siege ever since it got about that I'm a magician who can cure consumption with a drop of serum. [To EMMY] Dont come to me again about people who have no appointments. I tell you I can see nobody.

EMMY   Well, I'll tell her to wait a bit.

RIDGEON [*furious*]   Youll tell her I cant see her, and send her away: do you hear?

EMMY [*unmoved*]   Well, will you see Mr Cutler Walpole? He dont want a cure: he only wants to congratulate you.

RIDGEON   Of course. Shew him up. [*She turns to go*]. Stop. [*To SIR PATRICK*] I want two minutes more with you between ourselves. [*To EMMY*] Emmy: ask Mr Walpole to wait just two minutes, while I finish a consultation.

EMMY   Oh, he'll wait all right. He's talking to the poor lady. [*She goes out*].

SIR PATRICK   Well? what is it?

RIDGEON   Dont laugh at me. I want your advice.

SIR PATRICK   Professional advice?

RIDGEON   Yes. Theres something the matter with me. I dont know what it is.

SIR PATRICK   Neither do I. I suppose youve been sounded.

RIDGEON   Yes, of course. Theres nothing wrong with any of the organs: nothing special, anyhow. But I have a curious aching: I dont know where: I cant localize it. Sometimes I think it's my heart: sometimes I suspect my spine. It doesnt exactly hurt me; but it unsettles me completely. I feel that something is going to happen. And there are other symptoms. Scraps of tunes come into my head that seem to me very pretty, though theyre quite commonplace.

SIR PATRICK   Do you hear voices?

RIDGEON   No.

SIR PATRICK   I'm glad of that. When my patients tell me that theyve made a greater discovery than Harvey, and that they hear voices, I lock them up.

RIDGEON   You think I'm mad! Thats just the suspicion that has come across me once or twice. Tell me the truth: I can bear it.

SIR PATRICK   Youre sure there are no voices?

RIDGEON   Quite sure.

SIR PATRICK   Then it's only foolishness.

RIDGEON   Have you ever met anything like it before in your practice?

SIR PATRICK   Oh, yes: often. It's very common between the ages of seventeen and twenty-two. It sometimes comes on again at forty or thereabouts. Youre a bachelor, you see. It's not serious—if youre careful.

RIDGEON   About my food?

SIR PATRICK   No: about your behavior. Theres nothing wrong with your spine; and theres nothing wrong with your heart; but theres something wrong with your common sense. Youre not going to die; but you may be going to make a fool of yourself. So be careful.

RIDGEON   I see you dont believe in my discovery. Well, sometimes I dont believe in it myself. Thank you all the same. Shall we have Walpole up?

SIR PATRICK   Oh, have him up. [*RIDGEON rings*]. He's a clever operator, is Walpole, though he's only one of your chloroform surgeons. In my early days, you made your man drunk; and the porters and students held him down; and you had to set your teeth and finish the job fast. Nowadays you work at your ease; and the pain doesnt come until afterwards, when youve taken your cheque and rolled up your bag and left the house. I tell you, Colly, chloroform has done a lot of mischief. It's enabled every fool to be a surgeon.

RIDGEON [*to EMMY, who answers the bell*] Shew Mr Walpole up.

EMMY   He's talking to the lady.

RIDGEON [*exasperated*] Did I not tell you—

EMMY goes out without heeding him. He gives it up, with a shrug, and plants himself with his back to the console, leaning resignedly against it.

SIR PATRICK   I know your Cutler Walpoles and their like. Theyve found out that a man's body's full of bits and scraps of old organs he has no mortal use for. Thanks to chloroform, you can cut half a dozen of them out without leaving him any the worse, except for the illness and the guineas it costs him. I knew the Walpoles well fifteen years ago. The father used to snip off the ends of people's uvulas for fifty guineas, and paint throats with caustic every day for a year at two guineas a time. His brother-in-law extirpated tonsils for two hundred guineas until he took up women's cases at double the fees. Cutler himself worked hard at anatomy to find something fresh to operate on; and at last he got hold of something he calls the nuciform sac,* which he's made quite the fashion. People pay him five hundred guineas to cut it out. They might as well get their hair cut for all the difference it makes; but I suppose they feel important after it. You cant go out to dinner now without your neighbor bragging to you of some useless operation or other.

EMMY [*announcing*]   Mr Cutler Walpole. [*She goes out*].

CUTLER WALPOLE is an energetic, unhesitating man of forty, with a cleanly modelled face, very decisive and symmetrical about the short-ish, salient, rather pretty nose, and the three trimly turned corners made by his chin and jaws. In comparison with RIDGEON's delicate broken lines, and SIR PATRICK's softly rugged aged ones, his face looks machine-made and beeswaxed; but his scrutinizing, daring eyes give it life and force. He seems never at a loss, never in doubt: one feels that if he made a mistake he would make it thoroughly and firmly. He has neat, well-nourished hands, short arms, and is built for strength and compactness rather than for height. He is smartly dressed with a fancy waistcoat, a richly colored scarf secured by a handsome ring, ornaments on his watch chain, spats on his shoes, and a general air of the well-to-do sportsman about him. He goes straight across to RIDGEON and shakes hands with him.

WALPOLE   My dear Ridgeon, best wishes! heartiest congratu-lations! You deserve it.

RIDGEON   Thank you.

---

*Nut-shaped mass of tissue.

WALPOLE   As a man, mind you. You deserve it as a man. The opsonin is simple rot, as any capable surgeon can tell you; but we're all delighted to see your personal qualities officially recognized. Sir Patrick: how are you? I sent you a paper lately about a little thing I invented: a new saw. For shoulder blades.

SIR PATRICK [*meditatively*]   Yes: I got it. It's a good saw: a useful, handy instrument.

WALPOLE [*confidently*]   I knew youd see its points.

SIR PATRICK   Yes: I remember that saw sixty-five years ago.

WALPOLE   What!

SIR PATRICK   It was called a cabinetmaker's jimmy then.

WALPOLE   Get out! Nonsense! Cabinetmaker be—

RIDGEON   Never mind him, Walpole. He's jealous.

WALPOLE   By the way, I hope I'm not disturbing you two in anything private.

RIDGEON   No no. Sit down. I was only consulting him. I'm rather out of sorts. Overwork, I suppose.

WALPOLE [*swiftly*]   I know whats the matter with you. I can see it in your complexion. I can feel it in the grip of your hand.

RIDGEON   What is it?

WALPOLE   Blood-poisoning.

RIDGEON   Blood-poisoning! Impossible.

WALPOLE   I tell you, blood-poisoning. Ninety-five per cent of the human race suffer from chronic blood-poisoning, and die of it. It's as simple as A.B.C. Your nuciform sac is full of decaying matter—undigested food and waste products—rank ptomaines.* Now you take my advice, Ridgeon. Let me cut it out for you. You'll be another man afterwards.

SIR PATRICK   Dont you like him as he is?

WALPOLE   No I dont. I dont like any man who hasnt a healthy circulation. I tell you this: in an intelligently governed coun-

---

*Poisonous bacteria that can cause food poisoning.

try people wouldnt be allowed to go about with nuciform sacs, making themselves centres of infection. The operation ought to be compulsory: it's ten times more important than vaccination.

SIR PATRICK   Have you had your own sac removed, may I ask?

WALPOLE [*triumphantly*]   I havnt got one. Look at me! Ive no symptoms. I'm as sound as a bell. About five per cent of the population havnt got any; and I'm one of the five per cent. I'll give you an instance. You know Mrs Jack Foljambe: the smart Mrs Foljambe? I operated at Easter on her sister-in-law, Lady Gorran, and found she had the biggest sac I ever saw: it held about two ounces. Well, Mrs. Foljambe had the right spirit— the genuine hygienic instinct. She couldnt stand her sister-in-law being a clean, sound woman, and she simply a whited sepulchre.* So she insisted on my operating on her, too. And by George, sir, she hadnt any sac at all. Not a trace! Not a rudiment! ! I was so taken aback—so interested, that I forgot to take the sponges out, and was stitching them up inside her when the nurse missed them. Somehow, I'd made sure she'd have an exceptionally large one. [*He sits down on the couch, squaring his shoulders and shooting his hands out of his cuffs as he sets his knuckles akimbo*].

EMMY [*looking in*]   Sir Ralph Bloomfleld Bonington.

A long and expectant pause follows this announcement. All look to the door; but there is no SIR RALPH.

RIDGEON [*at last*]   Where is he?

EMMY [*looking back*]   Drat him, I thought he was following me. He's stayed down to talk to that lady.

RIDGEON [*exploding*]   I told you to tell that lady— [*EMMY vanishes*].

WALPOLE [*jumping up again*]   Oh, by the way, Ridgeon, that reminds me. Ive been talking to that poor girl. It's her hus-

---

*Appearing moral, but being immoral (see the Bible, Matthew 23:27, KJV).

band; and she thinks it's a case of consumption: the usual wrong diagnosis: these damned general practitioners ought never to be allowed to touch a patient except under the orders of a consultant.* She's been describing his symptoms to me; and the case is as plain as a pikestaff: bad blood-poisoning. Now she's poor. She cant afford to have him operated on. Well, you send him to me: I'll do it for nothing. Theres room for him in my nursing home. I'll put him straight, and feed him up and make her happy. I like making people happy. [*He goes to the chair near the window*].

EMMY [*looking in*]   Here he is.

SIR RALPH BLOOMFIELD BONINGTON *wafts himself into the room. He is a tall man, with a head like a tall and slender egg. He has been in his time a slender man; but now, in his sixth decade, his waistcoat has filled out somewhat. His fair eyebrows arch good-naturedly and uncritically. He has a most musical voice; his speech is a perpetual anthem; and he never tires of the sound of it. He radiates an enormous self-satisfaction, cheering, reassuring, healing by the mere incompatibility of disease or anxiety with his welcome presence. Even broken bones, it is said, have been known to unite at the sound of his voice: he is a born healer, as independent of mere treatment and skill as any Christian scientist. When he expands into oratory or scientific exposition, he is as energetic as WALPOLE; but it is with a bland, voluminous, atmospheric energy, which envelops its subject and its audience, and makes interruption or inattention impossible, and imposes veneration and credulity on all but the strongest minds. He is known in the medical world as B. B.; and the envy roused by his success in practice is softened by the conviction that he is, scientifically considered, a colossal humbug: the fact being that, though he knows just as much (and just as little) as his contemporaries, the qualifications that pass muster in common men reveal their weakness when hung on his egregious personality.*

---

*Specialist.

B. B.   Aha! Sir Colenso. Sir Colenso, eh? Welcome to the order of knighthood.

RIDGEON [*shaking hands*]   Thank you, B. B.

B. B.   What! Sir Patrick! And how are we to-day? A little chilly? a little stiff? but hale and still the cleverest of us all. [*SIR PATRICK grunts*]. What! Walpole! the absent-minded beggar:[7] eh?

WALPOLE   What does that mean?

B. B. Have you forgotten the lovely opera singer I sent you to have that growth taken off her vocal cords?

WALPOLE [*springing to his feet*]   Great heavens, man, you dont mean to say you sent her for a throat operation!

B. B. [*archly*]   Aha! Ha ha! Aha! [*trilling like a lark as he shakes his finger at WALPOLE*]. You removed her nuciform sac. Well, well! force of habit! force of habit! Never mind, ne-e-e-ver mind. She got back her voice after it, and thinks you the greatest surgeon alive; and so you are, so you are, so you are.

WALPOLE [*in a tragic whisper, intensely serious*]   Blood-poisoning. I see. I see. [*He sits down again*].

SIR PATRICK   And how is a certain distinguished family getting on under your care, Sir Ralph?

B. B. Our friend Ridgeon will be gratified to hear that I have tried his opsonin treatment on little Prince Henry with complete success.

RIDGEON [*startled and anxious*]   But how——

B. B. [*continuing*]   I suspected typhoid: the head gardener's boy had it; so I just called at St Anne's one day and got a tube of your very excellent serum. You were out, unfortunately.

RIDGEON   I hope they explained to you carefully——

B. B. [*waving away the absurd suggestion*]   Lord bless you, my dear fellow, I didnt need any explanations. I'd left my wife in the carriage at the door; and I'd no time to be taught my business by your young chaps. I know all about it. Ive handled these anti-toxins ever since they first came out.

RIDGEON   But theyre not anti-toxins; and theyre dangerous unless you use them at the right time.

B. B.   Of course they are. Everything is dangerous unless you take it at the right time. An apple at breakfast does you good: an apple at bedtime upsets you for a week. There are only two rules for anti-toxins. First, dont be afraid of them: second, inject them a quarter of an hour before meals, three times a day.

RIDGEON [*appalled*]   Great heavens, B. B., no, no, no.

B. B. [*sweeping on irresistibly*]   Yes, yes, yes, Colly. The proof of the pudding is in the eating, you know. It was an immense success. It acted like magic on the little prince. Up went his temperature; off to bed I packed him; and in a week he was all right again, and absolutely immune from typhoid for the rest of his life. The family were very nice about it: their gratitude was quite touching; but I said they owed it all to you, Ridgeon; and I am glad to think that your knighthood is the result.

RIDGEON   I am deeply obliged to you. [*Overcome, he sits down on the chair near the couch*].

B. B.   Not at all, not at all. Your own merit. Come! come! come! dont give way.

RIDGEON   It's nothing. I was a little giddy just now. Overwork, I suppose.

WALPOLE   Blood-poisoning.

B. B.   Overwork! Theres no such thing. I do the work of ten men. Am I giddy? No. NO. If youre not well, you have a disease. It may be a slight one; but it's a disease. And what is a disease? The lodgment in the system of a pathogenic germ, and the multiplication of that germ. What is the remedy? A very simple one. Find the germ and kill it.

SIR PATRICK   Suppose theres no germ?

B. B.   Impossible, Sir Patrick: there m u s t be a germ: else how could the patient be ill?

SIR PATRICK   Can you shew me the germ of overwork?

B. B.   No; but why? Why? Because, my dear Sir Patrick, though the germ is there, it's invisible. Nature has given it no danger signal for us. These germs—these bacilli—are translucent bodies, like glass, like water. To make them visible you must stain them. Well, my dear Paddy, do what you will, some of them wont stain. They wont take cochineal: they wont take methylene blue; they wont take gentian violet: they wont take any coloring matter. Consequently, though we know, as scientific men, that they exist, we cannot see them. But can you disprove their existence? Can you conceive the disease existing without them? Can you, for instance, shew me a case of diphtheria without the bacillus?

SIR PATRICK   No; but I'll shew you the same bacillus, without the disease, in your own throat.

B. B.   No, not the same, Sir Patrick. It is an entirely different bacillus; only the two are, unfortunately, so exactly alike that you cannot see the difference. You must understand, my dear Sir Patrick, that every one of these interesting little creatures has an imitator. Just as men imitate each other, germs imitate each other. There is the genuine diphtheria bacillus discovered by Lœffler; and there is the pseudo-bacillus, exactly like it, which you could find, as you say, in my own throat.

SIR PATRICK   And how do you tell one from the other?

B. B.   Well, obviously, if the bacillus is the genuine Lœffler, you have diphtheria; and if it's the pseudo-bacillus, youre quite well. Nothing simpler. Science is always simple and always profound. It is only the half-truths that are dangerous. Ignorant faddists pick up some superficial information about germs; and they write to the papers and try to discredit science. They dupe and mislead many honest and worthy people. But science has a perfect answer to them on every point.

A little learning is a dangerous thing;
Drink deep; or taste not the Pierian spring.*

I mean no disrespect to your generation, Sir Patrick: some of you old stagers did marvels through sheer professional intuition and clinical experience; but when I think of the average men of your day, ignorantly bleeding and cupping and purging, and scattering germs over their patients from their clothes and instruments, and contrast all that with the scientific certainty and simplicity of my treatment of the little prince the other day, I cant help being proud of my own generation: the men who were trained on the germ theory, the veterans of the great struggle over Evolution in the seventies. We may have our faults; but at least we are men of science. That is why I am taking up your treatment, Ridgeon, and pushing it. It's scientific. [*He sits down on the chair near the couch*].

EMMY [*at the door, announcing*]   Dr Blenkinsop.

DR BLENKINSOP is in very different case from the others. He is clearly not a prosperous man. He is flabby and shabby, cheaply fed and cheaply clothed. He has the lines made by a conscience between his eyes, and the lines made by continual money worries all over his face, cut all the deeper as he has seen better days, and hails his well-to-do colleagues as their contemporary and old hospital friend, though even in this he has to struggle with the diffidence of poverty and relegation to the poorer middle class.

RIDGEON   How are you, Blenkinsop?

BLENKINSOP   Ive come to offer my humble congratulations. Oh dear! all the great guns are before me.

B. B. [*patronizing, but charming*]   How d'ye do, Blenkinsop? How d'ye do?

---

*Quotation from Alexander Pope's "Essay on Criticism," this time accurate (see footnote to page 196).

BLENKINSOP   And Sir Patrick, too! [*SIR PATRICK grunts*].

RIDGEON   Youve met Walpole, of course?

WALPOLE   How d'ye do?

BLENKINSOP   It's the first time Ive had that honor. In my poor little practice there are no chances of meeting you great men. I know nobody but the St Anne's men of my own day. [*To RIDGEON*] And so youre Sir Colenso. How does it feel?

RIDGEON   Foolish at first. Dont take any notice of it.

BLENKINSOP   I'm ashamed to say I havnt a notion what your great discovery is; but I congratulate you all the same for the sake of old times.

B. B. [*shocked*]   But, my dear Blenkinsop, you used to be rather keen on science.

BLENKINSOP   Ah, I used to be a lot of things. I used to have two or three decent suits of clothes, and flannels to go up the river on Sundays. Look at me now: this is my best; and it must last till Christmas. What can I do? Ive never opened a book since I was qualified thirty years ago. I used to read the medical papers at first; but you know how soon a man drops that; besides, I cant afford them; and what are they after all but trade papers, full of advertisements? Ive forgotten all my science: whats the use of my pretending I havnt? But I have great experience: clinical experience; and bedside experience is the main thing, isnt it?

B. B.   No doubt; always provided, mind you, that you have a sound scientific theory to correlate your observations at the bedside. Mere experience by itself is nothing. If I take my dog to the bedside with me, he sees what I see. But he learns nothing from it. Why? Because he's not a scientific dog.

WALPOLE   It amuses me to hear you physicians and general practitioners talking about clinical experience. What do you see at the bedside but the outside of the patient? Well: it isnt his outside thats wrong, except perhaps in skin cases. What you want is a daily familiarity with people's insides; and that you can only get at the operating table. I know what I'm talking about: Ive been a surgeon and a consultant for twenty years; and Ive never known a general practitioner right in his diagnosis yet. Bring them a perfectly simple case; and they diagnose cancer, and arthritis, and appendicitis, and every other itis, when any really experienced surgeon can see that it's a plain case of blood-poisoning.

BLENKINSOP   Ah, it's easy for you gentlemen to talk; but what would you say if you had my practice? Except for the workmen's clubs, my patients are all clerks and shopmen. They darent be ill: they cant afford it. And when they break down, what can I do for them? Y o u can send your people to St Moritz or to Egypt, or recommend horse exercise or motoring or champagne jelly or complete change and rest for six months. *I* might as well order my people a slice of the moon. And the worst of it is, I'm too poor to keep well myself on the cooking I have to put up with. Ive such a wretched digestion; and I look it. How am I to inspire confidence? [*He sits disconsolately on the couch*].

RIDGEON [*restlessly*]   Dont, Blenkinsop: it's too painful. The most tragic thing in the world is a sick doctor.

WALPOLE   Yes, by George: its like a bald-headed man trying to sell a hair restorer. Thank God I'm a surgeon!

B. B. [*sunnily*]   I am never sick. Never had a day's illness in my life. Thats what enables me to sympathize with my patients.

WALPOLE [*interested*]   What! youre never ill?

B. B.   Never.

WALPOLE   Thats interesting. I believe you have no nuciform sac. If you ever do feel at all queer, I should very much like to have a look.

B. B.   Thank you, my dear fellow; but I'm too busy just now.

RIDGEON   I was just telling them when you came in, Blenkinsop, that I have worked myself out of sorts.

BLENKINSOP   Well, it seems presumptuous of me to offer a

prescription to a great man like you; but still I have great experience; and if I might recommend a pound of ripe greengages every day half an hour before lunch, I'm sure youd find a benefit. Theyre very cheap.

RIDGEON   What do you say to that B. B.?

B. B. [*encouragingly*]   Very sensible, Blenkinsop: very sensible indeed. I'm delighted to see that you disapprove of drugs.

SIR PATRICK [*grunts*]!

B. B. [*archly*]   Aha! Haha! Did I hear from the fireside armchair the bow-wow of the old school defending its drugs? Ah, believe me, Paddy, the world would be healthier if every chemist's shop in England were demolished. Look at the papers! full of scandalous advertisements of patent medicines! a huge commercial system of quackery and poison. Well, whose fault is it? Ours. I say, ours. We set the example. We spread the superstition. We taught the people to believe in bottles of doctor's stuff; and now they buy it at the stores instead of consulting a medical man.

WALPOLE   Quite true. Ive not prescribed a drug for the last fifteen years.

B. B.   Drugs can only repress symptoms: they cannot eradicate disease. The true remedy for all diseases is Nature's remedy. Nature and Science are at one, Sir Patrick, believe me; though you were taught differently. Nature has provided, in the white corpuscles as you call them—in the phagocytes as we call them—a natural means of devouring and destroying all disease germs. There is at bottom only one genuinely scientific treatment for all diseases, and that is to stimulate the phagocytes. Stimulate the phagocytes. Drugs are a delusion. Find the germ of the disease; prepare from it a suitable anti-toxin; inject it three times a day quarter of an hour before meals; and what is the result? The phagocytes are stimulated; they devour the disease; and the patient recovers—unless, of course, he's too far gone. That, I take it, is the essence of Ridgeon's discovery.

SIR PATRICK [*dreamily*]   As I sit here, I seem to hear my poor old father talking again.

B. B. [*rising in incredulous amazement*]   Your father! But, Lord bless my soul, Paddy, your father must have been an older man than you.

SIR PATRICK   Word for word almost, he said what you say. No more drugs. Nothing but inoculation.

B. B. [*almost contemptuously*]   Inoculation! Do you mean smallpox inoculation?

SIR PATRICK   Yes. In the privacy of our circle, sir, my father used to declare his belief that pox inoculation was good, not only for smallpox, but for all fevers.

B. B. [*suddenly rising to the new idea with immense interest and excitement*]   What! Ridgeon: did you hear that? Sir Patrick: I am more struck by what you have just told me than I can well express. Your father, sir, anticipated a discovery of my own. Listen, Walpole. Blenkinsop: attend one moment. You will all be intensely interested in this. I was put on the track by accident. I had a typhoid case and a tetanus case side by side in the hospital: a beadle and a city missionary. Think of what that meant for them, poor fellows! Can a beadle be dignified with typhoid? Can a missionary be eloquent with lockjaw? No. NO. Well, I got some typhoid anti-toxin from Ridgeon and a tube of Muldooley's anti-tetanus serum. But the missionary jerked all my things off the table in one of his paroxysms; and in replacing them I put Ridgeon's tube where Muldooley's ought to have been. The consequence was that I inoculated the typhoid case for tetanus and the tetanus case for typhoid. [*The doctors look greatly concerned. B. B., undamped, smiles triumphantly*]. Well, they recovered. THEY RECOVERED. Except for a touch of St Vitus's dance the missionary's as well to-day as ever; and the beadle's ten times the man he was.

BLENKINSOP   Ive known things like that happen. They cant be explained.

B. B. [*severely*]   Blenkinsop: there is nothing that cannot be explained by science. What did I do? Did I fold my hands helplessly and say that the case could not be explained? By no means. I sat down and used my brains. I thought the case out on scientific principles. I asked myself why didnt the missionary die of typhoid on top of tetanus, and the beadle of tetanus on top of typhoid? Theres a problem for you, Ridgeon. Think, Sir Patrick. Reflect, Blenkinsop. Look at it without prejudice, Walpole. What is the real work of the anti-toxin? Simply to stimulate the phagocytes. Very well. But so long as you stimulate the phagocytes, what does it matter which particular sort of serum you use for the purpose? Haha! Eh? Do you see? Do you grasp it? Ever since that Ive used all sorts of anti-toxins absolutely indiscriminately, with perfectly satisfactory results. I inoculated the little prince with your stuff, Ridgeon, because I wanted to give you a lift; but two years ago I tried the experiment of treating a scarlet fever case with a sample of hydrophobia serum from the Pasteur Institute, and it answered capitally. It stimulated the phagocytes; and the phagocytes did the rest. That is why Sir Patrick's father found that inoculation cured all fevers. It stimulated the phagocytes. [*He throws himself into his chair, exhausted with the triumph of his demonstration, and beams magnificently on them*].

EMMY [*looking in*]   Mr Walpole: your motor's come for you; and it's frightening Sir Patrick's horses; so, come along quick.

WALPOLE [*rising*]   Good-bye, Ridgeon.

RIDGEON   Good-bye; and many thanks.

B. B.   You see my point, Walpole?

EMMY   He cant wait, Sir Ralph. The carriage will be into the area if he dont come.

WALPOLE   I'm coming. [*To B. B.*] Theres nothing in your point: phagocytosis is pure rot: the cases are all blood-poisoning; and the knife is the real remedy. Bye-bye, Sir Paddy. Happy to have met you, Mr. Blenkinsop. Now, Emmy. [*He goes out, followed by EMMY*].

B. B. [*sadly*]   Walpole has no intellect. A mere surgeon. Wonderful operator; but, after all, what is operating? Only manual labor. Brain——BRAIN remains master of the situation. The nuciform sac is utter nonsense: theres no such organ. It's a mere accidental kink in the membrane, occurring in perhaps two-and-a-half per cent of the population. Of course I'm glad for Walpole's sake that the operation is fashionable; for he's a dear good fellow; and after all, as I always tell people, the operation will do them no harm: indeed, Ive known the nervous shake-up and the fortnight in bed do people a lot of good after a hard London season; but still it's a shocking fraud. [*Rising*] Well, I must be toddling. Good-bye, Paddy [*SIR PATRICK grunts*] good-bye, good-bye. Good-bye, my dear Blenkinsop, good-bye! Good-bye, Ridgeon. Dont fret about your health: you know what to do: if your liver is sluggish, a little mercury never does any harm. If you feel restless, try bromide. If that doesnt answer, a stimulant, you know: a little phosphorus and strychnine. If you cant sleep, trional, trional, trion——

SIR PATRICK [*drily*]   But no drugs, Colly, remember that.

B. B. [*firmly*]   Certainly not. Quite right, Sir Patrick. As temporary expedients, of course; but as treatment, no, NO. Keep away from the chemist's shop, my dear Ridgeon, whatever you do.

RIDGEON [*going to the door with him*]   I will. And thank you for the knighthood. Good-bye.

B. B. [*stopping at the door, with the beam in his eye twinkling a little*] By the way, who's your patient?

RIDGEON   Who?

B. B.   Downstairs. Charming woman. Tuberculous husband.

RIDGEON   Is she there still?

EMMY [*looking in*]   Come on, Sir Ralph: your wife's waiting in the carriage.

B. B. [*suddenly sobered*]   Oh! Good-bye. [*He goes out almost precipitately*].

RIDGEON   Emmy: is that woman there still? If so, tell her once for all that I cant and wont see her. Do you hear?

EMMY   Oh, she aint in a hurry: she doesnt mind how long she waits. [*She goes out*].

BLENKINSOP   I must be off, too: every half-hour I spend away from my work costs me eighteenpence. Good-bye, Sir Patrick.

SIR PATRICK   Good-bye. Good-bye.

RIDGEON   Come to lunch with me some day this week.

BLENKINSOP   I cant afford it, dear boy; and it would put me off my own food for a week. Thank you all the same.

RIDGEON [*uneasy at BLENKINSOP's poverty*]   Can I do nothing for you?

BLENKINSOP   Well, if you have an old frock-coat to spare? you see what would be an old one for you would be a new one for me; so remember the next time you turn out your wardrobe. Good-bye. [*He hurries out*].

RIDGEON [*looking after him*]   Poor chap! [*Turning to SIR PATRICK*] So thats why they made me a knight! And thats the medical profession!

SIR PATRICK   And a very good profession, too, my lad. When you know as much as I know of the ignorance and superstition of the patients, youll wonder that we're half as good as we are.

RIDGEON   We're not a profession: we're a conspiracy.

SIR PATRICK   All professions are conspiracies against the laity. And we cant all be geniuses like you. Every fool can get ill; but every fool cant be a good doctor: there are not enough good ones to go round. And for all you know, Bloomfield Bonington kills less people than you do.

RIDGEON   Oh, very likely. But he really ought to know the difference between a vaccine and an anti-toxin. Stimulate the phagocytes! The vaccine doesnt affect the phagocytes at all.

He's all wrong: hopelessly, dangerously wrong. To put a tube of serum into his hands is murder: simple murder.

EMMY [*returning*]   Now, Sir Patrick. How long more are you going to keep them horses standing in the draught?

SIR PATRICK   Whats that to you, you old catamaran?

EMMY   Come, come, now! none of your temper to me. And it's time for Colly to get to his work.

RIDGEON   Behave yourself, Emmy. Get out.

EMMY   Oh, I learnt how to behave myself before I learnt you to do it. I know what doctors are: sitting talking together about themselves when they ought to be with their poor patients. And I know what horses are, Sir Patrick. I was brought up in the country. Now be good; and come along.

SIR PATRICK [*rising*]   Very well, very well, very well. Goodbye, Colly. [*He pats RIDGEON on the shoulder and goes out, turning for a moment at the door to look meditatively at EMMY and say, with grave conviction*] You *are* an ugly old devil, and no mistake.

EMMY [*highly indignant, calling after him*]   Youre no beauty yourself. [*To RIDGEON, much flustered*] Theyve no manners: they think they can say what they like to me; and you set them on, you do. I'll teach them their places. Here now: are you going to see that poor thing or are you not?

RIDGEON   I tell you for the fiftieth time I wont see anybody. Send her away.

EMMY   Oh, I'm tired of being told to send her away. What good will that do her?

RIDGEON   Must I get angry with you, Emmy?

EMMY [*coaxing*]   Come now: just see her for a minute to please me: theres a good boy. She's given me half-a-crown. She thinks it's life and death to her husband for her to see you.

RIDGEON   Values her husband's life at half-a-crown!

EMMY   Well, it's all she can afford, poor lamb. Them others think nothing of half-a-sovereign just to talk about themselves to you, the sluts! Besides, she'll put you in a good temper for the day, because it's a good deed to see her; and she's the sort that gets round you.

RIDGEON   Well, she hasnt done so badly. For half-a-crown she's had a consultation with Sir Ralph Bloomfield Bonington and Cutler Walpole. Thats six guineas' worth to start with. I dare say she's consulted Blenkinsop too: thats another eighteenpence.

EMMY   Then youll see her for me, wont you?

RIDGEON   Oh, send her up and be hanged. [*EMMY trots out, satisfied. RIDGEON calls*] Redpenny!

REDPENNY [*appearing at the door*]   What is it?

RIDGEON   Theres a patient coming up. If she hasnt gone in five minutes, come in with an urgent call from the hospital for me. You understand: she's to have a strong hint to go.

REDPENNY   Right O! [*He vanishes*].

RIDGEON goes to the glass, and arranges his tie a little.

EMMY [*announcing*]   Mrs Doobidad [*RIDGEON leaves the glass and goes to the writing-table*].

The lady comes in. EMMY goes out and shuts the door. RIDGEON, who has put on an impenetrable and rather distant professional manner, turns to the lady, and invites her, by a gesture, to sit down on the couch.

MRS DUBEDAT is beyond all demur an arrestingly good-looking young woman. She has something of the grace and romance of a wild creature, with a good deal of the elegance and dignity of a fine lady. RIDGEON, who is extremely susceptible to the beauty of women, instinctively assumes the defensive at once, and hardens his manner still more. He has an impression that she is very well dressed; but she has a figure on which any dress would look well, and carries herself with the unaffected distinction of a woman who has never in her life suffered from those doubts and fears as to her social position which spoil the manners of most middling people. She is tall, slender, and strong; has dark hair, dressed so as to look like hair and not like a bird's nest or a pantaloon's wig (fashion wavering just then between these two models); has unexpectedly narrow, subtle, dark-fringed eyes that alter her expression disturbingly when she is excited and flashes them wide open; is softly impetuous in her speech and swift in her movements; and is just now in mortal anxiety. She carries a portfolio.

MRS DUBEDAT [*in low urgent tones*]   Doctor——

RIDGEON [*curtly*]   Wait. Before you begin, let me tell you at once that I can do nothing for you. My hands are full. I sent you that message by my old servant. You would not take that answer.

MRS DUBEDAT   How could I?

RIDGEON   You bribed her.

MRS DUBEDAT   I——

RIDGEON   That doesnt matter. She coaxed me to see you. Well, you must take it from me now that with all the good will in the world, I cannot undertake another case.

MRS DUBEDAT   Doctor: you must save my husband. You must. When I explain to you, you will see that you must. It is not an ordinary case, not like any other case. He is not like anybody else in the world: oh, believe me, he is not. I can prove it to you: [*fingering her portfolio*] I have brought some things to shew you. And you can save him: the papers say you can.

RIDGEON   Whats the matter? Tuberculosis?

MRS DUBEDAT   Yes. His left lung——

RIDGEON   Yes: you neednt tell me about that.

MRS DUBEDAT   You can cure him, if only you will. It is true that you can, isnt it? [*In great distress*] Oh, tell me, please.

RIDGEON [*warningly*]   You are going to be quiet and self-possessed, arnt you?

MRS DUBEDAT   Yes. I beg your pardon. I know I shouldnt—— [*Giving way again*] Oh, please, say that you c a n; and then I shall be all right.

RIDGEON [*huffily*]   I am not a curemonger: if you want cures, you must go to the people who sell them. [*Recovering himself, ashamed of the tone of his own voice*] But I have at the hospital ten tuberculous patients whose lives I believe I can save.

MRS DUBEDAT   Thank God!

RIDGEON   Wait a moment. Try to think of those ten patients as ten shipwrecked men on a raft—a raft that is barely large enough to save them—that will not support one more. Another head bobs up through the waves at the side. Another man begs to be taken aboard. He implores the captain of the raft to save him. But the captain can only do that by pushing one of his ten off the raft and drowning him to make room for the new comer. That is what you are asking me to do.

MRS DUBEDAT   But how can that be? I dont understand. Surely—

RIDGEON   You must take my word for it that it is so. My laboratory, my staff, and myself are working at full pressure. We are doing our utmost. The treatment is a new one. It takes time, means, and skill; and there is not enough for another case. Our ten cases are already chosen cases. Do you understand what I mean by chosen?

MRS DUBEDAT   Chosen. No: I cant understand.

RIDGEON [*sternly*]   You m u s t understand. Youve got to understand and to face it. In every single one of those ten cases I have had to consider, not only whether the man could be saved, but whether he was worth saving. There were fifty cases to choose from; and forty had to be condemned to death. Some of the forty had young wives and helpless children. If the hardness of their cases could have saved them they would have been saved ten times over. Ive no doubt your case is a hard one: I can see the tears in your eyes [*she hastily wipes her eyes*]: I know that you have a torrent of entreaties ready for me the moment I stop speaking; but it's no use. You must go to another doctor.

MRS DUBEDAT   But can you give me the name of another doctor who understands your secret?

RIDGEON   I have no secret: I am not a quack.

MRS DUBEDAT   I beg your pardon: I didnt mean to say anything wrong. I dont understand how to speak to you. Oh, pray dont be offended.

RIDGEON [*again a little ashamed*]   There! there! never mind. [*He relaxes and sits down*]. After all, I'm talking nonsense: I daresay I am a quack, a quack with a qualification. But my discovery is not patented.

MRS DUBEDAT   Then can any doctor cure my husband? Oh, why dont they do it? I have tried so many: I have spent so much. If only you would give me the name of another doctor.

RIDGEON   Every man in this street is a doctor. But outside myself and the handful of men I am training at St Anne's, there is nobody as yet who has mastered the opsonin treatment. And we are f u l l up? I'm sorry; but that is all I can say. [*Rising*] Good morning.

MRS DUBEDAT [*suddenly and desperately taking some drawings from her portfolio*]   Doctor: look at these. You understand drawings: you have good ones in your waiting-room. Look at them. They are his work.

RIDGEON   It's no use my looking. [*He looks, all the same*]. Hallo! [*He takes one to the window and studies it*]. Yes: this is the real thing. Yes, yes. [*He looks at another and returns to her*]. These are very clever. Theyre unfinished, arnt they?

MRS DUBEDAT   He gets tired so soon. But you see, dont you, what a genius he is? You see that he is worth saving. Oh, doctor, I married him just to help him to begin: I had money enough to tide him over the hard years at the beginning—to enable him to follow his inspiration until his genius was recognized. And I was useful to him as a model: his drawings of me sold quite quickly.

RIDGEON   Have you got one?

MRS DUBEDAT [*producing another*]   Only this one. It was the first.

RIDGEON [*devouring it with his eyes*]   Thats a wonderful drawing. Why is it called Jennifer?

MRS DUBEDAT   My name is Jennifer.

RIDGEON   A strange name.

MRS DUBEDAT   Not in Cornwall. I am Cornish. It's only what you call Guinevere.

RIDGEON [*repeating the names with a certain pleasure in them*] Guinevere. Jennifer. [*Looking again at the drawing*] Yes: it's really a wonderful drawing. Excuse me; but may I ask is it for sale? I'll buy it.

MRS DUBEDAT   Oh, take it. It's my own: he gave it to me. Take it. Take them all. Take everything; ask anything; but save him. You can: you will: you must.

REDPENNY [*entering with every sign of alarm*]   Theyve just telephoned from the hospital that youre to come instantly—a patient on the point of death. The carriage is waiting.

RIDGEON [*intolerantly*]   Oh, nonsense: get out. [*Greatly annoyed*] What do you mean by interrupting me like this?

REDPENNY   But—

RIDGEON   Chut! cant you see I'm engaged? Be off.

REDPENNY, bewildered, vanishes.

MRS DUBEDAT [*rising*]   Doctor: one instant only before you go—

RIDGEON   Sit down. It's nothing.

MRS DUBEDAT   But the patient. He said he was dying.

RIDGEON   Oh, he's dead by this time. Never mind. Sit down.

MRS DUBEDAT [*sitting down and breaking down*]   Oh, you none of you care. You see people die every day.

RIDGEON [*petting her*]   Nonsense! it's nothing: I told him to come in and say that. I thought I should want to get rid of you.

MRS DUBEDAT [*shocked at the falsehood*]   Oh!

RIDGEON [*continuing*]   Dont look so bewildered: theres nobody dying.

MRS DUBEDAT   My husband is.

RIDGEON [*pulling himself together*]   Ah, yes: I had forgotten your husband. Mrs Dubedat: you are asking me to do a very serious thing?

MRS DUBEDAT   I am asking you to save the life of a great man.

RIDGEON   You are asking me to kill another man for his sake; for as surely as I undertake another case, I shall have to hand back one of the old ones to the ordinary treatment. Well, I dont shrink from that. I have had to do it before; and I will do it again if you can convince me that his life is more important than the worst life I am now saving. But you must convince me first.

MRS DUBEDAT   He made those drawings; and they are not the best—nothing like the best; only I did not bring the really best: so few people like them. He is twenty-three: his whole life is before him. Wont you let me bring him to you? wont you speak to him? wont you see for yourself?

RIDGEON   Is he well enough to come to a dinner at the Star and Garter at Richmond?

MRS DUBEDAT   Oh yes. Why?

RIDGEON   I'll tell you. I am inviting all my old friends to a dinner to celebrate my knighthood—youve seen about it in the papers, havnt you?

MRS DUBEDAT   Yes, oh yes. That was how I found out about you.

RIDGEON   It will be a doctors' dinner; and it was to have been a bachelors' dinner. I'm a bachelor. Now if you will entertain for me, and bring your husband, he will meet me; and he will meet some of the most eminent men in my profession: Sir Patrick Cullen, Sir Ralph Bloomfield Bonington, Cutler Walpole, and others. I can put the case to them; and your husband will have to stand or fall by what we think of him. Will you come?

MRS DUBEDAT   Yes, of course I will come. Oh, thank you,

thank you. And may I bring some of his drawings—the really good ones?

RIDGEON   Yes. I will let you know the date in the course of to-morrow. Leave me your address.

MRS DUBEDAT   Thank you again and again. You have made me so happy: I know you will admire him and like him. This is my address. [*She gives him her card*].

RIDGEON   Thank you. [*He rings*].

MRS DUBEDAT [*embarrassed*]   May I—is there—should I—I mean— [*she blushes and stops in confusion*].

RIDGEON   Whats the matter?

MRS DUBEDAT   Your fee for this consultation?

RIDGEON   Oh, I forgot that. Shall we say a beautiful drawing of his favorite model for the whole treatment, including the cure?

MRS DUBEDAT   You are very generous. Thank you. I know you will cure him. Good-bye.

RIDGEON   I will. Good-bye. [*They shake hands*]. By the way, you know, dont you, that tuberculosis is catching. You take every precaution, I hope.

MRS DUBEDAT   I am not likely to forget it. They treat us like lepers at the hotels.

EMMY [*at the door*]   Well, deary: have you got round him?

RIDGEON   Yes. Attend to the door and hold your tongue.

EMMY   Thats a good boy. [*She goes out with MRS. DUBEDAT*].

RIDGEON [*alone*]   Consultation free. Cure guaranteed. [*He heaves a great sigh*].

ACT II

After dinner on the terrace at the Star and Garter,
Richmond. Cloudless summer night; nothing disturbs the
stillness except from time to time the long trajectory of a
distant train and the measured clucking of oars coming up
from the Thames in the valley below. The dinner is over;
and three of the eight chairs are empty. Sir Patrick, with
his back to the view, is at the head of the square table with
Ridgeon. The two chairs opposite them are empty. On their
right come, first, a vacant chair, and then one very fully
occupied by B. B., who basks blissfully in the moonbeams.
On their left, Schutzmacher and Walpole. The entrance to
the hotel is on their right, behind B.B.. The five men are
silently enjoying their coffee and cigarets, full of food, and
not altogether void of wine.

Mrs Dubedat, wrapped up for departure, comes in. They
rise, except Sir Patrick; but she takes one of the vacant
places at the foot of the table, next B. B.; and they sit
down again.

MRS DUBEDAT [as she enters]   Louis will be here presently. He
is shewing Dr Blenkinsop how to work the telephone. [She
sits]. Oh, I am so sorry we have to go. It seems such a shame,
this beautiful night. And we have enjoyed ourselves so much.

RIDGEON   I dont believe another half-hour would do Mr
Dubedat a bit of harm.

SIR PATRICK   Come now, Colly, come! come! none of that.
You take your man home, Mrs Dubedat; and get him to bed
before eleven.

B. B.   Yes, yes. Bed before eleven. Quite right, quite right. Sorry to lose you, my dear lady; but Sir Patrick's orders are the laws of——er——of Tyre and Sidon.*

WALPOLE   Let me take you home in my motor.

SIR PATRICK   No. You ought to be ashamed of yourself, Walpole. Your motor will take Mr and Mrs Dubedat to the station, and quite far enough too for an open carriage at night.

MRS DUBEDAT   Oh, I am sure the train is best.

RIDGEON   Well, Mrs Dubedat, we have had a most enjoyable evening.

WALPOLE   { Most enjoyable.

B. B.   { Delightful. Charming. Unforgettable.

MRS DUBEDAT [*with a touch of shy anxiety*]   What did you think of Louis? Or am I wrong to ask?

RIDGEON   Wrong! Why, we are all charmed with him.

WALPOLE   Delighted.

B. B.   Most happy to have met him. A privilege, a real privilege.

SIR PATRICK [*grunts*]!

MRS DUBEDAT [*quickly*]   Sir Patrick: are y o u uneasy about him?

SIR PATRICK [*discreetly*]   I admire his drawings greatly, maam.

MRS DUBEDAT   Yes; but I meant——

RIDGEON   You shall go away quite happy. He's worth saving. He must and shall be saved.

MRS DUBEDAT rises and gasps with delight, relief, and gratitude. They all rise except SIR PATRICK and SCHUTZMACHER, and come reassuringly to her.

B. B.   Certainly, c e r-tainly.

WALPOLE   Theres no real difficulty, if only you know what to do.

MRS DUBEDAT   Oh, how can I ever thank you! From this

---

*B.B.'s memory of the laws of Medes and Persians from the Bible (see Daniel 6:8–15) fails, so he improvises.

night I can begin to be happy at last. You dont know what I feel.

She sits down in tears. They crowd about her to console her.

B. B.   My dear lady: come come! come come! [*very persuasively*] c o m e come!

WALPOLE   Dont mind us. Have a good cry.

RIDGEON   No: dont cry. Your husband had better not know that weve been talking about him.

MRS DUBEDAT [*quickly pulling herself together*]   No, of course not. Please dont mind me. What a glorious thing it must be to be a doctor! [*They laugh*]. Dont laugh. You dont know what youve done for me. I never knew until now how deadly afraid I was—how I had come to dread the worst. I never dared let myself know. But now the relief has come: now I know.

LOUIS DUBEDAT comes from the hotel, in his overcoat, his throat wrapped in a shawl. He is a slim young man of 23, physically still a stripling, and pretty, though not effeminate. He has turquoise blue eyes, and a trick of looking you straight in the face with them, which, combined with a frank smile, is very engaging. Although he is all nerves, and very observant and quick of apprehension, he is not in the least shy. He is younger than JENNIFER; but he patronizes her as a matter of course. The doctors do not put him out in the least: neither SIR PATRICK's years nor BLOOMFIELD BONINGTON's majesty have the smallest apparent effect on him: he is as natural as a cat: he moves among men as most men move among things, though he is intentionally making himself agreeable to them on this occasion. Like all people who can be depended on to take care of themselves, he is welcome company; and his artist's power of appealing to the imagination gains him credit for all sorts of qualities and powers, whether he possesses them or not.

LOUIS [*pulling on his gloves behind RIDGEON's chair*]   Now, Jinny-Gwinny: the motor has come round.

RIDGEON   Why do you let him spoil your beautiful name like that, Mrs Dubedat?

MRS DUBEDAT   Oh, on grand occasions I am Jennifer.

B. B.   You are a bachelor: you do not understand these things, Ridgeon. Look at me [*They look*]. I also have two names. In moments of domestic worry, I am simple Ralph. When the sun shines in the home, I am Beedle-Deedle-Dumkins. Such is married life! Mr Dubedat: may I ask you to do me a favor before you go. Will you sign your name to this menu card, under the sketch you have made of me?

WALPOLE   Yes; and mine too, if you will be so good.

LOUIS   Certainly. [*He sits down and signs the cards*].

MRS DUBEDAT   Wont you sign Dr Schutzmacher's for him, Louis?

LOUIS   I dont think Dr Schutzmacher is pleased with his portrait. I'll tear it up. [*He reaches across the table for Schutzmacher's menu card, and is about to tear it. Schutzmacher makes no sign*].

RIDGEON   No, no: if Loony doesnt want it, I do.

LOUIS   I'll sign it for you with pleasure. [*He signs and hands it to RIDGEON*]. Ive just been making a little note of the river tonight: it will work up into something good [*he shews a pocket sketch-book*]. I think I'll call it the Silver Danube.

B. B.   Ah, charming, charming.

WALPOLE   Very sweet. Youre a nailer at pastel.

LOUIS coughs, first out of modesty, then from tuberculosis.

SIR PATRICK   Now then, Mr Dubedat: youve had enough of the night air. Take him home, maam.

MRS DUBEDAT   Yes. Come, Louis.

RIDGEON   Never fear. Never mind. I'll make that cough all right.

B. B.   We will stimulate the phagocytes. [*With tender effusion, shaking her hand*] G o o d-night, Mrs Dubedot. Good-night. Good-night.

WALPOLE   If the phagocytes fail, come to me. I'll put you right.

LOUIS   Good-night, Sir Patrick. Happy to have met you.

SIR PATRICK   'Night [*half a grunt*].

MRS DUBEDAT   Good-night, Sir Patrick.

SIR PATRICK   Cover yourself well up. Dont think your lungs are made of iron because theyre better than his. Good-night.

MRS DUBEDAT   Thank you. Thank you. Nothing hurts me. Good-night.

LOUIS goes out through the hotel without noticing SCHUTZ-MACHER. MRS DUBEDAT hesitates, then bows to him. SCHUTZ-MACHER rises and bows formally, German fashion. She goes out, attended by RIDGEON. The rest resume their seats, ruminating or smoking quietly.

B. B.   [*harmoniously*] Dee-lightful couple! Charming woman! Gifted lad! Remarkable talent! Graceful outlines! Perfect evening! Great success! Interesting case! Glorious night! Exquisite scenery! Capital dinner! Stimulating conversation! Restful outing! Good wine! Happy ending! Touching gratitude! Lucky Ridgeon——

RIDGEON [*returning*]   Whats that? Calling me, B. B.? [*He goes back to his seat next SIR PATRICK*].

B. B.   No, no. Only congratulating you on a most successful evening! Enchanting woman! Thorough breeding! Gentle nature! Refined——

BLENKINSOP comes from the hotel and takes the empty chair next RIDGEON.

BLENKINSOP   I'm so sorry to have left you like this, Ridgeon; but it was a telephone message from the police. Theyve found half a milkman at our level crossing with a prescription of mine in its pocket. Wheres Mr Dubedat?

RIDGEON   Gone.

BLENKINSOP [*rising, very pale*]   Gone!

RIDGEON   Just this moment——

BLENKINSOP   Perhaps I could overtake him—— [*he rushes into the hotel*].

WALPOLE [*calling after him*]   He's in the motor, man, miles off. You can— [*giving it up*]. No use.

RIDGEON   Theyre really very nice people. I confess I was afraid the husband would turn out an appalling bounder. But he's almost as charming in his way as she is in hers. And theres no mistake about his being a genius. It's something to have got a case really worth saving. Somebody else will have to go; but at all events it will be easy to find a worse man.

SIR PATRICK   How do you know?

RIDGEON   Come now, Sir Paddy, no growling. Have something more to drink.

SIR PATRICK   No, thank you.

WALPOLE   Do y o u see anything wrong with Dubedat, B. B.?

B. B.   Oh, a charming young fellow. Besides, after all, what c o u l d be wrong with him? L o o k at him. What c o u l d be wrong with him?

SIR PATRICK   There are two things that can be wrong with any man. One of them is a cheque. The other is a woman. Until you know that a man's sound on these two points, you know nothing about him.

B. B.   Ah, cynic, cynic!

WALPOLE   He's all right as to the cheque, for a while at all events. He talked to me quite frankly before dinner as to the pressure of money difficulties on an artist. He says he has no vices and is very economical, but that theres one extravagance he cant afford and yet cant resist; and that is dressing his wife prettily. So I said, bang plump out, "Let me lend you twenty pounds, and pay me when your ship comes home." He was really very nice about it. He took it like a man; and it was a pleasure to see how happy it made him, poor chap.

B. B.   [*who has listened to WALPOLE with growing perturbation*] But—but—but—when was this, may I ask?

WALPOLE   When I joined you that time down by the river.

B. B.   But, my dear Walpole, he had just borrowed ten pounds from me.

WALPOLE   What!

SIR PATRICK [*grunts*]!

B. B. [*indulgently*]   Well, well, it was really hardly borrowing; for he said heaven only knew when he could pay me. I couldnt refuse. It appears that Mrs Dubedat has taken a sort of fancy to me—

WALPOLE [*quickly*]   No: it was to me.

B. B.   Certainly not. Your name was never mentioned between us. He is so wrapped up in his work that he has to leave her a good deal alone; and the poor innocent young fellow—he has of course no idea of my position or how busy I am—actually wanted me to call occasionally and talk to her.

WALPOLE   Exactly what he said to me!

B. B.   Pooh! Pooh pooh! Really, I must say.
Much disturbed, he rises and goes up to the balustrade, contemplating the landscape vexedly.

WALPOLE   Look here, Ridgeon! this is beginning to look serious.
BLENKINSOP, very anxious and wretched, but trying to look unconcerned, comes back.

RIDGEON   Well, did you catch him?

BLENKINSOP   No. Excuse my running away like that. [*He sits down at the foot of the table, next BLOOMFIELD BONINGTON's chair*].

WALPOLE   Anything the matter?

BLENKINSOP   Oh no. A trifle—something ridiculous. It cant be helped. Never mind.

RIDGEON   Was it anything about Dubedat?

BLENKINSOP [*almost breaking down*]   I ought to keep it to myself, I know. I cant tell you, Ridgeon, how ashamed I am of dragging my miserable poverty to your dinner after all your kindness. It's not that you wont ask me again; but it's so humiliating. And I did so look forward to one evening in my dress clothes (t h e y r e still presentable, you see) with all my troubles left behind, just like old times.

RIDGEON   But what has happened?

BLENKINSOP   Oh, nothing. It's too ridiculous. I had just scraped up four shillings for this little outing; and it cost me one-and-fourpence to get here. Well, Dubedat asked me to lend him half-a-crown to tip the chambermaid of the room his wife left her wraps in, and for the cloakroom. He said he only wanted it for five minutes, as she had his purse. So of course I lent it to him. And he's forgotten to pay me. Ive just tuppence to get back with.

RIDGEON   Oh, never mind that—

BLENKINSOP [*stopping him resolutely*]   No: I know what youre going to say; but I wont take it. Ive never borrowed a penny; and I never will. Ive nothing left but my friends; and I wont sell them. If none of you were to be able to meet me without being afraid that my civility was leading up to the loan of five shillings, there would be an end of everything for me. I'll take your old clothes, Colly, sooner than disgrace you by talking to you in the street in my own; but I wont borrow money. I'll train it as far as the twopence will take me; and I'll tramp the rest.

WALPOLE   Youll do the whole distance in my motor. [*They are all greatly relieved; and WALPOLE hastens to get away from the painful subject by adding*] Did he get anything out of y o u, Mr Schutzmacher?

SCHUTZMACHER [*shakes his head in a most expressive negative*].

WALPOLE   You didnt appreciate his drawing, I think.

SCHUTZMACHER   Oh yes I did. I should have liked very much to have kept the sketch and got it autographed.

B. B.   But why didnt you?

SCHUTZMACHER   Well, the fact is, when I joined Dubedat after his conversation with Mr Walpole, he said the Jews were the only people who knew anything about art, and that though he had to put up with your Philistine twaddle, as he called it, it was what I said about the drawings that really pleased him. He also said that his wife was greatly struck with my knowledge, and that she always admired Jews. Then he asked me to advance him £50 on the security of the drawings.

B. B.		No, no. Positively! Seriously!
WALPOLE	[*All exclaiming*	What! Another fifty!
BLENKINSOP	*together*]	Think of that!
SIR PATRICK		[*grunts*]!

SCHUTZMACHER   Of course I couldnt lend money to a stranger like that.

B. B.   I envy you the power to say No, Mr Schutzmacher. Of course, I knew I oughtnt to lend money to a young fellow in that way; but I simply hadnt the nerve to refuse. I couldnt very well, you know, could I?

SCHUTZMACHER   I dont understand that. *I* felt that I couldnt very well lend it.

WALPOLE   What did he say?

SCHUTZMACHER   Well, he made a very uncalled-for remark about a Jew not understanding the feelings of a gentleman. I must say you Gentiles are very hard to please. You say we are no gentlemen when we lend money; and when we refuse to lend it you say just the same. I didnt mean to behave badly. As I told him, I might have lent it to him if he had been a Jew himself.

SIR PATRICK [*with a grunt*]   And what did he say to that?

SCHUTZMACHER   Oh, he began trying to persuade me that he was one of the chosen people—that his artistic faculty shewed it, and that his name was as foreign as my own. He said he didnt really want £50; that he was only joking; that all he wanted was a couple of sovereigns.

B. B.   No, no, Mr Schutzmacher. You invented that last touch. Seriously, now?

SCHUTZMACHER   No. You cant improve on Nature in telling stories about gentlemen like Mr Dubedat.

BLENKINSOP   You certainly do stand by one another, you chosen people, Mr Schutzmacher.

SCHUTZMACHER   Not at all. Personally, I like Englishmen better than Jews, and always associate with them. Thats only natural, because, as I am a Jew, theres nothing interesting in a Jew to me, whereas there is always something interesting and foreign in an Englishman. But in money matters it's quite different. You see, when an Englishman borrows, all he knows or cares is that he wants money; and he'll sign anything to get it, without in the least understanding it, or intending to carry out the agreement if it turns out badly for him. In fact, he thinks you a cad if you ask him to carry it out under such circumstances. Just like the Merchant of Venice, you know. But if a Jew makes an agreement, he means to keep it and expects you to keep it. If he wants money for a time, he borrows it and knows he must pay it at the end of the time. If he knows he cant pay, he begs it as a gift.

RIDGEON   Come, Loony! do you mean to say that Jews are never rogues and thieves?

SCHUTZMACHER   Oh, not at all. But I was not talking of criminals. I was comparing honest Englishmen with honest Jews.

One of the hotel maids, a pretty, fair-haired woman of about 25, comes from the hotel, rather furtively. She accosts RIDGEON.

THE MAID   I beg your pardon, sir—

RIDGEON   Eh?

THE MAID   I beg pardon, sir. It's not about the hotel. I'm not allowed to be on the terrace; and I should be discharged if I were seen speaking to you, unless you were kind enough to say you called me to ask whether the motor has come back from the station yet.

WALPOLE   Has it?

THE MAID   Yes, sir.

RIDGEON   Well, what do you want?

THE MAID   Would you mind, sir, giving me the address of the gentleman that was with you at dinner?

RIDGEON [sharply]   Yes, of course I should mind very much. You have no right to ask.

THE MAID   Yes, sir, I know it looks like that. But what am I to do?

SIR PATRICK   Whats the matter with you?

THE MAID   Nothing, sir. I want the address: thats all.

B. B.   You mean the young gentleman?

THE MAID   Yes, sir: that went to catch the train with the woman he brought with him.

RIDGEON   The woman! Do you mean the l a d y who dined here? the gentleman's wife?

THE MAID   Dont believe them, sir. She cant be his wife. I'm his wife.

B. B.   ⎫⎧ [in amazed remonstrance] My good girl!

RIDGEON ⎬⎨ You his wife!

WALPOLE ⎭⎩ What! whats that? Oh, this is getting perfectly fascinating, Ridgeon.

THE MAID   I could run upstairs and get you my marriage lines* in a minute, sir, if you doubt my word. He's Mr Louis Dubedat, isnt he?

RIDGEON   Yes.

THE MAID   Well, sir, you may believe me or not; but I'm the lawful Mrs Dubedat.

SIR PATRICK   And why arnt you living with your husband?

THE MAID   We couldnt afford it, sir. I had thirty pounds saved; and we spent it all on our honeymoon in three weeks, and a lot more that he borrowed. Then I had to go back into service, and he went to London to get work at his drawing;

---

*Informal marriage certificate.

and he never wrote me a line or sent me an address. I never saw nor heard of him again until I caught sight of him from the window going off in the motor with that woman.

SIR PATRICK   Well, thats two wives to start with.

B. B.   Now upon my soul I dont want to be uncharitable; but really I'm beginning to suspect that our young friend is rather careless.

SIR PATRICK   Beginning to think! How long will it take you, man, to find out that he's a damned young blackguard?

BLENKINSOP   Oh, thats severe, Sir Patrick, very severe. Of course it's bigamy; but still he's very young; and she's very pretty. Mr Walpole: may I spunge on you for another of those nice cigarets of yours? [*He changes his seat for the one next WALPOLE*].

WALPOLE   Certainly. [*He feels in his pockets*]. Oh bother! Where——? [*Suddenly remembering*] I say: I recollect now: I passed my cigaret case to Dubedat and he didnt return it. It was a gold one.

THE MAID   He didnt mean any harm: he never thinks about things like that, sir. I'll get it back for you, sir, if youll tell me where to find him.

RIDGEON   What am I to do? Shall I give her the address or not?

SIR PATRICK   Give her your own address; and then we'll see. [*To the maid*] Youll have to be content with that for the present, my girl. [*RIDGEON gives her his card*]. Whats your name?

THE MAID   Minnie Tinwell, sir.

SIR PATRICK   Well, you write him a letter to care of this gentleman; and it will be sent on. Now be off with you.

THE MAID   Thank you, sir. I'm sure you wouldnt see me wronged. Thank you all, gentlemen; and excuse the liberty.

She goes into the hotel. They watch her in silence.

RIDGEON [*when she is gone*]   Do you realize, you chaps, that we have promised Mrs Dubedat to save this fellow's life?

BLENKINSOP   Whats the matter with him?

RIDGEON   Tuberculosis.

BLENKINSOP [*interested*]   And can you cure that?

RIDGEON   I believe so.

BLENKINSOP   Then I wish youd cure me. My right lung is
touched, I'm sorry to say.

RIDGEON			What! your lung is going!
B. B.			My dear Blenkinsop, what do you tell me? [*full of concern for BLENKINSOP, he comes back from the balustrade*].
	[*all together*]		
SIR PATRICK			Eh? Eh? whats that?
WALPOLE			Hullo! you mustnt neglect this, you know.

BLENKINSOP [*putting his fingers in his ears*]   No, no: it's no
use. I know what youre going to say: Ive said it often to others. I cant afford to take care of myself; and theres an end
of it. If a fortnight's holiday would save my life, I'd have to
die. I shall get on as others have to get on. We cant all go
to St Moritz or to Egypt, you know, Sir Ralph. Dont talk
about it.

Embarrassed silence.

SIR PATRICK [*grunts and looks hard at RIDGEON*]!

SCHUTZMACHER [*looking at his watch and rising*]   I must go.
It's been a very pleasant evening, Colly. You might let me have
my portrait if you dont mind. I'll send Mr Dubedat that couple of sovereigns for it.

RIDGEON [*giving him the menu card*]   Oh dont do that, Loony. I
dont think he'd like that.

SCHUTZMACHER   Well, of course I shant if you feel that way
about it. But I dont think you understand Dubedat. However,
perhaps thats because I'm a Jew. Good-night, Dr Blenkinsop
[*shaking hands*].

BLENKINSOP   Good-night, sir—I mean—Good-night.

SCHUTZMACHER [*waving his hand to the rest*]   Good-night, everybody.

WALPOLE
B. B.   } Good-night.
SIR PATRICK
RIDGEON

B. B. repeats the salutation several times, in varied musical tones. SCHUTZMACHER goes out.

SIR PATRICK   It's time for us all to move. [*He rises and comes between BLENKINSOP and WALPOLE. RIDGEON also rises*]. Mr Walpole: take Blenkinsop home: he's had enough of the open air cure for to-night. Have you a thick overcoat to wear in the motor, Dr Blenkinsop?

BLENKINSOP   Oh, theyll give me some brown paper in the hotel; and a few thicknesses of brown paper across the chest are better than any fur coat.

WALPOLE   Well, come along. Good-night, Colly. Youre coming with us, arnt you, B. B.?

B. B.   Yes: I'm coming. [*WALPOLE and BLENKINSOP go into the hotel*]. Good-night, my dear Ridgeon [*shaking hands affectionately*]. Dont let us lose sight of your interesting patient and his very charming wife. We must not judge him too hastily, you know. [*With unction*] G o o o o o o o o d-night, Paddy. Bless you, dear old chap. [*SIR PATRICK utters a formidable grunt. B. B. laughs and pats him indulgently on the shoulder*]. Good-night. Good-night. Good-night. Good-night. [*He good-nights himself into the hotel*].

The others have meanwhile gone without ceremony. RIDGEON and SIR PATRICK are left alone together. RIDGEON, deep in thought, comes down to SIR PATRICK.

SIR PATRICK   Well, Mr Savior of Lives: which is it to be? that honest decent man Blenkinsop, or that rotten blackguard of an artist, eh?

RIDGEON   It's not an easy case to judge, is it? Blenkinsop's an honest decent man; but is he any use? Dubedat's a rotten blackguard; but he's a genuine source of pretty and pleasant and good things.

SIR PATRICK   What will he be a source of for that poor innocent wife of his, when she finds him out?

RIDGEON   Thats true. Her life will be a hell.

SIR PATRICK   And tell me this. Suppose you had this choice put before you: either to go through life and find all the pictures bad but all the men and women good, or to go through life and find all the pictures good and all the men and women rotten. Which would you choose?

RIDGEON   Thats a devilishly difficult question, Paddy. The pictures are so agreeable, and the good people so infernally disagreeable and mischievous, that I really cant undertake to say offhand which I should prefer to do without.

SIR PATRICK   Come come! none of your cleverness with me: I'm too old for it. Blenkinsop isnt that sort of good man; and you know it.

RIDGEON   It would be simpler if Blenkinsop could paint Dubedat's pictures.

SIR PATRICK   It would be simpler still if Dubedat had some of Blenkinsop's honesty. The world isnt going to be made simple for you, my lad: you must take it as it is. Youve to hold the scales between Blenkinsop and Dubedat. Hold them fairly.

RIDGEON   Well, I'll be as fair as I can. I'll put into one scale all the pounds Dubedat has borrowed, and into the other all the half-crowns that Blenkinsop hasnt borrowed.

SIR PATRICK   And youll take out of Dubedat's scale all the faith he has destroyed and the honor he has lost, and youll put into Blenkinsop's scale all the faith he has justified and the honor he has created.

RIDGEON   Come come, Paddy! none of your claptrap with me: I'm too sceptical for it. I'm not at all convinced that the world wouldnt be a better world if everybody behaved as Dubedat does than it is now that everybody behaves as Blenkinsop does.

SIR PATRICK   Then why dont y o u behave as Dubedat does?

RIDGEON   Ah, that beats me. Thats the experimental test. Still, it's a dilemma. It's a dilemma. You see theres a complication we havnt mentioned.

SIR PATRICK   Whats that?

RIDGEON   Well, if I let Blenkinsop die, at least nobody can say I did it because I wanted to marry his widow.

SIR PATRICK   Eh? Whats that?

RIDGEON   Now if I let Dubedat die, I'll marry his widow.

SIR PATRICK   Perhaps she wont have you, you know.

RIDGEON [with a self-assured shake of the head]   I've a pretty good flair for that sort of thing. I know when a woman is interested in me. She is.

SIR PATRICK   Well, sometimes a man knows best; and sometimes he knows worst. Youd much better cure them both.

RIDGEON   I cant. I'm at my limit. I can squeeze in one more case, but not two. I must choose.

SIR PATRICK   Well, you must choose as if she didnt exist: thats clear.

RIDGEON   Is that clear to you? Mind: it's not clear to me. She troubles my judgment.

SIR PATRICK   To me, it's a plain choice between a man and a lot of pictures.

RIDGEON   It's easier to replace a dead man than a good picture.

SIR PATRICK   Colly: when you live in an age that runs to pictures and statues and plays and brass bands because its men and women are not good enough to comfort its poor aching soul, you should thank Providence that you belong to a profession which is a high and great profession because its business is to heal and mend men and women.

RIDGEON   In short, as a member of a high and great profession, I'm to kill my patient.

SIR PATRICK   Dont talk wicked nonsense. You cant kill him. But you can leave him in other hands.

RIDGEON   In B. B.'s, for instance: eh? [*looking at him significantly*].

SIR PATRICK [*demurely facing his look*]   Sir Ralph Bloomfield Bonington is a very eminent physician.

RIDGEON   He is.

SIR PATRICK   I'm going for my hat.

RIDGEON strikes the bell as SIR PATRICK makes for the hotel. A waiter comes.

RIDGEON [*to the waiter*]   My bill, please.

WAITER   Yes, sir.

He goes for it.

ACT III

In Dubedat's studio. Viewed from the large window the outer door is in the wall on the left at the near end. The door leading to the inner rooms is in the opposite wall, at the far end. The facing wall has neither window nor door. The plaster on all the walls is uncovered and undecorated, except by scrawlings of charcoal sketches and memoranda. There is a studio throne (a chair on a dais) a little to the left, opposite the inner door, and an easel to the right, opposite the outer door, with a dilapidated chair at it. Near the easel and against the wall is a bare wooden table with bottles and jars of oil and medium, paint-smudged rags, tubes of color, brushes, charcoal, a small lay figure,* a kettle and spirit-lamp,† and other odds and ends. By the table is a sofa, littered with drawing blocks, sketch-books, loose sheets of paper, newspapers, books, and more smudged rags. Next the outer door is an umbrella and hat stand, occupied partly by Louis' hats and cloak and muffler, and partly by odds and ends of costumes. There is an old piano stool on the near side of this door. In the corner near the inner door is a little tea-table. A lay figure, in a cardinal's robe and hat, with an hour-glass in one hand and a scythe slung on its back, smiles with inane malice at Louis, who, in a milkman's smock much smudged with colors, is painting a piece of brocade which he has draped about his

---

*Life-size dummy with movable limbs.

†Lamp that burns volatile liquid fuel such as alcohol, sometimes in conjunction with a container, for heating substances.

wife. She is sitting on the throne, not interested in the painting, and appealing to him very anxiously about another matter.

MRS DUBEDAT   Promise.

LOUIS [*putting on a touch of paint with notable skill and care and answering quite perfunctorily*]   I promise, my darling.

MRS DUBEDAT   When you want money, you will always come to me.

LOUIS   But it's so sordid, dearest. I hate money. I cant keep always bothering you for money, money, money. Thats what drives me sometimes to ask other people, though I hate doing it.

MRS DUBEDAT   It is far better to ask me, dear. It gives people a wrong idea of you.

LOUIS   But I want to spare your little fortune, and raise money on my own work. Dont be unhappy, love: I can easily earn enough to pay it all back. I shall have a one-man-show next season; and then there will be no more money troubles. [*Putting down his palette*] There! I mustnt do any more on that until it's bone-dry; so you may come down.

MRS DUBEDAT [*throwing off the drapery as she steps down, and revealing a plain frock of tussore silk*]*   But you have promised, remember, seriously and faithfully, never to borrow again until you have first asked me.

LOUIS   Seriously and faithfully. [*Embracing her*] Ah, my love, how right you are! how much it means to me to have you by me to guard me against living too much in the skies. On my solemn oath, from this moment forth I will never borrow another penny.

MRS DUBEDAT [*delighted*]   Ah, thats right. Does his wicked worrying wife torment him and drag him down from the

---

*Heavy brownish silk fabric.

clouds. [*She kisses him*]. And now, dear, wont you finish those drawings for Maclean?

LOUIS   Oh, they dont matter. Ive got nearly all the money from him in advance.

MRS DUBEDAT   But, dearest, that is just the reason why you should finish them. He asked me the other day whether you really intended to finish them.

LOUIS   Confound his impudence! What the devil does he take me for? Now that just destroys all my interest in the beastly job. Ive a good mind to throw up the commission, and pay him back his money.

MRS DUBEDAT   We cant afford that, dear. You had better finish the drawings and have done with them. I think it is a mistake to accept money in advance.

LOUIS   But how are we to live?

MRS DUBEDAT   Well, Louis, it is getting hard enough as it is, now that they are all refusing to pay except on delivery.

LOUIS   Damn those fellows! they think of nothing and care for nothing but their wretched money.

MRS DUBEDAT   Still, if they pay us, they ought to have what they pay for.

LOUIS [*coaxing*]   There now: thats enough lecturing for to-day. Ive promised to be good, havnt I?

MRS DUBEDAT [*putting her arms round his neck*]   You know that I hate lecturing, and that I dont for a moment misunderstand you, dear, dont you?

LOUIS [*fondly*]   I know. I know. I'm a wretch; and youre an angel. Oh, if only I were strong enough to work steadily, I'd make my darling's house a temple, and her shrine a chapel more beautiful than was ever imagined. I cant pass the shops without wrestling with the temptation to go in and order all the really good things they have for you.

MRS DUBEDAT   I want nothing but you, dear. [*She gives him a caress, to which he responds so passionately that she disengages her-*

self]. There! be good now: remember that the doctors are coming this morning. Isnt it extraordinarily kind of them, Louis, to insist on coming? all of them, to consult about you?

LOUIS [*coolly*]   Oh, I daresay they think it will be a feather in their cap to cure a rising artist. They wouldnt come if it didnt amuse them, anyhow. [*Someone knocks at the door*]. I say: it's not time yet, is it?

MRS DUBEDAT   No, not quite yet.

LOUIS [*opening the door and finding RIDGEON there*]   Hello, Ridgeon. Delighted to see you. Come in.

MRS DUBEDAT [*shaking hands*]   It's so good of you to come, doctor.

LOUIS   Excuse this place, wont you? It's only a studio, you know: theres no real convenience for living here. But we pig along somehow, thanks to Jennifer.

MRS DUBEDAT   Now I'll run away. Perhaps later on, when youre finished with Louis, I may come in and hear the verdict. [*RIDGEON bows rather constrainedly*]. Would you rather I didnt?

RIDGEON   Not at all. Not at all.

MRS DUBEDAT looks at him, a little puzzled by his formal manner; then goes into the inner room.

LOUIS [*flippantly*]   I say: dont look so grave. Theres nothing awful going to happen, is there?

RIDGEON   No.

LOUIS   Thats all right. Poor Jennifer has been looking forward to your visit more than you can imagine. She's taken quite a fancy to you, Ridgeon. The poor girl has nobody to talk to: I'm always painting. [*Taking up a sketch*] Theres a little sketch I made of her yesterday.

RIDGEON   She shewed it to me a fortnight ago when she first called on me.

LOUIS [*quite unabashed*]   Oh! did she? Good Lord! how time does fly! I could have sworn I'd only just finished it. It's hard for her here, seeing me piling up drawings and nothing coming in for them. Of course I shall sell them next year fast enough, after my one-man-show; but while the grass grows the steed starves. I hate to have her coming to me for money, and having none to give her. But what can I do?

RIDGEON   I understood that Mrs Dubedat had some property of her own.

LOUIS   Oh yes, a little; but how could a man with any decency of feeling touch that? Suppose I did, what would she have to live on if I died? I'm not insured: cant afford the premiums. [*Picking out another drawing*] How do you like that?

RIDGEON [*putting it aside*]   I have not come here to-day to look at your drawings. I have more serious and pressing business with you.

LOUIS   You want to sound my wretched lung. [*With impulsive candor*] My dear Ridgeon: I'll be frank with you. Whats the matter in this house isnt lungs but bills. It doesnt matter about me; but Jennifer has actually to economize in the matter of food. Youve made us feel that we can treat you as a friend. Will you lend us a hundred and fifty pounds?

RIDGEON   No.

LOUIS [*surprised*]   Why not?

RIDGEON   I am not a rich man; and I want every penny I can spare and more for my researches.

LOUIS   You mean youd want the money back again.

RIDGEON   I presume people sometimes have that in view when they lend money.

LOUIS [*after a moment's reflection*]   Well, I can manage that for you. I'll give you a cheque—or see here: theres no reason why you shouldnt have your bit too: I'll give you a cheque for two hundred.

RIDGEON   Why not cash the cheque at once without trou-bling me?

LOUIS   Bless you! they wouldnt cash it: I'm overdrawn as it is. No: the way to work it is this. I'll post-date the cheque next

October. In October Jennifer's dividends come in. Well, you present the cheque. It will be returned marked "refer to drawer" or some rubbish of that sort. Then you can take it to Jennifer, and hint that if the cheque isnt taken up at once I shall be put in prison. She'll pay you like a shot. Youll clear £50; and youll do me a real service; for I do want the money very badly, old chap, I assure you.

RIDGEON [staring at him]   You see no objection to the transaction; and you anticipate none from me!

LOUIS   Well, what objection can there be? It's quite safe. I can convince you about the dividends.

RIDGEON   I mean on the score of its being——shall I say dishonorable?

LOUIS   Well, of course I shouldnt suggest it if I didnt want the money.

RIDGEON   Indeed! Well, you will have to find some other means of getting it.

LOUIS   Do you mean that you refuse?

RIDGEON   Do I mean——! [letting his indignation loose] Of course I refuse, man. What do you take me for? How dare you make such a proposal to me?

LOUIS   Why not?

RIDGEON   Faugh! You would not understand me if I tried to explain. Now, once for all, I will not lend you a farthing. I should be glad to help your wife; but lending you money is no service to her.

LOUIS   Oh well, if youre in earnest about helping her, I'll tell you what you might do. You might get your patients to buy some of my things, or to give me a few portrait commissions.

RIDGEON   My patients call me in as a physician, not as a commercial traveller.

A knock at the door. LOUIS goes unconcernedly to open it, pursuing the subject as he goes.

LOUIS   But you must have great influence with them. You must know such lots of things about them—private things that they wouldnt like to have known. They wouldnt dare to refuse you.

RIDGEON [*exploding*]   Well, upon my—

LOUIS opens the door, and admits SIR PATRICK, SIR RALPH, and WALPOLE.

RIDGEON [*proceeding furiously*]   Walpole: Ive been here hardly ten minutes; and already he's tried to borrow £150 from me. Then he proposed that I should get the money for him by blackmailing his wife; and youve just interrupted him in the act of suggesting that I should blackmail my patients into sitting to him for their portraits.

LOUIS   Well, Ridgeon, if this is what you call being an honorable man! I spoke to you in confidence.

SIR PATRICK   We're all going to speak to you in confidence, young man.

WALPOLE [*hanging his hat on the only peg left vacant on the hat-stand*]   We shall make ourselves at home for half an hour, Dubedat. Dont be alarmed: youre a most fascinating chap; and we love you.

LOUIS   Oh, all right, all right. Sit down—anywhere you can. Take this chair, Sir Patrick [*indicating the one on the throne*]. Up-z-z-z! [*helping him up: SIR PATRICK grunts and enthrones himself*]. Here you are, B. B. [*SIR RALPH glares at the familiarity; but LOUIS, quite undisturbed, puts a big book and a sofa cushion on the dais, on SIR PATRICK's right; and B. B. sits down, under protest*]. Let me take your hat. [*He takes B. B.'s hat unceremoniously, and substitutes it for the cardinal's hat on the head of the lay figure, thereby ingeniously destroying the dignity of the conclave. He then draws the piano stool from the wall and offers it to WALPOLE*]. You dont mind this, Walpole, do you? [*WALPOLE accepts the stool, and puts his hand into his pocket for his cigaret case. Missing it, he is reminded of his loss*].

WALPOLE   By the way, I'll trouble you for my cigaret case, if you dont mind?

LOUIS   What cigaret case?

WALPOLE   The gold one I lent you at the Star and Garter.

LOUIS [surprised]   Was that yours?

WALPOLE   Yes.

LOUIS   I'm awfully sorry, old chap. I wondered whose it was. I'm sorry to say this is all thats left of it. [He hitches up his smock; produces a card from his waistcoat pocket; and hands it to Walpole].

WALPOLE   A pawn ticket!

LOUIS [reassuringly]   It's quite safe: he cant sell it for a year, you know. I say, my dear Walpole, I am sorry. [He places his hand ingenuously on Walpole's shoulder and looks frankly at him].

WALPOLE [sinking on the stool with a gasp]   Dont mention it. It adds to your fascination.

RIDGEON [who has been standing near the easel]   Before we go any further, you have a debt to pay, Mr Dubedat.

LOUIS   I have a precious lot of debts to pay, Ridgeon. I'll fetch you a chair. [He makes for the inner door].

RIDGEON [stopping him]   You shall not leave the room until you pay it. It's a small one; and pay it you must and shall. I dont so much mind your borrowing £10 from one of my guests and £20 from the other—

WALPOLE   I walked into it, you know. I offered it.

RIDGEON   —they could afford it. But to clean poor Blenkinsop out of his last half-crown was damnable. I intend to give him that half-crown and to be in a position to pledge him my word that you paid it. I'll have that out of you, at all events.

B. B.   Quite right, Ridgeon. Quite right. Come, young man! down with the dust.* Pay up.

LOUIS   Oh, you neednt make such a fuss about it. Of course I'll pay it. I had no idea the poor fellow was hard up. I'm as shocked as any of you about it. [Putting his hand into his pocket]

---

*Meaning "pay up"; a term derived from a mining practice of payment by gold dust.

Here you are. [*Finding his pocket empty*] Oh, I say, I havnt any money on me just at present. Walpole: would you mind lending me half-a-crown just to settle this.

WALPOLE   Lend you half—[*his voice faints away*].

LOUIS   Well, if you dont, Blenkinsop wont get it; for I havnt a rap: you may search my pockets if you like.

WALPOLE   Thats conclusive. [*He produces half-a-crown*].

LOUIS [*passing it to Ridgeon*]   There! I'm really glad thats settled: it was the only thing that was on my conscience. Now I hope youre all satisfied.

SIR PATRICK   Not quite, Mr Dubedat. Do you happen to know a young woman named Minnie Tinwell?

LOUIS   Minnie! I should think I do; and Minnie knows me too. She's a really nice good girl, considering her station. Whats become of her?

WALPOLE   It's no use b l u f f i n g, Dubedat. Weve seen Minnie's marriage lines.

LOUIS [*coolly*]   Indeed? Have you seen Jennifer's?

RIDGEON [*rising in irrepressible rage*]   Do you dare insinuate that Mrs Dubedat is living with you without being married to you?

LOUIS   Why not?

B. B.   ⎧ [*echoing him in* ⎫ Why not!
SIR PATRICK   ⎬ *various tones of* ⎬ Why not!
RIDGEON   ⎨ *scandalized* ⎨ Why not!
WALPOLE   ⎩ *amazement*] ⎭ Why not!

LOUIS   Yes, why not? Lots of people do it: just as good people as you. Why dont you learn to t h i n k, instead of bleating and baahing like a lot of sheep when you come up against anything youre not accustomed to? [*Contemplating their amazed faces with a chuckle*] I say: I should like to draw the lot of you now: you do look jolly foolish. Especially you, Ridgeon. I had you that time, you know.

RIDGEON   How, pray?

LOUIS   Well, you set up to appreciate Jennifer, you know. And you despise me, dont you?

RIDGEON [*curtly*]   I loathe you. [*He sits down again on the sofa*].

LOUIS   Just so. And yet you believe that Jennifer is a bad lot because you think I told you so.

RIDGEON   Were you lying?

LOUIS   No; but you were smelling out a scandal instead of keeping your mind clean and wholesome. I can just play with people like you. I only asked you had you seen Jennifer's marriage lines; and you concluded straight away that she hadnt got any. You dont know a lady when you see one.

B. B. [*majestically*]   What do you mean by that, may I ask?

LOUIS   Now, I'm only an immoral artist; but if y o u d told me that Jennifer wasnt married, I'd have had the gentlemanly feeling and artistic instinct to say that she carried her marriage certificate in her face and in her character. But y o u are all moral men; and Jennifer is only an artist's wife—probably a model; and morality consists in suspecting other people of not being legally married. Arnt you ashamed of yourselves? Can one of you look me in the face after it?

WALPOLE   It's very hard to look you in the face, Dubedat; you have such a dazzling cheek. What about Minnie Tinwell, eh?

LOUIS   Minnie Tinwell is a young woman who has had three weeks of glorious happiness in her poor little life, which is more than most girls in her position get, I can tell you. Ask her whether she'd take it back if she could. She's got her name into history, that girl. My little sketches of her will be fought by collectors at Christie's. She'll have a page in my biography. Pretty good, that, for a still-room maid* at a seaside hotel, I think. What have you fellows done for her to compare with that?

---

*Maid in charge of the room where liqueurs and cakes are stored.

RIDGEON   We havnt trapped her into a mock marriage and deserted her.

LOUIS   No: you wouldnt have the pluck. But dont fuss yourselves. *I* didnt desert little Minnie. We spent all our money—

WALPOLE   All h e r money. Thirty pounds.

LOUIS   I said all o u r money: hers and mine too. Her thirty pounds didnt last three days. I had to borrow four times as much to spend on her. But I didnt grudge it; and she didnt grudge her few pounds either, the brave little lassie. When we were cleaned out, we'd had enough of it: you can hardly suppose that we were fit company for longer than that: I an artist, and she quite out of art and literature and refined living and everything else. There was no desertion, no misunderstanding, no police court or divorce court sensation for you moral chaps to lick your lips over at breakfast. We just said, Well, the money's gone: weve had a good time that can never be taken from us; so kiss; part good friends; and she back to service, and I back to my studio and my Jennifer, both the better and happier for our holiday.

WALPOLE   Quite a little poem, by George!

B. B.   If you had been scientifically trained, Mr Dubedat, you would know how very seldom an actual case bears out a principle. In medical practice a man may die when, scientifically speaking, he ought to have lived. I have actually known a man die of a disease from which he was scientifically speaking, immune. But that does not affect the fundamental truth of science. In just the same way, in moral cases, a man's behavior may be quite harmless and even beneficial, when he is morally behaving like a scoundrel. And he may do great harm when he is morally acting on the highest principles. But that does not affect the fundamental truth of morality.

SIR PATRICK   And it doesnt affect the criminal law on the subject of bigamy.

LOUIS   Oh bigamy! bigamy! bigamy! What a fascination anything connected with the police has for you all, you moralists! Ive proved to you that you were utterly wrong on the moral point: now I'm going to shew you that youre utterly wrong on the legal point; and I hope it will be a lesson to you not to be so jolly cocksure next time.

WALPOLE   Rot! You were married already when you married her; and that settles it.

LOUIS   Does it! Why cant you t h i n k? How do you know she wasnt married already too?

B. B.	[all	Walpole! Ridgeon!
RIDGEON	crying	This is beyond everything!
WALPOLE	out	Well, damn me!
SIR PATRICK	together]	You young rascal.

LOUIS [ignoring their outcry]   She was married to the steward of a liner. He cleared out and left her; and she thought, poor girl, that it was the law that if you hadnt heard of your husband for three years you might marry again. So as she was a thoroughly respectable girl and refused to have anything to say to me un- less we were married I went through the ceremony to please her and to preserve her self-respect.

RIDGEON   Did you tell her you were already married?

LOUIS   Of course not. Dont you see that if she had known, she wouldnt have considered herself my wife? You dont seem to understand, somehow.

SIR PATRICK   You let her risk imprisonment in her ignorance of the law?

LOUIS   Well, I risked imprisonment for her sake. I could have been had up for it just as much as she. But when a man makes a sacrifice of that sort for a woman, he doesnt go and brag about it to her; at least, not if he's a gentleman.

WALPOLE   What a r e we to do with this daisy?

LOUIS [impatiently]   Oh, go and do whatever the devil you please. Put Minnie in prison. Put me in prison. Kill Jennifer with the disgrace of it all. And then, when youve done all the mischief you can, go to church and feel good about it. [*He sits down pettishly on the old chair at the easel, and takes up a sketching block, on which he begins to draw*].

WALPOLE   He's got us.

SIR PATRICK [*grimly*]   He has.

B. B.   But is he to be allowed to defy the criminal law of the land?

SIR PATRICK   The criminal law is no use to decent people. It only helps blackguards to blackmail their families. What are we family doctors doing half our time but conspiring with the family solicitor to keep some rascal out of jail and some family out of disgrace?

B. B.   But at least it will punish him.

SIR PATRICK   Oh, yes: itll punish him. Itll punish not only him but everybody connected with him, innocent and guilty alike. Itll throw his board and lodging on our rates and taxes for a couple of years, and then turn him loose on us a more dangerous blackguard than ever. Itll put the girl in prison and ruin her: itll lay his wife's life waste. You may put the criminal law out of your head once for all: it's only fit for fools and savages.

LOUIS   Would you mind turning your face a little more this way, Sir Patrick. [*SIR PATRICK turns indignantly and glares at him*]. Oh, thats too much.

SIR PATRICK   Put down your foolish pencil, man; and think of your position. You can defy the laws made by men; but there are other laws to reckon with. Do know that youre going to die?

LOUIS   We're all going to die, arnt we?

WALPOLE   We're not all going to die in six months.

LOUIS   How do you know?

This for B. B. is the last straw. He completely loses his temper and begins to walk excitedly about.

B. B.   Upon my soul, I will not stand this. It is in questionable taste under any circumstances or in any company to harp on the subject of death; but it is a dastardly advantage to take of a medical man. [*Thundering at Dubedat*] I will not allow it, do you hear?

LOUIS   Well, I didnt begin it: you chaps did. It's always the way with the inartistic professions: when theyre beaten in argument they fall back on intimidation. I never knew a lawyer who didnt threaten to put me in prison sooner or later. I never knew a parson who didnt threaten me with damnation. And now you threaten me with death. With all your talk youve only one real trump in your hand, and thats Intimidation. Well, I'm not a coward; so it's no use with me.

B. B. [*advancing upon him*]   I'll tell you what you are, sir. Youre a scoundrel.

LOUIS   Oh, I dont mind you calling me a scoundrel a bit. It's only a word: a word that you dont know the meaning of. What is a scoundrel?

B. B.   You are a scoundrel, sir.

LOUIS   Just so. What is a scoundrel? I am. What am I? A scoundrel. It's just arguing in a circle. And you imagine youre a man of science!

B. B.   I—I—I—I have a good mind to take you by the scruff of your neck, you infamous rascal, and give you a sound thrashing.

LOUIS   I wish you would. Youd pay me something handsome to keep it out of court afterwards. [*B. B., baffled, flings away from him with a snort*]. Have you any more civilities to address to me in my own house? I should like to get them over before my wife comes back. [*He resumes his sketching*].

RIDGEON   My mind's made up. When the law breaks down, honest men must find a remedy for themselves. I will not lift a finger to save this reptile.

B. B.   That is the word I was trying to remember. Reptile.

WALPOLE   I cant help rather liking you, Dubedat. But you certainly are a thoroughgoing specimen.

SIR PATRICK   You know our opinion of you now, at all events.

LOUIS [*patiently putting down his pencil*]   Look here. All this is no good. You dont understand. You imagine that I'm simply an ordinary criminal.

WALPOLE   Not an ordinary one, Dubedat. Do yourself justice.

LOUIS   Well youre on the wrong tack altogether. I'm not a criminal. All your moralizings have no value for me. I dont believe in morality. I'm a disciple of Bernard Shaw.[8]

SIR PATRICK
B. B.   } } { [*puzzled*] Eh?
{ [*waving his hand as if the subject were now disposed of*] Thats enough: I wish to hear no more.

LOUIS   Of course I havnt the ridiculous vanity to set up to be exactly a Superman; but still, it's an ideal that I strive towards just as any other man strives towards his ideal.

B. B. [*intolerant*]   Dont trouble to explain. I now understand you perfectly. Say no more, please. When a man pretends to discuss science, morals, and religion, and then avows himself a follower of a notorious and avowed anti-vaccinationist, there is nothing more to be said. [*Suddenly putting in an effusive saving clause in parenthesis to RIDGEON*] Not, my dear Ridgeon, that I believe in vaccination in the popular sense any more than you do: I neednt tell you that. But there are things that place a man socially; and anti-vaccination is one of them. [*He resumes his seat on the dais*].

SIR PATRICK   Bernard Shaw? I never heard of him. He's a Methodist preacher, I suppose.

LOUIS [*scandalized*]   No, no. He's the most advanced man now living: he isnt anything.*

SIR PATRICK   I assure you, young man, my father learnt the

---

*Does not represent any particular religion.

doctrine of deliverance from sin from John Wesley's own lips before you or Mr. Shaw were born. It used to be very popular as an excuse for putting sand in sugar and water in milk. Youre a sound Methodist, my lad; only you dont know it.

LOUIS [*seriously annoyed for the first time*]   It's an intellectual insult. I dont believe theres such a thing as sin.

SIR PATRICK   Well, sir, there are people who dont believe theres such a thing as disease either. They call themselves Christian Scientists, I believe. Theyll just suit your complaint. We can do nothing for you. [*He rises*]. Good afternoon to you.

LOUIS [*running to him piteously*]   Oh dont get up, Sir Patrick. Dont go. Please dont. I didnt mean to shock you, on my word. Do sit down again. Give me another chance. Two minutes more: thats all I ask.

SIR PATRICK [*surprised by this sign of grace, and a little touched*] Well— [*He sits down*]—

LOUIS [*gratefully*]   Thanks awfully.

SIR PATRICK [*continuing*]   —I dont mind giving you two minutes more. But dont address yourself to me; for Ive retired from practice; and I dont pretend to be able to cure your complaint. Your life is in the hands of these gentlemen.

RIDGEON   Not in mine. My hands are full. I have no time and no means available for this case.

SIR PATRICK   What do you say, Mr. Walpole?

WALPOLE   Oh, I'll take him in hand: I dont mind. I feel perfectly convinced that this is not a moral case at all: it's a physical one. Theres something abnormal about his brain. That means, probably, some morbid condition affecting the spinal cord. And that means the circulation. In short, it's clear to me that he's suffering from an obscure form of blood-poisoning, which is almost certainly due to an accumulation of ptomaines in the nuciform sac. I'll remove the sac—

LOUIS [*changing color*]   Do you mean, operate on me? Ugh! No, thank you.

WALPOLE   Never fear: you wont feel anything. Youll be under an anæsthetic, of course. And it will be extraordinarily interesting.

LOUIS   Oh, well, if it would interest you, and if it wont hurt, thats another matter. How much will you give me to let you do it?

WALPOLE [*rising indignantly*]   How much! What do you mean?

LOUIS   Well, you dont expect me to let you cut me up for nothing, do you?

WALPOLE   Will you paint my portrait for nothing?

LOUIS   No; but I'll give you the portrait when it's painted; and you can sell it afterwards for perhaps double the money. But I cant sell my nuciform sac when youve cut it out.

WALPOLE   Ridgeon: did you ever hear anything like this! [*To LOUIS*] Well, you can keep your nuciform sac, and your tubercular lung, and your diseased brain: Ive done with you. One would think I was not conferring a favor on the fellow! [*He returns to his stool in high dudgeon*].*

SIR PATRICK   That leaves only one medical man who has not withdrawn from your case, Mr. Dubedat. You have nobody left to appeal to now but Sir Ralph Bloomfield Bonington.

WALPOLE   If I were you, B. B., I shouldnt touch him with a pair of tongs. Let him take his lungs to the Brompton Hospital. They wont cure him; but theyll teach him manners.

B. B.   My weakness is that I have never been able to say No, even to the most thoroughly undeserving people. Besides, I am bound to say that I dont think it is possible in medical practice to go into the question of the value of the lives we save. Just consider, Ridgeon. Let me put it to you, Paddy. Clear your mind of cant, Walpole.

WALPOLE [*indignantly*]   My mind is clear of cant.

B. B.   Quite so. Well now, look at my practice. It is what I sup-

---

*Indignation; resentment.

pose you would call a fashionable practice, a smart practice, a practice among the best people. You ask me to go into the question of whether my patients are of any use either to themselves or anyone else. Well, if you apply any scientific test known to me, you will achieve a reductio ad absurdum. You will be driven to the conclusion that the majority of them would be, as my friend Mr J. M. Barrie has tersely phrased it, better dead. Better dead.*There are exceptions, no doubt. For instance, there is the court, an essentially social-democratic institution, supported out of public funds by the public because the public wants it and likes it. My court patients are hardworking people who give satisfaction, undoubtedly. Then I have a duke or two whose estates are probably better managed than they would be in public hands. But as to most of the rest, if I once began to argue about them, unquestionably the verdict would be, Better dead. When they actually do die, I sometimes have to offer that consolation, thinly disguised, to the family. [*Lulled by the cadences of his own voice, he becomes drowsier and drowsier*]. The fact that they spend money so extravagantly on medical attendance really would not justify me in wasting my talents—such as they are—in keeping them alive. After all, if my fees are high, I have to spend heavily. My own tastes are simple: a camp bed, a couple of rooms, a crust, a bottle of wine; and I am happy and contented. My wife's tastes are perhaps more luxurious; but even she deplores an expenditure the sole object of which is to maintain the state my patients require from their medical attendant. The—er—er—er—[*suddenly waking up*] I have lost the thread of these remarks. What was I talking about, Ridgeon?

RIDGEON   About Dubedat.

B. B.   Ah yes. Precisely. Thank you. Dubedat, of course. Well,

---

*Scottish novelist and dramatist J.M. Barrie, best known for his character Peter Pan, was a friend of Shaw; *Better Dead* (1887) is his first novel.

what is our friend Dubedat? A vicious and ignorant young man with a talent for drawing.

LOUIS   Thank you. Dont mind me.

B. B.   But then, what are many of my patients? Vicious and ignorant young men without a talent for anything. If I were to stop to argue about their merits I should have to give up three-quarters of my practice. Therefore I have made it a rule not so to argue. Now, as an honorable man, having made that rule as to paying patients, can I make an exception as to a patient who, far from being a paying patient, may more fitly be described as a borrowing patient? No. I say No. Mr Dubedat: your moral character is nothing to me. I look at you from a purely scientific point of view. To me you are simply a field of battle in which an invading army of tubercle bacilli struggles with a patriotic force of phagocytes. Having made a promise to your wife, which my principles will not allow me to break, to stimulate those phagocytes, I will stimulate them. And I take no further responsibility. [He flings himself back in his seat exhausted].

SIR PATRICK   Well, Mr Dubedat, as Sir Ralph has very kindly offered to take charge of your case, and as the two minutes I promised you are up, I must ask you excuse me. [He rises].

LOUIS   Oh, certainly. Ive quite done with you. [Rising and holding up the sketch block] There! While youve been talking, Ive been doing. What is there left of your moralizing? Only a little carbonic acid gas which makes the room unhealthy. What is there left of my work? That. Look at it [RIDGEON rises to look at it].

SIR PATRICK [who has come down to him from the throne]   You young rascal, was it drawing me you were?

LOUIS   Of course. What else?

SIR PATRICK [takes the drawing from him and grunts approvingly] Thats rather good. Dont you think so, Colly?

RIDGEON   Yes. So good that I should like to have it.

SIR PATRICK   Thank you; but I should like to have it myself. What d'ye think, Walpole?

WALPOLE [*rising and coming over to look*]   No, by Jove: *I* must have this.

LOUIS   I wish I could afford to give it to you, Sir Patrick. But I'd pay five guineas sooner than part with it.

RIDGEON   Oh, for that matter, I will give you six for it.

WALPOLE   Ten.

LOUIS   I think Sir Patrick is morally entitled to it, as he sat for it. May I send it to your house, Sir Patrick, for twelve guineas?

SIR PATRICK   Twelve guineas! Not if you were President of the Royal Academy, young man. [*He gives him back the drawing decisively and turns away, taking up his hat*].

LOUIS [*to B. B.*]   Would you like to take it at twelve, Sir Ralph?

B. B. [*coming between LOUIS and WALPOLE*]   Twelve guineas? Thank you: I'll take it at that. [*He takes it and presents it to SIR PATRICK*]. Accept it from me, Paddy; and may you long be spared to contemplate it.

SIR PATRICK   Thank you. [*He puts the drawing into his hat*].

B. B.   I neednt settle with you now, Mr Dubedat: my fees will come to more than that. [*He also retrieves his hat*].

LOUIS [*indignantly*]   Well, of all the mean—[*words fail him*]! I'd let myself be shot sooner than do a thing like that. I consider youve stolen that drawing.

SIR PATRICK [*drily*]   So weve converted you to a belief in morality after all, eh?

LOUIS   Yah! [*To WALPOLE*] I'll do another one for you, Walpole, if youll let me have the ten you promised.

WALPOLE   Very good. I'll pay on delivery.

LOUIS   Oh! What do you take me for? Have you no confidence in my honor?

WALPOLE   None whatever.

LOUIS   Oh well, of course if you feel that way, you cant help it. Before you go, Sir Patrick, let me fetch Jennifer. I know she'd like to see you, if you dont mind. [*He goes to the inner door*]. And now, before she comes in, one word. Youve all been talking here pretty freely about me——in my own house too. *I* dont mind that: I'm a man and can take care of myself. But when Jennifer comes in, please remember that she's a lady, and that you are supposed to be gentlemen. [*He goes out*].

WALPOLE   Well!!! [*He gives the situation up as indescribable, and goes for his hat*].

RIDGEON   Damn his impudence!

B. B.   I shouldnt be at all surprised to learn that he's well connected. Whenever I meet dignity and self-possession without any discoverable basis, I diagnose good family.

RIDGEON   Diagnose artistic genius, B. B. Thats what saves his self-respect.

SIR PATRICK   The world is made like that. The decent fellows are always being lectured and put out of countenance by the snobs.

B. B. [*altogether refusing to accept this*]   *I* am not out of countenance. I should like, by Jupiter, to see the man who could put me out of countenance. [*Jennifer comes in*]. Ah, Mrs. Dubedat! And how are we to-day?

MRS DUBEDAT [*shaking hands with him*]   Thank you all so much for coming. [*She shakes WALPOLE's hand*]. Thank you, Sir Patrick [*she shakes SIR PATRICK's*]. Oh, life has been worth living since I have known you. Since Richmond I have not known a moment's fear. And it used to be nothing but fear. Wont you sit down and tell me the result of the consultation?

WALPOLE   I'll go, if you dont mind, Mrs. Dubedat. I have an appointment. Before I go, let me say that I am quite agreed with my colleagues here as to the character of the case. As to the cause and the remedy, thats not my business: I'm only a surgeon; and these gentlemen are physicians and will advise you. I may have my own views: in fact I h a v e them; and they are perfectly well known to my colleagues. If I am needed——

and needed I shall be finally——they know where to find me; and I am always at your service. So for to-day, good-bye. [*He goes out, leaving JENNIFER much puzzled by his unexpected withdrawal and formal manner*].

SIR PATRICK   I also will ask you to excuse me, Mrs Dubedat.

RIDGEON [*anxiously*]   Are you going?

SIR PATRICK   Yes: I can be of no use here; and I must be getting back. As you know, maam, I'm not in practice now; and I shall not be in charge of the case. It rests between Sir Colenso Ridgeon and Sir Ralph Bloomfield Bonington. They know my opinion. Good afternoon to you, maam. [*He bows and makes for the door*].

MRS DUBEDAT [*detaining him*]   Theres nothing wrong, is there? You dont think Louis is worse, do you?

SIR PATRICK   No: he's not worse. Just the same as at Richmond.

MRS DUBEDAT   Oh, thank you: you frightened me. Excuse me.

SIR PATRICK   Dont mention it, maam. [*He goes out*].

B. B.   Now, Mrs Dubedat, if I am to take the patient in hand——

MRS DUBEDAT [*apprehensively, with a glance at RIDGEON*]   You! But I thought that Sir Colenso——

B. B. [*beaming with the conviction that he is giving her a most gratifying surprise*]   My dear lady, your husband shall have Me.

MRS DUBEDAT   But——

B. B.   Not a word: it is a pleasure to me, for your sake. Sir Colenso Ridgeon will be in his proper place, in the bacteriological laboratory. *I* shall be in my proper place, at the bedside. Your husband shall be treated exactly as if he were a member of the royal family. [*MRS DUBEDAT uneasy, again is about to protest*]. No gratitude: it would embarrass me, I assure you. Now, may I ask whether you are particularly tied to these apartments. Of course, the motor has annihilated distance;

but I confess that if you were rather nearer to me, it would be a little more convenient.

MRS DUBEDAT   You see, this studio and flat are self-contained. I have suffered so much in lodgings. The servants are so frightfully dishonest.

B. B.   Ah! Are they? Are they? Dear me!

MRS DUBEDAT   I was never accustomed to lock things up. And I missed so many small sums. At last a dreadful thing happened. I missed a five-pound note. It was traced to the housemaid; and she actually said Louis had given it to her. And he wouldnt let me do anything: he is so sensitive that these things drive him mad.

B. B.   Ah—hm—ha—yes—say no more, Mrs. Dubedat: you shall not move. If the mountain will not come to Mahomet, Mahomet must come to the mountain.* Now I must be off. I will write and make an appointment. We shall begin stimulating the phagocytes on—on—probably on Tuesday next; but I will let you know. Depend on me; dont fret; eat regularly; sleep well; keep your spirits up; keep the patient cheerful; hope for the best; no tonic like a charming woman; no medicine like cheerfulness; no resource like science; good-bye, good-bye, good-bye. [Having shaken hands—she being too overwhelmed to speak—he goes out, stopping to say to RIDGEON] On Tuesday morning send me down a tube of some really stiff anti-toxin. Any kind will do. Dont forget. Good-bye, Colly. [He goes out].

RIDGEON   You look quite discouraged again. [She is almost in tears]. What's the matter? Are you disappointed?

MRS DUBEDAT   I know I ought to be very grateful. Believe me, I am very grateful. But—but—

*Proverbial saying that derives from English author Francis Bacon's essay "On Boldness" (from *Essays*, 1625).

RIDGEON   Well?

MRS DUBEDAT   I had set my heart on y o u r curing Louis.

RIDGEON   Well, Sir Ralph Bloomfield Bonington——

MRS DUBEDAT   Yes, I know, I know. It is a great privilege to have him. But oh, I wish it had been you. I know it's unreasonable; I cant explain; but I had such a strong instinct that you would cure him. I dont—I cant feel the same about Sir Ralph. You promised me. Why did you give Louis up?

RIDGEON   I explained to you. I cannot take another case.

MRS DUBEDAT   But at Richmond?

RIDGEON   At Richmond I thought I could make room for one more case. But my old friend Dr Blenkinsop claimed that place. His lung is attacked.

MRS DUBEDAT [*attaching no importance whatever to BLENKINSOP*] Do you mean that elderly man—that rather silly——

RIDGEON [*sternly*]   I mean the gentleman that dined with us: an excellent and honest man, whose life is as valuable as anyone else's. I have arranged that I shall take his case, and that Sir Ralph Bloomfield Bonington shall take Mr Dubedat's.

MRS DUBEDAT [*turning indignantly on him*]   I see what it is. Oh! it is envious, mean, cruel. And I thought that you would be above such a thing.

RIDGEON   What do you mean?

MRS DUBEDAT   Oh, do you think I dont know? do you think it has never happened before? Why does everybody turn against him? Can you not forgive him for being superior to you? for being cleverer? for being braver? for being a great artist?

RIDGEON   Yes: I can forgive him for all that.

MRS DUBEDAT   Well, have you anything to say against him? I have challenged everyone who has turned against him—challenged them face to face to tell me any wrong thing he has done, any ignoble thought he has uttered. They have always confessed that they could not tell me one. I challenge you now. What do you accuse him of?

RIDGEON   I am like all the rest. Face to face, I cannot tell you one thing against him.

MRS DUBEDAT [*not satisfied*]   But your manner is changed. And you have broken your promise to me to make room for him as your patient.

RIDGEON   I think you are a little unreasonable. You have had the very best medical advice in London for him; and his case has been taken in hand by a leader of the profession. Surely——

MRS DUBEDAT   Oh, it is so cruel to keep telling me that. It seems all right; and it puts me in the wrong. But I am not in the wrong. I have faith in you; and I have no faith in the others. We have seen so many doctors: I have come to know at last when they are only talking and can do nothing. It is different with you. I feel that you know. You must listen to me, doctor. [*With sudden misgiving*] Am I offending you by calling you doctor instead of remembering your title?

RIDGEON   Nonsense. I a m a doctor. But mind you, dont call Walpole one.

MRS DUBEDAT   I dont care about Mr Walpole: it is you who must befriend me. Oh, will you please sit down and listen to me just for a few minutes. [*He assents with a grave inclination, and sits on the sofa. She sits on the easel chair*]. Thank you. I wont keep you long; but I must tell you the whole truth. Listen. I know Louis as nobody else in the world knows him or ever can know him. I am his wife. I know he has little faults: impatiences, sensitivenesses, even little selfishnesses that are too trivial for him to notice. I know that he sometimes shocks people about money because he is so utterly above it, and cant understand the value ordinary people set on it. Tell me: did he——did he borrow any money from you?

RIDGEON   He asked me for some——once.

MRS DUDEBAT [*tears again in her eyes*]   Oh, I am so sorry——so sorry. But he will never do it again: I pledge you my word for that. He has given me his promise: here in this room just before you came; and he is incapable of breaking his word. That was his only real weakness; and now it is conquered and done with for ever.

RIDGEON   Was that really his only weakness?

MRS DUBEDAT   He is perhaps sometimes weak about women, because they adore him so, and are always laying traps for him. And of course when he says he doesnt believe in morality, ordinary pious people think he must be wicked. You can understand, cant you, how all this starts a great deal of gossip about him, and gets repeated until even good friends get set against him?

RIDGEON   Yes: I understand.

MRS DUDEBAT   Oh, if you only knew the other side of him as I do! Do you know, doctor, that if Louis dishonored himself by a really bad action, I should kill myself.

RIDGEON   Come! dont exaggerate.

MRS DUBEDAT   I should. You dont understand that, you east country people.

RIDGEON   You did not see much of the world in Cornwall, did you?

MRS DUBEDAT [*naïvely*]   Oh yes. I saw a great deal every day of the beauty of the world—more than you ever see here in London. But I saw very few people, if that is what you mean. I was an only child.

RIDGEON   That explains a good deal.

MRS DUBEDAT   I had a great many dreams; but at last they all came to one dream.

RIDGEON [*with half a sigh*]   Yes, the usual dream.

MRS DUBEDAT [*surprised*]   Is it usual?

RIDGEON   As I guess. You havnt yet told me what it was.

MRS DUBEDAT   I didnt want to waste myself. I could do nothing myself; but I had a little property and I could help with it. I had even a little beauty: dont think me vain for knowing it. I knew that men of genius always had a terrible struggle with poverty and neglect at first. My dream was to save one of them from that, and bring some charm and happiness into his life. I prayed Heaven to send me one. I firmly believe that Louis was guided to me in answer to my prayer. He was no more like the other men I had met than the Thames Embankment is like our Cornish coasts. He saw everything that I saw, and drew it for me. He understood everything. He came to me like a child. Only fancy, doctor: he never even wanted to marry me: he never thought of the things other men think of! I had to propose it myself. Then he said he had no money. When I told him I had some, he said "Oh, all right," just like a boy. He is still like that, quite unspoiled, a man in his thoughts, a great poet and artist in his dreams, and a child in his ways. I gave him myself and all I had that he might grow to his full height with plenty of sunshine. If I lost faith in him, it would mean the wreck and failure of my life. I should go back to Cornwall and die. I could show you the very cliff I should jump off. You must cure him: you must make him quite well again for me. I know that you can do it and that nobody else can. I implore you not to refuse what I am going to ask you to do. Take Louis yourself; and let Sir Ralph cure Dr Blenkinsop.

RIDGEON [slowly]   Mrs Dubedat: do you really believe in my knowledge and skill as you say you do?

MRS DUBEDAT   Absolutely. I do not give my trust by halves.

RIDGEON   I know that. Well, I am going to test you—hard. Will you believe me when I tell you that I understand what you have just told me; that I have no desire but to serve you in the most faithful friendship; and that your hero must be preserved to you.

MRS DUBEDAT   Oh forgive me. Forgive what I said. You will preserve him to me.

RIDGEON   At all hazards. [*She kisses his hand. He rises hastily*].
No: you have not heard the rest. [*She rises too*]. You must believe me when I tell you that the one chance of preserving the
hero lies in Louis being in the care of Sir Ralph.

MRS DUBEDAT [*firmly*]   You say so: I have no more doubt: I
believe you. Thank you.

RIDGEON   Good-bye. [*She takes his hand*]. I hope this will be a
lasting friendship.

MRS DUBEDAT   It will. My friendships end only with death.

RIDGEON   Death ends everything, doesnt it? Good-bye.

*With a sigh and a look of pity at her which she does not understand,
he goes.*

ACT IV

The studio. The easel is pushed back to the wall. Cardinal Death, holding his scythe and hour-glass like a sceptre and globe, sits on the throne. On the hat-stand hang the hats of Sir Patrick and Bloomfield Bonington. Walpole, just come in, is hanging up his beside them. There is a knock. He opens the door and finds Ridgeon there.

WALPOLE   Hallo, Ridgeon!
They come into the middle of the room together, taking off their gloves.
RIDGEON   Whats the matter! Have you been sent for, too?
WALPOLE   Weve all been sent for. Ive only just come: I havnt seen him yet. The charwoman says that old Paddy Cullen has been here with B. B. for the last half-hour. [*SIR PATRICK, with bad news in his face, enters from the inner room*]. Well: whats up?
SIR PATRICK   Go in and see. B. B. is in there with him.
WALPOLE goes. RIDGEON is about to follow him; but SIR PATRICK stops him with a look.
RIDGEON   What has happened?
SIR PATRICK   Do you remember Jane Marsh's arm?
RIDGEON   Is that whats happened?
SIR PATRICK   Thats whats happened. His lung has gone like Jane's arm. I never saw such a case. He has got through three months galloping consumption in three days.
RIDGEON   B. B. got in on the negative phase.
SIR PATRICK   Negative or positive, the lad's done for. He wont last out the afternoon. He'll go suddenly: Ive often seen it.

RIDGEON   So long as he goes before his wife finds him out, *I* dont care. I fully expected this.

SIR PATRICK [*drily*]   It's a little hard on a lad to be killed because his wife has too high an opinion of him. Fortunately few of us are in any danger of that.

SIR RALPH comes from the inner room and hastens between them, humanely concerned, but professionally elate and communicative.

B. B.   Ah, here you are, Ridgeon. Paddy's told you, of course.

RIDGEON   Yes.

B. B.   It's an enormously interesting case. You know, Colly, by Jupiter, if I didnt know as a matter of scientific fact that I'd been stimulating the phagocytes, I should say I'd been stimulating the other things. What is the explanation of it, Sir Patrick? How do you account for it, Ridgeon? Have we overstimulated the phagocytes? Have they not only eaten up the bacilli, but attacked and destroyed the red corpuscles as well? a possibility suggested by the patient's pallor. Nay, have they finally begun to prey on the lungs themselves? Or on one another? I shall write a paper about this case.

WALPOLE comes back, very serious, even shocked. He comes between B. B. and RIDGEON.

WALPOLE   Whew! B. B.: youve done it this time.

B. B.   What do you mean?

WALPOLE   Killed him. The worst case of neglected blood-poisoning I ever saw. It's too late now to do anything. He'd die under the anæsthetic.

B. B. [*offended*]   Killed! Really, Walpole, if your monomania were not well known, I should take such an expression very seriously.

SIR PATRICK   Come come! When youve both killed as many people as I have in my time youll feel humble enough about it. Come and look at him, Colly.

RIDGEON and SIR PATRICK go into the inner room.

WALPOLE   I apologize, B. B. But it's blood-poisoning.

B. B. [*recovering his irresistible good nature*] My dear Walpole, e v e r y t h i n g is blood-poisoning. But upon my soul, I shall not use any of that stuff of Ridgeon's again. What made me so sensitive about what you said just now is that, strictly between ourselves, Ridgeon has cooked our young friend's goose.

JENNIFER, worried and distressed, but always gentle, comes between them from the inner room. She wears a nurse's apron.

MRS DUBEDAT   Sir Ralph: what am I to do? That man who insisted on seeing me, and sent in word that his business was important to Louis, is a newspaper man. A paragraph appeared in the paper this morning saying that Louis is seriously ill; and this man wants to interview him about it. How can people be so brutally callous?

WALPOLE [*moving vengefully towards the door*]   You just leave me to deal with him!

MRS DUBEDAT [*stopping him*]   But Louis insists on seeing him: he almost began to cry about it. And he says he cant bear his room any longer. He says he wants to [*she struggles with a sob*] —to die in his studio. Sir Patrick says let him have his way: it can do no harm. What shall we do?

B. B. [*encouragingly*]   Why, follow Sir Patrick's excellent advice, of course. As he says, it can do him no harm; and it will no doubt do him good—a great deal of good. He will be much the better for it.

MRS DUBEDAT [*a little cheered*]   Will you bring the man up here, Mr Walpole, and tell him that he may see Louis, but that he mustnt exhaust him by talking? [*WALPOLE nods and goes out by the outer door*]. Sir Ralph, dont be angry with me; but Louis will die if he stays here. I must take him to Cornwall. He will recover there.

B. B. [*brightening wonderfully, as if Dubedat were already saved*] Cornwall! The very place for him! Wonderful for the lungs. Stupid of me not to think of it before. You are his best physician after all, dear lady. An inspiration! Cornwall: of course, yes, yes, yes.

MRS DUBEDAT [*comforted and touched*]   You are so kind, Sir Ralph. But dont give me m u c h hope or I shall cry; and Louis cant bear that.

B. B. [*gently putting his protecting arm round her shoulders*]   Then let us come back to him and help to carry him in. Cornwall! of course, of course. The very thing! [*They go together into the bedroom*].

WALPOLE returns with the NEWSPAPER MAN, a cheerful, affable young man who is disabled for ordinary business pursuits by a congenital erroneousness which renders him incapable of describing accurately anything he sees, or understanding or reporting accurately anything he hears. As the only employment in which these defects do not matter is journalism (for a newspaper, not having to act on its description and reports, but only to sell them to idly curious people, has nothing but honor to lose by inaccuracy and unveracity), he has perforce become a journalist, and has to keep up an air of high spirits through a daily struggle with his own illiteracy and the precariousness of his employment. He has a note-book, and occasionally attempts to make a note; but as he cannot write shorthand, and does not write with ease in any hand, he generally gives it up as a bad job before he succeeds in finishing a sentence.

THE NEWSPAPER MAN [*looking round and making indecisive attempts at notes*]   This is the studio, I suppose.

WALPOLE   Yes.

THE NEWSPAPER MAN [*wittily*]   Where he has his models, eh?

WALPOLE [*grimly irresponsive*]   No doubt.

THE NEWSPAPER MAN   Cubicle, you said it was?

WALPOLE   Yes, tubercle.

THE NEWSPAPER MAN   Which way do you spell it: is it c-u-b-i-c-a-l or c-l-e?

WALPOLE   Tubercle, man, not cubical. [*Spelling it for him*] T-u-b-e-r-c-l-e.

THE NEWSPAPER MAN   Oh! tubercle. Some disease, I suppose. I thought he had consumption. Are you one of the family or the doctor?

WALPOLE   I'm neither one nor the other. I am M i s t e r Cutler Walpole. Put that down. Then put down Sir Colenso Ridgeon.

THE NEWSPAPER MAN   Pigeon?

WALPOLE   Ridgeon. [*Contemptuously snatching his book*] Here: youd better let me write the names down for you: youre sure to get them wrong. That comes of belonging to an illiterate profession, with no qualifications and no public register.* [*He writes the particulars*].

THE NEWSPAPER MAN   Oh, I say: you h a v e got your knife into us, havnt you?

WALPOLE [*vindictively*]   I wish I had: I'd make a better man of you. Now attend. [*Shewing him the book*] These are the names of the three doctors. This is the patient. This is the address. This is the name of the disease. [*He shuts the book with a snap which makes the journalist blink, and returns it to him*]. Mr Dubedat will be brought in here presently. He wants to see you because he doesnt know how bad he is. We'll allow you to wait a few minutes to humor him; but if you talk to him, out you go. He may die at any moment.

THE NEWSPAPER MAN [*interested*]   Is he as bad as that? I say: I a m in luck to-day. Would you mind letting me photograph you? [*He produces a camera*]. Could you have a lancet or something in your hand?

WALPOLE   Put it up. If you want my photograph you can get it in Baker Street† in any of the series of celebrities.

THE NEWSPAPER MAN   But theyll want to be paid. If you wouldnt mind [*fingering the camera*]——?

---

*No license is required to practice journalism.

†Street in London where professional photographers had their shops.

WALPOLE   I would. Put it up, I tell you. Sit down there and be quiet.

The NEWSPAPER MAN quickly sits down on the piano stool as DUBEDAT, in an invalid's chair, is wheeled in by MRS DUBEDAT and SIR RALPH. They place the chair between the dais and the sofa, where the easel stood before. LOUIS is not changed as a robust man would be; and he is not scared. His eyes look larger; and he is so weak physically that he can hardly move, lying on his cushions with complete languor; but his mind is active; it is making the most of his condition, finding voluptuousness in languor and drama in death. They are all impressed, in, spite of themselves, except RIDGEON, who is implacable. B. B. is entirely sympathetic and forgiving. RIDGEON follows the chair with a tray of milk and stimulants. SIR PATRICK, who accompanies him, takes the tea-table from the corner and places it behind the chair for the tray. B. B. takes the easel chair and places it for JENNIFER at DUBEDAT's side, next the dais, from which the lay figure ogles the dying artist. B. B. then returns to DUBEDAT's left. JENNIFER sits. WALPOLE sits down on the edge of the dais. RIDGEON stands near him.

LOUIS [*blissfully*]   Thats happiness. To be in a studio! Happiness!

MRS DUBEDAT   Yes, dear. Sir Patrick says you may stay here as long as you like.

LOUIS   Jennifer.

MRS DUBEDAT   Yes, my darling.

LOUIS   Is the newspaper man here?

THE NEWSPAPER MAN [*glibly*]   Yes, Mr Dubedat: I'm here, at your service. I represent the press. I thought you might like to let us have a few words about—about—er—well, a few words on your illness, and your plans for the season.

LOUIS   My plans for the season are very simple. I'm going to die.

MRS DUBEDAT [*tortured*]   Louis—dearest—

LOUIS   My darling: I'm very weak and tired. Dont put on me the horrible strain of pretending that I dont know. Ive been lying there listening to the doctors—laughing to myself. They know. Dearest: dont cry. It makes you ugly; and I cant bear that. [*She dries her eyes and recovers herself with a proud effort*]. I want you to promise me something.

MRS DUBEDAT   Yes, yes: you know I will. [*Imploringly*] Only, my love, my love, dont talk: it will waste your strength.

LOUIS   No: it will only use it up. Ridgeon: give me something to keep me going for a few minutes—not one of your confounded anti-toxins, if you dont mind. I have some things to say before I go.

RIDGEON [*looking at SIR PATRICK*]   I suppose it can do no harm? [*He pours out some spirit, and is about to add soda water when SIR PATRICK corrects him*].

SIR PATRICK   In milk. Dont set him coughing.

LOUIS [*after drinking*]   Jennifer.

MRS DUBEDAT   Yes, dear.

LOUIS   If theres one thing I hate more than another, it's a widow. Promise me that youll never be a widow.

MRS DUBEDAT   My dear, what do you mean?

LOUIS   I want you to look beautiful. I want people to see in your eyes that you were married to me. The people in Italy used to point at Dante and say "There goes the man who has been in hell." I want them to point at you and say "There goes a woman who has been in heaven." It h a s been heaven, darling, hasnt it—sometimes?

MRS DUBEDAT   Oh yes, yes. Always, always.

LOUIS   If you wear black and cry, people will say "Look at that miserable woman: her husband made her miserable."

MRS DUBEDAT   No, never. You are the light and the blessing of my life. I never lived until I knew you.

LOUIS [*his eyes glistening*]   Then you must always wear beautiful dresses and splendid magic jewels. Think of all the wonderful pictures I shall never paint. [*She wins a terrible victory over a sob*]. Well, you must be transfigured with all the beauty of those pictures. Men must get such dreams from seeing you as they never could get from any daubing with paints and brushes. Painters must paint you as they never painted any mortal woman before. There must be a great tradition of beauty, a great atmosphere of wonder and romance. That is what men must always think of when they think of me. That is the sort of immortality I want. You can make that for me, Jennifer. There are lots of things you dont understand that every woman in the street understands; but you can understand that and do it as nobody else can. Promise me that immortality. Promise me you will not make a little hell of crape and crying and undertaker's horrors and withering flowers and all that vulgar rubbish.

MRS DUBEDAT   I promise. But all that is far off, dear. You are to come to Cornwall with me and get well. Sir Ralph says so.

LOUIS   Poor old B. B.

B. B. [*affected to tears, turns away and whispers to* SIR PATRICK] Poor fellow! Brain going.

LOUIS   Sir Patrick's there, isnt he?

SIR PATRICK   Yes, yes. I'm here.

LOUIS   Sit down, wont you? It's a shame to keep you standing about.

SIR PATRICK   Yes, yes. Thank you. All right.

LOUIS   Jennifer.

MRS DUBEDAT   Yes, dear.

LOUIS [*with a strange look of delight*]   Do you remember the burning bush?

MRS DUBEDAT   Yes, yes. Oh, my dear, how it strains my heart to remember it now!

LOUIS   Does it? It fills me with joy. Tell them about it.

MRS DUBEDAT   It was nothing—only that once in my old Cornish home we lit the first fire of the winter; and when we looked through the window we saw the flames dancing in a bush in the garden.

LOUIS   Such a color! Garnet color. Waving like silk. Liquid lovely flame flowing up through the bay leaves, and not burning them. Well, I shall be a flame like that. I'm sorry to disappoint the poor little worms; but the last of me shall be the flame in the burning bush. Whenever you see the flame, Jennifer, that will be me. Promise me that I shall be burnt.

MRS DUBEDAT   Oh, if I might be with you, Louis!

LOUIS   No: you must always be in the garden when the bush flames. You are my hold on the world: you are my immortality. Promise.

MRS DUBEDAT   I'm listening. I shall not forget. You know that I promise.

LOUIS   Well, thats about all; except that you are to hang my pictures at the one-man show. I can trust your eye. You wont let anyone else touch them.

MRS DUBEDAT   You can trust me.

LOUIS   Then theres nothing more to worry about, is there? Give me some more of that milk. I'm fearfully tired; but if I stop talking I shant begin again. [*SIR RALPH gives him a drink. He takes it and looks up quaintly*]. I say, B. B., do you think anything would stop y o u talking?

B. B. [*almost unmanned*]   He confuses me with you, Paddy. Poor fellow! Poor fellow!

LOUIS [*musing*]   I used to be awfully afraid of death; but now it's come I have no fear; and I'm perfectly happy. Jennifer.

MRS DUBEDAT   Yes, dear?

LOUIS   I'll tell you a secret. I used to think that our marriage was all an affectation, and that I'd break loose and run away some day. But now that I'm going to be broken loose whether I like it or not, I'm perfectly fond of you, and perfectly satisfied because I'm going to live as part of you and not as my troublesome self.

MRS DUBEDAT [*heartbroken*]   Stay with me, Louis. Oh, dont leave me, dearest.

LOUIS   Not that I'm selfish. With all my faults I dont think Ive ever been really selfish. No artist can: Art is too large for that. You will marry again, Jennifer.

MRS DUBEDAT   Oh, how c a n you, Louis?

LOUIS [*insisting childishly*]   Yes, because people who have found marriage happy always marry again. Ah, *I* shant be jealous. [*Slyly*] But dont talk to the other fellow too much about me: he wont like it. [*Almost chuckling*] I shall be your lover all the time; but it will be a secret from him, poor devil!

SIR PATRICK   Come! youve talked enough. Try to rest awhile.

LOUIS [*wearily*]   Yes: I'm fearfully tired; but I shall have a long rest presently. I have something to say to you fellows. Youre all there, arnt you? I'm too weak to see anything but Jennifer's bosom. That promises rest.

RIDGEON   We are all here.

LOUIS [*startled*]   That voice sounded devilish. Take care, Ridgeon: my ears hear things that other people's ears cant. Ive been thinking——thinking. I'm cleverer than you imagine.

SIR PATRICK [*whispering to RIDGEON*]   Youve got on his nerves, Colly. Slip out quietly.

RIDGEON [*apart to SIR PATRICK*]   Would you deprive the dying actor of his audience?

LOUIS [*his face lighting up faintly with mischievous glee*]   I heard that, Ridgeon. That was good. Jennifer, dear: be kind to Ridgeon always; because he was the last man who amused me.

RIDGEON [*relentless*]   Was I?

LOUIS   But it's not true. It's you who are still on the stage. I'm half way home already.

MRS DUBEDAT [*to RIDGEON*]   What did you say?

LOUIS [*answering for him*]   Nothing, dear. Only one of those little secrets that men keep among themselves. Well, all you chaps have thought pretty hard things of me, and said them.

B. B. [*quite overcome*]   No, no, Dubedat. Not at all.

LOUIS   Yes, you have. I know what you all think of me. Dont imagine I'm sore about it. I forgive you.

WALPOLE [*involuntarily*]   Well, damn me! [*Ashamed*] I beg your pardon.

LOUIS   That was old Walpole, I know. Dont grieve, Walpole. I'm perfectly happy. I'm not in pain. I dont want to live. Ive escaped from myself. I'm in heaven, immortal in the heart of my beautiful Jennifer. I'm not afraid, and not ashamed. [*Reflectively, puzzling it out for himself weakly*] I know that in an accidental sort of way, struggling through the unreal part of life, I havnt always been able to live up to my ideal. But in my own real world I have never done anything wrong, never denied my faith, never been untrue to myself. Ive been threatened and blackmailed and insulted and starved. But Ive played the game. Ive fought the good fight. And now it's all over, theres an indescribable peace. [*He feebly folds his hands and utters his creed*]. I believe in Michael Angelo, Velasquez, and Rembrandt; in the might of design, the mystery of color, the redemption of all things by Beauty everlasting, and the message of Art that has made these hands blessed. Amen. Amen.[9] [*He closes his eyes and lies still*].

MRS DUBEDAT [*breathless*]   Louis: are you—
WALPOLE rises and comes quickly to see whether he is dead.

LOUIS   Not yet, dear. Very nearly, but not yet. I should like to rest my head on your bosom; only it would tire you.

MRS DUBEDAT   No, no, no, darling: how could you tire me? [*She lifts him so that he lies on her bosom*].

LOUIS   Thats good. Thats real.

MRS DUBEDAT   Dont spare me, dear. Indeed, indeed you will not tire me. Lean on me with all your weight.

LOUIS [*with a sudden half return of his normal strength and comfort*] Jinny Gwinny: I think I shall recover after all. [*SIR PATRICK looks significantly at RIDGEON, mutely warning him that this is the end*].

MRS DUBEDAT [*hopefully*]   Yes, yes: you shall.

LOUIS   Because I suddenly want to sleep. Just an ordinary sleep.

MRS DUBEDAT [*rocking him*]   Yes, dear. Sleep. [*He seems to go to sleep. WALPOLE makes another movement. She protests*]. Sh-sh: please dont disturb him. [*His lips move*]. What did you say, dear? [*In great distress*] I cant listen without moving him. [*His lips move again: WALPOLE bends down and listens*].

WALPOLE   He wants to know is the newspaper man here.

THE NEWSPAPER MAN [*excited; for he has been enjoying himself enormously*]   Yes, Mr Dubedat. Here I am.

WALPOLE raises his hand warningly to silence him. SIR RALPH sits down quietly on the sofa and frankly buries his face in his handkerchief.

MRS DUBEDAT [*with great relief*]   Oh thats right, dear: dont spare me: lean with all your weight on me. Now you are really resting.

SIR PATRICK quickly comes forward and feels LOUIS's pulse; then takes him by the shoulders.

SIR PATRICK   Let me put him back on the pillow, maam. He will be better so.

MRS DUBEDAT [*piteously*]   Oh no, please, p l e a s e, doctor. He is not tiring me; and he will be so hurt when he wakes if he finds I have put him away.

SIR PATRICK   He will never wake again. [*He takes the body from her and replaces it in the chair. RIDGEON, unmoved, lets down the back and makes a bier of it*].

MRS DUBEDAT [*who has unexpectedly sprung to her feet, and stands dry-eyed and stately*]   Was that death?

WALPOLE   Yes.

MRS DUBEDAT [*with complete dignity*]   Will you wait for me a moment? I will come back. [*She goes out*].

WALPOLE   Ought we to follow her? Is she in her right senses?

SIR PATRICK [*with quiet conviction*]   Yes. She's all right. Leave her alone. She'll come back.

RIDGEON [*callously*]   Let us get this thing out of the way before she comes.

B. B. [*rising, shocked*]   My dear Colly! The poor lad! He died splendidly.

SIR PATRICK   Aye! that is how the wicked die.

> For there are no bands in their death;
> But their strength is firm:
> They are not in trouble as other men.*

No matter: it's not for us to judge. He's in another world now.

WALPOLE   Borrowing his first five-pound note there, probably.

RIDGEON   I said the other day that the most tragic thing in the world is a sick doctor. I was wrong. The most tragic thing in the world is a man of genius who is not also a man of honor.

RIDGEON and WALPOLE wheel the chair into the recess.

THE NEWSPAPER MAN [*to SIR RALPH*]   I thought it shewed a very nice feeling, his being so particular about his wife going into proper mourning for him and making her promise never to marry again.

B. B. [*impressively*]   Mrs Dubedat is not in a position to carry the interview any further. Neither are we.

SIR PATRICK   Good afternoon to you.

THE NEWSPAPER MAN   Mrs Dubedat said she was coming back.

B. B.   After you have gone.

---

*Quotation from the Bible, Psalm 73:4–5 (KJV).

THE NEWSPAPER MAN   Do you think she would give me a few words on How It Feels to be a Widow? Rather a good title for an article, isnt it?

B. B.   Young man: if you wait until Mrs Dubedat comes back, you will be able to write an article on How It Feels to be Turned Out of the House.

THE NEWSPAPER MAN [*unconvinced*]   You think she'd rather not—

B. B. [*cutting him short*]   Good day to you. [*Giving him a visiting-card*] Mind you get my name correctly. Good day.

THE NEWSPAPER MAN   Good day. Thank you. [*Vaguely trying to read the card*] Mr—

B. B.   No, not Mister. This is your hat, I think [*giving it to him*]. Gloves? No, of course: no gloves. Good day to you. [*He edges him out at last; shuts the door on him; and returns to SIR PATRICK as RIDGEON and WALPOLE come back from the recess, WALPOLE crossing the room to the hat-stand, and Ridgeon coming between SIR RALPH and SIR PATRICK*]. Poor fellow! Poor young fellow! How well he died! I feel a better man, really.

SIR PATRICK   When youre as old as I am, youll know that it matters very little how a man dies. What matters is, how he lives. Every fool that runs his nose against a bullet is a hero nowadays, because he dies for his country. Why dont he live for it to some purpose?

B. B.   No, please, Paddy: dont be hard on the poor lad. Not now, not now. After all, was he so bad? He had only two failings: money and women. Well, let us be honest. Tell the truth, Paddy. Dont be hypocritical, Ridgeon. Throw off the mask, Walpole. Are these two matters so well arranged at present that a disregard of the usual arrangements indicates real depravity?

WALPOLE   I dont mind his disregarding the usual arrangements. Confound the usual arrangements! To a man of science theyre beneath contempt both as to money and women. What I mind is his disregarding everything except his own pocket and his own fancy. He didnt disregard the usual arrangements when they paid him. Did he give us his pictures for nothing? Do you suppose he'd have hesitated to blackmail me if I'd compromised myself with his wife? Not he.

SIR PATRICK   Dont waste your time wrangling over him. A blackguard's a blackguard; an honest man's an honest man; and neither of them will ever be at a loss for a religion or a morality to prove that their ways are the right ways. It's the same with nations, the same with professions, the same all the world over and always will be.

B. B.   Ah, well, perhaps, perhaps, perhaps. Still, d e m o r - t u i s   n i l   n i s i   b o n u m.* He died extremely well, remarkably well. He has set us an example: let us endeavor to follow it rather than harp on the weaknesses that have perished with him. I think it is Shakespear who says that the good that most men do lives after them: the evil lies inter- réd with their bones. Yes: interréd with their bones. Believe me, Paddy, we are all mortal. It is the common lot, Ridgeon. Say what you will, Walpole, Nature's debt must be paid. If tis not to-day, twill be to-morrow.

> To-morrow and to-morrow and to-morrow
> After life's fitful fever they sleep well
> And like this insubstantial bourne from which
> No traveller returns
> Leave not a wrack behind.

WALPOLE is about to speak, but B. B., suddenly and vehemently pro- ceeding, extinguishes him.

---

*Of the dead [say] nothing but good (Latin).

Out, out, brief candle:

For nothing canst thou to damnation add

The readiness is all.[10]

WALPOLE [*gently; for B. B's feeling, absurdly expressed as it is, is too sincere and humane to be ridiculed*]   Yes, B. B. Death makes people go on like that. I dont know why it should; but it does. By the way, what are we going to do? Ought we to clear out; or had we better wait and see whether Mrs Dubedat will come back?

SIR PATRICK   I think we'd better go. We can tell the charwoman what to do.

They take their hats and go to the door.

MRS DUBEDAT [*coming from the inner door wonderfully and beautifully dressed, and radiant, carrying a great piece of purple silk, handsomely embroidered, over her arm*]   I'm so sorry to have kept you waiting.

SIR PATRICK	[*amazed, all	Dont mention it, madam.
B. B.	*together in*	Not at all, not at all.
RIDGEON	*a confused*	By no means.
WALPOLE	*murmur*]	It doesnt matter in the least.

MRS DUBEDAT [*coming to them*]   I felt that I must shake hands with his friends once before we part to-day. We have shared together a great privilege and a great happiness. I dont think we can ever think of ourselves as ordinary people again. We have had a wonderful experience; and that gives us a common faith, a common ideal, that nobody else can quite have. Life will always be beautiful to us: death will always be beautiful to us. May we shake hands on that?

SIR PATRICK [*shaking hands*]   Remember: all letters had better be left to your solicitor. Let him open everything and settle everything. Thats the law, you know.

MRS DUBEDAT   Oh, thank you: I didnt know. [*SIR PATRICK goes*].

WALPOLE   Good-bye. I blame myself: I should have insisted on operating. [*He goes*].

B. B.   I will send the proper people: they will know what to do: you shall have no trouble. Good-bye, my dear lady. [*He goes*].

RIDGEON   Good-bye. [*He offers his hand*].

MRS DUBEDAT [*drawing back with gentle majesty*]   I said his f r i e n d s, Sir Colenso. [*He bows and goes*].

She unfolds the great piece of silk, and goes into the recess to cover her dead.

ACT V

One of the smaller Bond Street* Picture Galleries. The entrance is from a picture shop. Nearly in the middle of the gallery there is a writing-table, at which the Secretary, fashionably dressed, sits with his back to the entrance, correcting catalogue proofs. Some copies of a new book are on the desk, also the Secretary's shining hat and a couple of magnifying glasses. At the side, on his left, a little behind him, is a small door marked PRIVATE. *Near the same side is a cushioned bench parallel to the walls, which are covered with Dubedat's works. Two screens, also covered with drawings, stand near the corners right and left of the entrance.*

Jennifer, beautifully dressed and apparently very happy and prosperous, comes into the gallery through the private door.

JENNIFER   Have the catalogues come yet, Mr Danby?

THE SECRETARY   Not yet.

JENNIFER   What a shame! It's a quarter past: the private view will begin in less than half an hour.

THE SECRETARY   I think I'd better run over to the printers to hurry them up.

JENNIFER   Oh, if you would be so good, Mr Danby. I'll take your place while youre away.

THE SECRETARY   If anyone should come before the time

---

*Expensive shopping area in London.

dont take any notice. The commissionaire wont let anyone through unless he knows him. We have a few people who like to come before the crowd—people who really buy; and of course we're glad to see them. Have you seen the notices in Brush and Crayon and in The Easel?

JENNIFER [*indignantly*]   Yes: most disgraceful. They write quite patronizingly, as if they were Mr Dubedat's superiors. After all the cigars and sandwiches they had from us on the press day, and all they drank, I really think it is infamous that they should write like that. I hope you have not sent them tickets for to-day.

THE SECRETARY   Oh, they wont come again: theres no lunch to-day. The advance copies of your book have come. [*He indicates the new books*].

JENNIFER [*pouncing on a copy, wildly excited*]   Give it to me. Oh! excuse me a moment [*she runs away with it through the private door*].
The SECRETARY takes a mirror from his drawer and smartens himself before going out. RIDGEON comes in.

RIDGEON   Good morning. May I look round, as usual, before the doors open?

THE SECRETARY   Certainly, Sir Colenso. I'm sorry the catalogues have not come: I'm just going to see about them. Heres my own list, if you dont mind.

RIDGEON   Thanks. Whats this? [*He takes up one of the new books*].

THE SECRETARY   Thats just come in. An advance copy of Mrs Dubedat's Life of her late husband.

RIDGEON [*reading the title*]   The Story of a King of Men. By His Wife. [*He looks at the portrait frontis-piece*]. Ay: there he is. You knew him here, I suppose.

THE SECRETARY   Oh, we knew him. Better than she did, Sir Colenso, in some ways, perhaps.

RIDGEON   So did I. [*They look significantly at one another*]. I'll take a look round.

The SECRETARY puts on the shining hat and goes out. RIDGEON begins looking at the pictures. Presently he comes back to the table for a magnifying glass, and scrutinizes a drawing very closely. He sighs; shakes his head, as if constrained to admit the extraordinary fascination and merit of the work; then marks the SECRETARY's list. Proceeding with his survey, he disappears behind round the screen. JENNIFER comes back with her book. A look round satisfies her that she is alone. She seats herself at the table and admires the memoir— her first printed book—to her heart's content. RIDGEON re-appears, face to the wall, scrutinizing the drawings. After using his glass again, he steps back to get a more distant view of one of the larger pictures. She hastily closes the book at the sound; looks round; recognizes him; and stares, petrified. He takes a further step back which brings him nearer to her.

RIDGEON [*shaking his head as before, ejaculates*]   Clever brute! [*She flushes as though he had struck her. He turns to put the glass down on the desk, and finds himself face to face with her intent gaze*]. I beg your pardon. I thought I was alone.

JENNIFER [*controlling herself, and speaking steadily and meaningly*] I am glad we have met, Sir Colenso Ridgeon. I met Dr Blenkinsop yesterday. I congratulate you on a wonderful cure.

RIDGEON [*can find no words: makes an embarrassed gesture of assent after a moment's silence, and puts down the glass and the SECRETARY's list on the table*].

JENNIFER   He looked the picture of health and strength and prosperity. [*She looks for a moment at the walls, contrasting BLENKINSOP's fortune with the artist's fate*].

RIDGEON [*in low tones, still embarrassed*]   He has been fortunate.

JENNIFER   V e r y fortunate. His life has been spared.

RIDGEON   I mean that he has been made a Medical Officer of Health. He cured the Chairman of the Borough Council very successfully.

JENNIFER   With y o u r medicines?

RIDGEON   No. I believe it was with a pound of ripe greengages.

JENNIFER [*with deep gravity*]   Funny!

RIDGEON   Yes. Life does not cease to be funny when people die any more than it ceases to be serious when people laugh.

JENNIFER   Dr Blenkinsop said one very strange thing to me.

RIDGEON   What was that?

JENNIFER   He said that private practice in medicine ought to be put down by law. When I asked him why, he said that private doctors were ignorant licensed murderers.

RIDGEON   That is what the public doctor always thinks of the private doctor. Well, Blenkinsop ought to know. He was a private doctor long enough himself. Come! you have talked at me long enough. Talk to me. You have something to reproach me with. There is reproach in your face, in your voice: you are full of it. Out with it.

JENNIFER   It is too late for reproaches now. When I turned and saw you just now, I wondered how you could come here coolly to look at his pictures. You answered the question. To you, he was only a clever brute.

RIDGEON [*quivering*]   Oh, dont. You know I did not know you were here.

JENNIFER [*raising her head a little with a quite gentle impulse of pride*]   You think it only mattered because I heard it. As if it could touch me, or touch him! Dont you see that what is really dreadful is that to you living things have no souls.

RIDGEON [*with a sceptical shrug*]   The soul is an organ I have not come across in the course of my anatomical work.

JENNIFER   You know you would not dare to say such a silly thing as that to anybody but a woman whose mind you despise. If you dissected me you could not find my conscience. Do you think I have got none?

RIDGEON   I have met people who had none.

JENNIFER   Clever brutes? Do you know, doctor, that some of the dearest and most faithful friends I ever had were only brutes! You would have vivisected them. The dearest and greatest of all my friends had a sort of beauty and affectionateness that only animals have. I hope you may never feel what I felt when I had to put him into the hands of men who defend the torture of animals because they are only brutes.

RIDGEON   Well, did you find us so very cruel, after all? They tell me that though you have dropped me, you stay for weeks with the Bloomfield Boningtons and the Walpoles. I think it must be true, because they never mention you to me now.

JENNIFER   The animals in Sir Ralph's house are like spoiled children. When Mr Walpole had to take a splinter out of the mastiff's paw, I had to hold the poor dog myself; and Mr Walpole had to turn Sir Ralph out of the room. And Mrs Walpole has to tell the gardener not to kill wasps when Mr Walpole is looking. But there are doctors who are naturally cruel; and there are others who get used to cruelty and are callous about it. They blind themselves to the souls of animals; and that blinds them to the souls of men and women. You made a dreadful mistake about Louis; but you would not have made it if you had not trained yourself to make the same mistake about dogs. You saw nothing in them but dumb brutes; and so you could see nothing in him but a clever brute.

RIDGEON [*with sudden resolution*]   I made no mistake whatever about him.

JENNIFER   Oh, doctor!

RIDGEON [*obstinately*]   I made no mistake whatever about him.

JENNIFER   Have you forgotten that he died?

RIDGEON [*with a sweep of his hand towards the pictures*]   He is not dead. He is there. [*Taking up the book*] And there.

JENNIFER [*springing up with blazing eyes*]   Put that down. How dare you touch it?

RIDGEON, amazed at the fierceness of the outburst, puts it down with a deprecatory shrug. She takes it up and looks at it as if he had profaned a relic.

RIDGEON   I am very sorry. I see I had better go.

JENNIFER [*putting the book down*]   I beg your pardon. I—I forgot myself. But it is not yet—it is a private copy.

RIDGEON   But for me it would have been a very different book.

JENNIFER   But for you it would have been a longer one.

RIDGEON   You know then that I killed him?

JENNIFER [*suddenly moved and softened*]   Oh, doctor, if you acknowledge that—if you have confessed it to yourself—if you realize what you have done, then there is forgiveness. I trusted in your strength instinctively at first; then I thought I had mistaken callousness for strength. Can you blame me? But if it was really strength—if it was only such a mistake as we all make sometimes—it will make me so happy to be friends with you again.

RIDGEON   I tell you I made no mistake. I cured Blenkinsop: was there any mistake there?

JENNIFER   He recovered. Oh, dont be foolishly proud, doctor. Confess to a failure, and save our friendship. Remember, Sir Ralph gave Louis your medicine; and it made him worse.

RIDGEON   I cant be your friend on false pretences. Something has got me by the throat: the truth must come out. I used that medicine myself on Blenkinsop. It did not make him worse. It is a dangerous medicine: it cured Blenkinsop: it killed Louis Dubedat. When I handle it, it cures. When another man handles it, it kills—sometimes.

JENNIFER [*naïvely: not yet taking it all in*]   Then why did you let Sir Ralph give it to Louis?

RIDGEON   I'm going to tell you. I did it because I was in love with you.

JENNIFER [*innocently surprised*]   In lo—You! an elderly man!

RIDGEON [*thunderstruck, raising his fists to heaven*]   Dubedat: thou
art avenged! [*He drops his hands and collapses on the bench*]. I never
thought of that. I suppose I appear to you a ridiculous old fogey.

JENNIFER   But surely—I did not mean to offend you, indeed—but you must be at least twenty years older than I am.

RIDGEON   Oh, quite. More, perhaps. In twenty years you will
understand how little difference that makes.

JENNIFER   But even so, how could you think that I—his
wife—could ever think of y o u—

RIDGEON [*stopping her with a nervous waving of his fingers*]   Yes,
yes, yes, yes: I quite understand: you neednt rub it in.

JENNIFER   But—oh, it is only dawning on me now—I was so
surprised at first—do you dare to tell me that it was to gratify a miserable jealousy that you deliberately—oh! oh! you
murdered him.

RIDGEON   I think I did. It really comes to that.

> Thou shalt not kill, but needst not strive
> Officiously to keep alive.*

I suppose—yes: I killed him.

JENNIFER   And you tell me that! to my face! callously! You are
not afraid!

RIDGEON   I am a doctor: I have nothing to fear. It is not an in-
dictable offence to call in B. B. Perhaps it ought to be; but it
isnt.

JENNIFER   I did not mean that. I meant afraid of my taking the
law into my own hands, and killing you.

RIDGEON   I am so hopelessly idiotic about you that I should
not mind it a bit. You would always remember me if you did
that.

---

*Quotation from "The Latest Decalogue," by English poet Arthur Hugh Clough
(1819–1861).

JENNIFER   I shall remember you always as a little man who tried to kill a great one.

RIDGEON   Pardon me. I succeeded.

JENNIFER [*with quiet conviction*]   No. Doctors think they hold the keys of life and death; but it is not their will that is fulfilled. I dont believe you made any difference at all.

RIDGEON   Perhaps not. But I intended to.

JENNIFER [*looking at him amazedly: not without pity*]   And you tried to destroy that wonderful and beautiful life merely because you grudged him a woman whom you could never have expected to care for you!

RIDGEON   Who kissed my hands. Who believed in me. Who told me her friendship lasted until death.

JENNIFER   And whom you were betraying.

RIDGEON   No. Whom I was saving.

JENNIFER [*gently*]   Pray, doctor, from what?

RIDGEON   From making a terrible discovery. From having your life laid waste.

JENNIFER   How?

RIDGEON   No matter. I h a v e saved you. I have been the best friend you ever had. You are happy. You are well. His works are an imperishable joy and pride for you.

JENNIFER   And you think that is y o u r doing. Oh doctor, doctor! Sir Patrick is right: you do think you are a little god. How can you be so silly? Y o u did not paint those pictures which are my imperishable joy and pride: y o u did not speak the words that will always be heavenly music in my ears. I listen to them now whenever I am tired or sad. That is why I am always happy.

RIDGEON   Yes, now that he is dead. Were you always happy when he was alive?

JENNIFER [*wounded*]   Oh, you are cruel, cruel. When he was alive I did not know the greatness of my blessing. I worried meanly about little things. I was unkind to him. I was unworthy of him.

RIDGEON [*laughing bitterly*]   Ha!

JENNIFER   Dont insult me: dont blaspheme. [*She snatches up the book and presses it to her heart in a paroxysm of remorse, exclaiming*] Oh, my King of Men!

RIDGEON   King of Men! Oh, this is too monstrous, too grotesque. We cruel doctors have kept the secret from you faithfully; but it is like all secrets: it will not not keep itself. The buried truth germinates and breaks through to the light.

JENNIFER   What truth?

RIDGEON   What truth! Why, that Louis Dubedat, King of Men, was the most entire and perfect scoundrel, the most miraculously mean rascal, the most callously selfish blackguard that ever made a wife miserable.

JENNIFER [*unshaken: calm and lovely*]   He made his wife the happiest woman in the world, doctor.

RIDGEON   No: by all thats true on earth, he made his w i d o w the happiest woman in the world; but it was I who made her a widow. And her happiness is my justification and my reward. Now you know what I did and what I thought of him. Be as angry with me as you like: at least you know me as I really am. If you ever come to care for an elderly man, you will know what you are caring for.

JENNIFER [*kind and quiet*]   I am not angry with you any more, Sir Colenso. I knew quite well that you did not like Louis; but it is not your fault: you dont understand: that is all. You never could have believed in him. It is just like your not believing in my religion: it is a sort of sixth sense that you have not got. And [*with a gentle reassuring movement towards him*] dont think that you have shocked me so dreadfully. I know quite well what you mean by his selfishness. He sacrificed everything for his art. In a certain sense he had even to sacrifice everybody—

RIDGEON   Everybody except himself. By keeping that back he lost the right to sacrifice you, and gave me the right to sacrifice him. Which I did.

JENNIFER [*shaking her head, pitying his error*]   He was one of the men who know what women know: that self-sacrifice is vain and cowardly.

RIDGEON   Yes, when the sacrifice is rejected and thrown away. Not when it becomes the food of godhead.

JENNIFER   I dont understand that. And I cant argue with you: you are clever enough to puzzle me, but not to shake me. You are so utterly, so wildly wrong; so incapable of appreciating Louis—

RIDGEON   Oh! [*taking up the SECRETARY's list*] I have marked five pictures as sold to me.

JENNIFER   They will not be sold to you. Louis' creditors insisted on selling them; but this is my birthday; and they were all bought in for me this morning by my husband.

RIDGEON   By whom?!!!

JENNIFER   By my husband.

RIDGEON [*gabbling and stuttering*]   What husband? Whose husband? Which husband? Whom? how? what? Do you mean to say that you have married again?

JENNIFER   Do you forget that Louis disliked widows, and that people who have married happily once always marry again?

RIDGEON   Then I have committed a purely disinterested murder!

The SECRETARY returns with a pile of catalogues.

THE SECRETARY   Just got the first batch of catalogues in time. The doors are open.

JENNIFER [*to RIDGEON, politely*]   So glad you like the pictures, Sir Colenso. Good morning.

RIDGEON   Good morning. [*He goes towards the door; hesitates; turns to say something more; gives it up as a bad job; and goes*].

PYGMALION

PREFACE TO PYGMALION
A PROFESSOR OF PHONETICS

A s will be seen later on, Pygmalion needs, not a preface, but a sequel, which I have supplied in its due place.

The English have no respect for their language, and will not teach their children to speak it. They spell it so abominably that no man can teach himself what it sounds like. It is impossible for an Englishman to open his mouth without making some other Englishman hate or despise him. German and Spanish are accessible to foreigners: English is not accessible even to Englishmen. The reformer England needs today is an energetic phonetic enthusiast: that is why I have made such a one the hero of a popular play. There have been heroes of that kind crying in the wilderness for many years past. When I became interested in the subject towards the end of the eighteen-seventies, Melville Bell[1] was dead; but Alexander J. Ellis* was still a living patriarch, with an impressive head always covered by a velvet skull cap, for which he would apologize to public meetings in a very courtly manner. He and Tito Pagliardini,† another phonetic veteran, were men whom it was impossible to dislike. Henry Sweet, then a young man, lacked their sweetness of character: he was about as conciliatory to conventional mortals as Ibsen or Samuel Butler. His great ability as a

---

*English philologist and mathematician (1814–1890); an advocate of spelling reform.

†Italian singer (1817–1895) who taught French in England and advocated a phonetic alphabet.

phonetician (he was, I think, the best of them all at his job) would have entitled him to high official recognition, and perhaps enabled him to popularize his subject, but for his Satanic contempt for all academic dignitaries and persons in general who thought more of Greek than of phonetics. Once, in the days when the Imperial Institute* rose in South Kensington, and Joseph Chamberlain was booming the Empire, I induced the editor of a leading monthly review to commission an article from Sweet on the imperial importance of his subject. When it arrived, it contained nothing but a savagely derisive attack on a professor of language and literature whose chair Sweet regarded as proper to a phonetic expert only. The article, being libelous, had to be returned as impossible; and I had to renounce my dream of dragging its author into the limelight. When I met him afterwards, for the first time for many years, I found to my astonishment that he, who had been a quite tolerably presentable young man, had actually managed by sheer scorn to alter his personal appearance until he had become a sort of walking repudiation of Oxford and all its traditions. It must have been largely in his own despite that he was squeezed into something called a Readership of phonetics there. The future of phonetics rests probably with his pupils, who all swore by him; but nothing could bring the man himself into any sort of compliance with the university, to which he nevertheless clung by divine right in an intensely Oxonian way. I daresay his papers, if he has left any, include some satires that may be published without too destructive results fifty years hence. He was, I believe, not in the least an illnatured man: very much the opposite, I should say; but he would not suffer fools gladly.

Those who knew him will recognize in my third act the allusion to the patent shorthand in which he used to write postcards, and

---

*Institute founded in 1887 to conduct research into resources and raw materials of the British Empire, and to make the growing Empire understandable to the British people.

which may be acquired from a four and six-penny manual* published by the Clarendon Press. The postcards which Mrs. Higgins
describes are such as I have received from Sweet. I would decipher
a sound which a cockney would represent by *zerr*, and a Frenchman
by *seu*, and then write demanding with some heat what on earth it
meant. Sweet, with boundless contempt for my stupidity, would
reply that it not only meant but obviously was the word Result, as
no other word containing that sound, and capable of making sense
with the context, existed in any language spoken on earth. That less
expert mortals should require fuller indications was beyond
Sweet's patience. Therefore, though the whole point of his "Current Shorthand" is that it can express every sound in the language
perfectly, vowels as well as consonants, and that your hand has to
make no stroke except the easy and current ones with which you
write m, n, and u, l, p, and q, scribbling them at whatever angle
comes easiest to you, his unfortunate determination to make this
remarkable and quite legible script serve also as a shorthand reduced it in his own practice to the most inscrutable of cryp-
tograms. His true objective was the provision of a full, accurate,
legible script for our noble but ill-dressed language; but he was led
past that by his contempt for the popular Pitman system of shorthand,† which he called the Pitfall system. The triumph of Pitman
was a triumph of business organization: there was a weekly paper
to persuade you to learn Pitman: there were cheap textbooks and
exercise books and transcripts of speeches for you to copy, and
schools where experienced teachers coached you up to the necessary proficiency. Sweet could not organize his market in that fashion. He might as well have been the Sybil who tore up the leaves of
prophecy that nobody would attend to.‡ The four and six-penny
manual, mostly in his lithographed handwriting, that was never

---

*Reference to *A Manual of Current Shorthand* (1892).

†Named after its inventor, Sir Isaac Pitman (1813–1897).

‡Amalthaea, the Sibyl of Cumae, was a legendary prophetess of ancient Rome who
destroyed six of nine prophetic books when the Roman king refused to pay for them.

vulgarly advertized, may perhaps some day be taken up by a syndicate and pushed upon the public as The Times pushed the Ency-
clopædia Britannica; but until then it will certainly not prevail
against Pitman. I have bought three copies of it during my lifetime;
and I am informed by the publishers that its cloistered existence is
still a steady and healthy one. I actually learned the system two several times; and yet the shorthand in which I am writing these lines
is Pitman's. And the reason is, that my secretary cannot transcribe
Sweet, having been perforce taught in the schools of Pitman.
Therefore, Sweet railed at Pitman as vainly as Thersites railed at
Ajax: his raillery, however it may have eased his soul, gave no popular vogue to Current Shorthand.

Pygmalion Higgins is not a portrait of Sweet, to whom the adventure of Eliza Doolittle would have been impossible; still, as will
be seen, there are touches of Sweet in the play. With Higgins's
physique and temperament Sweet might have set the Thames on
fire. As it was, he impressed himself professionally on Europe to
an extent that made his comparative personal obscurity, and the
failure of Oxford to do justice to his eminence, a puzzle to foreign
specialists in his subject. I do not blame Oxford, because I think
Oxford is quite right in demanding a certain social amenity from
its nurslings (heaven knows it is not exorbitant in its requirements!); for although I well know how hard it is for a man of genius with a seriously underrated subject to maintain serene and
kindly relations with the men who underrate it, and who keep all
the best places for less important subjects which they profess
without originality and sometimes without much capacity for
them, still, if he overwhelms them with wrath and disdain, he cannot expect them to heap honors on him.

Of the later generations of phoneticians I know little. Among
them towers the Poet Laureate,* to whom perhaps Higgins may

---

*Robert Bridges, poet laureate of England (1913–1930) and author of *Milton's
Prosody* (1893), practiced spelling reform.

owe his Miltonic sympathies, though here again I must disclaim all portraiture. But if the play makes the public aware that there are such people as phoneticians, and that they are among the most important people in England at present, it will serve its turn.

I wish to boast that Pygmalion has been an extremely successful play all over Europe and North America as well as at home. It is so intensely and deliberately didactic, and its subject is esteemed so dry, that I delight in throwing it at the heads of the wiseacres who repeat the parrot cry that art should never be didactic. It goes to prove my contention that art should never be anything else.

Finally, and for the encouragement of people troubled with accents that cut them off from all high employment, I may add that the change wrought by Professor Higgins in the flower girl is neither impossible nor uncommon. The modern concierge's daughter who fulfils her ambition by playing the Queen of Spain in Ruy Blas* at the Théâtre Français is only one of many thousands of men and women who have sloughed off their native dialects and acquired a new tongue. But the thing has to be done scientifically, or the last state of the aspirant may be worse than the first. An honest and natural slum dialect is more tolerable than the attempt of a phonetically untaught person to imitate the vulgar dialect of the golf club; and I am sorry to say that in spite of the efforts of our Academy of Dramatic Art, there is still too much sham golfing English on our stage, and too little of the noble English of Forbes Robertson.

*The valet who passes as a nobleman in Victor Hugo's 1838 verse drama of the same name.

PYGMALION

ACT I

Covent Garden at 11.15 p.m. Torrents of heavy summer rain. Cab whistles blowing frantically in all directions. Pedestrians running for shelter into the market and under the portico of St. Paul's Church,[2] where there are already several people, among them a lady and her daughter in evening dress. They are all peering out gloomily at the rain, except one man with his back turned to the rest, who seems wholly preoccupied with a notebook in which he is writing busily.

The church clock strikes the first quarter.

THE DAUGHTER [*in the space between the central pillars, close to the one on her left*]   I'm getting chilled to the bone. What can Freddy be doing all this time? Hes been gone twenty minutes.

THE MOTHER [*on her daughter's right*]   Not so long. But he ought to have got us a cab by this.

A BYSTANDER [*on the lady's right*]   He wont get no cab not until half-past eleven, missus, when they come back after dropping their theatre fares.

THE MOTHER   But we must have a cab. We cant stand here until half-past eleven. It's too bad.

THE BYSTANDER   Well, it aint my fault, missus.

THE DAUGHTER   If Freddy had a bit of gumption, he would have got one at the theatre door.

THE MOTHER   What could he have done, poor boy?

THE DAUGHTER   Other people got cabs. Why couldnt he?

FREDDY rushes in out of the rain from the Southampton Street side, and comes between them closing a dripping umbrella. He is a young man of twenty, in evening dress, very wet around the ankles.

THE DAUGHTER   Well, havnt you got a cab?

FREDDY   Theres not one to be had for love or money.

THE MOTHER   Oh, Freddy, there must be one. You cant have tried.

THE DAUGHTER   It's too tiresome. Do you expect us to go and get one ourselves?

FREDDY   I tell you theyre all engaged. The rain was so sudden: nobody was prepared; and everybody had to take a cab. Ive been to Charing Cross one way and nearly to Ludgate Circus the other; and they were all engaged.

THE MOTHER   Did you try Trafalgar Square?

FREDDY   There wasnt one at Trafalgar Square.

THE DAUGHTER   Did you try?

FREDDY   I tried as far as Charing Cross Station. Did you expect me to walk to Hammersmith?

THE DAUGHTER   You havnt tried at all.

THE MOTHER   You really are very helpless, Freddy. Go again; and dont come back until you have found a cab.

FREDDY   I shall simply get soaked for nothing.

THE DAUGHTER   And what about us? Are we to stay here all night in this draught, with next to nothing on. You selfish pig—

FREDDY   Oh, very well: I'll go, I'll go. [*He opens his umbrella and dashes off Strandwards, but comes into collision with a flower girl, who is hurrying in for shelter, knocking her basket out of her hands. A blinding flash of lightning, followed instantly by a rattling peal of thunder, orchestrates the incident*].

THE FLOWER GIRL   Nah then, Freddy: look wh' y' gowin, deah.

FREDDY   Sorry [*he rushes off*].

THE FLOWER GIRL [*picking up her scattered flowers and replacing them in the basket*]   Theres menners f' yer! Te-oo banches o voylets trod into the mad.* [*She sits down on the plinth of the column, sorting her flowers, on the lady's right. She is not at all an attractive person.†* *She is perhaps eighteen, perhaps twenty, hardly older. She wears a little sailor hat of black straw that has long been exposed to the dust and soot of London and has seldom if ever been brushed. Her hair needs washing rather badly: its mousy color can hardly be natural. She wears a shoddy black coat that reaches nearly to her knees and is shaped to her waist. She has a brown skirt with a coarse apron. Her boots are much the worse for wear. She is no doubt as clean as she can afford to be; but compared to the ladies she is very dirty. Her features are no worse than theirs; but their condition leaves something to be desired; and she needs the services of a dentist*].

THE MOTHER   How do you know that my son's name is Freddy, pray?

THE FLOWER GIRL   Ow, eez ye-ooa san, is e? Wal, fewd dan y' de-ooty bawmz a mather should, eed now bettern to spawl a pore gel's flahrzn than ran away athaht pyin. Will ye-oo py me f'them?[3] [*Here, with apologies, this desperate attempt to represent her dialect without a phonetic alphabet must be abandoned as unintelligible outside London.*]

THE DAUGHTER   Do nothing of the sort, mother. The idea!

THE MOTHER   Please allow me, Clara. Have you any pennies?

THE DAUGHTER   No. I've nothing smaller than sixpence.

THE FLOWER GIRL [*hopefully*]   I can give you change for a tanner,‡ kind lady.

THE MOTHER [*to CLARA*]   Give it to me. [*CLARA parts reluctantly*]. Now [*to the girl*] this is for your flowers.

THE FLOWER GIRL   Thank you kindly, lady.

---

*That is, "Two bunches of violets trod in the mud."
†Shaw later revised this phrase to "a romantic figure."
‡Sixpence coin (slang).

THE DAUGHTER Make her give you the change. These things are only a penny a bunch.

THE MOTHER Do hold your tongue, Clara. [*To the girl*] You can keep the change.

THE FLOWER GIRL Oh, thank you, lady.

THE MOTHER Now tell me how you know that young gentleman's name.

THE FLOWER GIRL I didnt.

THE MOTHER I heard you call him by it. Dont try to deceive me.

THE FLOWER GIRL [*protesting*] Whos trying to deceive you? I called him Freddy or Charlie same as you might yourself if you was talking to a stranger and wished to be pleasant. [*She sits down beside her basket*].

THE DAUGHTER Sixpence thrown away! Really, mamma, you might have spared Freddy that. [*She retreats in disgust behind the pillar*].

An elderly gentleman of the amiable military type rushes into shelter, and closes a dripping umbrella. He is in the same plight as FREDDY, very wet about the ankles. He is in evening dress, with a light overcoat. He takes the place left vacant by the daughter's retirement.

THE GENTLEMAN Phew!

THE MOTHER [*to the gentleman*] Oh, sir, is there any sign of its stopping?

THE GENTLEMAN I'm afraid not. It started worse than ever about two minutes ago. [*He goes to the plinth beside the flower girl; puts up his foot on it; and stoops to turn down his trouser ends*].*

THE MOTHER Oh, dear! [*She retires sadly and joins her daughter*].

THE FLOWER GIRL [*taking advantage of the military gentleman's proximity to establish friendly relations with him*] If it's worse it's

---

*Having turned them up due to the rain.

a sign it's nearly over. So cheer up, Captain; and buy a flower off a poor girl.

THE GENTLEMAN   I'm sorry, I havnt any change.

THE FLOWER GIRL   I can give you change, Captain.

THE GENTLEMAN   For a sovereign? Ive nothing less.

THE FLOWER GIRL   Garn! Oh do buy a flower off me, Captain. I can change half-a-crown. Take this for tuppence.

THE GENTLEMAN   Now dont be troublesome: theres a good girl. [*Trying his pockets*] I really havnt any change—Stop: heres three hapence, if thats any use to you [*he retreats to the other pillar*].

THE FLOWER GIRL [*disappointed, but thinking three halfpence better than nothing*]   Thank you, sir.

THE BYSTANDER [*to the girl*]   You be careful: give him a flower for it. Theres a bloke here behind taking down every blessed word youre saying. [*All turn to the man who is taking notes*].

THE FLOWER GIRL [*springing up terrified*]   I aint done nothing wrong by speaking to the gentleman. Ive a right to sell flowers if I keep off the kerb. [*Hysterically*] I'm a respectable girl: so help me, I never spoke to him except to ask him to buy a flower off me. [*General hubbub, mostly sympathetic to the flower girl, but deprecating her excessive sensibility. Cries of* Dont start hollerin. Whos hurting you? Nobody's going to touch you. Whats the good of fussing? Steady on. Easy, easy, etc., *come from the elderly staid spectators, who pat her comfortingly. Less patient ones bid her shut her head, or ask her roughly what is wrong with her. A remoter group, not knowing what the matter is, crowd in and increase the noise with question and answer:* Whats the row? What she do? Where is he? A tec* taking her down. What! him? Yes: him over there: Took money off the gentleman, etc. *The flower girl, distraught and mobbed, breaks through them to the gentleman, crying*

---

*Detective.

wildly] Oh, sir, dont let him charge me.* You dunno what it means to me. Theyll take away my character and drive me on the streets for speaking to gentlemen. They—

THE NOTE TAKER [*coming forward on her right, the rest crowding after him*]   There, there, there, there! whos hurting you, you silly girl? What do you take me for?

THE BYSTANDER   It's all right: hes a gentleman: look at his boots. [*Explaining to the note taker*] She thought you was a copper's nark,[†] sir.

THE NOTE TAKER [*with quick interest*]   Whats a copper's nark?

THE BYSTANDER [*inapt at definition*]   It's a—well, it's a copper's nark, as you might say. What else would you call it? A sort of informer.

THE FLOWER GIRL [*still hysterical*]   I take my Bible oath I never said a word—

THE NOTE TAKER [*overbearing but good-humored*]   Oh, shut up, shut up. Do I look like a policeman?

THE FLOWER GIRL [*far from reassured*]   Then what did you take down my words for? How do I know whether you took me down right? You just shew me what youve wrote about me. [*The note taker opens his book and holds it steadily under her nose, though the pressure of the mob trying to read it over his shoulders would upset a weaker man*]. Whats that? That aint proper writing. I cant read that.

THE NOTE TAKER   I can. [*Reads, reproducing her pronunciation exactly*] "Cheer ap, Keptin; n' baw ya flahr orf a pore gel."

THE FLOWER GIRL [*much distressed*]   It's because I called him Captain. I meant no harm. [*To the gentleman*] Oh, sir, dont let him lay a charge agen me for a word like that. You—

---

*That is, with soliciting for prostitution.
†Police informant.

THE GENTLEMAN   Charge! I make no charge. [*To the note taker*] Really, sir, if you are a detective, you need not begin protecting me against molestation by young women until I ask you. Anybody could see that the girl meant no harm.

THE BYSTANDERS GENERALLY [*demonstrating against police espionage*]   Course they could. What business is it of yours? You mind your own affairs. He wants promotion, he does. Taking down people's words! Girl never said a word to him. What harm if she did? Nice thing a girl cant shelter from the rain without being insulted, etc., etc., etc. [*She is conducted by the more sympathetic demonstrators back to her plinth, where she resumes her seat and struggles with her emotion.*]

THE BYSTANDER   He aint a tec. Hes a blooming busybody: thats what he is. I tell you, look at his boots.

THE NOTE TAKER [*turning on him genially*]   And how are all your people down at Selsey?

THE BYSTANDER [*suspiciously*]   Who told you my people come from Selsey?

THE NOTE TAKER   Never you mind. They did. [*To the girl*] How do you come to be up so far east? You were born in Lisson Grove.

THE FLOWER GIRL [*appalled*]   Oh, what harm is there in my leaving Lisson Grove? It wasnt fit for a pig to live in; and I had to pay four-and-six a week. [*In tears*] Oh, boo—hoo—oo—

THE NOTE TAKER   Live where you like; but stop that noise.

THE GENTLEMAN [*to the girl*]   Come, come! he cant touch you: you have a right to live where you please.

A SARCASTIC BYSTANDER [*thrusting himself between the note taker and the gentleman*]   Park Lane, for instance. Id like to go into the Housing Question with you, I would.

THE FLOWER GIRL [*subsiding into a brooding melancholy over her basket, and talking very low-spiritedly to herself*]   I'm a good girl, I am.

THE SARCASTIC BYSTANDER [*not attending to her*]   Do you know where *I* come from?

THE NOTE TAKER [*promptly*]   Hoxton.

Titterings. Popular interest in the note taker's performance increases.

THE SARCASTIC ONE [*amazed*]   Well, who said I didnt? Bly me!* You know everything, you do.

THE FLOWER GIRL [*still nursing her sense of injury*]   Aint no call to meddle with me, he aint.

THE BYSTANDER [*to her*]   Of course he aint. Dont you stand it from him. [*To the note taker*] See here: what call have you to know about people what never offered to meddle with you? Wheres your warrant?

SEVERAL BYSTANDERS [*encouraged by this seeming point of law*]   Yes: wheres your warrant?

THE FLOWER GIRL   Let him say what he likes. I dont want to have no truck with him.

THE BYSTANDER   You take us for dirt under your feet, dont you? Catch you taking liberties with a gentleman!

THE SARCASTIC BYSTANDER   Yes: tell him where he come from if you want to go fortune-telling.

THE NOTE TAKER   Cheltenham, Harrow, Cambridge, and India.

THE GENTLEMAN   Quite right. [*Great laughter. Reaction in the note taker's favor. Exclamations of* He knows all about it. Told him proper. Hear him tell the toff where he come from? etc.]. May I ask, sir, do you do this for your living at a music hall?[4]

THE NOTE TAKER   Ive thought of that. Perhaps I shall some day.

The rain has stopped; and the persons on the outside of the crowd begin to drop off.

THE FLOWER GIRL [*resenting the reaction*]   Hes no gentleman, he aint, to interfere with a poor girl.

---

*Slang expression equivalent to "damn me"; probably from "blind me."

THE DAUGHTER [*out of patience, pushing her way rudely to the front and displacing the gentleman, who politely retires to the other side of the pillar*]   What on earth is Freddy doing? I shall get pneumonia if I stay in this draught any longer.

THE NOTE TAKER [*to himself, hastily making a note of her pronunciation of "monia"*]   Earlscourt.

THE DAUGHTER [*violently*]   Will you please keep your impertinent remarks to yourself?

THE NOTE TAKER   Did I say that out loud? I didnt mean to. I beg your pardon. Your mother's Epsom, unmistakeably.

THE MOTHER [*advancing between her daughter and the note taker*]   How very curious! I was brought up in Largelady Park, near Epsom.

THE NOTE TAKER [*uproariously amused*]   Ha! ha! What a devil of a name! Excuse me. [*To the daughter*] You want a cab, do you?

THE DAUGHTER   Dont dare speak to me.

THE MOTHER   Oh, please, please Clara. [*Her daughter repudiates her with an angry shrug and retires haughtily*]. We should be so grateful to you, sir, if you found us a cab. [*The note taker produces a whistle*]. Oh, thank you. [*She joins her daughter*].

The note taker blows a piercing blast.

THE SARCASTIC BYSTANDER   There! I knowed he was a plain-clothes copper.

THE BYSTANDER   That aint a police whistle: thats a sporting whistle.

THE FLOWER GIRL [*still preoccupied with her wounded feelings*]   Hes no right to take away my character. My character is the same to me as any lady's.

THE NOTE TAKER   I dont know whether youve noticed it; but the rain stopped about two minutes ago.

THE BYSTANDER   So it has. Why didnt you say so before?

and us losing our time listening to your silliness. [*He walks off towards the Strand*].

THE SARCASTIC BYSTANDER   I can tell where you come from. You come from Anwell.* Go back there.

THE NOTE TAKER [*helpfully*]   Hanwell.

THE SARCASTIC BYSTANDER [*affecting great distinction of speech*]   Thenk you, teacher. Haw haw! So long [*he touches his hat with mock respect and strolls off*].

THE FLOWER GIRL   Frightening people like that! How would he like it himself.

THE MOTHER   It's quite fine now, Clara. We can walk to a motor bus. Come. [*She gathers her skirts above her ankles and hurries off towards the Strand*].

THE DAUGHTER   But the cab— [*her mother is out of hearing*]. Oh, how tiresome! [*She follows angrily*].

All the rest have gone except the note taker, the gentleman, and the flower girl, who sits arranging her basket, and still pitying herself in murmurs.

THE FLOWER GIRL   Poor girl! Hard enough for her to live without being worrited and chivied.†

THE GENTLEMAN [*returning to his former place on the note taker's left*]   How do you do it, if I may ask?

THE NOTE TAKER   Simply phonetics. The science of speech. Thats my profession: also my hobby. Happy is the man who can make a living by his hobby! You can spot an Irishman or a Yorkshireman by his brogue. *I* can place any man within six miles. I can place him within two miles in London. Sometimes within two streets.

THE FLOWER GIRL   Ought to be ashamed of himself, unmanly coward!

THE GENTLEMAN   But is there a living in that?

---

*Hanwell County Asylum for the insane.

†That is, worried and chased.

THE NOTE TAKER   Oh yes. Quite a fat one. This is an age of upstarts. Men begin in Kentish Town* with £80 a year, and end in Park Lane with a hundred thousand. They want to drop Kentish Town; but they give themselves away every time they open their mouths. Now I can teach them——

THE FLOWER GIRL   Let him mind his own business and leave a poor girl——

THE NOTE TAKER [*explosively*]   Woman: cease this detestable boohooing instantly; or else seek the shelter of some other place of worship.

THE FLOWER GIRL [*with feeble defiance*]   Ive a right to be here if I like, same as you.

THE NOTE TAKER   A woman who utters such depressing and disgusting sounds has no right to be anywhere—no right to live. Remember that you are a human being with a soul and the divine gift of articulate speech: that your native language is the language of Shakespear and Milton and The Bible; and dont sit there crooning like a bilious† pigeon.

THE FLOWER GIRL [*quite overwhelmed, and looking up at him in mingled wonder and deprecation without daring to raise her head*] Ah-ah-ah-ow-ow-ow-oo!

THE NOTE TAKER [*whipping out his book*]   Heavens! what a sound! [*He writes; then holds out the book and reads, reproducing her vowels exactly*] Ah-ah-ah-ow-ow-ow-oo!

THE FLOWER GIRL [*tickled by the performance, and laughing in spite of herself*]   Garn!

THE NOTE TAKER   You see this creature with her kerbstone English: the English that will keep her in the gutter to the end of her days. Well, sir, in three months I could pass that girl off as a duchess at an ambassador's garden party. I could even get her a place as lady's maid or shop assistant, which requires

---

*Working-class district of London; a slum area in the mid to late 1800s.
†Peevish, or ill-natured.

better English. Thats the sort of thing I do for commercial millionaires. And on the profits of it I do genuine scientific work in phonetics, and a little as a poet on Miltonic lines.

THE GENTLEMAN   I am myself a student of Indian dialects; and——

THE NOTE TAKER [*eagerly*]   Are you? Do you know Colonel Pickering, the author of Spoken Sanscrit?

THE GENTLEMAN   I am Colonel Pickering. Who are you?

THE NOTE TAKER   Henry Higgins, author of Higgins's Universal Alphabet.

PICKERING [*with enthusiasm*]   I came from India to meet you.

HIGGINS   I was going to India to meet you.

PICKERING   Where do you live?

HIGGINS   27A Wimpole Street. Come and see me to-morrow.

PICKERING   I'm at the Carlton. Come with me now and lets have a jaw over some supper.

HIGGINS   Right you are.

THE FLOWER GIRL [*to PICKERING, as he passes her*]   Buy a flower, kind gentleman. I'm short for my lodging.

PICKERING   I really havnt any change. I'm sorry [*he goes away*].

HIGGINS [*shocked at girl's mendacity*]   Liar. You said you could change half-a-crown.

THE FLOWER GIRL [*rising in desperation*]   You ought to be stuffed with nails, you ought. [*Flinging the basket at his feet*] Take the whole blooming basket for sixpence.

The church clock strikes the second quarter.

HIGGINS [*hearing in it the voice of God, rebuking him for his Pharisaic* want of charity to the poor girl*]   A reminder. [*He raises his hat solemnly; then throws a handful of money into the basket and follows Pickering*].

THE FLOWER GIRL [*picking up a half-crown*]   Ah-ow-ooh! [*Picking up a couple of florins*] Aaah-ow-ooh! [*Picking up several coins*]

---

*Relating to the Pharisees, a sect often portrayed in the Bible as hypocritical.

Aaaaaah-ow-ooh! [*Picking up a half-sovereign*] Aaaaaaaaaaaah-ow-ooh!!!

FREDDY [*springing out of a taxicab*]   Got one at last. Hallo! [*To the girl*] Where are the two ladies that were here?

THE FLOWER GIRL   They walked to the bus when the rain stopped.

FREDDY   And left me with a cab on my hands. Damnation!

THE FLOWER GIRL [*with grandeur*]   Never you mind, young man. I'm going home in a taxi. [*She sails off to the cab. The driver puts his hand behind him and holds the door firmly shut against her. Quite understanding his mistrust, she shews him her handful of money.* Eightpence aint no object to me, Charlie. [*He grins and opens the door*]. Angel Court, Drury Lane, round the corner of Micklejohn's oil shop. Lets see how fast you can make her hop it. [*She gets in and pulls the door to with a slam as the taxicab starts*].

FREDDY   Well, I'm dashed!

ACT II

Next day at 11 a.m. Higgins's laboratory in Wimpole Street. It is a room on the first floor, looking on the street, and was meant for the drawing-room. The double doors are in the middle of the back wall; and persons entering find in the corner to their right two tall file cabinets at right angles to one another against the walls. In this corner stands a flat writing-table, on which are a phonograph, a laryngoscope, a row of tiny organ pipes with a bellows, a set of lamp chimneys for singing flames* with burners attached to a gas plug in the wall by an indiarubber tube, several tuning-forks of different sizes, a life-size image of half a human head, showing in section the vocal organs, and a box containing a supply of wax cylinders† for the phonograph.

Further down the room, on the same side, is a fireplace, with a comfortable leather-covered easy-chair at the side of the hearth nearest the door, and a coal-scuttle. There is a clock on the mantelpiece. Between the fireplace and the phonograph table is a stand for newspapers.

On the other side of the central door, to the left of the visitor, is a cabinet of shallow drawers. On it is a telephone and the telephone directory. The corner beyond, and most

---

*Lamp chimneys are glass tubes around the wick of an oil lamp that keep the flame steady; flames in the tube that resonate to the human voice are called "singing flames."

†Used in the earliest phonographs as a medium for recording and replaying sound.

of the side wall, is occupied by a grand piano, with the keyboard at the end furthest from the door, and a bench for the player extending the full length of the keyboard. On the piano is a dessert dish heaped with fruit and sweets, mostly chocolates.

The middle of the room is clear. Besides the easy-chair, the piano bench, and two chairs at the phonograph table, there is one stray chair. It stands near the fireplace. On the walls, engravings; mostly Piranesis[5] and mezzotint portraits.* No paintings.

Pickering is seated at the table, putting down some cards and a tuning-fork which he has been using. Higgins is standing up near him, closing two or three file drawers which are hanging out. He appears in the morning light as a robust, vital, appetizing sort of man of forty or thereabouts, dressed in a professional-looking black frock-coat with a white linen collar and black silk tie. He is of the energetic, scientific type, heartily, even violently interested in everything that can be studied as a scientific subject, and careless about himself and other people, including their feelings. He is, in fact, but for his years and size, rather like a very impetuous baby "taking notice" eagerly and loudly, and requiring almost as much watching to keep him out of unintended mischief. His manner varies from genial bullying when he is in a good humor to stormy petulance when anything goes wrong; but he is so entirely frank and void of malice that he remains likeable even in his least reasonable moments.

HIGGINS [as he shuts the last drawer]   Well, I think thats the whole show.

---

*Portraits engraved on copper or steel; Higgins prefers their austerity to voluptuous color.

PICKERING   It's really amazing. I havnt taken half of it in, you
know.

HIGGINS   Would you like to go over any of it again?

PICKERING [*rising and coming to the fireplace, where he plants himself with his back to the fire*]   No, thank you; not now. I'm quite
done up for this morning.

HIGGINS [*following him, and standing beside him on his left*]   Tired
of listening to sounds?

PICKERING   Yes. It's a fearful strain. I rather fancied myself
because I can pronounce twenty-four distinct vowel sounds;
but your hundred and thirty beat me. I cant hear a bit of difference between most of them.

HIGGINS [*chuckling, and going over to the piano to eat sweets*]   Oh,
that comes with practice. You hear no difference at first; but
you keep on listening, and presently you find theyre all as different as A from B. [*Mrs. Pearce looks in: she is Higgins's housekeeper*] Whats the matter?

MRS. PEARCE [*hesitating, evidently perplexed*]   A young woman
wants to see you, sir.

HIGGINS   A young woman! What does she want?

MRS. PEARCE   Well, sir, she says youll be glad to see her
when you know what shes come about. Shes quite a common
girl, sir. Very common indeed. I should have sent her away,
only I thought perhaps you wanted her to talk into your machines. I hope Ive not done wrong; but really you see such
queer people sometimes—youll excuse me, I'm sure, sir—

HIGGINS   Oh, thats all right, Mrs. Pearce. Has she an interesting accent?

MRS. PEARCE   Oh, something dreadful, sir, really. I dont
know how you can take an interest in it.

HIGGINS [*to PICKERING*]   Lets have her up. Shew her up, Mrs.
Pearce [*he rushes across to his working table and picks out a cylinder to use on the phonograph*].

MRS. PEARCE [*only half resigned to it*]   Very well, sir. It's for you to say. [*She goes downstairs*].

HIGGINS   This is rather a bit of luck. I'll shew you how I make records. We'll set her talking; and I'll take it down first in Bell's visible Speech; then in broad Romic;* and then we'll get her on the phonograph so that you can turn her on as often as you like with the written transcript before you.

MRS. PEARCE [*returning*]   This is the young woman, sir.

The flower girl enters in state. She has a hat with three ostrich feathers, orange, sky-blue, and red. She has a nearly clean apron, and the shoddy coat has been tidied a little. The pathos of this deplorable figure, with its innocent vanity and consequential air, touches PICKERING, who has already straightened himself in the presence of MRS. PEARCE. But as to HIGGINS, the only distinction he makes between men and women is that when he is neither bullying nor exclaiming to the heavens against some featherweight cross, he coaxes women as a child coaxes its nurse when it wants to get anything out of her.

HIGGINS [*brusquely, recognizing her with unconcealed disappointment, and at once, babylike, making an intolerable grievance of it*]   Why, this is the girl I jotted down last night. Shes no use: Ive got all the records I want of the Lisson Grove lingo; and I'm not going to waste another cylinder on it. [*To the girl*] Be off with you: I dont want you.

THE FLOWER GIRL   Dont you be so saucy. You aint heard what I come for yet. [*To MRS. PEARCE, who is waiting at the door for further instruction*] Did you tell him I come in a taxi?

MRS. PEARCE   Nonsense, girl! what do you think a gentleman like Mr. Higgins cares what you came in?

THE FLOWER GIRL   Oh, we are proud! He aint above giving lessons, not him: I heard him say so. Well, I aint come here

---

*System of phonetic notation devised by English phonetician Henry Sweet (1845–1912).

to ask for any compliment; and if my money's not good enough I can go elsewhere.

HIGGINS   Good enough for what?

THE FLOWER GIRL   Good enough for ye-oo. Now you know, dont you? I'm come to have lessons, I am. And to pay for em too: make no mistake.

HIGGINS [*stupent*]*   W e l l ! ! ! [*Recovering his breath with a gasp*] What do you expect me to say to you?

THE FLOWER GIRL   Well, if you was a gentleman, you might ask me to sit down, I think. Dont I tell you I'm bringing you business?

HIGGINS   Pickering: shall we ask this baggage† to sit down or shall we throw her out of the window?

THE FLOWER GIRL [*running away in terror to the piano, where she turns at bay*]   Ah-ah-ah-ow-ow-ow-oo! [*Wounded and whimpering*] I wont be called a baggage when Ive offered to pay like any lady.

Motionless, the two men stare at her from the other side of the room, amazed.

PICKERING [*gently*]   What is it you want, my girl?

THE FLOWER GIRL   I want to be a lady in a flower shop stead of selling at the corner of Tottenham Court Road. But they wont take me unless I can talk more genteel. He said he could teach me. Well, here I am ready to pay him——not asking any favor——and he treats me as if I was dirt.

MRS. PEARCE   How can you be such a foolish ignorant girl as to think you could afford to pay Mr. Higgins?

THE FLOWER GIRL   Why shouldnt I? I know what lessons cost as well as you do; and I'm ready to pay.

---

*Astonished; this Latinate word suits Higgins, who is a Milton aficionado (see note 7 for this play).

†Pejorative word for a woman, ranging in meaning from a pert (saucy, or forward) woman to a prostitute.

HIGGINS   How much?

THE FLOWER GIRL [*coming back to him, triumphant*]   Now youre talking! I thought youd come off it when you saw a chance of getting back a bit of what you chucked at me last night. [*Confidentially*] Youd had a drop in, hadnt you?

HIGGINS [*peremptorily*]   Sit down.

THE FLOWER GIRL   Oh, if youre going to make a compliment of it—

HIGGINS [*thundering at her*]   Sit down.

MRS. PEARCE [*severely*]   Sit down, girl. Do as youre told. [*She places the stray chair near the hearthrug between Higgins and Pickering, and stands behind it waiting for the girl to sit down*].

THE FLOWER GIRL   Ah-ah-ah-ow-ow-oo! [*She stands, half rebellious, half bewildered*].

PICKERING [*very courteous*]   Wont you sit down?

THE FLOWER GIRL [*coyly*]   Dont mind if I do. [*She sits down. Pickering returns to the hearthrug*].

HIGGINS   Whats your name?

THE FLOWER GIRL   Liza Doolittle.

HIGGINS [*declaiming gravely*]

> Eliza, Elizabeth, Betsy and Bess,
> They went to the woods to get a birds nes':

PICKERING   They found a nest with four eggs in it:

HIGGINS   They took one apiece, and left three in it.

They laugh heartily at their own wit.

LIZA   Oh, dont be silly.

MRS. PEARCE   You mustnt speak to the gentleman like that.

LIZA   Well, why wont he speak sensible to me?

HIGGINS   Come back to business. How much do you propose to pay me for the lessons?

LIZA   Oh, I know whats right. A lady friend of mine gets French lessons for eighteenpence an hour from a real French gentleman. Well, you wouldnt have the face to ask me the same for teaching me my own language as you would for French; so I wont give more than a shilling. Take it or leave it.

HIGGINS [*walking up and down the room, rattling his keys and his cash in his pockets*]   You know, Pickering, if you consider a shilling, not as a simple shilling, but as a percentage of this girl's income, it works out as fully equivalent to sixty or seventy guineas from a millionaire.

PICKERING   How so?

HIGGINS   Figure it out. A millionaire has about £150 a day. She earns about half-a-crown.

LIZA [*haughtily*]   Who told you I only——

HIGGINS [*continuing*]   She offers me two-fifths of her day's income for a lesson. Two-fifths of a millionaire's income for a day would be somewhere about £60. It's handsome. By George, it's enormous! it's the biggest offer I ever had.

LIZA [*rising, terrified*]   Sixty pounds! What are you talking about? I never offered you sixty pounds. Where would I get——

HIGGINS   Hold your tongue.

LIZA [*weeping*]   But I aint got sixty pounds. Oh——

MRS. PEARCE   Dont cry, you silly girl. Sit down. Nobody is going to touch your money.

HIGGINS   Somebody is going to touch you, with a broomstick, if you dont stop snivelling. Sit down.

LIZA [*obeying slowly*]   Ah-ah-ah-ow-oo-o! One would think you was my father.

HIGGINS   If I decide to teach you, I'll be worse than two fathers to you. Here [*he offers her his silk handkerchief*]!

LIZA   Whats this for?

HIGGINS   To wipe your eyes. To wipe any part of your face that feels moist. Remember: thats your handkerchief; and thats your sleeve. Dont mistake the one for the other if you wish to become a lady in a shop.

LIZA, utterly bewildered, stares helplessly at him.

MRS. PEARCE It's no use talking to her like that, Mr. Higgins: she doesnt understand you. Besides, youre quite wrong: she doesnt do it that way at all [*she takes the handkerchief*].

LIZA [*snatching it*] Here! You give me that handkerchief. He give it to me, not to you.

PICKERING [*laughing*] He did. I think it must be regarded as her property, Mrs. Pearce.

MRS. PEARCE [*resigning herself*] Serve you right, Mr. Higgins.

PICKERING Higgins: I'm interested. What about the ambassador's garden party? I'll say youre the greatest teacher alive if you make that good. I'll bet you all the expenses of the experiment you cant do it. And I'll pay for the lessons.

LIZA Oh, you are real good. Thank you, Captain.

HIGGINS [*tempted, looking at her*] It's almost irresistible. Shes so deliciously low—so horribly dirty—

LIZA [*protesting extremely*] Ah-ah-ah-ah-ow-ow-oo-oo!!! I aint dirty: I washed my face and hands afore I come, I did.

PICKERING Youre certainly not going to turn her head with flattery, Higgins.

MRS. PEARCE [*uneasy*] Oh, dont say that, sir: theres more ways than one of turning a girl's head; and nobody can do it better than Mr. Higgins, though he may not always mean it. I do hope, sir, you wont encourage him to do anything foolish.

HIGGINS [*becoming excited as the idea grows on him*] What is life but a series of inspired follies? The difficulty is to find them to do. Never lose a chance: it doesnt come every day. I shall make a duchess of this draggle-tailed guttersnipe.*

LIZA [*strongly deprecating this view of her*] Ah-ah-ah-ow-ow-oo!

HIGGINS [*carried away*] Yes: in six months—in three if she has a good ear and a quick tongue—I'll take her anywhere and pass her off as anything. We'll start to-day: now! this moment!

---

*Woman who wears a skirt that is dirty from being dragged over wet ground and who searches the street for usable things.

Take her away and clean her, Mrs. Pearce. Monkey Brand,* if it wont come off any other way. Is there a good fire in the kitchen?

MRS. PEARCE [*protesting*]   Yes; but—

HIGGINS [*storming on*]   Take all her clothes off and burn them. Ring up Whiteley† or somebody for new ones. Wrap her up in brown paper til they come.

LIZA   Youre no gentleman, youre not, to talk of such things. I'm a good girl, I am; and I know what the like of you are, I do.

HIGGINS   We want none of your Lisson Grove prudery here, young woman. Youve got to learn to behave like a duchess. Take her away, Mrs. Pearce. If she gives you any trouble wallop her.

LIZA [*springing up and running between PICKERING and MRS. PEARCE for protection*]   No! I'll call the police, I will.

MRS. PEARCE   But Ive no place to put her.

HIGGINS   Put her in the dustbin.

LIZA   Ah-ah-ah-ow-ow-oo!

PICKERING   Oh come, Higgins! be reasonable.

MRS. PEARCE [*resolutely*]   You must be reasonable, Mr. Higgins: really you must. You cant walk over everybody like this.
HIGGINS, thus scolded, subsides. The hurricane is succeeded by a zephyr of amiable surprise.

HIGGINS [*with professional exquisiteness of modulation*]   I walk over everybody! My dear Mrs. Pearce, my dear Pickering, I never had the slightest intention of walking over anyone. All I propose is that we should be kind to this poor girl. We must help her to prepare and fit herself for her new station in life. If I did not express myself clearly it was because I did not wish to hurt her delicacy, or yours.
LIZA, reassured, steals back to her chair.

---

*Strong scouring soap with a wrapper bearing the image of a monkey looking into a mirror.

†London department store.

MRS. PEARCE [*to PICKERING*]   Well, did you ever hear anything like that, sir?

PICKERING [*laughing heartily*]   Never, Mrs. Pearce: never.

HIGGINS [*patiently*]   Whats the matter?

MRS. PEARCE   Well, the matter is, sir, that you cant take a girl up like that as if you were picking up a pebble on the beach.

HIGGINS   Why not?

MRS. PEARCE   Why not! But you dont know anything about her. What about her parents? She may be married.

LIZA   Garn!

HIGGINS   There! As the girl very properly says, Garn! Married indeed! Dont you know that a woman of that class looks a worn out drudge of fifty a year after shes married.

LIZA   Whood marry me?

HIGGINS [*suddenly resorting to the most thrillingly beautiful low tones in his best elocutionary style*]   By George, Eliza, the streets will be strewn with the bodies of men shooting themselves for your sake before Ive done with you.

MRS. PEARCE   Nonsense, sir. You mustnt talk like that to her.

LIZA [*rising and squaring herself determinedly*]   I'm going away. He's off his chump,* he is. I dont want no balmies† teaching me.

HIGGINS [*wounded in his tenderest point by her insensibility to his elocution*]   Oh, indeed! I'm mad, am I? Very well, Mrs. Pearce: you neednt order the new clothes for her. Throw her out.

LIZA [*whimpering*]   Nah-ow. You got no right to touch me.

MRS. PEARCE   You see now what comes of being saucy. [*Indicating the door*] This way, please.

LIZA [*almost in tears*]   I didnt want no clothes. I wouldnt have taken them [*she throws away the handkerchief*]. I can buy my own clothes.

HIGGINS [*deftly retrieving the handkerchief and intercepting her on*

---

*Off his head; crazy.

†Crazy people.

her reluctant way to the door]   Youre an ungrateful wicked girl. This is my return for offering to take you out of the gutter and dress you beautifully and make a lady of you.

MRS. PEARCE   Stop, Mr. Higgins. I wont allow it. It's you that are wicked. Go home to your parents, girl; and tell them to take better care of you.

LIZA   I aint got no parents. They told me I was big enough to earn my own living and turned me out.

MRS. PEARCE   Wheres your mother?

LIZA   I aint got no mother. Her that turned me out was my sixth stepmother. But I done without them. And I'm a good girl, I am.

HIGGINS   Very well, then, what on earth is all this fuss about? The girl doesnt belong to anybody—is no use to anybody but me. [*He goes to MRS. PEARCE and begins coaxing*]. You can adopt her, Mrs. Pearce: I'm sure a daughter would be a great amusement to you. Now dont make any more fuss. Take her downstairs; and——

MRS. PEARCE   But whats to become of her? Is she to be paid anything? Do be sensible, sir.

HIGGINS   Oh, pay her whatever is necessary: put it down in the housekeeping book. [*Impatiently*] What on earth will she want with money? She'll have her food and her clothes. She'll only drink if you give her money.

LIZA [*turning on him*]   Oh you are a brute. It's a lie: nobody ever saw the sign of liquor on me. [*She goes back to her chair and plants herself there defiantly*].

PICKERING [*in good-humored remonstrance*]   Does it occur to you, Higgins, that the girl has some feelings?

HIGGINS [*looking critically at her*]   Oh no, I dont think so. Not any feelings that we need bother about. [*Cheerily*] Have you, Eliza?

LIZA   I got my feelings same as anyone else.

HIGGINS [*to PICKERING, reflectively*]   You see the difficulty?

PICKERING   Eh? What difficulty?

HIGGINS   To get her to talk grammar. The mere pronunciation is easy enough.

LIZA   I dont want to talk grammar. I want to talk like a lady.

MRS. PEARCE   Will you please keep to the point, Mr. Higgins. I want to know on what terms the girl is to be here. Is she to have any wages? And what is to become of her when youve finished your teaching? You must look ahead a little.

HIGGINS [*impatiently*]   Whats to become of her if I leave her in the gutter? Tell me that, Mrs. Pearce.

MRS. PEARCE   Thats her own business, not yours, Mr. Higgins.

HIGGINS   Well, when Ive done with her, we can throw her back into the gutter; and then it will be her own business again; so thats all right.

LIZA   Oh, youve no feeling heart in you: you dont care for nothing but yourself [*she rises and takes the floor resolutely*]. Here! Ive had enough of this. I'm going [*making for the door*]. You ought to be ashamed of yourself, you ought.

HIGGINS [*snatching a chocolate cream from the piano, his eyes suddenly beginning to twinkle with mischief*]   Have some chocolates, Eliza.

LIZA [*halting, tempted*]   How do I know what might be in them? Ive heard of girls being drugged by the like of you.

HIGGINS whips out his penknife; cuts a chocolate in two; puts one half into his mouth and bolts it; and offers her the other half.

HIGGINS   Pledge of good faith, Eliza. I eat one half: you eat the other. [*LIZA opens her mouth to retort: he pops the half chocolate into it*]. You shall have boxes of them, barrels of them, every day. You shall live on them. Eh?

LIZA [*who has disposed of the chocolate after being nearly choked by it*]   I wouldnt have ate it, only I'm too ladylike to take it out of my mouth.

HIGGINS   Listen, Eliza. I think you said you came in a taxi.

LIZA   Well, what if I did? Ive as good a right to take a taxi as anyone else.

HIGGINS   You have, Eliza; and in future you shall have as many taxis as you want. You shall go up and down and round the town in a taxi every day. Think of that, Eliza.

MRS. PEARCE   Mr. Higgins: youre tempting the girl. It's not right. She should think of the future.

HIGGINS   At her age! Nonsense! Time enough to think of the future when you havnt any future to think of. No, Eliza: do as this lady does: think of other people's futures; but never think of your own. Think of chocolates, and taxis, and gold, and diamonds.

LIZA   No: I dont want no gold and no diamonds. I'm a good girl, I am. [*She sits down again, with an attempt at dignity*].

HIGGINS   You shall remain so, Eliza, under the care of Mrs. Pearce. And you shall marry an officer in the Guards, with a beautiful moustache: the son of a marquis, who will disinherit him for marrying you, but will relent when he sees your beauty and goodness—

PICKERING   Excuse me, Higgins; but I really must interfere. Mrs. Pearce is quite right. If this girl is to put herself in your hands for six months for an experiment in teaching, she must understand thoroughly what shes doing.

HIGGINS   How can she? Shes incapable of understanding anything. Besides, do any of us understand what we are doing? If we did, would we ever do it?

PICKERING   Very clever, Higgins; but not sound sense. [*To ELIZA*] Miss Doolittle—

LIZA [*overwhelmed*]   Ah-ah-ow-oo!

HIGGINS   There! Thats all you get out of Eliza. Ah-ah-ow-oo! No use explaining. As a military man you ought to know that. Give her her orders: thats what she wants. Eliza: you are to live here for the next six months, learning how to speak beautifully, like a lady in a florist's shop. If youre good and do whatever youre told, you shall sleep in a proper bedroom, and have lots to eat, and money to buy chocolates and take rides in taxis. If youre naughty and idle you will sleep in the back kitchen among the black beetles, and be walloped by Mrs. Pearce with a broomstick. At the end of six months you shall go to Buckingham Palace in a carriage, beautifully dressed. If the King finds out youre not a lady, you will be taken by the police to the Tower of London, where your head will be cut off as a warning to other presumptuous flower girls. If you are not found out, you shall have a present of seven-and-sixpence to start life with as a lady in a shop. If you refuse this offer you will be a most ungrateful and wicked girl; and the angels will weep for you. [*To PICKERING*] Now are you satisfied, Pickering? [*To MRS. PEARCE*] Can I put it more plainly and fairly, Mrs. Pearce?

MRS. PEARCE [*patiently*]   I think youd better let me speak to the girl properly in private. I dont know that I can take charge of her or consent to the arrangement at all. Of course I know you dont mean her any harm; but when you get what you call interested in people's accents, you never think or care what may happen to them or you. Come with me, Eliza.

HIGGINS   Thats all right. Thank you, Mrs. Pearce. Bundle her off to the bath-room.

LIZA [*rising reluctantly and suspiciously*]   Youre a great bully, you are. I wont stay here if I dont like. I wont let nobody wallop me. I never asked to go to Buckingham Palace, I didnt. I was never in trouble with the police, not me. I'm a good girl—

MRS. PEARCE   Dont answer back, girl. You dont understand the gentleman. Come with me. [*She leads the way to the door, and holds it open for ELIZA*].

LIZA [*as she goes out*]   Well, what I say is right. I wont go near the king, not if I'm going to have my head cut off. If I'd known what I was letting myself in for, I wouldnt have come here. I always been a good girl; and I never offered to say a word to him; and I dont owe him nothing; and I dont care; and I wont be put upon; and I have my feelings the same as anyone else— *MRS. PEARCE shuts the door; and ELIZA's plaints are no longer audible. PICKERING comes from the hearth to the chair and sits astride it with his arms on the back.*

PICKERING   Excuse the straight question, Higgins. Are you a man of good character where women are concerned?

HIGGINS [*moodily*]   Have you ever met a man of good character where women are concerned?

PICKERING   Yes: very frequently.

HIGGINS [*dogmatically, lifting himself on his hands to the level of the piano, and sitting on it with a bounce*]   Well, I havnt. I find that the moment I let a woman make friends with me, she becomes jealous, exacting, suspicious, and a damned nuisance. I find that the moment I let myself make friends with a woman, I become selfish and tyrannical. Women upset everything. When you let them into your life, you find that the woman is driving at one thing and youre driving at another.

PICKERING   At what, for example?

HIGGINS [*coming off the piano restlessly*]   Oh, Lord knows! I suppose the woman wants to live her own life; and the man wants to live his; and each tries to drag the other on to the wrong track. One wants to go north and the other south; and the result is that both have to go east, though they both hate the east wind. [*He sits down on the bench at the keyboard*]. So here I am, a confirmed old bachelor, and likely to remain so.

PICKERING [*rising and standing over him gravely*]   Come, Higgins! You know what I mean. If I'm to be in this business I shall feel responsible for that girl. I hope it's understood that no advantage is to be taken of her position.

HIGGINS   What! That thing! Sacred, I assure you. [*Rising to explain*] You see, she'll be a pupil; and teaching would be impossible unless pupils were sacred. Ive taught scores of American millionairesses how to speak English: the best look-

ing women in the world. I'm seasoned. They might as well be
blocks of wood. *I* might as well be a block of wood. It's—
MRS. PEARCE opens the door. She has ELIZA's hat in her hand.
PICKERING retires to the easy-chair at the hearth and sits down.

HIGGINS [*eagerly*]   Well, Mrs. Pearce: is it all right?

MRS. PEARCE [*at the door*]   I just wish to trouble you with a
word, if I may, Mr. Higgins.

HIGGINS   Yes, certainly. Come in. [*She comes forward*]. Dont burn
that, Mrs. Pearce. I'll keep it as a curiosity. [*He takes the hat*].

MRS. PEARCE   Handle it carefully, sir, please. I had to promise
her not to burn it; but I had better put it in the oven for a while.

HIGGINS [*putting it down hastily on the piano*]   Oh! thank you.
Well, what have you to say to me?

PICKERING   Am I in the way?

MRS. PEARCE   Not at all, sir. Mr. Higgins: will you please be
very particular what you say before the girl?

HIGGINS [*sternly*]   Of course. I'm always particular about what
I say. Why do you say this to me?

MRS. PEARCE [*unmoved*]   No, sir: youre not at all particular
when youve mislaid anything or when you get a little impatient. Now it doesnt matter before me: I'm used to it. But you
really must not swear before the girl.

HIGGINS [*indignantly*]   *I* swear! [*Most emphatically*] I never
swear. I detest the habit. What the devil do you mean?

MRS. PEARCE [*stolidly*]   Thats what I mean, sir. You swear a
great deal too much. I dont mind your damning and blasting,
and what the devil and where the devil and who the devil—

HIGGINS   Mrs. Pearce: this language from your lips! Really!

MRS. PEARCE [*not to be put off*]   —but there is a certain word
I must ask you not to use. The girl has just used it herself because the bath was too hot. It begins with the same letter as
bath. She knows no better: she learnt it at her mother's knee.
But she must not hear it from your lips.

HIGGINS [*loftily*]   I cannot charge myself with having ever uttered it, Mrs. Pearce. [*She looks at him steadfastly. He adds, hiding an uneasy conscience with a judicial air*] Except perhaps in a moment of extreme and justifiable excitement.

MRS. PEARCE   Only this morning, sir, you applied it to your boots, to the butter, and to the brown bread.

HIGGINS   Oh, that! Mere alliteration, Mrs. Pearce, natural to a poet.

MRS. PEARCE   Well, sir, whatever you choose to call it, I beg you not to let the girl hear you repeat it.

HIGGINS   Oh, very well, very well. Is that all?

MRS. PEARCE   No, sir. We shall have to be very particular with this girl as to personal cleanliness.

HIGGINS   Certainly. Quite right. Most important.

MRS. PEARCE   I mean not to be slovenly about her dress or untidy in leaving things about.

HIGGINS [*going to her solemnly*]   Just so. I intended to call your attention to that [*he passes on to PICKERING, who is enjoying the conversation immensely*]. It is these little things that matter, Pickering. Take care of the pence and the pounds will take care of themselves is as true of personal habits as of money. [*He comes to anchor on the hearthrug, with the air of a man in an unassailable position*].

MRS. PEARCE   Yes, sir. Then might I ask you not to come down to breakfast in your dressing-gown, or at any rate not to use it as a napkin to the extent you do, sir. And if you would be so good as not to eat everything off the same plate, and to remember not to put the porridge saucepan out of your hand on the clean tablecloth, it would be a better example to the girl. You know you nearly choked yourself with a fishbone in the jam only last week.

HIGGINS [*routed from the hearthrug and drifting back to the piano*] I may do these things sometimes in absence of mind; but surely I dont do them habitually. [*Angrily*] By the way: my dressing-gown smells most damnably of benzine.

MRS. PEARCE   No doubt it does, Mr. Higgins. But if you will wipe your fingers—

HIGGINS [*yelling*]   Oh very well, very well: I'll wipe them in my hair in future.

MRS. PEARCE   I hope youre not offended, Mr. Higgins.

HIGGINS [*shocked at finding himself thought capable of an unamiable sentiment*]   Not at all, not at all. Youre quite right, Mrs. Pearce: I shall be particularly careful before the girl. Is that all?

MRS. PEARCE   No, sir. Might she use some of those Japanese dresses you brought from abroad? I really cant put her back into her old things.

HIGGINS   Certainly. Anything you like. Is that all?

MRS. PEARCE   Thank you, sir. Thats all. [*She goes out*].

HIGGINS   You know, Pickering, that woman has the most extraordinary ideas about me. Here I am, a shy, diffident sort of man. Ive never been able to feel really grown-up and tremendous, like other chaps. And yet shes firmly persuaded that I'm an arbitrary overbearing bossing kind of person. I cant account for it.[6]

MRS. PEARCE returns.

MRS. PEARCE   If you please, sir, the trouble's beginning already. Theres a dustman* downstairs, Alfred Doolittle, wants to see you. He says you have his daughter here.

PICKERING [*rising*]   Phew! I say! [*He retreats to the hearthrug*].

HIGGINS [*promptly*]   Send the blackguard† up.

MRS. PEARCE   Oh, very well, sir. [*She goes out*].

PICKERING   He may not be a blackguard, Higgins.

HIGGINS   Nonsense. Of course hes a blackguard.

PICKERING   Whether he is or not, I'm afraid we shall have some trouble with him.

---

*Garbage man (sanitation worker).

†Old-fashioned term for an immoral scoundrel.

HIGGINS [*confidently*]   Oh no: I think not. If theres any trouble he shall have it with me, not I with him. And we are sure to get something interesting out of him.

PICKERING   About the girl?

HIGGINS   No. I mean his dialect.

PICKERING   Oh!

MRS. PEARCE [*at the door*]   Doolittle, sir. [*She admits DOOLIT-TLE and retires*].

ALFRED DOOLITTLE is an elderly but vigorous dustman, clad in the costume of his profession, including a hat with a back brim covering his neck and shoulders. He has well marked and rather interesting features, and seems equally free from fear and conscience. He has a re-markably expressive voice, the result of a habit of giving vent to his feelings without reserve. His present pose is that of wounded honor and stern resolution.

DOOLITTLE [*at the door, uncertain which of the two gentlemen is his man*]   Professor Higgins?

HIGGINS   Here. Good morning. Sit down.

DOOLITTLE   Morning, Governor. [*He sits down magisterially*] I come about a very serious matter, Governor.

HIGGINS [*to PICKERING*]   Brought up in Hounslow. Mother Welsh, I should think. [*DOOLITTLE opens his mouth, amazed. HIGGINS continues*] What do you want, Doolittle?

DOOLITTLE [*menacingly*]   I want my daughter: thats what I want. See?

HIGGINS   Of course you do. Youre her father, arnt you? You dont suppose anyone else wants her, do you? I'm glad to see you have some spark of family feeling left. Shes upstairs. Take her away at once.

DOOLITTLE [*rising, fearfully taken aback*]   What!

HIGGINS   Take her away. Do you suppose I'm going to keep your daughter for you?

DOOLITTLE [*remonstrating*]   Now, now, look here, Governor. Is this reasonable? Is it fairity to take advantage of a man like this? The girl belongs to me. You got her. Where do I come in? [*He sits down again*].

HIGGINS   Your daughter had the audacity to come to my house and ask me to teach her how to speak properly so that she could get a place in a flower-shop. This gentleman and my housekeeper have been here all the time. [*Bullying him*] How dare you come here and attempt to blackmail me? You sent her here on purpose.

DOOLITTLE [*protesting*]   No, Governor.

HIGGINS   You must have. How else could you possibly know that she is here?

DOOLITTLE   Dont take a man up like that, Governor.

HIGGINS   The police shall take you up. This is a plant—a plot to extort money by threats. I shall telephone for the police [*he goes resolutely to the telephone and opens the directory*].

DOOLITTLE   Have I asked you for a brass farthing? I leave it to the gentleman here: have I said a word about money?

HIGGINS [*throwing the book aside and marching down on Doolittle with a poser*]   What else did you come for?

DOOLITTLE [*sweetly*]   Well, what would a man come for? Be human, Governor.

HIGGINS [*disarmed*]   Alfred: did you put her up to it?

DOOLITTLE   So help me, Governor, I never did. I take my Bible oath I aint seen the girl these two months past.

HIGGINS   Then how did you know she was here?

DOOLITTLE ["*most musical, most melancholy*"]*   I'll tell you, Governor, if youll only let me get a word in. I'm willing to tell you. I'm wanting to tell you. I'm waiting to tell you.

HIGGINS   Pickering: this chap has a certain natural gift of rhetoric. Observe the rhythm of his native woodnotes wild.[7] "I'm willing to tell you: I'm wanting to tell you: I'm waiting to tell

---

*Quotation from Milton's "Il Penseroso": "Sweet Bird that shunn'st the noise of folly, / Most musicall, most melancholy!" (lines 61–62).

you." Sentimental rhetoric! thats the Welsh strain in him. It also accounts for his mendacity and dishonesty.

PICKERING   Oh, p l e a s e, Higgins: I'm west country my-self. [*To DOOLITTLE*] How did you know the girl was here if you didnt send her?

DOOLITTLE   It was like this, Governor. The girl took a boy in the taxi to give him a jaunt. Son of her landlady, he is. He hung about on the chance of her giving him another ride home. Well, she sent him back for her luggage when she heard you was willing for her to stop here. I met the boy at the corner of Long Acre and Endell Street.

HIGGINS   Public house. Yes?

DOOLITTLE   The poor man's club, Governor: why shouldnt I?

PICKERING   Do let him tell his story, Higgins.

DOOLITTLE   He told me what was up. And I ask you, what was my feelings and my duty as a father? I says to the boy, "You bring me the luggage," I says—

PICKERING   Why didnt you go for it yourself?

DOOLITTLE   Landlady wouldnt have trusted me with it, Gov-ernor. Shes that kind of woman: you know. I had to give the boy a penny afore he trusted me with it, the little swine. I brought it to her just to oblige you like, and make myself agreeable. Thats all.

HIGGINS   How much luggage?

DOOLITTLE   Musical instrument, Governor. A few pictures, a trifle of jewelry, and a bird-cage. She said she didnt want no clothes. What was I to think from that, Governor? I ask you as a parent what was I to think?

HIGGINS   So you came to rescue her from worse than death, eh?

DOOLITTLE [*appreciatively: relieved at being so well understood*] Just so, Governor. Thats right.

PICKERING   But why did you bring her luggage if you in-tended to take her away?

DOOLITTLE   Have I said a word about taking her away? Have I now?

HIGGINS [*determinedly*]   Youre going to take her away, double quick. [*He crosses to the hearth and rings the bell*].

DOOLITTLE [*rising*]   No, Governor. Dont say that. I'm not the man to stand in my girl's light. Heres a career opening for her, as you might say; and—

MRS. PEARCE opens the door and awaits orders.

HIGGINS   Mrs. Pearce: this is Eliza's father. He has come to take her away. Give her to him. [*He goes back to the piano, with an air of washing his hands of the whole affair*].

DOOLITTLE   No. This is a misunderstanding. Listen here—

MRS. PEARCE   He cant take her away, Mr. Higgins: how can he? You told me to burn her clothes.

DOOLITTLE   Thats right. I cant carry the girl through the streets like a blooming monkey, can I? I put it to you.

HIGGINS   You have put it to me that you want your daughter. Take your daughter. If she has no clothes go out and buy her some.

DOOLITTLE [*desperate*]   Wheres the clothes she come in? Did I burn them or did your missus here?

MRS. PEARCE   I am the housekeeper, if you please. I have sent for some clothes for your girl. When they come you can take her away. You can wait in the kitchen. This way, please.

DOOLITTLE, much troubled; accompanies her to the door; then hesitates; finally turns confidentially to HIGGINS.

DOOLITTLE   Listen here, Governor. You and me is men of the world, aint we?

HIGGINS   Oh! Men of the world, are we? Youd better go, Mrs. Pearce.

MRS. PEARCE   I think so, indeed, sir. [*She goes, with dignity*].

PICKERING   The floor is yours, Mr. Doolittle.

DOOLITTLE [*to PICKERING*]   I thank you, Governor.

[*To HIGGINS, who takes refuge on the piano bench, a little overwhelmed by the proximity of his visitor; for DOOLITTLE has a professional flavor of dust about him*]. Well, the truth is, Ive taken a sort of fancy to you, Governor; and if you want the girl, I'm not so set on having her back home again but what I might be open to an arrangement. Regarded in the light of a young woman, shes a fine handsome girl. As a daughter shes not worth her keep; and so I tell you straight. All I ask is my rights as a father; and youre the last man alive to expect me to let her go for nothing; for I can see youre one of the straight sort, Governor. Well, whats a five pound note to you? And whats Eliza to me? [*He returns to his chair and sits down judicially*].

PICKERING   I think you ought to know, Doolittle, that Mr. Higgins's intentions are entirely honorable.

DOOLITTLE   Course they are, Governor. If I thought they wasnt, Id ask fifty.

HIGGINS [*revolted*]   Do you mean to say, you callous rascal, that you would sell your daughter for £50?

DOOLITTLE   Not in a general way I wouldnt; but to oblige a gentleman like you I'd do a good deal, I do assure you.

PICKERING   Have you no morals, man?

DOOLITTLE [*unabashed*]   Cant afford them, Governor. Neither could you if you was as poor as me. Not that I mean any harm, you know. But if Liza is going to have a bit out of this, why not me too?

HIGGINS [*troubled*]   I dont know what to do, Pickering. There can be no question that as a matter of morals it's a positive crime to give this chap a farthing. And yet I feel a sort of rough justice in his claim.

DOOLITTLE   Thats it, Governor. Thats all I say. A father's heart, as it were.

PICKERING   Well, I know the feeling; but really it seems hardly right—

DOOLITTLE   Dont say that, Governor. Dont look at it that

way. What am I, Governors both? I ask you, what am I? I'm one of the undeserving poor: thats what I am. Think of what that means to a man. It means that hes up agen middle class morality all the time. If theres anything going, and I put in for a bit of it, it's always the same story: "Youre undeserving; so you cant have it." But my needs is as great as the most deserving widow's that ever got money out of six different charities in one week for the death of the same husband. I dont need less than a deserving man: I need more. I dont eat less hearty than him; and I drink a lot more. I want a bit of amusement, cause I'm a thinking man. I want cheerfulness and a song and a band when I feel low. Well, they charge me just the same for everything as they charge the deserving. What is middle class morality? Just an excuse for never giving me anything. Therefore, I ask you, as two gentlemen, not to play that game on me. I'm playing straight with you. I aint pretending to be deserving. I'm undeserving; and I mean to go on being undeserving. I like it; and thats the truth. Will you take advantage of a man's nature to do him out of the price of his own daughter what hes brought up and fed and clothed by the sweat of his brow until shes growed big enough to be interesting to you two gentlemen? Is five pounds unreasonable? I put it to you; and I leave it to you.

HIGGINS [*rising, and going over to PICKERING*]   Pickering: if we were to take this man in hand for three months, he could choose between a seat in the Cabinet and a popular pulpit in Wales.

PICKERING   What do you say to that, Doolittle?

DOOLITTLE   Not me, Governor, thank you kindly. Ive heard all the preachers and all the prime ministers—for I'm a thinking man and game for politics or religion or social reform same as all the other amusements—and I tell you it's a dog's life anyway you look at it. Undeserving poverty is my line. Taking one station in society with another, it's—it's—well, it's the only one that has any ginger in it, to my taste.

HIGGINS   I suppose we must give him a fiver.

PICKERING   He'll make a bad use of it, I'm afraid.

DOOLITTLE   Not me, Governor, so help me I wont. Dont you be afraid that I'll save it and spare it and live idle on it. There wont be a penny of it left by Monday: I'll have to go to work same as if I'd never had it. It wont pauperize me, you bet. Just one good spree for myself and the missus, giving pleasure to ourselves and employment to others, and satisfaction to you to think it's not been throwed away. You couldnt spend it better.

HIGGINS [*taking out his pocket book and coming between* DOOLITTLE *and the piano*]   This is irresistible. Lets give him ten. [*He offers two notes to the dustman*].

DOOLITTLE   No, Governor. She wouldnt have the heart to spend ten; and perhaps I shouldnt neither. Ten pounds is a lot of money: it makes a man feel prudent like; and then goodbye to happiness. You give me what I ask you, Governor: not a penny more, and not a penny less.

PICKERING   Why dont you marry that missus of yours? I rather draw the line at encouraging that sort of immorality.

DOOLITTLE   Tell her so, Governor: tell her so. *I'm* willing. It's me that suffers by it. Ive no hold on her. I got to be agreeable to her. I got to give her presents. I got to buy her clothes something sinful. I'm a slave to that woman, Governor, just because I'm not her lawful husband. And she knows it too. Catch her marrying me! Take my advice, Governor: marry Eliza while shes young and dont know no better. If you dont youll be sorry for it after. If you do, she'll be sorry for it after; but better you than her, because youre a man, and shes only a woman and dont know how to be happy anyhow.

HIGGINS   Pickering: if we listen to this man another minute, we shall have no convictions left. [*To* DOOLITTLE] Five pounds I think you said.

DOOLITTLE   Thank you kindly, Governor.

HIGGINS   Youre sure you wont take ten?

DOOLITTLE   Not now. Another time, Governor.

HIGGINS [*handing him a five-pound note*]   Here you are.

DOOLITTLE   Thank you, Governor. Good morning. [*He hurries to the door, anxious to get away with his booty. When he opens it he is confronted with a dainty and exquisitely clean young Japanese lady in a simple blue cotton kimono printed cunningly with small white jasmine blossoms. MRS. PEARCE is with her. He gets out of her way deferentially and apologizes*]. Beg pardon, miss.

THE JAPANESE LADY   Garn! Dont you know your own daughter?

DOOLITTLE   } *exclaiming* { Bly me! it's Eliza!
HIGGINS   } *simul-* { Whats that! This!
PICKERING   } *taneously* { By Jove!

LIZA   Dont I look silly?

HIGGINS   Silly?

MRS. PEARCE [*at the door*]   Now, Mr. Higgins, please dont say anything to make the girl conceited about herself.

HIGGINS [*conscientiously*]   Oh! Quite right, Mrs. Pearce. [*To ELIZA*] Yes: damned silly.

MRS. PEARCE   Please, sir.

HIGGINS [*correcting himself*]   I mean extremely silly.

LIZA   I should look all right with my hat on. [*She takes up her hat; puts it on; and walks across the room to the fireplace with a fashionable air*].

HIGGINS   A new fashion, by George! And it ought to look horrible!

DOOLITTLE [*with fatherly pride*]   Well, I never thought she'd clean up as good looking as that, Governor. Shes a credit to me, aint she?

LIZA   I tell you, it's easy to clean up here. Hot and cold water on tap, just as much as you like, there is. Woolly towels, there is; and a towel horse so hot, it burns your fingers. Soft brushes to scrub yourself, and a wooden bowl of soap smelling like primroses. Now I know why ladies is so clean. Washing's a treat for them. Wish they saw what it is for the like of me!

HIGGINS   I'm glad the bath-room met with your approval.

LIZA   It didnt: not all of it; and I dont care who hears me say it. Mrs. Pearce knows.

HIGGINS   What was wrong, Mrs. Pearce?

MRS. PEARCE [*blandly*]   Oh, nothing, sir. It doesnt matter.

LIZA   I had a good mind to break it. I didnt know which way to look. But I hung a towel over it, I did.

HIGGINS   Over what?

MRS. PEARCE   Over the looking-glass, sir.

HIGGINS   Doolittle: you have brought your daughter up too strictly.

DOOLITTLE   Me! I never brought her up at all, except to give her a lick of a strap now and again. Dont put it on me, Governor. She aint accustomed to it, you see: thats all. But she'll soon pick up your free-and-easy ways.

LIZA   I'm a good girl, I am; and I wont pick up no free and easy ways.

HIGGINS   Eliza: if you say again that youre a good girl, your father shall take you home.

LIZA   Not him. You dont know my father. All he come here for was to touch you for some money to get drunk on.

DOOLITTLE   Well, what else would I want money for? To put into the plate in church, I suppose. [*She puts out her tongue at him. He is so incensed by this that PICKERING presently finds it necessary to step between them*]. Dont you give me none of your lip; and dont let me hear you giving this gentleman any of it neither, or youll hear from me about it. See?

HIGGINS   Have you any further advice to give her before you go, Doolittle? Your blessing, for instance.

DOOLITTLE   No, Governor: I aint such a mug as to put up my children to all I know myself. Hard enough to hold them in without that. If you want Eliza's mind improved, Governor, you do it yourself with a strap. So long, gentlemen. [*He turns to go*].

HIGGINS [*impressively*]   Stop. Youll come regularly to see your daughter. It's your duty, you know. My brother is a clergyman; and he could help you in your talks with her.

DOOLITTLE [*evasively*]   Certainly. I'll come, Governor. Not just this week, because I have a job at a distance. But later on you may depend on me. Afternoon, gentlemen. Afternoon, maam. [*He takes off his hat to MRS. PEARCE, who disdains the salutation and goes out. He winks at HIGGINS, thinking him probably a fellow-sufferer from MRS. PEARCE's difficult disposition, and follows her*].

LIZA   Dont you believe the old liar. He'd as soon you set a bull-dog on him as a clergyman. You wont see him again in a hurry.

HIGGINS   I dont want to, Eliza. Do you?

LIZA   Not me. I dont want never to see him again, I dont. Hes a disgrace to me, he is, collecting dust, instead of working at his trade.

PICKERING   What is his trade, Eliza?

LIZA   Talking money out of other people's pockets into his own. His proper trade's a navvy;* and he works at it some-times too—for exercise—and earns good money at it. Aint you going to call me Miss Doolittle any more?

PICKERING   I beg your pardon, Miss Doolittle. It was a slip of the tongue.

LIZA   Oh, I dont mind; only it sounded so genteel. I should just like to take a taxi to the corner of Tottenham Court Road and get out there and tell it to wait for me, just to put the girls in their place a bit. I wouldnt speak to them, you know.

PICKERING   Better wait til we get you something really fash-ionable.

HIGGINS   Besides, you shouldnt cut your old friends now that you have risen in the world. Thats what we call snobbery.

---

*Manual laborer; ditch-digger.

LIZA   You dont call the like of them my friends now, I should hope. Theyve took it out of me often enough with their ridicule when they had the chance; and now I mean to get a bit of my own back. But if I'm to have fashionable clothes, I'll wait. I should like to have some. Mrs. Pearce says youre going to give me some to wear in bed at night different to what I wear in the daytime; but it do seem a waste of money when you could get something to shew. Besides, I never could fancy changing into cold things on a winter night.

MRS. PEARCE [*coming back*]   Now, Eliza. The new things have come for you to try on.

LIZA   Ah-ow-oo-ooh! [*She rushes out*].

MRS. PEARCE [*following her*]   Oh, dont rush about like that, girl. [*She shuts the door behind her*].

HIGGINS   Pickering: we have taken on a stiff job.

PICKERING [*with conviction*]   Higgins: we have.

ACT III

*It is Mrs. Higgins's at-home day. Nobody has yet arrived.
Her drawing-room, in a flat on Chelsea* embankment, has
three windows looking on the river; and the ceiling is not
so lofty as it would be in an older house of the same
pretension. The windows are open, giving access to a
balcony with flowers in pots. If you stand with your face to
the windows, you have the fireplace on your left and the
door in the right-hand wall close to the corner nearest the
windows.*

*Mrs. Higgins was brought up on Morris and Burne
Jones; and her room, which is very unlike her son's room in
Wimpole Street, is not crowded with furniture and little
tables and nicknacks. In the middle of the room there is a
big ottoman; and this, with the carpet, the Morris wall-
papers, and the Morris chintz window curtains and
brocade covers of the ottoman and its cushions, supply all
the ornament, and are much too handsome to be hidden by
odds and ends of useless things. A few good oil-paintings
from the exhibitions in the Grosvenor Gallery thirty years
ago (the Burne Jones, not the Whistler⁸ side of them) are
on the walls. The only landscape is a Cecil Lawson† on the
scale of a Rubens. There is a portrait of Mrs. Higgins as
she was when she defied fashion in her youth in one of the*

---

*Artists' quarter in London.

†English landscape painter (1851–1882), whose best-known work, "The Minister's Garden," was exhibited in 1878 at the Grosvenor Gallery in London.

beautiful Rossettian costumes which, when caricatured by
people who did not understand, led to the absurdities of
popular estheticism in the eighteen-seventies.*

*In the corner diagonally opposite the door Mrs.
Higgins, now over sixty and long past taking the trouble
to dress out of the fashion, sits writing at an elegantly
simple writing-table with a bell button within reach of her
hand. There is a Chippendale chair further back in the
room between her and the window nearest her side. At the
other side of the room, further forward, is an Elizabethan
chair roughly carved in the taste of Inigo Jones. On the
same side a piano in a decorated case. The corner between
the fireplace and the window is occupied by a divan
cushioned in Morris chintz.*

It is between four and five in the afternoon.

The door is opened violently; and Higgins enters with his hat on.

MRS. HIGGINS [*dismayed*]   Henry [*scolding him*]! What are you
doing here to-day? It is my at-home day:[†] you promised not to
come. [*As he bends to kiss her, she takes his hat off, and presents it
to him*].

HIGGINS   Oh bother! [*He throws the hat down on the table*].

MRS. HIGGINS   Go home at once.

HIGGINS [*kissing her*]   I know, mother. I came on purpose.

MRS. HIGGINS   But you mustnt. I'm serious, Henry. You offend all my friends: they stop coming whenever they meet
you.

HIGGINS   Nonsense! I know I have no small talk; but people
dont mind. [*He sits on the settee*].

---

*After the English poet and painter Dante Gabriel Rossetti (1828–1882), who
painted medieval religious and fantasy subjects.

†Particular day reserved for casual visits from acquaintances.

MRS. HIGGINS   Oh! dont they? Small talk indeed! What about your large talk? Really, dear, you mustnt stay.

HIGGINS   I must. Ive a job for you. A phonetic job.

MRS. HIGGINS   No use, dear. I'm sorry; but I cant get round your vowels; and though I like to get pretty postcards in your patent shorthand, I always have to read the copies in ordinary writing you so thoughtfully send me.

HIGGINS   Well, this isnt a phonetic job.

MRS. HIGGINS   You said it was.

HIGGINS   Not your part of it. Ive picked up a girl.

MRS. HIGGINS   Does that mean that some girl has picked you up?

HIGGINS   Not at all. I dont mean a love affair.

MRS. HIGGINS   What a pity!

HIGGINS   Why?

MRS. HIGGINS   Well, you never fall in love with anyone under forty-five. When will you discover that there are some rather nice-looking young women about?

HIGGINS   Oh, I cant be bothered with young women. My idea of a loveable woman is something as like you as possible.[9] I shall never get into the way of seriously liking young women: some habits lie too deep to be changed. [*Rising abruptly and walking about, jingling his money and his keys in his trouser pockets*] Besides, theyre all idiots.

MRS. HIGGINS   Do you know what you would do if you really loved me, Henry?

HIGGINS   Oh bother! What? Marry, I suppose?

MRS. HIGGINS   No. Stop fidgeting and take your hands out of your pockets. [*With a gesture of despair, he obeys and sits down again*]. Thats a good boy. Now tell me about the girl.

HIGGINS   Shes coming to see you.

MRS. HIGGINS   I dont remember asking her.

HIGGINS   You didnt. *I* asked her. If youd known her you wouldnt have asked her.

MRS. HIGGINS   Indeed! Why?

HIGGINS   Well, it's like this. Shes a common flower girl. I picked her off the kerbstone.

MRS. HIGGINS   And invited her to my at-home!

HIGGINS [*rising and coming to her to coax her*]   Oh, thatll be all right. Ive taught her to speak properly; and she has strict orders as to her behavior. Shes to keep to two subjects: the weather and everybody's health—Fine day and How do you do, you know—and not to let herself go on things in general. That will be safe.

MRS. HIGGINS   Safe! To talk about our health! about our insides! perhaps about our outsides! How could you be so silly, Henry?

HIGGINS [*impatiently*]   Well, she must talk about something. [*He controls himself and sits down again*]. Oh, she'll be all right: dont you fuss. Pickering is in it with me. Ive a sort of bet on that I'll pass her off as a duchess in six months. I started on her some months ago; and shes getting on like a house on fire. I shall win my bet. She has a quick ear; and shes been easier to teach than my middle-class pupils because shes had to learn a complete new language. She talks English almost as you talk French.

MRS. HIGGINS   Thats satisfactory, at all events.

HIGGINS   Well, it is and it isnt.

MRS. HIGGINS   What does that mean?

HIGGINS   You see, Ive got her pronunciation all right; but you have to consider not only how a girl pronounces, but what she pronounces; and thats where—

They are interrupted by the parlor-maid, announcing guests.

THE PARLOR-MAID   Mrs. and Miss Eynsford Hill. [*She withdraws*].

HIGGINS   Oh Lord! [*He rises; snatches his hat from the table; and makes for the door; but before he reaches it his mother introduces him*].

MRS. and MISS EYNSFORD HILL are the mother and daughter who sheltered from the rain in Covent Garden. The mother is well bred, quiet, and has the habitual anxiety of straitened means. The daughter has acquired a gay air of being very much at home in society: the bravado of genteel poverty.

MRS. EYNSFORD HILL [*to MRS. HIGGINS*]   How do you do? [*They shake hands*].

MISS EYNSFORD HILL   How d'you do? [*She shakes*].

MRS. HIGGINS [*introducing*]   My son Henry.

MRS. EYNSFORD HILL   Your celebrated son! I have so longed to meet you, Professor Higgins.

HIGGINS [*glumly, making no movement in her direction*]   Delighted. [*He backs against the piano and bows brusquely*].

MISS EYNSFORD HILL [*going to him with confident familiarity*] How do you do?

HIGGINS [*staring at her*]   Ive seen you before somewhere. I havnt the ghost of a notion where; but Ive heard your voice. [*Drearily*] It doesnt matter. Youd better sit down.

MRS. HIGGINS   I'm sorry to say that my celebrated son has no manners. You mustnt mind him.

MISS EYNSFORD HILL [*gaily*]   I dont. [*She sits in the Elizabethan chair*].

MRS. EYNSFORD HILL [*a little bewildered*]   Not at all. [*She sits on the ottoman between her daughter and MRS. HIGGINS, who has turned her chair away from the writing-table*].

HIGGINS   Oh, have I been rude? I didnt mean to be.

He goes to the central window, through which, with his back to the company, he contemplates the river and the flowers in Battersea Park on the opposite bank as if they were a frozen desert.

The parlor-maid returns, ushering in Pickering.

THE PARLOR-MAID   Colonel Pickering [*she withdraws*].

PICKERING   How do you do, Mrs. Higgins?

MRS. HIGGINS   So glad youve come. Do you know Mrs. Eynsford Hill——Miss Eynsford Hill? [*Exchange of bows. The*

Colonel brings the Chippendale chair a little forward between MRS. HILL and MRS. HIGGINS, and sits down].

PICKERING   Has Henry told you what weve come for?

HIGGINS [*over his shoulder*]   We were interrupted: damn it!

MRS. HIGGINS   Oh Henry, Henry, really!

MRS. EYNSFORD HILL [*half rising*]   Are we in the way?

MRS. HIGGINS [*rising and making her sit down again*]   No, no. You couldnt have come more fortunately: we want you to meet a friend of ours.

HIGGINS [*turning hopefully*]   Yes, by George! We want two or three people. Youll do as well as anybody else.

The parlor-maid returns, ushering FREDDY.

THE PARLOR-MAID   Mr. Eynsford Hill.

HIGGINS [*almost audibly, past endurance*]   God of Heaven! another of them.

FREDDY [*shaking hands with MRS. HIGGINS*]   Ahdedo?*

MRS. HIGGINS   Very good of you to come. [*Introducing*] Colonel Pickering.

FREDDY [*bowing*]   Ahdedo?

MRS. HIGGINS   I dont think you know my son, Professor Higgins.

FREDDY [*going to Higgins*]   Ahdedo?

HIGGINS [*looking at him much as if he were a pickpocket*]   I'll take my oath Ive met you before somewhere. Where was it?

FREDDY   I dont think so.

HIGGINS [*resignedly*]   It dont matter, anyhow. Sit down.

He shakes FREDDY's hand, and almost slings him on the ottoman with his face to the windows; then comes round to the other side of it.

HIGGINS   Well, here we are, anyhow! [*He sits down on the ottoman next MRS. EYNSFORD HILL, on her left*]. And now, what the devil are we going to talk about until Eliza comes?

MRS. HIGGINS   Henry: you are the life and soul of the Royal

---

*That is, "How do you do?"

Society's soirées; but really youre rather trying on more commonplace occasions.

HIGGINS   Am I? Very sorry. [*Beaming suddenly*] I suppose I am, you know. [*Uproariously*] Ha, ha!

MISS EYNSFORD HILL [*who considers HIGGINS quite eligible matrimonially*]   I sympathize. *I* havnt any small talk. If people would only be frank and say what they really think!

HIGGINS [*relapsing into gloom*]   Lord forbid!

MRS. EYNSFORD HILL [*taking up her daughter's cue*]   But why?

HIGGINS   What they think they ought to think is bad enough, Lord knows; but what they really think would break up the whole show. Do you suppose it would be really agreeable if I were to come out now with what *I* really think?

MISS EYNSFORD HILL [*gaily*]   Is it so very cynical?

HIGGINS   Cynical! Who the dickens said it was cynical? I mean it wouldnt be decent.

MRS. EYNSFORD HILL [*seriously*]   Oh! I'm sure you dont mean that, Mr. Higgins.

HIGGINS   You see, we're all savages, more or less. We're supposed to be civilized and cultured—to know all about poetry and philosophy and art and science, and so on; but how many of us know even the meanings of these names? [*To MISS HILL*] What do you know of poetry? [*To MRS. HILL*] What do you know of science? [*Indicating FREDDY*] What does he know of art or science or anything else? What the devil do you imagine I know of philosophy?

MRS. HIGGINS [*warningly*]   Or of manners, Henry?

THE PARLOR-MAID [*opening the door*]   Miss Doolittle. [*She withdraws*].

HIGGINS [*rising hastily and running to MRS. HIGGINS*]   Here she is, mother. [*He stands on tiptoe and makes signs over his mother's head to ELIZA to indicate to her which lady is her hostess*].

ELIZA, who is exquisitely dressed, produces an impression of such remarkable distinction and beauty as she enters that they all rise, quite fluttered. Guided by HIGGINS's signals, she comes to MRS. HIGGINS with studied grace.

LIZA [*speaking with pedantic correctness of pronunciation and great beauty of tone*]   How do you do, Mrs. Higgins? [*She gasps slightly in making sure of the H in Higgins, but is quite successful*]. Mr. Higgins told me I might come.

MRS. HIGGINS [*cordially*]   Quite right: I'm very glad indeed to see you.

PICKERING   How do you do, Miss Doolittle?

LIZA [*shaking hands with him*]   Colonel Pickering, is it not?

MRS. EYNSFORD HILL   I feel sure we have met before, Miss Doolittle. I remember your eyes.

LIZA   How do you do? [*She sits down on the ottoman gracefully in the place just left vacant by Higgins*].

MRS. EYNSFORD HILL [*introducing*]   My daughter Clara.

LIZA   How do you do?

CLARA [*impulsively*]   How do you do? [*She sits down on the ottoman beside Eliza, devouring her with her eyes*].

FREDDY [*coming to their side of the ottoman*]   Ive certainly had the pleasure.

MRS. EYNSFORD HILL [*introducing*]   My son Freddy.

LIZA   How do you do?

FREDDY bows and sits down in the Elizabethan chair, infatuated.

HIGGINS [*suddenly*]   By George, yes: it all comes back to me! [*They stare at him*]. Covent Garden! [*Lamentably*] What a damned thing!

MRS. HIGGINS   Henry, please! [*He is about to sit on the edge of the table*]. Dont sit on my writing-table: youll break it.

HIGGINS [*sulkily*]   Sorry.

He goes to the divan, stumbling into the fender and over the fire-irons on his way; extricating himself with muttered imprecations; and finishing his disastrous journey by throwing himself so impatiently on the divan that he almost breaks it. MRS. HIGGINS looks at him, but controls herself and says nothing.

A long and painful pause ensues.

MRS. HIGGINS [*at last, conversationally*]   Will it rain, do you
  think?

LIZA   The shallow depression* in the west of these islands is
  likely to move slowly in an easterly direction. There are no indications of any great change in the barometrical situation.

FREDDY   Ha! ha! how awfully funny!

LIZA   What is wrong with that, young man? I bet I got it right.

FREDDY   Killing!

MRS. EYNSFORD HILL   I'm sure I hope it wont turn cold.
  Theres so much influenza about. It runs right through our
  whole family regularly every spring.

LIZA [*darkly*]   My aunt died of influenza: so they said.

MRS. EYNSFORD HILL [*clicks her tongue sympathetically*]!!!

LIZA [*in the same tragic tone*]   But it's my belief they done the old
  woman in.

MRS. HIGGINS [*puzzled*]   Done her in?

LIZA   Y-e-e-e-es, Lord love you! Why should she die of influenza? She come through diphtheria right enough the year
  before. I saw her with my own eyes. Fairly blue with it, she
  was. They all thought she was dead; but my father he kept
  ladling gin down her throat til she came to so sudden that she
  bit the bowl off the spoon.

MRS. EYNSFORD HILL [*startled*]   Dear me!

LIZA [*piling up the indictment*]   What call would a woman with
  that strength in her have to die of influenza? What become
  of her new straw hat that should have come to me? Somebody pinched it; and what I say is, them as pinched it done
  her in.

MRS. EYNSFORD HILL   What does doing her in mean?

HIGGINS [*hastily*]   Oh, thats the new small talk. To do a person
  in means to kill them.

---

*Area of low pressure.

MRS. EYNSFORD HILL [*to ELIZA, horrified*]   You surely dont believe that your aunt was killed?

LIZA   Do I not! Them she lived with would have killed her for a hat-pin, let alone a hat.

MRS. EYNSFORD HILL   But it cant have been right for your father to pour spirits down her throat like that. It might have killed her.

LIZA   Not her. Gin was mother's milk to her. Besides, he'd poured so much down his own throat that he knew the good of it.

MRS. EYNSFORD HILL   Do you mean that he drank?

LIZA   Drank! My word! Something chronic.

MRS. EYNSFORD HILL   How dreadful for you!

LIZA   Not a bit. It never did him no harm what I could see. But then he did not keep it up regular. [*Cheerfully*] On the burst, as you might say, from time to time. And always more agreeable when he had a drop in. When he was out of work, my mother used to give him fourpence and tell him to go out and not come back until he'd drunk himself cheerful and loving-like. Theres lots of women has to make their husbands drunk to make them fit to live with. [*Now quite at her ease*] You see, it's like this. If a man has a bit of a conscience, it always takes him when he's sober; and then it makes him low-spirited. A drop of booze just takes that off and makes him happy. [*To FREDDY, who is in convulsions of suppressed laughter*] Here! what are you sniggering at?

FREDDY   The new small talk. You do it so awfully well.

LIZA   If I was doing it proper, what was you laughing at? [*To HIGGINS*] Have I said anything I oughtnt?

MRS. HIGGINS [*interposing*]   Not at all, Miss Doolittle.

LIZA   Well, thats a mercy, anyhow. [*Expansively*] What I always say is—

HIGGINS [*rising and looking at his watch*]   Ahem!

LIZA [*looking round at him; taking the hint; and rising*]   Well: I must go. [*They all rise. FREDDY goes to the door*]. So pleased to have met you. Good-bye. [*She shakes hands with MRS. HIG-GINS*].

MRS. HIGGINS   Good-bye.

LIZA   Good-bye, Colonel Pickering.

PICKERING   Good-bye, Miss Doolittle. [*They shake hands*].

LIZA [*nodding to the others*]   Good-bye, all.

FREDDY [*opening the door for her*]   Are you walking across the Park, Miss Doolittle? If so—

LIZA   Walk! Not bloody[10] likely. [*Sensation*]. I am going in a taxi. [*She goes out*].

PICKERING gasps and sits down. FREDDY goes out on the balcony to catch another glimpse of ELIZA.

MRS. EYNSFORD HILL [*suffering from shock*]   Well, I really cant get used to the new ways.

CLARA [*throwing herself discontentedly into the Elizabethan chair*] Oh, it's all right, mamma, quite right. People will think we never go anywhere or see anybody if you are so old-fashioned.

MRS. EYNSFORD HILL   I daresay I am very old-fashioned; but I do hope you wont begin using that expression, Clara. I have got accustomed to hear you talking about men as rotters,* and calling everything filthy and beastly;† though I do think it horrible and unladylike. But this last is really too much. Dont you think so, Colonel Pickering?

PICKERING   Dont ask me. Ive been away in India for several years; and manners have changed so much that I sometimes dont know whether I'm at a respectable dinner-table or in a ship's forecastle.‡

CLARA   It's all a matter of habit. Theres no right or wrong in it. Nobody means anything by it. And it's so quaint, and gives

---

*Objectionable males.

†Offensively dirty and badly behaved.

‡Crew's quarters in a ship's bow.

such a smart emphasis to things that are not in themselves very witty. I find the new small talk delightful and quite innocent.

MRS. EYNSFORD HILL [*rising*]   Well, after that, I think it's time for us to go.

PICKERING and HIGGINS rise.

CLARA [*rising*]   Oh yes: we have three at-homes to go to still. Good-bye, Mrs. Higgins. Good-bye, Colonel Pickering. Good-bye, Professor Higgins.

HIGGINS [*coming grimly at her from the divan, and accompanying her to the door*]   Good-bye. Be sure you try on that small talk at the three at-homes. Dont be nervous about it. Pitch it in strong.

CLARA [*all smiles*]   I will. Good-bye. Such nonsense, all this early Victorian prudery!

HIGGINS [*tempting her*]   Such damned nonsense!

CLARA   Such bloody nonsense!

MRS. EYNSFORD HILL [*convulsively*]   Clara!

CLARA   Ha! ha! [*She goes out radiant, conscious of being thoroughly up to date, and is heard descending the stairs in a stream of silvery laughter*].

FREDDY [*to the heavens at large*]   Well, I ask you— [*He gives it up, and comes to MRS. HIGGINS*]. Good-bye.

MRS. HIGGINS [*shaking hands*]   Good-bye. Would you like to meet Miss Doolittle again?

FREDDY [*eagerly*]   Yes, I should, most awfully.

MRS. HIGGINS   Well, you know my days.

FREDDY   Yes. Thanks awfully. Good-bye. [*He goes out*].

MRS. EYNSFORD HILL   Good-bye, Mr. Higgins.

HIGGINS   Good-bye. Good-bye.

MRS. EYNSFORD HILL [*to PICKERING*]   It's no use. I shall never be able to bring myself to use that word.

PICKERING   Dont. It's not compulsory, you know. Youll get on quite well without it.

MRS. EYNSFORD HILL   Only, Clara is so down on me if I am not positively reeking with the latest slang. Good-bye.

PICKERING   Good-bye [*They shake hands*].

MRS. EYNSFORD HILL [*to MRS. HIGGINS*]   You mustnt mind Clara. [*PICKERING, catching from her lowered tone that this is not meant for him to hear, discreetly joins HIGGINS at the window*]. We're so poor! and she gets so few parties, poor child! She doesnt quite know. [*MRS. HIGGINS, seeing that her eyes are moist, takes her hand sympathetically and goes with her to the door*]. But the boy is nice. Dont you think so?

MRS. HIGGINS   Oh, quite nice. I shall always be delighted to see him.

MRS. EYNSFORD HILL   Thank you, dear. Good-bye. [*She goes out*].

HIGGINS [*eagerly*]   Well? Is Eliza presentable [*he swoops on his mother and drags her to the ottoman, where she sits down in ELIZA's place with her son on her left*]?

PICKERING returns to his chair on her right.

MRS. HIGGINS   You silly boy, of course shes not presentable. Shes a triumph of your art and of her dressmaker's; but if you suppose for a moment that she doesnt give herself away in every sentence she utters, you must be perfectly cracked about her.

PICKERING   But dont you think something might be done? I mean something to eliminate the sanguinary element from her conversation.

MRS. HIGGINS   Not as long as she is in Henry's hands.

HIGGINS [*aggrieved*]   Do you mean that my language is improper?

MRS. HIGGINS   No, dearest: it would be quite proper—say on a canal barge; but it would not be proper for her at a garden party.

HIGGINS [*deeply injured*]   Well I must say—

PICKERING [*interrupting him*]   Come, Higgins: you must learn to know yourself. I havnt heard such language as yours since we used to review the volunteers in Hyde Park twenty years ago.

HIGGINS [*sulkily*]   Oh, well, if you say so, I suppose I dont always talk like a bishop.

MRS. HIGGINS [*quieting Henry with a touch*]   Colonel Pickering: will you tell me what is the exact state of things in Wimpole Street?

PICKERING [*cheerfully: as if this completely changed the subject*]   Well, I have come to live there with Henry. We work together at my Indian Dialects; and we think it more convenient—

MRS. HIGGINS   Quite so. I know all about that: it's an excellent arrangement. But where does this girl live?

HIGGINS   With us, of course. Where would she live?

MRS. HIGGINS   But on what terms? Is she a servant? If not, what is she?

PICKERING [*slowly*]   I think I know what you mean, Mrs. Higgins.

HIGGINS   Well, dash me if *I* do! Ive had to work at the girl every day for months to get her to her present pitch. Besides, shes useful. She knows where my things are, and remembers my appointments and so forth.

MRS. HIGGINS   How does your housekeeper get on with her?

HIGGINS   Mrs. Pearce? Oh, shes jolly glad to get so much taken off her hands; for before Eliza came, she used to have to find things and remind me of my appointments. But shes got some silly bee in her bonnet about Eliza. She keeps saying "You dont think, sir": doesnt she, Pick?

PICKERING   Yes: thats the formula. "You dont think, sir." Thats the end of every conversation about Eliza.

HIGGINS   As if I ever stop thinking about the girl and her confounded vowels and consonants. I'm worn out, thinking about her, and watching her lips and her teeth and her tongue, not to mention her soul, which is the quaintest of the lot.

MRS. HIGGINS   You certainly are a pretty pair of babies, playing with your live doll.

HIGGINS   Playing! The hardest job I ever tackled: make no mistake about that, mother. But you have no idea how frightfully interesting it is to take a human being and change her into a quite different human being by creating a new speech for her. It's filling up the deepest gulf that separates class from class and soul from soul.

PICKERING [*drawing his chair closer to MRS. HIGGINS and bending over to her eagerly*]   Yes: it's enormously interesting. I assure you, Mrs. Higgins, we take Eliza very seriously. Every week— every day almost—there is some new change. [*Closer again*] We keep records of every stage—dozens of gramophone disks and photographs—

HIGGINS [*assailing her at the other ear*]   Yes, by George: it's the most absorbing experiment I ever tackled. She regularly fills our lives up; doesnt she, Pick?

PICKERING   We're always talking Eliza.

HIGGINS   Teaching Eliza.

PICKERING   Dressing Eliza.

MRS. HIGGINS   What!

HIGGINS   Inventing new Elizas.

HIGGINS   [*speaking together*] { You know, she has the most extraordinary quickness of ear:

PICKERING   { I assure you, my dear Mrs. Higgins, that girl

HIGGINS   { just like a parrot. Ive tried her with every

PICKERING	is a genius. She can play the piano quite beautifully.
HIGGINS	possible sort of sound that a human being can make—
PICKERING	We have taken her to classical concerts and to music
HIGGINS	Continental dialects, African dialects, Hottentot
PICKERING	halls; and it's all the same to her: she plays everything
HIGGINS	clicks, things it took me years to get hold of; and
PICKERING	she hears right off when she comes home, whether it's
HIGGINS	she picks them up like a shot, right away, as if she had
PICKERING	Beethoven and Brahms or Lehar* and Lionel Monckton;[11]
HIGGINS	been at it all her life.
PICKERING	though six months ago, she'd never as much as touched a piano—

MRS. HIGGINS [*putting her fingers in her ears, as they are by this time shouting one another down with an intolerable noise*]   Sh-sh-sh—sh! [*They stop*].

PICKERING   I beg your pardon. [*He draws his chair back apologetically*].

HIGGINS   Sorry. When Pickering starts shouting nobody can get a word in edgeways.

MRS. HIGGINS   Be quiet, Henry. Colonel Pickering: dont you realize that when Eliza walked into Wimpole Street, something walked in with her?

---

*Franz Lehár (1870–1948), Hungarian composer of operettas; a contemporary of Shaw.

PICKERING   Her father did. But Henry soon got rid of him.

MRS. HIGGINS   It would have been more to the point if her mother had. But as her mother didnt something else did.

PICKERING   But what?

MRS. HIGGINS [*unconsciously dating herself by the word*]   A problem.

PICKERING   Oh, I see. The problem of how to pass her off as a lady.

HIGGINS   I'll solve that problem. Ive half solved it already.

MRS. HIGGINS   No, you two infinitely stupid male creatures: the problem of what is to be done with her afterwards.

HIGGINS   I dont see anything in that. She can go her own way, with all the advantages I have given her.

MRS. HIGGINS   The advantages of that poor woman who was here just now! The manners and habits that disqualify a fine lady from earning her own living without giving her a fine lady's income! Is that what you mean?

PICKERING [*indulgently, being rather bored*]   Oh, that will be all right, Mrs. Higgins. [*He rises to go*].

HIGGINS [*rising also*]   We'll find her some light employment.

PICKERING   Shes happy enough. Dont you worry about her. Good-bye. [*He shakes hands as if he were consoling a frightened child, and makes for the door*].

HIGGINS   Anyhow, theres no good bothering now. The things done. Good-bye, mother. [*He kisses her, and follows PICKERING*].

PICKERING [*turning for a final consolation*]   There are plenty of openings. We'll do whats right. Good-bye.

HIGGINS [*to PICKERING as they go out together*]   Let's take her to the Shakespear exhibition at Earls Court.

PICKERING   Yes: lets. Her remarks will be delicious.

HIGGINS   She'll mimic all the people for us when we get home.

PICKERING   Ripping. [*Both are heard laughing as they go downstairs*].

MRS. HIGGINS [*rises with an impatient bounce, and returns to her work at the writing-table. She sweeps a litter of disarranged papers out of her way; snatches a sheet of paper from her stationery case; and tries resolutely to write. At the third line she gives it up; flings down her pen; grips the table angrily and exclaims*]   Oh, men! men!! men!!!

ACT IV

The Wimpole Street laboratory. Midnight. Nobody in the room. The clock on the mantelpiece strikes twelve. The fire is not alight: it is a summer night.

Presently Higgins and Pickering are heard on the stairs.

HIGGINS [*calling down to PICKERING*]   I say, Pick: lock up, will you. I shant be going out again.

PICKERING   Right. Can Mrs. Pearce go to bed? We dont want anything more, do we?

HIGGINS   Lord, no!

ELIZA opens the door and is seen on the lighted landing in opera cloak, brilliant evening dress, and diamonds, with fan, flowers, and all accessories. She comes to the hearth, and switches on the electric lights there. She is tired: her pallor contrasts strongly with her dark eyes and hair; and her expression is almost tragic. She takes off her cloak; puts her fan and flowers on the piano; and sits down on the bench, brooding and silent. HIGGINS, in evening dress, with overcoat and hat, comes in, carrying a smoking jacket* which he has picked up downstairs. He takes off the hat and overcoat; throws them carelessly on the newspaper stand; disposes of his coat in the same way; puts on the smoking jacket; and throws himself wearily into the easy-chair at the hearth. PICKERING, similarly attired, comes in. He also takes off his hat and overcoat, and is about to throw them on HIGGINS's when he hesitates.

PICKERING   I say: Mrs. Pearce will row if we leave these things lying about in the drawing-room.

---

*Loose-fitting jacket for wear when relaxing at home.

HIGGINS   Oh, chuck them over the bannisters into the hall. She'll find them there in the morning and put them away all right. She'll think we were drunk.

PICKERING   We are, slightly. Are there any letters?

HIGGINS   I didnt look. [*PICKERING takes the overcoats and hats and goes downstairs. HIGGINS begins half singing half yawning an air from La Fanciulla del Golden West.*[12] *Suddenly he stops and exclaims*] I wonder where the devil my slippers are!

ELIZA looks at him darkly; then rises suddenly and leaves the room.

HIGGINS yawns again, and resumes his song.

PICKERING returns, with the contents of the letter-box in his hand.

PICKERING   Only circulars, and this coroneted billet-doux* for you. [*He throws the circulars into the fender, and posts himself on the hearthrug, with his back to the grate*].

HIGGINS [*glancing at the billet-doux*]   Money-lender. [*He throws the letter after the circulars*].

ELIZA returns with a pair of large down-at-heel slippers. She places them on the carpet before HIGGINS, and sits as before without a word.

HIGGINS [*yawning again*]   Oh Lord! What an evening! What a crew! What a silly tomfoollery! [*He raises his shoe to unlace it, and catches sight of the slippers. He stops unlacing and looks at them as if they had appeared there of their own accord*]. Oh! theyre there, are they?

PICKERING [*stretching himself*]   Well, I feel a bit tired. It's been a long day. The garden party, a dinner party, and the opera! Rather too much of a good thing. But you've won your bet, Higgins. Eliza did the trick, and something to spare, eh?

HIGGINS [*fervently*]   Thank God it's over!

ELIZA flinches violently; but they take no notice of her; and she recovers herself and sits stonily as before.

---

*Love letter with a crest embossed on it; Pickering is speaking ironically.

PICKERING   Were you nervous at the garden party? *I* was. Eliza didnt seem a bit nervous.

HIGGINS   Oh, she wasnt nervous. I knew she'd be all right. No: it's the strain of putting the job through all these months that has told on me. It was interesting enough at first, while we were at the phonetics; but after that I got deadly sick of it. If I hadnt backed myself to do it I should have chucked the whole thing up two months ago. It was a silly notion: the whole thing has been a bore.

PICKERING   Oh come! the garden party was frightfully exciting. My heart began beating like anything.

HIGGINS   Yes, for the first three minutes. But when I saw we were going to win hands down, I felt like a bear in a cage, hanging about doing nothing. The dinner was worse: sitting gorging there for over an hour, with nobody but a damned fool of a fashionable woman to talk to! I tell you, Pickering, never again for me. No more artificial duchesses. The whole thing has been simple purgatory.

PICKERING   Youve never been broken in properly to the social routine. [*Strolling over to the piano*] I rather enjoy dipping into it occasionally myself: it makes me feel young again. Anyhow, it was a great success: an immense success. I was quite frightened once or twice because Eliza was doing it so well. You see, lots of the real people cant do it at all: theyre such fools that they think style comes by nature to people in their position; and so they never learn. Theres always something professional about doing a thing superlatively well.

HIGGINS   Yes: thats what drives me mad: the silly people dont know their own silly business.* [*Rising*] However, it's over and done with; and now I can go to bed at last without dreading tomorrow.

---

*Higgins is repeating a well-known saying by English theologian and logician Richard Whately (1787–1863).

ELIZA's beauty becomes murderous.

PICKERING   I think I shall turn in too. Still, it's been a great occasion: a triumph for you. Good-night. [*He goes*].

HIGGINS [*following him*]   Good-night. [*Over his shoulder, at the door*] Put out the lights, Eliza; and tell Mrs. Pearce not to make coffee for me in the morning: I'll take tea. [*He goes out*].

ELIZA tries to control herself and feel indifferent as she rises and walks across to the hearth to switch off the lights. By the time she gets there she is on the point of screaming. She sits down in Higgins's chair and holds on hard to the arms. Finally she gives way and flings herself furiously on the floor raging.

HIGGINS [*in despairing wrath outside*]   What the devil have I done with my slippers? [*He appears at the door*].

LIZA [*snatching up the slippers, and hurling them at him one after the other with all her force*]   There are your slippers. And there. Take your slippers; and may you never have a day's luck with them!

HIGGINS [*astounded*]   What on earth——! [*He comes to her*]. Whats the matter? Get up. [*He pulls her up*]. Anything wrong?

LIZA [*breathless*]   Nothing wrong—with y o u. Ive won your bet for you, havnt I? Thats enough for you. *I* dont matter, I suppose.

HIGGINS   Y o u won my bet! You! Presumptuous insect! *I* won it. What did you throw those slippers at me for?

LIZA   Because I wanted to smash your face. I'd like to kill you, you selfish brute. Why didnt you leave me where you picked me out of—in the gutter? You thank God it's all over, and that now you can throw me back again there, do you? [*She crisps her fingers frantically*].

HIGGINS [*looking at her in cool wonder*]   The creature* i s nervous, after all.

---

*Allusion to Mary Shelley's 1818 novel *Frankenstein*, in which Dr. Frankenstein refers to the monster he creates as the "creature."

LIZA [*gives a suffocated scream of fury, and instinctively darts her nails at his face*]!!

HIGGINS [*catching her wrists*]   Ah! would you? Claws in, you cat. How dare you shew your temper to me? Sit down and be quiet. [*He throws her roughly into the easy-chair*].

LIZA [*crushed by superior strength and weight*]   Whats to become of me? Whats to become of me?

HIGGINS   How the devil do I know whats to become of you? What does it matter what becomes of you?

LIZA   You dont care. I know you dont care. You wouldnt care if I was dead. I'm nothing to you—not so much as them slippers.

HIGGINS [*thundering*]   T h o s e slippers.

LIZA [*with bitter submission*]   Those slippers. I didnt think it made any difference now.

A pause. ELIZA hopeless and crushed. HIGGINS a little uneasy.

HIGGINS [*in his loftiest manner*]   Why have you begun going on like this? May I ask whether you complain of your treatment here?

LIZA   No.

HIGGINS   Has anybody behaved badly to you? Colonel Pickering? Mrs. Pearce? Any of the servants?

LIZA   No.

HIGGINS   I presume you dont pretend that I have treated you badly.

LIZA   No.

HIGGINS   I am glad to hear it. [*He moderates his tone*]. Perhaps youre tired after the strain of the day. Will you have a glass of champagne? [*He moves towards the door*].

LIZA   No. [*Recollecting her manners*] Thank you.

HIGGINS [*good-humored again*]   This has been coming on you for some days. I suppose it was natural for you to be anxious about the garden party. But thats all over now [*He pats her kindly on the shoulder. She writhes*]. Theres nothing more to worry about.

LIZA   No. Nothing more for y o u to worry about. [*She suddenly rises and gets away from him by going to the piano bench, where she sits and hides her face*]. Oh God! I wish I was dead.

HIGGINS [*staring after her in sincere surprise*]   Why? in heaven's name, why? [*Reasonably, going to her*] Listen to me, Eliza. All this irritation is purely subjective.

LIZA   I dont understand. I'm too ignorant.

HIGGINS   It's only imagination. Low spirits and nothing else. Nobody's hurting you. Nothing's wrong. You go to bed like a good girl and sleep it off. Have a little cry and say your prayers: that will make you comfortable.

LIZA   I heard y o u r prayers. "Thank God it's all over!"

HIGGINS [*impatiently*]   Well, dont you thank God it's all over? Now you are free and can do what you like.

LIZA [*pulling herself together in desperation*]   What am I fit for? What have you left me fit for? Where am I to go? What am I to do? Whats to become of me?

HIGGINS [*enlightened, but not at all impressed*]   Oh, thats whats worrying you, is it? [*He thrusts his hands into his pockets, and walks about in his usual manner, rattling the contents of his pockets, as if condescending to a trivial subject out of pure kindness*]. I shouldnt bother about it if I were you. I should imagine you wont have much difficulty in settling yourself somewhere or other, though I hadnt quite realized that you were going away. [*She looks quickly at him: he does not look at her, but examines the dessert stand on the piano and decides that he will eat an apple*]. You might marry, you know. [*He bites a large piece out of the apple, and munches it noisily*]. You see, Eliza, all men are not confirmed old bachelors like me and the Colonel. Most men are the marrying sort (poor devils!); and youre not bad-looking; it's quite a pleasure to look at you sometimes—not now, of course, because youre crying and looking as ugly as the very devil; but when youre all right and quite yourself, youre what I should call attractive. That is, to the people in the marrying line, you understand. You go to bed and have a good nice rest; and then get up and look at yourself in the glass; and you wont feel so cheap.

ELIZA again looks at him, speechless, and does not stir.

The look is quite lost on him: he eats his apple with a dreamy expression of happiness, as it is quite a good one.

HIGGINS [*a genial afterthought occurring to him*]   I daresay my mother could find some chap or other who would do very well.

LIZA   We were above that at the corner of Tottenham Court Road.

HIGGINS [*waking up*]   What do you mean?

LIZA   I sold flowers. I didnt sell myself. Now youve made a lady of me I'm not fit to sell anything else. I wish youd left me where you found me.

HIGGINS [*slinging the core of the apple decisively into the grate*]*
Tosh, Eliza. Dont you insult human relations by dragging all this cant† about buying and selling into it. You neednt marry the fellow if you dont like him.

LIZA   What else am I to do?

HIGGINS   Oh, lots of things. What about your old idea of a florist's shop? Pickering could set you up in one: hes lots of money. [*Chuckling*] He'll have to pay for all those togs you have been wearing today; and that, with the hire of the jewellery, will make a big hole in two hundred pounds. Why, six months ago you would have thought it the millennium to have a flower shop of your own. Come! youll be all right. I must clear off to bed: I'm devilish sleepy. By the way, I came down for something: I forget what it was.

LIZA   Your slippers.

HIGGINS   Oh yes, of course. You shied them at me. [*He picks them up, and is going out when she rises and speaks to him*].

---

*Fireplace.

†Jargon; insincere speech.

LIZA   Before you go, sir—

HIGGINS [*dropping the slippers in his surprise at her calling him Sir*] Eh?

LIZA   Do my clothes belong to me or to Colonel Pickering?

HIGGINS [*coming back into the room as if her question were the very climax of unreason*]   What the devil use would they be to Pickering?

LIZA   He might want them for the next girl you pick up to experiment on.

HIGGINS [*shocked and hurt*]   Is t h a t the way you feel towards us?

LIZA   I dont want to hear anything more about that. All I want to know is whether anything belongs to me. My own clothes were burnt.

HIGGINS   But what does it matter? Why need you start bothering about that in the middle of the night?

LIZA   I want to know what I may take away with me. I dont want to be accused of stealing.

HIGGINS [*now deeply wounded*]   Stealing! You shouldnt have said that, Eliza. That shews a want of feeling.

LIZA   I'm sorry. I'm only a common ignorant girl; and in my station I have to be careful. There cant be any feelings between the like of you and the like of me. Please will you tell me what belongs to me and what doesn't?

HIGGINS [*very sulky*]   You may take the whole damned houseful if you like. Except the jewels. Theyre hired. Will that satisfy you? [*He turns on his heel and is about to go in extreme dudgeon*].*

LIZA [*drinking in his emotion like nectar, and nagging him to provoke a further supply*]   Stop, please. [*She takes off her jewels*]. Will you take these to your room and keep them safe? I dont want to run the risk of their being missing.

HIGGINS [*furious*]   Hand them over. [*She puts them into his*

*Resentment; indignation.

hands]. If these belonged to me instead of to the jeweler, I'd ram them down your ungrateful throat. [*He perfunctorily thrusts them into his pockets, unconsciously decorating himself with the protruding ends of the chains*].

LIZA [*taking a ring off*]   This ring isnt the jeweler's: it's the one you bought me in Brighton. I dont want it now. [*Higgins dashes the ring violently into the fireplace, and turns on her so threateningly that she crouches over the piano with her hands over her face, and exclaims*] Dont you hit me.

HIGGINS   Hit you! You infamous creature, how dare you accuse me of such a thing? It is you who have hit me. You have wounded me to the heart.

LIZA [*thrilling with hidden joy*]   I'm glad. Ive got a little of my own back, anyhow.

HIGGINS [*with dignity, in his finest professional style*]   You have caused me to lose my temper: a thing that has hardly ever happend to me before. I prefer to say nothing more tonight. I am going to bed.

LIZA [*pertly*]   Youd better leave a note for Mrs. Pearce about the coffee; for she wont be told by me.

HIGGINS [*formally*]   Damn Mrs. Pearce; and damn the coffee; and damn you; and damn my own folly in having lavished hard-earned knowledge and the treasure of my regard and intimacy on a heartless guttersnipe. [*He goes out with impressive decorum, and spoils it by slamming the door savagely*].

ELIZA smiles for the first time; expresses her feelings by a wild pantomime in which an imitation of HIGGINS's exit is confused with her own triumph; and finally goes down on her knees on the hearthrug to look for the ring.[13]

ACT V

Mrs. Higgins's drawing-room. She is at her writing-table as before. The parlor-maid comes in.

THE PARLOR-MAID [*at the door*]   Mr. Henry, mam, is downstairs with Colonel Pickering.

MRS. HIGGINS   Well, shew them up.

THE PARLOR-MAID   Theyre using the telephone, mam. Telephoning to the police, I think.

MRS. HIGGINS   What!

THE PARLOR-MAID [*coming further in and lowering her voice*] Mr. Henry's in a state, mam. I thought I'd better tell you.

MRS. HIGGINS   If you had told me that Mr. Henry was not in a state it would have been more surprising. Tell them to come up when theyve finished with the police. I suppose hes lost something.

THE PARLOR-MAID   Yes, mam [*going*].

MRS. HIGGINS   Go upstairs and tell Miss Doolittle that Mr. Henry and the Colonel are here. Ask her not to come down till I send for her.

THE PARLOR-MAID   Yes, mam.

HIGGINS bursts in. He is, as the parlor-maid has said, in a state.

HIGGINS   Look here, mother: heres a confounded thing!

MRS. HIGGINS   Yes, dear. Good-morning. [*He checks his impatience and kisses her, whilst the parlor-maid goes out*]. What is it?

HIGGINS   Eliza's bolted.*

---

*Slang for "ran away."

MRS. HIGGINS [*calmly continuing her writing*]   You must have frightened her.

HIGGINS   Frightened her! nonsense! She was left last night, as usual, to turn out the lights and all that; and instead of going to bed she changed her clothes and went right off: her bed wasnt slept in. She came in a cab for her things before seven this morning; and that fool Mrs. Pearce let her have them without telling me a word about it. What am I to do?

MRS. HIGGINS   Do without, I'm afraid, Henry. The girl has a perfect right to leave if she chooses.

HIGGINS [*wandering distractedly across the room*]   But I cant find anything. I dont know what appointments Ive got. I'm— [*PICKERING comes in. MRS. HIGGINS puts down her pen and turns away from the writing-table*].

PICKERING [*shaking hands*]   Good-morning, Mrs. Higgins. Has Henry told you? [*He sits down on the ottoman*].

HIGGINS   What does that ass of an inspector say? Have you offered a reward?

MRS. HIGGINS [*rising in indignant amazement*]   You dont mean to say you have set the police after Eliza?

HIGGINS   Of course. What are the police for? What else could we do? [*He sits in the Elizabethan chair*].

PICKERING   The inspector made a lot of difficulties. I really think he suspected us of some improper purpose.

MRS. HIGGINS   Well, of course he did. What right have you to go to the police and give the girl's name as if she were a thief, or a lost umbrella, or something? Really! [*She sits down again, deeply vexed*].

HIGGINS   But we want to find her.

PICKERING   We cant let her go like this, you know, Mrs. Higgins. What were we to do?

MRS. HIGGINS   You have no more sense, either of you, than two children. Why—

The parlor-maid comes in and breaks off the conversation.

THE PARLOR-MAID   Mr. Henry: a gentleman wants to see you very particular. Hes been sent on from Wimpole Street.

HIGGINS   Oh, bother! I cant see anyone now. Who is it?

THE PARLOR-MAID   A Mr. Doolittle, sir.

PICKERING   Doolittle! Do you mean the dustman?

THE PARLOR-MAID   Dustman! Oh no, sir: a gentleman.

HIGGINS [*springing up excitedly*]   By George, Pick, it's some relative of hers that shes gone to. Somebody we know nothing about. [*To the parlor-maid*] Send him up, quick.

THE PARLOR-MAID   Yes, sir. [*She goes*].

HIGGINS [*eagerly, going to his mother*]   Genteel relatives! now we shall hear something. [*He sits down in the Chippendale chair*].

MRS. HIGGINS   Do you know any of her people?

PICKERING   Only her father: the fellow we told you about.

THE PARLOR-MAID [*announcing*]   Mr. Doolittle. [*She withdraws*].

DOOLITTLE enters. He is brilliantly dressed in a new fashionable frock-coat, with white waistcoat and grey trousers. A flower in his buttonhole, a dazzling silk hat, and patent leather shoes complete the effect. He is too concerned with the business he has come on to notice MRS. HIGGINS. He walks straight to Higgins, and accosts him with vehement reproach.

DOOLITTLE [*indicating his own person*]   See here! Do you see this? You done this.

HIGGINS   Done what, man?

DOOLITTLE   This, I tell you. Look at it. Look at this hat. Look at this coat.

PICKERING   Has Eliza been buying you clothes?

DOOLITTLE   Eliza! not she. Not half. Why would she buy me clothes?

MRS. HIGGINS   Good-morning, Mr. Doolittle. Wont you sit down?

DOOLITTLE [*taken aback as he becomes conscious that he has forgotten his hostess*]   Asking your pardon, maam. [*He approaches her and shakes her proffered hand].* Thank you. [*He sits down on the ottoman, on PICKERING's right*]. I am that full of what has happened to me that I cant think of anything else.

HIGGINS   What the dickens has happened to you?

DOOLITTLE   I shouldnt mind if it had only happened to me: anything might happen to anybody and nobody to blame but Providence, as you might say. But this is something that you done to me: yes, you, Henry Higgins.

HIGGINS   Have you found Eliza? Thats the point.

DOOLITTLE   Have you lost her?

HIGGINS   Yes.

DOOLITTLE   You have all the luck, you have. I aint found her; but she'll find me quick enough now after what you done to me.

MRS. HIGGINS   But what has my son done to you, Mr. Doolittle?

DOOLITTLE   Done to me! Ruined me. Destroyed my happiness. Tied me up and delivered me into the hands of middle class morality.

HIGGINS [*rising intolerantly and standing over DOOLITTLE*] Youre raving. Youre drunk. Youre mad. I gave you five pounds. After that I had two conversations with you, at half-a-crown an hour. Ive never seen you since.

DOOLITTLE   Oh! Drunk! am I? Mad! am I? Tell me this. Did you or did you not write a letter to an old blighter* in America that was giving five millions to found Moral Reform Societies all over the world, and that wanted you to invent a universal language for him?

HIGGINS   What! Ezra D. Wannafeller!† Hes dead. [*He sits down again carelessly*].

---

*Fellow; rascal.

†Parody of "Rockefeller"; John D. Rockefeller (1839–1937) was an American industrialist and philanthropist.

DOOLITTLE   Yes: hes dead; and I'm done for. Now did you or did you not write a letter to him to say that the most original moralist at present in England, to the best of your knowledge, was Alfred Doolittle, a common dustman.

HIGGINS   Oh, after your last visit I remember making some silly joke of the kind.

DOOLITTLE   Ah! you may well call it a silly joke. It put the lid on me right enough. Just give him the chance he wanted to shew that Americans is not like us: that they recognize and re-spect merit in every class of life, however humble. Them words is in his blooming will, in which, Henry Higgins, thanks to your silly joking, he leaves me a share in his Pre-digested Cheese Trust worth three thousand a year on condi-tion that I lecture for his Wannafeller Moral Reform World League as often as they ask me up to six times a year.

HIGGINS   The devil he does! Whew! [Brightening suddenly] What a lark!

PICKERING   A safe thing for you, Doolittle. They wont ask you twice.

DOOLITTLE   It aint the lecturing I mind. I'll lecture them blue in the face, I will, and not turn a hair. It's making a gen-tleman of me that I object to. Who asked him to make a gen-tleman of me? I was happy. I was free. I touched pretty nigh everybody for money when I wanted it, same as I touched you, Henry Higgins. Now I am worrited; tied neck and heels; and everybody touches me for money. It's a fine thing for you, says my solicitor. Is it? says I. You mean it's a good thing for you, I says. When I was a poor man and had a solicitor once when they found a pram in the dust cart, he got me off, and got shut of me and got me shut of him as quick as he could. Same with the doctors: used to shove me out of the hospital before I could hardly stand on my legs, and nothing to pay. Now they finds out that I'm not a healthy man and cant live unless they looks after me twice a day. In the house I'm not let do a hand's turn for myself: somebody else must do it and touch me* for it. A year ago I hadnt a relative in the world except two or three that wouldnt speak to me. Now Ive fifty, and not a decent week's wages among the lot of them. I have to live for others and not for myself: thats middle class morality. You talk of losing Eliza. Dont you be anxious: I bet shes on my doorstep by this: she that could support herself easy by selling flowers if I wasnt respectable. And the next one to touch me will be you, Henry Higgins. I'll have to learn to speak middle class language from you, instead of speaking proper English. Thats where youll come in; and I daresay thats what you done it for.

MRS. HIGGINS   But, my dear Mr. Doolittle, you need not suffer all this if you are really in earnest. Nobody can force you to accept this bequest. You can repudiate it. Isnt that so, Colonel Pickering?

PICKERING   I believe so.

DOOLITTLE [*softening his manner in deference to her sex*]   Thats the tragedy of it, maam. It's easy to say chuck it; but I havent the nerve. Which of us has? We're all intimidated. Intimidated, maam: thats what we are. What is there for me if I chuck it but the workhouse in my old age? I have to dye my hair already to keep my job as a dustman. If I was one of the deserving poor, and had put by a bit, I could chuck it; but then why should I, acause the deserving poor might as well be millionaires for all the happiness they ever has. They dont know what happiness is. But I, as one of the undeserving poor, have nothing between me and the pauper's uniform but this here blasted three thousand a year that shoves me into the middle class. (Excuse the expression, maam: youd use it yourself if you had my provocation). Theyve got you every way you turn: it's a choice between the Skilly of the workhouse and the Char

---

*That is, get money out of me.

Bydis of the middle class;[14] and I havnt the nerve for the workhouse. Intimidated: thats what I am. Broke. Bought up. Happier men than me will call for my dust, and touch me for their tip; and I'll look on helpless, and envy them. And thats what your son has brought me to. [*He is overcome by emotion*].

MRS. HIGGINS   Well, I'm very glad youre not going to do anything foolish, Mr. Doolittle. For this solves the problem of Eliza's future. You can provide for her now.

DOOLITTLE [*with melancholy resignation*]   Yes, maam: I'm expected to provide for everyone now, out of three thousand a year.

HIGGINS [*jumping up*]   Nonsense! he cant provide for her. He shant provide for her. She doesnt belong to him. I paid him five pounds for her. Doolittle: either youre an honest man or a rogue.

DOOLITTLE [*tolerantly*]   A little of both, Henry, like the rest of us: a little of both.

HIGGINS   Well, you took that money for the girl; and you have no right to take her as well.

MRS. HIGGINS   Henry: dont be absurd. If you really want to know where Eliza is, she is upstairs.

HIGGINS [*amazed*]   Upstairs!!! Then I shall jolly soon fetch her downstairs. [*He makes resolutely for the door*].

MRS. HIGGINS [*rising and following him*]   Be quiet, Henry. Sit down.

HIGGINS   I—

MRS. HIGGINS   Sit down, dear; and listen to me.

HIGGINS   Oh very well, very well, very well. [*He throws himself ungraciously on the ottoman, with his face towards the windows*]. But I think you might have told me this half an hour ago.

MRS. HIGGINS   Eliza came to me this morning. She passed the night partly walking about in a rage, partly trying to throw herself into the river and being afraid to, and partly in the

Carlton Hotel. She told me of the brutal way you two treated her.

HIGGINS [*bounding up again*]   What!

PICKERING [*rising also*]   My dear Mrs. Higgins, shes been telling you stories. We didnt treat her brutally. We hardly said a word to her; and we parted on particularly good terms. [*Turning on HIGGINS*] Higgins did you bully her after I went to bed?

HIGGINS   Just the other way about. She threw my slippers in my face. She behaved in the most outrageous way. I never gave her the slightest provocation. The slippers came bang into my face the moment I entered the room——before I had uttered a word. And used perfectly awful language.

PICKERING [*astonished*]   But why? What did we do to her?

MRS. HIGGINS   I think I know pretty well what you did. The girl is naturally rather affectionate, I think. Isnt she, Mr. Doolittle?

DOOLITTLE   Very tender-hearted, maam. Takes after me.

MRS. HIGGINS   Just so. She had become attached to you both. She worked very hard for you, Henry! I dont think you quite realize what anything in the nature of brain work means to a girl like that. Well, it seems that when the great day of trial came, and she did this wonderful thing for you without making a single mistake, you two sat there and never said a word to her, but talked together of how glad you were that it was all over and how you had been bored with the whole thing. And then you were surprised because she threw your slippers at you! *I* should have thrown the fire-irons at you.

HIGGINS   We said nothing except that we were tired and wanted to go to bed. Did we, Pick?

PICKERING [*shrugging his shoulders*]   That was all.

MRS. HIGGINS [*ironically*]   Quite sure?

PICKERING   Absolutely. Really, that was all.

MRS. HIGGINS   You didn't thank her, or pet her, or admire her, or tell her how splendid she'd been.

HIGGINS [*impatiently*]   But she knew all about that. We didnt make speeches to her, if thats what you mean.

PICKERING [*conscience stricken*]   Perhaps we were a little inconsiderate. Is she very angry?

MRS. HIGGINS [*returning to her place at the writing-table*]   Well, I'm afraid she wont go back to Wimpole Street, especially now that Mr. Doolittle is able to keep up the position you have thrust on her; but she says she is quite willing to meet you on friendly terms and to let bygones be bygones.

HIGGINS [*furious*]   Is she, by George? Ho!

MRS. HIGGINS   If you promise to behave yourself, Henry, I'll ask her to come down. If not, go home; for you have taken up quite enough of my time.

HIGGINS   Oh, all right. Very well. Pick: you behave yourself. Let us put on our best Sunday manners for this creature that we picked out of the mud. [*He flings himself sulkily into the Elizabethan chair*].

DOOLITTLE [*remonstrating*]   Now, now, Henry Higgins! have some consideration for my feelings as a middle class man.

MRS. HIGGINS   Remember your promise, Henry. [*She presses the bell-button on the writing-table*]. Mr. Doolittle: will you be so good as to step out on the balcony for a moment. I dont want Eliza to have the shock of your news until she has made it up with these two gentlemen. Would you mind?

DOOLITTLE   As you wish, lady. Anything to help Henry to keep her off my hands. [*He disappears through the window*].

The parlor-maid answers the bell. PICKERING sits down in DOOLITTLE's place.

MRS. HIGGINS   Ask Miss Doolittle to come down, please.

THE PARLOR-MAID   Yes, mam. [*She goes out*].

MRS. HIGGINS   Now, Henry: be good.

HIGGINS   I am behaving myself perfectly.

PICKERING   He is doing his best, Mrs. Higgins.

> *A pause. HIGGINS throws back his head; stretches out his legs; and begins to whistle.*

MRS. HIGGINS   Henry, dearest, you dont look at all nice in that attitude.

HIGGINS [*pulling himself together*]   I was not trying to look nice, mother.

MRS. HIGGINS   It doesnt matter, dear. I only wanted to make you speak.

HIGGINS   Why?

MRS. HIGGINS   Because you cant speak and whistle at the same time. Higgins groans. Another very trying pause.

HIGGINS [*springing up, out of patience*]   Where the devil is that girl? Are we to wait here all day?

> *ELIZA enters, sunny, self-possessed, and giving a staggeringly convincing exhibition of ease of manner. She carries a little work-basket, and is very much at home. PICKERING is too much taken aback to rise.*

LIZA   How do you do, Professor Higgins? Are you quite well?

HIGGINS [*choking*]   Am I— [*He can say no more*].

LIZA   But of course you are: you are never ill. So glad to see you again, Colonel Pickering. [*He rises hastily; and they shake hands*]. Quite chilly this morning, isnt it? [*She sits down on his left. He sits beside her*].

HIGGINS   Dont you dare try this game on me. I taught it to you; and it doesnt take me in. Get up and come home; and dont be a fool.

> *ELIZA takes a piece of needlework from her basket, and begins to stitch at it, without taking the least notice of this outburst.*

MRS. HIGGINS   Very nicely put, indeed, Henry. No woman could resist such an invitation.

HIGGINS   You let her alone, mother. Let her speak for herself. You will jolly soon see whether she has an idea that I havnt put into her head or a word that I havnt put into her mouth. I tell you I have created this thing out of the squashed cabbage leaves of Covent Garden; and now she pretends to play the fine lady with me.

MRS. HIGGINS [*placidly*]   Yes, dear; but youll sit down, wont you?

HIGGINS sits down again, savagely.

LIZA [*to Pickering, taking no apparent notice of Higgins, and working away deftly*]   Will you drop me altogether now that the experiment is over, Colonel Pickering?

PICKERING   Oh dont. You mustnt think of it as an experiment. It shocks me, somehow.

LIZA   Oh, I'm only a squashed cabbage leaf—

PICKERING [*impulsively*]   No.

LIZA [*continuing quietly*]   —but I owe so much to you that I should be very unhappy if you forgot me.

PICKERING   It's very kind of you to say so, Miss Doolittle.

LIZA   It's not because you paid for my dresses. I know you are generous to everybody with money. But it was from you that I learnt really nice manners; and that is what makes one a lady, isnt it? You see it was so very difficult for me with the example of Professor Higgins always before me. I was brought up to be just like him, unable to control myself, and using bad language on the slightest provocation. And I should never have known that ladies and gentlemen didnt behave like that if you hadnt been there.

HIGGINS   Well!!

PICKERING   Oh, thats only his way, you know. He doesnt mean it.

LIZA   Oh, *I* didnt mean it either, when I was a flower girl. It was only my way. But you see I did it; and thats what makes the difference after all.

PICKERING   No doubt. Still, he taught you to speak; and I couldnt have done that, you know.

LIZA [*trivially*]   Of course: that is his profession.

HIGGINS Damnation!

LIZA [*continuing*] It was just like learning to dance in the fashionable way: there was nothing more than that in it. But do you know what began my real education?

PICKERING What?

LIZA [*stopping her work for a moment*] Your calling me Miss Doolittle that day when I first came to Wimpole Street. That was the beginning of self-respect for me. [*She resumes her stitching*]. And there were a hundred little things you never noticed, because they came naturally to you. Things about standing up and taking off your hat and opening door—

PICKERING Oh, that was nothing.

LIZA Yes: things that shewed you thought and felt about me as if I were something better than a scullery-maid; though of course I know you would have been just the same to a scullery-maid if she had been let in the drawing-room. You never took off your boots in the dining room when I was there.

PICKERING You mustnt mind that. Higgins takes off his boots all over the place.

LIZA I know. I am not blaming him. It is his way, isnt it? But it made such a difference to me that you didnt do it. You see, really and truly, apart from the things anyone can pick up (the dressing and the proper way of speaking, and so on), the difference between a lady and a flower girl is not how she behaves, but how shes treated. I shall always be a flower girl to Professor Higgins, because he always treats me as a flower girl, and always will; but I know I can be a lady to you, because you always treat me as a lady, and always will.

MRS. HIGGINS Please dont grind your teeth, Henry.

PICKERING Well, this is really very nice of you, Miss Doolittle.

LIZA I should like you to call me Eliza, now, if you would.

PICKERING Thank you. Eliza, of course.

LIZA   And I should like Professor Higgins to call me Miss Doolittle.

HIGGINS   I'll see you damned first.

MRS. HIGGINS   Henry! Henry!

PICKERING [*laughing*]   Why dont you slang back at him? Dont stand it. It would do him a lot of good.

LIZA   I cant. I could have done it once; but now I cant go back to it. Last night, when I was wandering about, a girl spoke to me; and I tried to get back into the old way with her; but it was no use. You told me, you know, that when a child is brought to a foreign country, it picks up the language in a few weeks, and forgets its own. Well, I am a child in your country. I have forgotten my own language, and can speak nothing but yours. Thats the real break-off with the corner of Tottenham Court Road. Leaving Wimpole Street finishes it.

PICKERING [*much alarmed*]   Oh! but youre coming back to Wimpole Street, arnt you? Youll forgive Higgins?

HIGGINS [*rising*]   Forgive! Will she, by George! Let her go. Let her find out how she can get on without us. She will relapse into the gutter in three weeks without me at her elbow.

DOOLITTLE appears at the centre window. With a look of dignified reproach at HIGGINS, he comes slowly and silently to his daughter, who, with her back to the window, is unconscious of his approach.

PICKERING   Hes incorrigible, Eliza. You wont relapse, will you?

LIZA   No: Not now. Never again. I have learnt my lesson. I dont believe I could utter one of the old sounds if I tried. [*DOOLIT-TLE touches her on her left shoulder. She drops her work, losing her self-possession utterly at the spectacle of her father's splendor*] A-a-a-a-a-ah-ow-ooh!

HIGGINS [*with a crow of triumph*]   Aha! Just so. A-a-a-a-ahowooh! A-a-a-a-ahowooh! A-a-a-a-ahowooh! Victory! Victory! [*He throws himself on the divan, folding his arms, and spraddling arrogantly*].

DOOLITTLE· Can you blame the girl? Dont look at me like that, Eliza. It aint my fault. Ive come into some money.

LIZA   You must have touched a millionaire this time, dad.

DOOLITTLE   I have. But I'm dressed something special today. I'm going to St. George's, Hanover Square.*Your stepmother is going to marry me.

LIZA [*angrily*]   Youre going to let yourself down to marry that low common woman!

PICKERING [*quietly*]   He ought to, Eliza. [*To DOOLITTLE*] Why has she changed her mind?

DOOLITTLE [*sadly*]   Intimidated. Governor. Intimidated. Middle class morality claims its victim. Wont you put on your hat, Liza, and come and see me turned off?

LIZA   If the Colonel says I must, I—I'll [*almost sobbing*] I'll demean myself. And get insulted for my pains, like enough.

DOOLITTLE   Dont be afraid: she never comes to words with anyone now, poor woman! respectability has broke all the spirit out of her.

PICKERING [*squeezing ELIZA's elbow gently*]   Be kind to them, Eliza. Make the best of it.

LIZA [*forcing a little smile for him through her vexation*]   Oh well, just to shew theres no ill feeling. I'll be back in a moment. [*She goes out*].

DOOLITTLE [*sitting down beside PICKERING*]   I feel uncommon nervous about the ceremony, Colonel. I wish youd come and see me through it.

PICKERING   But youve been through it before, man. You were married to Eliza's mother.

DOOLITTLE   Who told you that, Colonel?

PICKERING   Well, nobody told me. But I concluded—naturally—

DOOLITTLE   No: that aint the natural way, Colonel: it's only

---

*Church where wealthy people married.

the middle class way. My way was always the undeserving way. But dont say nothing to Eliza. She dont know: I always had a delicacy about telling her.

PICKERING   Quite right. We'll leave it so, if you dont mind.

DOOLITTLE   And youll come to the church, Colonel, and put me through straight?

PICKERING   With pleasure. As far as a bachelor can.

MRS. HIGGINS   May I come, Mr. Doolittle? I should be very sorry to miss your wedding.

DOOLITTLE   I should indeed be honored by your condescension, maam; and my poor old woman would take it as a tremenjous compliment. Shes been very low, thinking of the happy days that are no more.

MRS. HIGGINS [rising]   I'll order the carriage and get ready. [The men rise, except HIGGINS]. I shant be more than fifteen minutes. [As she goes to the door ELIZA comes in, hatted and buttoning her gloves]. I'm going to the church to see your father married, Eliza. You had better come in the brougham* with me. Colonel Pickering can go on with the bridegroom.

MRS. HIGGINS goes out. ELIZA comes to the middle of the room between the centre window and the ottoman. Pickering joins her.

DOOLITTLE   Bridegroom! What a word! It makes a man realize his position, somehow. [He takes up his hat and goes towards the door].

PICKERING   Before I go, Eliza, do forgive him and come back to us.

LIZA   I dont think papa would allow me. Would you, dad?

DOOLITTLE [sad but magnanimous]   They played you off very cunning, Eliza, them two sportsmen. If it had been only one of them, you could have nailed him. But you see, there was two; and one of them chaperoned the other, as you might say. [To PICKERING] It was artful of you, Colonel; but I bear no

*Horse-drawn closed carriage with the driver outside in front.

malice: I should have done the same myself. I been the victim
of one woman after another all my life; and I dont grudge you
two getting the better of Eliza. I shant interfere. It's time for
us to go, Colonel. So long, Henry. See you in St. George's,
Eliza. [*He goes out*].

PICKERING [*coaxing*]   Do stay with us, Eliza. [*He follows Doolittle*].

*ELIZA goes out on the balcony to avoid being alone with HIGGINS.
He rises and joins her there. She immediately comes back into the
room and makes for the door; but he goes along the balcony quickly
and gets his back to the door before she reaches it.*

HIGGINS   Well, Eliza, youve had a bit of your own back, as you
call it. Have you had enough? and are you going to be reasonable? Or do you want any more?

LIZA   You want me back only to pick up your slippers and put
up with your tempers and fetch and carry for you.

HIGGINS   I havnt said I wanted you back at all.

LIZA   Oh, indeed. Then what are we talking about?

HIGGINS   About you, not about me. If you come back I shall
treat you just as I have always treated you. I cant change my
nature; and I dont intend to change my manners. My manners
are exactly the same as Colonel Pickering's.

LIZA   Thats not true. He treats a flower girl as if she was a
duchess.

HIGGINS   And I treat a duchess as if she was a flower girl.

LIZA   I see. [*She turns away composedly, and sits on the ottoman, facing the window*]. The same to everybody.

HIGGINS   Just so.

LIZA   Like father.

HIGGINS [*grinning, a little taken down*]   Without accepting the
comparison at all points, Eliza, it's quite true that your father
is not a snob, and that he will be quite at home in any station
of life to which his eccentric destiny may call him. [*Seriously*]
The great secret, Eliza, is not having bad manners or good

manners or any other particular sort of manners, but having the same manner for all human souls: in short, behaving as if you were in Heaven, where there are no third-class carriages, and one soul is as good as another.

LIZA   Amen. You are a born preacher.

HIGGINS [*irritated*]   The question is not whether I treat you rudely, but whether you ever heard me treat anyone else better.

LIZA [*with sudden sincerity*]   I dont care how you treat me. I dont mind your swearing at me. I dont mind a black eye: Ive had one before this. But [*standing up and facing him*] I wont be passed over.

HIGGINS   Then get out of my way; for I wont stop for you. You talk about me as if I were a motor bus.

LIZA   So you are a motor bus: all bounce and go, and no consideration for anyone. But I can do without you: dont think I cant.

HIGGINS   I know you can. I told you you could.

LIZA [*wounded, getting away from him to the other side of the ottoman with her face to the hearth*]   I know you did, you brute. You wanted to get rid of me.

HIGGINS   Liar.

LIZA   Thank you. [*She sits down with dignity*].

HIGGINS   You never asked yourself, I suppose, whether *I* could do without y o u.

LIZA [*earnestly*]   Dont you try to get round me. Youll h a v e to do without me.

HIGGINS [*arrogant*]   I can do without anybody. I have my own soul: my own spark of divine fire. But [*with sudden humility*] I shall miss you, Eliza. [*He sits down near her on the ottoman*]. I have learnt something from your idiotic notions: I confess that humbly and gratefully. And I have grown accustomed to your voice and appearance. I like them, rather.

LIZA   Well, you have both of them on your gramophone and in your book of photographs. When you feel lonely without me, you can turn the machine on. It's got no feelings to hurt.

HIGGINS   I cant turn your soul on. Leave me those feelings; and you can take away the voice and the face. They are not you.

LIZA   Oh, you a r e a devil. You can twist the heart in a girl as easy as some could twist her arms to hurt her. Mrs. Pearce warned me. Time and again she has wanted to leave you; and you always got round her at the last minute. And you dont care a bit for her. And you dont care a bit for me.

HIGGINS   I care for life, for humanity; and you are a part of it that has come my way and been built into my house. What more can you or anyone ask?

LIZA   I wont care for anybody that doesnt care for me.

HIGGINS   Commercial principles, Eliza. Like [*reproducing her Covent Garden pronunciation with professional exactness*] s'yollin voylets [selling violets], isnt it?

LIZA   Dont sneer at me. It's mean to sneer at me.

HIGGINS   I have never sneered in my life. Sneering doesnt become either the human face or the human soul. I am expressing my righteous contempt for Commercialism. I dont and wont trade in affection. You call me a brute because you couldnt buy a claim on me by fetching my slippers and finding my spectacles. You were a fool: I think a woman fetching a man's slippers is a disgusting sight: did I ever fetch y o u r slippers? I think a good deal more of you for throwing them in my face. No use slaving for me and then saying you want to be cared for: who cares for a slave? If you come back, come back for the sake of good fellowship; for youll get nothing else. Youve had a thousand times as much out of me as I have out of you; and if you dare to set up your little dog's tricks of fetching and carrying slippers against my creation of a Duchess Eliza, I'll slam the door in your silly face.

LIZA   What did you do it for if you didnt care for me?

HIGGINS [*heartily*]   Why, because it was my job.

LIZA   You never thought of the trouble it would make for me.

HIGGINS   Would the world ever have been made if its maker
had been afraid of making trouble? Making life means making
trouble. Theres only one way of escaping trouble; and thats
killing things. Cowards, you notice, are always shrieking to
have troublesome people killed.

LIZA   I'm no preacher: I dont notice things like that. I notice
that you dont notice me.

HIGGINS [*jumping up and walking about intolerantly*]   Eliza: youre
an idiot. I waste the treasures of my Miltonic mind* by
spreading them before you. Once for all, understand that I go
my way and do my work without caring twopence what happens to either of us. I am not intimidated, like your father and
your stepmother. So you can come back or go to the devil:
which you please.

LIZA   What am I to come back for?

HIGGINS [*bouncing up on his knees on the ottoman and leaning over
it to her*]   For the fun of it. Thats why I took you on.

LIZA [*with averted face*]   And you may throw me out tomorrow
if I dont do everything you want me to?

HIGGINS   Yes; and you may walk out tomorrow if I dont do
everything y o u want me to.

LIZA   And live with my stepmother?

HIGGINS   Yes, or sell flowers.

LIZA   Oh! if I only c o u l d go back to my flower basket! I
should be independent of both you and father and all the
world! Why did you take my independence from me? Why did
I give it up? I'm a slave now, for all my fine clothes.

HIGGINS   Not a bit. I'll adopt you as my daughter and settle
money on you if you like. Or would you rather marry Pickering?

---

*Higgins is explicitly identifying himself with Milton (see note 7 for this play).

LIZA [*looking fiercely round at him*]   I wouldnt marry y o u if you asked me; and youre nearer my age than what he is.

HIGGINS [*gently*]   Than he is: not "than what he is."

LIZA [*losing her temper and rising*]   I'll talk as I like. Youre not my teacher now.

HIGGINS [*reflectively*]   I dont suppose Pickering would, though. Hes as confirmed an old bachelor as I am.

LIZA   Thats not what I want; and dont you think it. Ive always had chaps enough wanting me that way. Freddy Hill writes to me twice and three times a day, sheets and sheets.

HIGGINS [*disagreeably surprised*]   Damn his impudence! [*He recoils and finds himself sitting on his heels*].

LIZA   He has a right to if he likes, poor lad. And he does love me.

HIGGINS [*getting off the ottoman*]   You have no right to encourage him.

LIZA   Every girl has a right to be loved.

HIGGINS   What! By fools like that?

LIZA   Freddy's not a fool. And if hes weak and poor and wants me, may be hed make me happier than my betters that bully me and dont want me.

HIGGINS   Can he m a k e anything of you? Thats the point.

LIZA   Perhaps I could make something of him. But I never thought of us making anything of one another; and you never think of anything else. I only want to be natural.

HIGGINS   In short, you want me to be as infatuated about you as Freddy? Is that it?

LIZA   No I dont. Thats not the sort of feeling I want from you. And dont you be too sure of yourself or of me. I could have been a bad girl if I'd liked. Ive seen more of some things than you, for all your learning. Girls like me can drag gentlemen down to make love to them easy enough. And they wish each other dead the next minute.

HIGGINS   Of course they do. Then what in thunder are we quarrelling about?

LIZA [*much troubled*]   I want a little kindness. I know I'm a common ignorant girl, and you a book-learned gentleman; but I'm not dirt under your feet. What I done [*correcting herself*] what I did was not for the dresses and the taxis: I did it because we were pleasant together and I come—came—to care for you; not to want you to make love to me, and not forgetting the difference between us, but more friendly like.

HIGGINS   Well, of course. Thats just how I feel. And how Pickering feels. Eliza: youre a fool.

LIZA   Thats not a proper answer to give me [*she sinks on the chair at the writing-table in tears*].

HIGGINS   It's all youll get until you stop being a common idiot. If youre going to be a lady, youll have to give up feeling neglected if the men you know dont spend half their time snivelling over you and the other half giving you black eyes. If you cant stand the coldness of my sort of life, and the strain of it, go back to the gutter. Work til you are more a brute than a human being; and then cuddle and squabble and drink til you fall asleep. Oh, it's a fine life, the life of the gutter. It's real: it's warm: it's violent: you can feel it through the thickest skin: you can taste it and smell it without any training or any work. Not like Science and Literature and Classical Music and Philosophy and Art. You find me cold, unfeeling, selfish, dont you? Very well: be off with you to the sort of people you like. Marry some sentimental hog or other with lots of money, and a thick pair of lips to kiss you with and a thick pair of boots to kick you with. If you cant appreciate what youve got, youd better get what you can appreciate.

LIZA [*desperate*]   Oh, you are a cruel tyrant. I cant talk to you: you turn everything against me: I'm always in the wrong. But you know very well all the time that youre nothing but a bully. You know I cant go back to the gutter, as you call it, and that I have no real friends in the world but you and the Colonel. You know well I couldnt bear to live with a low common man after you two; and it's wicked and cruel of you to insult me by pretending I could. You think I must go back to Wimpole Street because I have nowhere else to go but father's. But dont you be too sure that you have me under your feet to be trampled on and talked down. I'll marry Freddy, I will, as soon as hes able to support me.

HIGGINS [*sitting down beside her*]   Rubbish! you shall marry an ambassador. You shall marry the Governor-General of India or the Lord-Lieutenant of Ireland, or somebody who wants a deputy-queen. I'm not going to have my masterpiece thrown away on Freddy.

LIZA   You think I like you to say that. But I havnt forgot what you said a minute ago; and I wont be coaxed round as if I was a baby or a puppy. If I cant have kindness, I'll have independence.

HIGGINS   Independence? Thats middle class blasphemy. We are all dependent on one another, every soul of us on earth.

LIZA [*rising determinedly*]   I'll let you see whether I'm dependent on you. If you can preach, I can teach. I'll go and be a teacher.

HIGGINS   Whatll you teach, in heaven's name?

LIZA   What you taught me. I'll teach phonetics.

HIGGINS   Ha! Ha! Ha!

LIZA   I'll offer myself as an assistant to Professor Nepean.

HIGGINS [*rising in a fury*]   What! That impostor! that humbug! that toadying ignoramus! Teach him my methods! my discoveries! You take one step in his direction and I'll wring your neck. [*He lays hands on her*]. Do you hear?

LIZA [*defiantly non-resistant*]   Wring away. What do I care? I knew youd strike me some day. [*He lets her go, stamping with rage at having forgotten himself, and recoils so hastily that he stumbles back into his seat on the ottoman*]. Aha! Now I know how to deal with you. What a fool I was not to think of it before! You cant take away the knowledge you gave me. You said I had a finer ear than you. And I can be civil and kind to people, which is more than you can. Aha! Thats done you, Henry Higgins, it has. Now I dont care that [*snapping her fingers*] for your bullying and your big talk. I'll advertize it in the papers that your duchess is only a flower girl that you taught, and that she'll teach anybody to be a duchess just the same in six months for a thousand guineas. Oh, when I think of myself crawling under your feet and being trampled on and called names, when all the time I had only to lift up my finger to be as good as you, I could just kick myself.

HIGGINS [*wondering at her*]   You damned impudent slut, you! But it's better than snivelling; better than fetching slippers and finding spectacles, isnt it? [*Rising*] By George, Eliza, I said I'd make a woman of you; and I have. I like you like this.

LIZA   Yes: you turn round and make up to me now that I'm not afraid of you, and can do without you.

HIGGINS   Of course I do, you little fool. Five minutes ago you were like a millstone round my neck. Now youre a tower of strength: a consort battleship. You and I and Pickering will be three old bachelors together instead of only two men and a silly girl.

MRS. HIGGINS returns, dressed for the wedding. ELIZA instantly becomes cool and elegant.

MRS. HIGGINS   The carriage is waiting, Eliza. Are you ready?

LIZA   Quite. Is the Professor coming?

MRS. HIGGINS   Certainly not. He cant behave himself in church. He makes remarks out loud all the time on the clergyman's pronunciation.

LIZA   Then I shall not see you again, Professor. Good-bye. [*She goes to the door*].

MRS. HIGGINS [*coming to HIGGINS*]   Good-bye, dear.

HIGGINS   Good-bye, mother. [*He is about to kiss her, when he recollects something*]. Oh, by the way, Eliza, order a ham and a Stilton cheese, will you? And buy me a pair of reindeer gloves,

number eights, and a tie to match that new suit of mine, at
Eale & Binman's. You can choose the color. [*His cheerful, careless, vigorous voice shows that he is incorrigible*].

LIZA [*disdainfully*]   Buy them yourself. [*She sweeps out*].

MRS. HIGGINS   I'm afraid youve spoiled that girl, Henry. But
never mind, dear: I'll buy you the tie and gloves.

HIGGINS [*sunnily*]   Oh, dont bother. She'll buy em all right
enough. Good-bye.

*They kiss. MRS. HIGGINS runs out. HIGGINS, left alone, rattles his
cash in his pocket; chuckles; and disports himself in a highly self-
satisfied manner.*[15]

*   *   *   *   *   *   *   *   *   *

The rest of the story need not be shown in action, and indeed,
would hardly need telling if our imaginations were not so enfee-
bled by their lazy dependence on the ready-mades and reach-me-
downs of the ragshop in which Romance keeps its stock of "happy
endings" to misfit all stories. Now, the history of Eliza Doolittle,
though called a romance because of the transfiguration it records
seems exceedingly improbable, is common enough. Such transfig-
urations have been achieved by hundreds of resolutely ambitious
young women since Nell Gwynne* set them the example by playing queens and fascinating kings in the theatre in which she began
by selling oranges. Nevertheless, people in all directions have assumed, for no other reason than that she became the heroine of a
romance, that she must have married the hero of it. This is unbearable, not only because her little drama, if acted on such a
thoughtless assumption, must be spoiled, but because the true sequel is patent to anyone with a sense of human nature in general,
and of feminine instinct in particular.

Eliza, in telling Higgins she would not marry him if he asked

---

*Eleanor Gwynne (1650–1687), English actress and mistress of King Charles II.

her, was not coquetting: she was announcing a well-considered decision. When a bachelor interests, and dominates, and teaches, and becomes important to a spinster, as Higgins with Eliza, she always, if she has character enough to be capable of it, considers very seriously indeed whether she will play for becoming that bachelor's wife, especially if he is so little interested in marriage that a determined and devoted woman might capture him if she set herself resolutely to do it. Her decision will depend a good deal on whether she is really free to choose; and that, again, will depend on her age and income. If she is at the end of her youth, and has no security for her livelihood, she will marry him because she must marry anybody who will provide for her. But at Eliza's age a good-looking girl does not feel that pressure: she feels free to pick and choose. She is therefore guided by her instinct in the matter. Eliza's instinct tells her not to marry Higgins. It does not tell her to give him up. It is not in the slightest doubt as to his remaining one of the strongest personal interests in her life. It would be very sorely strained if there was another woman likely to supplant her with him. But as she feels sure of him on that last point, she has no doubt at all as to her course, and would not have any, even if the difference of twenty years in age, which seems so great to youth, did not exist between them.

As our own instincts are not appealed to by her conclusion, let us see whether we cannot discover some reason in it. When Higgins excused his indifference to young women on the ground that they had an irresistible rival in his mother, he gave the clue to his inveterate old-bachelordom. The case is uncommon only to the extent that remarkable mothers are uncommon. If an imaginative boy has a sufficiently rich mother who has intelligence, personal grace, dignity of character without harshness, and a cultivated sense of the best art of her time to enable her to make her house beautiful, she sets a standard for him against which very few women can struggle, besides effecting for him a disengagement of his affections, his sense of beauty, and his idealism from his specifically sexual impulses. This makes him a standing puzzle to the huge number of uncultivated people who have been brought up in tasteless homes by commonplace or disagreeable parents, and to whom, consequently, literature, painting, sculpture, music, and affectionate personal relations come as modes of sex if they come at all. The word passion means nothing else to them; and that Higgins could have a passion for phonetics and idealize his mother instead of Eliza, would seem to them absurd and unnatural. Nevertheless, when we look round and see that hardly anyone is too ugly or disagreeable to find a wife or a husband if he or she wants one, whilst many old maids and bachelors are above the average in quality and culture, we cannot help suspecting that the disentanglement of sex from the associations with which it is so commonly confused, a disentanglement which persons of genius achieve by sheer intellectual analysis, is sometimes produced or aided by parental fascination.

Now, though Eliza was incapable of thus explaining to herself Higgins's formidable powers of resistance to the charm that prostrated Freddy at the first glance, she was instinctively aware that she could never obtain a complete grip of him, or come between him and his mother (the first necessity of the married woman). To put it shortly, she knew that for some mysterious reason he had not the makings of a married man in him, according to her conception of a husband as one to whom she would be his nearest and fondest and warmest interest. Even had there been no mother-rival, she would still have refused to accept an interest in herself that was secondary to philosophic interests. Had Mrs. Higgins died, there would still have been Milton and the Universal Alphabet. Landor's remark that to those who have the greatest power of loving, love is a secondary affair, would not have recommended Landor to Eliza. Put that along with her resentment of Higgins's domineering superiority, and her mistrust of his coaxing cleverness in getting round her and evading her wrath when he had gone too far with his impetuous bullying, and you will see that

Eliza's instinct had good grounds for warning her not to marry her Pygmalion.

And now, whom did Eliza marry? For if Higgins was a predestinate old bachelor, she was most certainly not a predestinate old maid. Well, that can be told very shortly to those who have not guessed it from the indications she has herself given them.

Almost immediately after Eliza is stung into proclaiming her considered determination not to marry Higgins, she mentions the fact that young Mr. Frederick Eynsford Hill is pouring out his love for her daily through the post. Now Freddy is young, practically twenty years younger than Higgins: he is a gentleman (or, as Eliza would qualify him, a toff),* and speaks like one; he is nicely dressed, is treated by the Colonel as an equal, loves her unaffectedly, and is not her master, nor ever likely to dominate her in spite of his advantage of social standing. Eliza has no use for the foolish romantic tradition that all women love to be mastered, if not actually bullied and beaten. "When you go to women," says Nietzsche, "take your whip with you." Sensible despots have never confined that precaution to women: they have taken their whips with them when they have dealt with men, and been slavishly idealized by the men over whom they have flourished the whip much more than by women. No doubt there are slavish women as well as slavish men; and women, like men, admire those that are stronger than themselves. But to admire a strong person and to live under that strong person's thumb are two different things. The weak may not be admired and hero-worshipped; but they are by no means disliked or shunned; and they never seem to have the least difficulty in marrying people who are too good for them. They may fail in emergencies; but life is not one long emergency: it is mostly a string of situations for which no exceptional strength is needed, and with which even rather weak people can cope if they have a stronger partner to help them out. Accordingly, it is a

---

*Slang for a member of the upper class whose clothes indicate his status.

truth everywhere in evidence that strong people, masculine or feminine, not only do not marry stronger people, but do not shew any preference for them in selecting their friends. When a lion meets another with a louder roar "the first lion thinks the last a bore." The man or woman who feels strong enough for two, seeks for every other quality in a partner than strength.

The converse is also true. Weak people want to marry strong people who do not frighten them too much; and this often leads them to make the mistake we describe metaphorically as "biting off more than they can chew." They want too much for too little; and when the bargain is unreasonable beyond all bearing, the union becomes impossible: it ends in the weaker party being either discarded or borne as a cross, which is worse. People who are not only weak, but silly or obtuse as well, are often in these difficulties.

This being the state of human affairs, what is Eliza fairly sure to do when she is placed between Freddy and Higgins? Will she look forward to a lifetime of fetching Higgins's slippers or to a lifetime of Freddy fetching hers? There can be no doubt about the answer. Unless Freddy is biologically repulsive to her, and Higgins biologically attractive to a degree that overwhelms all her other instincts, she will, if she marries either of them, marry Freddy.

And that is just what Eliza did.

Complications ensued; but they were economic, not romantic. Freddy had no money and no occupation. His mother's jointure,* a last relic of the opulence of Largelady Park, had enabled her to struggle along in Earlscourt with an air of gentility, but not to procure any serious secondary education for her children, much less give the boy a profession. A clerkship at thirty shillings a week was beneath Freddy's dignity, and extremely distasteful to him besides. His prospects consisted of a hope that if he kept up appearances

---

*Condition of marriage whereby a widow can draw income from her husband's estate.

somebody would do something for him. The something appeared vaguely to his imagination as a private secretaryship or a sinecure of some sort. To his mother it perhaps appeared as a marriage to some lady of means who could not resist her boy's niceness. Fancy her feelings when he married a flower girl who had become déclassée under extraordinary circumstances which were now notorious!

It is true that Eliza's situation did not seem wholly ineligible. Her father, though formerly a dustman, and now fantastically disclassed, had become extremely popular in the smartest society by a social talent which triumphed over every prejudice and every disadvantage. Rejected by the middle class, which he loathed, he had shot up at once into the highest circles by his wit, his dustmanship (which he carried like a banner), and his Nietzschean transcendence of good and evil. At intimate ducal dinners he sat on the right hand of the Duchess; and in country houses he smoked in the pantry and was made much of by the butler when he was not feeding in the dining-room and being consulted by cabinet ministers. But he found it almost as hard to do all this on four thousand a year as Mrs. Eynsford Hill to live in Earlscourt on an income so pitiably smaller that I have not the heart to disclose its exact figure. He absolutely refused to add the last straw to his burden by contributing to Eliza's support.

Thus Freddy and Eliza, now Mr. and Mrs. Eynsford Hill, would have spent a penniless honeymoon but for a wedding present of £500 from the Colonel to Eliza. It lasted a long time because Freddy did not know how to spend money, never having had any to spend, and Eliza, socially trained by a pair of old bachelors, wore her clothes as long as they held together and looked pretty, without the least regard to their being many months out of fashion. Still, £500 will not last two young people for ever; and they both knew, and Eliza felt as well, that they must shift for themselves in the end. She could quarter herself on Wimpole Street because it had come to be her home; but she was quite aware that she ought not to quarter Freddy there, and that it would not be good for his character if she did.

Not that the Wimpole Street bachelors objected. When she consulted them, Higgins declined to be bothered about her housing problem when that solution was so simple. Eliza's desire to have Freddy in the house with her seemed of no more importance than if she had wanted an extra piece of bedroom furniture. Pleas as to Freddy's character, and the moral obligation on him to earn his own living, were lost on Higgins. He denied that Freddy had any character, and declared that if he tried to do any useful work some competent person would have the trouble of undoing it: a procedure involving a net loss to the community, and great unhappiness to Freddy himself, who was obviously intended by Nature for such light work as amusing Eliza, which, Higgins declared, was a much more useful and honorable occupation than working in the city. When Eliza referred again to her project of teaching phonetics, Higgins abated not a jot of his violent opposition to it. He said she was not within ten years of being qualified to meddle with his pet subject; and as it was evident that the Colonel agreed with him, she felt she could not go against them in this grave matter, and that she had no right, without Higgins's consent, to exploit the knowledge he had given her; for his knowledge seemed to her as much his private property as his watch: Eliza was no communist. Besides, she was superstitiously devoted to them both, more entirely and frankly after her marriage than before it.

It was the Colonel who finally solved the problem, which had cost him much perplexed cogitation. He one day asked Eliza, rather shyly, whether she had quite given up her notion of keeping a flower shop. She replied that she had thought of it, but had put it out of her head, because the Colonel had said, that day at Mrs. Higgins's, that it would never do. The Colonel confessed that when he said that, he had not quite recovered from the dazzling impression of the day before. They broke the matter to Higgins that evening. The sole comment vouchsafed by him very nearly led to a serious quarrel with Eliza. It was to the effect that she would have in Freddy an ideal errand boy.

Freddy himself was next sounded on the subject. He said he had been thinking of a shop himself; though it had presented itself to his pennilessness as a small place in which Eliza should sell tobacco at one counter whilst he sold newspapers at the opposite one. But he agreed that it would be extraordinarily jolly to go early every morning with Eliza to Covent Garden and buy flowers on the scene of their first meeting: a sentiment which earned him many kisses from his wife. He added that he had always been afraid to propose anything of the sort, because Clara would make an awful row about a step that must damage her matrimonial chances, and his mother could not be expected to like it after clinging for so many years to that step of the social ladder on which retail trade is impossible.

This difficulty was removed by an event highly unexpected by Freddy's mother. Clara, in the course of her incursions into those artistic circles which were the highest within her reach, discovered that her conversational qualifications were expected to include a grounding in the novels of Mr. H. G. Wells. She borrowed them in various directions so energetically that she swallowed them all within two months. The result was a conversion of a kind quite common today. A modern Acts of the Apostles* would fill fifty whole Bibles if anyone were capable of writing it.

Poor Clara, who appeared to Higgins and his mother as a disagreeable and ridiculous person, and to her own mother as in some inexplicable way a social failure, had never seen herself in either light; for, though to some extent ridiculed and mimicked in West Kensington like everybody else there, she was accepted as a rational and normal—or shall we say inevitable?—sort of human being. At worst they called her The Pusher; but to them no more

---

*New Testament book that recounts the proselytizing travels of Saints Peter and Paul.

than to herself had it ever occurred that she was pushing the air, and pushing it in a wrong direction. Still, she was not happy. She was growing desperate. Her one asset, the fact that her mother was what the Epsom greengrocer called a carriage lady had no exchange value, apparently. It had prevented her from getting educated, because the only education she could have afforded was education with the Earlscourt greengrocer's daughter. It had led her to seek the society of her mother's class; and that class simply would not have her, because she was much poorer than the greengrocer, and, far from being able to afford a maid, could not afford even a housemaid, and had to scrape along at home with an illiberally treated general servant. Under such circumstances nothing could give her an air of being a genuine product of Largelady Park. And yet its tradition made her regard a marriage with anyone within her reach as an unbearable humiliation. Commercial people and professional people in a small way were odious to her. She ran after painters and novelists; but she did not charm them; and her bold attempts to pick up and practise artistic and literary talk irritated them. She was, in short, an utter failure, an ignorant, incompetent, pretentious, unwelcome, penniless, useless little snob; and though she did not admit these disqualifications (for nobody ever faces unpleasant truths of this kind until the possibility of a way out dawns on them) she felt their effects too keenly to be satisfied with her position.

Clara had a startling eyeopener when, on being suddenly wakened to enthusiasm by a girl of her own age who dazzled her and produced in her a gushing desire to take her for a model, and gain her friendship, she discovered that this exquisite apparition had graduated from the gutter in a few months' time. It shook her so violently, that when Mr. H. G. Wells lifted her on the point of his puissant pen, and placed her at the angle of view from which the life she was leading and the society to which she clung appeared in its true relation to real human needs and worthy social structure, he effected a conversion and a conviction of sin comparable to the most sensational feats of General Booth or Gypsy Smith. Clara's snobbery went bang. Life suddenly began to move with her. Without knowing how or why, she began to make friends and enemies. Some of the acquaintances to whom she had been a tedious or indifferent or ridiculous affliction, dropped her: others became cordial. To her amazement she found that some "quite nice" people were saturated with Wells, and that this accessibility to ideas was the secret of their niceness. People she had thought deeply religious, and had tried to conciliate on that tack with disastrous results, suddenly took an interest in her, and revealed a hostility to conventional religion which she had never conceived possible except among the most desperate characters. They made her read Galsworthy; and Galsworthy exposed the vanity of Largelady Park and finished her. It exasperated her to think that the dungeon in which she had languished for so many unhappy years had been unlocked all the time, and that the impulses she had so carefully struggled with and stifled for the sake of keeping well with society, were precisely those by which alone she could have come into any sort of sincere human contact. In the radiance of these discoveries, and the tumult of their reaction, she made a fool of herself as freely and conspicuously as when she so rashly adopted Eliza's expletive in Mrs. Higgins's drawing-room; for the new-born Wellsian had to find her bearings almost as ridiculously as a baby; but nobody hates a baby for its ineptitudes, or thinks the worse of it for trying to eat the matches; and Clara lost no friends by her follies. They laughed at her to her face this time; and she had to defend herself and fight it out as best she could.

When Freddy paid a visit to Earlscourt (which he never did when he could possibly help it) to make the desolating announcement that he and his Eliza were thinking of blackening the Largelady scutcheon by opening a shop, he found the little household already convulsed by a prior announcement from Clara that she also was going to work in an old furniture shop in Dover Street, which had been started by a fellow Wellsian. This appointment

Clara owed, after all, to her old social accomplishment of Push. She had made up her mind that, cost what it might, she would see Mr. Wells in the flesh; and she had achieved her end at a garden party. She had better luck than so rash an enterprise deserved. Mr. Wells came up to her expectations. Age had not withered him, nor could custom stale his infinite variety[16] in half an hour. His pleasant neatness and compactness, his small hands and feet, his teeming ready brain, his unaffected accessibility, and a certain fine apprehensiveness which stamped him as susceptible from his topmost hair to his tipmost toe, proved irresistible. Clara talked of nothing else for weeks and weeks afterwards. And as she happened to talk to the lady of the furniture shop, and that lady also desired above all things to know Mr. Wells and sell pretty things to him, she offered Clara a job on the chance of achieving that end through her.

And so it came about that Eliza's luck held, and the expected opposition to the flower shop melted away. The shop is in the arcade of a railway station not very far from the Victoria and Albert Museum; and if you live in that neighborhood you may go there any day and buy a buttonhole from Eliza.

Now here is a last opportunity for romance. Would you not like to be assured that the shop was an immense success, thanks to Eliza's charms and her early business experience in Covent Garden? Alas! the truth is the truth: the shop did not pay for a long time, simply because Eliza and her Freddy did not know how to keep it. True, Eliza had not to begin at the very beginning: she knew the names and prices of the cheaper flowers; and her elation was unbounded when she found that Freddy, like all youths educated at cheap, pretentious, and thoroughly inefficient schools, knew a little Latin. It was very little, but enough to make him appear to her a Porson or Bentley,* and to put him at his ease with

---

*Richard Porson (1759–1808) and Richard Bentley (1662–1742) were noted English classical scholars; Bentley, as Milton's first editor, foolishly rewrote lines in *Paradise Lost*.

botanical nomenclature. Unfortunately he knew nothing else; and Eliza, though she could count money up to eighteen shillings or so, and had acquired a certain familiarity with the language of Milton from her struggles to qualify herself for winning Higgins's bet, could not write out a bill without utterly disgracing the establishment. Freddy's power of stating in Latin that Balbus* built a wall and that Gaul was divided into three parts did not carry with it the slightest knowledge of accounts or business: Colonel Pickering had to explain to him what a cheque book and a bank account meant. And the pair were by no means easily teachable. Freddy backed up Eliza in her obstinate refusal to believe that they could save money by engaging a bookkeeper with some knowledge of the business. How, they argued, could you possibly save money by going to extra expense when you already could not make both ends meet? But the Colonel, after making the ends meet over and over again, at last gently insisted; and Eliza, humbled to the dust by having to beg from him so often, and stung by the uproarious derision of Higgins, to whom the notion of Freddy succeeding at anything was a joke that never palled, grasped the fact that business, like phonetics, has to be learned.

On the piteous spectacle of the pair spending their evenings in shorthand schools and polytechnic classes, learning bookkeeping and typewriting with incipient junior clerks, male and female, from the elementary schools, let me not dwell. There were even classes at the London School of Economics, and a humble personal appeal to the director of that institution to recommend a course bearing on the flower business. He, being a humorist, explained to them the method of the celebrated Dickensian essay on Chinese Metaphysics by the gentleman who read an article on China and an article on Metaphysics and combined the information. He suggested that they should combine the London School with Kew Gardens. Eliza, to whom the procedure of the Dickensian gentle-

---

*Lucius Cornelius Balbus (first century B.C.), Julius Caesar's chief of engineers.

man seemed perfectly correct (as in fact it was) and not in the least funny (which was only her ignorance) took his advice with entire gravity. But the effort that cost her the deepest humiliation was a request to Higgins, whose pet artistic fancy, next to Milton's verse, was calligraphy, and who himself wrote a most beautiful Italian hand, that he would teach her to write. He declared that she was congenitally incapable of forming a single letter worthy of the least of Milton's words; but she persisted; and again he suddenly threw himself into the task of teaching her with a combination of stormy intensity, concentrated patience, and occasional bursts of interesting disquisition on the beauty and nobility, the august mission and destiny, of human handwriting. Eliza ended by acquiring an extremely uncommercial script which was a positive extension of her personal beauty, and spending three times as much on stationery as anyone else because certain qualities and shapes of paper became indispensable to her. She could not even address an envelope in the usual way because it made the margins all wrong.

Their commercial school days were a period of disgrace and despair for the young couple. They seemed to be learning nothing about flower shops. At last they gave it up as hopeless, and shook the dust of the shorthand schools, and the polytechnics, and the London School of Economics from their feet for ever. Besides, the business was in some mysterious way beginning to take care of itself. They had somehow forgotten their objections to employing other people. They came to the conclusion that their own way was the best, and that they had really a remarkable talent for business. The Colonel, who had been compelled for some years to keep a sufficient sum on current account at his bankers to make up their deficits, found that the provision was unnecessary: the young people were prospering. It is true that there was not quite fair play between them and their competitors in trade. Their week-ends in the country cost them nothing, and saved them the price of their Sunday dinners; for the motor car was the Colonel's; and he and Higgins paid the hotel bills. Mr. F. Hill, florist and greengrocer (they soon discovered that there was money in asparagus; and asparagus led to other vegetables), had an air which stamped the business as classy; and in private life he was still Frederick Eynsford Hill, Esquire. Not that there was any swank* about him: nobody but Eliza knew that he had been christened Frederick Challoner. Eliza herself swanked like anything.

That is all. That is how it has turned out. It is astonishing how much Eliza still manages to meddle in the housekeeping at Wimpole Street in spite of the shop and her own family. And it is notable that though she never nags her husband, and frankly loves the Colonel as if she were his favorite daughter, she has never got out of the habit of nagging Higgins that was established on the fatal night when she won his bet for him. She snaps his head off on the faintest provocation, or on none. He no longer dares to tease her by assuming an abysmal inferiority of Freddy's mind to his own. He storms and bullies and derides; but she stands up to him so ruthlessly that the Colonel has to ask her from time to time to be kinder to Higgins; and it is the only request of his that brings a mulish expression into her face. Nothing but some emergency or calamity great enough to break down all likes and dislikes, and throw them both back on their common humanity—and may they be spared any such trial!—will ever alter this. She knows that Higgins does not need her, just as her father did not need her. The very scrupulousness with which he told her that day that he had become used to having her there, and dependent on her for all sorts of little services, and that he should miss her if she went away (it would never have occurred to Freddy or the Colonel to say anything of the sort) deepens her inner certainty that she is "no more to him than them slippers," yet she has a sense, too, that his indifference is deeper than the infatuation of commoner souls. She is immensely interested in him. She has even secret mischievous moments in which she wishes she could get him alone, on a desert is-

---

*Air of superiority; pretentiousness.

land, away from all ties and with nobody else in the world to consider, and just drag him off his pedestal and see him making love
like any common man. We all have private imaginations of that
sort. But when it comes to business, to the life that she really leads
as distinguished from the life of dreams and fancies, she likes
Freddy and she likes the Colonel; and she does not like Higgins
and Mr. Doolittle. Galatea never does quite like Pygmalion: his relation to her is too godlike to be altogether agreeable.

HEARTBREAK HOUSE

HEARTBREAK HOUSE AND HORSEBACK HALL[1]

WHERE HEARTBREAK HOUSE STANDS

HEARTBREAK HOUSE IS not merely the name of the play which follows this preface. It is cultured, leisured Europe before the war. When the play was begun not a shot had been fired; and only the professional diplomatists and the very few amateurs whose hobby is foreign policy even knew that the guns were loaded. A Russian playwright, Tchekov, had produced four fascinating dramatic studies of Heartbreak House, of which three, The Cherry Orchard, Uncle Vanya, and The Seagull, had been performed in England. Tolstoy, in his Fruits of Enlightenment, had shown us through it in his most ferociously contemptuous manner. Tolstoy did not waste any sympathy on it: it was to him the house in which Europe was stifling its soul; and he knew that our utter enervation and futilization in that overheated drawing-room atmosphere was delivering the world over to the control of ignorant and soulless cunning and energy, with the frightful consequences which have now overtaken it. Tolstoy was no pessimist: he was not disposed to leave the house standing if he could bring it down about the ears of its pretty and amiable voluptuaries; and he wielded the pickaxe with a will. He treated the case of the inmates as one of opium poisoning, to be dealt with by seizing the patients roughly and exercising them violently until they were broad awake. Tchekov, more of a fatalist, had no faith in these charming people extricating themselves. They would, he thought, be sold up and sent adrift by the bailiffs; and he therefore had no scruple in exploiting and even flattering their charm.

THE INHABITANTS

Tchekov's plays, being less lucrative than swings and roundabouts, got no further in England, where theatres are only ordinary commercial affairs, than a couple of performances by the Stage Society. We stared and said, "How Russian!" They did not strike me in that way. Just as Ibsen's intensely Norwegian plays exactly fitted every middle and professional class suburb in Europe, these intensely Russian plays fitted all the country houses in Europe in which the pleasures of music, art, literature, and the theatre had supplanted hunting, shooting, fishing, flirting, eating, and drinking. The same nice people, the same utter futility. The nice people could read; some of them could write; and they were the sole repositories of culture who had social opportunities of contact with our politicians, administrators, and newspaper proprietors, or any chance of sharing or influencing their activities. But they shrank from that contact. They hated politics. They did not wish to realize Utopia for the common people: they wished to realize their favorite fictions and poems in their own lives; and, when they could, they lived without scruple on incomes which they did nothing to earn. The women in their girlhood made themselves look like variety theatre stars, and settled down later into the types of beauty imagined by the previous generation of painters. They took the only part of our society in which there was leisure for high culture, and made it an economic, political, and, as far as practicable, a moral vacuum; and as Nature, abhorring the vacuum, immediately filled it up with sex and with all sorts of refined pleasures, it was a very delightful place at its best for moments of relaxation. In other moments it was disastrous. For prime ministers and their like, it was a veritable Capua.

HORSEBACK HALL

But where were our front benchers to nest if not here? The alternative to Heartbreak House was Horseback Hall, consisting of a prison for horses with an annex for the ladies and gentlemen who rode them, hunted them, talked about them, bought them and sold them, and gave nine-tenths of their lives to them, dividing the other tenth between charity, churchgoing (as a substitute for religion), and conservative electioneering (as a substitute for politics). It is true that the two establishments got mixed at the edges. Exiles from the library, the music room, and the picture gallery would be found languishing among the stables, miserably discontented; and hardy horsewomen who slept at the first chord of Schumann were born, horribly misplaced, into the garden of Klingsor;[2] but sometimes one came upon horsebreakers and heartbreakers who could make the best of both worlds. As a rule, however, the two were apart and knew little of one another; so the prime minister folk had to choose between barbarism and Capua. And of the two atmospheres it is hard to say which was the more fatal to statesmanship.

REVOLUTION ON THE SHELF

Heartbreak House was quite familiar with revolutionary ideas on paper. It aimed at being advanced and freethinking, and hardly ever went to church or kept the Sabbath except by a little extra fun at week-ends. When you spent a Friday to Tuesday in it you found on the shelf in your bedroom not only the books of poets and novelists, but of revolutionary biologists and even economists. Without at least a few plays by myself and Mr Granville Barker, and a few stories by Mr H. G. Wells, Mr Arnold Bennett, and Mr John Galsworthy, the house would have been out of the movement. You would find Blake among the poets, and beside him Bergson, Butler, Scott Haldane,* the poems of Meredith and

---

*John Scott Haldane (1860–1936), Scottish writer and physiologist.

Thomas Hardy, and, generally speaking, all the literary imple-
ments for forming the mind of the perfect modern Socialist and
Creative Evolutionist.* It was a curious experience to spend Sunday in dipping into these books, and on Monday morning to read
in the daily paper that the country had just been brought to the
verge of anarchy because a new Home Secretary or chief of police
without an idea in his head that his great-grandmother might not
have had to apologize for, had refused to "recognize" some powerful Trade Union, just as a gondola might refuse to recognize a
20,000-ton liner.

In short, power and culture were in separate compartments.
The barbarians were not only literally in the saddle, but on the
front bench in the House of Commons, with nobody to correct
their incredible ignorance of modern thought and political science
but upstarts from the counting-house, who had spent their lives
furnishing their pockets instead of their minds. Both, however,
were practised in dealing with money and with men, as far as acquiring the one and exploiting the other went; and although this
is as undesirable an expertness as that of the medieval robber
baron, it qualifies men to keep an estate or a business going in its
old routine without necessarily understanding it, just as Bond
Street tradesmen and domestic servants keep fashionable society
going without any instruction in sociology.

THE CHERRY ORCHARD

The Heartbreak people neither could nor would do anything of
the sort. With their heads as full of the Anticipations† of Mr H. G.
Wells as the heads of our actual rulers were empty even of the an-
ticipations of Erasmus or Sir Thomas More, they refused the
drudgery of politics, and would have made a very poor job of it if

---

*One who believes evolution has direction and purpose; a follower of French
philosopher Henri Bergson (1859–1941) or Shaw.

†Collection of essays published in 1902.

they had changed their minds. Not that they would have been allowed to meddle anyhow, as only through the accident of being a hereditary peer can anyone in these days of Votes for Everybody get into parliament if handicapped by a serious modern cultural equipment; but if they had, their habit of living in a vacuum would have left them helpless and ineffective in public affairs. Even in private life they were often helpless wasters of their inheritance, like the people in Tchekov's Cherry Orchard. Even those who lived within their incomes were really kept going by their solicitors and agents, being unable to manage an estate or run a business without continual prompting from those who have to learn how to do such things or starve.

From what is called Democracy no corrective to this state of things could be hoped. It is said that every people has the Government it deserves. It is more to the point that every Government has the electorate it deserves; for the orators of the front bench can edify or debauch an ignorant electorate at will. Thus our democracy moves in a vicious circle of reciprocal worthiness and unworthiness.

NATURE'S LONG CREDITS

Nature's way of dealing with unhealthy conditions is unfortunately not one that compels us to conduct a solvent hygiene on a cash basis. She demoralizes us with long credits and reckless overdrafts, and then pulls us up cruelly with catastrophic bankruptcies. Take, for example, common domestic sanitation. A whole city generation may neglect it utterly and scandalously, if not with absolute impunity, yet without any evil consequences that anyone thinks of tracing to it. In a hospital two generations of medical students may tolerate dirt and carelessness, and then go out into general practice to spread the doctrine that fresh air is a fad, and sanitation an imposture set up to make profits for plumbers. Then suddenly Nature takes her revenge. She strikes at the city with a pestilence and at the hospital with an epidemic of hospital gangrene, slaughtering right and left until the innocent young have paid for the guilty old, and the account is balanced. And then she goes to sleep again and gives another period of credit, with the same result.

This is what has just happened in our political hygiene. Political science has been as recklessly neglected by Governments and electorates during my lifetime as sanitary science was in the days of Charles the Second. In international relations diplomacy has been a boyishly lawless affair of family intrigues, commercial and territorial brigandage, torpors of pseudo-goodnature produced by laziness and spasms of ferocious activity produced by terror. But in these islands we muddled through. Nature gave us a longer credit than she gave to France or Germany or Russia. To British centenarians who died in their beds in 1914, any dread of having to hide underground in London from the shells of an enemy seemed more remote and fantastic than a dread of the appearance of a colony of cobras and rattlesnakes in Kensington Gardens. In the prophetic works of Charles Dickens we were warned against many evils which have since come to pass; but of the evil of being slaughtered by a foreign foe on our own doorsteps there was no shadow. Nature gave us a very long credit; and we abused it to the utmost. But when she struck at last she struck with a vengeance. For four years she smote our first-born and heaped on us plagues of which Egypt never dreamed. They were all as preventible as the great Plague of London, and came solely because they had not been prevented. They were not undone by winning the war. The earth is still bursting with the dead bodies of the victors.

THE WICKED HALF CENTURY

It is difficult to say whether indifference and neglect are worse than false doctrine; but Heartbreak House and Horseback Hall unfortunately suffered from both. For half a century before the war civilization had been going to the devil very precipitately under the influence of a pseudo-science as disastrous as the blackest Calvinism. Calvinism taught that as we are predestinately saved or damned, nothing that we can do can alter our destiny. Still, as Calvinism gave the individual no clue as to whether he had drawn a lucky number or an unlucky one, it left him a fairly strong interest in encouraging his hopes of salvation and allaying his fear of damnation by behaving as one of the elect might be expected to behave rather than as one of the reprobate. But in the middle of the nineteenth century naturalists and physicists assured the world, in the name of Science, that salvation and damnation are all nonsense, and that predestination is the central truth of religion, inasmuch as human beings are produced by their environment, their sins and good deeds being only a series of chemical and mechanical reactions over which they have no control. Such figments as mind, choice, purpose, conscience, will, and so forth, are, they taught, mere illusions, produced because they are useful in the continual struggle of the human machine to maintain its environment in a favorable condition, a process incidentally involving the ruthless destruction or subjection of its competitors for the supply (assumed to be limited) of subsistence available. We taught Prussia this religion; and Prussia bettered our instruction so effectively that we presently found ourselves confronted with the necessity of destroying Prussia to prevent Prussia destroying us. And that has just ended in each destroying the other to an extent doubtfully reparable in our time.

It may be asked how so imbecile and dangerous a creed ever came to be accepted by intelligent beings. I will answer that question more fully in my next volume of plays,* which will be entirely devoted to the subject. For the present I will only say that there were better reasons than the obvious one that such sham science as this opened a scientific career to very stupid men, and all the other careers to shameless rascals, provided they were indus-

---

*Reference to *Back to Methuselah* (1921), a cycle of five plays by Shaw that revisit the themes of evolution and human destiny.

trious enough. It is true that this motive operated very powerfully; but when the new departure in scientific doctrine which is associated with the name of the great naturalist Charles Darwin began, it was not only a reaction against a barbarous pseudo-evangelical teleology intolerably obstructive to all scientific progress, but was accompanied, as it happened, by discoveries of extraordinary interest in physics, chemistry, and that lifeless method of evolution which its investigators called Natural Selection. Howbeit, there was only one result possible in the ethical sphere, and that was the banishment of conscience from human affairs, or, as Samuel Butler vehemently put it, "of mind from the universe."

HYPOCHONDRIA

Now Heartbreak House, with Butler and Bergson and Scott Haldane alongside Blake and the other major poets on its shelves (to say nothing of Wagner and the tone poets),* was not so completely blinded by the doltish materialism of the laboratories as the uncultured world outside. But being an idle house it was a hypochondriacal house, always running after cures. It would stop eating meat, not on valid Shelleyan† grounds, but in order to get rid of a bogey called Uric Acid; and it would actually let you pull all its teeth out to exorcise another demon named Pyorrhea.‡ It was superstitious, and addicted to table-rapping, materialization seances, clairvoyance, palmistry, crystal-gazing and the like to such an extent that it may be doubted whether ever before in the history of the world did soothsayers, astrologers, and unregistered therapeutic specialists of all sorts flourish as they did during this half century of the drift to the abyss. The registered doctors and surgeons were hard put to it to compete with the unregistered.

---

*Composers of symphonic poems, such as Nikolay Rimsky-Korsakov (1844–1908).

†Like the English poet Percy Bysshe Shelley (1792–1822), Shaw was a vegetarian.

‡Gum disease.

They were not clever enough to appeal to the imagination and sociability of the Heartbreakers by the arts of the actor, the orator, the poet, the winning conversationalist. They had to fall back coarsely on the terror of infection and death. They prescribed inoculations and operations. Whatever part of a human being could be cut out without necessarily killing him they cut out; and he often died (unnecessarily of course) in consequence. From such trifles as uvulas and tonsils they went on to ovaries and appendices until at last no one's inside was safe. They explained that the human intestine was too long, and that nothing could make a child of Adam healthy except short circuiting the pylorus* by cutting a length out of the lower intestine and fastening it directly to the stomach. As their mechanist theory taught them that medicine was the business of the chemist's laboratory, and surgery of the carpenter's shop, and also that Science (by which they meant their practices) was so important that no consideration for the interests of any individual creature, whether frog or philosopher, much less the vulgar commonplaces of sentimental ethics, could weigh for a moment against the remotest off-chance of an addition to the body of scientific knowledge, they operated and vivisected and inoculated and lied on a stupendous scale, clamoring for and actually acquiring such legal powers over the bodies of their fellow-citizens as neither king, pope, nor parliament dare ever have claimed. The Inquisition itself was a Liberal institution compared to the General Medical Council.

THOSE WHO DO NOT KNOW HOW TO LIVE MUST MAKE A MERIT OF DYING

Heartbreak House was far too lazy and shallow to extricate itself from this palace of evil enchantment. It rhapsodized about love; but it believed in cruelty. It was afraid of the cruel people; and it saw that cruelty was at least effective. Cruelty did things that

---

*Opening from the stomach into the intestine.

made money, whereas Love did nothing but prove the soundness of Larochefoucauld's saying that very few people would fall in love if they had never read about it. Heartbreak House, in short, did not know how to live, at which point all that was left to it was the boast that at least it knew how to die: a melancholy accomplishment which the outbreak of war presently gave it practically unlimited opportunities of displaying. Thus were the firstborn of Heartbreak House smitten; and the young, the innocent, the hopeful expiated the folly and worthlessness of their elders.

WAR DELIRIUM

Only those who have lived through a first-rate war, not in the field, but at home, and kept their heads, can possibly understand the bitterness of Shakespeare and Swift, who both went through this experience. The horror of Peer Gynt* in the madhouse, when the lunatics, exalted by illusions of splendid talent and visions of a dawning millennium, crowned him as their emperor, was tame in comparison. I do not know whether anyone really kept his head completely except those who had to keep it because they had to conduct the war at first hand. I should not have kept my own (as far as I did keep it) if I had not at once understood that as a scribe and speaker I too was under the most serious public obligation to keep my grip on realities; but this did not save me from a considerable degree of hyperaesthesia.† There were of course some happy people to whom the war meant nothing: all political and general matters lying outside their little circle of interest. But the ordinary war-conscious civilian went mad, the main symptom being a conviction that the whole order of nature had been reversed. All foods, he felt, must now be adulterated. All schools must be closed. No advertisements must be sent to the newspapers, of which new editions must appear and be bought up

---

*Eponymous hero of Henrik Ibsen's Faustian verse drama of 1867.

†Abnormal physical or emotional sensitivity.

every ten minutes. Travelling must be stopped, or, that being impossible, greatly hindered. All pretences about fine art and culture
and the like must be flung off as an intolerable affectation; and the
picture galleries and museums and schools at once occupied by
war workers. The British Museum itself was saved only by a hair's
breadth. The sincerity of all this, and of much more which would
not be believed if I chronicled it, may be established by one conclusive instance of the general craziness. Men were seized with the
illusion that they could win the war by giving away money. And
they not only subscribed millions to Funds of all sorts with no discoverable object, and to ridiculous voluntary organizations for
doing what was plainly the business of the civil and military authorities, but actually handed out money to any thief in the street
who had the presence of mind to pretend that he (or she) was "collecting" it for the annihilation of the enemy. Swindlers were em-
boldened to take offices; label themselves Anti-Enemy Leagues;
and simply pocket the money that was heaped on them. Attrac-
tively dressed young women found that they had nothing to do but
parade the streets, collecting-box in hand, and live gloriously on
the profits. Many months elapsed before, as a first sign of returning sanity, the police swept an Anti-Enemy secretary into prison
pour encourager les autres,* and the passionate penny collecting of
the Flag Days was brought under some sort of regulation.

MADNESS IN COURT

The demoralization did not spare the Law Courts. Soldiers were
acquitted, even on fully proved indictments for wilful murder,
until at last the judges and magistrates had to announce that what
was called the Unwritten Law, which meant simply that a soldier
could do what he liked with impunity in civil life, was not the law
of the land, and that a Victoria Cross did not carry with it a perpetual plenary indulgence. Unfortunately the insanity of the juries

---

*As a warning to others; literally, "to encourage others" (French).

and magistrates did not always manifest itself in indulgence. No person unlucky enough to be charged with any sort of conduct, however reasonable and salutary, that did not smack of war delirium, had the slightest chance of acquittal. There were in the country, too, a certain number of people who had conscientious objections to war as criminal or unchristian. The Act of Parliament introducing Compulsory Military Service thoughtlessly exempted these persons, merely requiring them to prove the genuineness of their convictions. Those who did so were very ill-advised from the point of view of their own personal interest; for they were persecuted with savage logicality in spite of the law; whilst those who made no pretence of having any objection to war at all, and had not only had military training in Officers' Training Corps, but had proclaimed on public occasions that they were perfectly ready to engage in civil war on behalf of their political opinions, were allowed the benefit of the Act on the ground that they did not approve of this particular war. For the Christians there was no mercy. In cases where the evidence as to ther being killed by ill treatment was so unequivocal that the verdict would certainly have been one of wilful murder had the prejudice of the coroner's jury been on the other side, their tormentors were gratuitously declared to be blameless. There was only one virtue, pugnacity: only one vice, pacifism. That is an essential condition of war; but the Government had not the courage to legislate accordingly; and its law was set aside for Lynch law.

The climax of legal lawlessness was reached in France. The greatest Socialist statesman in Europe, Jaurès,* was shot and killed by a gentleman who resented his efforts to avert the war. M. Clemenceau† was shot by another gentleman of less popular opinions, and happily came off no worse than having to spend a pre-

---

*Socialist leader Jean Jaurès, who defended Alfred Dreyfus (accused of treason), was assassinated by a fanatical patriot on July 13, 1914.

†Georges Clemenceau (1841–1929) served twice as premier of France.

cautionary couple of days in bed. The slayer of Jaurès was recklessly acquitted: the would-be slayer of M. Clemenceau was carefully found guilty. There is no reason to doubt that the same thing
would have happened in England if the war had begun with a successful attempt to assassinate Keir Hardie,* and ended with an unsuccessful one to assassinate Mr Lloyd George.[3]

THE LONG ARM OF WAR

The pestilence which is the usual accompaniment of war was
called influenza. Whether it was really a war pestilence or not was
made doubtful by the fact that it did its worst in places remote
from the battlefields, notably on the west coast of North America
and in India. But the moral pestilence, which was unquestionably
a war pestilence, reproduced this phenomenon. One would have
supposed that the war fever would have raged most furiously in
the countries actually under fire, and that the others would be
more reasonable. Belgium and Flanders, where over large districts
literally not one stone was left upon another as the opposed
armies drove each other back and forward over it after terrific
preliminary bombardments, might have been pardoned for reliev-
ing their feelings more emphatically than by shrugging their shoulders and saying, "C'est la guerre."† England, inviolate for so many
centuries that the swoop of war on her homesteads had long
ceased to be more credible than a return of the Flood, could
hardly be expected to keep her temper sweet when she knew at
last what it was to hide in cellars and underground railway sta-
tions, or lie quaking in bed, whilst bombs crashed, houses crumbled, and aircraft guns distributed shrapnel on friend and foe alike
until certain shop windows in London, formerly full of fashionable hats, were filled with steel helmets. Slain and mutilated

---

*James Keir Hardie (1856–1915), first leader of the Labour Party in Parlia-
ment.

†That's war (French).

women and children, and burnt and wrecked dwellings, excuse a
good deal of violent language, and produce a wrath on which
many suns go down before it is appeased. Yet it was in the United
States of America, where nobody slept the worse for the war, that
the war fever went beyond all sense and reason. In European
Courts there was vindictive illegality: in American Courts there
was raving lunacy. It is not for me to chronicle the extravagances
of an Ally: let some candid American do that. I can only say that to
us sitting in our gardens in England, with the guns in France making themselves felt by a throb in the air as unmistakeable as an audible sound, or with tightening hearts studying the phases of the
moon in London in their bearing on the chances whether our
houses would be standing or ourselves alive next morning, the
newspaper accounts of the sentences American Courts were passing on young girls and old men alike for the expression of opinions which were being uttered amid thundering applause before
huge audiences in England, and the more private records of the
methods by which the American War Loans were raised, were so
amazing that they put the guns and the possibilities of a raid clean
out of our heads for the moment.

THE RABID WATCHDOGS OF LIBERTY

Not content with these rancorous abuses of the existing law, the
war maniacs made a frantic rush to abolish all constitutional guarantees of liberty and well-being. The ordinary law was superseded
by Acts under which newspapers were seized and their printing
machinery destroyed by simple police raids *à la Russe*,* and persons arrested and shot without any pretence of trial by jury or
publicity of procedure or evidence. Though it was urgently necessary that production should be increased by the most scientific organization and economy of labor, and though no fact was better
established than that excessive duration and intensity of toil re-

---

*Russian-style (French).

duces production heavily instead of increasing it, the factory laws
were suspended, and men and women recklessly over-worked
until the loss of their efficiency became too glaring to be ignored.
Remonstrances and warnings were met either with an accusation
of pro-Germanism or the formula, "Remember that we are at war
now." I have said that men assumed that war had reversed the
order of nature, and that all was lost unless we did the exact opposite of everything we had found necessary and beneficial in
peace. But the truth was worse than that. The war did not change
men's minds in any such impossible way. What really happened
was that the impact of physical death and destruction, the one reality that every fool can understand, tore off the masks of education, art, science and religion from our ignorance and barbarism,
and left us glorying grotesquely in the licence suddenly accorded
to our vilest passions and most abject terrors. Ever since Thucyd-
ides wrote his history, it has been on record that when the angel
of death sounds his trumpet the pretences of civilization are blown
from men's heads into the mud like hats in a gust of wind. But
when this scripture was fulfilled among us, the shock was not the
less appalling because a few students of Greek history were not
surprised by it. Indeed these students threw themselves into the
orgy as shamelessly as the illiterate. The Christian priest joining in
the war dance without even throwing off his cassock first, and the
respectable school governor expelling the German professor with
insult and bodily violence, and declaring that no English child
should ever again be taught the language of Luther and Goethe,
were kept in countenance by the most impudent repudiations of
every decency of civilization and every lesson of political experience on the part of the very persons who, as university professors,
historians, philosophers, and men of science, were the accredited
custodians of culture. It was crudely natural, and perhaps necessary for recruiting purposes, that German militarism and German
dynastic ambition should be painted by journalists and recruiters
in black and red as European dangers (as in fact they are), leaving

it to be inferred that our own militarism and our own political constitution are millennially* democratic (which they certainly are not); but when it came to frantic denunciations of German chemistry, German biology, German poetry, German music, German literature, German philosophy, and even German engineering, as malignant abominations standing towards British and French chemistry and so forth in the relation of heaven to hell, it was clear that the utterers of such barbarous ravings had never really understood or cared for the arts and sciences they professed and were profaning, and were only the appallingly degenerate descendants of the men of the seventeenth and eighteenth centuries who, recognizing no national frontiers in the great realm of the human mind, kept the European comity of that realm loftily and even ostentatiously above the rancors of the battle-field. Tearing the Garter from the Kaiser's leg, striking the German dukes from the roll of our peerage, changing the King's illustrious and historically appropriate surname (for the war was the old war of Guelph against Ghibelline,[4] with the Kaiser as Arch-Ghibelline) to that of a traditionless locality. One felt that the figure of St. George and the Dragon on our coinage should be replaced by that of the soldier driving his spear through Archimedes.[†] But by that time there was no coinage: only paper money in which ten shillings called itself a pound as confidently as the people who were disgracing their country called themselves patriots.

THE SUFFERINGS OF THE SANE

The mental distress of living amid the obscene din of all these carmagnoles and corobberies[‡] was not the only burden that lay on

---

*Ideally.

†Shaw uses the third-century B.C. Greek geometrician and engineer to symbolize reason.

‡Carmagnoles are songs and dances popular during the French Revolution; corroberries (usually "corroborees") are Australian Aborigine festivities with songs and dances.

sane people during the war. There was also the emotional strain, complicated by the offended economic sense, produced by the casualty lists. The stupid, the selfish, the narrow-minded, the callous and unimaginative were spared a great deal. "Blood and destruction shall be so in use that mothers shall but smile when they behold their infantes quartered by the hands of war,"* was a Shakespearean prophecy that very nearly came true; for when nearly every house had a slaughtered son to mourn, we should all have gone quite out of our senses if we had taken our own and our friend's bereavements at their peace value. It became necessary to give them a false value; to proclaim the young life worthily and gloriously sacrificed to redeem the liberty of mankind, instead of to expiate the heedlessness and folly of their fathers, and expiate it in vain. We had even to assume that the parents and not the children had made the sacrifice, until at last the comic papers were driven to satirize fat old men, sitting comfortably in club chairs, and boasting of the sons they had "given" to their country.

No one grudged these anodynes to acute personal grief; but they only embittered those who knew that the young men were having their teeth set on edge because their parents had eaten sour political grapes.† Then think of the young men themselves! Many of them had no illusions about the policy that led to the war: they went clear-sighted to a horribly repugnant duty. Men essentially gentle and essentially wise, with really valuable work in hand, laid it down voluntarily and spent months forming fours‡ in the barrack yard, and stabbing sacks of straw in the public eye, so that they might go out to kill and maim men as gentle as themselves. These men, who were perhaps, as a class, our most efficient soldiers (Frederick Keeling,§ for example), were not duped for a

---

*Near quotation of Marc Antony in Shakespeare's *Julius Caesar* (act 3, scene 1).
†Allusion to the Bible, Ezekiel 18:2.
‡Military drill in which soldiers arrange themselves into files four deep.
§Promising young intellectual and Fabian socialist who was killed in 1916.

moment by the hypocritical melodrama that consoled and stimulated the others. They left their creative work to drudge at destruction, exactly as they would have left it to take their turn at
the pumps in a sinking ship. They did not, like some of the conscientious objectors, hold back because the ship had been neglected by its officers and scuttled by its wreckers. The ship had
to be saved, even if Newton had to leave his fluxions and Michael
Angelo his marbles to save it; so they threw away the tools of
their beneficent and ennobling trades, and took up the blood-
stained bayonet and the murderous bomb, forcing themselves to
pervert their divine instinct for perfect artistic execution to the
effective handling of these diabolical things, and their economic
faculty for organization to the contriving of ruin and slaughter.
For it gave an ironic edge to their tragedy that the very talents
they were forced to prostitute made the prostitution not only effective, but even interesting; so that some of them were rapidly
promoted, and found themselves actually becoming artists in
war, with a growing relish for it, like Napoleon and all the other
scourges of mankind, in spite of themselves. For many of them
there was not even this consolation. They "stuck it," and hated it,
to the end.

EVIL IN THE THRONE OF GOOD

This distress of the gentle was so acute that those who shared it in
civil life, without having to shed blood with their own hands, or
witness destruction with their own eyes, hardly care to obtrude
their own woes. Nevertheless, even when sitting at home in safety,
it was not easy for those who had to write and speak about the war
to throw away their highest conscience, and deliberately work to
a standard of inevitable evil instead of to the ideal of life more
abundant. I can answer for at least one person who found the
change from the wisdom of Jesus and St. Francis to the morals of
Richard III and the madness of Don Quixote extremely irksome.
But that change had to be made; and we are all the worse for it,

except those for whom it was not really a change at all, but only a relief from hypocrisy.

Think, too, of those who, though they had neither to write nor to fight, and had no children of their own to lose, yet knew the inestimable loss to the world of four years of the life of a generation wasted on destruction. Hardly one of the epoch-making works of the human mind might not have been aborted or destroyed by taking their authors away from their natural work for four critical years. Not only were Shakespeares and Platos being killed outright; but many of the best harvests of the survivors had to be sown in the barren soil of the trenches. And this was no mere British consideration. To the truly civilized man, to the good European, the slaughter of the German youth was as disastrous as the slaughter of the English. Fools exulted in "German losses." They were our losses as well. Imagine exulting in the death of Beethoven because Bill Sykes* dealt him his death blow!

STRAINING AT THE GNAT AND SWALLOWING THE CAMEL

But most people could not comprehend these sorrows. There was a frivolous exultation in death for its own sake, which was at bottom an inability to realize that the deaths were real deaths and not stage ones. Again and again, when an air raider dropped a bomb which tore a child and its mother limb from limb, the people who saw it, though they had been reading with great cheerfulness of thousands of such happenings day after day in their newspapers, suddenly burst into furious imprecations on "the Huns" as murderers, and shrieked for savage and satisfying vengeance. At such moments it became clear that the deaths they had not seen meant no more to them than the mimic death of the cinema screen. Sometimes it was not necessary that death should be actually witnessed: it had only to take place under circumstances of sufficient

---

*Brutal criminal in Charles Dickens's novel *Oliver Twist* (1837–1838).

novelty and proximity to bring it home almost as sensationally and effectively as if it had been actually visible.

For example, in the spring of 1915 there was an appalling slaughter of our young soldiers at Neuve Chapelle and at the Gallipoli landing. I will not go so far as to say that our civilians were delighted to have such exciting news to read at breakfast. But I cannot pretend that I noticed either in the papers, or in general intercourse, any feeling beyond the usual one that the cinema show at the front was going splendidly, and that our boys were the bravest of the brave. Suddenly there came the news that an Atlantic liner, the Lusitania, had been torpedoed, and that several well-known first-class passengers, including a famous theatrical manager and the author of a popular farce,* had been drowned, among others. The others included Sir Hugh Lane;† but as he had only laid the country under great obligations in the sphere of the fine arts, no great stress was laid on that loss.

Immediately an amazing frenzy swept through the country. Men who up to that time had kept their heads now lost them utterly. "Killing saloon passengers! What next?" was the essence of the whole agitation; but it is far too trivial a phrase to convey the faintest notion of the rage which possessed us. To me, with my mind full of the hideous cost of Neuve Chapelle, Ypres, and the Gallipoli landing, the fuss about the Lusitania seemed almost a heartless impertinence, though I was well acquainted personally with the three best-known victims, and understood, better perhaps than most people, the misfortune of the death of Lane. I even found a grim satisfaction, very intelligible to all soldiers, in the fact that the civilians who found the war such splendid British sport should get a sharp taste of what it was to the actual combatants. I expressed my impatience very freely, and found that my

---

*The manager is American theatrical producer Charles Frohman (1860–1915); the author is Charles Klein, who co-wrote the 1910 farce *Potash and Perlmutter*.

†Irish art dealer (1875–1915); director of the National Gallery of Ireland.

\

very straightforward and natural feeling in the matter was received as a monstrous and heartless paradox. When I asked those who gaped at me whether they had anything to say about the holocaust of Festubert, they gaped wider than before, having totally forgotten it, or rather, having never realized it. They were not heartless any more than I was; but the big catastrophe was too big for them to grasp, and the little one had been just the right size for them. I was not surprised. Have I not seen a public body for just the same reason pass a vote for £30,000 without a word, and then spend three special meetings, prolonged into the night, over an item of seven shillings for refreshments?

LITTLE MINDS AND BIG BATTLES

Nobody will be able to understand the vagaries of public feeling during the war unless they bear constantly in mind that the war in its entire magnitude did not exist for the average civilian. He could not conceive even a battle, much less a campaign. To the suburbs the war was nothing but a suburban squabble. To the miner and navvy it was only a series of bayonet fights between German champions and English ones. The enormity of it was quite beyond most of us. Its episodes had to be reduced to the dimensions of a railway accident or a shipwreck before it could produce any effect on our minds at all. To us the ridiculous bombardments of Scarborough and Ramsgate were colossal tragedies, and the battle of Jutland a mere ballad. The words "after thorough artillery preparation" in the news from the front meant nothing to us; but when our seaside trippers learned that an elderly gentleman at breakfast in a week-end marine hotel had been interrupted by a bomb dropping into his egg-cup, their wrath and horror knew no bounds. They declared that this would put a new spirit into the army, and had no suspicion that the soldiers in the trenches roared with laughter over it for days, and told each other that it would do the blighters at home good to have a taste of what the army was up against. Sometimes the smallness of view was pathetic. A man would work at home regardless of the call "to make the world safe for democracy."* His brother would be killed at the front. Immediately he would throw up his work and take up the war as a family blood feud against the Germans. Sometimes it was comic. A wounded man, entitled to his discharge, would return to the trenches with a grim determination to find the Hun who had wounded him and pay him out for it.

It is impossible to estimate what proportion of us, in khaki or out of it, grasped the war and its political antecedents as a whole in the light of any philosophy of history or knowledge of what war is. I doubt whether it was as high as our proportion of higher mathematicians. But there can be no doubt that it was prodigiously outnumbered by the comparatively ignorant and childish. Remember that these people had to be stimulated to make the sacrifices demanded by the war, and that this could not be done by appeals to a knowledge which they did not possess, and a comprehension of which they were incapable. When the armistice at last set me free to tell the truth about the war at the following general election, a soldier said to a candidate whom I was supporting, "If I had known all that in 1914, they would never have got me into khaki." And that, of course, was precisely why it had been necessary to stuff him with a romance that any diplomatist would have laughed at. Thus the natural confusion of ignorance was increased by a deliberately propagated confusion of nursery bogey stories and melodramatic nonsense, which at last overreached itself and made it impossible to stop the war before we had not only achieved the triumph of vanquishing the German army and thereby overthrowing its militarist monarchy, but made the very serious mistake of ruining the centre of Europe, a thing that no sane European State could afford to do.

---

*Paraphrase of a line in President Woodrow Wilson's April 2, 1917, address to Congress upon the United States entering World War I.

THE DUMB CAPABLES AND THE NOISY INCAPABLES

Confronted with this picture of insensate delusion and folly, the critical reader will immediately counter-plead that England all this time was conducting a war which involved the organization of several millions of fighting men and of the workers who were supplying them with provisions, munitions, and transport, and that this could not have been done by a mob of hysterical ranters. This is fortunately true. To pass from the newspaper offices and political platforms and club fenders and suburban drawing-rooms to the Army and the munition factories was to pass from Bedlam to the busiest and sanest of workaday worlds. It was to rediscover England, and find solid ground for the faith of those who still believed in her. But a necessary condition of this efficiency was that those who were efficient should give all their time to their business and leave the rabble raving to its heart's content. Indeed the raving was useful to the efficient, because, as it was always wide of the mark, it often distracted attention very conveniently from operations that would have been defeated or hindered by publicity. A precept which I endeavored vainly to popularize early in the war, "If you have anything to do go and do it: if not, for heaven's sake get out of the way," was only half carried out. Certainly the capable people went and did it; but the incapables would by no means get out of the way: they fussed and bawled and were only prevented from getting very seriously into the way by the blessed fact that they never knew where the way was. Thus whilst all the efficiency of England was silent and invisible, all its imbecility was deafening the heavens with its clamor and blotting out the sun with its dust. It was also unfortunately intimidating the Government by its blusterings into using the irresistible powers of the State to intimidate the sensible people, thus enabling a despicable minority of would-be lynchers to set up a reign of terror which could at any time have been broken by a single stern word from a responsible minister. But our ministers had not that sort of courage: neither Heartbreak House nor Horseback Hall had bred it, much less the suburbs. When matters at last came to the looting of shops by criminals under patriotic pretexts, it was the police force and not the Government that put its foot down. There was even one deplorable moment, during the submarine scare, in which the Government yielded to a childish cry for the maltreatment of naval prisoners of war, and, to our great disgrace, was forced by the enemy to behave itself. And yet behind all this public blundering and misconduct and futile mischief, the effective England was carrying on with the most formidable capacity and activity. The ostensible England was making the empire sick with its incontinences, its ignorances, its ferocities, its panics, and its endless and intolerable blarings of Allied national anthems in season and out. The esoteric England was proceeding irresistibly to the conquest of Europe.

THE PRACTICAL BUSINESS MEN

From the beginning the useless people set up a shriek for "practical business men." By this they meant men who had become rich by placing their personal interests before those of the country, and measuring the success of every activity by the pecuniary profit it brought to them and to those on whom they depended for their supplies of capital. The pitiable failure of some conspicuous samples from the first batch we tried of these poor devils helped to give the whole public side of the war an air of monstrous and hopeless farce. They proved not only that they were useless for public work, but that in a well-ordered nation they would never have been allowed to control private enterprise.

HOW THE FOOLS SHOUTED THE WISE MEN DOWN

Thus, like a fertile country flooded with mud, England showed no sign of her greatness in the days when she was putting forth all her

strength to save herself from the worst consequences of her littleness. Most of the men of action, occupied to the last hour of their
time with urgent practical work, had to leave to idler people, or
to professional rhetoricians, the presentation of the war to the
reason and imagination of the country and the world in speeches,
poems, manifestoes, picture posters, and newspaper articles. I
have had the privilege of hearing some of our ablest commanders
talking about their work; and I have shared the common lot of
reading the accounts of that work given to the world by the newspapers. No two experiences could be more different. But in the
end the talkers obtained a dangerous ascendancy over the rank and
file of the men of action; for though the great men of action are
always inveterate talkers and often very clever writers, and therefore cannot have their minds formed for them by others, the average man of action, like the average fighter with the bayonet, can
give no account of himself in words even to himself, and is apt to
pick up and accept what he reads about himself and other people
in the papers, except when the writer is rash enough to commit
himself on technical points. It was not uncommon during the war
to hear a soldier, or a civilian engaged on war work, describing
events within his own experience that reduced to utter absurdity
the ravings and maunderings of his daily paper, and yet echo the
opinions of that paper like a parrot. Thus, to escape from the pre-
vailing confusion and folly, it was not enough to seek the company
of the ordinary man of action: one had to get into contact with the
master spirits. This was a privilege which only a handful of people
could enjoy. For the unprivileged citizen there was no escape. To
him the whole country seemed mad, futile, silly, incompetent,
with no hope of victory except the hope that the enemy might be
just as mad. Only by very resolute reflection and reasoning could
he reassure himself that if there was nothing more solid beneath
these appalling appearances the war could not possibly have gone
on for a single day without a total breakdown of its organization.

THE MAD ELECTION

Happy were the fools and the thoughtless men of action in those days. The worst of it was that the fools were very strongly represented in parliament, as fools not only elect fools, but can persuade men of action to elect them too. The election that immediately followed the armistice was perhaps the maddest that has ever taken place. Soldiers who had done voluntary and heroic service in the field were defeated by persons who had apparently never run a risk or spent a farthing that they could avoid, and who even had in the course of the election to apologize publicly for bawling Pacifist or Pro-German at their opponent. Party leaders seek such followers, who can always be depended on to walk tamely into the lobby at the party whip's orders, provided the leader will make their seats safe for them by the process which was called, in derisive reference to the war rationing system, "giving them the coupon." Other incidents were so grotesque that I cannot mention them without enabling the reader to identify the parties, which would not be fair, as they were no more to blame than thousands of others who must necessarily be nameless. The general result was patently absurd; and the electorate, disgusted at its own work, instantly recoiled to the opposite extreme, and cast out all the coupon candidates at the earliest bye-elections by equally silly majorities. But the mischief of the general election could not be undone; and the Government had not only to pretend to abuse its European victory as it had promised, but actually to do it by starving the enemies who had thrown down their arms. It had, in short, won the election by pledging itself to be thriftlessly wicked, cruel, and vindictive; and it did not find it as easy to escape from this pledge as it had from nobler ones. The end, as I write, is not yet; but it is clear that this thoughtless savagery will recoil on the heads of the Allies so severely that we shall be forced by the sternest necessity to take up our share of healing the Europe we have wounded almost to death instead of attempting to complete her destruction.

THE YAHOO AND THE ANGRY APE

Contemplating this picture of a state of mankind so recent that no denial of its truth is possible, one understands Shakespeare comparing Man to an angry ape,* Swift describing him as a Yahoo rebuked by the superior virtue of the horse, and Wellington declaring that the British can behave themselves neither in victory nor defeat. Yet none of the three had seen war as we have seen it. Shakespeare blamed great men, saying that "Could great men thunder as Jove himself does, Jove would ne'er be quiet; for every pelting petty officer would use his heaven for thunder: nothing but thunder."† What would Shakespeare have said if he had seen something far more destructive than thunder in the hand of every village laborer, and found on the Messines Ridge the craters of the nineteen volcanoes that were let loose there at the touch of a finger that might have been a child's finger without the result being a whit less ruinous? Shakespeare may have seen a Stratford cottage struck by one of Jove's thunderbolts, and have helped to extinguish the lighted thatch and clear away the bits of the broken chimney. What would he have said if he had seen Ypres as it is now, or returned to Stratford, as French peasants are returning to their homes to-day, to find the old familiar signpost inscribed "To Stratford, 1 mile," and at the end of the mile nothing but some holes in the ground and a fragment of a broken churn here and there? Would not the spectacle of the angry ape endowed with powers of destruction that Jove never pretended to, have beggared even his command of words?

And yet, what is there to say except that war puts a strain on

---

*Isabella makes this comparison in Shakespeare's *Measure for Measure* (act 2, scene 2).

†Quotation of more of Isabella's speech.

human nature that breaks down the better half of it, and makes the worse half a diabolical virtue? Better for us if it broke it down altogether, for then the warlike way out of our difficulties would be barred to us, and we should take greater care not to get into them. In truth, it is, as Byron said, "not difficult to die," and enormously difficult to live: that explains why, at bottom, peace is not only better than war, but infinitely more arduous. Did any hero of the war face the glorious risk of death more bravely than the traitor Bolo* faced the ignominious certainty of it? Bolo taught us all how to die: can we say that he taught us all how to live? Hardly a week passes now without some soldier who braved death in the field so recklessly that he was decorated or specially commended for it, being haled before our magistrates for having failed to resist the paltriest temptations of peace, with no better excuse than the old one that "a man must live." Strange that one who, sooner than do honest work, will sell his honor for a bottle of wine, a visit to the theatre, and an hour with a strange woman, all obtained by passing a worthless cheque, could yet stake his life on the most desperate chances of the battle-field! Does it not seem as if, after all, the glory of death were cheaper than the glory of life? If it is not easier to attain, why do so many more men attain it? At all events it is clear that the kingdom of the Prince of Peace has not yet become the kingdom of this world. His attempts at invasion have been resisted far more fiercely than the Kaiser's. Successful as that resistance has been, it has piled up a sort of National Debt that is not the less oppressive because we have no figures for it and do not intend to pay it. A blockade that cuts off "the grace of our Lord" is in the long run less bearable than the blockades which merely cut off raw materials; and against that blockade our Armada is impotent. In the blockader's house, he has assured us, there are

*Reference to the French traitor Paul Bolo, who was accused of spying on his country and executed in 1918.

many mansions; but I am afraid they do not include either Heartbreak House or Horseback Hall.

PLAGUE ON BOTH YOUR HOUSES!

Meanwhile the Bolshevist picks and petards* are at work on the foundations of both buildings; and though the Bolshevists may be buried in the ruins, their deaths will not save the edifices. Unfortunately they can be built again. Like Doubting Castle, they have been demolished many times by successive Greathearts, and rebuilt by Simple, Sloth, and Presumption, by Feeble Mind and Much Afraid, and by all the jurymen of Vanity Fair.† Another generation of "secondary education" at our ancient public schools and the cheaper institutions that ape them will be quite sufficient to keep the two going until the next war.

For the instruction of that generation I leave these pages as a record of what civilian life was during the war: a matter on which history is usually silent. Fortunately it was a very short war. It is true that the people who thought it could not last more than six months were very signally refuted by the event. As Sir Douglas Haig‡ has pointed out, its Waterloos lasted months instead of hours. But there would have been nothing surprising in its lasting thirty years. If it had not been for the fact that the blockade achieved the amazing feat of starving out Europe, which it could not possibly have done had Europe been properly organized for war, or even for peace, the war would have lasted until the belligerents were so tired of it that they could no longer be compelled to compel themselves to go on with it. Considering its magnitude, the war of 1914–18 will certainly be classed as the

---

*Explosives used to breach a gate or wall.

†All of these are allegorical places or persons in John Bunyan's *Pilgram's Progress* (1678), which Shaw admired for its hopefulness.

‡This commander in chief of the British forces (1914–1921) provided Shaw with a demonstration of experimental weapons.

shortest in history. The end came so suddenly that the combatant literally stumbled over it; and yet it came a full year later than it should have come if the belligerents had not been far too afraid of one another to face the situation sensibly. Germany, having failed to provide for the war she began, failed again to surrender before she was dangerously exhausted. Her opponents, equally improvi-dent, went as much too close to bankruptcy as Germany to star-vation. It was a bluff at which both were bluffed. And, with the usual irony of war, it remains doubtful whether Germany and Russia, the defeated, will not be the gainers; for the victors are al-ready busy fastening on themselves the chains they have struck from the limbs of the vanquished.

HOW THE THEATRE FARED

Let us now contract our view rather violently from the European theatre of war to the theatre in which the fights are sham fights, and the slain, rising the moment the curtain has fallen, go com-fortably home to supper after washing off their rose-pink wounds. It is nearly twenty years since I was last obliged to introduce a play in the form of a book for lack of an opportunity of presenting it in its proper mode by a performance in a theatre. The war has thrown me back on this expedient. Heartbreak House has not yet reached the stage. I have withheld it because the war has com-pletely upset the economic conditions which formerly enabled se-rious drama to pay its way in London. The change is not in the theatres nor in the management of them, nor in the authors and actors, but in the audiences. For four years the London theatres were crowded every night with thousands of soldiers on leave from the front. These soldiers were not seasoned London playgo-ers. A childish experience of my own gave me a clue to their con-dition. When I was a small boy I was taken to the opera. I did not then know what an opera was, though I could whistle a good deal of opera music. I had seen in my mother's album photographs of all the great opera singers, mostly in evening dress. In the theatre

I found myself before a gilded balcony filled with persons in evening dress whom I took to be the opera singers. I picked out one massive dark lady as Alboni,* and wondered how soon she would stand up and sing. I was puzzled by the fact that I was made to sit with my back to the singers instead of facing them. When the curtain went up, my astonishment and delight were unbounded.

THE SOLDIER AT THE THEATRE FRONT

In 1915, I saw in the theatres men in khaki in just the same predicament. To everyone who had my clue to their state of mind it was evident that they had never been in a theatre before and did not know what it was. At one of our great variety theatres I sat beside a young officer, not at all a rough specimen, who, even when the curtain rose and enlightened him as to the place where he had to look for his entertainment, found the dramatic part of it utterly incomprehensible. He did not know how to play his part of the game. He could understand the people on the stage singing and dancing and performing gymnastic feats. He not only understood but intensely enjoyed an artist who imitated cocks crowing and pigs squeaking. But the people who pretended that they were somebody else, and that the painted picture behind them was real, bewildered him. In his presence I realized how very sophisticated the natural man has to become before the conventions of the theatre can be easily acceptable, or the purpose of the drama obvious to him.

Well, from the moment when the routine of leave for our soldiers was established, such novices, accompanied by damsels (called flappers) often as innocent as themselves, crowded the theatres to the doors. It was hardly possible at first to find stuff crude enough to nurse them on. The best music-hall comedians ransacked their memories for the oldest quips and the most childish antics to avoid carrying the military spectators out of their depth.

---

*Marietta Alboni (1823–1894), Italian contralto opera singer.

I believe that this was a mistake as far as the novices were concerned. Shakespeare, or the dramatized histories of George Barnwell, Maria Martin, or the Demon Barber of Fleet Street,* would probably have been quite popular with them. But the novices were only a minority after all. The cultivated soldier, who in time of peace would look at nothing theatrical except the most advanced post-Ibsen plays in the most artistic settings, found himself, to his own astonishment, thirsting for silly jokes, dances, and brainlessly sensuous exhibitions of pretty girls. The author of some of the most grimly serious plays of our time told me that after enduring the trenches for months without a glimpse of the female of his species, it gave him an entirely innocent but delightful pleasure merely to see a flapper. The reaction from the battle-field produced a condition of hyper-aesthesia in which all the theatrical values were altered. Trivial things gained intensity and stale things novelty. The actor, instead of having to coax his audiences out of the boredom which had driven them to the theatre in an ill humor to seek some sort of distraction, had only to exploit the bliss of smiling men who were no longer under fire and under military discipline, but actually clean and comfortable and in a mood to be pleased with anything and everything that a bevy of pretty girls and a funny man, or even a bevy of girls pretending to be pretty and a man pretending to be funny, could do for them.

Then could be seen every night in the theatres old-fashioned farcical comedies, in which a bedroom, with four doors on each side and a practicable window in the middle, was understood to resemble exactly the bedroom in the flats beneath and above, all three inhabited by couples consumed with jealousy. When these people came home drunk at night; mistook their neighbor's flats

---

*George Barnwell is a sinner in George Lillo's middle-class sentimental tragedy *The London Merchant* (1731); Maria Martin is the heroine of *Maria Martin, or the Red Barn Mystery*, about her murder by her lover in 1827; Sweeney Todd is the legendary "Demon Barber" of London, who slit his customers' throats.

for their own; and in due course got into the wrong beds, it was not only the novices who found the resulting complications and scandals exquisitely ingenious and amusing, nor their equally verdant flappers who could not help squealing in a manner that astonished the oldest performers when the gentleman who had just come in drunk through the window pretended to undress, and allowed glimpses of his naked person to be descried from time to time. Men who had just read the news that Charles Wyndham* was dying, and were thereby sadly reminded of Pink Dominos† and the torrent of farcical comedies that followed it in his heyday until every trick of that trade had become so stale that the laughter they provoked turned to loathing: these veterans also, when they returned from the field, were as much pleased by what they knew to be stale and foolish as the novices by what they thought fresh and clever.

COMMERCE IN THE THEATRE

Wellington said that an army moves on its belly. So does a London theatre. Before a man acts he must eat. Before he performs plays he must pay rent. In London we have no theatres for the welfare of the people: they are all for the sole purpose of producing the utmost obtainable rent for the proprietor. If the twin flats and twin beds produce a guinea more than Shakespeare, out goes Shakespeare and in come the twin flats and the twin beds. If the brainless bevy of pretty girls and the funny man outbid Mozart, out goes Mozart.

UNSER SHAKESPEARE

Before the war an effort was made to remedy this by establishing a national theatre in celebration of the tercentenary of the death of Shakespeare. A committee was formed; and all sorts of illustri-

---

*Actor-manager of the period (1837–1919).

†French farce adapted into English by James Alberry (1838–1899).

ous and influential persons lent their names to a grand appeal to our national culture. My play, The Dark Lady of The Sonnets, was one of the incidents of that appeal. After some years of effort the result was a single handsome subscription from a German gentleman.* Like the celebrated swearer in the anecdote when the cart containing all his household goods lost its tailboard at the top of the hill and let its contents roll in ruin to the bottom, I can only say, "I cannot do justice to this situation," and let it pass without another word.

THE HIGHER DRAMA PUT OUT OF ACTION

The effect of the war on the London theatres may now be imagined. The beds and the bevies drove every higher form of art out of it. Rents went up to an unprecedented figure. At the same time prices doubled everywhere except at the theatre pay-boxes, and raised the expenses of management to such a degree that unless the houses were quite full every night, profit was impossible. Even bare solvency could not be attained without a very wide popularity. Now what had made serious drama possible to a limited extent before the war was that a play could pay its way even if the theatre were only half full until Saturday and three-quarters full then. A manager who was an enthusiast and a desperately hard worker, with an occasional grant-in-aid from an artistically disposed millionaire, and a due proportion of those rare and happy accidents by which plays of the higher sort turn out to be potboilers as well, could hold out for some years, by which time a relay might arrive in the person of another enthusiast. Thus and not otherwise occurred that remarkable revival of the British drama at the beginning of the century which made my own career as a playwright possible in England. In America I had already es-

---

*Reference to Sir Carl Meyer, who donated £70,000 to the National Theatre in 1908.

tablished myself, not as part of the ordinary theatre system, but in association with the exceptional genius of Richard Mansfield. In Germany and Austria I had no difficulty: the system of publicly aided theatres there, Court and Municipal, kept drama of the kind I dealt in alive; so that I was indebted to the Emperor of Austria for magnificent productions of my works at a time when the sole official attention paid me by the British Courts was the announcement to the English-speaking world that certain plays of mine were unfit for public performance, a substantial set-off against this being that the British Court,* in the course of its private play-going, paid no regard to the bad character given me by the chief officer of its household.

Howbeit, the fact that my plays effected a lodgment on the London stage, and were presently followed by the plays of Granville Barker, Gilbert Murray, John Masefield, St. John Hankin, Laurence Housman, Arnold Bennett, John Galsworthy, John Drinkwater, and others which would in the nineteenth century have stood rather less chance of production at a London theatre than the Dialogues of Plato, not to mention revivals of the ancient Athenian drama and a restoration to the stage of Shakespeare's plays as he wrote them, was made economically possible solely by a supply of theatres which could hold nearly twice as much money as it cost to rent and maintain them. In such theatres work appealing to a relatively small class of cultivated persons, and therefore attracting only from half to three-quarters as many spectators as the more popular pastimes, could nevertheless keep going in the hands of young adventurers who were doing it for its own sake, and had not yet been forced by advancing age and responsibilities to consider the commercial value of their time and energy too closely. The war struck this foundation away in the manner I have just described. The expenses of running the cheapest west-

---

*In the person of King Edward VII, who attended Shaw's play *John Bull's Other Island* (1904).

end theatres rose to a sum which exceeded by twenty-five per cent the utmost that the higher drama can, as an ascertained matter of fact, be depended on to draw. Thus the higher drama, which has never really been a commercially sound speculation, now became an impossible one. Accordingly, attempts are being made to provide a refuge for it in suburban theatres in London and repertory theatres in the provinces. But at the moment when the army has at last disgorged the survivors of the gallant band of dramatic pioneers whom it swallowed, they find that the economic conditions which formerly made their work no worse than precarious now put it out of the question altogether, as far as the west end of London is concerned.

CHURCH AND THEATRE

I do not suppose many people care particularly. We are not brought up to care; and a sense of the national importance of the theatre is not born in mankind: the natural man, like so many of the soldiers at the beginning of the war, does not know what a theatre is. But please note that all these soldiers who did not know what a theatre was, knew what a church was. And they had been taught to respect churches. Nobody had ever warned them against a church as a place where frivolous women paraded in their best clothes; where stories of improper females like Potiphar's wife, and erotic poetry like the Song of Songs, were read aloud; where the sensuous and sentimental music of Schubert, Mendelssohn, Gounod, and Brahms was more popular than severe music by greater composers; where the prettiest sort of pretty pictures of pretty saints assailed the imagination and senses through stained-glass windows; and where sculpture and architecture came to the help of painting. Nobody ever reminded them that these things had sometimes produced such developments of erotic idolatry that men who were not only enthusiastic amateurs of literature, painting, and music, but famous practitioners of them, had actually exulted when mobs and even regular troops under express command had mutilated church statues, smashed church windows, wrecked church organs, and torn up the sheets from which the church music was read and sung. When they saw broken statues in churches, they were told that this was the work of wicked, godless rioters, instead of, as it was, the work partly of zealots bent on driving the world, the flesh, and the devil out of the temple, and partly of insurgent men who had become intolerably poor because the temple had become a den of thieves. But all the sins and perversions that were so carefully hidden from them in the history of the Church were laid on the shoulders of the Theatre: that stuffy, uncomfortable place of penance in which we suffer so much inconvenience on the slenderest chance of gaining a scrap of food for our starving souls. When the Germans bombed the Cathedral of Rheims the world rang with the horror of the sacrilege. When they bombed the Little Theatre in the Adelphi, and narrowly missed bombing two writers of plays* who lived within a few yards of it, the fact was not even mentioned in the papers. In point of appeal to the senses no theatre ever built could touch the fane[†] at Rheims: no actress could rival its Virgin in beauty, nor any operatic tenor look otherwise than a fool beside its David. Its picture glass was glorious even to those who had seen the glass of Chartres. It was wonderful in its very grotesques: who would look at the Blondin Donkey[‡] after seeing its leviathans? In spite of the Adam-Adelphian[§] decoration on which Miss Kingston had lavished so much taste and care, the Little Theatre was in comparison with Rheims the gloomiest of little conventicles: indeed the cathedral must, from the Puritan point of view, have debauched a million

---

*J. M. Barrie (see footnote to page 320) and Shaw, who were neighbors and friends.

†Cathedral.

‡Music-hall turn by the animal imitators the Brothers Griffiths that parodied the French tightrope walker Charles Blondin (1824–1897).

§The décor of the Adelphi Theatre was by Scottish architect Robert Adam (1728–1792).

voluptuaries for every one whom the Little Theatre had sent home thoughtful to a chaste bed after Mr Chesterton's Magic or Brieux's *Les Avariés*.* Perhaps that is the real reason why the Church is lauded and the Theatre reviled. Whether or no, the fact remains that the lady† to whose public spirit and sense of the national value of the theatre I owed the first regular public performance of a play of mine had to conceal her action as if it had been a crime, whereas if she had given the money to the Church she would have worn a halo for it. And I admit, as I have always done, that this state of things may have been a very sensible one. I have asked Londoners again and again why they pay half a guinea to go to a theatre when they can go to St. Paul's or Westminster Abbey for nothing. Their only possible reply is that they want to see something new and possibly something wicked; but the theatres mostly disappoint both hopes. If ever a revolution makes me Dictator, I shall establish a heavy charge for admission to our churches. But everyone who pays at the church door shall receive a ticket entitling him or her to free admission to one performance at any theatre he or she prefers. Thus shall the sensuous charms of the church service be made to subsidize the sterner virtue of the drama.

THE NEXT PHASE

The present situation will not last. Although the newspaper I read at breakfast this morning before writing these words contains a calculation that no less than twenty-three wars are at present being waged to confirm the peace, England is no longer in khaki; and a violent reaction is setting in against the crude theatrical fare of the four terrible years. Soon the rents of theatres will once more be fixed on the assumption that they cannot always be full,

---

*Play by French dramatist Eugène Brieux, adapted into English in 1914 as *Damaged Goods*, by John Pollock.

†Reference to English theater manager A. E. F. Horniman (1860–1937), who presented Shaw's first publicly produced play, *Arms and the Man*, in 1894.

nor even on the average half full week in and week out. Prices will change. The higher drama will be at no greater disadvantage than it was before the war; and it may benefit, first, by the fact that many of us have been torn from the fools' paradise in which the theatre formerly traded, and thrust upon the sternest realities and necessities until we have lost both faith in and patience with the theatrical pretences that had no root either in reality or necessity; second, by the startling change made by the war in the distribution of income. It seems only the other day that a millionaire was a man with £50,000 a year. To-day, when he has paid his income tax and super tax, and insured his life for the amount of his death duties, he is lucky if his net income is £10,000, though his nominal property remains the same. And this is the result of a Budget which is called "a respite for the rich." At the other end of the scale millions of persons have had regular incomes for the first time in their lives; and their men have been regularly clothed, fed, lodged, and taught to make up their minds that certain things have to be done, also for the first time in their lives. Hundreds of thousands of women have been taken out of their domestic cages and tasted both discipline and independence. The thoughtless and snobbish middle classes have been pulled up short by the very unpleasant experience of being ruined to an unprecedented extent. We have all had a tremendous jolt; and although the widespread notion that the shock of the war would automatically make a new heaven and a new earth, and that the dog would never go back to his vomit nor the sow to her wallowing in the mire,* is already seen to be a delusion, yet we are far more conscious of our condition than we were, and far less disposed to submit to it. Revolution, lately only a sensational chapter in history or a demagogic claptrap, is now a possibility so imminent that hardly by trying to suppress it in other countries by arms and defamation, and calling the process anti-Bolshevism, can our Government stave it off at home.

---

*Allusion to the Bible, 2 Peter 2:22.

Perhaps the most tragic figure of the day is the American President who was once a historian. In those days it became his task to tell us how, after that great war in America which was more clearly than any other war of our time a war for an idea, the conquerors, confronted with a heroic task of reconstruction, turned recreant, and spent fifteen years in abusing their victory under cover of pretending to accomplish the task they were doing what they could to make impossible. Alas! Hegel was right when he said that we learn from history that men never learn anything from history. With what anguish of mind the President sees that we, the new conquerors, forgetting everything we professed to fight for, are sitting down with watering mouths to a good square meal of ten years revenge upon and humiliation of our prostrate foe, can only be guessed by those who know, as he does, how hopeless is remonstrance, and how happy Lincoln was in perishing from the earth before his inspired messages became scraps of paper. He knows well that from the Peace Conference will come, in spite of his utmost, no edict on which he will be able, like Lincoln, to invoke "the considerate judgment of mankind, and the gracious favor of Almighty God."* He led his people to destroy the militarism of Zabern;[5] and the army they rescued is busy in Cologne imprisoning every German who does not salute a British officer; whilst the Government at home, asked whether it approves, replies that it does not propose even to discontinue this Zabernism when the Peace is concluded, but in effect looks forward to making Germans salute British officers until the end of the world. That is what war makes of men and women. It will wear off; and the worst it threatens is already proving impracticable; but before the humble and contrite heart† ceases to be despised, the President and I, being of the same age, will be dotards.

---

*Quotation from the Emancipation Proclamation, issued by United States President Abraham Lincoln on January 1, 1863.

†Ironic allusion to the Bible, Isaiah 57:15.

In the meantime there is, for him, another history to write; for me, another comedy to stage. Perhaps, after all, that is what wars are for, and what historians and playwrights are for. If men will not learn until their lessons are written in blood, why, blood they must have, their own for preference.

THE EPHEMERAL THRONES AND THE ETERNAL THEATRE

To the theatre it will not matter. Whatever Bastilles fall, the theatre will stand. Apostolic Hapsburg has collapsed; All Highest Hohenzollern languishes in Holland, threatened with trial on a capital charge of fighting for his country against England; Imperial Romanoff, said to have perished miserably by a more summary method of murder, is perhaps alive or perhaps dead: nobody cares more than if he had been a peasant; the lord of Hellas is level with his lackeys in republican Switzerland; Prime Ministers and Commanders-in-Chief have passed from a brief glory as Solons and Caesars into failure and obscurity[6] as closely on one another's heels as the descendants of Banquo;* but Euripides and Aristophanes, Shakespeare and Molière, Goethe and Ibsen remain fixed in their everlasting seats.

HOW WAR MUZZLES THE DRAMATIC POET

As for myself, why, it may be asked, did I not write two plays about the war instead of two pamphlets on it? The answer is significant. You cannot make war on war and on your neighbor at the same time. War cannot bear the terrible castigation of comedy, the ruthless light of laughter that glares on the stage. When men are heroically dying for their country, it is not the time to show their

---

*In Shakespeare's *Macbeth* (act 4, scene 1), when shown the descendants of the murdered Banquo in a vision, Macbeth asks if their line will "stretch out to the crack of doom?"

lovers and wives and fathers and mothers how they are being sacrificed to the blunders of boobies, the cupidity of capitalists, the
ambition of conquerors, the electioneering of demagogues, the
Pharisaism of patriots, the lusts and lies and rancors and blood-
thirsts that love war because it opens their prison doors, and sets
them in the thrones of power and popularity. For unless these
things are mercilessly exposed they will hide under the mantle of
the ideals on the stage just as they do in real life.

And though there may be better things to reveal, it may not,
and indeed cannot, be militarily expedient to reveal them whilst
the issue is still in the balance. Truth telling is not compatible with
the defence of the realm. We are just now reading the revelations
of our generals and admirals, unmuzzled at last by the armistice.
During the war, General A, in his moving despatches from the
field, told how General B had covered himself with deathless glory
in such and such a battle. He now tells us that General B came
within an ace of losing us the war by disobeying his orders on that
occasion, and fighting instead of running away as he ought to have
done. An excellent subject for comedy now that the war is over,
no doubt; but if General A had let this out at the time, what would
have been the effect on General B's soldiers? And had the stage
made known what the Prime Minister and the Secretary of State
for War who overruled General A thought of him, and what he
thought of them, as now revealed in raging controversy, what
would have been the effect on the nation? That is why comedy,
though sorely tempted, had to be loyally silent; for the art of the
dramatic poet knows no patriotism; recognizes no obligation but
truth to natural history; cares not whether Germany or England
perish; is ready to cry with Brynhild, "Lass'uns verderben, lachend
zu grunde geh'n"[7] sooner than deceive or be deceived; and thus
becomes in time of war a greater military danger than poison,
steel, or trinitrotoluene.* That is why I had to withhold Heart-

---

*The explosive TNT.

break House from the footlights during the war; for the Germans might on any night have turned the last act from play into earnest, and even then might not have waited for their cues.[8]

June, 1919.

HEARTBREAK HOUSE

ACT I

The hilly country in the middle of the north edge of Sussex, looking very pleasant on a fine evening at the end of September, is seen through the windows of a room which has been built so as to resemble the after part of an old-fashioned high-pooped ship with a stern gallery;* for the windows are ship built with heavy timbering, and run right across the room as continuously as the stability of the wall allows. A row of lockers under the windows provides an unupholstered window-seat interrupted by twin glass doors, respectively half-way between the stern post and the sides. Another door strains the illusion a little by being apparently in the ship's port side, and yet leading, not to the open sea, but to the entrance hall of the house. Between this door and the stern gallery are bookshelves. There are electric light switches beside the door leading to the hall and the glass doors in the stern gallery. Against the starboard wall is a carpenter's bench. The vice has a board in its jaws; and the floor is littered with shavings, over-flowing from a waste-paper basket. A couple of planes and a centrebit† are on the bench. In the same wall, between the bench and the windows, is a narrow doorway with a half door, above which a glimpse of the room beyond shows that it is a shelved pantry with bottles and kitchen crockery.

---

*Balcony-like platform projecting from the stern of a ship.
†Usually spelled "centerbit"; tool for making cylindrical holes.

On the starboard side, but close to the middle, is a plain oak drawing-table with drawing-board, T-square, straight-edges, set squares,* mathematical instruments, saucers of water color, a tumbler of discolored water, Indian ink, pencils, and brushes on it. The drawing-board is set so that the draughtsman's chair has the window on its left hand. On the floor at the end of the table, on his right, is a ship's fire bucket. On the port side of the room, near the bookshelves, is a sofa with its back to the windows. It is a sturdy mahogany article, oddly upholstered in sailcloth, including the bolster, with a couple of blankets hanging over the back. Between the sofa and the drawing-table is a big wicker chair, with broad arms and a low sloping back, with its back to the light. A small but stout table of teak, with a round top and gate legs,† stands against the port wall between the door and the bookcase. It is the only article in the room that suggests (not at all convincingly) a woman's hand in the furnishing. The uncarpeted floor of narrow boards is caulked and holystoned‡ like a deck.

The garden to which the glass doors lead dips to the south before the landscape rises again to the hills. Emerging from the hollow is the cupola of an observatory. Between the observatory and the house is a flagstaff on a little esplanade, with a hammock on the east side and a long garden seat on the west.

A young lady, gloved and hatted, with a dust coat on, is sitting in the window-seat with her body twisted to enable her to look out of the view. One hand props her chin: the other hangs down with a volume of the Temple

---

*T squares, straightedges, and set squares are types of rulers.
†Movable table legs that support table leaves.
‡Scrubbed with a piece of sandstone, as a ship's deck.

Shakespeare* in it, and her finger stuck in the page she has been reading.

A clock strikes six.

The young lady turns and looks at her watch. She rises with an air of one who waits and is almost at the end of her patience. She is a pretty girl, slender, fair, and intelligent looking, nicely but not expensively dressed, evidently not a smart idler.

With a sigh of weary resignation she comes to the draughtsman's chair; sits down; and begins to read Shakespeare. Presently the book sinks to her lap; her eyes close; and she dozes into a slumber.

An elderly womanservant comes in from the hall with three unopened bottles of rum on a tray. She passes through and disappears in the pantry without noticing the young lady. She places the bottles on the shelf and fills her tray with empty bottles. As she returns with these, the young lady lets her book drop, awakening herself, and startling the womanservant so that she all but lets the tray fall.

THE WOMANSERVANT   God bless us! [*The young lady picks up the book and places it on the table.*] Sorry to wake you, miss, I'm sure; but you are a stranger to me. What might you be waiting here for now?

THE YOUNG LADY   Waiting for somebody to show some signs of knowing that I have been invited here.

THE WOMANSERVANT   Oh, you're invited, are you? And has nobody come? Dear! dear!

THE YOUNG LADY   A wild-looking old gentleman came and looked in at the window; and I heard him calling out, "Nurse, there is a young and attractive female waiting in the poop. Go and see what she wants." Are you the nurse?

THE WOMANSERVANT   Yes, miss: I'm Nurse Guinness.

---

*New Temple Shakespeare was a popular series of Shakespeare's plays.

That was old Captain Shotover, Mrs Hushabye's father. I heard him roaring; but I thought it was for something else. I suppose it was Mrs Hushabye that invited you, ducky?

THE YOUNG LADY   I understood her to do so. But really I think I'd better go.

NURSE GUINNESS   Oh, don't think of such a thing, miss. If Mrs Hushabye has forgotten all about it, it will be a pleasant surprise for her to see you, won't it?

THE YOUNG LADY   It has been a very unpleasant surprise to me to find that nobody expects me.[9]

NURSE GUINNESS   You'll get used to it, miss: this house is full of surprises for them that don't know our ways.

CAPTAIN SHOTOVER [looking in from the hall suddenly: an ancient but still hardy man with an immense white beard, in a reefer jacket* with a whistle hanging from his neck]   Nurse, there is a hold-all and a handbag on the front steps for everybody to fall over. Also a tennis racquet. Who the devil left them there?

THE YOUNG LADY   They are mine, I'm afraid.

THE CAPTAIN [advancing to the drawing-table]   Nurse, who is this misguided and unfortunate young lady?

NURSE GUINNESS   She says Miss Hessy invited her, sir.

THE CAPTAIN   And had she no friend, no parents, to warn her against my daughter's invitations? This is a pretty sort of house, by heavens! A young and attractive lady is invited here. Her luggage is left on the steps for hours; and she herself is deposited in the poop and abandoned, tired and starving. This is our hospitality. These are our manners. No room ready. No hot water. No welcoming hostess. Our visitor is to sleep in the toolshed, and to wash in the duckpond.

NURSE GUINNESS   Now it's all right, Captain: I'll get the lady some tea; and her room shall be ready before she has fin-

---

*Naval officer's double-breasted blue jacket.

ished it. [*To the young lady.*] Take off your hat, ducky; and make yourself at home [*she goes to the door leading to the hall*].

THE CAPTAIN [*as she passes him*]   Ducky! Do you suppose, woman, that because this young lady has been insulted and neglected, you have the right to address her as you address my wretched children, whom you have brought up in ignorance of the commonest decencies of social intercourse?

NURSE GUINNESS   Never mind him, doty.* [*Quite unconcerned, she goes out into the hall on her way to the kitchen.*]

THE CAPTAIN   Madam, will you favor me with your name? [*He sits down in the big wicker chair.*]

THE YOUNG LADY   My name is Ellie Dunn.

THE CAPTAIN   Dunn! I had a boatswain whose name was Dunn. He was originally a pirate in China. He set up as a ship's chandler† with stores which I have every reason to believe he stole from me. No doubt he became rich. Are you his daughter?

ELLIE [*indignant*]   No, certainly not. I am proud to be able to say that though my father has not been a successful man, nobody has ever had one word to say against him. I think my father is the best man I have ever known.

THE CAPTAIN   He must be greatly changed. Has he attained the seventh degree of concentration?

ELLIE   I don't understand.

THE CAPTAIN   But how could he, with a daughter? I, madam, have two daughters. One of them is Hesione Hushabye, who invited you here. I keep this house: she upsets it. I desire to attain the seventh degree of concentration: she invites visitors and leaves me to entertain them. [*NURSE GUINNESS returns with the tea-tray, which she places on the teak table.*] I have a second daughter who is, thank God, in a remote part of the

---

*Idiosyncratic form of address (perhaps related to "dote").
†Dealer in supplies for ships.

Empire with her numskull of a husband. As a child she thought the figure-head of my ship, the Dauntless, the most beautiful thing on earth. He resembled it. He had the same expression: wooden yet enterprising. She married him, and will never set foot in this house again.

NURSE GUINNESS [*carrying the table, with the tea-things on it, to ELLIE's side*]   Indeed you never were more mistaken. She is in England this very moment. You have been told three times this week that she is coming home for a year for her health. And very glad you should be to see your own daughter again after all these years.

THE CAPTAIN   I am not glad. The natural term of the affection of the human animal for its offspring is six years. My daughter Ariadne was born when I was forty-six. I am now eighty-eight. If she comes, I am not at home. If she wants anything, let her take it. If she asks for me, let her be informed that I am extremely old, and have totally forgotten her.

NURSE GUINNESS   That's no talk to offer to a young lady. Here, ducky, have some tea; and don't listen to him [*she pours out a cup of tea*].

THE CAPTAIN [*rising wrathfully*]   Now before high heaven they have given this innocent child Indian tea: the stuff they tan their own leather insides with. [*He seizes the cup and the tea-pot and empties both into the leathern bucket.*]

ELLIE [*almost in tears*]   Oh, please! I am so tired. I should have been glad of anything.

NURSE GUINNESS   Oh, what a thing to do! The poor lamb is ready to drop.

THE CAPTAIN   You shall have some of my tea. Do not touch that fly-blown* cake: nobody eats it here except the dogs. [*He disappears into the pantry.*]

NURSE GUINNESS   There's a man for you! They say he sold

---

*Stale.

himself to the devil in Zanzibar before he was a captain; and the older he grows the more I believe them.

A WOMAN'S VOICE [*in the hall*] Is anyone at home? Hesione! Nurse! Papa! Do come, somebody; and take in my luggage.

Thumping heard, as of an umbrella, on the wainscot.

NURSE GUINNESS My gracious! It's Miss Addy, Lady Utterword, Mrs Hushabye's sister: the one I told the captain about. [*Calling.*] Coming, Miss, coming.

She carries the table back to its place by the door and is hurrying out when she is intercepted by LADY UTTERWORD, who bursts in much flustered. LADY UTTERWORD, a blonde, is very handsome, very well dressed, and so precipitate in speech and action that the first impression (erroneous) is one of comic silliness.

LADY UTTERWORD Oh, is that you, Nurse? How are you? You don't look a day older. Is nobody at home? Where is Hesione? Doesn't she expect me? Where are the servants? Whose luggage is that on the steps? Where's papa? Is everybody asleep? [*Seeing ELLIE.*] Oh! I beg your pardon. I suppose you are one of my nieces. [*Approaching her with outstretched arms.*] Come and kiss your aunt, darling.

ELLIE I'm only a visitor. It is my luggage on the steps.

NURSE GUINNESS I'll go get you some fresh tea, ducky. [*She takes up the tray.*]

ELLIE But the old gentleman said he would make some himself.

NURSE GUINNESS Bless you! he's forgotten what he went for already. His mind wanders from one thing to another.

LADY UTTERWORD Papa, I suppose?

NURSE GUINNESS Yes, Miss.

LADY UTTERWORD [*vehemently*] Don't be silly, Nurse. Don't call me Miss.

NURSE GUINNESS [*placidly*] No, lovey [*she goes out with the tea-tray*].

LADY UTTERWORD [*sitting down with a flounce on the sofa*] I

know what you must feel. Oh, this house, this house! I come
back to it after twenty-three years; and it is just the same: the
luggage lying on the steps, the servants spoilt and impossible,
nobody at home to receive anybody, no regular meals, nobody
ever hungry because they are always gnawing bread and butter or munching apples, and, what is worse, the same disorder in ideas, in talk, in feeling. When I was a child I was used
to it: I had never known anything better, though I was unhappy, and longed all the time—oh, how I longed!—to be respectable, to be a lady, to live as others did, not to have to
think of everything for myself. I married at nineteen to escape
from it. My husband is Sir Hastings Utterword, who has been
governor of all the crown colonies in succession. I have always
been the mistress of Government House. I have been so
happy: I had forgotten that people could live like this. I
wanted to see my father, my sister, my nephews and nieces
(one ought to, you know), and I was looking forward to it.
And now the state of the house! the way I'm received! the casual impudence of that woman Guinness, our old nurse! really
Hesione might at least have been here: *some* preparation might
have been made for me. You must excuse my going on in this
way; but I am really very much hurt and annoyed and disillusioned: and if I had realized it was to be like this, I wouldn't
have come. I have a great mind to go away without another
word [*she is on the point of weeping*].

ELLIE [*also very miserable*]   Nobody has been here to receive me
either. I thought I ought to go away too. But how can I, Lady
Utterword? My luggage is on the steps; and the station fly*
has gone.

*The captain emerges from the pantry with a tray of Chinese lacquer
and a very fine tea-set on it. He rests it provisionally on the end of
the table; snatches away the drawing-board, which he stands on the*

---

*Hired transportation to and from the train station.

*floor against table legs; and puts the tray in the space thus cleared.
ELLIE pours out a cup greedily.*

THE CAPTAIN   Your tea, young lady. What! another lady! I
must fetch another cup [*he makes for the pantry*].

LADY UTTERWORD [*rising from the sofa, suffused with emotion*]
Papa! Don't you know me? I'm your daughter.

THE CAPTAIN   Nonsense! my daughter's upstairs asleep. [*He
vanishes through the half door.*]

LADY UTTERWORD retires to the window to conceal her tears.

ELLIE [*going to her with the cup*]   Don't be so distressed. Have
this cup of tea. He is very old and very strange: he has been
just like that to me. I know how dreadful it must be: my own
father is all the world to me. Oh, I'm sure he didn't mean it.

The captain returns with another cup.

THE CAPTAIN   Now we are complete. [*He places it on the tray.*]

LADY UTTERWORD [*hysterically*]   Papa, you can't have forgotten me. I am Ariadne. I'm little Paddy Patkins. Won't you
kiss me? [*She goes to him and throws her arms round his neck.*]

THE CAPTAIN [*woodenly enduring her embrace*]   How can you be
Ariadne? You are a middle-aged woman: well preserved,
madam, but no longer young.

LADY UTTERWORD   But think of all the years and years I
have been away, Papa. I have had to grow old, like other people.

THE CAPTAIN [*disengaging himself*]   You should grow out of
kissing strange men: they may be striving to attain the seventh
degree of concentration.

LADY UTTERWORD   But I'm your daughter. You haven't
seen me for years.

THE CAPTAIN   So much the worse! When our relatives are at
home, we have to think of all their good points or it would be
impossible to endure them. But when they are away, we console ourselves for their absence by dwelling on their vices.
That is how I have come to think my absent daughter Ariadne

a perfect fiend; so do not try to ingratiate yourself here by impersonating her [*he walks firmly away to the other side of the room*].

LADY UTTERWORD   Ingratiating myself indeed! [*With dignity.*] Very well, papa. [*She sits down at the drawing-table and pours out tea for herself.*]

THE CAPTAIN   I am neglecting my social duties. You remember Dunn? Billy Dunn?

LADY UTTERWORD   Do you mean that villainous sailor who robbed you?

THE CAPTAIN [*introducing ELLIE*]   His daughter. [*He sits down on the sofa.*]

ELLIE [*protesting*]   No—

NURSE GUINNESS returns with fresh tea.

THE CAPTAIN   Take that hogwash away. Do you hear?

NURSE   You've actually remembered about the tea! [*To ELLIE.*] Oh, miss, he didn't forget you after all! You *have* made an impression.

THE CAPTAIN [*gloomily*]   Youth! beauty! novelty! They are badly wanted in this house. I am excessively old. Hesione is only moderately young. Her children are not youthful.

LADY UTTERWORD   How can children be expected to be youthful in this house? Almost before we could speak we were filled with notions that might have been all very well for pagan philosophers of fifty, but were certainly quite unfit for respectable people of any age.

NURSE   You were always for respectability, Miss Addy.

LADY UTTERWORD   Nurse, will you please remember that I am Lady Utterword, and not Miss Addy, nor lovey, nor darling, nor doty? Do you hear?

NURSE   Yes, ducky: all right. I'll tell them all they must call you My lady. [*She takes her tray out with undisturbed placidity.*]

LADY UTTERWORD   What comfort? what sense is there in having servants with no manners?

ELLIE [*rising and coming to the table to put down her empty cup*] Lady Utterword, do you think Mrs Hushabye really expects me?

LADY UTTERWORD   Oh, don't ask me. You can see for yourself that I've just arrived; her only sister, after twenty-three years' absence! and it seems that *I* am not expected.

THE CAPTAIN   What does it matter whether the young lady is expected or not? She is welcome. There are beds: there is food. I'll find a room for her myself [*he makes for the door*].

ELLIE [*following him to stop him*]   Oh, please——[*He goes out.*] Lady Utterword, I don't know what to do. Your father persists in believing that my father is some sailor who robbed him.

LADY UTTERWORD   You had better pretend not to notice it. My father is a very clever man; but he always forgot things; and now that he is old, of course he is worse. And I must warn you that it is sometimes very hard to feel quite sure that he really forgets.

MRS HUSHABYE bursts into the room tempestuously and embraces ELLIE. She is a couple of years older than LADY UTTERWORD, and even better looking. She has magnificent black hair, eyes like the fish pools of Heshbon, and a nobly modelled neck, short at the back and low between her shoulders in front. Unlike her sister she is uncorseted and dressed anyhow in a rich robe of black pile† that shows off her white skin and statuesque contour.*

MRS HUSHABYE   Ellie, my darling, my pettikins [*kissing her*], how long have you been here? I've been at home all the time: I was putting flowers and things in your room; and when I just sat down for a moment to try how comfortable the armchair was I went off to sleep. Papa woke me and told me you were here. Fancy your finding no one, and being neglected and abandoned. [*Kissing her again.*] My poor love! [*She deposits*

---

*Simile taken from the Bible, Song of Solomon 7:4.
†Velvety fabric.

ELLIE on the sofa. Meanwhile ARIADNE has left the table and come over to claim her share of attention.] Oh! you've brought some-one with you. Introduce me.

LADY UTTERWORD   Hesione, is it possible that you don't know me?

MRS HUSHABYE [*conventionally*]   Of course I remember your face quite well. Where have we met?

LADY UTTERWORD   Didn't Papa tell you I was here? Oh! this is really too much. [*She throws herself sulkily into the big chair.*]

MRS HUSHABYE   Papa!

LADY UTTERWORD   Yes, Papa. Our papa, you unfeeling wretch! [*Rising angrily.*] I'll go straight to a hotel.

MRS HUSHABYE [*seizing her by the shoulders*]   My goodness gracious goodness, you don't mean to say that you're Addy!

LADY UTTERWORD   I certainly am Addy; and I don't think I can be so changed that you would not have recognized me if you had any real affection for me. And Papa didn't think me even worth mentioning!

MRS HUSHABYE   What a lark! Sit down [*she pushes her back into the chair instead of kissing her, and posts herself behind it*]. You *do* look a swell. You're much handsomer than you used to be. You've made the acquaintance of Ellie, of course. She is going to marry a perfect hog of a millionaire for the sake of her father, who is as poor as a church mouse; and you must help me to stop her.

ELLIE   Oh, please, Hesione!

MRS HUSHABYE   My pettikins, the man's coming here today with your father to begin persecuting you; and everybody will see the state of the case in ten minutes; so what's the use of making a secret of it?

ELLIE   He is not a hog, Hesione. You don't know how wonder-fully good he was to my father, and how deeply grateful I am to him.

MRS HUSHABYE [*to LADY UTTERWORD*]. Her father is a very remarkable man, Addy. His name is Mazzini Dunn. Mazzini* was a celebrity of some kind who knew Ellie's grandparents. They were both poets, like the Brownings; and when her father came into the world Mazzini said, "Another soldier born for freedom!" So they christened him Mazzini; and he has been fighting for freedom in his quiet way ever since. That's why he is so poor.

ELLIE   I am proud of his poverty.

MRS HUSHABYE   Of course you are, pettikins. Why not leave him in it, and marry someone you love?

LADY UTTERWORD [*rising suddenly and explosively*]   Hesione, are you going to kiss me or are you not?

MRS HUSHABYE   What do you want to be kissed for?

LADY UTTERWORD   I *don't* want to be kissed; but I do want you to behave properly and decently. We are sisters. We have been separated for twenty-three years. You *ought* to kiss me.

MRS HUSHABYE   To-morrow morning, dear, before you make up. I hate the smell of powder.

LADY UTTERWOOD   Oh! you unfeeling— [*she is interrupted by the return of the captain*].

THE CAPTAIN [*to ELLIE*]   Your room is ready. [*ELLIE rises.*] The sheets were damp; but I have changed them [*he makes for the garden door on the port side*].

LADY UTTERWORD   Oh! What about *my* sheets?

THE CAPTAIN [*halting at the door*]   Take my advice: air them: or take them off and sleep in blankets. You shall sleep in Ariadne's old room.

LADY UTTERWORD   Indeed I shall do nothing of the sort. That little hole! I am entitled to the best spare room.

---

*Giuseppe Mazzini (1805–1872), an Italian revolutionary who sought to unify Italy under a republican government and who participated in Italy's struggle for independence from Austrian domination.

THE CAPTAIN [*continuing unmoved*]   She married a numskull. She told me she would marry anyone to get away from home.

LADY UTTERWORD   You are pretending not to know me on purpose. I will leave the house.

MAZZINI DUNN enters from the hall. He is a little elderly man with bulging credulous eyes and earnest manners. He is dressed in a blue serge jacket suit with an unbuttoned mackintosh over it, and carries a soft black hat of clerical cut.

ELLIE   At last! Captain Shotover, here is my father.

THE CAPTAIN   This! Nonsense! not a bit like him [*he goes away through the garden, shutting the door sharply behind him*].

LADY UTTERWORD   I will not be ignored and pretended to be somebody else. I will have it out with Papa now, this instant. [*To MAZZINI.*] Excuse me. [*She follows the captain out, making a hasty bow to MAZZINI, who returns it.*]

MRS HUSHABYE [*hospitably shaking hands*]   How good of you to come, Mr Dunn! You don't mind Papa, do you? He is as mad as a hatter, you know, but quite harmless and extremely clever. You will have some delightful talks with him.

MAZZINI   I hope so. [*To ELLIE.*] So here you are, Ellie, dear. [*He draws her arm affectionately through his.*] I must thank you, Mrs Hushabye, for your kindness to my daughter. I'm afraid she would have had no holiday if you had not invited her.

MRS HUSHABYE   Not at all. Very nice of her to come and attract young people to the house for us.

MAZZINI [*smiling*]   I'm afraid Ellie is not interested in young men, Mrs Hushabye. Her taste is on the graver, solider side.

MRS HUSHABYE [*with a sudden rather hard brightness in her manner*]   Won't you take off your overcoat, Mr Dunn? You will find a cupboard for coats and hats and things in the corner of the hall.

MAZZINI [*hastily releasing ELLIE*]   Yes—thank you—I had better— [*he goes out*].

MRS HUSHABYE [*emphatically*]   The old brute!

ELLIE   Who?

MRS HUSHABYE   Who! Him. He. It [*pointing after MAZZINI*]. "Graver, solider tastes," indeed!

ELLIE [*aghast*]   You don't mean that you were speaking like that of my father!

MRS HUSHABYE   I was. You know I was.

ELLIE [*with dignity*]   I will leave your house at once. [*She turns to the door.*]

MRS HUSHABYE   If you attempt it, I'll tell your father why.

ELLIE [*turning again*]   Oh! How can you treat a visitor like this, Mrs Hushabye?

MRS HUSHABYE   I thought you were going to call me Hesione.

ELLIE   Certainly not now?

MRS HUSHABYE   Very well: I'll tell your father.

ELLIE [*distressed*]   Oh!

MRS HUSHABYE   If you turn a hair—if you take his part against me and against your own heart for a moment, I'll give that born soldier of freedom a piece of my mind that will stand him on his selfish old head for a week.

ELLIE   Hesione! My father selfish! How little you know—

She is interrupted by MAZZINI, who returns, excited and perspiring.

MAZZINI   Ellie, Mangan has come: I thought you'd like to know. Excuse me, Mrs Hushabye, the strange old gentleman—

MRS HUSHABYE   Papa. Quite so.

MAZZINI   Oh, I beg your pardon, of course: I was a little confused by his manner. He is making Mangan help him with something in the garden; and he wants me too—

A powerful whistle is heard.

THE CAPTAIN'S VOICE   Bosun ahoy! [*the whistle is repeated*].

MAZZINI [*flustered*]   Oh dear! I believe he is whistling for me. [*He hurries out.*]

MRS HUSHABYE   Now *my* father is a wonderful man if you like.

ELLIE   Hesione, listen to me. You don't understand. My father and Mr Mangan were boys together. Mr Ma—

MRS HUSHABYE   I don't care what they were: we must sit down if you are going to begin as far back as that. [*She snatches at ELLIE's waist, and makes her sit down on the sofa beside her.*] Now, pettikins, tell me all about Mr Mangan. They call him Boss Mangan, don't they? He is a Napoleon of industry and disgustingly rich, isn't he? Why isn't your father rich?

ELLIE   My poor father should never have been in business. His parents were poets; and they gave him the noblest ideas; but they could not afford to give him a profession.

MRS HUSHABYE   Fancy your grandparents, with their eyes in fine frenzy rolling! And so your poor father had to go into business. Hasn't he succeeded in it?

ELLIE   He always used to say he could succeed if he only had some capital. He fought his way along, to keep a roof over our heads and bring us up well; but it was always a struggle: always the same difficulty of not having capital enough. I don't know how to describe it to you.

MRS HUSHABYE   Poor Ellie! I know. Pulling the devil by the tail.

ELLIE [*hurt*]   Oh, no. Not like that. It was at least dignified.

MRS HUSHABYE   That made it all the harder, didn't it? *I* shouldn't have pulled the devil by the tail with dignity. I should have pulled hard— [*between her teeth*] hard. Well? Go on.

ELLIE   At last it seemed that all our troubles were at an end. Mr Mangan did an extraordinarily noble thing out of pure friendship for my father and respect for his character. He asked him how much capital he wanted, and gave it to him. I don't mean that he lent it to him, or that he invested it in his business. He just simply made him a present of it. Wasn't that splendid of him?

MRS HUSHABYE   On condition that you married him?

ELLIE   Oh, no, no, no! This was when I was a child. He had never even seen me: he never came to our house. It was absolutely disinterested. Pure generosity.

MRS HUSHABYE   Oh! I beg the gentleman's pardon. Well, what became of the money?

ELLIE   We all got new clothes and moved into another house. And I went to another school for two years.

MRS HUSHABYE   Only two years?

ELLIE   That was all: for at the end of two years my father was utterly ruined.

MRS HUSHABYE   How?

ELLIE   I don't know. I never could understand. But it was dreadful. When we were poor my father had never been in debt. But when he launched out into business on a large scale, he had to incur liabilities. When the business went into liquidation he owed more money than Mr Mangan had given him.

MRS HUSHABYE   Bit off more than he could chew, I suppose.

ELLIE   I think you are a little unfeeling about it.

MRS HUSHABYE   My pettikins, you mustn't mind my way of talking. I was quite as sensitive and particular as you once; but I have picked up so much slang from the children that I am really hardly presentable. I suppose your father had no head for business, and made a mess of it.

ELLIE   Oh, that just shows how entirely you are mistaken about him. The business turned out a great success. It now pays forty-four per cent after deducting the excess profits tax.

MRS HUSHABYE   Then why aren't you rolling in money?

ELLIE   I don't know. It seems very unfair to me. You see, my father was made bankrupt. It nearly broke his heart, because he had persuaded several of his friends to put money into the business. He was sure it would succeed; and events proved that he was quite right. But they all lost their money. It was dreadful. I don't know what we should have done but for Mr Mangan.

MRS HUSHABYE   What! Did the Boss come to the rescue again, after all his money being thrown away?

ELLIE   He did indeed, and never uttered a reproach to my father. He bought what was left of the business—the buildings and the machinery and things—from the official trustee for enough money to enable my father to pay six and eightpence in the pound and get his discharge.* Everyone pitied papa so much, and saw so plainly that he was an honorable man, that they let him off at six-and-eight-pence instead of ten shillings. Then Mr Mangan started a company to take up the business, and made my father a manager in it to save us from starvation; for I wasn't earning anything then.

MRS HUSHABYE   Quite a romance. And when did the Boss develop the tender passion?

ELLIE   Oh, that was years after, quite lately. He took the chair one night at a sort of people's concert. I was singing there. As an amateur, you know: half a guinea for expenses and three songs with three encores. He was so pleased with my singing that he asked might he walk home with me. I never saw anyone so taken aback as he was when I took him home and introduced him to my father, his own manager. It was then that my father told me how nobly he had behaved. Of course it was considered a great chance for me, as he is so rich. And—and—we drifted into a sort of understanding—I suppose I should call it an engagement— [*she is distressed and cannot go on*].

MRS HUSHABYE [*rising and marching about*]   You may have drifted into it; but you will bounce out of it, my pettikins, if I am to have anything to do with it.

ELLIE [*hopelessly*]   No: it's no use. I am bound in honor and gratitude. I will go through with it.

MRS HUSHABYE [*behind the sofa, scolding down at her*]   You

---

*That is, from bankruptcy, so he could once again engage in business.

know, of course, that it's not honorable or grateful to marry a man you don't love. Do you love this Mangan man?

ELLIE   Yes. At least——

MRS HUSHABYE   I don't want to know about "at least": I want to know the worst. Girls of your age fall in love with all sorts of impossible people, especially old people.

ELLIE   I like Mr Mangan very much; and I shall always be——

MRS HUSHABYE [*impatiently completing the sentence and prancing away intolerantly to starboard*]   ——grateful to him for his kindness to dear father. I know. Anybody else?

ELLIE   What do you mean?

MRS HUSHABYE   Anybody else? Are you in love with anybody else?

ELLIE   Of course not.

MRS HUSHABYE   Humph! [*The book on the drawing-table catches her eye. She picks it up, and evidently finds the title very unexpected. She looks at ELLIE, and asks, quaintly*] Quite sure you're not in love with an actor?

ELLIE   No, no. Why? What put such a thing into your head?

MRS HUSHABYE   This is yours, isn't it? Why else should you be reading Othello?

ELLIE   My father taught me to love Shakespeare.

MRS HUSHABYE [*flinging the book down on the table*] Really! your father does seem to be about the limit.

ELLIE [*naïvely*]   Do you never read Shakespeare, Hesione? That seems to me so extraordinary. I like Othello.

MRS HUSHABYE   Do you, indeed? He was jealous, wasn't he?

ELLIE   Oh, not that. I think all the part about jealousy is horrible. But don't you think it must have been a wonderful experience for Desdemona, brought up so quietly at home, to meet a man who had been out in the world doing all sorts of brave things and having terrible adventures, and yet finding something in her that made him love to sit and talk with her and tell her about them?

MRS HUSHABYE   That's your idea of romance, is it?

ELLIE   Not romance, exactly. It might really happen.

ELLIE's eyes show that she is not arguing, but in a daydream. MRS HUSHABYE, watching her inquisitively, goes deliberately back to the sofa and resumes her seat beside her.

MRS HUSHABYE   Ellie darling, have you noticed that some of those stories that Othello told Desdemona couldn't have happened?

ELLIE   Oh, no. Shakespeare thought they could have happened.

MRS HUSHABYE   Um! Desdemona thought they could have happened. But they didn't.

ELLIE   Why do you look so enigmatic about it? You are such a sphinx: I never know what you mean.

MRS HUSHABYE   Desdemona would have found him out if she had lived, you know. I wonder was that why he strangled her!

ELLIE   Othello was not telling lies.

MRS HUSHABYE   How do you know?

ELLIE   Shakespeare would have said if he was. Hesione, there are men who have done wonderful things: men like Othello, only, of course, white, and very handsome, and—

MRS HUSHABYE   Ah! Now we're coming to it. Tell me all about him. I knew there must be somebody, or you'd never have been so miserable about Mangan: you'd have thought it quite a lark to marry him.

ELLIE [*blushing vividly*]   Hesione, you are dreadful. But I don't want to make a secret of it, though of course I don't tell everybody. Besides, I don't know him.

MRS HUSHABYE   Don't know him! What does that mean?

ELLIE   Well, of course I know him to speak to.

MRS HUSHABYE   But you want to know him ever so much more intimately, eh?

ELLIE   No, no: I know him quite—almost intimately.

MRS HUSHABYE   You don't know him; and you know him almost intimately. How lucid!

ELLIE   I mean that he does not call on us. I—I got into conversation with him by chance at a concert.

MRS HUSHABYE   You seem to have rather a gay time at your concerts, Ellie.

ELLIE   Not at all: we talk to everyone in the green-room waiting for our turns. I thought he was one of the artists: he looked so splendid. But he was only one of the committee. I happened to tell him that I was copying a picture at the National Gallery. I make a little money that way. I can't paint much; but as it's always the same picture I can do it pretty quickly and get two or three pounds for it. It happened that he came to the National Gallery one day.

MRS HUSHABYE   On students' day. Paid sixpence to stumble about through a crowd of easels, when he might have come in next day for nothing and found the floor clear! Quite by accident?

ELLIE [*triumphantly*]   No. On purpose. He liked talking to me. He knows lots of the most splendid people. Fashionable women who are all in love with him. But he ran away from them to see me at the National Gallery and persuade me to come with him for a drive round Richmond Park in a taxi.

MRS HUSHABYE   My pettikins, you have been going it. It's wonderful what you good girls can do without anyone saying a word.

ELLIE   I am not in society, Hesione. If I didn't make acquaintances in that way I shouldn't have any at all.

MRS HUSHABYE   Well, no harm if you know how to take care of yourself. May I ask his name?

ELLIE [*slowly and musically*]   Marcus Darnley.

MRS HUSHABYE [*echoing the music*]   Marcus Darnley! What a splendid name!

ELLIE   Oh, I'm so glad you think so. I think so too; but I was afraid it was only a silly fancy of my own.

MRS HUSHABYE   Hm! Is he one of the Aberdeen Darnleys?

ELLIE   Nobody knows. Just fancy! He was found in an antique chest—

MRS HUSHABYE   A what?

ELLIE   An antique chest, one summer morning in a rose garden, after a night of the most terrible thunderstorm.

MRS HUSHABYE   What on earth was he doing in the chest? Did he get into it because he was afraid of the lightning?

ELLIE   Oh, no, no: he was a baby. The name Marcus Darnley was embroidered on his baby clothes. And five hundred pounds in gold.

MRS HUSHABYE [*looking hard at her*]   Ellie!

ELLIE   The garden of the Viscount—

MRS HUSHABYE   —de Rougemont?*

ELLIE [*innocently*]   No: de Larochejaquelin. A French family. A vicomte. His life has been one long romance. A tiger—

MRS HUSHABYE   Slain by his own hand?

ELLIE   Oh, no: nothing vulgar like that. He saved the life of the tiger from a hunting party: one of King Edward's hunting parties in India. The King was furious: that was why he never had his military services properly recognized. But he doesn't care. He is a Socialist and despises rank, and has been in three revolutions fighting on the barricades.

MRS HUSHABYE   How can you sit there telling me such lies? You, Ellie, of all people! And I thought you were a perfectly simple, straightforward, good girl.

ELLIE [*rising, dignified but very angry*]   Do you mean to say you don't believe me?

---

*Louis de Rougemont is the assumed name of nineteenth-century Swiss adventurer Louis Grin (1847–1921), who wrote sensational, often bogus, accounts of his adventures; Hesione implies that "Marcus Darnley" (her husband's pseudonym) is a liar.

MRS HUSHABYE   Of course I don't believe you. You're inventing every word of it. Do you take me for a fool?

ELLIE stares at her. Her candor is so obvious that MRS HUSHABYE is puzzled.

ELLIE   Goodbye, Hesione. I'm very sorry. I see now that it sounds very improbable as I tell it. But I can't stay if you think that way about me.

MRS HUSHABYE [*catching her dress*]   You shan't go. I couldn't be so mistaken: I know too well what liars are like. Somebody has really told you all this.

ELLIE [*flushing*]   Hesione, don't say that you don't believe him. I couldn't bear that.

MRS HUSHABYE [*soothing her*]   Of course I believe him, dearest. But you should have broken it to me by degrees. [*Drawing her back to her seat.*] Now tell me all about him. Are you in love with him?

ELLIE   Oh, no. I'm not so foolish. I don't fall in love with people. I'm not so silly as you think.

MRS HUSHABYE   I see. Only something to think about—to give some interest and pleasure to life.

ELLIE   Just so. That's all, really.

MRS HUSHABYE   It makes the hours go fast, doesn't it? No tedious waiting to go to sleep at nights and wondering whether you will have a bad night. How delightful it makes waking up in the morning! How much better than the happiest dream! All life transfigured! No more wishing one had an interesting book to read, because life is so much happier than any book! No desire but to be alone and not to have to talk to anyone: to be alone and just think about it.

ELLIE [*embracing her*]   Hesione, you are a witch. How do you know? Oh, you are the most sympathetic woman in the world!

MRS HUSHABYE [*caressing her*]   Pettikins, my pettikins, how I envy you! and how I pity you!

ELLIE   Pity me! Oh, why?

A very handsome man of fifty, with mousquetaire moustaches, wearing a rather dandified curly brimmed hat, and carrying an elaborate walking-stick, comes into the room from the hall, and stops short at sight of the women on the sofa.

ELLIE [*seeing him and rising in glad surprise*]   Oh! Hesione: this is Mr Marcus Darnley.

MRS HUSHABYE [*rising*]   What a lark! He is my husband.

ELLIE   But now— [*she stops suddenly: then turns pale and sways*].

MRS HUSHABYE [*catching her and sitting down with her on the sofa*]   Steady, my pettikins.

THE MAN [*with a mixture of confusion and effrontery, depositing his hat and stick on the teak table*]   My real name, Miss Dunn, is Hector Hushabye. I leave you to judge whether that is a name any sensitive man would care to confess so. I never use it when I can possibly help it. I have been away for nearly a month; and I had no idea you knew my wife, or that you were coming here. I am none the less delighted to find you in our little house.

ELLIE [*in great distress*]   I don't know what to do. Please, may I speak to papa? Do leave me. I can't bear it.

MRS HUSHABYE   Be off, Hector.

HECTOR   I—

MRS HUSHABYE   Quick, quick. Get out.

HECTOR   If you think it better— [*he goes out, taking his hat with him but leaving the stick on the table*].

MRS HUSHABYE [*laying ELLIE down at the end of the sofa*]   Now, pettikins, he is gone. There's nobody but me. You can let yourself go. Don't try to control yourself. Have a good cry.

ELLIE [*raising her head*]   Damn!

MRS HUSHABYE   Splendid! Oh, what a relief! I thought you were going to be broken-hearted. Never mind me. Damn him again.

ELLIE   I am not damning him. I am damning myself for being such a fool. [*Rising.*] How could I let myself be taken in so? [*She begins prowling to and fro, her bloom gone, looking curiously older and harder.*]

MRS HUSHABYE [*cheerfully*]   Why not, pettikins? Very few young women can resist Hector. I couldn't when I was your age. He is really rather splendid, you know.

ELLIE [*turning on her*]   Splendid! Yes, splendid looking, of course. But how can you love a liar?

MRS HUSHABYE   I don't know. But you can, fortunately. Otherwise there wouldn't be much love in the world.

ELLIE   But to lie like that! To be a boaster! a coward!

MRS HUSHABYE [*rising in alarm*]   Pettikins, none of that, if you please. If you hint the slightest doubt of Hector's courage, he will go straight off and do the most horribly dangerous things to convince himself that he isn't a coward. He has a dreadful trick of getting out of one third-floor window and coming in at another, just to test his nerve. He has a whole drawerful of Albert Medals* for saving people's lives.

ELLIE   He never told me that.

MRS HUSHABYE   He never boasts of anything he really did: he can't bear it; and it makes him shy if anyone else does. All his stories are made-up stories.

ELLIE [*coming to her*]   Do you mean that he is really brave, and really has adventures, and yet tells lies about things that he never did and that never happened?

MRS HUSHABYE   Yes, pettikins, I do. People don't have their virtues and vices in sets: they have them anyhow: all mixed.

ELLIE [*staring at her thoughtfully*]   There's something odd about this house, Hesione, and even about you. I don't know why I'm talking to you so calmly. I have a horrible fear that my

---

*Awards, named for Prince Albert (1819–1861, husband of Queen Victoria), for altruistic rescues from injury or death.

heart is broken, but that heartbreak is not like what I thought it must be.

MRS HUSHABYE [*fondling her*]   It's only life educating you, pettikins. How do you feel about Boss Mangan now?

ELLIE [*disengaging herself with an expression of distaste*]   Oh, how can you remind me of him, Hesione?

MRS HUSHABYE   Sorry, dear. I think I hear Hector coming back. You don't mind now, do you, dear?

ELLIE   Not in the least. I am quite cured.

MAZZINI DUNN and HECTOR come in from the hall.

HECTOR [*as he opens the door and allows MAZZINI to pass in*] One second more, and she would have been a dead woman!

MAZZINI   Dear! dear! what an escape! Ellie, my love, Mr Hushabye has just been telling me the most extraordinary—

ELLIE   Yes, I've heard it [*she crosses to the other side of the room*].

HECTOR [*following her*]   Not this one: I'll tell it to you after dinner. I think you'll like it. The truth is I made it up for you, and was looking forward to the pleasure of telling it to you. But in a moment of impatience at being turned out of the room, I threw it away on your father.

ELLIE [*turning at bay with her back to the carpenter's bench, scornfully self-possessed*]   It was not thrown away. He believes it. I should not have believed it.

MAZZINI [*benevolently*]   Ellie is very naughty, Mr Hushabye. Of course she does not really think that. [*He goes to the bookshelves, and inspects the titles of the volumes.*]

BOSS MANGAN comes in from the hall, followed by the captain. MANGAN, carefully frock-coated as for church or for a directors' meeting, is about fifty-five, with a care-worn, mistrustful expression, standing a little on an entirely imaginary dignity, with a dull complexion, straight, lustreless hair, and features so entirely commonplace that it is impossible to describe them.

CAPTAIN SHOTOVER [*to MRS HUSHABYE, introducing the newcomer*]   Says his name is Mangan. Not able-bodied.

MRS HUSHABYE [*graciously*]   How do you do, Mr Mangan?

MANGAN [*shaking hands*]   Very pleased.

CAPTAIN SHOTOVER   Dunn's lost his muscle, but recovered his nerve. Men seldom do after three attacks of delirium tremens [*he goes into the pantry*].

MRS HUSHABYE   I congratulate you, Mr Dunn.

MAZZINI [*dazed*]   I am a lifelong teetotaler.

MRS HUSHABYE   You will find it far less trouble to let papa have his own way than try to explain.

MAZZINI   But three attacks of delirium tremens, really!

MRS HUSHABYE [*to MANGAN*]   Do you know my husband, Mr Mangan [*she indicates HECTOR*].

MANGAN [*going to HECTOR, who meets him with outstretched hand*]   Very pleased. [*Turning to ELLIE.*] I hope, Miss Ellie, you have not found the journey down too fatiguing. [*They shake hands.*]

MRS HUSHABYE   Hector, show Mr Dunn his room.

HECTOR   Certainly. Come along, Mr Dunn. [*He takes MAZZINI out.*]

ELLIE   You haven't shown me my room yet, Hesione.

MRS HUSHABYE   How stupid of me! Come along. Make yourself quite at home, Mr Mangan. Papa will entertain you. [*She calls to the captain in the pantry.*] Papa, come and explain the house to Mr Mangan.

She goes out with ELLIE. The captain comes from the pantry.

CAPTAIN SHOTOVER   You're going to marry Dunn's daughter. Don't. You're too old.

MANGAN [*staggered*]   Well! That's fairly blunt, Captain.

CAPTAIN SHOTOVER   It's true.

MANGAN   She doesn't think so.

CAPTAIN SHOTOVER   She does.

MANGAN   Older men than I have—

CAPTAIN SHOTOVER [*finishing the sentence for him*]   —made fools of themselves. That, also, is true.

MANGAN [*asserting himself*]   I don't see that this is any business of yours.

CAPTAIN SHOTOVER   It is everybody's business. The stars in their courses are shaken when such things happen.

MANGAN   I'm going to marry her all the same.

CAPTAIN SHOTOVER   How do you know?

MANGAN [*playing the strong man*]   I intend to. I mean to. See? I never made up my mind to do a thing yet that I didn't bring it off. That's the sort of man I am; and there will be a better understanding between us when you make up your mind to that, Captain.

CAPTAIN SHOTOVER   You frequent picture palaces.

MANGAN   Perhaps I do. Who told you?

CAPTAIN SHOTOVER   Talk like a man, not like a movy. You mean that you make a hundred thousand a year.

MANGAN   I don't boast. But when I meet a man that makes a hundred thousand a year, I take off my hat to that man, and stretch out my hand to him and call him brother.

CAPTAIN SHOTOVER   Then you also make a hundred thousand a year, hey?

MANGAN   No. I can't say that. Fifty thousand, perhaps.

CAPTAIN SHOTOVER   His half brother only [*he turns away from MANGAN with his usual abruptness, and collects the empty teacups on the Chinese tray*].

MANGAN [*irritated*]   See here, Captain Shotover. I don't quite understand my position here. I came here on your daughter's invitation. Am I in her house or in yours?

CAPTAIN SHOTOVER   You are beneath the dome of heaven, in the house of God. What is true within these walls is true outside them. Go out on the seas; climb the mountains; wander through the valleys. She is still too young.

MANGAN [*weakening*]   But I'm very little over fifty.

CAPTAIN SHOTOVER   You are still less under sixty. Boss

Mangan, you will not marry the pirate's child [*he carries the tray away into the pantry*].

MANGAN [*following him to the half door*]   What pirate's child? What are you talking about?

CAPTAIN SHOTOVER [*in the pantry*]   Ellie Dunn. You will not marry her.

MANGAN   Who will stop me?

CAPTAIN SHOTOVER [*emerging*]   My daughter [*he makes for the door leading to the hall*].

MANGAN [*following him*]   Mrs Hushabye! Do you mean to say she brought me down here to break it off?

CAPTAIN SHOTOVER [*stopping and turning on him*]   I know nothing more than I have seen in her eye. She will break it off. Take my advice: marry a West Indian negress: they make excellent wives. I was married to one myself for two years.

MANGAN   Well, I am damned!

CAPTAIN SHOTOVER   I thought so. I was, too, for many years. The negress redeemed me.

MANGAN [*feebly*]   This is queer. I ought to walk out of this house.

CAPTAIN SHOTOVER   Why?

MANGAN   Well, many men would be offended by your style of talking.

CAPTAIN SHOTOVER   Nonsense! It's the other sort of talking that makes quarrels. Nobody ever quarrels with me.

A gentleman, whose first-rate tailoring and frictionless manners proclaim the wellbred West Ender, comes in from the hall. He has an engaging air of being young and unmarried, but on close inspection is found to be at least over forty.

THE GENTLEMAN   Excuse my intruding in this fashion, but there is no knocker on the door and the bell does not seem to ring.

CAPTAIN SHOTOVER   Why should there be a knocker? Why should the bell ring? The door is open.

THE GENTLEMAN   Precisely. So I ventured to come in.

CAPTAIN SHOTOVER   Quite right. I will see about a room for you [*he makes for the door*].

THE GENTLEMAN [*stopping him*]   But I'm afraid you don't know who I am.

CAPTAIN SHOTOVER   Do you suppose that at my age I make distinctions between one fellowcreature and another? [*He goes out. MANGAN and the newcomer stare at one another.*]

MANGAN   Strange character, Captain Shotover, sir.

THE GENTLEMAN   Very.

CAPTAIN SHOTOVER [*shouting outside*]   Hesione, another person has arrived and wants a room. Man about town, well dressed, fifty.

THE GENTLEMAN   Fancy Hesione's feelings! May I ask are you a member of the family?

MANGAN   No.

THE GENTLEMAN   I am. At least a connection.

MRS HUSHABYE comes back.

MRS HUSHABYE   How do you do? How good of you to come!

THE GENTLEMAN   I am very glad indeed to make your acquaintance, Hesione. [*Instead of taking her hand he kisses her. At the same moment the captain appears in the doorway.*] You will excuse my kissing your daughter, Captain, when I tell you that—

CAPTAIN SHOTOVER   Stuff! Everyone kisses my daughter. Kiss her as much as you like [*he makes for the pantry*].

THE GENTLEMAN   Thank you. One moment, Captain. [*The captain halts and turns. The gentleman goes to him affably.*] Do you happen to remember—but probably you don't, as it occurred many years ago—that your younger daughter married a numskull?

CAPTAIN SHOTOVER   Yes. She said she'd marry anybody to get away from this house. I should not have recognized you:

your head is no longer like a walnut. Your aspect is softened. You have been boiled in bread and milk for years and years, like other married men. Poor devil! [*He disappears into the pantry.*]

MRS HUSHABYE [*going past MANGAN to the gentleman and scrutinizing him*]. I don't believe you are Hastings Utterword.

THE GENTLEMAN   I am not.

MRS HUSHABYE   Then what business had you to kiss me?

THE GENTLEMAN   I thought I would like to. The fact is, I am Randall Utterword, the unworthy younger brother of Hastings. I was abroad diplomatizing when he was married.

LADY UTTERWORD [*dashing in*]   Hesione, where is the key of the wardrobe in my room? My diamonds are in my dressing-bag: I must lock it up— [*recognizing the stranger with a shock*] Randall, how dare you? [*She marches at him past MRS HUSHABYE, who retreats and joins MANGAN near the sofa.*]

RANDALL   How dare I what? I am not doing anything.

LADY UTTERWORD   Who told you I was here?

RANDALL   Hastings. You had just left when I called on you at Claridge's; so I followed you down here. You are looking extremely well.

LADY UTTERWORD   Don't presume to tell me so.

MRS HUSHABYE   What is wrong with Mr Randall, Addy?

LADY UTTERWORD [*recollecting herself*]   Oh, nothing. But he has no right to come bothering you and papa without being invited [*she goes to the window-seat and sits down, turning away from them ill-humoredly and looking into the garden, where HECTOR and ELLIE are now seen strolling together*].

MRS HUSHABYE   I think you have not met Mr Mangan, Addy.

LADY UTTERWORD [*turning her head and nodding coldly to MANGAN*]   I beg your pardon. Randall, you have flustered me so: I make a perfect fool of myself.

MRS HUSHABYE   Lady Utterword. My sister. My younger sister.

MANGAN [*bowing*]   Pleased to meet you, Lady Utterword.

LADY UTTERWORD [*with marked interest*]   Who is that gentleman walking in the garden with Miss Dunn?

MRS HUSHABYE   I don't know. She quarrelled mortally with my husband only ten minutes ago; and I didn't know anyone else had come. It must be a visitor. [*She goes to the window to look.*] Oh, it is Hector. They've made it up.

LADY UTTERWORD   Your husband! That handsome man?

MRS HUSHABYE   Well, why shouldn't my husband be a handsome man?

RANDALL [*joining them at the window*]   One's husband never is, Ariadne [*he sits by LADY UTTERWORD, on her right*].

MRS HUSHABYE   One's sister's husband always is, Mr Randall.

LADY UTTERWORD   Don't be vulgar, Randall. And you, Hesione, are just as bad.

ELLIE and HECTOR come in from the garden by the starboard door. Randall rises. ELLIE retires into the corner near the pantry. HECTOR comes forward; and LADY UTTERWORD rises looking her very best.

MRS. HUSHABYE   Hector, this is Addy.

HECTOR [*apparently surprised*]   Not this lady.

LADY UTTERWORD [*smiling*]   Why not?

HECTOR [*looking at her with a piercing glance of deep but respectful admiration, his moustache bristling*]   I thought—[*pulling himself together*]. I beg your pardon, Lady Utterword. I am extremely glad to welcome you at last under our roof [*he offers his hand with grave courtesy*].

MRS HUSHABYE   She wants to be kissed, Hector.

LADY UTTERWORD   Hesione! [*But she still smiles.*]

MRS HUSHABYE   Call her Addy; and kiss her like a good brother-in-law; and have done with it. [*She leaves them to themselves.*]

HECTOR   Behave yourself, Hesione. Lady Utterword is entitled not only to hospitality but to civilization.

LADY UTTERWORD [*gratefully*] Thank you, Hector. [*They shake hands cordially.*]

MAZZINI DUNN is seen crossing the garden from starboard to port.

CAPTAIN SHOTOVER [*coming from the pantry and addressing ELLIE*] Your father has washed himself.

ELLIE [*quite self-possessed*] He often does, Captain Shotover.

CAPTAIN SHOTOVER A strange conversion! I saw him through the pantry window.

MAZZINI DUNN enters through the port window door, newly washed and brushed, and stops, smiling benevolently, between MANGAN and MRS HUSHABYE.

MRS HUSHABYE [*introducing*] Mr Mazzini Dunn, Lady Ut— oh, I forgot: you've met. [*Indicating ELLIE*] Miss Dunn.

MAZZINI [*walking across the room to take ELLIE's hand, and beaming at his own naughty irony*] I have met Miss Dunn also. She is my daughter. [*He draws her arm through his caressingly.*]

MRS HUSHABYE Of course: how stupid! Mr Utterword, my sister's—er—

RANDALL [*shaking hands agreeably*] Her brother-in-law, Mr Dunn. How do you do?

MRS HUSHABYE This is my husband.

HECTOR We have met, dear. Don't introduce us any more. [*He moves away to the big chair, and adds*] Won't you sit down, Lady Utterword? [*She does so very graciously.*]

MRS HUSHABYE Sorry. I hate it: it's like making people show their tickets.

MAZZINI [*sententiously*] How little it tells us, after all! The great question is, not who we are, but what we are.

CAPTAIN SHOTOVER Ha! What are you?

MAZZINI [*taken aback*] What am I?

CAPTAIN SHOTOVER A thief, a pirate, and a murderer.

MAZZINI I assure you you are mistaken.

CAPTAIN SHOTOVER An adventurous life; but what does it end in? Respectability. A ladylike daughter. The language and appearance of a city missionary. Let it be a warning to all of you [*he goes out through the garden*].

DUNN   I hope nobody here believes that I am a thief, a pirate, or a murderer. Mrs Hushabye, will you excuse me a moment? I must really go and explain. [*He follows the captain.*]

MRS HUSHABYE [*as he goes*]   It's no use. You'd really better— [*but DUNN has vanished*]. We had better all go out and look for some tea. We never have regular tea; but you can always get some when you want: the servants keep it stewing all day. The kitchen veranda is the best place to ask. May I show you? [*She goes to the starboard door.*]

RANDALL [*going with her*]   Thank you, I don't think I'll take any tea this afternoon. But if you will show me the garden—

MRS HUSHABYE   There's nothing to see in the garden except papa's observatory, and a gravel pit with a cave where he keeps dynamite and things of that sort. However, it's pleasanter out of doors; so come along.

RANDALL   Dynamite! Isn't that rather risky?

MRS HUSHABYE   Well, we don't sit in the gravel pit when there's a thunderstorm.

LADY UTTERWORD   That's something new. What is the dynamite for?

HECTOR   To blow up the human race if it goes too far. He is trying to discover a psychic ray that will explode all the explosive at the will of a Mahatma.*

ELLIE   The captain's tea is delicious, Mr Utterword.

MRS HUSHABYE [*stopping in the doorway*]   Do you mean to say that you've had some of my father's tea? that you got round him before you were ten minutes in the house?

ELLIE   I did.

MRS HUSHABYE   You little devil! [*She goes out with RANDALL.*]

MANGAN   Won't you come, Miss Ellie?

---

*Saintly sage.

ELLIE   I'm too tired. I'll take a book up to my room and rest a
little. [*She goes to the bookshelf.*]

MANGAN   Right. You can't do better. But I'm disappointed.
[*He follows RANDALL and MRS HUSHABYE.*]

*ELLIE, HECTOR, and LADY UTTERWORD are left. HECTOR is
close to LADY UTTERWORD. They look at ELLIE, waiting for her to
go.*

ELLIE [*looking at the title of a book*]   Do you like stories of adventure, Lady Utterword?

LADY UTTERWORD [*patronizingly*]   Of course, dear.

ELLIE   Then I'll leave you to Mr Hushabye. [*She goes out through
the hall.*]

HECTOR   That girl is mad about tales of adventure. The lies I
have to tell her!

LADY UTTERWORD [*not interested in ELLIE*]   When you saw
me what did you mean by saying that you thought, and then
stopping short? What did you think?

HECTOR [*folding his arms and looking down at her magnetically*]
May I tell you?

LADY UTTERWORD   Of course.

HECTOR   It will not sound very civil. I was on the point of saying, "I thought you were a plain woman."

LADY UTTERWORD   Oh, for shame, Hector! What right
had you to notice whether I am plain or not?

HECTOR   Listen to me, Ariadne. Until today I have seen only
photographs of you; and no photograph can give the strange
fascination of the daughters of that supernatural old man.
There is some damnable quality in them that destroys men's
moral sense, and carries them beyond honor and dishonor.
You know that, don't you?

LADY UTTERWORD   Perhaps I do, Hector. But let me warn
you once for all that I am a rigidly conventional woman. You
may think because I'm a Shotover that I'm a Bohemian, because we are all so horribly Bohemian. But I'm not. I hate and

loathe Bohemianism. No child brought up in a strict Puritan household ever suffered from Puritanism as I suffered from our Bohemianism.

HECTOR   Our children are like that. They spend their holidays in the houses of their respectable schoolfellows.

LADY UTTERWORD   I shall invite them for Christmas.

HECTOR   Their absence leaves us both without our natural chaperones.

LADY UTTERWORD   Children are certainly very inconvenient sometimes. But intelligent people can always manage, unless they are Bohemians.

HECTOR   You are no Bohemian; but you are no Puritan either: your attraction is alive and powerful. What sort of woman do you count yourself?

LADY UTTERWORD   I am a woman of the world, Hector; and I can assure you that if you will only take the trouble always to do the perfectly correct thing, and to say the perfectly correct thing, you can do just what you like. An ill-conducted, careless woman gets simply no chance. An ill-conducted, careless man is never allowed within arm's length of any woman worth knowing.

HECTOR   I see. You are neither a Bohemian woman nor a Puritan woman. You are a dangerous woman.

LADY UTTERWORD   On the contrary, I am a safe woman.

HECTOR   You are a most accursedly attractive woman. Mind, I am not making love to you. I do not like being attracted. But you had better know how I feel if you are going to stay here.

LADY UTTERWORD   You are an exceedingly clever lady-killer, Hector. And terribly handsome. I am quite a good player, myself, at that game. Is it quite understood that we are only playing?

HECTOR   Quite. I am deliberately playing the fool, out of sheer worthlessness.

LADY UTTERWORD   [rising brightly]   Well, you are my

brother-in-law. Hesione asked you to kiss me. [*He seizes her in his arms and kisses her strenuously.*] Oh! that was a little more than play, brother-in-law. [*She pushes him suddenly away.*] You shall not do that again.

HECTOR   In effect, you got your claws deeper into me than I intended.

MRS HUSHABYE [*coming in from the garden*]   Don't let me disturb you; I only want a cap to put on daddiest. The sun is setting; and he'll catch cold [*she makes for the door leading to the hall*].

LADY UTTERWORD   Your husband is quite charming, darling. He has actually condescended to kiss me at last. I shall go into the garden: it's cooler now [*she goes out by the port door*].

MRS HUSHABYE   Take care, dear child. I don't believe any man can kiss Addy without falling in love with her. [*She goes into the hall.*]

HECTOR [*striking himself on the chest*]   Fool! Goat!

MRS HUSHABYE comes back with the captain's cap.

HECTOR   Your sister is an extremely enterprising old girl. Where's Miss Dunn!

MRS HUSHABYE   Mangan says she has gone up to her room for a nap. Addy won't let you talk to Ellie: she has marked you for her own.

HECTOR   She has the diabolical family fascination. I began making love to her automatically. What am I to do? I can't fall in love; and I can't hurt a woman's feelings by telling her so when she falls in love with me. And as women are always falling in love with my moustache I get landed in all sorts of tedious and terrifying flirtations in which I'm not a bit in earnest.

MRS HUSHABYE   Oh, neither is Addy. She has never been in love in her life, though she has always been trying to fall in head over ears. She is worse than you, because you had one real go at least, with me.

HECTOR   That was a confounded madness. I can't believe that such an amazing experience is common. It has left its mark on me. I believe that is why I have never been able to repeat it.

MRS HUSHABYE [*laughing and caressing his arm*]   We were frightfully in love with one another, Hector. It was such an enchanting dream that I have never been able to grudge it to you or anyone else since. I have invited all sorts of pretty women to the house on the chance of giving you another turn. But it has never come off.

HECTOR   I don't know that I want it to come off. It was damned dangerous. You fascinated me; but I loved you; so it was heaven. This sister of yours fascinates me; but I hate her; so it is hell. I shall kill her if she persists.

MRS HUSHABYE   Nothing will kill Addy; she is as strong as a horse. [*Releasing him.*] Now *I* am going off to fascinate somebody.

HECTOR   The Foreign Office toff?* Randall?

MRS HUSHABYE   Goodness gracious, no! Why should I fascinate him?

HECTOR   I presume you don't mean the bloated capitalist, Mangan?

MRS HUSHABYE   Hm! I think he had better be fascinated by me than by Ellie. [*She is going into the garden when the captain comes in from it with some sticks in his hand.*] What have you got there, daddiest?

CAPTAIN SHOTOVER   Dynamite.

MRS HUSHABYE   You've been to the gravel pit. Don't drop it about the house, there's a dear. [*She goes into the garden, where the evening light is now very red.*]

HECTOR   Listen, O sage. How long dare you concentrate on a feeling without risking having it fixed in your consciousness all the rest of your life?

CAPTAIN SHOTOVER   Ninety minutes. An hour and a half. [*He goes into the pantry.*]

---

*Expensively dressed gentleman.

HECTOR, left alone, contracts his brows, and falls into a day-dream. He does not move for some time. Then he folds his arms. Then, throwing his hands behind him, and gripping one with the other, he strides tragically once to and fro. Suddenly he snatches his walking-stick from the teak table, and draws it; for it is a sword-stick. He fights a desperate duel with an imaginary antagonist, and after many vicissitudes runs him through the body up to the hilt. He sheathes his sword and throws it on the sofa, falling into another reverie as he does so. He looks straight into the eyes of an imaginary woman; seizes her by the arms; and says in a deep and thrilling tone, "Do you love me!" The captain comes out of the pantry at this moment; and HECTOR, caught with his arms stretched out and his fists clenched, has to account for his attitude by going through a series of gymnastic exercises.

CAPTAIN SHOTOVER   That sort of strength is no good. You will never be as strong as a gorilla.

HECTOR   What is the dynamite for?

CAPTAIN SHOTOVER   To kill fellows like Mangan.

HECTOR   No use. They will always be able to buy more dynamite than you.

CAPTAIN SHOTOVER   I will make a dynamite that he cannot explode.

HECTOR   And that you can, eh?

CAPTAIN SHOTOVER   Yes: when I have attained the seventh degree of concentration.

HECTOR   What's the use of that? You never do attain it.

CAPTAIN SHOTOVER   What then is to be done? Are we to be kept forever in the mud by these hogs to whom the universe is nothing but a machine for greasing their bristles and filling their snouts?

HECTOR   Are Mangan's bristles worse than Randall's love-locks?*

---

*Long locks of hair variously arranged, worn especially by men in the seventeenth and eighteenth centuries.

CAPTAIN SHOTOVER   We must win powers of life and death over them both. I refuse to die until I have invented the means.

HECTOR   Who are we that we should judge them?

CAPTAIN SHOTOVER   What are they that they should judge us? Yet they do, unhesitatingly. There is enmity between our seed and their seed. They know it and act on it, strangling our souls. They believe in themselves. When we believe in ourselves, we shall kill them.

HECTOR   It is the same seed. You forget that your pirate has a very nice daughter. Mangan's son may be a Plato: Randall's a Shelley. What was my father?

CAPTAIN SHOTOVER   The damndest scoundrel I ever met. [He replaces the drawing-board: sits down at the table; and begins to mix a wash of color.]

HECTOR   Precisely. Well, dare you kill his innocent grandchildren?

CAPTAIN SHOTOVER   They are mine also.

HECTOR   Just so. We are members one of another. [He throws himself carelessly on the sofa.] I tell you I have often thought of this killing of human vermin. Many men have thought of it. Decent men are like Daniel in the lion's den: their survival is a miracle; and they do not always survive. We live among the Mangans and Randalls and Billie Dunns as they, poor devils, live among the disease germs and the doctors and the lawyers and the parsons and the restaurant chefs and the tradesmen and the servants and all the rest of the parasites and blackmailers. What are our terrors to theirs? Give me the power to kill them; and I'll spare them in sheer——

CAPTAIN SHOTOVER [cutting in sharply]   Fellow feeling?

HECTOR   No. I should kill myself if I believed that. I must believe that my spark, small as it is, is divine, and that the red light over their door is hell fire. I should spare them in simple magnanimous pity.

CAPTAIN SHOTOVER   You can't spare them until you have the power to kill them. At present they have the power to kill you. There are millions of blacks over the water for them to train and let loose on us. They're going to do it. They're doing it already.

HECTOR   They are too stupid to use their power.

CAPTAIN SHOTOVER [*throwing down his brush and coming to the end of the sofa*]   Do not deceive yourself: they do use it. We kill the better half of ourselves every day to propitiate them. The knowledge that these people are there to render all our aspirations barren prevents us having the aspirations. And when we are tempted to seek their destruction they bring forth demons to delude us, disguised as pretty daughters, and singers and poets and the like, for whose sake we spare them.

HECTOR [*sitting up and leaning towards him*]   May not Hesione be such a demon, brought forth by you lest I should slay you?

CAPTAIN SHOTOVER   That is possible. She has used you up, and left you nothing but dreams, as some women do.

HECTOR   Vampire women, demon women.

CAPTAIN SHOTOVER   Men think the world well lost for them, and lose it accordingly. Who are the men that do things? The husbands of the shrew and of the drunkard, the men with the thorn in the flesh. [*Walking distractedly away towards the pantry.*] I must think these things out. [*Turning suddenly.*] But I go on with the dynamite none the less. I will discover a ray mightier than any X-ray: a mind ray that will explode the ammunition in the belt of my adversary before he can point his gun at me. And I must hurry. I am old: I have no time to waste in talk [*he is about to go into the pantry, and HECTOR is making for the hall, when HESIONE comes back*].

MRS HUSHABYE   Daddiest, you and Hector must come and help me to entertain all these people. What on earth were you shouting about?

HECTOR [*stopping in the act of turning the door handle*] He is madder than usual.

MRS HUSHABYE We all are.

HECTOR I must change [*he resumes his door opening*].

MRS HUSHABYE Stop, stop. Come back, both of you. Come back. [*They return, reluctantly.*] Money is running short.

HECTOR Money! Where are my April dividends?

MRS HUSHABYE Where is the snow that fell last year?

CAPTAIN SHOTOVER Where is all the money you had for that patent lifeboat I invented?

MRS HUSHABYE Five hundred pounds; and I have made it last since Easter!

CAPTAIN SHOTOVER Since Easter! Barely four months! Monstrous extravagance! I could live for seven years on £500.

MRS HUSHABYE Not keeping open house as we do here, daddiest.

CAPTAIN SHOTOVER Only £500 for that lifeboat! I got twelve thousand for the invention before that.

MRS HUSHABYE Yes, dear; but that was for the ship with the magnetic keel that sucked up submarines. Living at the rate we do, you cannot afford life-saving inventions. Can't you think of something that will murder half Europe at one bang?

CAPTAIN SHOTOVER No. I am ageing fast. My mind does not dwell on slaughter as it did when I was a boy. Why doesn't your husband invent something? He does nothing but tell lies to women.

HECTOR Well, that is a form of invention, is it not? However, you are right: I ought to support my wife.

MRS HUSHABYE Indeed you shall do nothing of the sort: I should never see you from breakfast to dinner. I want my husband.

HECTOR [*bitterly*] I might as well be your lapdog.

MRS HUSHABYE Do you want to be my breadwinner, like the other poor husbands?

HECTOR   No, by thunder! What a damned creature a husband is anyhow!

MRS HUSHABYE [*to the captain*]   What about that harpoon cannon?

CAPTAIN SHOTOVER   No use. It kills whales, not men.

MRS HUSHABYE   Why not? You fire the harpoon out of a cannon, it sticks in the enemy's general; you wind him in; and there you are.

HECTOR   You are your father's daughter, Hesione.

CAPTAIN SHOTOVER   There is something in it. Not to wind in generals: they are not dangerous. But one could fire a grapnel and wind in a machine gun or even a tank. I will think it out.

MRS HUSHABYE [*squeezing the captain's arm affectionately*]   Saved! You are a darling, daddiest. Now we must go back to these dreadful people and entertain them.

CAPTAIN SHOTOVER   They have had no dinner. Don't forget that.

HECTOR   Neither have I. And it is dark: it must be all hours.

MRS HUSHABYE   Oh, Guinness will produce some sort of dinner for them. The servants always take jolly good care that there is food in the house.

CAPTAIN SHOTOVER [*raising a strange wail in the darkness*]   What a house! What a daughter!

MRS HUSHABYE [*raving*]   What a father!

HECTOR [*following suit*]   What a husband!

CAPTAIN SHOTOVER   Is there no thunder in heaven?

HECTOR   Is there no beauty, no bravery, on earth?

MRS HUSHABYE   What do men want? They have their food, their firesides, their clothes mended, and our love at the end of the day. Why are they not satisfied? Why do they envy us the pain with which we bring them into the world, and make strange dangers and torments for themselves to be even with us?

CAPTAIN SHOTOVER [*weirdly chanting*]

I built a house for my daughters, and opened the doors
     thereof,
That men might come for their choosing, and their betters
     spring from their love;
But one of them married a numskull;

HECTOR [*taking up the rhythm*]

The other a liar wed;

MRS HUSHABYE [*completing the stanza*]

And now must she lie beside him, even as she made her bed.

LADY UTTERWORD [*calling from the garden*]   Hesione! He-
sione! Where are you?
HECTOR   The cat is on the tiles.*
MRS HUSHABYE   Coming, darling, coming [*she goes quickly
into the garden*].
     The captain goes back to his place at the table.
HECTOR [*going out into the hall*]   Shall I turn up the lights for
you?
CAPTAIN SHOTOVER   No. Give me deeper darkness.
Money is not made in the light.

---

*Meaning she is looking for a mate.

ACT II

The same room, with the lights turned up and the curtains drawn. Ellie comes in, followed by Mangan. Both are dressed for dinner. She strolls to the drawing-table. He comes between the table and the wicker chair.

MANGAN   What a dinner! I don't call it a dinner: I call it a meal.

ELLIE   I am accustomed to meals, Mr Mangan, and very lucky to get them. Besides, the captain cooked some maccaroni for me.

MANGAN [*shuddering liverishly*]   Too rich: I can't eat such things. I suppose it's because I have to work so much with my brain. That's the worst of being a man of business: you are always thinking, thinking, thinking. By the way, now that we are alone, may I take the opportunity to come to a little understanding with you?

ELLIE [*settling into the draughtsman seat*]   Certainly. I should like to.

MANGAN [*taken aback*]   Should you? That surprises me; for I thought I noticed this afternoon that you avoided me all you could. Not for the first time either.

ELLIE   I was very tired and upset. I wasn't used to the ways of this extraordinary house. Please forgive me.

MANGAN   Oh, that's all right: I don't mind. But Captain Shotover has been talking to me about you. You and me, you know.

ELLIE [*interested*]   The captain! What did he say?

MANGAN   Well, he noticed the difference between our ages.

ELLIE   He notices everything.

MANGAN   You don't mind, then?

ELLIE   Of course I know quite well that our engagement—

MANGAN   Oh! you call it an engagement.

ELLIE   Well, isn't it?

MANGAN   Oh, yes, yes: no doubt it is if you hold to it. This is the first time you've used the word; and I didn't quite know where we stood: that's all. [*He sits down in the wicker chair; and resigns himself to allow her to lead the conversation.*] You were saying—?

ELLIE   Was I? I forget. Tell me. Do you like this part of the country? I heard you ask Mr Hushabye at dinner whether there are any nice houses to let down here.

MANGAN   I like the place. The air suits me. I shouldn't be surprised if I settled down here.

ELLIE   Nothing would please me better. The air suits me too. And I want to be near Hesione.

MANGAN [*with growing uneasiness*]   The air may suit us; but the question is, should we suit one another? Have you thought about that?

ELLIE   Mr Mangan, we must be sensible, mustn't we? It's no use pretending that we are Romeo and Juliet. But we can get on very well together if we choose to make the best of it. Your kindness of heart will make it easy for me.

MANGAN [*leaning forward, with the beginning of something like deliberate unpleasantness in his voice*]   Kindness of heart, eh? I ruined your father, didn't I?

ELLIE   Oh, not intentionally.

MANGAN   Yes I did. Ruined him on purpose.

ELLIE   On purpose!

MANGAN   Not out of ill-nature, you know. And you'll admit that I kept a job for him when I had finished with him. But business is business; and I ruined him as a matter of business.

ELLIE   I don't understand how that can be. Are you trying to make me feel that I need not be grateful to you, so that I may choose freely?

MANGAN [*rising aggressively*]   No. I mean what I say.

ELLIE   But how could it possibly do you any good to ruin my father? The money he lost was yours.

MANGAN [*with a sour laugh*]   Was mine! It is mine, Miss Ellie, and all the money the other fellows lost too. [*He shoves his hands into his pockets and shows his teeth.*] I just smoked them out like a hive of bees. What do you say to that? A bit of shock, eh?

ELLIE   It would have been, this morning. Now! you can't think how little it matters. But it's quite interesting. Only, you must explain it to me. I don't understand it. [*Propping her elbows on the drawing-board and her chin on her hands, she composes herself to listen with a combination of conscious curiosity with unconscious contempt which provokes him to more and more unpleasantness, and an attempt at patronage of her ignorance.*]

MANGAN   Of course you don't understand: what do *you* know about business? You just listen and learn. Your father's business was a new business; and I don't start new businesses: I let other fellows start them. They put all their money and their friends' money into starting them. They wear out their souls and bodies trying to make a success of them. They're what you call enthusiasts. But the first dead lift of the thing is too much for them; and they haven't enough financial experience. In a year or so they have either to let the whole show go bust, or sell out to a new lot of fellows for a few deferred ordinary shares:* that is, if they're lucky enough to get anything at all. As likely as not the very same thing happens to the new lot. They put in more money and a couple of years more work; and then perhaps they have to sell out to a third lot. If it's

---

*Shares issued to the owners of a company, on which a dividend is paid at a later date.

really a big thing the third lot will have to sell out too, and leave their work and their money behind them. And that's where the real business man comes in: where *I* come in. But I'm cleverer than some: I don't mind dropping a little money to start the process. I took your father's measure. I saw that he had a sound idea, and that he would work himself silly for it if he got the chance. I saw that he was a child in business, and was dead certain to outrun his expenses and be in too great a hurry to wait for his market. I knew that the surest way to ruin a man who doesn't know how to handle money is to give him some. I explained my idea to some friends in the city, and they found the money; for I take no risks in ideas, even when they're my own. Your father and the friends that ventured their money with him were no more to me than a heap of squeezed lemons. You've been wasting your gratitude: my kind heart is all rot. I'm sick of it. When I see your father beaming at me with his moist, grateful eyes, regularly wallowing in gratitude, I sometimes feel I must tell him the truth or burst. What stops me is that I know he wouldn't believe me. He'd think it was my modesty, as you did just now. He'd think anything rather than the truth, which is that he's a blamed fool, and I am a man that knows how to take care of himself. [*He throws himself back into the big chair with large self-approval.*] Now what do you think of me, Miss Ellie?

ELLIE [*dropping her hands*]   How strange! that my mother, who knew nothing at all about business, should have been quite right about you! She always said—not before papa, of course, but to us children—that you were just that sort of man.

MANGAN [*sitting up, much hurt*]   Oh! did she? And yet she'd have let you marry me.

ELLIE   Well, you see, Mr Mangan, my mother married a very good man—for whatever you may think of my father as a man of business, he is the soul of goodness—and she is not at all keen on my doing the same.

MANGAN   Anyhow, you don't want to marry me now, do you?

ELLIE [*very calmly*]   Oh, I think so. Why not?

MANGAN [*rising aghast*]   Why not!

ELLIE   I don't see why we shouldn't get on very well together.

MANGAN   Well, but look here, you know— [*he stops, quite at a loss*].

ELLIE [*patiently*]   Well?

MANGAN   Well, I thought you were rather particular about people's characters.

ELLIE   If we women were particular about men's characters, we should never get married at all, Mr Mangan.

MANGAN   A child like you talking of "we women"! What next! You're not in earnest?

ELLIE   Yes, I am. Aren't you?

MANGAN   You mean to hold me to it?

ELLIE   Do you wish to back out of it?

MANGAN   Oh, no. Not exactly back out of it.

ELLIE   Well?

He has nothing to say. With a long whispered whistle, he drops into the wicker chair and stares before him like a beggared gambler. But a cunning look soon comes into his face. He leans over towards her on his right elbow, and speaks in a low steady voice.

MANGAN   Suppose I told you I was in love with another woman!

ELLIE [*echoing him*]   Suppose I told you I was in love with another man!

MANGAN [*bouncing angrily out of his chair*]   I'm not joking.

ELLIE   Who told you *I* was?

MANGAN   I tell you I'm serious. You're too young to be serious; but you'll have to believe me. I want to be near your friend Mrs Hushabye. I'm in love with her. Now the murder's out.

ELLIE   I want to be near your friend Mr Hushabye. I'm in love with him. [*She rises and adds with a frank air*] Now we are in one another's confidence, we shall be real friends. Thank you for telling me.

MANGAN [*almost beside himself*]   Do you think I'll be made a convenience of like this?

ELLIE   Come, Mr Mangan! you made a business convenience of my father. Well, a woman's business is marriage. Why shouldn't I make a domestic convenience of you?

MANGAN   Because I don't choose, see? Because I'm not a silly gull like your father. That's why.

ELLIE [*with serene contempt*]   You are not good enough to clean my father's boots, Mr Mangan; and I am paying you a great compliment in condescending to make a convenience of you, as you call it. Of course you are free to throw over our engagement if you like; but, if you do, you'll never enter Hesione' s house again: I will take care of that.

MANGAN [*gasping*]   You little devil, you've done me. [*On the point of collapsing into the big chair again he recovers himself.*] Wait a bit, though: you're not so cute as you think. You can't beat Boss Mangan as easy as that. Suppose I go straight to Mrs Hushabye and tell her that you're in love with her husband.

ELLIE   She knows it.

MANGAN   You told her!!!

ELLIE   She told me.

MANGAN [*clutching at his bursting temples*]   Oh, this is a crazy house. Or else I'm going clean off my chump. Is she making a swop with you—she to have your husband and you to have hers?

ELLIE   Well, you don't want us both, do you?

MANGAN [*throwing himself into the chair distractedly*]   My brain won't stand it. My head's going to split. Help! Help me to hold it. Quick: hold it: squeeze it. Save me. [*ELLIE comes behind his chair; clasps his head hard for a moment; then begins to draw her hands from his forehead back to his ears.*] Thank you. [*Drowsily.*]

That's very refreshing. [*Waking a little.*] Don't you hypnotize me, though. I've seen men made fools of by hypnotism.

ELLIE [*steadily*]   Be quiet. I've seen men made fools of without hypnotism.

MANGAN [*humbly*]   You don't dislike touching me, I hope. You never touched me before, I noticed.

ELLIE   Not since you fell in love naturally with a grown-up nice woman, who will never expect you to make love to her. And I will never expect him to make love to me.

MANGAN   He may, though.

ELLIE [*making her passes rhythmically*]   Hush. Go to sleep. Do you hear? You are to go to sleep, go to sleep, go to sleep; be quiet, deeply deeply quiet; sleep, sleep, sleep, sleep, sleep.

He falls asleep. ELLIE steals away; turns the light out; and goes into the garden.

NURSE GUINNESS opens the door and is seen in the light which comes in from the hall.

GUINNESS [*speaking to someone outside*]   Mr Mangan's not here, duckie: there's no one here. It's all dark.

MRS HUSHABYE [*without*]   Try the garden. Mr Dunn and I will be in my boudoir. Show him the way.

GUINNESS   Yes, ducky. [*She makes for the garden door in the dark; stumbles over the sleeping MANGAN and screams.*] Ahoo! O Lord, sir! I beg your pardon, I'm sure: I didn't see you in the dark. Who is it? [*She goes back to the door and turns on the light.*] Oh, Mr Mangan, sir, I hope I haven't hurt you plumping into your lap like that. [*Coming to him.*] I was looking for you, sir. Mrs Hushabye says will you please— [*noticing that he remains quite insensible*]. Oh, my good Lord, I hope I haven't killed him. Sir! Mr Mangan! Sir! [*She shakes him; and he is rolling inertly off the chair on the floor when she holds him up and props him against the cushion.*] Miss Hessy! Miss Hessy! Quick, doty darling. Miss Hessy! [*MRS HUSHABYE comes in from the hall, followed by MAZZINI DUNN.*] Oh, Miss Hessy, I've been and killed him.

MAZZINI runs round the back of the chair to MANGAN's right hand, and sees that the nurse's words are apparently only too true.

MAZZINI   What tempted you to commit such a crime, woman?

MRS HUSHABYE [*trying not to laugh*]   Do you mean you did it on purpose?

GUINNESS   Now is it likely I'd kill any man on purpose? I fell over him in the dark; and I'm a pretty tidy weight. He never spoke nor moved until I shook him; and then he would have dropped dead on the floor. Isn't it tiresome?

MRS HUSHABYE [*going past the nurse to MANGAN's side, and inspecting him less credulously than MAZZINI*]   Nonsense! he is not dead: he is only asleep. I can see him breathing.

GUINNESS   But why won't he wake?

MAZZINI [*speaking very politely into MANGAN's ear*]   Mangan! My dear Mangan! [*he blows into MANGAN's ear*].

MRS HUSHABYE   That's no good [*she shakes him vigorously*]. Mr Mangan, wake up. Do you hear? [*He begins to roll over.*] Oh! Nurse, nurse: he's falling: help me.

NURSE GUINNESS rushes to the rescue. With MAZZINI's assistance, MANGAN is propped safely up again.

GUINNESS [*behind the chair; bending over to test the case with her nose*]   Would he be drunk, do you think, pet?

MRS HUSHABYE   Had he any of papa's rum?

MAZZINI   It can't be that: he is most abstemious. I am afraid he drank too much formerly, and has to drink too little now. You know, Mrs Hushabye, I really think he has been hypnotized.

GUINNESS   Hip no what, sir?

MAZZINI   One evening at home, after we had seen a hypnotizing performance, the children began playing at it; and Ellie stroked my head. I assure you I went off dead asleep; and they had to send for a professional to wake me up after I had slept eighteen hours. They had to carry me upstairs; and as the poor children were not very strong, they let me slip; and I rolled right down the whole flight and never woke up. [*MRS HUSHABYE splutters.*] Oh, you may laugh, Mrs Hushabye; but I might have been killed.

MRS HUSHABYE   I couldn't have helped laughing even if you had been, Mr Dunn. So Ellie has hypnotized him. What fun!

MAZZINI   Oh no, no, no. It was such a terrible lesson to her: nothing would induce her to try such a thing again.

MRS HUSHABYE   Then who did it? *I* didn't.

MAZZINI   I thought perhaps the captain might have done it un-intentionally. He is so fearfully magnetic: I feel vibrations whenever he comes close to me.

GUINNESS   The captain will get him out of it anyhow, sir: I'll back him for that. I'll go fetch him [*she makes for the pantry*].

MRS HUSHABYE   Wait a bit. [*To MAZZINI.*] You say he is all right for eighteen hours?

MAZZINI   Well, *I* was asleep for eighteen hours.

MRS HUSHABYE   Were you any the worse for it?

MAZZINI   I don't quite remember. They had poured brandy down my throat, you see; and—

MRS HUSHABYE   Quite. Anyhow, you survived. Nurse, dar-ling: go and ask Miss Dunn to come to us here. Say I want to speak to her particularly. You will find her with Mr Hushabye probably.

GUINNESS   I think not, ducky: Miss Addy is with him. But I'll find her and send her to you. [*She goes out into the garden.*]

MRS HUSHABYE [*calling MAZZINI's attention to the figure on the chair*]   Now, Mr Dunn, look. Just look. Look hard. Do you still intend to sacrifice your daughter to that thing?

MAZZINI [*troubled*]   You have completely upset me, Mrs Hushabye, by all you have said to me. That anyone could imag-ine that I—I, a consecrated soldier of freedom, if I may say so—could sacrifice Ellie to anybody or anyone, or that I should ever have dreamed of forcing her inclinations in any way, is a most painful blow to my—well, I suppose you would say to my good opinion of myself.

MRS HUSHABYE [*rather stolidly*]   Sorry.

MAZZINI [*looking forlornly at the body*]   What is your objection to poor Mangan, Mrs Hushabye? He looks all right to me. But then I am so accustomed to him.

MRS HUSHABYE   Have you no heart? Have you no sense? Look at the brute! Think of poor weak innocent Ellie in the clutches of this slavedriver, who spends his life making thousands of rough violent workmen bend to his will and sweat for him: a man accustomed to have great masses of iron beaten into shape for him by steam-hammers! to fight with women and girls over a halfpenny an hour ruthlessly! a captain of industry, I think you call him, don't you? Are you going to fling your delicate, sweet, helpless child into such a beast's claws just because he will keep her in an expensive house and make her wear diamonds to show how rich he is?

MAZZINI [*staring at her in wide-eyed amazement*]   Bless you, dear Mrs Hushabye, what romantic ideas of business you have! Poor dear Mangan isn't a bit like that.

MRS HUSHABYE [*scornfully*]   Poor dear Mangan indeed!

MAZZINI   But he doesn't know anything about machinery. He never goes near the men: he couldn't manage them: he is afraid of them. I never can get him to take the least interest in the works: he hardly knows more about them than you do. People are cruelly unjust to Mangan: they think he is all rugged strength just because his manners are bad.

MRS HUSHABYE   Do you mean to tell me he isn't strong enough to crush poor little Ellie?

MAZZINI   Of course it's very hard to say how any marriage will turn out; but speaking for myself, I should say that he won't have a dog's chance against Ellie. You know, Ellie has remarkable strength of character. I think it is because I taught her to like Shakespeare when she was very young.

MRS HUSHABYE [*contemptuously*]   Shakespeare! The next thing you will tell me is that you could have made a great deal more money than Mangan. [*She retires to the sofa, and sits down at the port end of it in the worst of humors.*]

MAZZINI [*following her and taking the other end*]   No: I'm no good at making money. I don't care enough for it, somehow. I'm not ambitious! that must be it. Mangan is wonderful about money: he thinks of nothing else. He is so dreadfully afraid of being poor. I am always thinking of other things: even at the works I think of the things we are doing and not of what they cost. And the worst of it is, poor Mangan doesn't know what to do with his money when he gets it. He is such a baby that he doesn't know even what to eat and drink: he has ruined his liver eating and drinking the wrong things; and now he can hardly eat at all. Ellie will diet him splendidly. You will be surprised when you come to know him better: he is really the most helpless of mortals. You get quite a protective feeling towards him.

MRS HUSHABYE   Then who manages his business, pray?

MAZZINI   I do. And of course other people like me.

MRS HUSHABYE   Footling* people, you mean.

MAZZINI   I suppose you'd think us so.

MRS HUSHABYE   And pray why don't you do without him if you're all so much cleverer?

MAZZINI   Oh, we couldn't: we should ruin the business in a year. I've tried; and I know. We should spend too much on everything. We should improve the quality of the goods and make them too dear. We should be sentimental about the hard cases among the workpeople. But Mangan keeps us in order. He is down on us about every extra halfpenny. We could never do without him. You see, he will sit up all night thinking of how to save sixpence. Won't Ellie make him jump, though, when she takes his house in hand!

---

*Silly, or inconsequential.

MRS HUSHABYE   Then the creature is a fraud even as a captain of industry!

MAZZINI   I am afraid all the captains of industry are what *you* call frauds, Mrs Hushabye. Of course there are some manufacturers who really do understand their own works; but they don't make as high a rate of profit as Mangan does. I assure you Mangan is quite a good fellow in his way. He means well.

MRS HUSHABYE   He doesn't look well. He is not in his first youth, is he?

MAZZINI   After all, no husband is in his first youth for very long, Mrs Hushabye. And men can't afford to marry in their first youth nowadays.

MRS HUSHABYE   Now if *I* said that, it would sound witty. Why can't *you* say it wittily? What on earth is the matter with you? Why don't you inspire everybody with confidence? with respect?

MAZZINI [*humbly*]   I think that what is the matter with me is that I am poor. You don't know what that means at home. Mind: I don't say they have ever complained. They've all been wonderful: they've been proud of my poverty. They've even joked about it quite often. But my wife has had a very poor time of it. She has been quite resigned—

MRS HUSHABYE [*shuddering involuntarily*]!!

MAZZINI   There! You see, Mrs Hushabye. I don't want Ellie to live on resignation.

MRS HUSHABYE   Do you want her to have to resign herself to living with a man she doesn't love?

MAZZINI [*wistfully*]   Are you sure that would be worse than living with a man she did love, if he was a footling person?

MRS HUSHABYE [*relaxing her contemptuous attitude, quite interested in MAZZINI now*]   You know, I really think you must love Ellie very much; for you become quite clever when you talk about her.

MAZZINI   I didn't know I was so very stupid on other subjects.

MRS HUSHABYE   You are, sometimes.

MAZZINI [*turning his head away; for his eyes are wet*]   I have learnt a good deal about myself from you, Mrs Hushabye; and I'm afraid I shall not be the happier for your plain speaking. But if you thought I needed it to make me think of Ellie's happiness you were very much mistaken.

MRS HUSHABYE [*leaning towards him kindly*]   Have I been a beast?

MAZZINI [*pulling himself together*]   It doesn't matter about me, Mrs Hushabye. I think you like Ellie; and that is enough for me.

MRS HUSHABYE   I'm beginning to like you a little. I perfectly loathed you at first. I thought you the most odious, self-satisfied, boresome elderly prig I ever met.

MAZZINI [*resigned, and now quite cheerful*]   I daresay I am all that. I never have been a favorite with gorgeous women like you. They always frighten me.

MRS HUSHABYE [*pleased*]   Am I a gorgeous woman, Mazzini? I shall fall in love with you presently.

MAZZINI [*with placid gallantry*]   No, you won't, Hesione. But you would be quite safe. Would you believe it that quite a lot of women have flirted with me because I am quite safe? But they get tired of me for the same reason.

MRS HUSHABYE [*mischievously*]   Take care. You may not be so safe as you think.

MAZZINI   Oh yes, quite safe. You see, I have been in love really: the sort of love that only happens once. [*Softly.*] That's why Ellie is such a lovely girl.

MRS HUSHABYE   Well, really, you *are* coming out. Are you quite sure you won't let me tempt you into a second grand passion?

MAZZINI   Quite. It wouldn't be natural. The fact is, you don't strike on my box, Mrs Hushabye; and I certainly don't strike on yours.

MRS HUSHABYE   I see. Your marriage was a safety match.

MAZZINI   What a very witty application of the expression I used! I should never have thought of it.

ELLIE comes in from the garden, looking anything but happy.

MRS HUSHABYE [*rising*]   Oh! here is Ellie at last. [*She goes behind the sofa.*]

ELLIE [*on the threshold of the starboard door*]   Guinness said you wanted me: you and papa.

MRS HUSHABYE   You have kept us waiting so long that it almost came to—well, never mind. Your father is a very wonderful man [*she ruffles his hair affectionately*]: the only one I ever met who could resist me when I made myself really agreeable. [*She comes to the big chair, on MANGAN's left.*] Come here. I have something to show you. [*ELLIE strolls listlessly to the other side of the chair.*] Look.

ELLIE [*contemplating MANGAN without interest*]   I know. He is only asleep. We had a talk after dinner; and he fell asleep in the middle of it.

MRS HUSHABYE   You did it, Ellie. You put him asleep.

MAZZINI [*rising quickly and coming to the back of the chair*]   Oh, I hope not. Did you, Ellie?

ELLIE [*wearily*]   He asked me to.

MAZZINI   But it's dangerous. You know what happened to me.

ELLIE [*utterly indifferent*]   Oh, I daresay I can wake him. If not, somebody else can.

MRS HUSHABYE   It doesn't matter, anyhow, because I have at last persuaded your father that you don't want to marry him.

ELLIE [*suddenly coming out of her listlessness, much vexed*]   But why did you do that, Hesione? I do want to marry him. I fully intend to marry him.

MAZZINI   Are you quite sure, Ellie? Mrs Hushabye has made me feel that I may have been thoughtless and selfish about it.

ELLIE [*very clearly and steadily*]   Papa. When Mrs. Hushabye takes it on herself to explain to you what I think or don't think, shut your ears tight; and shut your eyes too. Hesione knows nothing about me: she hasn't the least notion of the sort of person I am, and never will. I promise you I won't do anything I don't want to do and mean to do for my own sake.

MAZZINI   You are quite, quite sure?

ELLIE   Quite, quite sure. Now you must go away and leave me to talk to Mrs Hushabye.

MAZZINI   But I should like to hear. Shall I be in the way?

ELLIE [*inexorable*]   I had rather talk to her alone.

MAZZINI [*affectionately*]   Oh, well, I know what a nuisance parents are, dear. I will be good and go. [*He goes to the garden door.*] By the way, do you remember the address of that professional who woke me up? Don't you think I had better telegraph to him?

MRS HUSHABYE [*moving towards the sofa*]   It's too late to telegraph tonight.

MAZZINI   I suppose so. I do hope he'll wake up in the course of the night. [*He goes out into the garden.*]

ELLIE [*turning rigorously on HESIONE the moment her father is out of the room*].   Hesione, what the devil do you mean by making mischief with my father about Mangan?

MRS HUSHABYE [*promptly losing her temper*]   Don't you dare speak to me like that, you little minx. Remember that you are in my house.

ELLIE   Stuff! Why don't you mind your own business? What is it to you whether I choose to marry Mangan or not?

MRS HUSHABYE   Do you suppose you can bully me, you miserable little matrimonial adventurer?

ELLIE   Every woman who hasn't any money is a matrimonial adventurer. It's easy for you to talk: you have never known what it is to want money; and you can pick up men as if they were daisies. I am poor and respectable—

MRS HUSHABYE [*interrupting*]   Ho! respectable! How did you pick up Mangan? How did you pick up my husband? You have the audacity to tell me that I am a——a——a——

ELLIE   A siren. So you are. You were born to lead men by the nose: if you weren't, Marcus would have waited for me, perhaps.

MRS HUSHABYE [*suddenly melting and half laughing*]   Oh, my poor Ellie, my pettikins, my unhappy darling! I am so sorry about Hector. But what can I do? It's not my fault: I'd give him to you if I could.

ELLIE   I don't blame you for that.

MRS HUSHABYE   What a brute I was to quarrel with you and call you names! Do kiss me and say you're not angry with me.

ELLIE [*fiercely*]   Oh, don't slop and gush and be sentimental. Don't you see that unless I can be hard—as hard as nails—I shall go mad? I don't care a damn about your calling me names: do you think a woman in my situation can feel a few hard words?

MRS HUSHABYE   Poor little woman! Poor little situation!

ELLIE   I suppose you think you're being sympathetic. You are just foolish and stupid and selfish. You see me getting a smasher right in the face that kills a whole part of my life: the best part that can never come again; and you think you can help me over it by a little coaxing and kissing. When I want all the strength I can get to lean on: something iron, something stony, I don't care how cruel it is, you go all mushy and want to slobber over me. I'm not angry; I'm not unfriendly; but for God's sake do pull yourself together; and don't think that because you're on velvet and always have been, women who are in hell can take it as easily as you.

MRS HUSHABYE [*shrugging her shoulders*]   Very well. [*She sits down on the sofa in her old place.*] But I warn you that when I am neither coaxing and kissing nor laughing, I am just wondering how much longer I can stand living in this cruel, damnable world. You object to the siren: well, I drop the siren. You want to rest your wounded bosom against a grindstone. Well [*folding her arms*], here is the grindstone.

ELLIE [*sitting down beside her, appeased*]   That's better: you really have the trick of falling in with everyone's mood; but you don't understand, because you are not the sort of woman for whom there is only one man and only one chance.

MRS HUSHABYE   I certainly don't understand how your marrying that object [*indicating MANGAN*] will console you for not being able to marry Hector.

ELLIE   Perhaps you don't understand why I was quite a nice girl this morning, and am now neither a girl nor particularly nice.

MRS HUSHABYE   Oh, yes, I do. It's because you have made up your mind to do something despicable and wicked.

ELLIE   I don't think so, Hesione. I must make the best of my ruined house.

MRS HUSHABYE   Pooh! You'll get over it. Your house isn't ruined.

ELLIE   Of course I shall get over it. You don't suppose I'm to sit down and die of a broken heart, I hope, or be an old maid living on a pittance from the Sick and Indigent Roomkeepers' Association. But my heart is broken, all the same. What I mean by that is that I know that what has happened to me with Marcus will not happen to me ever again. In the world for me there is Marcus and a lot of other men of whom one is just the same as another. Well, if I can't have love, that's no reason why I should have poverty. If Mangan has nothing else, he has money.

MRS HUSHABYE   And are there no *young* men with money.

ELLIE   Not within my reach. Besides, a young man would have the right to expect love from me, and would perhaps leave me when he found I could not give it to him. Rich young men can get rid of their wives, you know, pretty cheaply. But this object, as you call him, can expect nothing more from me than I am prepared to give him.

MRS HUSHABYE   He will be your owner, remember. If he

buys you, he will make the bargain pay him and not you. Ask your father.

ELLIE [*rising and strolling to the chair to contemplate their subject*] You need not trouble on that score, Hesione. I have more to give Boss Mangan than he has to give me: it is I who am buying him, and at a pretty good price too, I think. Women are better at that sort of bargain than men. I have taken the Boss's measure; and ten Boss Mangans shall not prevent me doing far more as I please as his wife than I have ever been able to do as a poor girl. [*Stooping to the recumbent figure.*] Shall they, Boss? I think not. [*She passes on to the drawing-table, and leans against the end of it, facing the windows.*] I shall not have to spend most of my time wondering how long my gloves will last, anyhow.

MRS HUSHABYE [*rising superbly*]   Ellie, you are a wicked, sordid little beast. And to think that I actually condescended to fascinate that creature there to save you from him! Well, let me tell you this: if you make this disgusting match, you will never see Hector again if I can help it.

ELLIE [*unmoved*]   I nailed Mangan by telling him that if he did not marry me he should never see you again [*she lifts herself on her wrists and seats herself on the end of the table*].

MRS HUSHABYE [*recoiling*]   Oh!

ELLIE   So you see I am not unprepared for your playing that trump against me. Well, you just try it: that's all. I should have made a man of Marcus, not a household pet.

MRS HUSHABYE [*flaming*]   You dare!

ELLIE [*looking almost dangerous*]   Set him thinking about me if *you* dare.

MRS HUSHABYE   Well, of all the impudent little fiends I ever met! Hector says there is a certain point at which the only answer you can give to a man who breaks all the rules is to knock him down. What would you say if I were to box your ears?

ELLIE [*calmly*]   I should pull your hair.

MRS HUSHABYE [*mischievously*] That wouldn't hurt me. Perhaps it comes off at night.

ELLIE [*so taken aback that she drops off the table and runs to her*] Oh, you don't mean to say, Hesione, that your beautiful black hair is false?

MRS HUSHABYE [*patting it*] Don't tell Hector. He believes in it.

ELLIE [*groaning*] Oh! Even the hair that ensnared him false! Everything false!

MRS HUSHABYE Pull it and try. Other women can snare men in their hair; but I can swing a baby on mine. Aha! you can't do that, Goldylocks.

ELLIE [*heartbroken*] No. You have stolen my babies.

MRS HUSHABYE Pettikins, don't make me cry. You know what you said about my making a household pet of him is a little true. Perhaps he ought to have waited for you. Would any other woman on earth forgive you?

ELLIE Oh, what right had you to take him all for yourself! [*Pulling herself together.*] There! You couldn't help it: neither of us could help it. He couldn't help it. No, don't say anything more: I can't bear it. Let us wake the object. [*She begins stroking MANGAN's head, reversing the movement with which she put him to sleep.*] Wake up, do you hear? You are to wake up at once. Wake up, wake up, wake—

MANGAN [*bouncing out of the chair in a fury and turning on them*] Wake up! So you think I've been asleep, do you? [*He kicks the chair violently back out of his way, and gets between them.*] You throw me into a trance so that I can't move hand or foot—I might have been buried alive! it's a mercy I wasn't—and then you think I was only asleep. If you'd let me drop the two times you rolled me about, my nose would have been flattened for life against the floor. But I've found you all out, anyhow. I know the sort of people I'm among now. I've heard every word you've said, you and your precious father, and [*to MRS*

HUSHABYE] you too. So I'm an object, am I? I'm a thing, am I? I'm a fool that hasn't sense enough to feed myself properly, am I? I'm afraid of the men that would starve if it weren't for the wages I give them, am I? I'm nothing but a disgusting old skinflint to be made a convenience of by designing women and fool managers of my works, am I? I'm——

MRS HUSHABYE [*with the most elegant aplomb*]   Sh-sh-sh-sh-sh! Mr Mangan, you are bound in honor to obliterate from your mind all you heard while you were pretending to be asleep. It was not meant for you to hear.

MANGAN   Pretending to be asleep! Do you think if I was only pretending that I'd have sprawled there helpless, and listened to such unfairness, such lies, such injustice and plotting and backbiting and slandering of me, if I could have up and told you what I thought of you! I wonder I didn't burst.

MRS HUSHABYE [*sweetly*]   You dreamt it all, Mr. Mangan. We were only saying how beautifully peaceful you looked in your sleep. That was all, wasn't it, Ellie? Believe me, Mr Mangan, all those unpleasant things came into your mind in the last half second before you woke. Ellie rubbed your hair the wrong way; and the disagreeable sensation suggested a disagreeable dream.

MANGAN [*doggedly*]   I believe in dreams.

MRS HUSHABYE   So do I. But they go by contraries,* don't they?

MANGAN [*depths of emotion suddenly welling up in him*]   I shan't forget, to my dying day, that when you gave me the glad eye that time in the garden, you were making a fool of me. That was a dirty low mean thing to do. You had no right to let me come near you if I disgusted you. It isn't my fault if I'm old and haven't a moustache like a bronze candlestick as your hus-

---

*That is, the reality is the opposite of the dream.

band has. There are things no decent woman would do to a man—like a man hitting a woman in the breast.

HESIONE, utterly shamed, sits down on the sofa and covers her face with her hands. MANGAN sits down also on his chair and begins to cry like a child. ELLIE stares at them. MRS HUSHABYE, at the distressing sound he makes, takes down her hands and looks at him. She rises and runs to him.

MRS HUSHABYE   Don't cry: I can't bear it. Have I broken your heart? I didn't know you had one. How could I?

MANGAN   I'm a man, ain't I?

MRS HUSHABYE [*half coaxing, half rallying, altogether tenderly*] Oh no: not what I call a man. Only a Boss: just that and nothing else. What business has a Boss with a heart?

MANGAN   Then you're not a bit sorry for what you did, nor ashamed?

MRS HUSHABYE   I was ashamed for the first time in my life when you said that about hitting a woman in the breast, and I found out what I'd done. My very bones blushed red. You've had your revenge, Boss. Aren't you satisfied?

MANGAN   Serve you right! Do you hear? Serve you right! You're just cruel. Cruel.

MRS HUSHABYE   Yes: cruelty would be delicious if one could only find some sort of cruelty that didn't really hurt. By the way [*sitting down beside him on the arm of the chair*], what's your name? It's not really Boss, is it?

MANGAN [*shortly*]   If you want to know, my name's Alfred.

MRS HUSHABYE [*springs up*]   Alfred!! Ellie, he was christened after Tennyson!!!

MANGAN [*rising*]   I was christened after my uncle, and never had a penny from him, damn him! What of it?

MRS HUSHABYE   It comes to me suddenly that you are a real person: that you had a mother, like anyone else. [*Putting her hands on his shoulders and surveying him.*] Little Alf!

MANGAN   Well, you have a nerve.

MRS HUSHABYE   And you have a heart, Alfy, a whimpering little heart, but a real one. [*Releasing him suddenly.*] Now run and make it up with Ellie. She has had time to think what to say to you, which is more than I had [*she goes out quickly into the garden by the port door*].

MANGAN   That woman has a pair of hands that go right through you.

ELLIE   Still in love with her, in spite of all we said about you?

MANGAN   Are all women like you two? Do they never think of anything about a man except what they can get out of him? You weren't even thinking that about me. You were only thinking whether your gloves would last.

ELLIE   I shall not have to think about that when we are married.

MANGAN   And you think I am going to marry you after what I heard there!

ELLIE   You heard nothing from me that I did not tell you before.

MANGAN   Perhaps you think I can't do without you.

ELLIE   I think you would feel lonely without us all, now, after coming to know us so well.

MANGAN [*with something like a yell of despair*]   Am I never to have the last word?

CAPTAIN SHOTOVER [*appearing at the starboard garden door*] There is a soul in torment here. What is the matter?

MANGAN   This girl doesn't want to spend her life wondering how long her gloves will last.

CAPTAIN SHOTOVER [*passing through*]   Don't wear any. I never do [*he goes into the pantry*].

LADY UTTERWORD [*appearing at the port garden door, in a handsome dinner dress*]   Is anything the matter?

ELLIE   This gentleman wants to know is he never to have the last word?

LADY UTTERWORD [*coming forward to the sofa*]   I should let him have it, my dear. The important thing is not to have the last word, but to have your own way.

MANGAN   She wants both.

LADY UTTERWORD   She won't get them, Mr Mangan. Providence always has the last word.

MANGAN [*desperately*]   Now you are going to come religion over me. In this house a man's mind might as well be a football. I'm going. [*He makes for the hall, but is stopped by a hail from the captain, who has just emerged from his pantry*].

CAPTAIN SHOTOVER   Whither away, Boss Mangan?

MANGAN   To hell out of this house: let that be enough for you and all here.

CAPTAIN SHOTOVER   You were welcome to come: you are free to go. The wide earth, the high seas, the spacious skies are waiting for you outside.

LADY UTTERWORD   But your things, Mr Mangan. Your bag, your comb and brushes, your pyjamas—

HECTOR [*who has just appeared in the port doorway in a handsome Arab costume*]   Why should the escaping slave take his chains with him?

MANGAN   That's right, Hushabye. Keep the pyjamas, my lady, and much good may they do you.

HECTOR [*advancing to LADY UTTERWORD's left hand*]   Let us all go out into the night and leave everything behind us.

MANGAN   You stay where you are, the lot of you. I want no company, especially female company.

ELLIE   Let him go. He is unhappy here. He is angry with us.

CAPTAIN SHOTOVER   Go, Boss Mangan; and when you have found the land where there is happiness and where there are no women, send me its latitude and longitude; and I will join you there.

LADY UTTERWORD   You will certainly not be comfortable without your luggage, Mr Mangan.

ELLIE [*impatient*]   Go, go: why don't you go? It is a heavenly night: you can sleep on the heath. Take my waterproof to lie on: it is hanging up in the hall.

588   GEORGE BERNARD SHAW

HECTOR   Breakfast at nine, unless you prefer to breakfast with the captain at six.

ELLIE   Good night, Alfred.

HECTOR   Alfred! [*He runs back to the door and calls into the garden.*] Randall, Mangan's Christian name is Alfred.

RANDALL [*appearing in the starboard doorway in evening dress*] Then Hesione wins her bet.

MRS HUSHABYE appears in the port doorway. She throws her left arm round HECTOR's neck: draws him with her to the back of the sofa: and throws her right arm round LADY UTTERWORD's neck.

MRS HUSHABYE   They wouldn't believe me, Alf.

They contemplate him.

MANGAN   Is there any more of you coming in to look at me, as if I was the latest thing in a menagerie?

MRS HUSHABYE   You are the latest thing in this menagerie.

Before MANGAN can retort, a fall of furniture is heard from upstairs: then a pistol shot, and a yell of pain. The staring group breaks up in consternation.

MAZZINI'S VOICE [*from above*]   Help! A burglar! Help!*

HECTOR [*his eyes blazing*]   A burglar!!!

MRS HUSHABYE   No, Hector: you'll be shot [*but it is too late; he has dashed out past MANGAN, who hastily moves towards the bookshelves out of his way*].

CAPTAIN SHOTOVER [*blowing his whistle*]   All hands aloft! [*He strides out after HECTOR.*]

LADY UTTERWORD   My diamonds! [*She follows the captain.*]

RANDALL [*rushing after her*]   No, Ariadne. Let me.

ELLIE   Oh, is papa shot? [*She runs out.*]

MRS HUSHABYE   Are you frightened, Alf?

MANGAN   No. It ain't my house, thank God.

---

*Shaw had rehearsed this sudden intrusion by a criminal into a country house in his earlier play *Misalliance* (1910).

MRS HUSHABYE   If they catch a burglar, shall we have to go into court as witnesses, and be asked all sorts of questions about our private lives?

MANGAN   You won't be believed if you tell the truth.

MAZZINI, terribly upset, with a duelling pistol in his hand, comes from the hall, and makes his way to the drawing-table.

MAZZINI   Oh, my dear Mrs Hushabye, I might have killed him. [*He throws the pistol on the table and staggers round to the chair.*] I hope you won't believe I really intended to.

HECTOR comes in, marching an old and villainous looking man before him by the collar. He plants him in the middle of the room and releases him.

ELLIE follows, and immediately runs across to the back of her father's chair and pats his shoulders.

RANDALL [*entering with a poker*]   Keep your eye on this door, Mangan. I'll look after the other [*he goes to the starboard door and stands on guard there*].

LADY UTTERWORD comes in after RANDALL, and goes between MRS HUSHABYE and MANGAN.

NURSE GUINNESS brings up the rear, and waits near the door, on MANGAN's left.

MRS HUSHABYE   What has happened?

MAZZINI   Your housekeeper told me there was somebody upstairs, and gave me a pistol that Mr Hushabye had been practising with. I thought it would frighten him; but it went off at a touch.

THE BURGLAR   Yes, and took the skin off my ear. Precious near took the top off my head. Why don't you have a proper revolver instead of a thing like that, that goes off if you as much as blow on it?

HECTOR   One of my duelling pistols. Sorry.

MAZZINI   He put his hands up and said it was a fair cop.*

---

*Meaning he was caught fair and square.

THE BURGLAR   So it was. Send for the police.

HECTOR   No, by thunder! It was not a fair cop. We were four to one.

MRS HUSHABYE   What will they do to him?

THE BURGLAR   Ten years. Beginning with solitary. Ten years off my life. I shan't serve it all: I'm too old. It will see me out.

LADY UTTERWORD   You should have thought of that before you stole my diamonds.

THE BURGLAR   Well, you've got them back, lady, haven't you? Can you give me back the years of my life you are going to take from me?

MRS HUSHABYE   Oh, we can't bury a man alive for ten years for a few diamonds.

THE BURGLAR   Ten little shining diamonds! Ten long black years!

LADY UTTERWORD   Think of what it is for us to be dragged through the horrors of a criminal court, and have all our family affairs in the papers! If you were a native, and Hastings could order you a good beating and send you away, I shouldn't mind; but here in England there is no real protection for any respectable person.

THE BURGLAR   I'm too old to be giv a hiding, lady. Send for the police and have done with it. It's only just and right you should.

RANDALL [*who has relaxed his vigilance on seeing the burglar so pacifically disposed, and comes forward swinging the poker between his fingers like a well-folded umbrella*]   It is neither just nor right that we should be put to a lot of inconvenience to gratify your moral enthusiasm, my friend. You had better get out, while you have the chance.

THE BURGLAR [*inexorably*]   No. I must work my sin off my conscience. This has come as a sort of call to me. Let me spend the rest of my life repenting in a cell. I shall have my reward above.

MANGAN [*exasperated*]   The very burglars can't behave naturally in this house.

HECTOR   My good sir, you must work out your salvation at somebody else's expense. Nobody here is going to charge you.

THE BURGLAR   Oh, you won't charge me, won't you?

HECTOR   No. I'm sorry to be inhospitable; but will you kindly leave the house?

THE BURGLAR   Right. I'll go to the police station and give myself up. [*He turns resolutely to the door: but HECTOR stops him.*]

HECTOR   Oh no. You mustn't do that.

RANDALL   No, no. Clear out, man, can't you; and don't be a fool.

MRS HUSHABYE   Don't be so silly. Can't you repent at home?

LADY UTTERWORD   You will have to do as you are told.

THE BURGLAR   It's compounding a felony, you know.

MRS HUSHABYE   This is utterly ridiculous. Are we to be forced to prosecute this man when we don't want to?

THE BURGLAR   Am I to be robbed of my salvation to save you the trouble of spending a day at the sessions?* Is that justice? Is it right? Is it fair to me?

MAZZINI [*rising and leaning across the table persuasively as if it were a pulpit desk or a shop counter*]   Come, come! let me show you how you can turn your very crimes to account. Why not set up as a locksmith? You must know more about locks than most honest men?

THE BURGLAR   That's true, sir. But I couldn't set up as a locksmith under twenty pounds.

RANDALL   Well, you can easily steal twenty pounds. You will find it in the nearest bank.

THE BURGLAR [*horrified*]   Oh, what a thing for a gentleman to put into the head of a poor criminal scrambling out of the

---

*Active court, when cases are being heard.

bottomless pit as it were! Oh, shame on you, sir! Oh, God forgive you! [*He throws himself into the big chair and covers his face as if in prayer.*]

LADY UTTERWORD   Really, Randall!

HECTOR   It seems to me that we shall have to take up a collection for this inopportunely contrite sinner.

LADY UTTERWORD   But twenty pounds is ridiculous.

THE BURGLAR [*looking up quickly*]   I shall have to buy a lot of tools, lady.

LADY UTTERWORD   Nonsense: you have your burgling kit.

THE BURGLAR   What's a jimmy and a centrebit and an acetylene welding plant* and a bunch of skeleton keys? I shall want a forge, and a smithy, and a shop, and fittings. I can't hardly do it for twenty.

HECTOR   My worthy friend, we haven't got twenty pounds.

THE BURGLAR [*now master of the situation*]   You can raise it among you, can't you?

MRS HUSHABYE   Give him a sovereign, Hector, and get rid of him.

HECTOR [*giving him a pound*]   There! Off with you.

THE BURGLAR [*rising and taking the money very ungratefully*]   I won't promise nothing. You have more on you than a quid: all the lot of you, I mean.

LADY UTTERWORD [*rigorously*]   Oh, let us prosecute him and have done with it. I have a conscience too, I hope; and I do not feel at all sure that we have any right to let him go, especially if he is going to be greedy and impertinent.

THE BURGLAR [*quickly*]   All right, lady, all right. I've no wish to be anything but agreeable. Good evening, ladies and gentlemen; and thank you kindly.

---

*Torch.

He is hurrying out when he is confronted in the doorway by CAPTAIN SHOTOVER.

CAPTAIN SHOTOVER [*fixing the burglar with a piercing regard*] What's this? Are there two of you?

THE BURGLAR [*falling on his knees before the captain in abject terror*]   Oh, my good Lord, what have I done? Don't tell me it's your house I've broken into, Captain Shotover.

The captain seizes him by the collar: drags him to his feet: and leads him to the middle of the group, HECTOR falling back beside his wife to make way for them.

CAPTAIN SHOTOVER [*turning him towards ELLIE*]   Is that your daughter? [*He releases him.*]

THE BURGLAR   Well, how do I know, Captain? You know the sort of life you and me has led. Any young lady of that age might be my daughter anywhere in the wide world, as you might say.

CAPTAIN SHOTOVER [*to MAZZINI*]   You are not Billy Dunn. This is Billy Dunn. Why have you imposed on me?

THE BURGLAR [*indignantly to MAZZINI*]   Have you been giving yourself out to be me? You, that nigh blew my head off! Shooting yourself, in a manner of speaking!

MAZZINI   My dear Captain Shotover, ever since I came into this house I have done hardly anything else but assure you that I am not Mr William Dunn, but Mazzini Dunn, a very different person.

THE BURGLAR   He don't belong to my branch, Captain. There's two sets in the family: the thinking Dunns and the drinking Dunns, each going their own ways. I'm a drinking Dunn: he's a thinking Dunn. But that didn't give him any right to shoot me.

CAPTAIN SHOTOVER   So you've turned burglar, have you?

THE BURGLAR   No, Captain: I wouldn't disgrace our old sea calling by such a thing. I am no burglar.

LADY UTTERWORD   What were you doing with my diamonds?

GUINNESS   What did you break into the house for if you're no burglar?

RANDALL   Mistook the house for your own and came in by the wrong window, eh?

THE BURGLAR   Well, it's no use my telling you a lie: I can take in most captains, but not Captain Shotover, because he sold himself to the devil in Zanzibar, and can divine water, spot gold, explode a cartridge in your pocket with a glance of his eye, and see the truth hidden in the heart of man. But I'm no burglar.

CAPTAIN SHOTOVER   Are you an honest man?

THE BURGLAR   I don't set up to be better than my fellow-creatures, and never did, as you well know, Captain. But what I do is innocent and pious. I enquire about for houses where the right sort of people live. I work it on them same as I worked it here. I break into the house; put a few spoons or diamonds in my pocket; make a noise; get caught; and take up a collection. And you wouldn't believe how hard it is to get caught when you're actually trying to. I have knocked over all the chairs in a room without a soul paying any attention to me. In the end I have had to walk out and leave the job.

RANDALL   When that happens, do you put back the spoons and diamonds?

THE BURGLAR   Well, I don't fly in the face of Providence, if that's what you want to know.

CAPTAIN SHOTOVER   Guinness, you remember this man?

GUINNESS   I should think I do, seeing I was married to him, the blackguard!

HESIONE ⎱ *exclaiming* ⎰ Married to him!
LADY UTTERWORD ⎰ *together* ⎱ Guinness! !

THE BURGLAR   It wasn't legal. I've been married to no end of women. No use coming that over me.

CAPTAIN SHOTOVER   Take him to the forecastle [*he flings him to the door with a strength beyond his years*].

GUINNESS   I suppose you mean the kitchen. They won't have him there. Do you expect servants to keep company with thieves and all sorts?

CAPTAIN SHOTOVER   Land-thieves and water-thieves are the same flesh and blood. I'll have no boatswain on my quarter-deck. Off with you both.

THE BURGLAR   Yes, Captain. [*He goes out humbly.*]

MAZZINI   Will it be safe to have him in the house like that?

GUINNESS   Why didn't you shoot him, sir? If I'd known who he was, I'd have shot him myself. [*She goes out.*]

MRS HUSHABYE   Do sit down, everybody. [*She sits down on the sofa*].

They all move except ELLIE. MAZZINI resumes his seat. RANDALL sits down in the window-seat near the starboard door, again making a pendulum of his poker, and studying it as Galileo might have done. HECTOR sits on his left, in the middle. MANGAN, forgotten, sits in the port corner. LADY UTTERWORD takes the big chair. CAPTAIN SHOTOVER goes into the pantry in deep abstraction. They all look after him: and LADY UTTERWORD coughs consciously.

MRS HUSHABYE   So Billy Dunn was poor nurse's little romance. I knew there had been somebody.

RANDALL   They will fight their battles over again and enjoy themselves immensely.

LADY UTTERWORD [*irritably*]   You are not married; and you know nothing about it, Randall. Hold your tongue.

RANDALL   Tyrant!

MRS HUSHABYE   Well, we have had a very exciting evening. Everything will be an anticlimax after it. We'd better all go to bed.

RANDALL   Another burglar may turn up.

MAZZINI   Oh, impossible! I hope not.

RANDALL   Why not? There is more than one burglar in England.

MRS HUSHABYE   What do you say, Alf?

MANGAN [*huffily*]   Oh, I don't matter. I'm forgotten. The burglar has put my nose out of joint. Shove me into a corner and have done with me.

MRS HUSHABYE [*jumping up mischievously, and going to him*] Would you like a walk on the heath, Alfred? With me?

ELLIE   Go, Mr Mangan. It will do you good. Hesione will soothe you.

MRS HUSHABYE [*slipping her arm under his and pulling him upright*]   Come, Alfred. There is a moon: it's like the night in Tristan and Isolde.[10] [*She caresses his arm and draws him to the port garden door.*]

MANGAN [*writing but yielding*]   How you can have the face— the heart— [*he breaks down and is heard sobbing as she takes him out*].

LADY UTTERWORD   What an extraordinary way to behave! What is the matter with the man?

ELLIE [*in a strangely calm voice, staring into an imaginary distance*] His heart is breaking: that is all. [*The captain appears at the pantry door, listening.*] It is a curious sensation: the sort of pain that goes mercifully beyond our powers of feeling. When your heart is broken, your boats are burned: nothing matters any more. It is the end of happiness and the beginning of peace.

LADY UTTERWORD [*suddenly rising in a rage, to the astonishment of the rest*]   How dare you?

HECTOR   Good heavens! What's the matter?

RANDALL [*in a warning whisper*]   Tch—tch—tch! Steady.

ELLIE [*surprised and haughty*]   I was not addressing you particularly, Lady Utterword. And I am not accustomed to being asked how dare I.

LADY UTTERWORD   Of course not. Anyone can see how badly you have been brought up.

MAZZINI   Oh, I hope not, Lady Utterword. Really!

LADY UTTERWORD   I know very well what you meant. The impudence!

ELLIE   What on earth do you mean?

CAPTAIN SHOTOVER [*advancing to the table*]   She means that her heart will not break. She has been longing all her life for someone to break it. At last she has become afraid she has none to break.

LADY UTTERWORD [*flinging herself on her knees and throwing her arms round him*]   Papa, don't say you think I've no heart.

CAPTAIN SHOTOVER [*raising her with grim tenderness*]   If you had no heart how could you want to have it broken, child?

HECTOR [*rising with a bound*]   Lady Utterword, you are not to be trusted. You have made a scene [*he runs out into the garden through the starboard door*].

LADY UTTERWORD   Oh! Hector, Hector! [*she runs out after him*].

RANDALL   Only nerves, I assure you. [*He rises and follows her, waving the poker in his agitation.*] Ariadne! Ariadne! For God's sake, be careful. You will— [*he is gone*].

MAZZINI [*rising*]   How distressing! Can I do anything, I wonder?

CAPTAIN SHOTOVER [*promptly taking his chair and setting to work at the drawing-board*]   No. Go to bed. Good-night.

MAZZINI [*bewildered*]   Oh! Perhaps you are right.

ELLIE   Good-night, dearest. [*She kisses him.*]

MAZZINI   Good-night, love. [*He makes for the door, but turns aside to the bookshelves.*] I'll just take a book [*he takes one*]. Good-night. [*He goes out, leaving ELLIE alone with the captain.*]
The captain is intent on his drawing. ELLIE, standing sentry over his chair, contemplates him for a moment.

ELLIE   Does nothing ever disturb you, Captain Shotover?

CAPTAIN SHOTOVER   I've stood on the bridge for eighteen hours in a typhoon. Life here is stormier; but I can stand it.

ELLIE   Do you think I ought to marry Mr Mangan?

CAPTAIN SHOTOVER [*never looking up*]   One rock is as good as another to be wrecked on.

ELLIE   I am not in love with him.

CAPTAIN SHOTOVER   Who said you were?

ELLIE   You are not surprised?

CAPTAIN SHOTOVER   Surprised! At my age!

ELLIE   It seems to me quite fair. He wants me for one thing: I want him for another.

CAPTAIN SHOTOVER   Money?

ELLIE   Yes.

CAPTAIN SHOTOVER   Well, one turns the cheek: the other kisses it. One provides the cash: the other spends it.

ELLIE   Who will have the best of the bargain, I wonder?

CAPTAIN SHOTOVER   You. These fellows live in an office all day. You will have to put up with him from dinner to breakfast; but you will both be asleep most of that time. All day you will be quit of him; and you will be shopping with his money. If that is too much for you, marry a seafaring man: you will be bothered with him only three weeks in the year, perhaps.

ELLIE   That would be best of all, I suppose.

CAPTAIN SHOTOVER   It's a dangerous thing to be married right up to the hilt, like my daughter's husband. The man is at home all day, like a damned soul in hell.

ELLIE   I never thought of that before.

CAPTAIN SHOTOVER   If you're marrying for business, you can't be too businesslike.

ELLIE   Why do women always want other women's husbands?

CAPTAIN SHOTOVER   Why do horse-thieves prefer a horse that is broken-in to one that is wild?

ELLIE [with a short laugh]   I suppose so. What a vile world it is!

CAPTAIN SHOTOVER   It doesn't concern me. I'm nearly out of it.

ELLIE   And I'm only just beginning.

CAPTAIN SHOTOVER   Yes; so look ahead.

ELLIE   Well, I think I am being very prudent.

CAPTAIN SHOTOVER   I didn't say prudent. I said look ahead.

ELLIE   What's the difference?

CAPTAIN SHOTOVER   It's prudent to gain the whole world and lose your own soul. But don't forget that your soul sticks to you if you stick to it; but the world has a way of slipping through your fingers.

ELLIE [*wearily, leaving him and beginning to wander restlessly about the room*]   I'm sorry, Captain Shotover; but it's no use talking like that to me. Old-fashioned people are no use to me. Old-fashioned people think you can have a soul without money. They think the less money you have, the more soul you have. Young people nowadays know better. A soul is a very expensive thing to keep: much more so than a motor car.

CAPTAIN SHOTOVER   Is it? How much does your soul eat?

ELLIE   Oh, a lot. It eats music and pictures and books and mountains and lakes and beautiful things to wear and nice people to be with. In this country you can't have them without lots of money: that is why our souls are so horribly starved.

CAPTAIN SHOTOVER   Mangan's soul lives on pig's food.

ELLIE   Yes: money is thrown away on him. I suppose his soul was starved when he was young. But it will not be thrown away on me. It is just because I want to save my soul that I am marrying for money. All the women who are not fools do.

CAPTAIN SHOTOVER   There are other ways of getting money. Why don't you steal it?

ELLIE   Because I don't want to go to prison.

CAPTAIN SHOTOVER   Is that the only reason? Are you quite sure honesty has nothing to do with it?

ELLIE   Oh, you are very very old-fashioned, Captain. Does any modern girl believe that the legal and illegal ways of getting money are the honest and dishonest ways? Mangan robbed my father and my father's friends. I should rob all the money back from Mangan if the police would let me. As they won't, I must get it back by marrying him.

CAPTAIN SHOTOVER   I can't argue: I'm too old: my mind is made up and finished. All I can tell you is that, old-fashioned or new-fashioned, if you sell yourself, you deal your soul a blow that all the books and pictures and concerts and scenery in the world won't heal [*he gets up suddenly and makes for the pantry*].

ELLIE [*running after him and seizing him by the sleeve*]   Then why did you sell yourself to the devil in Zanzibar?

CAPTAIN SHOTOVER [*stopping, startled*]   What?

ELLIE   You shall not run away before you answer. I have found out that trick of yours. If you sold yourself, why shouldn't I?

CAPTAIN SHOTOVER   I had to deal with men so degraded that they wouldn't obey me unless I swore at them and kicked them and beat them with my fists. Foolish people took young thieves off the streets; flung them into a training ship where they were taught to fear the cane instead of fearing God; and thought they'd made men and sailors of them by private subscription. I tricked these thieves into believing I'd sold myself to the devil. It saved my soul from the kicking and swearing that was damning me by inches.

ELLIE [*releasing him*]   I shall pretend to sell myself to Boss Mangan to save my soul from the poverty that is damning *me* by inches.

CAPTAIN SHOTOVER   Riches will damn you ten times deeper. Riches won't save even your body.

ELLIE   Old-fashioned again. We know now that the soul is the body, and the body the soul. They tell us they are different because they want to persuade us that we can keep our souls if we let them make slaves of our bodies. I am afraid you are no use to me, Captain.

CAPTAIN SHOTOVER   What did you expect? A Savior, eh? Are you old-fashioned enough to believe in that?

ELLIE   No. But I thought you were very wise, and might help me. Now I have found you out. You pretend to be busy, and think of fine things to say, and run in and out to surprise people by saying them, and get away before they can answer you.

CAPTAIN SHOTOVER   It confuses me to be answered. It discourages me. I cannot bear men and women. I *have* to run away. I must run away now [*he tries to*].

ELLIE [*again seizing his arm*]   You shall not run away from me. I can hypnotize you. You are the only person in the house I can say what I like to. I know you are fond of me. Sit down. [*She draws him to the sofa.*]

CAPTAIN SHOTOVER [*yielding*]   Take care: I am in my dotage. Old men are dangerous: it doesn't matter to them what is going to happen to the world.

They sit side by side on the sofa. She leans affectionately against him with her head on his shoulder and her eyes half closed.

ELLIE [*dreamily*]   I should have thought nothing else mattered to old men. They can't be very interested in what is going to happen to themselves.

CAPTAIN SHOTOVER   A man's interest in the world is only the overflow from his interest in himself. When you are a child your vessel is not yet full; so you care for nothing but your own affairs. When you grow up, your vessel overflows; and you are a politician, a philosopher, or an explorer and adventurer. In old age the vessel dries up: there is no overflow: you are a child again. I can give you the memories of my ancient wisdom: mere scraps and leavings; but I no longer really care for anything but my own little wants and hobbies. I sit here working out my old ideas as a means of destroying my fellow-creatures. I see my daughters and their men living foolish lives of romance and sentiment and snobbery. I see you, the younger generation, turning from their romance and sentiment and snobbery to money and comfort and hard common sense. I was ten times happier on the bridge in the typhoon, or frozen into Arctic ice for months in darkness, than you or they have ever been. You are looking for a rich husband. At your age I looked for hardship, danger, horror, and death, that I might feel the life in me more intensely. I did not let the fear of death govern my life; and my reward was, I had my life. You are going to let the fear of poverty govern your life; and your reward will be that you will eat, but you will not live.

ELLIE [*sitting up impatiently*]   But what can I do? I am not a sea captain: I can't stand on bridges in typhoons, or go slaughtering seals and whales in Greenland's icy mountains.* They won't let women be captains. Do you want me to be a stewardess?

CAPTAIN SHOTOVER   There are worse lives. The stewardesses could come ashore if they liked; but they sail and sail and sail.

ELLIE   What could they do ashore but marry for money? I don't want to be a stewardess: I am too bad a sailor. Think of something else for me.

CAPTAIN SHOTOVER   I can't think so long and continuously. I am too old. I must go in and out. [*He tries to rise.*]

ELLIE [*pulling him back*]   You shall not. You are happy here, aren't you?

CAPTAIN SHOTOVER   I tell you it's dangerous to keep me. I can't keep awake and alert.

ELLIE   What do you run away for? To sleep?

CAPTAIN SHOTOVER   No. To get a glass of rum.

ELLIE [*frightfully disillusioned*]   Is that it? How disgusting! Do you like being drunk?

CAPTAIN SHOTOVER   No: I dread being drunk more than anything in the world. To be drunk means to have dreams; to go soft; to be easily pleased and deceived; to fall into the

---

*Phrase from Bishop Reginald Herber's early-nineteenth-century "Missionary Hymn."

clutches of women. Drink does that for you when you are young. But when you are old: very very old, like me, the dreams come by themselves. You don't know how terrible that is: you are young: you sleep at night only, and sleep soundly. But later on you will sleep in the afternoon. Later still you will sleep even in the morning; and you will awake tired, tired of life. You will never be free from dozing and dreams; the dreams will steal upon your work every ten minutes unless you can awaken yourself with rum. I drink now to keep sober; but the dreams are conquering: rum is not what it was: I have had ten glasses since you came; and it might be so much water. Go get me another: Guinness knows where it is. You had better see for yourself the horror of an old man drinking.

ELLIE   You shall not drink. Dream. I like you to dream. You must never be in the real world when we talk together.

CAPTAIN SHOTOVER   I am too weary to resist, or too weak. I am in my second childhood. I do not see you as you really are. I can't remember what I really am. I feel nothing but the accursed happiness I have dreaded all my life long: the happiness that comes as life goes, the happiness of yielding and dreaming instead of resisting and doing, the sweetness of the fruit that is going rotten.

ELLIE   You dread it almost as much as I used to dread losing my dreams and having to fight and do things. But that is all over for me: my dreams are dashed to pieces. I should like to marry a very old, very rich man. I should like to marry you. I had much rather marry you than marry Mangan. Are you very rich?

CAPTAIN SHOTOVER   No. Living from hand to mouth. And I have a wife somewhere in Jamaica: a black one. My first wife. Unless she's dead.

ELLIE   What a pity! I feel so happy with you. [*She takes his hand, almost unconsciously, and pats it.*] I thought I should never feel happy again.

CAPTAIN SHOTOVER   Why?

ELLIE   Don't you know?

CAPTAIN SHOTOVER   No.

ELLIE   Heartbreak. I fell in love with Hector, and didn't know he was married.

CAPTAIN SHOTOVER   Heartbreak? Are you one of those who are so sufficient to themselves that they are only happy when they are stripped of everything, even of hope?

ELLIE [*gripping the hand*]   It seems so; for I feel now as if there was nothing I could not do, because I want nothing.

CAPTAIN SHOTOVER   That's the only real strength. That's genius. That's better than rum.

ELLIE [*throwing away his hand*]   Rum! Why did you spoil it?

HECTOR and RANDALL come in from the garden through the starboard door.

HECTOR   I beg your pardon. We did not know there was anyone here.

ELLIE [*rising*]   That means that you want to tell Mr Randall the story about the tiger. Come, Captain: I want to talk to my father; and you had better come with me.

CAPTAIN SHOTOVER [*rising*]   Nonsense! the man is in bed.

ELLIE   Aha! I've caught you. My real father has gone to bed; but the father you gave me* is in the kitchen. You knew quite well all along. Come. [*She draws him out into the garden with her through the port door.*]

HECTOR   That's an extraordinary girl. She has the Ancient Mariner on a string like a Pekinese dog.

RANDALL   Now that they have gone, shall we have a friendly chat?

HECTOR   You are in what is supposed to be my house. I am at your disposal.

---

*That is, Billy Dunn.

HECTOR sits down in the draughtsman's chair, turning it to face RANDALL, who remains standing, leaning at his ease against the carpenter's bench.

RANDALL   I take it that we may be quite frank. I mean about Lady Utterword.

HECTOR   You may. I have nothing to be frank about. I never met her until this afternoon.

RANDALL [*straightening up*]   What! But you are her sister's husband.

HECTOR   Well, if you come to that, you are her husband's brother.

RANDALL   But you seem to be on intimate terms with her.

HECTOR   So do you.

RANDALL   Yes: but I *am* on intimate terms with her. I have known her for years.

HECTOR   It took her years to get to the same point with you that she got to with me in five minutes, it seems.

RANDALL [*vexed*]   Really, Ariadne is the limit [*he moves away huffishly towards the windows*].

HECTOR [*coolly*]   She is, as I remarked to Hesione, a very enterprising woman.

RANDALL [*returning, much troubled*]   You see, Hushabye, you are what women consider a good-looking man.

HECTOR   I cultivated that appearance in the days of my vanity; and Hesione insists on my keeping it up. She makes me wear these ridiculous things [*indicating his Arab costume*] because she thinks me absurd in evening dress.

RANDALL   Still, you do keep it up, old chap. Now, I assure you I have not an atom of jealousy in my disposition—

HECTOR   The question would seem to be rather whether your brother has any touch of that sort.

RANDALL   What! Hastings! Oh, don't trouble about Hastings. He has the gift of being able to work sixteen hours a day at the dullest detail, and actually likes it. That gets him to the top wherever he goes. As long as Ariadne takes care that he is fed regularly, he is only too thankful to anyone who will keep her in good humor for him.

HECTOR   And as she has all the Shotover fascination, there is plenty of competition for the job, eh?

RANDALL [*angrily*]   She encourages them. Her conduct is perfectly scandalous. I assure you, my dear fellow, I haven't an atom of jealousy in my composition; but she makes herself the talk of every place she goes to by her thoughtlessness. It's nothing more: she doesn't really care for the men she keeps hanging about her; but how is the world to know that? It's not fair to Hastings. It's not fair to me.

HECTOR   Her theory is that her conduct is so correct—

RANDALL   Correct! She does nothing but make scenes from morning till night. *You* be careful, old chap. She will get you into trouble: that is, she would if she really cared for you.

HECTOR   Doesn't she?

RANDALL   Not a scrap. She may want your scalp to add to her collection; but her true affection has been engaged years ago. You had really better be careful.

HECTOR   Do you suffer much from this jealousy?

RANDALL   Jealousy! I jealous! My dear fellow, haven't I told you that there is not an atom of—

HECTOR   Yes. And Lady Utterword told me she never made scenes. Well, don't waste your jealousy on my moustache. Never waste jealousy on a real man: it is the imaginary hero that supplants us all in the long run. Besides, jealousy does not belong to your easy man-of-the-world pose, which you carry so well in other respects.

RANDALL   Really, Hushabye, I think a man may be allowed to be a gentleman without being accused of posing.

HECTOR   It is a pose like any other. In this house we know all the poses: our game is to find out the man under the pose. The man under your pose is apparently Ellie's favorite, Othello.

RANDALL   Some of your games in this house are damned annoying, let me tell you.

HECTOR   Yes: I have been their victim for many years. I used to writhe under them at first; but I became accustomed to them. At last I learned to play them.

RANDALL   If it's all the same to you I had rather you didn't play them on me. You evidently don't quite understand my character, or my notions of good form.

HECTOR   Is it your notion of good form to give away Lady Utterword?

RANDALL [*a childishly plaintive note breaking into his huff*]   I have not said a word against Lady Utterword. This is just the conspiracy over again.

HECTOR   What conspiracy?

RANDALL   You know very well, sir. A conspiracy to make me out to be pettish and jealous and childish and everything I am not. Everyone knows I am just the opposite.

HECTOR [*rising*]   Something in the air of the house has upset you. It often does have that effect. [*He goes to the garden door and calls LADY UTTERWORD with commanding emphasis.*] Ariadne!

LADY UTTERWORD [*at some distance*]   Yes.

RANDALL   What are you calling her for? I want to speak—

LADY UTTERWORD [*arriving breathless*]   Yes. You really are a terribly commanding person. What's the matter?

HECTOR   I do not know how to manage your friend Randall. No doubt you do.

LADY UTTERWORD   Randall: have you been making yourself ridiculous, as usual? I can see it in your face. Really, you are the most pettish* creature.

RANDALL   You know quite well, Ariadne, that I have not an ounce of pettishness in my disposition. I have made myself perfectly pleasant here. I have remained absolutely cool and

---

*Peevish, or fretful.

imperturbable in the face of a burglar. Imperturbability is almost too strong a point of mine. But [*putting his foot down with a stamp, and walking angrily up and down the room*] I *insist* on being treated with a certain consideration. I will not allow Hushabye to take liberties with me. I will not stand your encouraging people as you do.

HECTOR   The man has a rooted delusion that he is your husband.

LADY UTTERWORD   I know. He is jealous. As if he had any right to be! He compromises me everywhere. He makes scenes all over the place. Randall: I will not allow it. I simply will not allow it. You had no right to discuss me with Hector. I will not be discussed by men.

HECTOR   Be reasonable, Ariadne. Your fatal gift of beauty forces men to discuss you.

LADY UTTERWORD   Oh indeed! what about *your* fatal gift of beauty?

HECTOR   How can I help it?

LADY UTTERWORD   You could cut off your moustache: I can't cut off my nose. I get my whole life messed up with people falling in love with me. And then Randall says I run after men.

RANDALL   I—

LADY UTTERWORD   Yes you do: you said it just now. Why can't you think of something else than women? Napoleon was quite right when he said that women are the occupation of the idle man. Well, if ever there was an idle man on earth, his name is Randall Utterword.

RANDALL   Ariad—

LADY UTTERWORD [*overwhelming him with a torrent of words*] Oh yes you are: it's no use denying it. What have you ever done? What good are you? You are as much trouble in the house as a child of three. You couldn't live without your valet.

RANDALL   This is—

LADY UTTERWORD   Laziness! You are laziness incarnate. You are selfishness itself. You are the most uninteresting man on earth. You can't even gossip about anything but yourself and your grievances and your ailments and the people who have offended you. [*Turning to HECTOR.*] Do you know what they call him, Hector?

HECTOR   ⎱ [*speaking* ⎰ Please don't tell me.
RANDALL   ⎰ *together*] ⎱ I'll not stand it—

LADY UTTERWORD   Randall the Rotter: that is his name in good society.

RANDALL [*shouting*]   I'll not bear it, I tell you. Will you listen to me, you infernal— [*he chokes*].

LADY UTTERWORD   Well: go on. What were you going to call me? An infernal what? Which unpleasant animal is it to be this time?

RANDALL [*foaming*]   There is no animal in the world so hateful as a woman can be. You are a maddening devil. Hushabye, you will not believe me when I tell you that I have loved this demon all my life; but God knows I have paid for it [*he sits down in the draughtsman's chair, weeping*].

LADY UTTERWORD [*standing over him with triumphant contempt*]   Cry-baby!

HECTOR [*gravely, coming to him*]   My friend, the Shotover sisters have two strange powers over men. They can make them love; and they can make them cry. Thank your stars that you are not married to one of them.

LADY UTTERWORD [*haughtily*]   And pray, Hector—

HECTOR [*suddenly catching her round the shoulders: swinging her right round him and away from RANDALL: and gripping her throat with the other hand*]   Ariadne, if you attempt to start on me, I'll choke you: do you hear? The cat-and-mouse game with the other sex is a good game; but I can play your head off at it. [*He throws her, not at all gently, into the big chair, and proceeds, less fiercely but firmly.*] It is true that Napoleon said that woman is the occupation of the idle man. But he added that she is the relaxation of the warrior. Well, *I* am the warrior. So take care.

LADY UTTERWORD [*not in the least put out, and rather pleased by his violence*]   My dear Hector, I have only done what you asked me to do.

HECTOR   How do you make that out, pray?

LADY UTTERWORD   You called me in to manage Randall, didn't you? You said you couldn't manage him yourself.

HECTOR   Well, what if I did? I did not ask you to drive the man mad.

LADY UTTERWORD   He isn't mad. That's the way to manage him. If you were a mother, you'd understand.

HECTOR   Mother! What are you up to now?

LADY UTTERWORD   Its quite simple. When the children got nerves and were naughty, I smacked them just enough to give them a good cry and a healthy nervous shock. They went to sleep and were quite good afterwards. Well, I can't smack Randall: he is too big; so when he gets nerves and is naughty, I just rag him till he cries. He will be all right now. Look: he is half asleep already [*which is quite true*].

RANDALL [*waking up indignantly*]   I'm not. You are most cruel, Ariadne. [*Sentimentally.*] But I suppose I must forgive you, as usual [*he checks himself in the act of yawning*].

LADY UTTERWORD [*to HECTOR*]   Is the explanation satisfactory, dread warrior?

HECTOR   Some day I shall kill you, if you go too far. I thought you were a fool.

LADY UTTERWORD [*laughing*]   Everybody does, at first. But I am not such a fool as I look. [*She rises complacently.*] Now, Randall, go to bed. You will be a good boy in the morning.

RANDALL [*only very faintly rebellious*]   I'll go to bed when I like. It isn't ten yet.

LADY UTTERWORD   It is long past ten. See that he goes to bed at once, Hector. [*She goes into the garden.*]

HECTOR   Is there any slavery on earth viler than this slavery of men to women?

RANDALL [*rising resolutely*]   I'll not speak to her tomorrow. I'll not speak to her for another week. I'll give her *such* a lesson. I'll go straight to bed without bidding her good-night. [*He makes for the door leading to the hall.*]

HECTOR   You are under a spell, man. Old Shotover sold himself to the devil in Zanzibar. The devil gave him a black witch for a wife; and these two demon daughters are their mystical progeny. I am tied to Hesione's apron-string; but I'm her husband; and if I did go stark staring mad about her, at least we became man and wife. But why should *you* let yourself be dragged about and beaten by Ariadne as a toy donkey is dragged about and beaten by a child? What do you get by it? Are you her lover?

RANDALL   You must not misunderstand me. In a higher sense—in a Platonic sense—

HECTOR   Psha! Platonic sense! She makes you her servant; and when pay-day comes round, she bilks you: that is what you mean.

RANDALL [*feebly*]   Well, if I don't mind, I don't see what business it is of yours. Besides, I tell you I am going to punish her. You shall see: *I* know how to deal with women. I'm really very sleepy. Say good-night to Mrs Hushabye for me, will you, like a good chap. Good-night. [*He hurries out.*]

HECTOR   Poor wretch! Oh women! women! women! [*He lifts his fists in invocation to heaven.*] Fall. Fall and crush.[11] [*He goes out into the garden.*]

ACT III

In the garden, Hector, as he comes out through the glass door of the poop, finds Lady Utterword lying voluptuously in the hammock on the east side of the flagstaff, in the circle of light cast by the electric arc, which is like a moon in its opal globe. Beneath the head of the hammock, a campstool. On the other side of the flagstaff, on the long garden seat, Captain Shotover is asleep, with Ellie beside him, leaning affectionately against him on his right hand. On his left is a deck chair. Behind them in the gloom, Hesione is strolling about with Mangan. It is a fine still night, moonless.

LADY UTTERWORD   What a lovely night! It seems made for us.

HECTOR   The night takes no interest in us. What are we to the night? [*He sits down moodily in the deck chair.*]

ELLIE [*dreamily, nestling against the captain*]   Its beauty soaks into my nerves. In the night there is peace for the old and hope for the young.

HECTOR   Is that remark your own?

ELLIE   No. Only the last thing the captain said before he went to sleep.

CAPTAIN SHOTOVER   I'm not asleep.

HECTOR   Randall is. Also Mr Mazzini Dunn. Mangan, too, probably.

MANGAN   No.

HECTOR   Oh, you are there. I thought Hesione would have sent you to bed by this time.

MRS HUSHABYE [*coming to the back of the garden seat, into the light, with MANGAN*]   I think I shall. He keeps telling me he has a presentiment that he is going to die. I never met a man so greedy for sympathy.

MANGAN [*plaintively*]   But I have a presentiment. I really have. And you wouldn't listen.

MRS HUSHABYE   I was listening for something else. There was a sort of splendid drumming in the sky. Did none of you hear it? It came from a distance and then died away.

MANGAN   I tell you it was a train.

MRS HUSHABYE   And *I* tell *you*, Alf, there is no train at this hour. The last is nine forty-five.

MANGAN   But a goods train.

MRS HUSHABYE   Not on our little line. They tack a truck on to the passenger train. What can it have been, Hector?

HECTOR   Heaven's threatening growl of disgust at us useless futile creatures. [*Fiercely.*] I tell you, one of two things must happen. Either out of that darkness some new creation will come to supplant us as we have supplanted the animals, or the heavens will fall in thunder and destroy us.

LADY UTTERWORD [*in a cool instructive manner, wallowing comfortably in her hammock*]   We have not supplanted the animals, Hector. Why do you ask heaven to destroy this house, which could be made quite comfortable if Hesione had any notion of how to live? Don't you know what is wrong with it?

HECTOR   We are wrong with it. There is no sense in us. We are useless, dangerous, and ought to be abolished.

LADY UTTERWORD   Nonsense! Hastings told me the very first day he came here, nearly twenty-four years ago, what is wrong with the house.

CAPTAIN SHOTOVER   What! The numskull said there was something wrong with my house!

LADY UTTERWORD   I said Hastings said it; and he is not in the least a numskull.

CAPTAIN SHOTOVER   What's wrong with my house?

LADY UTTERWORD   Just what is wrong with a ship, papa. Wasn't it clever of Hastings to see that?

CAPTAIN SHOTOVER   The man's a fool. There's nothing wrong with a ship.

LADY UTTERWORD   Yes, there is.

MRS HUSHABYE   But what is it? Don't be aggravating, Addy.

LADY UTTERWORD   Guess.

HECTOR   Demons. Daughters of the witch of Zanzibar. Demons.

LADY UTTERWORD   Not a bit. I assure you, all this house needs to make it a sensible, healthy, pleasant house, with good appetites and sound sleep in it, is horses.

MRS HUSHABYE   Horses! What rubbish!

LADY UTTERWORD   Yes: horses. Why have we never been able to let this house? Because there are no proper stables. Go anywhere in England where there are natural, wholesome, contented, and really nice English people; and what do you always find? That the stables are the real centre of the household; and that if any visitor wants to play the piano the whole room has to be upset before it can be opened, there are so many things piled on it. I never lived until I learned to ride; and I shall never ride really well because I didn't begin as a child. There are only two classes in good society in England: the equestrian classes and the neurotic classes. It isn't mere convention: everybody can see that the people who hunt are the right people and the people who don't are the wrong ones.

CAPTAIN SHOTOVER   There is some truth in this. My ship made a man of me; and a ship is the horse of the sea.

LADY UTTERWORD   Exactly how Hastings explained your being a gentleman.

CAPTAIN SHOTOVER   Not bad for a numskull. Bring the man here with you next time: I must talk to him.

LADY UTTERWORD   Why is Randall such an obvious rotter? He is well bred; he has been at a public school and a university; he has been in the Foreign Office; he knows the best people and has lived all his life among them. Why is he so unsatisfactory, so contemptible? Why can't he get a valet to stay with him longer than a few months? Just because he is too lazy and pleasure-loving to hunt and shoot. He strums the piano, and sketches, and runs after married women, and reads literary books and poems. He actually plays the flute; but I never let him bring it into my house. If he would only— [*she is interrupted by the melancholy strains of a flute coming from an open window above. She raises herself indignantly in the hammock*]. Randall, you have not gone to bed. Have you been listening? [*The flute replies pertly.*]

How vulgar! Go to bed instantly, Randall: how dare you? [*The window is slammed down. She subsides.*] How can anyone care for such a creature!

MRS HUSHABYE   Addy: do you think Ellie ought to marry poor Alfred merely for his money?

MANGAN [*much alarmed*]   What's that? Mrs Hushabye, are my affairs to be discussed like this before everybody?

LADY UTTERWORD   I don't think Randall is listening now.

MANGAN   Everybody is listening. It isn't right.

MRS HUSHABYE   But in the dark, what does it matter? Ellie doesn't mind. Do you, Ellie?

ELLIE   Not in the least. What is your opinion, Lady Utterword? You have so much good sense.

MANGAN   But it isn't right. It— [*MRS HUSHABYE puts her hand on his mouth.*]   Oh, very well.

616   GEORGE BERNARD SHAW

LADY UTTERWORD   How much money have you, Mr. Mangan?

MANGAN   Really—No: I can't stand this.

LADY UTTERWORD   Nonsense, Mr Mangan! It all turns on your income, doesn't it?

MANGAN   Well, if you come to that, how much money has she?

ELLIE   None.

LADY UTTERWORD   You are answered, Mr Mangan. And now, as you have made Miss Dunn throw her cards on the table, you cannot refuse to show your own.

MRS HUSHABYE   Come, Alf! out with it! How much?

MANGAN [*baited out of all prudence*]   Well, if you want to know, I have no money and never had any.

MRS HUSHABYE   Alfred, you mustn't tell naughty stories.

MANGAN   I'm not telling you stories. I'm telling you the raw truth.

LADY UTTERWORD   Then what do you live on, Mr Mangan?

MANGAN   Travelling expenses. And a trifle of commission.

CAPTAIN SHOTOVER   What more have any of us but travelling expenses for our life's journey?

MRS HUSHABYE   But you have factories and capital and things?

MANGAN   People think I have. People think I'm an industrial Napoleon. That's why Miss Ellie wants to marry me. But I tell you I have nothing.

ELLIE   Do you mean that the factories are like Marcus's tigers? That they don't exist?

MANGAN   They exist all right enough. But they're not mine. They belong to syndicates and shareholders and all sorts of lazy good-for-nothing capitalists. I get money from such people to start the factories. I find people like Miss Dunn's father to work them, and keep a tight hand so as to make them pay.

Of course I make them keep me going pretty well; but it's a dog's life; and I don't own anything.

MRS HUSHABYE   Alfred, Alfred, you are making a poor mouth of it* to get out of marrying Ellie.

MANGAN   I'm telling the truth about my money for the first time in my life; and it's the first time my word has ever been doubted.

LADY UTTERWORD   How sad! Why don't you go in for politics, Mr Mangan?

MANGAN   Go in for politics! Where have you been living? I *am* in politics.

LADY UTTERWORD   I'm sure I beg your pardon. I never heard of you.

MANGAN   Let me tell you, Lady Utterword, that the Prime Minister of this country asked me to join the Government without even going through the nonsense of an election, as the dictator of a great public department.

LADY UTTERWORD   As a Conservative or a Liberal?

MANGAN   No such nonsense. As a practical business man. [*They all burst out laughing.*] What are you all laughing at?

MRS HUSHABYE   Oh, Alfred, Alfred!

ELLIE   You! who have to get my father to do everything for you!

MRS HUSHABYE   You! who are afraid of your own workmen!

HECTOR   You! with whom three women have been playing cat and mouse all the evening!

LADY UTTERWORD   You must have given an immense sum to the party funds, Mr Mangan.

MANGAN   Not a penny out of my own pocket. The syndicate found the money: they knew how useful I should be to them in the Government.

LADY UTTERWORD   This is most interesting and unex-

---

*Meaning he is deliberately downplaying his assets.

pected, Mr Mangan. And what have your administrative achievements been, so far?

MANGAN   Achievements? Well, I don't know what you call achievements; but I've jolly well put a stop to the games of the other fellows in the other departments. Every man of them thought he was going to save the country all by himself, and do me out of the credit and out of my chance of a title. I took good care that if they wouldn't let me do it they shouldn't do it themselves either. I may not know anything about my own machinery; but I know how to stick a ramrod into the other fellow's. And now they all look the biggest fools going.

HECTOR   And in heaven's name, what do you look like?

MANGAN   I look like the fellow that was too clever for all the others, don't I? If that isn't a triumph of practical business, what is?

HECTOR   Is this England, or is it a madhouse?

LADY UTTERWORD   Do you expect to save the country, Mr Mangan?

MANGAN   Well, who else will? Will your Mr Randall save it?

LADY UTTERWORD   Randall the rotter! Certainly not.

MANGAN   Will your brother-in-law save it with his moustache and his fine talk?

HECTOR   Yes, if they will let me.

MANGAN [sneering]   Ah! *Will* they let you?

HECTOR   No. They prefer you.

MANGAN   Very well then, as you're in a world where I'm appreciated and you're not, you'd best be civil to me, hadn't you? Who else is there but me?

LADY UTTERWORD   There is Hastings. Get rid of your ridiculous sham democracy; and give Hastings the necessary powers, and a good supply of bamboo to bring the British native to his senses: he will save the country with the greatest ease.

CAPTAIN SHOTOVER   It had better be lost. Any fool can govern with a stick in his hand. *I* could govern that way. It is not God's way. The man is a numskull.

LADY UTTERWORD   The man is worth all of you rolled into one. What do you say, Miss Dunn?

ELLIE   I think my father would do very well if people did not put upon him and cheat him and despise him because he is so good.

MANGAN [*contemptuously*]   I think I see Mazzini Dunn getting into parliament or pushing his way into the Government. We've not come to that yet, thank God! What do you say, Mrs Hushabye?

MRS HUSHABYE   Oh, *I* say it matters very little which of you governs the country so long as we govern you.

HECTOR   We? Who is we, pray?

MRS HUSHABYE   The devil's granddaughters, dear. The lovely women.

HECTOR [*raising his hands as before*]   Fall, I say, and deliver us from the lures of Satan!

ELLIE   There seems to be nothing real in the world except my father and Shakespeare. Marcus's tigers are false; Mr Mangan's millions are false; there is nothing really strong and true about Hesione but her beautiful black hair; and Lady Utterword's is too pretty to be real. The one thing that was left to me was the Captain's seventh degree of concentration; and that turns out to be—

CAPTAIN SHOTOVER   Rum.

LADY UTTERWORD [*placidly*]   A good deal of my hair is quite genuine. The Duchess of Dithering offered me fifty guineas for this [*touching her forehead*] under the impression that it was a transformation; but it is all natural except the color.

MANGAN [*wildly*]   Look here: I'm going to take off all my clothes [*he begins tearing off his coat*].

LADY UTTERWORD		Mr Mangan!
CAPTAIN SHOTOVER	[*in	What's that?
HECTOR	consterna-	Ha! ha! Do. Do.
ELLIE	tion*]	Please don't.

MRS HUSHABYE [*catching his arm and stopping him*]   Alfred, for shame! Are you mad?

MANGAN   Shame! What shame is there in this house? Let's all strip stark naked. We may as well do the thing thoroughly when we're about it. We've stripped ourselves morally naked: well, let us strip ourselves physically naked as well, and see how we like it. I tell you I can't bear this. I was brought up to be respectable. I don't mind the women dyeing their hair and the men drinking: it's human nature. But it's not human nature to tell everybody about it. Every time one of you opens your mouth I go like this [*he cowers as if to avoid a missile*], afraid of what will come next. How are we to have any self-respect if we don't keep it up that we're better than we really are?

LADY UTTERWORD   I quite sympathize with you, Mr Mangan. I have been through it all; and I know by experience that men and women are delicate plants and must be cultivated under glass. Our family habit of throwing stones in all directions and letting the air in is not only unbearably rude, but positively dangerous. Still, there is no use catching physical colds as well as moral ones; so please keep your clothes on.

MANGAN   I'll do as I like: not what you tell me. Am I a child or a grown man? I won't stand this mothering tyranny. I'll go back to the city, where I'm respected and made much of.

MRS HUSHABYE   Goodbye, Alf. Think of us sometimes in the city. Think of Ellie's youth!

ELLIE   Think of Hesione's eyes and hair!

CAPTAIN SHOTOVER   Think of this garden in which you are not a dog barking to keep the truth out!

HECTOR   Think of Lady Utterword's beauty! her good sense! her style!

LADY UTTERWORD   Flatterer. Think, Mr. Mangan, whether you can really do any better for yourself elsewhere: that is the essential point, isn't it?

MANGAN [*surrendering*]   All right: all right. I'm done. Have it your own way. Only let me alone. I don't know whether I'm on my head or my heels when you all start on me like this. I'll stay. I'll marry her. I'll do anything for a quiet life. Are you satisfied now?

ELLIE   No. I never really intended to make you marry me, Mr Mangan. Never in the depths of my soul. I only wanted to feel my strength: to know that you could not escape if I chose to take you.

MANGAN [*indignantly*]   What! Do you mean to say you are going to throw me over after my acting so handsome?

LADY UTTERWORD   I should not be too hasty, Miss Dunn. You can throw Mr Mangan over at any time up to the last moment. Very few men in his position go bankrupt. You can live very comfortably on his reputation for immense wealth.

ELLIE   I cannot commit bigamy, Lady Utterword.

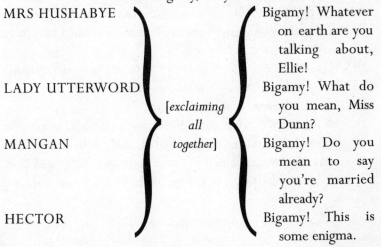

MRS HUSHABYE   Bigamy! Whatever on earth are you talking about, Ellie!

LADY UTTERWORD   [*exclaiming all together*]   Bigamy! What do you mean, Miss Dunn?

MANGAN   Bigamy! Do you mean to say you're married already?

HECTOR   Bigamy! This is some enigma.

ELLIE   Only half an hour ago I became Captain Shotover's white wife.

MRS HUSHABYE   Ellie! What nonsense! Where?

ELLIE   In heaven, where all true marriages are made.

LADY UTTERWORD   Really, Miss Dunn! Really, papa!

MANGAN   He told me *I* was too old! And him a mummy!

HECTOR [*quoting Shelley*]

> "Their altar the grassy earth outspread:
> And their priest the muttering wind."*

ELLIE   Yes: I, Ellie Dunn, give my broken heart and my strong sound soul to its natural captain, my spiritual husband and second father.

She draws the captain's arm through hers, and pats his hand. The captain remains fast asleep.

MRS HUSHABYE   Oh, that's very clever of you, pettikins. Very clever. Alfred, you could never have lived up to Ellie. You must be content with a little share of me.

MANGAN [*sniffing and wiping his eyes*]   It isn't kind— [*his emotion chokes him.*].

LADY UTTERWORD   You are well out of it, Mr Mangan. Miss Dunn is the most conceited young woman I have met since I came back to England.

MRS HUSHABYE   Oh, Ellie isn't conceited. Are you, pettikins?

ELLIE   I know my strength now, Hesione.

MANGAN   Brazen, I call you. Brazen.

MRS HUSHABYE   Tut, tut, Alfred: don't be rude. Don't you feel how lovely this marriage night is, made in heaven? Aren't you happy, you and Hector? Open your eyes: Addy and Ellie look beautiful enough to please the most fastidious man: we

---

*Near quotation from "Rosalind and Helen: A Modern Eclogue," by English poet Percy Bysshe Shelley (1792–1822); Shaw has changed "our" to "their."

live and love and have not a care in the world. We women have managed all that for you. Why in the name of common sense do you go on as if you were two miserable wretches?

CAPTAIN SHOTOVER   I tell you happiness is no good. You can be happy when you are only half alive. I am happier now I am half dead than ever I was in my prime. But there is no blessing on my happiness.

ELLIE [*her face lighting up*]   Life with a blessing! that is what I want. Now I know the real reason why I couldn't marry Mr Mangan: there would be no blessing on our marriage. There is a blessing on my broken heart. There is a blessing on your beauty, Hesione. There is a blessing on your father's spirit. Even on the lies of Marcus there is a blessing; but on Mr Mangan's money there is none.

MANGAN   I don't understand a word of that.

ELLIE   Neither do I. But I know it means something.

MANGAN   Don't say there was any difficulty about the blessing. I was ready to get a bishop to marry us.

MRS HUSHABYE   Isn't he a fool, pettikins?

HECTOR [*fiercely*]   Do not scorn the man. We are all fools.

MAZZINI, in pyjamas and a richly colored silk dressing-gown, comes from the house, on LADY UTTERWORD's side.

MRS HUSHABYE   Oh! here comes the only man who ever resisted me. What's the matter, Mr Dunn? Is the house on fire?

MAZZINI   Oh, no: nothing's the matter: but really it's impossible to go to sleep with such an interesting conversation going on under one's window, and on such a beautiful night too. I just had to come down and join you all. What has it all been about?

MRS HUSHABYE   Oh, wonderful things, soldier of freedom.

HECTOR   For example, Mangan, as a practical business man, has tried to undress himself and has failed ignominiously; whilst you, as an idealist, have succeeded brilliantly.

MAZZINI   I hope you don't mind my being like this, Mrs Hushabye. [*He sits down on the campstool.*]

MRS HUSHABYE   On the contrary, I could wish you always like that.

LADY UTTERWORD   Your daughter's match is off, Mr Dunn. It seems that Mr Mangan, whom we all supposed to be a man of property, owns absolutely nothing.

MAZZINI   Well, of course I knew that, Lady Utterword. But if people believe in him and are always giving him money, whereas they don't believe in me and never give me any, how can I ask poor Ellie to depend on what I can do for her?

MANGAN   Don't you run away with this idea that I have nothing. I—

HECTOR   Oh, don't explain. We understand. You have a couple of thousand pounds in exchequer bills, 50,000 shares worth tenpence a dozen, and half a dozen tabloids of cyanide of potassium to poison yourself with when you are found out. That's the reality of your millions.

MAZZINI   Oh no, no, no. He is quite honest: the businesses are genuine and perfectly legal.

HECTOR [disgusted]   Yah! Not even a great swindler!

MANGAN   So you think. But I've been too many for some honest men, for all that.

LADY UTTERWORD   There is no pleasing you, Mr Mangan. You are determined to be neither rich nor poor, honest nor dishonest.

MANGAN   There you go again. Ever since I came into this silly house I have been made to look like a fool, though I'm as good a man in this house as in the city.

ELLIE [musically]   Yes: this silly house, this strangely happy house, this agonizing house, this house without foundations. I shall call it Heartbreak House.

MRS HUSHABYE   Stop, Ellie; or I shall howl like an animal.[12]

MANGAN   [breaks into a low snivelling]!!!

MRS HUSHABYE   There! you have set Alfred off.

ELLIE   I like him best when he is howling.

CAPTAIN SHOTOVER   Silence! [*MANGAN subsides into silence.*] I say, let the heart break in silence.

HECTOR   Do you accept that name for your house?

CAPTAIN SHOTOVER   It is not my house: it is only my kennel.

HECTOR   We have been too long here. We do not live in this house: we haunt it.

LADY UTTERWORD [*heart torn*]   It is dreadful to think how you have been here all these years while I have gone round the world. I escaped young; but it has drawn me back. It wants to break my heart too. But it shan't. I have left you and it behind. It was silly of me to come back. I felt sentimental about papa and Hesione and the old place. I felt them calling to me.

MAZZINI   But what a very natural and kindly and charming human feeling, Lady Utterword!

LADY UTTERWORD   So I thought, Mr Dunn. But I know now that it was only the last of my influenza. I found that I was not remembered and not wanted.

CAPTAIN SHOTOVER   You left because you did not want us. Was there no heartbreak in that for your father?[13] You tore yourself up by the roots; and the ground healed up and brought forth fresh plants and forgot you. What right had you to come back and probe old wounds?

MRS HUSHABYE   You were a complete stranger to me at first, Addy; but now I feel as if you had never been away.

LADY UTTERWORD   Thank you, Hesione; but the influenza is quite cured. The place may be Heartbreak House to you, Miss Dunn, and to this gentleman from the city who seems to have so little self-control; but to me it is only a very ill-regulated and rather untidy villa without any stables.

HECTOR   Inhabited by——?

ELLIE   A crazy old sea captain and a young singer who adores him.

MRS HUSHABYE   A sluttish female, trying to stave off a double chin and an elderly spread, vainly wooing a born soldier of freedom.

MAZZINI   Oh, really, Mrs Hushabye—

MANGAN   A member of His Majesty's Government that everybody sets down as a nincompoop: don't forget him, Lady Utterword.

LADY UTTERWORD   And a very fascinating gentleman whose chief occupation is to be married to my sister.

HECTOR   All heartbroken imbeciles.

MAZZINI   Oh no. Surely, if I may say so, rather a favorable specimen of what is best in our English culture. You are very charming people, most advanced, unprejudiced, frank, humane, unconventional, democratic, free-thinking, and everything that is delightful to thoughtful people.

MRS HUSHABYE   You do us proud, Mazzini.

MAZZINI   I am not flattering, really. Where else could I feel perfectly at ease in my pyjamas? I sometimes dream that I am in very distinguished society, and suddenly I have nothing on but my pyjamas! Sometimes I haven't even pyjamas. And I always feel overwhelmed with confusion. But here, I don't mind in the least: it seems quite natural.

LADY UTTERWORD   An infallible sign that you are now not in really distinguished society, Mr Dunn. If you were in my house, you would feel embarrassed.

MAZZINI   I shall take particular care to keep out of your house, Lady Utterword.

LADY UTTERWORD   You will be quite wrong, Mr Dunn. I should make you very comfortable; and you would not have the trouble and anxiety of wondering whether you should wear your purple and gold or your green and crimson dressing-gown at dinner. You complicate life instead of simplifying it by doing these ridiculous things.

ELLIE   Your house is not Heartbreak House: is it, Lady Utterword?

HECTOR   Yet she breaks hearts, easy as her house is. That poor devil upstairs with his flute howls when she twists his heart, just as Mangan howls when my wife twists his.

LADY UTTERWORD   That is because Randall has nothing to do but have his heart broken. It is a change from having his head shampooed. Catch anyone breaking Hastings' heart!

CAPTAIN SHOTOVER   The numskull wins, after all.

LADY UTTERWORD   I shall go back to my numskull with the greatest satisfaction when I am tired of you all, clever as you are.

MANGAN [*huffily*]   I never set up to be clever.

LADY UTTERWORD   I forgot you, Mr Mangan.

MANGAN   Well, I don't see that quite, either.

LADY UTTERWORD   You may not be clever, Mr Mangan; but you are successful.

MANGAN   But I don't want to be regarded merely as a successful man. I have an imagination like anyone else. I have a presentiment——

MRS HUSHABYE   Oh, you are impossible, Alfred. Here I am devoting myself to you; and you think of nothing but your ridiculous presentiment. You bore me. Come and talk poetry to me under the stars. [*She drags him away into the darkness.*]

MANGAN [*tearfully, as he disappears*]   Yes: it's all very well to make fun of me; but if you only knew——

HECTOR [*impatiently*]   How is all this going to end?

MAZZINI   It won't end, Mr Hushabye. Life doesn't end: it goes on.

ELLIE   Oh, it can't go on forever. I'm always expecting something. I don't know what it is; but life must come to a point sometime.

LADY UTTERWORD   The point for a young woman of your age is a baby.

HECTOR   Yes, but, damn it, I have the same feeling; and *I* can't have a baby.

LADY UTTERWORD   By deputy, Hector.

HECTOR   But I *have* children. All that is over and done with for
me: and yet I too feel that this can't last. We sit here talking,
and leave everything to Mangan and to chance and to the devil.
Think of the powers of destruction that Mangan and his mutual
admiration gang wield! It's madness: it's like giving a torpedo
to a badly brought up child to play at earthquakes with.

MAZZINI   I know. I used often to think about that when I was
young.

HECTOR   Think! What's the good of thinking about it? Why
didn't you do something?

MAZZINI   But I did. I joined societies and made speeches and
wrote pamphlets. That was all I could do. But, you know,
though the people in the societies thought they knew more
than Mangan, most of them wouldn't have joined if they had
known as much. You see they had never had any money to
handle or any men to manage. Every year I expected a revolution, or some frightful smash-up: it seemed impossible that
we could blunder and muddle on any longer. But nothing
happened, except, of course, the usual poverty and crime
and drink that we are used to. Nothing ever does happen. It's
amazing how well we get along, all things considered.

LADY UTTERWORD   Perhaps somebody cleverer than you
and Mr Mangan was at work all the time.

MAZZINI   Perhaps so. Though I was brought up not to believe
in anything, I often feel that there is a great deal to be said for
the theory of an over-ruling Providence, after all.

LADY UTTERWORD   Providence! I meant Hastings.

MAZZINI   Oh, I beg your pardon, Lady Utterword.

CAPTAIN SHOTOVER   Every drunken skipper trusts to
Providence. But one of the ways of Providence with drunken
skippers is to run them on the rocks.

MAZZINI   Very true, no doubt, at sea. But in politics, I assure
you, they only run into jellyfish. Nothing happens.

CAPTAIN SHOTOVER   At sea nothing happens to the sea.

Nothing happens to the sky. The sun comes up from the east and goes down to the west. The moon grows from a sickle to an arc lamp, and comes later and later until she is lost in the light as other things are lost in the darkness. After the typhoon, the flying-fish glitter in the sunshine like birds. It's amazing how they get along, all things considered. Nothing happens, except something not worth mentioning.

ELLIE   What is that, O Captain, my captain?*

CAPTAIN SHOTOVER [*savagely*]   Nothing but the smash of the drunken skipper's ship on the rocks, the splintering of her rotten timbers, the tearing of her rusty plates, the drowning of the crew like rats in a trap.

ELLIE   Moral: don't take rum.

CAPTAIN SHOTOVER [*vehemently*]   That is a lie, child. Let a man drink ten barrels of rum a day, he is not a drunken skipper until he is a drifting skipper. Whilst he can lay his course and stand on his bridge and steer it, he is no drunkard. It is the man who lies drinking in his bunk and trusts to Providence that I call the drunken skipper, though he drank nothing but the waters of the River Jordan.

ELLIE   Splendid! And you haven't had a drop for an hour. You see you don't need it: your own spirit is not dead.

CAPTAIN SHOTOVER   Echoes: nothing but echoes. The last shot was fired years ago.

HECTOR   And this ship that we are all in? This soul's prison we call England?

CAPTAIN SHOTOVER   The captain is in his bunk, drinking bottled ditch-water; and the crew is gambling in the forecastle. She will strike and sink and split. Do you think the laws of God will be suspended in favor of England because you were born in it?

---

*Allusion to Walt Whitman's poem "O Captain! My Captain!" written in response to the assassination of President Abraham Lincoln in 1865.

HECTOR   Well, I don't mean to be drowned like a rat in a trap. I still have the will to live. What am I to do?

CAPTAIN SHOTOVER   Do? Nothing simpler. Learn your business as an Englishman.

HECTOR   And what may my business as an Englishman be, pray?

CAPTAIN SHOTOVER   Navigation. Learn it and live; or leave it and be damned.

ELLIE   Quiet, quiet: you'll tire yourself.

MAZZINI   I thought all that once, Captain; but I assure you nothing will happen.

A dull distant explosion is heard.

HECTOR [*starting up*]   What was that?

CAPTAIN SHOTOVER   Something happening [*he blows his whistle*]. Breakers ahead!

The light goes out.

HECTOR [*furiously*]   Who put that light out? Who dared put that light out?

NURSE GUINNESS [*running in from the house to the middle of the esplanade*]   I did, sir. The police have telephoned to say we'll be summoned if we don't put that light out: it can be seen for miles.

HECTOR   It shall be seen for a hundred miles [*he dashes into the house*].

NURSE GUINNESS   The rectory is nothing but a heap of bricks, they say. Unless we can give the rector a bed he has nowhere to lay his head this night.

CAPTAIN SHOTOVER   The Church is on the rocks, breaking up. I told him it would unless it headed for God's open sea.

NURSE GUINNESS   And you are all to go down to the cellars.

CAPTAIN SHOTOVER   Go there yourself, you and all the crew. Batten down the hatches.

NURSE GUINNESS   And hide beside the coward I married!

I'll go on the roof first. [*The lamp lights up again.*] There! Mr
Hushabye's turned it on again.

THE BURGLAR [*hurrying in and appealing to NURSE GUINNESS*]
Here: where's the way to that gravel pit? The boot-boy says
there's a cave in the gravel pit. Them cellars is no use. Where's
the gravel pit, Captain?

NURSE GUINNESS   Go straight on past the flagstaff until you
fall into it and break your dirty neck. [*She pushes him contemptuously towards the flagstaff, and herself goes to the foot of the hammock and waits there, as it were by Ariadne's cradle.*]

*Another and louder explosion is heard. The burglar stops and stands
trembling.*

ELLIE [*rising*]   That was nearer.

CAPTAIN SHOTOVER   The next one will get us. [*He rises.*]
Stand by, all hands, for judgment.

THE BURGLAR   Oh my Lordy God! [*He rushes away frantically
past the flagstaff into the gloom.*]

MRS HUSHABYE [*emerging panting from the darkness*]   Who was
that running away? [*She comes to ELLIE.*] Did you hear the explosions? And the sound in the sky: it's splendid: it's like an or-
chestra: it's like Beethoven.

ELLIE   By thunder, Hesione: it is Beethoven.

*She and HESIONE throw themselves into one another's arms in wild
excitement. The light increases.*

MAZZINI [*anxiously*]   The light is getting brighter.

NURSE GUINNESS [*looking up at the house*]   It's Mr Hushabye
turning on all the lights in the house and tearing down the
curtains.

RANDALL [*rushing in in his pyjamas, distractedly waving a flute*]
Ariadne, my soul, my precious, go down to the cellars: I beg
and implore you, go down to the cellars!

LADY UTTERWORD [*quite composed in her hammock*]   The
governor's wife in the cellars with the servants! Really, Randall!

632 GEORGE BERNARD SHAW

RANDALL   But what shall I do if you are killed?

LADY UTTERWORD   You will probably be killed, too, Randall. Now play your flute to show that you are not afraid; and be good. Play us "Keep the home fires burning."

NURSE GUINNESS [*grimly*]   *They'll* keep the home fires burning for us: them up there.

RANDALL [*having tried to play*]   My lips are trembling. I can't get a sound.

MAZZINI   I hope poor Mangan is safe.

MRS HUSHABYE   He is hiding in the cave in the gravel pit.

CAPTAIN SHOTOVER   My dynamite drew him there. It is the hand of God.

HECTOR [*returning from the house and striding across to his former place*]   There is not half light enough. We should be blazing to the skies.

ELLIE [*tense with excitement*]   Set fire to the house, Marcus.

MRS HUSHABYE   My house! No.

HECTOR   I thought of that; but it would not be ready in time.

CAPTAIN SHOTOVER   The judgment has come. Courage will not save you; but it will show that your souls are still live.

MRS HUSHABYE   Sh-sh! Listen: do you hear it now? It's magnificent.

They all turn away from the house and look up, listening.

HECTOR [*gravely*]   Miss Dunn, you can do no good here. We of this house are only moths flying into the candle. You had better go down to the cellar.

ELLIE [*scornfully*]   I don't think.

MAZZINI   Ellie, dear, there is no disgrace in going to the cellar. An officer would order his soldiers to take cover. Mr Hushabye is behaving like an amateur. Mangan and the burglar are acting very sensibly; and it is they who will survive.

ELLIE   Let them. I shall behave like an amateur. But why should you run any risk?

MAZZINI   Think of the risk those poor fellows up there are running!

NURSE GUINNESS   Think of *them*, indeed, the murdering blackguards! What next?

A terrific explosion shakes the earth. They reel back into their seats, or clutch the nearest support. They hear the falling of the shattered glass from the windows.

MAZZINI   Is anyone hurt?

HECTOR   Where did it fall?

NURSE GUINNESS [*in hideous triumph*]   Right in the gravel pit: I seen it. Serve un right! I seen it [*she runs away towards the gravel pit, laughing harshly*].

HECTOR   One husband gone.

CAPTAIN SHOTOVER   Thirty pounds of good dynamite wasted.

MAZZINI   Oh, poor Mangan!

HECTOR   Are you immortal that you need pity him? Our turn next.

They wait in silence and intense expectation. HESIONE and ELLIE hold each other's hand tight.

A distant explosion is heard.

MRS HUSHABYE [*relaxing her grip*]   Oh! they have passed us.

LADY UTTERWORD   The danger is over, Randall. Go to bed.

CAPTAIN SHOTOVER   Turn in, all hands. The ship is safe. [*He sits down and goes asleep.*]

ELLIE [*disappointedly*]   Safe!

HECTOR [*disgustedly*]   Yes, safe. And how damnably dull the world has become again suddenly! [*He sits down.*]

MAZZINI [*sitting down*]   I was quite wrong, after all. It is we who have survived; and Mangan and the burglar——

HECTOR   ——the two burglars——

LADY UTTERWORD   ——the two practical men of business——

MAZZINI   —both gone. And the poor clergyman will have to get a new house.

MRS HUSHABYE   But what a glorious experience! I hope they'll come again tomorrow night.

ELLIE [*radiant at the prospect*]   Oh, I hope so.

RANDALL at last succeeds in keeping the home fires burning* on his flute.

---

*Allusion to English composer Ivor Novello's popular World War I song "Keep the Home Fires Burning" (1915).

ENDNOTES

For many of the footnotes and endnotes of this edition, and especially where I have not been able to track a reference myself, I have relied mainly on two sources: the series of selected Shaw plays (*Major Barbara, The Doctor's Dilemma, Pygmalion, Heartbreak House*) annotated by A. C. Ward in the 1950s and 1960s, published by Longmans, Green and Co; and *The Complete Prefaces*, vols. 1 and 2, annotated by Dan H. Laurence and Daniel J. Leary, published by Allen Lane, Penguin Press, 1993, 1995.

MAJOR BARBARA

1. (p. 5) *they conclude that I am echoing Schopenhauer, Nietzsche, Ibsen, Strindberg, Tolstoy:* Shaw is naming several controversial figures of his time: German philosophers Arthur Schopenhauer (1788–1860) and Friedrich Wilhelm Nietzsche (1844–1900); Norwegian playwright and poet Henrik Johan Ibsen (1828–1906); Swedish playwright and novelist August Strindberg (1849–1912); and Russian novelist Leo Tolstoy (1828–1910).

2. (p. 6) *though I already knew all about Alnaschar and Don Quixote and Simon Tappertit and many another romantic hero mocked by reality:* Shaw lists three fictional romantic heroes: In "The Barber's Fifth Brother," a tale from *The Arabian Nights' Entertainments*, Alnaschar is a dreamer who invests in glassware in a scheme to become rich and marry the vizier's daughter, but then shatters the glass in a rage against his imaginary wife; Don Quixote is the idealistic romantic hero of the satirical romance of that name by Spanish novelist Miguel de Cervantes

(1547–1616); Simon Tappertit, in Charles Dickens's novel *Barnaby Rudge* (1841), is a locksmith's apprentice given to ambitious and romantic delusions.

3. (p. 10) *Nietzsche, like Schopenhauer, is the victim in England of a single much quoted sentence containing the phrase "big blonde beast":* The phrase, from Nietzsche's *The Genealogy of Morals* (1887; First Essay, section 11), refers to the noble animal element that reemerges from time to time in heroic peoples. "Blonde," according to Nietzsche's translator, Walter Kaufmann, refers not to the Teutonic races but to a lion's mane.

4. (p. 15) *His [Undershaft's] conduct stands the Kantian test:* The reference is to the categorical imperative—universal rule of ethical conduct—of German philosopher Immanuel Kant (1724–1804): Act as if the maxim from which you act were to become a universal law.

5. (p. 20) *I am met with nothing but vague cacklings about Ibsen and Nietzsche, and am only too thankful that they are not about Alfred de Musset and Georges Sand:* Shaw uses French writers (and lovers) Alfred de Musset (1810–1857) and George Sand (1804–1876; pen name of Amandine-Aurore-Lucile Dudevant) as representatives of outmoded Romantic thought.

6. (p. 26) *a flag with Blood and Fire on it is unfurled, not in murderous rancor, but because fire is beautiful and blood a vital and splendid red:* The Salvation Army motto, which appears on its flag, is "Blood and Fire." Shaw explains here that the Blood and Fire are not literal but rather figurative of the beauty and energy of life and joy; like the English artist and poet William Blake (1757–1827), Shaw appreciated the power and exuberance of vital energy.

7. (p. 28) *like Frederick's grenadier, the Salvationist wants to live for ever:* During the Seven Years War (1756–1763), in his failed attack on Kolin (June 18, 1757), King Frederick II of Prussia (known as Frederick the Great) is said to have turned to his

hesitant soldiers and urged them on with the taunt, "You scoundrels! Do you want to live forever?"

8. (p. 38) *he launches his sixpennorth of fulminate, missing his mark, but . . . slaying twenty-three persons, besides wounding ninety-nine. . . . Had he blown all Madrid to atoms, . . . not one could have escaped the charge of being an accessory, . . . themselves also:* Unfortunately, Shaw here seems to sympathize with Morral's terrorist act (see note on page 37); at the least, he refuses to judge it as something worse than stupidity: The deaths of twenty-three innocent people and the injuring of ninety-nine others provoke him only to note that as participants in a repressive and exploitative capitalist society, they along with everyone else were guilty of allowing that society to continue its evil. It is an abhorrent view. And if it does not sound strange to our ears, that is because we heard this explanation of terrorism often enough after the terrorist attacks on the New York World Trade Center and the Pentagon on September 11, 2001.

9. (p. 38) *Bonapart's pounding of the Paris mob to pieces in 1795, called in playful approval by our respectable classes "the whiff of grapeshot":* "The Whiff of Grapeshot" is the title of chapter 7 in Scottish historian Thomas Carlyle's 1837 work *The French Revolution* (book 3, part 7). In the chapter Carlyle recounts how Napoleon fired with cannons upon a crowd of insurrectionists, killing 200 of them; he asserts that this action marked the end of the French Revolution.

10. (p. 39) *who can doubt that all over the world proletarians of the ducal kidney are now revelling in "the whiff of dynamite":* Shaw's analogy creates a false moral equivalence between a crowd using violence to seize power and in turn being met with violence to a crowd witnessing a wedding and being blown up.

11. (p. 39) *we are a civilized and merciful people, and, however much we may regret it, must not treat him as Ravaillac and Damiens:* François Ravaillac (1578–1610) assassinated King Henry IV of France

(Henry of Navarre); Robert-François Damiens (1715–1757) attempted to assassinate King Louis XV of France. Both men were tortured and executed.

12. (p. 40) *Think of him setting out to find a gentleman and a Christian in the multitude of human wolves howling for his blood:* The outcry against Morral and Nakens (see note on page 40) must have been extraordinary for Shaw to display anger as he does here. One hopes that Shaw's appellation (howling wolves) was not meant to apply to the families of the twenty-three people killed by Morral, who might justifiably speak against Nakens for harboring a terrorist.

13. (p. 45) *It would be far more sensible to put up with their vices . . . until they give more trouble than they are worth, at which point we should . . . place them in the lethal chamber:* Shaw was a man of ideas: Many were good; several were bad. The idea of executing incorrigible lawbreakers is an example of the latter. Shaw believed that execution should be reserved only for those criminals who are not capable of reform; he considered that system of dealing with crime to be morally superior for three reasons: He saw punishment of any kind as morally reprehensible and repugnant; he considered capital punishment to be murder and revenge dressed in solemn ritual; and he believed that capital punishment degrades the souls of the executors. Furthermore, he felt repeat offenders should be executed in a nonpunitive way rather than imprisoned because imprisonment is extraordinarily cruel punishment and therefore morally indefensible.

14. (p. 49) Lady Britomart: Lady Britomart is named after Edmund Spenser's knight-heroine in book 3 of *The Faerie Queene* (1590) to indicate her formidable strength of character. The name also suggests a range of meanings and associations: British, Mars (god of war in classical mythology), and markets (capitalism).

15. (p. 54) *"Do you think Bismarck or Gladstone or Disraeli could*

*have openly defied every social and moral obligation all their lives
as your father has?"*: Otto von Bismarck (1815–1898),
known as the Iron Chancellor, was the first chancellor of
Germany; rivals William Gladstone (1809–1898) and Benjamin Disraeli (1804–1881) were successive prime ministers of Britain.

16. (p. 57) *"history tells us of only two successful institutions: one the
Undershaft firm, and the other the Roman Empire under the Antonines"*: Antonines is the collective name of the second-
century Roman emperors Antoninus Pius and his sons, who
succeeded him. Undershaft has borrowed this opinion about
the age of the Antonines from English historian Edward Gib-
bon's *The History of the Decline and Fall of the Roman Empire*
(1776–1788).

17. (p. 60) Adolphus Cusins: Shaw based the character of Cusins
in part on his friend Gilbert Murray (1866–1957), a noted
scholar of the religion and literature of ancient Greece. Murray's translations of Euripides (later much criticized by T. S.
Eliot for wordiness) were performed alongside Shaw's plays at
the Court Theatre in the first decade of the twentieth century.

18. (p. 63) *"pukinon domon elthein" [transliterated from the Greek]*:
The phrase, which means "to enter the thick (compact) house,"
is adapted from a passage about the theft of a helmet by Autolycus (son of the messenger god Mercury, in Greek mythology) in book 10 of the *Iliad*, the epic poem about the siege of
Troy attributed to the Greek poet Homer. Gilbert Murray (see
note 17, above) furnished Shaw with this gag in a letter of October 7, 1905, by suggesting that the line could also mean that
it was a bit thick of Autolycus to break into the house.

19. (p. 78) *"Romola"*: Romola is the eponymous heroine of the
1863 novel by English novelist George Eliot. By his own admission, Shaw "almost venerated" Eliot in his youth; but he
later came to regard her as too lacking in hope. By associating
Snobby with the Chartists (see note on p. 77) and Rummy

with George Eliot, Shaw is distinguishing himself from the previous generation of social reformers.

20. (p. 82) *striking her with his fist in the face:* Though there are episodes of farcical violence in Shaw, this extended episode of realistic violence is unique. In spite of its realism, however, Bill Walker's violence toward women has the literary model of Bill Sykes's brutal treatment of Nancy in Charles Dickens's novel *Oliver Twist* (1837–1838). The connection between the two Bills was made even more apparent when Robert Newton played both characters in the respective film versions: David Lean, who had been the film editor of *Major Barbara* in 1941, cast Newton as Bill Sykes in the *Oliver Twist* he directed in 1948.

21. (p. 85) *"coroner's inquest on me daughter":* As the father of a daughter who has died, Peter Shirley foreshadows Undershaft in his later figurative loss of Barbara.

22. (p. 96) *"Dionysos":* In Greek mythology, Dionysus, the god of wine, is not one of the original Olympian gods and is consequently something of an outsider—a foundling god, one might say. The Greeks associated Dionysus with wine-drinking and ecstatic reveling, hence with the abandonment (or transcendence) of reason and rational restraint of the appetites. Gilbert Murray's translation of Euripides' *The Bacchae*, which depicts the seduction and destruction of the young ruler Pentheus by Dionysus, influenced the writing of *Major Barbara*, as did Shaw's friendship and collegial relationship with Murray. Murray's translation of Euripides' *Hippolytus* was performed at the Court Theatre the same year *Major Barbara* was performed there.

23. (p. 96) *"One and another / In money and guns may outpass his brother; . . . / But whoe'er can know . . . / That to live is happy, has found his heaven":* Shaw has Cusins quote from Murray's translation of *The Bacchae*, but he substitutes "money and guns" for Murray's "gold and power."

24. (p. 97) *"Is it so hard a thing to see . . . / And shall not Barbara be loved for ever?"*: Cusins continues to quote from *The Bacchae*, substituting "Fate" for "Hate" in Murray's original and, as he goes on to indicate, "Barbara" in place of "loveliness."

25. (p. 106) *"That will make the standard price to buy anybody who's for sale. I'm not; and the Army's not"*: In a Wildean example of life imitating art, in 2002 a Florida chapter of the Salvation Army refused a large donation from an individual who had won the state lottery on the grounds that it would be hypocritical to accept the winnings because many of the Army's clients had gambled away their families' financial means of support.

26. (p. 107) *incidentally stealing the sovereign on his way out by picking up his cap from the drum*: Snobby's deft theft of Bill's sovereign parallels Undershaft's stealthy "removal" of Barbara's ability to rely on the Salvation Army, which he is in the process of accomplishing underneath the surface of the action.

27. (p. 114) *the band strikes up the march, which rapidly becomes more distant as the procession moves briskly away*: Shaw controls the mood and emotion of this moment through stagecraft. Having gradually crowded the scene from the beginning of the act to the climax here, he now swiftly removes almost everyone from the stage to enact the sense of Barbara's feeling of abandonment and loss. Everyone (save Peter Shirley) and everything fades away from her, including the sound of the Salvation Army band, leaving her bewildered and desolate.

28. (p. 114) *"'My ducats and my daughter'!"*: Undershaft ironically quotes Shylock in Shakespeare's *The Merchant of Venice* on the subject of losing both his daughter and the money she stole from him while eloping with Lorenzo (act 2, scene 8). At this moment, Undershaft has "lost" his daughter by deliberately alienating her from her vocation as a Salvation Army savior of souls; and he has lost his money by donating a large sum to the Salvation Army.

29. (p. 115) The mug smashes against the door and falls in fragments: Here Shaw creates in the action a realistic and striking analogue to the shattering of Barbara's sense of self.

30. (p. 116) *"a Rowton doss":* This is a step up from a flophouse: A doss is a crude or makeshift bed; in the late nineteenth century, an organization chaired by English philanthropist Baron Rowton made good, inexpensive lodgings available to the poor.

31. (p. 116) *"Tell me about Tom Paine's books and Bradlaugh's lectures":* American political philosopher Thomas Paine (1737–1809) and English reformer Charles Bradlaugh (1833–1891) were radical left-wing thinkers; they appeal to Peter Shirley because of their antireligious (Paine) and unorthodox religious (Bradlaugh) views. Shaw implies that Barbara now needs to rethink how to channel her own deeply religious impulses.

32. (p. 137) *"Did you know that, Undershaft?":* Lomax's presumptuously familiar form of address here is underlined by Undershaft's pointedly formal address in his response: "Mr. Lomax." Lomax's carelessness with matches extends to his manners and, Shaw implies, to his intellectual exercises as well.

33. (p. 138) *"William Morris Labor Church":* William Morris (1834–1896), socialist and aestheticist, was one of Shaw's heroes. That Morris has inspired the founding of a Labor church is a Shaw joke.

34. (p. 144) UNDERSHAFT *(enigmatically) "A will of which I am a part."* BARBARA *(startled) "Father! Do you know what you are saying; or are you laying a snare for my soul?":* Barbara's response indicates that she interprets her father's enigmatic statement to mean that God's mysterious will drives the munitions works. But Shaw has made Undershaft's self-explanation resemble closely that of Mephistopheles in Johann Wolfgang von Goethe's nineteenth-century poetic drama *Faust* (part 1): "I am a part of the part [Chaos] that originally was all there was."

Shaw thus preserves the ambiguity of Undershaft's agency—that is, whether it is divine or devilish.

THE DOCTOR'S DILEMMA

1. (p. 178) *equipage (or autopage):* Shaw here coins the latter term (referring to keeping an automobile) in imitation of the former, which means a horse-drawn carriage and the expenses and employees associated with keeping it.

2. (p. 181) *every piano-tuner a Helmholtz, every Old Bailey barrister a Solon, every Seven Dials pigeon dealer a Darwin, . . . every locomotive engine a miracle, and its driver no less wonderful than George Stephenson:* Hermann L. F. von Helmholtz (1821–1894) was a renowned German physiologist and physicist; Old Bailey is London's main criminal court building; Greek statesman Solon (c.600 B.C.), one of the Seven Wise Men of Greece, was renowned as a wise lawgiver; Seven Dials, a meeting point of seven roads in London and a poor area in Victorian times, is an unglamorous locale; English inventor George Stephenson (1781–1848) invented the railway locomotive engine.

3. (p. 208) *Bluebeard:* Bluebeard, the serial wife-killer of Charles Perrault's fairy tale in *Contes de ma mere l'oye* (*Mother Goose Tales*, 1697), is presumably based on the real-life figure of Gilles de Rais, a fifteenth-century homosexual pederast and serial killer of young boys. Shaw would use the historical character in his play *Saint Joan* (1923).

4. (p. 226) *I was reproached during the performances of The Doctor's Dilemma at the Court Theatre in 1907:* The Court Theatre is where many of Shaw's plays were first performed between 1904 and 1907. These productions consolidated his reputation as an accomplished, provocative, entertaining modern playwright. This preface to *The Doctor's Dilemma* was written after it had been rehearsed and performed at the Court Theatre. Shaw always advised readers to attend to his prefaces after they had seen or read the play.

5. (p. 253) His combination of soft manners and responsive kindliness, with a certain unseizable reserve and a familiar yet foreign chiselling of feature, reveal the Jew: Although Shaw's observations here of racial characteristics are without self-consciousness or prejudice, his calling attention to Doctor Schutzmacher's racial identity was deemed too controversial when a film version of the play was made in 1958: The character was omitted in the adaptation.

6. (p. 258) "What is it the old cardinal says in Browning's play? 'I have known four and twenty leaders of revolt'": The "old cardinal" is the papal legate Ogniben (Everygood in Italian), in English playwright Robert Browning's A Soul's Tragedy (1846); in the play, Ogniben cynically manipulates the protagonist, Chiappino, into demonstrating how unreal his political idealism is. Sir Patrick plays a somewhat analogous role in Ridgeon's adventure of self-discovery. (Shaw had been a member of the Browning Society and knew Browning's verse dramas well.)

7. (p. 267) "Walpole! the absent-minded beggar": The reference is to English writer Rudyard Kipling's 1899 poem "The Absent-minded Beggar." The accent in the delivery of B.B.'s line falls on "absent-minded"; "beggar" is used here figuratively to mean "fellow," not an actual "beggar."

8. (p. 317) "I don't believe in morality. I'm a disciple of Bernard Shaw": Michael Holroyd reports in his biography of Shaw (Bernard Shaw, vol. 2; see "For Further Reading") that a blackmailer once tried to justify his criminal behavior by claiming he was a disciple of Shaw. Such a misuse of his works, Shaw felt, was due mainly to journalistic misrepresentations of his ideas.

9. (p. 341) "I believe in Michael Angelo, Velasquez, and Rembrandt; . . . Amen": Shaw indicated that Louis's prayer derives from a story by German composer and writer Richard Wagner, "An End in Paris" (1841), in which the composer-protagonist professes a similar creed, but with "God, Mozart, and Beethoven" where Louis has his trinity of great artists.

10. (p. 346) *"I think it is Shakespear who says . . . The readiness is all"*:
Shaw said that this hilarious mismatching and mangling of
lines from Shakespeare's plays was inspired by the duke's fearful version of Hamlet's "To be or not to be" soliloquy in Mark
Twain's 1884 novel *Adventures of Huckleberry Finn* (chapter 21).
First, B.B. switches the order of "good" and "evil" in Marc
Antony's famous observation, "The evil that men do lives after
them, / The good is oft interred with their bones" (*Julius Caesar,* act 3, scene 2). "If tis not today, twil be tomorrow" ap-
proximates Hamlet's "If it be not now, yet it will come"
(*Hamlet,* act 5, scene 2). "Tomorrow and tomorrow and to-
morrow" is from Macbeth's despairing speech (*Macbeth,* act 5,
scene 5). B.B. next comes close to Macbeth's words about
Duncan: "After life's fitful fever he sleeps well" (act 3, scene
2). "And like this insubstantial bourne . . . wrack behind"
combines Hamlet's "from whose bourne no traveler returns"
(act 3, scene 1) with Prospero's "And like this insubstantial
pageant faded / Leave not a rack [cloud] behind" (*The Tempest,*
act 4, scene 1). "Out, out, brief candle" is Macbeth's speech
(act 5, scene 5). "Nothing canst thou to damnation add" is
Othello to Iago (*Othello,* act 3, scene 3). Finally, B.B. returns
to Hamlet's same speech about Providence for "The readiness
is all" (act 5, scene 5).

PYGMALION

1. (p. 361) *Melville Bell:* The reference is to American teacher of
elocution Alexander Melville Bell (1819–1905); inspired by
his wife's deafness, he invented "visible speech," a system of
written sounds, to help deaf-mutes communicate.

2. (p. 367) St. Paul's Church: In later editions Shaw specified,
"Not Wren's cathedral but Inigo Jones' church." Inigo Jones
(1573–1652) and Sir Christopher Wren (1632–1723) were
renowned English architects. Jones restored Saint Paul's
Church in 1634; Wren designed the new Saint Paul's Cathe-

dral after it was destroyed in the Great Fire of London in
1666.

3. (p. 369) *"Ow, eez ye-ooa san, is e? Wal, fewd dan y' de-ooty bawmz a
mather should, eed now bettern to spawl a pore gel's flahrzn than ran
awy athaht pyin. Will ye-oo py me f 'them"*: That is, "Oh, he's your
son, is he? Well, if you'd done your duty by him as a mother
should, he'd know better than to spoil a poor girl's flowers
and then run away without paying. Will you pay me for them?"

4. (p. 374) *"May I ask, sir, do you do this for your living at a music
hall?"*: The origin of this episode in the play can be found in a
letter Shaw wrote to *The Morning Leader* (August 16, 1901)
about his having been invited to the docks to explain elocution to the laborers. When Shaw instead explained to them the
"phonetic alphabet," they were amused and called him "a
quick-change artist." Also, though they recognized the difference between their pronunciation and that of educated people, "the nature of that difference—which they earnestly
desired to remove—was a mystery to them."

5. (p. 381) On the walls, engravings; mostly Piranesis: Giovanni
Battista Piranesi (1720–1778) was an Italian architect and en-
graver; his *Carceri* (Prisons) engravings depict enormous and
labyrinthine structures that, as geometric displays, appeal to
Higgins's scientific taste.

6. (p. 397) *"You know, Pickering, that woman has the most extraordinary ideas about me. . . . I cant account for it"*: Higgins's lack of
self-knowledge in regard to his domineering nature is comparable to Lady Britomart's similar disingenuousness in *Major
Barbara*. Ultimately, though, Shaw's comic motif of willful
egotists who fail to recognize themselves as such probably derives from Sir Anthony Absolute (in Richard Sheridan's *The
Rivals*, 1775), who, in the midst of a passionate fury, asks his
son Jack to be "cool" like his father.

7. (p. 399) *"his native woodnotes wild"*: English poet John Milton
(1608–1674) refers thus to Shakespeare in his poem "L'Alle-

gro" (line 134) in order to distinguish his own art as sophisticated and premeditated from Shakespeare's spontaneous products of the imagination. Shaw made a similar distinction between himself and Shakespeare, whom he considered to be the master of word music, but poor in ideas. By recalling Milton's lines here Shaw makes Higgins, the figurative version of himself, a Miltonist; like Milton, Shaw was anxious about his own originality in comparison to Shakespeare. Milton and his creation Satan (in *Paradise Lost*) and Shaw and his creation Higgins all want to be the authors of themselves.

8. (p. 409) Mrs. Higgins was brought up on Morris and Burne Jones; and her room . . . is not crowded with furniture and little tables and nicknacks. . . . the Morris wall-papers, and the Morris chintz window curtains and brocade covers. . . . A few good oil-paintings . . . (the Burne Jones, not the Whistler): English poet and artist William Morris (1834–1896), a friend of Shaw, introduced the idea of designing homes and furnishings according to aesthetic principles; he designed wallpaper, chintzes, and the like. Mrs. Higgins rejects Victorian *horror vacui* ("fear of empty spaces") by not crowding her drawing room with "furniture and little tables and nicknacks"; in doing so, she proclaims her modernity. Edward Burne-Jones (1833–1898) was a pre-Raphaelite painter and an associate of Morris; Mrs. Higgins's embrace of Burne-Jones shows that her modernity stops short of Shaw's contemporaries, for she has no paintings in the more modern manner of Whistler.

9. (p. 411) *"My idea of a loveable woman is something as like you as possible"*: Shaw refers to Higgins as having a "mother-fixation," and as such he must be accounted as one of the earliest literary characters created from a consciousness of the Oedipus complex (a child's sexual attraction to the parent of the opposite sex and jealousy of the parent of the same sex), a theory developed by Sigmund Freud (1856–1939). Shaw was

familiar with Freud's theories and wrote about them extensively to Gilbert Murray on March 14, 1911.

10. (p. 419) *"bloody"*: No one knows precisely why this particular adjective became taboo in British English, but it did. Its casual application seems to have been considered blasphemous or sacrilegious, or at least too vulgar for polite conversation. It was unheard on the British stage until Eliza uttered it in 1914; it provoked tidal waves of laughter, as much at the breaking of a taboo as at the enormity of Eliza's social gaffe. Since there are no more verbal taboos on our stage, except politically incorrect ones, the original effect is not reproducible.

11. (p. 424) *"Lionel Monckton"*: This English composer (1861–1924) wrote the hit musical comedy *The Arcadians*, which ran in London from 1909 to 1911; Monckton's most popular airs would have been familiar to Londoners like Higgins and Eliza.

12. (p. 428) La Fanciulla del Golden West: Italian composer Giacomo Puccini's great opera is actually titled *La Fanciulla del West* (The Girl of the West, 1910); Shaw has conflated its title with that of its play-source, *The Girl of the Golden West* (1905), by American playwright David Belasco. The aria Higgins is "half-singing" is most likely "Ch'ella mi creda libero e lontano" (Let her think that I am free and far away).

13. (p. 435) and finally goes down on her knees on the hearthrug to look for the ring: The hearthrug is in front of the fireplace where Higgins had flung the ring. By having Eliza search there among the ashes, Shaw is playing on the story of Cinderella. In later editions Shaw added that Eliza then puts the ring on the dessert stand, where she knows Higgins will find it because of his fondness for sweets.

14. (pp. 441–442) *"it's a choice between the Skilly of the workhouse and the Char Bydis of the middle class"*: In Greek legend Scylla, a sea monster, and Charybdis, a whirlpool, occupied oppo-

site sides of the Strait of Messina, through which Odysseus had to sail without being capsized by either. The phrase "between Scylla and Charybdis" means between two equal difficulties.

15. (p. 459) Higgins, left alone, rattles his cash in his pocket; chuckles; and disports himself in a highly self-satisfied manner: Since the first performance of *Pygmalion* in England, actors and audiences have rebelled against the unresolved ending of Shaw's first version of the play, used in this edition. In Shaw's later revision, Higgins "roars with laughter" as he informs his mother that Eliza is going to "marry Freddy." In so doing, Higgins conforms to the prose narrative Shaw appended to the published version of the play.

16. (p. 469) *Age had not withered him, nor could custom stale his infinite variety:* Shaw's application of Enobarbus's famous ascription of immortal vitality to Cleopatra (in Shakespeare's *Antony and Cleopatra*, act 2, scene 2) shows his great affection and friendship for Wells, as do the sentences that follow.

HEARTBREAK HOUSE

1. (p. 477) *Heartbreak House and Horseback Hall:* With these two categories—metaphors, really Shaw indicates a division of the upper classes. Heartbreak House, as he goes on to explain, symbolizes the socially liberal, artistic, and intellectual but apolitical and self-absorbed group; Horseback Hall is the pro forma conservative, anti-intellectual, anti-artistic, but pro-leisure-sports and self-absorbed group. Shaw points out that neither group provided a good pool for political leaders.

2. (p. 479) *the garden of Klingsor:* Shaw uses this image as a symbol of sensuous self-indulgence. In German composer Richard Wagner's 1882 opera *Parsifal*, the eponymous hero is tempted to such self-indulgence by the flower maidens in the magical garden of the evil magician Klingsor.

3. (p. 489) *unsuccessful [attempt] to assassinate Mr Lloyd George:*
David Lloyd George (1863–1945) was prime minister of
Great Britain during the last two years of World War I, and
thereafter for four more years. Louis Cottin, an anarchist, attempted to assassinate him but only wounded him.

4. (p. 492) *Tearing the Garter from the Kaiser's leg, . . . changing the
King's illustrious and historically appropriate surname (for the war
was the old war of Guelph against Ghibelline):* The Order of the
Garter is an order of chivalry founded in 1348 by King Edward III; at the start of World War I, Kaiser Wilhelm II, emperor of Germany and king of Prussia (1888 to 1918), was
stripped of this high British honor. Also at the start of the war,
Britain's King George V changed his family name from the
German Saxe-Coburg-Gotha to the English Windsor. The
Guelphs and the Ghibellines were two warring political parties in Italy during the twelfth to the fourteenth centuries; the
Guelphs, the papal and popular party, opposed the authority
of the German emperors in Italy, while the aristocratic Ghibellines supported the German emperors.

5. (p. 516) *to destroy the militarism of Zabern:* Zabern, usually
spelled Saverne, in northeastern France in the region of
Alsace-Lorraine, was the site of conflict between the German
military and local citizens that contributed to the motivation
for World War I.

6. (p. 517) *Apostolic Hapsburg has collapsed; All Highest Hohenzollern
languishes in Holland, . . . Imperial Romanoff, said to have perished
miserably by a more summary method of murder, . . . the lord of
Hellas is level with his lackeys in republican Switzerland; . . .
Commanders-in-Chief have passed from a brief glory as Solons and
Caesars into failure and obscurity:* Hapsburg is the name of the
ruling family of Austria that gained ascendancy over much of
Europe during the sixteenth century. Hohenzollern is the
royal family name of Kaiser Wilhelm II (see note 4, above),
who abdicated to Holland on November 9, 1918. Czar

Nicholas II of Russia (1868–1918), a member of the Romanoff (or Romanov) Russian dynasty and the last czar of
Russia, was murdered with all his family by the Bolsheviks during the Russian Revolution. Constantine I, king of Greece
(1913–1917, 1920–1922), known as king of the Hellenes, did
not support the Allied forces during World War I and consequently was deposed; he sought refuge in Switzerland. The
Greek statesman Solon (c.600 B.C.), one of the Seven Wise
Men of Greece, was renowned as a wise lawgiver.

7. (p. 518) *"Lass' uns verderben, lachend zu grunde geh'n":* The English translation is "Laughing let us be destroyed, laughing let
us go to our graves"; the quotation is from the ecstatic love
duet between Brünnhilde and Siegfried that concludes
Richard Wagner's 1871 opera *Siegfried.*

8. (pp. 518–519) *That is why I had to withhold Heartbreak House
from the footlights during the war; for the Germans might . . . not
have waited for their cues:* In a letter of October 5, 1916, to Sidney and Beatrice Webb (fellow members of the Fabian Society), Shaw recounts his experience with two zeppelins that
passed over his country home in Ayot St. Lawrence; the experience was the inspiration for the end of the play. In the letter,
Shaw writes: "The sound of the Zepp's engines was so fine,
and its voyage through the stars so enchanting, that I positively
caught myself hoping next night that there would be another
raid." Clearly, Shaw transmuted these feelings into Ellie and
Hesione's emotions at the end of the play. Shaw adds the following observation in the letter after he notes the human suffering caused by the bringing down of one of the zeppelins
and the gleeful response of some of the onlookers, as well as
his own ability to get right to sleep: "Pretty lot of animals we
are!"

9. (p. 524) *"It has been a very unpleasant surprise to me to find that
nobody expects me":* It is a common motif in dreams that one arrives at a place where one is not known or expected. *Heart-*

break House begins with Ellie's falling asleep, and with Nurse Guinness's just managing to prevent a crash of bottles to the floor. These two actions frame the play as a circular dream: The entire play may be seen as Ellie's dream; at the end of the play, the motif of the bottles that do not fall is replicated on a grander scale by the house's escaping destruction.

10. (p. 596) *"it's like the night in Tristan and Isolde"*: In Wagner's opera *Tristan und Isolde* (1859), the lovers are drawn to the night as the realm where a true and complete union can take place between them.

11. (p. 611) *"Fall and crush"*: Hector echoes Albany's line, "Fall, and cease" in the last scene of Shakespeare's *King Lear*. As Albany sees the ancient Lear carrying in Cordelia's murdered body, he expresses his sense that the world should collapse and end in the face of such evil. Likewise, through Hector's sense of futility here, Shaw is expressing his own anger at the carnage and stupidity of a world gone war-mad between 1914 and 1918.

12. (p. 624) *"Stop, Ellie; or I shall howl like an animal"*: Through Hesione's near-breakdown, Shaw is alluding (again) to the final scene of *King Lear*, when Lear enters with the body of Cordelia in his arms and commands everyone to "Howl, howl, howl." Lear is reduced to a grieving animal howling out its raw pain. It is such grief over the cataclysm of the war that keeps threatening to break through the surface of the play, as here in Hesione's attempt to suppress her despair.

13. (p. 625) *"Was there no heartbreak in that for your father?"*: Shotover's humiliation here in the confession of how his daughter Addy's leaving home broke his heart shows how deeply Shaw has embedded *King Lear* in *Heartbreak House*; just as Lear's denial of his own mortality manifests itself in his incestuous impulse to keep his daughter Cordelia to himself, so too does Captain Shotover's resistance to crashing the ship of state on the rocks manifest itself in his spiritual marriage to Ellie, who,

as befits the dream-like state of the action, can be both his daughter and his wife. The issue of Ellie's marrying the older Mangan, a man her adored father's age, is Shaw' s version of the first part of *King Lear*, where Cordelia must first reject her father's demands on her.

INSPIRED BY <u>PYGMALION</u> AND THREE OTHER PLAYS

My Fair Lady, with book and lyrics by Alan Jay Lerner and music by Frederick Loewe, opened on Broadway on March 15, 1956, to overwhelming applause from audiences and critics alike. The original production starred Rex Harrison as Henry Higgins and the incandescent Julie Andrews as Eliza Doolittle. Eliza gets things started memorably with "Wouldn't It Be Loverly?" in which she daydreams for a "room somewhere / far away from the cold night air." The roster of songs, which all became hits, includes "Just You Wait," "I Could Have Danced All Night," "On the Street Where You Live," and "I've Grown Accustomed to Her Face."

Lerner and Loewe had attempted to turn *Pygmalion* into a musical in 1952 but found the task impossible. For this production they made several cuts to Shaw's drama, most conspicuously changing Shaw's ending into an unambiguously happy one. At the beginning of the libretto, Lerner inserted the phrase, "I have omitted [Shaw's epilogue] because in it Shaw explains how Eliza ends not with Higgins but with Freddy and—Shaw and Heaven forgive me!—I am not certain he is right." Thus *My Fair Lady* closes with Higgins's famous: "Eliza? Where the devil are my slippers?"

My Fair Lady quickly became a phenomenon in American theater. The Broadway production was a great commercial success, earned ten Tony nominations, and has been called the greatest stage musical of all time. On June 13, 1961, *My Fair Lady* beat out Rodgers and Hammerstein's *Oklahoma!* as history's longest-running Broadway play, and the best-selling original cast recording is still in demand. At the 1957 Tony Awards, Harrison earned a statue for his performance, and Andrews was nominated for hers (she spent a total of forty-eight months playing Eliza on the stage). *My Fair Lady* also won Tonys for best director (Moss Hart), best conductor and musical director (Franz Allers), best scenic designer (Oliver Smith), best costume designer (Cecil Beaton), and best musical.

Part of *My Fair Lady*'s commercial success was the multimillion-dollar sale of the movie rights. George Cukor (*The Philadelphia Story* and *David Copperfield*) directed the lavish screen adaptation, produced by movie mogul Jack L. Warner. Rex Harrison reprised his stage role as phonetics professor Henry Higgins, and Audrey Hepburn replaced Julie Andrews, with songs voiced by Marni Nixon (who also sang Natalie Wood's part in *West Side Story*). The 1964 film opens with a dazzling sequence of close-ups of flowers lining a brilliantly recreated Covent Garden Opera House. Hepburn's waifish and unwashed Eliza stands by, selling flowers to the fabulously dressed, upper-class operagoers. Without delay, Harrison sidles up and begins to abuse Hepburn for her deplorable accent, giving vent to barbed dialogue that is indebted to Shaw's original. Some of the more acerbic insults include "A woman who utters such disgusting and depressing noise has no right to be anywhere, no right to live," and "Don't sit there crooning like a bilious pigeon." So begins one of cinema's most intelligent romances, one in which the principal players neither touch nor kiss.

Cukor's *My Fair Lady* was nominated for twelve Academy Awards. The film earned Oscars for best actor (Harrison); director; cinematography and color (Harry Stradling); art and set direction; sound; music and score adaptation (André Previn); and costume design (Cecil Beaton), as well as best picture. Oddly enough, Julie Andrews, who is generally agreed to be sorely missing from Cukor's film, won the best actress Oscar for her performance in that year's *Mary Poppins*.

The stage success of *My Fair Lady* in New York and London inspired MGM to produce a lavish widescreen film of *The Doctor's*

Dilemma (1958). Directed by Anthony Asquith (who had co-directed with Leslie Howard the highly successful 1938 film of *Pygmalion*), it stars Dirk Bogarde and Leslie Caron, and features the experienced Shavian actors Robert Morley and Alastair Sim, who play two incompetent doctors with great comedic zest and skill.

Major Barbara was memorably filmed in 1941 while German bombs fell on London, inconveniencing the production greatly. The director of record is Gabriel Pascal, but the editor, David Lean, seems to have had a large part in putting the film together. Wendy Hiller, who effectively created the role of Eliza Doolittle on screen three years earlier, plays Barbara. Rex Harrison is an attractive Cusins, while Robert Morley makes a delightfully devilish Undershaft.

Heartbreak House has never been filmed, but Rex Harrison and Amy Irving starred in an excellent television adaptation in 1986. Harrison as Captain Shotover proves himself once again the premier Shavian actor of his time, while Amy Irving finds the emotional depth Shaw meant the role of Ellie to have.

COMMENTS & QUESTIONS

In this section, we aim to provide the reader with an array of perspectives on the text, as well as questions that challenge those perspectives. The commentary has been culled from sources as diverse as reviews contemporaneous with the works, letters written by the author, literary criticism of later generations, and appreciations written throughout the works' history. Following the commentary, a series of questions seeks to filter George Bernard Shaw's Pygmalion and Three Other Plays *through a variety of points of view and bring about a richer understanding of these enduring works.*

COMMENTS

George Bernard Shaw

Every time one of my new plays is first produced the critics declare it is rotten, though they are always willing to admit that the next to the last play is the greatest thing I've done. I have educated the critics up to an appreciation of the next to the last of my plays.

—*New York Times* (May 5, 1907)

H. L. Mencken

If we divest ourselves of the idea that Shaw is trying to preach some rock-ribbed doctrine in each of his plays, instead of merely setting forth human events as he sees them, we may find his dramas much easier of comprehension. True enough, in his prefaces and stage directions, he delivers himself of many wise saws and elaborate theories. But upon the stage, fortunately, prefaces and stage directions are no longer read to audiences, as they were in

Shakespeare's time, and so, if they are ever to discharge their natural functions, the Shaw dramas must stand as simple plays. . . .

Shaw himself, a follower of Ibsen, has shown variations sufficiently marked to bring him followers of his own. In all the history of the English stage, no man has exceeded him in technical resources nor in nimbleness of wit. Some of his scenes are fairly irresistible, and throughout his plays his avoidance of the old-fashioned machinery of the drama gives even his wildest extravagances an air of reality.

—*George Bernard Shaw: His Plays* (1905)

A. B. Walkley

In perfect innocence Mr. Shaw puts his apology into the mouth of one of the people in *Major Barbara*. "Andrew, this is not the place for making speeches"; and Andrew replies, "I know no other way of expressing myself." Exactly! Here is a dramatist who knows no other way of expressing himself in drama than the essentially undramatic way of speech-making. He never knew any other way, but in his earlier plays he did make an effort to conceal the fact. In his earlier plays there was some pretence of dramatic form, unity, coherence. In *Major Barbara* there is none.

—*Drama and Life* (1907)

The Nation

"The Doctor's Dilemma"—the nature of the dilemma need not be specified here—is one long tirade against the medical profession. The supposed indictment is fortified by reckless misstatement, gross exaggeration, unscrupulous pleading, suppression of the truth, malicious suggestion, and dogmatic assertion. Occasional instances of maltreatment are quoted as general examples. A quasi-scientific gloss is imparted to fluent nonsense by the use of technical phraseology. In his preface he coolly writes: "I deal with the subject as an economist, a politician, and a citizen, exercising my common sense," common sense being the one quality of which his fallacious illustrations are conspicuously devoid. He does not explain why an economist or a politician should be an infallible judge of medical ethics, practice, and ability. Never were methods more unscientific than those which he employs. Unfortunately the adroitness of his whimsical humor often distracts attention from his own malpractice. He does not always talk pernicious rubbish. His advocacy of sunshine and soap, for instance, as sanitary agents, is perfectly sound. But his wise edicts are mere platitudes. Some of his conclusions are indisputable, but when he points out the way to reform he shatters his pretence of being an economist. He ruins his case by his unjust perversity, dishonesty, and egotism. But his humorous caricatures of different types of physicians and surgeons are delicious, as is his possibly unintended exposure of the humbug of the so-called "artistic temperament" in the person of the fascinating rascal Dubedat. Mr. Shaw knows something about shams.

—March 30, 1911

The Drama

A new book by George Bernard Shaw is always hailed by a multitude of readers; even the worst of the Shaw of today is so much better than the best of many writers that the bookbuyer's enthusiasm will not be seriously dampened by *Heartbreak House*. It is probably the worst of Shaw. . . .

For the characters are not typical, and the situations are often absurd. The workmanship is frequently slipshod, not in the old way which was Mr. Shaw's clever flouting of conventional technique, but in pure carelessness. In some cases one smarts from the unadulterated theatrical hoakum.

—November 1919

James Agate

If a man can be partaker of God's theatre, he shall likewise be partaker of God's rest, says Bacon. But if truth be the thing which

Shaw will have most, rest is that which he will have not at all. If we will be partakers of Shaw's theatre we must be prepared to be partakers of his fierce unrest.

But then no thinker would ever desire to lay up any other reward. When Whitman writes: "I have said that the soul is not more than the body, And I have said that the body is not more than the soul, And nothing, not God, is greater to one than oneself is," we must either assent or dissent. Simply to cry out "Whitmanesque!" is no way out of the difficulty. When Ibsen writes a play to prove that building happy homes for happy human beings is not the highest peak of human endeavour, leaving us to find out what higher summit there may be, he intends us to use our brains. It is beside the point to cry out "How like Ibsen!" *Heartbreak House* is a restatement of these two themes. You have to get Ibsen thoroughly in mind if you are not to find the Zeppelin at the end of Shaw's play merely monstrous. It has already destroyed the people who achieve; it is to come again to lighten the talkers' darkness, and at the peril of all the happy homes in the neighbourhood. You will do well to keep Whitman in mind when you hear the old sea-captain bellowing with a thousand different intonations and qualities of emphasis: Be yourself, do not sleep. I do not mean, of course, that Shaw had these two themes actually in mind when he set about this rather maundering, Tchekovian rhapsody. But they have long been part of his mental make-up, and he cannot escape them or their implications. The difficulty seems to be in the implications. Is a man to persist in being himself if that self runs counter to God or the interests of parish, nation, the community at large? The characters in this play are nearer to apes and goats than to men and women. Shall they nevertheless persist in being themselves, or shall they pray to be Zeppelin-destroyed and born again? The tragedy of the women is the very ordinary one of having married the wrong man. But all these men—liars and humbugs, ineffectual, hysterical, neurasthenic—are wrong men. The play, in so far as it has a material plot, is an affair of grotesque and horrid ac-

couplements. It is monstrous for the young girl to mate in any natural sense with a, superficially considered, rather disgusting old
man. Shall she take him in the spirit as a spiritual mate? Shaw holds
that she shall, and that in the theater even spiritual truth shall prevail over formal prettiness.

—*Alarums and Excursions* (1922)

QUESTIONS

1. Shaw was an active member of the Fabian Society, a reformist,
   quasi-socialist organization. Do you see evidence of this affiliation in the plays in this volume?
2. Consider Shaw's treatment of strong-minded, unconventional
   young women. Do they seem real flesh and blood, or mere
   mouthpieces for Shaw's ideas? What do you make of their
   usual association with older men?
3. What are the most common butts of Shaw's humor?
4. Do you feel that the primary effect of Shaw's prefaces is to il-
   luminate the plays? What else do they do?
5. Shaw is a notorious polemicist. But are the endings of these
   four plays polemical? Do they make a point or argue a cause
   in an unequivocal way? Or are they ambiguous, suggestive
   rather than explicit?

FOR FURTHER READING

WORKS BY SHAW

Collected Plays with Their Prefaces: Vols. 1–7. Edited by Dan H. Laurence. New York: Dodd, Mead, 1975.

The Collected Screenplays of Bernard Shaw. Edited by Bernard F. Dukore. Athens: University of Georgia Press, 1980.

Collected Letters. Edited by Dan H. Laurence. Vol. 1, 1874–1897, New York: Dodd, Mead, 1965; Vol. 2, 1898–1910, New York: Dodd, Mead, 1972; Vol. 3, 1911–1925, New York: Viking Press, 1985; Vol. 4, 1926–1950. New York: Viking Press, 1988.

The Drama Observed. Edited by Bernard F. Dukore. Vol. 1:1880–1895; Vol. 2:1895–1897; Vol. 3:1897–1911; Vol. 4:1911–1950. University Park: Pennsylvania State University Press, 1993. An invaluable collection of all Shaw's writings about theater.

Shaw's Music: The Complete Musical Criticism in Three Volumes. Edited by Dan H. Laurence. Vol. 1:1876–1890; Vol. 2:1890–1893; Vol. 3:1893–1850. New York: Dodd, Mead, 1981.

BIOGRAPHY

Ervine, St. John G. *Bernard Shaw: His Life, Work, and Friends.* New York: William Morrow, 1956. The most sympathetic and fair biography of Shaw.

Henderson, Archibald. *George Bernard Shaw: Man of the Century.* New York: Appleton-Century-Crofts, 1956.

Holroyd, Michael. *Bernard Shaw, Vol. 1, 1856–1898: The Search for Love,* New York: Random House, 1988. *Bernard Shaw, Vol. 2, 1898–1918: The Pursuit of Power.* New York: Random House,

1989. *Bernard Shaw, Vol. 3, 1918–1950: The Lure of Fantasy.* New York: Random House, 1991. *Bernard Shaw, Vol. 4, 1950–1991: The Last Laugh.* New York: Random House, 1992. The most detailed and comprehensive biography. A condensed version is available: *Bernard Shaw: The One-Volume Definitive Edition.* New York: Random House, 1998.

Shaw, George Bernard. *Interviews and Recollections.* Edited by A. M. Gibbs. Iowa City: University of Iowa Press, 1990. An indispensable record of first-hand personal views of and by Shaw.

CRITICAL WORKS

Bentley, Eric. *Bernard Shaw.* New York: New Directions, 1947.

Berst, Charles A. *Bernard Shaw and the Art of Drama.* Champaign-Urbana: University of Illinois Press, 1973.

Bertolini, John A. *The Playwrighting Self of Bernard Shaw.* Carbondale and Edwardsville: University of Southern Illinois Press, 1991.

Crompton, Louis. *Shaw the Dramatist.* Lincoln: University of Nebraska Press, 1969.

Dukore, Bernard. *Shaw's Theatre.* Gainesville: University Press of Florida, 2000.

Evans, T. F., ed. *Shaw: The Critical Heritage.* London: Routledge, 1976.

Gibbs, A. M. *The Art and Mind of Shaw.* New York: Macmillan, 1983.

Gordon, David J. *Bernard Shaw and the Comic Sublime.* New York: St. Martin's Press, 1990.

Holroyd, Michael, ed. *The Genius of Shaw.* New York: Holt, Rinehart and Winston, 1979.

Meisel, Martin. *Shaw and the Nineteenth-Century Theater.* Princeton, NJ: Princeton University Press, 1963. A brilliant and delightful account of Shaw's relationship to the theater of his youth.

Morgan, Margery M. *The Shavian Playground.* London: Methuen, 1972.

Shaw: The Annual of Bernard Shaw Studies: Vols. 1–22 successive. General editors: Stanley Weintraub, Fred D. Crawford, Gale K. Larson. University Park: Pennsylvania State University Press, 1981–2003.

Turco, Alfred, Jr. *Shaw's Moral Vision.* Ithaca, NY: Cornell University Press, 1976.

Valency, Maurice. *The Cart and the Trumpet.* New York: Oxford University Press, 1973.

Watson, Barbara Bellow. *A Shavian Guide to the Intelligent Woman.* New York: W. W. Norton, 1972. Still the best case for Shaw as a feminist.

Wisenthal, J. L. *The Marriage of Contraries.* Cambridge, MA: Harvard University Press, 1974.